Милым моим соседям Розочке и Саше

с пожеланием хорошего здоровья и долгой интересной жизни.

С уважением

Фира.

22. III. 18.

J. Z. GASSKO

PAIN ON TRIAL

Edited by Deanna Boddie

Boston • 2017

Jane Gassko *Pain on Trial*

Edited by Deanna Boddie

ISBN 978-1940220659
Library of Congress Control Number: 2017907579

Published by M•Graphics Publishing
www.mgraphics-publishing.com
mgraphics.books@gmail.com

Text Layout by M·Graphics © 2017
Cover Design by Natali Cohen © 2017

Printed in the United States of America

For people who suffer from pain
and live with it day in and day out

PREFACE

PAIN ON TRIAL IS BASED ON a true story, even though it's written in a fictional format. Not a single fact is distorted or made up. The names of the protagonist and other characters in thc story have been changed to protect their privacy.

Although the problems associated with illegal prescriptions and drug abuse in the United States continue to grow, another significant problem is the undertreatment of chronic pain, which is almost forgotten. People in different degrees of pain are desperately looking for consistent and effective care, and too often they can't find it. Primary care physicians and specialists are struggling to provide meaningful pain relief to people in need, but their efforts are often restricted by draconian government regulations and fear to be persecuted.

Although the World Health Organization named opioids as the gold standard for treating severe pain (2000), in the present environment, physicians who prescribe adequate amount of opioids to their patients are in danger of losing their licenses and ending up in prison. As a result of the witch hunts that the DEA, FBI, and other agencies have conducted in relation to opioid prescriptions, millions of American people who suffer from lasting and often unbearable pain are denied adequate pain relief.

Through Dr. Holden's dramatic story, the reader will learn about the complex issues associated with treating chronic pain as well as the obstacles that frequently deprive chronic pain patients of a normal life. For this publication, the particular facts related to treatment of chronic pain, drug dependence, recreational drug abuse, and addiction to opioids are consistent with the medical knowledge that was available from 1995 through the summer of 2007. State and national guidelines, regulations, and policies regarding opioid prescription also correlate with the same time period.

Prologue

May 2015

JUDGE ADLER ENTERED THE COURTROOM, HER expression more somber than usual.

"Good afternoon, everyone. Please sit down and remain seated," she stated and turned to her clerk. "Please invite the jury to come in."

The jurors walked in. They looked solemn, their faces unreadable.

Judge Adler turned to the jury box. "Members of the jury, have you reached a verdict?"

"Yes, we have, Your Honor," answered the foreperson, a tall, dark-haired woman in spectacles.

"Was it unanimous?"

"Yes, Your Honor."

Chapter One

February 2007

It had been a long day. Ben's last patient was just leaving when the phone rang, loud and persistent. Another emergency. Ben sighed and slowly picked up the phone. By the end of the working day, he was usually so tired that even talking on the phone seemed an arduous task.

It was Sandra, his secretary, who would never bother him if it weren't important.

"Sorry, Doctor. I know it's past your working hours, but you'll probably have to see this one."

"Sciatica or something more exciting?" Ben sighed.

"You never miss a chance to joke, Doctor," Sandra shook her head. "Well, this time it looks like it's something more exciting."

"Knee arthritis?"

"No," Sandra smiled. "An ABC-TV producer."

"He must have knocked on the wrong door. The psychiatrist is on the second floor."

"Doctor, please. The man is working on a feature called *ABC Chronicles* to make a program on advanced medical services in the area, and he wants to talk to you. Actually, he called a few days ago and asked to meet with you, but it was in the middle of your work day, and I didn't want to disturb you, and then I completely forgot about him. I'm sorry."

"All right, let him in."

A tall, slim, dark-haired man in his late forties with an affable smile walked into Ben's office.

"Harry Olson," the producer introduced himself.

"Good to meet you," Ben shook his hand.

"Doctor, you must be tired, so I'll skip pleasantries and cut to the chase. We are working on the program, "American Health Front," and planning to show a segment on a cutting edge treatment for chronic pain. We want people to see what can be done for these complicated and widespread problems, and we heard that your pain center provides incredible services for people in pain. Would you mind if in a week or so we videotape activities in your office and interview your staff, yourself, and some of your patients who will agree to appear on *Chronicles*?"

"No, I wouldn't mind. I don't think it will hurt anyone to be featured on ABC."

"No, it won't," laughed the producer.

A week later, in early March, Harry Olson was back with a young ponytailed cameraman, introducing himself as Gene Kinsey, who promptly set up his equipment, and the interview began.

"Doctor Holden, could you please tell us about your specialty? Are you a pain physician?"

"Yes, I am. Quite a few years ago, I was trained in PM&R, which stands for Physical Medicine and Rehabilitation, and I developed a special interest in helping people in pain. I've taken multiple pain-related courses and training sessions, and actually, I still continue taking them a few times a year."

"Doctor, are you board-certified?"

"Yes, I am."

"Are you specializing in any particular field?"

"I'm focused on a wide spectrum of painful musculoskeletal conditions, mainly severe and chronic in nature. We offer a variety of treatments, both conventional and alternative."

"Can you give us a few examples?" asked Olson.

"Of course. Have you ever heard of the Lordex decompression table?"

"No, we haven't," replied the producer.

"Do you know anything about alpha wave stimulation treatment?"

"No, I don't," said Olson. "Do you, Gene?"

"No," Kinsey admitted reluctantly. "What is that?"

"I'll show you and explain it to you later. How about prolotherapy?"

"No idea," both visitors responded simultaneously.

"Well, let me tell a little about each of them first, and then I'll walk you around and show what we do."

Ben was watching their faces while he was talking. Both of his guests seemed to immediately grasp and approve Ben's concept of healing people who were suffering from all kinds of pain, often for years, by using an entire spectrum of conventional and alternative treatments. However, even before Ben was halfway through his enthusiastic description of their numerous office services, the producer, who had been patiently waiting for a pause, interrupted.

"Dr. Holden, can I schedule an appointment for my mother? She is over eighty, suffers from terrible back pain, and no one has been able to help her so far."

"Of course!" Ben instantly felt excited. A challenging case was always a gratifying experience. "If she needs help badly, we can schedule her for tomorrow morning before my first patient."

"She may not make it on time," the producer smiled. "She lives in Georgia."

"Can't ABC send her a private jet?" Ben asked with a straight face.

The producer laughed.

"Your mother is welcome to come whenever she can. Just give us a call beforehand. We never refuse to treat people in pain, and we try to see them as soon as we can. Besides, it may be a good excuse for her to visit her son, right?"

"That's true," Harry Olson suppressed a smile. "Can we interview some of your patients now?"

"Sure."

They stepped into the waiting room.

"Hi, Brad," Dr. Holden walked up to a tall broad-shouldered man. "Let me introduce you to Mr. Olson and Mr. Kinsey. They are working on a segment for an ABC health program and want to interview some of my patients. Would you mind talking to them?"

"No, I wouldn't mind," Brad cast a shy smile.

"Why are you here, Brad?" Harry Olson asked gently.

"I had eight back surgeries over the past eleven years. They didn't help much, to say the least. Anyway, eventually I developed a failed back syndrome. Three years ago, I arrived at Dr. Holden's office as an invalid."

"And now? Are you feeling better?" asked Olson.

"You bet. Now I work full time, take an hour commute to my job, and feel like a completely new man."

Olson and Kinsey exchanged incredulous glances. Over the next twenty minutes, both of them talked to a few more patients to get a better understanding of what this place was about.

The producer and the cameraman videotaped the Lordex Decompression Machine and the Tranquility Room with non-invasive alpha-wave treatment for the program. They also videotaped tai-chi and yoga instructors working with Dr. Holden's patients in the spacious exercise room.

The ABC men, polite and professional, charmed the whole staff. They finished their work in three hours and left with a promise to send a copy of the video as soon as it was ready. And they kept their promise.

By coincidence, the ABC program was scheduled to be aired on Ben's birthday. Their friends joked that Ben must have cast a spell on the ABC producer to arrange it. On a cool April night in 2007, Ben, his wife, Emma, and their closest friends gathered at their home, and after a scrumptious dinner, they all moved into the living room to watch *Chronicles*.

The program comprised several segments, including an advanced surgical center and its innovative heart surgery techniques, an infertility clinic, and Ben's pain management center. This segment, just like the ones before it, was short but showed the essence of Ben's comprehensive approach and, what was even more important, delivered a clear message: this is the place where the doctors and everyone else on the staff take good care of people with severe pain.

"Ben, you looked handsome!" Danielle, Emma's best friend, gushed to Ben and hugged him.

"Handsome is not the right word. He was magnificent!" Gail, Emma's other friend, hugged him too.

"Ladies, have you listened to a word of what he and his staff said? Or did you just pay attention to Ben's good looks?" interrupted Max, Danielle's husband. "I think Ben's center is unique. I wonder if there is another one like his in the area."

"It's a unique place for those who suffer from chronic pain," said Michael. "My brother, who has chronic arthritis in his knees, is a patient at this clinic. I know what I'm talking about."

"I believe Ben is unique specialist!" added Tina. "Emma, don't you think so?"

"I think..." Emma paused. "I think that if you guys don't stop singing his praises, he will develop a *chronic* superiority complex impossible to cure."

She sent her husband a playful smile and then turned serious.

"ABC did a truly good job, Ben. The people who suffer from pain should know what your center can do for them."

On that joyful mid-April night, neither Ben nor Emma could even imagine how dramatic a turn their fortune would take a month later.

Chapter Two

A Month Later

It was one of those almost perfect spring days when the brightness of the sun was quite promising, and the air was still fresh and chilly. Trees and flowers were already in bloom, and despite the smell of car fumes from the highway nearby, their scent was gentle and teasing.

That morning Emma was driving their friend Mark to her husband's medical office for his next treatment. Mark was suffering from intense backache, and none of the conventional treatments had helped him in the past. Because of his severe spinal stenosis and multiple herniated discs, driving was now out of the question for Mark. His friend told him that if anyone could help him, it would be Dr. Holden, who had a reputation as a knowledgeable and caring physician. A stubborn man who hated going to doctors, Mark finally agreed to see him.

At his first appointment two weeks earlier, Dr. Holden offered him a fairly new treatment, which involved gradual stretching of the spine by a spinal decompression device. At each treatment session, the machine slowly decompressed his herniated discs, releasing pressure on his sciatic nerves, and now Mark was feeling much better.

The treatment course was to be twenty-five sessions in a row. Because Mark wasn't allowed to drive, Emma offered to take him to the office and back, yet each time she brought him to the office, another patient or someone from Ben's staff would offer him a ride home as Mark lived close by.

That morning when she picked him up, Mark handed her a plastic bag with a small cardboard box inside, a smile on his jovial face.

"My wife's pastries," he explained proudly. "Sheila baked them last night for you and Ben."

"She shouldn't do that," Emma started impulsively and then smiled. "You have to be insane to refuse her pastries."

Emma dropped Mark off next to the office entry, and when he was leaving, he turned to her and smiled gratefully.

"This back stretching machine is really something. I wish I had listened to my friend and gone to Dr. Holden sooner."

"I'm glad this treatment helps." Emma paused. "By the way, who will drive you back home today?"

"Don't worry. Someone will. They always find me a ride. Each person on Ben's staff is a 3-carat diamond. Where did Ben find them?"

"I don't know, Tiffany's?"

Mark smiled broadly.

"You don't mind, if I drive you home today?"

"Oh, you don't have to," Mark shook his head, but Emma could see he was pleased.

"Call me when you're done."

"I will. Thank you, Emma. How can I ever repay you?"

"You already have. I bet the pastry is out of this world."

Mark smiled and, leaning heavily on his cane, shuffled to the office entrance.

* * *

Emma was driving home and thinking about the book she was writing. It was coming along quite well, and she was feeling that whirling excitement she usually experienced before getting to her desk. A few more minutes, and she would be home.

The lilacs in front of their house were blooming madly, and Emma instantly thought that she should get some lilacs for Sheila. She entered the house, grabbed the garden scissors, and rushed back outside.

Emma closed the front door and instantly froze, dismally staring at her hands. No key, no cell phone, just a pair of useless scissors. Lilac branches are much easier to break than to clip. Emma automatically walked to the lilac bushes and began breaking bough after bough, thinking about what to do next. Who invented these fancy locks that shut the doors the second you walked outside? The neighbors, who had the spare key, were not home, and she didn't even have her cell phone!

A man and a woman were walking down the street, talking animatedly and laughing.

"I'm sorry to interrupt you," Emma approached them tentatively. "You wouldn't happen to have a cell phone? I'm locked out and need to call my husband."

"Please," the woman reached into her pocket and handed Emma her cell phone.

Ben answered her call right away. It meant his first patient hadn't arrived yet.

"Ben, I'm sorry to bother you, but I walked outside... I'm locked out." Emma tried to sound composed. "Could you please send someone with your key?"

"Listen, my first patient arrived a little earlier than I expected. Everyone at the front desk is very busy for the moment. But let me talk to Greg, I don't think he would mind bringing you the key. His first patient just canceled. If he agrees, he'll bring you the key in about twenty minutes. Can you last that long?"

"Sure. Thank you." She hung up.

Greg was a new physical therapist, and Emma had met him only once. He was a gallant middle-aged man, and everyone in the office liked him.

Emma thanked the woman and returned her the phone. The couple wished her good luck and moved on.

It's all right, Emma thought, pacing back and forth down the street. She was getting a little cold. In twenty minutes Greg will be here, and I'll be at my desk.

Twenty minutes passed, but no one showed up. Thirty minutes passed. Then forty minutes. It was a sunny, but rather cold and windy morning, and Emma was freezing. She was also getting anxious and upset. What was taking Greg so long? Where was he? Was he driving here via the North Pole? Her frustration, which was reaching the boiling point, morphed into worry. What if something bad happened to Greg on his way here? She sighed heavily and at that moment saw a navy-blue Honda, unhurriedly turning around the corner and moving toward their house.

"Finally!" Emma dashed to the car. "Greg, are you all right?"

"Me? Of course. Why?"

"I expected you a little earlier."

"Oh, you know, I like to drive the familiar roads. It's much faster that way."

"Really?" Emma stifled a smile. "Thank you, Greg. You are my savior."

Greg handed her the key and drove away.

Emma picked up the lilacs and went inside. The moment she stepped into the kitchen to put the flowers into a vase, the phone rang. It was her friend Danielle.

"Hi, Emma. How is your life going?"

"Not so good, Dani. I was locked out, frozen to death. I've been pacing our street for more than an hour!"

"But the rest is fine?" Danielle's question had an unfamiliar note.

"Oh, the rest is fine."

"Are you sure?" Danielle's voice sounded odd.

"What do you mean?"

"Is everything all right in Ben's office?"

"Yes. I was there about an hour ago. Everything was fine. Why?"

"Emma, my colleague had an appointment with Ben scheduled for this morning. She arrived at the parking lot of his office..." Danielle faltered. "The police stopped her and didn't let her in."

"The police? That's ridiculous! Is it her first visit?"

"I think so," said Danielle.

"She must have come to the wrong place. There are no police there. Why would the police be there?"

"I don't know."

"Don't worry, Dani. It's some mistake. Listen, I just stepped in, hungry as a wolf, and I need a cup of hot tea right now. You don't mind if I call you later?"

"Sure," Danielle said hesitantly.

Emma was halfway to the kitchen when the phone rang again.

This time it was her mother-in-law.

"Emma, something is wrong at Ben's office. Do you know that?" Martha's voice was tense, if not terrified.

"Martha, who told you that?"

"One of my neighbors just arrived for her appointment," Martha was breathing heavily. "She called me... She said police... many policemen were there."

Must be the same confused woman, Emma thought.

"Martha, don't worry. I'll call Ben's secretary and call you back."

Emma hung up. She was now getting that weird feeling in her stomach, the one she used to get before some tough exams in college, an apprehension she hadn't felt in years.

She dialed Sandra's cell phone number, the only way to reach Ben's secretary immediately.

Sandra picked up right away.

"Sandra, it's me, Emma. Is everything all right in the office?"

"No, Mrs. Holden. Things are bad. Really bad. People in blue are everywhere. All over the place. Sorry, I can't talk any longer."

"Do you know what happened?"

"Not a clue."

"Sandra, please, don't hang up. Do you think I can talk to Ben?"

"I doubt it."

"Sandra, stay calm. I'm on my way."

* * *

That morning as always around 7:30 a.m. Sandra arrived at the office to prepare for a day of intensive work. She had already pulled the medical charts for the doctors the night before, yet she still had to take care of quite a few things, including returning messages and answering phone calls that usually came as early as eight o'clock. The office was officially open at 9:30 a.m., but Dr. Holden usually arrived around 8:00 a.m. to complete routine paperwork and to see emergency patients who had called him the night before. Almost every day, they got phone calls from people with severe pain—often out-of-control pain—who needed urgent attention, and Dr. Holden never said "no." He would often agree to see them early in the morning before his scheduled patients arrived.

When Sandra started working for Dr. Holden, she was astounded to learn how many people were suffering from all sorts of pain. Quite a few of them were handicapped or crippled after car- or job-related accidents; some were disabled due to failed surgeries, while others had been improperly treated or undertreated for years.

Sandra observed that the lucky ones who came to their center soon enough to be cured recovered rather quickly, because Dr. Holden offered them multiple treatments they could rarely find elsewhere. Dr. Holden and Julia Lander, the nurse practitioner, frequently attended pain conferences and workshops, educating themselves about modern advances in their specialty and learning new techniques. Dr. Holden regularly acquired new equipment and was always looking for specialists who could make his practice even more diversified and effective. Their center already included a pain psychologist, a psychiatrist, a neurologist, and an acupuncturist. A year earlier, Dr. Holden decided to build an exercise room with hardwood floors and wall-sized mirrors. Once the project was finished, he hired yoga, tai-chi, and Pilates instructors to work with patients who might benefit from these exercises.

"Exercise is your best remedy," he told his patients. "No drowsiness or nausea. No side effects."

Holden didn't need to advertise. Almost every day, Sandra booked at least three or four new patients referred by their physicians, coworkers, relatives, or friends. They would often start with these comments: "My brother told me, if anyone can help you, that will be Dr. Holden," or "My colleague said, if you want your suffering stopped, go to Dr. Holden's center. They are the best."

At the end of their first visits, quite a few of them would say, "Doctor, you are the first physician who *listened* to me" or "You are the first doctor who really cared." Every year at Christmas time, thank you cards poured into their office.

Coming early to the office every day, Sandra was allowed to leave two hours before the office closed. The other secretary, Anita, who arrived by 9:30 a.m., would stay until the end of the day. Sandra liked to spend her free afternoon with her three-year-old daughter, whom she adored.

Sandra put away her purse and turned on the computer.

I can't wait to see my little devil's face when she learns we are going to the Children's Museum this Saturday with her grandma, Sandra thought. She will go nuts. And so will Grandma.

By 9:30 a.m. four more members of Dr. Holden's staff arrived: Julia Lander, the nurse practitioner; Dr. White, the neurologist; Greg Hawthorn, the physical therapist; and Anita, a new secretary, who had joined Dr. Holden's team a few months earlier. Anita helped Sandra to prepare the paperwork for the day, and by 9:30 a.m. the staff was ready to take its first patients. One of them, Bill Green, who had an appointment with Julia Lander, was already sitting in the waiting room. Another patient, Hector Brady, had just walked in. Sandra knew him quite well; Hector lived in New Hampshire and would never request an urgent appointment unless it was something serious. Mr. Brady smiled apologetically and slowly moved to the front desk. He greeted Sandra with a courteous smile, handed her his insurance card and limped to his seat.

A proud man, thought Sandra, always well mannered and composed. He must be in severe pain today, otherwise he wouldn't be here before the office opened.

Dr. Holden invited Hector into his office. Twenty minutes later, Hector walked back into the waiting room, and Dr. Holden called his next patient, Roger Higgins. Roger was scheduled for his regular prolotherapy injections, which worked wonders for his injured back.

Julia Lander emerged from her office, as always in high spirits, and invited Bill Green, a former marine officer and war veteran to come into her office. The daily routine was getting into full swing.

Sandra reviewed the notes she took the day before so as not to miss anything important. Work in Dr. Holden's office was complex and intense, at times very stressful, but she liked it a great deal. Sandra knew she was working in a place where each member of the staff was taking care of every patient the best way possible. These suffering people were coming from all over the area, a few even from other states. It was the first job in Sandra's life where she felt both comfortable and important.

Suddenly, Sandra heard the front door yanked open. She automatically looked up to see which patient was making such a rowdy entrance. A beefy, square-jawed man in a navy-blue jacket briskly walked through the door. He was followed by another stocky, younger man in navy blue. The younger one stopped at the door and blocked the entrance. Square Jaw moved toward the front desk and speared Sandra and Anita with his narrow watery-gray eyes.

"Step away from the computers!" he barked. "Nobody move!"

The front door swung wide open and about thirty or forty strangers, many of them armed, stormed into the office. Most of them were dressed in dark-blue uniforms with different signs on the back such as DEA, FBI, State Police, and IRS.

The blue-jackets flooded the premises like a tsunami, some of them instantly disappearing in the doctors' offices and examination rooms. Others were roaming the hall and the waiting room, searching for something in every corner of the office.

With rising terror, Sandra and Anita watched them silently. What was going on? Who were these people and what were they doing here?

September 11 was still fresh in Anita's mind, and she instantly thought that this squad arrived to rescue them from a terrorist act. But Sandra's thoughts rushed in a different direction. She was a refugee from the Soviet Union, and these men reminded her of something else from her past life. At that time she was working in a small medical office in St. Petersburg, formerly Leningrad, and one cold winter afternoon, a group of ski-masked people with automatic guns barged in their office and terrorized its tiny staff for hours. As they learned later, it was a special police squad that was looking for millions of rubles in this small medical practice. They found nothing, and with no explanation or apology, they left as abruptly as they appeared and never came back. The memory of that afternoon invasion still made her shudder. These blue-uniformed people were not masked, but many of them were armed, and their barking commands sounded as harsh and terrifying as the commands of that Russian police squad.

If not for their fluent English, flashed through Sandra's mind, this armed unit could have easily passed for a Russian hit squad. What was it all about? Why didn't they introduce themselves? And why didn't they explain to us what was going on?

The door from Dr. Holden's office banged open, and Roger Higgins walked out of it, his face blazing with anger. One of the blue-jackets, a burly man with small, darting eyes, put his hefty hand on Roger's shoulder and said something to him in a low voice. Roger pushed his hand away, his glance tense and fuming.

"I'm not talking to you, sir. I'm Dr. Holden's patient, and I came here for my injections, not for an interrogation. You disgust me!"

While Roger was walking to the exit, the burly blue-jacket leaned toward a young man in a police uniform standing next to him. "Go and get his plate numbers."

Square Jaw peered at Sandra.

"Where is the money?" he snapped.

"What money?" Sandra was confused.

"Cash! Where is the cash?" Square Jaw's stern glance meant serious business.

Sandra reached into the safe and took all the cash stored there. A ten-dollar bill that was Mr. Green's co-payment. She handed the bill to the officer. "Is it what you are looking for?"

Square Jaw seemed to be on the verge of exploding.

"Is this all? Where is the rest? Give me all money! We are not playing games here!" he yelled.

"This is all I have. And you don't have to scream into my ear; my hearing is still pretty good," Sandra replied calmly.

The man rushed to the safe and stared into its open belly. A few prescription pads, nothing else.

"Don't worry. We'll find it," he muttered grimly.

Sandra shrugged and didn't answer.

"Now, you two, give me your handbags," Square Jaw demanded, his cold, menacing eyes drilling through Sandra and Anita.

They obeyed the command and gave him their handbags. Fright was flooding Anita's body. A swarm of questions was whirling in her head, but she didn't dare to ask any of them.

"Officer, do you have a search warrant?" She heard Sandra's voice coming from afar. Sandra was getting back her nerve, and she sounded angry.

"Yes, we do," Square Jaw said, not stopping his wild rummaging of her handbag. He obviously had no intention of showing them any warrants.

"Sir, could you please be so kind as to treat my belongings with some respect?" Sandra said indignantly.

"Why?" The thug didn't even hide his arrogance. "Who are you to demand respect?"

"I'm Dr. Holden's assistant. I'm not a criminal."

"That remains to be seen." Square Jaw smirked and cast a long look at both Sandra and Anita.

"Now, both of you, get up and follow me," he ordered and moved to the waiting area.

"Sit tight and don't talk to each other," he pointed to the chairs across from the fish tank and left.

The waiting area looked unusually deserted. The only other person there was a middle-aged man of nondescript appearance that Sandra and Anita had not seen before.

"Are you a new patient?" Sandra asked sympathetically. "Do you need any help?"

"No, thank you. I'm all set," the man assured her and stared at the window. It looked like he didn't want to be bothered.

Sandra and Anita sat silently. Sandra wondered who this lonely stranger could be and why he was the only one in the waiting room. She could sense he was not a patient. Who was he?

Anita wasn't thinking about this man. She was frightened. Her thoughts were thousands of miles away, in Baku in January 1990, when ruthless fanatics barged into the homes of Armenians, beating them up, torturing and killing the old, the young, and the babies. Within a few days, every Armenian who had survived the pogroms left Baku for good. To stay meant to die.

Anita, her husband, and their children were accepted as refugees in the United States, their new motherland. They were now safe and free. The clot of fear—the residue of the massacre—was gradually waning and turning into a tiny flicker burning somewhere deep inside, a flicker she was learning to suppress.

After working at a few jobs, Anita finally found the one that felt exactly right. At Dr. Holden's center, everyone worked with ceaseless enthusiasm. Busy every single minute of the day, Anita never felt tired. Dr. Holden's contagious sense of humor kept everyone in high spirits, and Anita often caught herself smiling, even when she was occupied with something that was far from funny.

Anita was hired as a secretary, but Dr. Holden thought it was important for all his staff to be educated in the basics of pain management, and he frequently invited her to his professional presentations to local physicians or to individuals at senior centers. After each presentation, he would ask Anita for her comments and suggestions. For the first time, Anita felt truly respected and happy.

But now gloomy memories were pressing heavily on her brain. Her heart was pounding so loudly she thought everyone who was passing by could hear it. She didn't feel happy anymore. And she didn't feel safe. Something very wrong was happening here. She knew it was an awful mistake. But how much would they have to endure before this mess would be straightened out?

Her thoughts were interrupted by Sandra's voice.

"Sir, I have a severe headache. I need my medication. Could you please bring me my handbag?"

"You'll have to wait," a police officer replied unhurriedly.

"I've been waiting for the past hour," Sandra said. "The headache is getting worse. Please bring me my handbag."

The officer, a big, slightly stooped man in his early forties with a dull look, didn't move.

"I have a prescription. My name is on the bottle."

The officer was motionless.

"My medication is just an Extra Strength Tylenol," Sandra pleaded.

"I'm not a doctor," the officer cast Sandra a cold look. "I don't know nothing about this stuff, and I don't want to hear you whining about your headache anymore. Honestly," he smirked, "I don't give a shit."

Chapter Three

That morning, Ben's first scheduled patient was Roger Higgins, one of his favorites. A slender, athletic, forty-eight-year-old man, he'd arrived at Dr. Holden's office two years before with a history of lower back pain, and Ben treated it with periodic injections of 25% dextrose. These injections of concentrated sugar solution were meant to restore degenerated ligaments in Roger's lumbar area and make them strong and durable again. The treatment was working well, and recently Roger had even resumed his gym exercises.

As always, Roger was extremely polite and appreciative. Knowing the injection ritual only too well by now, he positioned himself on the treatment table and exposed his lower back for the spinal injection. Ben aspirated the conventional amount of the therapeutic solution and was about to give his usual words of comfort that helped patients to relax, when the door sprang open. Ben hadn't heard any knocking on the door, nor had anyone asked his permission to come in. It was so unusual that he was more surprised than upset. They had a firm rule at the office: no one was allowed to interrupt a session with a patient, not even the office manager, unless it was a matter of extreme importance. Let alone without knocking.

Ben turned to the door and went numb. Five or six burly men, some in uniforms and some in civilian clothes, barged into his examination room. The closest one to Ben yelled, "Don't move! Take everything out of your pockets!"

The man rushed to Ben and thoroughly searched him.

"Do you have any guns or illegal drugs on your premises?" he barked.

"No, I do not," Ben responded calmly.

Another uniformed man dashed to Roger Higgins.

"Get dressed and get out!" he ordered.

"Sorry, Roger," Ben said regretfully. "We'll call you later."

Without the slightest sign of fear, Roger pulled on his shirt, shook Ben's hand, and unhurriedly moved to the door.

Another man, in his late fifties, entered the room. He was wearing a navy blue blazer, a white shirt, and a gray tie, and he looked less intimidating than the rest of the crowd. He smiled, showed Ben his FBI badge, and handed him his business card. "James Grafton, Senior FBI Agent," read the card.

He shook Ben's hand in a friendly manner and introduced himself.

Ben was still more puzzled than scared by the scene, but to his surprise, he suddenly felt his hands tremble and his lips twitch. His voice, however, remained calm.

"Please sit down, Mr. Grafton," said Ben, and took a seat. "Can you tell me please what this is all about?"

"First of all," started Mr. Grafton, "let me assure you that you are not under arrest. We are just conducting a thorough investigation of your practice, and so far we are not pressing any charges. I'm afraid, however, that you won't be able to see your scheduled patients today. And, of course, we have many questions to ask."

Ben felt his agitation subside, and he was now feeling more like himself.

"Please ask me any questions you like." Ben met the agent's gaze calmly. "I'll be more than happy to answer."

Sure that he hadn't done anything wrong, Ben completely forgot the basic rule, "Never talk to law officers without your attorney present." He didn't have an attorney. Besides, if he talked to these agents, Ben believed he would have a chance to explain to them that their arrival was an obvious mistake. Whoever had sent them to his office was definitely misled.

Ben cast a glance at the still-open door of his office and saw many more people in uniform and civilian clothes roaming in the hallway, talking to his staff and taking pictures. The magnitude of the operation was slowly dawning on him. What exactly were they looking for? What could be of any interest to them in his clinic?

Mr. Grafton was now asking Ben about his practice, his patients, and his preferred ways of treating pain. Yet Ben had a strong feeling that Mr. Grafton was not much interested in the *content* of his answers. He was cagily watching Ben, trying to measure his level of fear and read what was *unsaid*.

Gradually their conversation shifted to Ben's family. It became more interactive, even to the point that Agent Grafton shared with Ben some information about his own daughter, who was the same age as Ben's younger daughter and who was "so much interested in art." Finally, they both came to the conclusion that as parents they were very lucky to have such accomplished and sensible children. To any stranger, they probably looked like a couple of old buddies, comparing notes on the hardships and rewards of their children's upbringing. Ben wondered if Agent Grafton was going to invite him and Emma to dinner or at least ask for his home phone number to bring their "bonding" to the next level.

Suddenly, their conversation was brought to an end by a youngish, broad-chested, gritty man in a blue DEA jacket. He introduced himself as Special Agent Luis and asked Ben to follow him to the small area that served as a lunchroom for the office staff. Luis explained to Ben that the reason for the relocation was the need for a search of his office.

"Can we expect to find anything funny?" The DEA man offered a painted smile.

"I have some funny gifts from my patients there. Are they what you are looking for?" Ben stifled a smile.

The agent opened his mouth to answer but instantly shut it, at a loss for words.

For some inexplicable reason, Ben's mind wandered to his recent flea market discovery, a porcelain hippopotamus. That day at the market, Ben believed that the hippo was sadly staring at him and silently begging to be adopted. For the last six months, the hippo—Ben had named it Hugo—was resting comfortably on the windowsill in Ben's office, peering at Ben and his patients through his half-sleepy eyes. On the toughest days, Hugo's phlegmatic smile was a true comfort. Now Ben wondered what his pal Hugo would think of these fervent "researchers."

In the lunchroom Ben was offered a seat and introduced to another determined-looking DEA agent with an exceptionally strong handshake and to a young woman, a stocky blonde, too young to be a seasoned agent. During the next two hours of the interrogation, the young woman didn't say a word and served mostly as a recorder while Special Agent Luis bombarded Ben with questions regarding his prescription patterns and his reasons for starting his patients on certain medications, especially painkillers. Then he gradually moved on to discuss specific patients.

Ben knew many of his patients by their first names and usually remembered even the nuances of their health problems. Quite a few of the patients confided their personal problems to him and sought his advice on both medical and personal issues. There were a few patients who even went to college or changed their vocations to ones more suitable for their health conditions as a result of Ben's recommendations. Many of his new patients had arrived at his center depressed, and Ben referred them to a psychiatrist or pain psychologist, both of whom worked on the premises. His patients' emotional condition was always his primary concern.

One of the patients that Ken Luis was especially interested in was a famous hockey player, Paul Campbell, who had been under Ben's care for the past four years. By now the man was well over fifty, but he still played for the National Hockey Veterans Team. Last December he called Ben from Red Square in Moscow right after his team had won a game against the Russian veterans and wished Ben a Merry Christmas. Upon his return from Russia, he brought Ben a big colorful poster with photographs of both teams. Paul's bold signature across the whole poster read, "With respect and appreciation, from Moscow. Paul Campbell."

Paul, known for his strong character and unmatched audacity on the hockey rink, sustained so many injuries and had so many surgeries that he had lost count. His shoulders and knees were covered with scars, and the MRI of his back made Ben sad. Still, under Ben's care, Paul's life was as normal as it could be, considering his condition. He was traveling all over Europe with a team of veteran hockey players, and he scored a goal or two in almost every game. Treated with injections and pain medications, Paul was happy that despite his trauma-inflicted arthritis he could still enjoy the passion of his life.

Luis's questions about Paul Campbell were suddenly interrupted by the man who had personally searched Ben a few hours ago. He entered the lunchroom carrying a plastic bottle half-filled with yellow-brownish liquid. The agent's face had the triumphant expression of a predator who had just cornered its prey and was about to devour it.

"Doctor, can you explain to us what this bottle of urine is doing in your medical cabinet?" Sarcasm was spouting from his every pore.

Ben was puzzled. He was certain that no one from his staff would leave anything like that in his office, or any other room in their clinic, for that matter. Was it somebody's foul joke? Was the bottle planted? Then it hit him. It wasn't urine. It was a mixture of virgin olive oil and three different herbal extracts that he had bought at Whole Foods. Mixed in the right proportion and rubbed into achy joints, the neck, or the back, this blend worked almost magically for relieving pain and muscle spasms. Ben had found the recipe in the book titled *Ancient Healing Secrets* and tried it himself first to make sure it was safe and effective. It turned out to be extremely potent yet free of side effects. Clearly ancient Greek and Roman physicians weren't ignoramuses and knew a thing or two. This mixture had quite a pleasant smell and could not be confused with the smells of body fluids, especially urine.

"What makes you think it is urine?" asked Ben.

"No kidding! What else?" the man smirked.

"It's an herbal-essence mixture I use to treat my patients. Please uncork the bottle and sniff it."

"No way! I'm not going to do *that*." The man secured the bottle in an orange plastic bag with a sign, *BIOHAZARDS*, and walked out of the room. Ben wondered how long it would take their forensic chemists to figure out what this mixture consists of. Poor guy, he will be so disappointed.

The briefly interrupted interrogation continued. A new team of investigators walked into the lunch room and replaced Ken Luis, his colleague, and the blonde woman. Two muscular men in their mid-forties—both with grayish hair and menacing looks—introduced themselves as Agents Bruce Powers and Thomas Stone.

"Doctor, let's get straight to the point," Bruce cast Ben a probing look. "There are about fifty medical offices in this area, and you and your staff prescribe more narcotic medicine than any of them. How would you explain that?"

Ben couldn't believe how uninformed these agents were. Most of the doctors who had their practices in neighboring towns didn't treat patients with chronic pain—that was why they rarely or never prescribed painkillers. Those few doctors who did provide pain management often focused on interventional procedures and rarely prescribed any medications.

"Well, when patients come to a primary care physician with an infection, they usually get a prescription for antibiotics," Ben explained patiently. "Asthma patients expect to get refills for inhalers or steroids, and people with high blood pressure get beta blockers and diuretics. Almost all of *my* patients are people suffering from severe chronic pain, and for pain, at least over the last four thousand years or so, nothing has worked better than opioid medications, especially in combination with other treatments."

Ben looked at the interrogators and saw that his explanation was totally lost on them. They apparently didn't know even the basics of pain management. He had to educate them and put an end to this unfortunate misunderstanding.

"Chronic pain," Ben continued, "is similar to any other chronic medical condition; it commonly lasts for years and sometimes becomes a lifelong ordeal. When people come to our center with a history of chronic pain, we very seldom can promise them a cure. However, what we can do is to provide them with effective relief from their suffering. We offer our patients a whole variety of treatments, including injections, osteopathic treatments, acupuncture, and others. We refer them to all kinds of physical therapy and exercise, but very often their pain still needs to be controlled with medications. And as you probably know, opioids are the most effective treatment and have fewer side effects than any other pain-relievers or most other medications in general."

Most of his friends and relatives knew that whenever pain was mentioned in a conversation, Ben would get wound up, and no one could stop him.

"Do you know that there are fifty to seventy million chronic pain patients in our country?"

The men shook their heads.

"Are you aware that most of the chronic patients in this country are *undertreated*, while some don't get any treatment *at all*. Do you know how many families are ruined and how many careers are crushed because of inadequate pain control? Those who are in lasting pain not only lose their sleep and their jobs, they lose their relationships and their hopes. Pain eventually turns them into depressed, angry, and desperate creatures who have nothing to look forward to anymore, and at this stage they are much more prone to drinking, abusing street drugs and even suicide. When they hit bottom, they become outcasts of society. The goal of our center is to prevent this from happening. It's not easy. But you won't believe what the combination of right treatments can do even for the most difficult patients."

"What *can* it do?" Bruce winked at his colleague. "Give them access to free drugs to abuse them or sell?"

Ben ignored the sarcasm. The man's question pushed him toward his favorite topic.

"You know, when people come to the bank, they normally come for the usual financial transactions, yet there are some who come to rob. It happens. But it doesn't mean that everyone who comes to the bank should be regarded and treated as a potential bank robber. Would you agree with that?" Ben forced a smile.

The men didn't smile back and didn't seem to have an answer.

"Do you know that some of your pain patients sell your prescriptions?" asked Bruce.

"No, I don't know that." Ben paused. "If this is the case, it's truly regrettable. But I know that the overwhelming majority of our patients are honest, hard-working people who, just like you and me, deserve to live a normal life. Isn't it enough that they are afflicted by incurable suffering? Does our society, including law enforcement, expect physicians to act as zealous policemen and exacerbate their patients' misery by unfair suspicions? Or should doctors observe the Hippocratic Oath and *treat* their patients to the best of their abilities and try to alleviate their pain?"

Ben knew the agent's sarcastic question implied that some of his patients deceived him, that they were faking pain in order to get narcotic medications, but he also knew that research showed that it was practically impossible to tell who was suffering from real pain and who was not. There were no reliable tests or devices to register the intensity of pain or even its mere presence. The research also showed that even the most experienced physicians couldn't tell if their patients were drug addicts or if they had severe, poorly controlled pain. In either case, the patient's behavior and actions could be almost identical. Most physicians didn't want to assume the roles of policemen and treat their pain patients as potential criminals. Still, he knew some doctors who refused to prescribe their suffering patients opioids because they were fearful of possible persecution.

Ben broke the silence.

"Gentlemen, can you imagine that you have an asthma attack and your doctor refuses you an inhaler or oxygen? Or you suffer from chest pain and your physician informs you that he is not comfortable prescribing nitro or digoxin?"

Ben asked the question and all of a sudden realized that it wasn't rhetorical. The fifty patients scheduled today to be treated by his staff, including a few new ones, were being deprived of their treatments. They would not receive physical therapy, injections, prescriptions, exercises, or opportunities to discuss their immediate problems with their doctors. Every visit to the pain center for each of these patients was critical. What were they punished for? Was this even legal?

"Do you sincerely believe that all our patients are drug addicts and common criminals?"

The agents kept silent.

"Are you aware that more than seventy percent of our patients are senior citizens? And most of the younger patients had multiple surgeries—often failed surgeries—and yet they try their best to keep their jobs."

The agents shared a swift look.

"So, what do you think?" Ben insisted.

"We think," Bruce replied after a slight hesitation, "that you are an intelligent and... passionate physician."

Ben couldn't help but notice that their facial expressions had mellowed slightly.

Without adding a word, the agents shook his hand and left. Ben looked at his watch. It was 5:35 p.m. The work day was over. The longest day ever in his practice, and he had only seen one patient.

* * *

Julia Lander, the nurse practitioner and Ben's assistant, walked into the examination room with a big smile. Could she ever dream of any occupation so exciting and gratifying? Her first patient, Bill Green, a former marine officer and war veteran, took a seat while Julia opened Bill's medical chart.

"How are you feeling, Bill? You look so relaxed today. Have you been sleeping better lately?"

Bill smiled gently and parted his lips to answer when the door was kicked open and a stout, ruddy-faced man in a police uniform barged into the room, followed by a dark-haired athletic woman in her late thirties. The woman was in a navy blue uniform with a big FBI sign on it, a shotgun on her left side. "Must be left-handed," flashed in Julia's mind. The woman didn't introduce herself, just said, "We need to talk. Take a seat." Julia slowly sank onto her chair, and the agent sat down next to her. Julia didn't notice when and how Bill and the policeman disappeared.

While the FBI woman engaged Julia in conversation, the policeman silently walked up to Bill, grabbed him by the shoulder, and firmly pushed him out of the room. Bill was so stunned by the intrusion that he didn't even react to the insolence. He was taken aback even more by the expression on Julia's face when the door to her examination room was opened by the kick of a boot. Never in his life had he seen a woman so terrified. He knew that Julia was Jewish, and the first thought that came to mind was, "That's probably how Jewish women felt when Nazis forced their way into their homes."

Once outside, Bill instantly recovered from the shock and brushed the policeman's hand off his shoulder. Bill knew he was losing control, but he couldn't help it. Why should he, a former marine officer and war veteran, tolerate this insult?

"You, you... How could you do this to a woman? To a nurse? Who do you think you are?"

The policeman, his face ablaze with fury, turned Bill around, skillfully locked handcuffs on Bill's wrists, and shoved him to the exit.

"You will be charged with resisting arrest!" he croaked.

"Oh, you treat me like a criminal?" yelled Bill. "And what is my crime exactly? The fact that I've defended my country? Or that I was wounded in Iraq?"

His questions hung in the air, never answered.

* * *

The FBI woman was polite. She didn't ask any questions about Julia's work in the office. Instead, she was curious about her husband and her grown-up daughter. What did they do for a living? What were their hobbies? She was interested in the vacation trips Julia and her husband had taken and their future plans for traveling. Julia tried to answer each question honestly and at the same time figure out why this woman was in her office and why she was so interested in Julia's personal life. Yet the conversation ran like a rapid mountain stream, and Julia didn't have a second to focus on anything but the agent's questions.

At some point the woman's cell phone rang. She picked it up.

"I can't talk right now," she said. "I'm in the middle of an interview."

"Interview?" Echoed in Julia's head. She thought it was just a talk.

Julia tried to stay calm, but she was now feeling some discomfort, and a small tight knot had formed inside her body, pressing in all directions. The whole situation seemed surreal, as if Julia was transported to some movie set and was acting in a role she hadn't auditioned for, the role that someone else had chosen for her and now was forcing her to play. She, a grown-up woman, who had been married for quite a while, raised children, had earned bachelor's and master's degrees, worked hard and was always respected, felt that her life was spinning out of control.

The door opened once again, and a young man in a navy blue suit walked in to join the "interview." He too was friendly, and their conversation seemed purely social. But Julia didn't believe it was small talk anymore.

"Why are you here?" Julia asked. "What happened?"

"We're just checking some information," the young man explained. "If everything is fine, tomorrow your office will be back to normal, and everyone will forget it ever happened."

"*What* happened?" Julia wanted to ask, but the question stuck in her throat. It was such a simple and appropriate question, but she couldn't force herself to utter it.

"May I go to the restroom?" Julia asked instead. A self-confident person, Julia addressed the question to the agent, who was almost half her age, feeling as if the woman were her classroom teacher and Julia was a first-grader who needed permission.

The woman nodded. She opened the door and followed Julia to the facility. When they reached the restroom, the woman hastily passed by Julia, walked into the restroom first and closed the door behind her. In a minute or two she walked out and let Julia in. When Julia left the restroom, the woman walked in again, inspected the room, then walked out and accompanied Julia back to her office. Julia suddenly felt short of breath. The tight knot inside was now pressing harder and harder.

When they returned to the examination room, the woman told Julia that now she would be interviewed by another agent, Margo.

"Margo is very nice," the woman said. "You'll like her."

The woman handed Julia her business card and left.

She never introduced herself, thought Julia, and she was about to look at the card when the door opened, and two new people walked in. A young, long-faced woman and a heavyset, dark-skinned man with grim brown eyes. They both were in civilian dress. The woman said "hello" and introduced herself, "Agent Margo Stroller." The man just nodded and pierced Julia with a hard, inquisitive look.

Margo asked Julia a few questions about their pain management center and seemed pleased with her answers. She *was* very nice, just as the FBI woman had described her. But when Julia was in the middle of replying to her third question, the stocky man interrupted her.

"Ms. Lander, tell me, what do you do when you *object* to Dr. Holden's medical decisions?" He drilled Julia with another hard stare.

"How could I object to them? I'm a nurse practitioner, in practice for seven years, only three of them in pain management, and he is an extremely knowledgeable physician with more than twenty-five years of experience. How could I object to his decisions?"

"But when you *don't* agree with him, what do you do?" The man's gaze was purely hostile.

Julia felt short of breath again, as if she had just dashed up to the fifth floor in one huge leap.

"I never disagreed with him. I respect his opinion. He is a very good doctor, and he cares about his patients like no one else."

Margo cast a long look at the grim man, and then turned to Julia.

"Ms. Lander, how long have you been working with Dr. Holden?" Margo's voice was sweet and friendly.

"Three years."

"Do you like working with him?" Margo's greenish-blue eyes were filled with genuine interest.

"Very much," Julia exhaled.

Questions were flying from Agent Margo's mouth one after another, prompt and simple, and Julia tried to answer all of them as sincerely as possible. Margo was about to ask her next question when Mr. Gloom passed by her and posed his question first.

"Ms. Lander, do you value your nursing license?"

"Of course, I do! You probably know how hard you have to study and work to get it."

"Then why do you sacrifice it so easily?" The man narrowed his dark eyes, vile sparkles madly dancing in the slots.

"What do you mean 'sacrifice'?" Julia felt confused.

"If the doctor does something wrong and you disagree with him, then he is guilty and you are not. But if you always agree with him, then you are as guilty as he is. Do you understand what I'm saying, Ms. Lander?"

Julia nodded pensively. What a fool she was. They had been trying to force on her this vicious role of traitor for a few hours now, and she didn't get it! All their questions, and especially these "disagree questions," had one purpose and one purpose only: to turn her against Dr. Holden. *Divide and conquer!* What an odd pair, this Sweetheart Margo and Mr. Gloom. Dr. Jekyll and Mr. Hyde?

"So, Ms. Lander, once again, did you ever object to Dr. Holden's medical decisions?"

Julia firmly met the man's stony gaze.

"I believe I have already answered your question, sir. Any other subjects you want to discuss?"

The man's eyes were fuming.

"No more questions." He paused. "For now," he added mockingly and moved to the door with agent Margo silently marching in tow.

When they both vanished behind the door, Julia looked at her watch for the first time since she had entered her examination room. The watch showed 5:40 p.m. Had it been a regular day, she would either be seeing her last patient or doing her paperwork. She came to the office early in the morning, and over the past eight hours never felt hungry or thirsty. It was rather odd, yet at the moment it wasn't relevant. Something else was even more odd but much more relevant. Over all these hours she hadn't seen a single patient. None of the twenty-three chronic pain patients that had been scheduled with her today were examined or treated, and none of them received their vitally needed medications. They were left to suffer, and who knows for how long! How could that happen? Why was she spending her workday answering meaningless questions? She heard a knock on the door.

"Come in," Julia said wearily.

The door opened, and Dr. Holden walked in. He silently sank onto the chair next to her desk. Julia was used to the doctor's habit of walking into her examination room after their last patients were gone. Even when their workday was long and exhausting, he would crack a joke and cheer her up. His dry humor worked unfailingly, but now his tired gray eyes were devoid of any humor.

Awfully sad eyes, Julia thought, and suddenly felt an odd pain in her chest as if it were being squeezed by a powerful hand.

"Something really bad is going on, right, Doctor?" She knew her question was rhetorical, but she couldn't help it.

Ben didn't answer, just grinned sorrowfully and nodded.

Chapter Four

Grace, the office manager, started her morning as usual, going through her to-do list for the day and waiting for the physical therapist to stop by and get his first patient's medical chart. Frank was supposed to have arrived fifteen minutes ago, and Grace was getting a little worried. She grabbed the chart to bring it to Frank, stepped out of her office, and stopped, dumbfounded. The office premises were unrecognizable, swarmed by strangers in navy blue uniforms. State police, FBI, and DEA agents darted in front of her eyes in incomprehensible disarray.

"What's going on?" Grace froze like Lot's wife.

"Ma'am, the folder please." Before she could utter a word, a stranger in blue forcefully pulled the chart out of her hands.

"Follow me," he ordered, walking her to the waiting room and pointing to a chair. "Take a seat and don't talk to anyone."

"Someone had planted a bomb in our office," floated in Grace's head. "This is an anti-terrorist squad. These people are here to save us!"

She looked around. In the waiting room, besides herself, there were only Sandra, Anita, and a man she had never seen before.

"Girls, what is going on? A terrorist attack? A bomb?"

Sandra cast a quick look at the stranger, then a longer one at Grace.

"We have no idea," she said gravely, "but it doesn't look good. Actually, it looks quite crazy."

"What do you think it's all about?" Grace was confused.

"I don't know," Sandra said worriedly. "All I know is that something bad has happened... scary... and disgusting."

The stranger was peering outside the window, but Sandra couldn't be fooled so easily. This guy may feign his aloofness as much as he wanted, she thought, but he was here on purpose.

Anita got up and headed to the restroom. She didn't make it to the hall—an FBI officer blocked her way.

"Where are you going?" he asked, his voice terse and belligerent.

"To the restroom," said Anita, feeling her legs trembling.

"Not so fast." The man motioned to a young woman in navy blue.

"Agent Clark," he ordered, "take this woman to the facility."

The two women silently moved toward the restroom.

"Wait here," the agent said to Anita, and disappeared inside.

A few minutes later, the agent walked out and sized up Anita from tip to toe as if she was about to place a price tag on her.

"You may go in."

This woman acts and sounds like a robot, Anita thought with sympathy. Why would anyone choose such a nasty job, taking people to restrooms?

When Anita left the restroom, the agent dashed in again. To check if I've put down the toilet seat, Anita grinned, but then suddenly felt burning salty tingling in her eyes.

She returned to the waiting area. It was empty, and she was about to get back to her chair when she heard a stern voice right behind her back, "Follow me, ma'am. We need to talk." Anita turned around and saw a slightly stooped middle-aged man dressed in a navy blue uniform. Another "friendly" character, Anita thought, in this nauseating spectacle.

* * *

Sandra was taken to the vacant office of their psychiatrist, who didn't take patients on Thursdays. A big, dark-skinned man and a young, long-faced woman were already there, but neither of them were in uniform. The interrogation started without any overture. The two didn't introduce themselves, didn't tell Sandra what agencies they represented, and didn't explain to her what had happened and why they were questioning her. They asked for her name, her position in the practice, and then they immediately switched to a different sort of question.

"How are you paid for your work?" Before Sandra could answer the question, the man helpfully offered, "Cash?"

"I'm always paid by a *check*," Sandra said with assurance.

"And a nice chunk under the table, right?" The man was drilling Sandra with his spiky dark-brown eyes.

"I am *always* paid by a check only," Sandra boldly returned his look. "And, in case you are interested, I pay taxes on what I make, and over the seven years that I've been working in the United States, I have never had a single problem with the IRS."

"How many patients a day do you usually book?" It was the first question the woman asked.

"It depends on how many specialists work on that particular day. Each specialist usually takes twenty to twenty-five patients a day."

Sandra felt calm and confident. She had nothing to hide. She was certain that neither Dr. Holden nor anyone else on his staff ever did anything wrong. Whenever she would ask him about office policy, he would always say, "Sandra, by the book only, and on this particular subject, the rules are..."

"What health insurances do you take?" continued the woman.

Sandra named as many as she could remember at the moment.

"Do you take patients without insurance?" the man took over.

"Sometimes we do. As you know, not everyone has health coverage. Besides, some services and procedures, such as prolotherapy or lumbar decompression treatments, are not covered by any insurance, which is a real shame."

"Shame?"

"Yes, it's a shame insurances doesn't cover them. These treatments work really well."

"So those who don't have insurance or use these treatments pay cash, right?" The man was watching Sandra intently.

"Some pay with cash, some with a check, and some with a credit card."

"Do you have any out-of-state patients?" The man's glance was getting heavier, as if he used it as a press to squeeze deeply hidden, clandestine thoughts from her.

"Yes, we do. We have an excellent reputation. About a month ago, our center was featured on ABC as one of the most advanced practices in the area."

The agents ignored her last comments and continued the questioning. Sandra was getting more and more irritated by the questions and especially by the agents' haughty demeanor. Their intent was becoming clear, and if she wasn't becoming concerned about Dr. Holden, it would seem laughable to her. No, it was not laughable at all. The agents obviously wanted to harm Dr. Holden. That was the main purpose of their "conversation." And these people were representing the government? Their government?

Since the day she arrived in America, Sandra had felt nothing but love, gratitude, and respect for this country. Had she overlooked something? Was she ill-informed all these years? Or blind? Or maybe this ambush was sanctioned by some misguided madman who had no idea what an important job her office staff was doing?

Sandra wasn't a pushover, but she knew she didn't have any control over what was going on now. The only thing she could do was to answer the questions and answer them honestly. So she did. The agents were jotting something down in their notepads but didn't show Sandra what they had written and didn't explain anything to her, even though one aspect of their conversation was clear to Sandra: her answers didn't please them. The minute the questioning stopped, Sandra inhaled deeply and plunged on.

"Could you please tell me what is happening? I've been working here for a few years, and I truly believe it's an excellent medical center. Why are you asking me all these questions? What is happening?" she spilled out this volley of questions and instantly felt pangs of anxiety.

The stocky man, his eyes full of spite, seemed eager to reply.

"It's none of your business," he said sternly. "You can go now."

Sandra was taken back to the waiting area, joining Anita and Grace, who had already returned from their interrogations. They were all permitted to talk now, but they were not in a hurry to share their thoughts as the stranger was sitting close by, still feigning aloofness.

Finally Anita and Grace were allowed to leave the premises, and then they could talk freely and compare notes, although there was not much to share. The scenarios of their interrogations were similar, and the answers the interrogators received from Dr. Holden's staff seemed to disappoint them. No matter how hard the agents tried to intimidate them, they didn't utter a single unfavorable remark about either Dr. Holden or Nurse Lander.

* * *

Sandra hated idleness. If only she could get back to her work. That day fifty-three patients were scheduled to see Dr. Holden, Julia Lander, and Dr. White, the neurologist. Nineteen more were scheduled to come for physical therapy, yoga, and other exercises. Seventy-two patients arrived at the office that day to get relief from their pain, Sandra noted, and these heartless bastards didn't allow them to have it!

Sandra instinctively turned to the front desk, which was her daily residence, and froze in disbelief. The police officers and FBI agents were fumbling through the office medical charts, piling them one after another into plastic crates and taking them away. The charts, always stored in perfect order, were now in complete disarray. How dare they mess everything up! How is their office going to function tomorrow without charts? Sandra jumped from her seat in the waiting room to try to stop the barbaric intrusion when a stab of fear glued her to the chair.

* * *

Patients had been arriving one after another all day long, but each one was stopped by the police at the entrance to the office. The policemen didn't introduce themselves and didn't show their badges. Some patients were searched, and all of them were interrogated.

"Who did you come to see?" an elderly man with a cane was asked.

"Dr. Holden."

"Take your hands out of your pockets!"

"What's going on, officer?"

"It's me who asks questions here, not you. What's your medical problem?"

"That is private information, isn't it?"

"What medication are you on?"

"I don't think I have to report that to anybody."

"You drug addicts came to the wrong place. Go to DETOX."

"Me? To DETOX? Why do you say that? I don't even take any medication! I'm here for physical therapy!"

"You'll have to skip it. Scram! Your visit is over."

* * *

Sandra was watching the agents scanning their lists and frantically searching for particular charts. She made a fairly educated guess why they couldn't locate some of them. There were patients who got married and changed their last names and those who moved out of state and stopped coming. Over the years a few patients died, and their files were stored in a different place. Sandra saw that the agents were getting frustrated, even angry. Who knows? Sandra thought, they may think that some of the charts had "conveniently" disappeared. Sandra fleetingly debated about what to do and finally walked straight to the stooped, gloomy-faced man who was frantically scuffling through the files.

"Would you like me to help you?" Sandra offered nervously.

The man frowned. Sandra could feel he was trying to weigh the advantages of the offer versus the risks of accepting it.

"Go ahead," he blurted, then handed her the list and stepped aside.

Until the end of the working day, Sandra helped him to find the charts, her every move vigilantly watched. Crate after crate was loaded with the medical charts—a thousand of them were removed from the office along with all the official and personal papers agents could find. No one said a word about when they would be returned. Their only offer was to make copies of the medical charts. Sandra received copies of the first five hundred charts a week later. The FBI charged 19 cents a page, rather than the usual price of 5 to 10 cents per page at any copy center. The copies were accompanied by the bill, which was a total of $6,000.

Dr. Holden's certificates for attending conferences and workshops, the rent agreement, all financial documents, papers vitally important to office functioning, and everything else that the agents could put their hands on were snatched. As a parting gift for the shaken office staff and to make up for the inconvenience of the intrusion, the agents, on their way out, decorated the walls of the pain management center with sticky flyers that read *ADDICTED? GO TO DETOX.*

* * *

When Emma arrived at the parking lot, she barely recognized it. She slowed down before entering the driveway when a man in police uniform dashed to her car and stopped her.

"Where are you going, ma'am?"

"To Dr. Holden's office."

"Do you have an appointment?" The officer was polite but tense.

"No, I don't. I am his wife." The man was hesitant for a moment.

"Please park over here." He pointed to the parking space on his left. "Someone will be with you shortly."

Emma parked the car, shut down the engine, and examined the parking lot more closely. It was covered with police cars, vans, and people in uniforms. The signs on their backs read, State police, Boston Police, FBI, IRS, DEA, and some others. Agents and officers were moving around the parking area in a complex, incomprehensible choreography. Looks like a crime scene from *Law and Order,* Emma thought. She cast a glance at the other side of the street and saw three men and a woman, each with a TV camera, watching the whole scene with dismal gravity.

The scene looked so weird that Emma didn't even try to make any sense of it. She was sitting in her car, lightheaded, waiting for someone to explain to her what this bizarre scene was about. Why did all these agencies suddenly get interested in her husband's business? Why were all these people here? What did the DEA signs mean? She had never seen these signs before.

A young man with the FBI logo on his uniform approached her car and invited Emma to step inside the building. The moment Emma entered the hallway, she saw more people dressed in navy blue uniforms swarming around, their sober faces bearing an impression of vital importance. Emma didn't have a second to process the scene as she was instantly ushered into the manager's office, where two men, both a little older and higher in rank, were waiting for her.

They greeted her politely, but their cold looks were unnerving.

"Don't worry, ma'am. Nobody here was arrested," the older one assured her. "And no charges were pressed. We are just investigating."

"Investigating what?"

"Your husband's practice."

"Why?"

"We have our reasons."

"I see." Emma was trying to think of another question, but her thoughts were wandering around her head in complete disarray.

"Did you know that your husband was under investigation?" the taller man asked.

"No. Why would he be?"

The men didn't answer, just exchanged telling looks. They asked her a few more questions about her husband's hobbies and their vacations that had nothing to do with his practice.

Emma had no problem answering the questions, yet she was puzzled. Why were they so curious about their personal life?

"Do *you* have any questions, madam?" the shorter one suddenly asked.

Emma thought for a moment and then remembered something.

"What do the DEA signs mean?"

The men exchanged funny glances.

"You don't know?" the younger one asked.

"No, I have never seen them before."

"DEA means Drug Enforcement Agency," the younger man explained, and turned to the older one with a mocking smile.

"Anything else you'd like to know?" the older man asked.

"No, that's all," said Emma. She suddenly felt tired and completely incapable of thinking.

The older man rose from his chair, and the younger one followed him. The meeting was over. Emma walked into the hallway, moved toward the exit, and stopped abruptly. Someone in the waiting room was crying. Was she hallucinating? Or was it real? She couldn't tell anymore. She felt that all of her energy had been sucked out of her by the surreal scene unfolding in Ben's office and that stupid, meaningless conversation with the agents. She wanted to go home, to be far away from this building invaded by these uniformed people.

* * *

By the time Emma arrived home, she felt nauseous. She made herself a cup of tea with lemon and walked to the bedroom to lie down. A few hours later, she noticed that the light on the answering machine was blinking. She pressed the button.

"Hi. I'm Harry Moral, producer from Channel 25. We are going to run a piece on Dr. Holden in the news tonight. If he would like to tell us his side of the story, he can call me at 781-555-3344."

Emma instantly remembered the gloomy faces of the people with cameras on the sidewalk. She dialed Ben's cell phone number, almost sure he wouldn't pick up. To her surprise, Ben answered her call on the second ring.

"Ben, how are you doing?" Emma asked, and immediately thought that this trivial, often futile question that people ask each other every day, quite often not even expecting any answer, carried an entirely new meaning now.

"I'm all right, darling. And you?"

"I'm OK. When do you think you'll be home?"

"In about an hour or so."

"A producer from Channel 25 called. He wants your side of the story. Would you talk to him?"

"Why not? What's his number?"

Ben and Emma had stopped watching the local TV news a few years ago because nothing positive was ever shown. It seemed like murders, fires, and all sorts of other horrific accidents were the core of people's lives nowadays, as if nothing good ever happened in their city and there was nothing else of any value or any interest to the public. Although Ben called the producer and told him his side of the story, neither Ben nor Emma watched Channel 25 news that night. They were too tired, and they had enough news for the day.

* * *

The next morning, Emma woke up later than usual at 7:30 a.m. Ben had already left for the gym. She sat up in bed, an odd lightness in her head. The memories of the day before began slowly surfacing in her still-sleepy brain. She saw uniformed agents swarming the office parking lot with FBI, DEA, IRS, and Police signs on their backs. Agents roamed through Ben's office. Two men snickered at her questions. Someone was crying. Was it just her nightmare or had something bad really happened? She was still sleepy and felt confused. No, such horrible things do not happen in this country. Emma forced herself to concentrate. She was motionless for a long moment. Don't kid yourself. It did happen. You saw it with your own eyes. Emma took a deep breath. Still, there is no reason to panic. It's some kind of an error. It will be fixed—

The phone rang.

"Emma, I just left the gym. I'm heading to the office."

"I'll meet you there." Emma grabbed her jacket and rushed to the car.

Chapter Five

On Friday, the doctors didn't take patients in Ben's center, but different therapies and exercise classes were available. A few patients were sitting in the waiting room, reading books or magazines and waiting for their turn. Emma walked to the front desk. Sandra was sitting at her regular place, with a phone in her right hand pressed to her ear, her face tense, and her lips trembling.

She hung up and looked at Emma.

"They call one after another. The patients," she explained. "They are stunned. Some are furious. They cannot believe it has happened. This woman... Andrea... was crying and asked me what to do. If they shut down this office, how will she live without Dr. Holden's care? He was the only doctor who found a way to help her. What should I tell them?"

Emma walked to Sandra and put her arms around her.

"Sandra, even government agencies sometimes make mistakes. It may take a little while for them to realize that—"

"It's horrible. Just horrible. I came to this country from the Soviet Union where raids like that were commonplace. But here?" Sandra let out a long sigh. "Should I emigrate again? They say there is life on Mars after all. Do you know when they are going to sell the tickets?"

"It may be quite a long trip," Emma smiled, "and a really nasty jetlag after it. Let's not panic. It was simply a mistake. We'll find a way to fix it."

"A mistake? Mrs. Holden, did you and Dr. Holden watch the Channel 25 news last night?"

"No, we didn't."

"Let's go online. You have to see it."

Sandra walked Emma to her computer and pressed "enter." The scene in the office parking lot flashed on the screen, accompanied by the Channel 25 journalist's report about the raid of the seven agencies on Dr. Holden's office. Then a big, stout man in a baseball cap appeared on the screen, his face in the shade but still recognizable. The man said that a while ago he came to Dr. Holden's practice with severe back pain, and Dr. Holden turned him into a drug addict.

"What is the word about Dr. Holden on the street?" asked the journalist.

"The word is that he prescribes drugs to those who do not need them. You can come to his office, pay a $150 and get any prescription you want. Some people call him 'Doctor Feel Good'."

"When Dr. Holden was asked for comments," added the journalist, "he said that he had never done anything illegal in his job. The only goal of his practice is to help people with pain."

Emma was dumbstruck.

"I recognized the man," said Sandra. "He *was* our patient and Dr. Holden dismissed him about a year ago. He was a "doctor-shopper."

"A 'doctor-shopper'?"

"A person who goes to different doctors to get prescriptions, and none of them is aware that this patient sees other physicians, so they might independently prescribe narcotic pain killers. Then these crooks use some meds to alleviate their pain and sell the rest. That's how some people make money these days," explained Sandra. "They are criminals."

"So this man insists that because of Ben he became a drug addict, right? So he is not only a drug addict, but he could be a drug dealer too?"

"Most likely he is."

"And he is Channel 25's star witness?" gasped Emma.

"It looks like he is their *only* witness."

"Sandra, could it be that we are having the same horrible dream?"

"I had that feeling all day long yesterday. Not anymore. You know that they took a thousand of our medical records? How are we going to see patients next week? They said they could make us copies, but how many copies will they make over the weekend? Some records are more than a hundred pages long! Any idea how much it will cost?"

"A fortune, I guess," a familiar voice replied.

Emma and Sandra turned around. It was Julia Lander.

It was Julia all right, but a different Julia. Usually smiley and radiant, she was now strained and sad. It wasn't the woman who used every chance she had to tell everyone how lucky and privileged she was to have this job.

"Julia, it's just a terrible, terrible mistake, and it will be fixed. Do you hear me?" Emma stroked Julia's shoulder.

Julia nodded, her eyes full of sorrow and skepticism.

And then it struck Emma, "Julia, Ben is registered for a workshop in San Francisco this weekend to learn a new injection technique. It starts tomorrow. How can he leave now?"

"We just spoke about that. I told him it would be wiser to cancel the trip, but he insisted on going. I think, what he needs to do now is to find a good lawyer."

"A lawyer?" winced Emma.

Emma found Ben in his office sitting at his desk, staring at papers spread in front of him, his mind somewhere else.

"Ben, are you still planning to leave for San Francisco tomorrow?"

He didn't answer right away. "I want to," he said finally. "I'm really interested in this new approach. It requires X-ray guidance, and I've bought this extremely expensive equipment and already paid $5,000 to set up the room for it, and I really want to learn the technique."

"Ben, you can learn it some other time when the situation is cleared up. I'm sure there will be other workshops like that. Please cancel the trip. Sandra and I will help you with the cancellations."

For a few minutes, Ben was looking at Emma and not seeing her. Then, as if forcing himself back into the room, he glanced at her with that serious look he used to have when he was telling a joke. Yet this time Emma was sure it was not a joke he was about to tell.

"You think I don't know I shouldn't be going? I do. I just wanted it so badly." Ben was silent for a long moment. "All right, let's cancel it."

"Good move. One more thing, Ben. We cannot pretend that what happened yesterday was not serious. You need an attorney, a really good one."

"I was already thinking about that. I'm about to call Rachel Leigh. She may know someone."

"Who is Rachel Leigh?"

"She is a legal expert in pain management. A nationally recognized expert. I met her at a pain conference a few years back. She may know some good lawyers around here. I want to talk to her before I hire anyone."

"Go ahead, call her, and don't worry about the workshop. Sandra and I will take care of it."

Emma returned to the front desk and asked Sandra to cancel the workshop. She was on her way to the vacant room where she could make a phone call to cancel Ben's flight when she saw Julia sitting in the waiting room reading a newspaper. Emma stopped and waited for Julia to finish reading.

"Ben agreed to cancel the trip," she said as soon as Julia was done with the article.

"Good," Julia replied without any enthusiasm. "The mailman just brought this," she added, handing Emma the *Boston Veritas*.

"Read this one."

Emma got the paper, took a seat, and immersed herself in the article. When she finished, she didn't know what to make of it, except that it seemed absolutely ridiculous. The reporter described the raid on Ben's office, listed all the agencies that participated in the planned ambush, and then described Ben's office, yet did not include any information about the numerous services that were offered or that it was featured a month before as one of the most advanced practices in the area. The reporter quoted her interview with the office landlord, who said that Ben was a good tenant and paid his rent on time. The reporter also quoted someone who worked in the office next door and said that Ben's patients had walked into his office a few times by accident, and once someone even asked for a cup of coffee. That was the most insightful comment that Emma found in the article. She shook her head in disbelief; this was journalism at its best.

"A ridiculous article." Emma turned to Julia. "Actually, it's good that it is so shallow and foolish. It means they have absolutely nothing incriminating to write about Ben's practice, otherwise they would have. You know what the media likes best? A scandal. To sling mud at people whenever it has a chance. This article shows that yesterday's raid was absurd. Nothing more than a stupid mistake."

"It *was* absurd," agreed Julia. "No, it was repellent. It was humiliating to us and our patients. The patients have been calling here all morning, upset, devastated, and angry. Many of them said they had already called Channel 25. This raid and this TV show were disgusting and outrageous. These agents repeatedly said no charges were pressed. No one was arrested either. And look what they did! They interrogated us. They searched our purses. They accompanied us to the restroom as if we were criminals! They removed all the office documents, every single piece of paper, even our personal notes, everything they could lay their hands on.

And they took away a thousand files of medical records! How can we see our patients now? And this is what they call justice?"

"Julia, listen, mistakes happen," Emma replied. "It's an awful, awful misunderstanding. But in a few days everything will be straightened out. And our lives will be back to normal. I'm sure they will." The phones in the office were ringing continually. Emma could hear Sandra and Anita talking to patients, trying to calm them down and to comfort them. Now the phone rang again, but this time it wasn't a patient. It was someone from Channel 25. He wanted to talk to Dr. Holden. He said they were getting endless phone calls from his patients, and now he wanted to hear what the doctor had to say.

* * *

Ben was lucky to reach Rachel Leigh on his first try. She listened to his story without interruption.

"Ben, please describe the whole incident in writing and fax it to me immediately. Meanwhile, I'll try to find you a good lawyer in Boston. I'll call you back in about an hour. And don't talk to any media guys. They are not your friends, no matter what they say."

Emma gently opened the door of Ben's office. Ben was sitting at his desk, motionless, his eyes half-closed, his thoughts far away. He didn't even notice her.

"Ben, someone from Channel 25 is on the phone. He wants to talk to you. He says their phones have been ringing all morning. It's your patients. He didn't elaborate on what they said, but he wanted an interview."

"Tell him I am busy and can't talk. Not today and not tomorrow either, end of story."

He paused, collecting his thoughts.

"Could you please help me type a short description of what happened yesterday? For Rachel. I need to fax it to her right now."

"Sure. Let me just get rid of the media guy."

A few minutes later Emma came back, sat at the computer, and began typing. *"On Thursday, May 17, 2007, without any warnings, seven agencies, including the DEA, FBI, IRS, state health department, state police, Boston police, and local police..."*

Half an hour later she walked to the front desk to ask Sandra to fax the report to Rachel Leigh.

Leigh called an hour later.

"Ben, I found you a lawyer. Please call Parker & Brown; it's a very reputable firm. Your lawyer's name is Edward Gould. He was recommended to me by a friend. She said he was very good. Call him and fax him the report you sent to me. Here is his phone number. He expects your call. Good luck. And please keep me posted."

"I will. Thanks, Rachel." Ben took a long pause. "I just got a phone call from the Medical Board. They asked me to come for a meeting on Monday. Do you think it's serious?"

"I'm afraid it's more serious than it may seem to you. But let's talk after you meet with Mr. Gould."

Ben hung up and dialed Attorney Gould's number.

"Edward Gould speaking."

"Hi, Mr. Gould. I'm Dr. Holden. Rachel Leigh told me you would expect my call."

"That's true, but we'd better meet in person. Can you meet me today at 4 p.m.?"

"Yes, I can. Mr. Gould, do you mind if I bring my wife?"

"Not at all. See you at 4 p.m."

Ben looked at his watch. It was almost 3 p.m. Driving from his office to downtown Boston on Friday afternoon might be an ordeal.

Emma was sitting next to Sandra. The phones rang one after another, and Sandra and Anita were patiently explaining to the callers that the office was not closed and that they would be seen by the doctor and the other specialists of the center next week, and that they could still come for acupuncture, yoga, tai-chi, and Pilates as well. The center was not shut down.

Ben walked up to Emma, who was sitting silently, half-listening to the secretaries' conversation and at the same time thinking about something else.

"Emma, the lawyer expects us at 4:00, and we can't afford to be late. We have to leave right now. The traffic on the Mass Pike will be horrendous."

Emma cast a long, sad glance at Sandra and Anita, slowly got up, and moved to the door.

* * *

Ben and Emma hadn't been in that part of downtown for ages. The traffic, as Ben had predicted, was awful. When they thought they were close to the destination, they parked in the first garage they saw, which turned out to be quite a distance away from the firm's building. On that windy and rainy afternoon, their fifteen-minute walk felt far from pleasurable.

The office was located in a skyscraper with a spacious lobby and a fast-speed elevator. The firm's secretary, an elegant, middle-aged woman, welcomed them with a friendly smile and asked for their names.

"Please take a seat. Mr. Gould will be with you shortly. Would you like some tea, coffee, or water?"

"Thank you. Water will be good," said Emma, and they both sat in big, comfortable chairs, for the first time that day with no tasks to perform.

They had some experience with real estate lawyers, Ben reminisced, and it was not always enjoyable. He heaved a lengthy sigh. Let's hope this one will be at least bearable.

As if reading his thoughts, Emma turned to Ben and whispered,

"I hope this lawyer that Rachel Leigh found for us is as good as..."

She didn't finish the sentence, when two good-looking, casually dressed men, one in his mid-forties, the other a few years younger, walked straight toward Ben and Emma.

"Edward Gould," the older lawyer introduced himself and shook their hands. "And this is my colleague, Anthony Minnelli. He specializes in medical law, and I'm a criminal attorney."

At the word "criminal" Emma shuddered. Until this day, they had not had any trouble with the law. Actually, none of their relatives had any trouble either. For the first time in their family history, someone was in need of a criminal defense attorney. And apparently one lawyer wasn't enough. They needed two. No chance to wake up from the nightmare. *This* was their new life.

The lawyers took them to a brightly lit room and offered them seats.

"We apologize for our dress," smiled Mr. Gould. "In our office Friday is a casual day."

"It's all right," Ben smiled back. "In our office Friday is casual too."

Their first meeting lasted about two hours. The lawyers wanted to know about the day of the raid and about Ben's practice. They took notes and were attentive, and both of them appeared friendly and sympathetic.

"Dr. Holden," Edward Gould looked Ben straight in the eye. "Have you ever done anything that could incriminate you? Anything? Even if you think it is trifle, please tell us about it. It's really important for us to know everything."

"I have never done anything illegal," said Ben decisively.

"Good," said the attorney. "You mentioned that you are invited to the Board of Medicine on Monday. We'll go with you. You will not speak there. I will. I don't want to frighten you, but from what you told us, your situation is rather serious. You have to stay as composed as you can, and we'll do whatever it takes to help you."

"Thank you. And don't worry, I'm composed. And not scared. Actually, I view the whole situation as kind of... a new experience. And it's not in my nature to give in." Ben smiled.

The lawyers smiled back politely. Yet if Ben were more suspicious, he might have noticed a gloomy shade of doubt in their well-mannered smiles.

On the way to the parking garage, Ben and Emma got lost. The streets were poorly lit, and the couple was greeted with cold rain and heavy blasts of raging wind. Ben's effort to shield them with the umbrella the pouring rain proved fruitless. By the time they found the garage, they were soaked to the skin, and yet they barely noticed it.

* * *

At home the answering machine showed seventeen messages. Emma pressed the button.

"Hi, Emma and Ben. This is Danielle and Max. We saw the Channel 25 show. It's sickening. Absolutely disgusting. But it won't ruin you. We won't let it happen. We love you very much."

"Hi, guys. This is Martha. Greg and I are calling to say that we are with you. This is a terrible mistake, and it will be fixed in no time. Stay strong. We'll help in any way possible."

"Ben and Emma, this is Irene and Alex. Guys, we read the paper. The article is the most stupid thing ever written. Don't pay attention to this trash. Please let us know how we can help. Anything. We love you, guys."

Seventeen messages. Relatives, close friends, and even friends whom they had seen only once in a while. They couldn't remember ever receiving so many loving words in one gulp. Emma was listening to the recordings, one tear after another streaming down her anguished face.

* * *

Day after day they were getting more and more phone calls from their friends who found out what had happened. Not many of their friends read the *Boston Veritas,* and very few of them watched Channel 25, but the news was spreading, and every single day Ben and Emma were getting new phone calls and finding new cheering messages on the answering machine. They had a few relatives living in the area and plenty of friends; no one of these plenty let them down. Almost no one.

* * *

Monday morning was sunny and warm. The meeting at the Medical Board was scheduled for 11 a.m. They easily found the building, and five minutes later, at 10:55, Edward Gould and Anthony Minnelli arrived; this time they were dressed in tailored suits, white dress shirts, and ties.

"Your complaint counsel is Accalia Sharket," Gould said after greeting them. "She is a former prosecutor. From my experience, not the most compassionate person on earth. Let's go and meet her."

They entered the building, Edward checked in at the front desk, and they took their seats in the grim, empty hallway. Ten minutes passed, then twenty. Thirty minutes later they were still sitting in the barren waiting area unacknowledged.

"Each time you come here, they make you wait," said Minnelli. "It's their way to let you know who is in charge."

"We'll wait," Ben said half-heartedly. "I am not in a rush. I had to cancel all appointments with my patients anyway."

He tried to look calm, but Emma could see that he was nervous and sad. Ten minutes later, Accalia Sharket showed up and introduced herself. She didn't apologize for keeping them waiting, although she tried to show some sort of politeness. Her thin lips forced a minuscule smile, but the smile didn't match well her cold, stinging glance. The woman was thickset, with ash-blonde hair, and walked with a military gait. She was in her early forties and was taking great pains to look fully in charge.

"I want to talk to Mr. Gould first," she said tersely, and disappeared behind the door of her office as quickly as she had appeared. Gould cast a telling grin to Ben and Emma and followed Ms. Sharket.

For the next forty-five minutes, Anthony entertained Ben and Emma with funny stories from his professional past, while both of them were doing their best to feign sincere interest.

Finally Gould walked out of the room. He looked like a general who had won a bloody battle, but the victory was too costly to call for a celebration.

"Let's get out of here. Let's talk outside," he said, and moved determinedly toward the exit.

The bright, sunny day was in stark contrast to Edward's looks.

"This woman..." Edward paused, searching for the right word to define the Medical Board attorney and seemingly failed. "She wanted to interrogate you regarding fourteen of your patients, right now. She had their medical charts ready on her desk. Can you believe it? The woman... Fourteen charts! Some of them look as thick as *Webster's Dictionary*, and she wanted to discuss them before you'd even had a chance to reexamine them! This is outrageous!"

Ben felt perplexed. "Fourteen patients' charts? What could be possibly wrong with them?"

"I said no," continued Edward. "We are not discussing them now. I was trying to convince her to give me the charts so that I could make copies for you. And then all of us would go over them, and only *after* that, we'll meet and talk. It took me forty minutes to get her to agree."

"Thank you, Edward," said Ben. "You are right; it's much more reasonable and productive to go over these charts first and then discuss them with Ms. Sharket."

"Let's meet tomorrow at your office, Ben," said Gould. "I'll bring the copies of these medical files. Also, Anthony and I would like to take a look at your medical center and meet your staff, if you don't mind."

"Not at all. We would be honored," said Ben.

* * *

Ben and Emma were walking to the car silently, holding hands as they often did even after twenty years of marriage. Ben was thinking about the fourteen charts. What could possibly be in there that had attracted the board's zealous attention? Four days ago that ambush squad took away a thousand charts, and now the board already had fourteen to discuss? It looked... odd.

Emma was thinking about how lucky they were to come here with the lawyers. Ben was so trusting, sometimes to a fault. If not for Edward, Ben would immediately agree to discuss the charts, and who knows what snares this blonde trickster had in store for him. Paying for the top-notch legal counsel would probably cost them an arm and a leg, but if they didn't have professionals like Gould and Minnelli in their corner, it could cost them... Emma didn't even want to finish the thought. Ben was still naive and overly optimistic, Emma pondered sadly. They were both a couple of rookies, taking first lessons on the rules of the game. Were they even close to grasping the full scope of the unfolding crisis?

* * *

At home the answering machine was blinking its fiery eye. Twelve new messages. Emma mechanically moved closer and stopped. What if some angry viewers of Channel 25 or some indignant readers of the *Boston Veritas* had called to insult Ben? Well, they have to listen to their messages anyway. She hesitantly pressed the button.

"Hi, guys. It's Mike. I just learned about this awful thing. Please let me know if I can help. You can call me anytime, I have insomnia anyway."

"Emma, Ben, we are calling to say how much we love you and how much we hate all these vicious people who are after Ben. It's a witch-hunt, nothing else. And if you need help, don't procrastinate, call us right away!"

They listened to all twelve messages. Not a single word of resentment. Only sympathy and support. One message was even from a couple they met only a month ago.

"Ben and Emma, this is Roger and Irene, your new friends. What you are going through is horrible. If we can help with anything, please let us know. Actually, how about coming over to dinner tomorrow night?"

Ben patted Emma on the shoulder.

"Perk up, darling! With such an army of cheerleaders we are doomed to be all right."

* * *

The next morning, Edward Gould and Anthony Minnelli showed up at Ben's pain management center at 9:00 a.m. sharp. They found the place thoughtfully designed and pleasantly decorated, and they could see that the staff functioned in an orderly and courteous manner. They were also impressed by all the equipment and procedures that were available for patients. Anthony, whose primary practice was to deal with medical malpractice cases, had been to scores of doctors' offices and a few pain clinics. Some of them looked much fancier than Ben's, but none of them offered such a diversity of treatments for people suffering from debilitating pain.

Gould and Minnelli sat down in Ben's office and went over the fourteen charts reluctantly surrendered by Accalia Sharket. They didn't find anything wrong with the treatments or documentation in any of those files, but Minnelli strongly recommended refraining from discussing them with Sharket before board members explained their concerns about the charts. It sounded like a sensible piece of advice, and Ben instantly accepted it.

While Minelli and Ben reviewed the charts, Edward Gould walked around the clinic, talking to the staff and trying to get a sense of what this pain management center was about. When his tour was over, he dialed Ms. Sharket's number.

"Hello, Ms. Sharket. Edward Gould. I'm calling from Dr. Holden's office. I've spent a few hours here, and I have to say that it's a very impressive clinic. I strongly recommend you visit it."

"You do?" Sharket's voice sounded surprised and ironic.

"I'm positive. Believe me, your visit will give you a new perspective on the case."

"Thank you, Mr. Gould. I'll think about it."

And Ms. Sharket did *think* about it. She even called twice to schedule her visit. But she never showed up. And none of the Medical Board members bothered to come either.

Chapter Six

THE NEXT WEEK AND THE WEEK after, everyone in the center worked longer hours to accommodate the patients not seen on May 17. Almost everyone on the staff believed that this mistake would be straightened out in no time. Patients, who'd come for their appointments one after another, offered their help while many more called the office with the same offer. "What can I do to get the doctor out of trouble? Can I testify on his behalf?" "No," Sandra or Anita replied patiently. "No charges have been pressed." "Can I write a letter in his support?" "Yes, your letter would be helpful."

Letters poured into the office, and staff who worked there used every free minute to rush to the front desk and read them. Emma stopped by with some comfort food and to cheer up Ben's employees, and she wanted to read the letters too. She took the pile, read the first line of the top letter, and turned to Sandra.

"Who wrote this letter?" she asked in a low voice.

Sandra silently pointed at the smartly-dressed man in his forties, sitting next to the fish tank.

Emma read the letter.

I'm writing this letter in response to false allegations that have been directed at Dr. Holden and his state-of-the-art treatment programs. I have been his patient for about five years, and his treatments help me tremendously to deal with my chronic pain. I am very fortunate to be treated by such a talented physician, who is constantly looking out for his patients' well-being.

On May 17, when I showed up for my appointment with Dr. Holden, I was stopped by the police and interrogated about my health condition and my treatments. I was treated as a criminal. I thought I would be arrested for showing up for my appointment on time.

The manner in which Dr. Holden is portrayed by the media and treated by the authorities is nothing less than a crime, a real witch hunt.

I have never met a doctor that is more professional, caring, and compassionate, and I'll be more than happy to testify on his behalf.

Emma opened the next letter.

A few days ago, I came across an article about Dr. Holden in the* Boston Veritas *and was dismayed to see the terrible accusation that just could not be true. Over the eight years he has been treating me, I have always known him as an honest and hard-working doctor. I feel very lucky to have him as my doctor because on countless occasions it was solely through his consultation that I finally received the right diagnosis and the proper treatment. His mastery of medicine can't be unnoticed. I am absolutely sure that this excellent doctor and honest man will be cleared of all wrong-doings.

Emma finished reading the letter and turned to Anita.

"Anita, could you please make me copies of the whole pile. I want to take them home."

At home, Emma opened the folder and reached for her reading glasses. The first letter in the pile was from the man who had two failed lower back surgeries. His orthopedic surgeon gave up on him. He said he couldn't do anything else. Then someone referred him to Ben's pain management center and he became Ben's patient. Emma continued reading.

This letter is simply to let you know how thankful and grateful I am for what you and your staff have done for me. You have treated me with more respect and professionalism than any other doctor has before. You have helped me to manage my chronic back pain, which has not only given me a better quality of life, but most of all you have given me HOPE.

Emma stopped reading for a moment and tried to picture the man who wrote the letter. He must be young. She felt deep sympathy for all chronically ill people, keenly aware that their suffering would not go away. If they were properly treated, their pain could be managed, but it would never go away. Still, among all these suffering people, the young ones would have to endure more than the rest; and there were many of them coming to Ben's center. Some were injured at their jobs or in a car accident, some were athletes with professional traumas, and some showed up after adventurous activities that turned bad. Unlike the older patients, who, no matter how reluctantly, had to accept the fact that aging, besides other troubles, is also a *painful* process, these young ones were struck by misfortune or in some cases even by tragedy that was not a natural ingredient of youth. Their whole lives were still ahead of them, but they would never be pain free.

Emma returned to the letter.

With your treatment and individual concern, you have helped me more than I could ever express to you. You are a great physician who truly understands pain and who is RESPECTED by MANY. Thank you for giving my life back to me!

Emma took a deep breath and started on the next letter. It was from a woman she met only once in the office. She still remembered her bright blue eyes and shy smile.

I am writing this letter to ask for your help in clearing the good name of a wonderful doctor. Once you take a close look at his practice, you will discover that he is a gift to his patients, a doctor whose profound knowledge and constant search for better treatments is a blessing for people in pain. Dr. Holden is a person of high integrity and impeccable honor. I hope you will be able to help clear his good name, because the threatening cloud hanging over him makes my heart ache.

Emma stopped reading and looked out of the window. The lilac bushes were still in full bloom as spring marched on and as if nothing had happened. Well, nothing had happened to **them**, but how would the government raid affect all these suffering people? They had finally found a place where they were given a chance to live normal lives, and now...

Emma took the next letter.

My name is Steve McGovern. Ever since I was in a car accident a few years ago and had rods and screws put in my spine, I thought my life was over. I was in pain 24 hours a day, seven days a week. Dr. Holden gave me a new lease on life. He is not only a great doctor; he is a great man who cares about the people he helps.

He had turned my life around 180 degrees. I went from sitting at home suffering on the couch to a rising star at my job. Under Dr. Holden's care I have had 3 promotions at my job. If not for his help, it would have not been possible to do my work. He has also

given me hope in the future to have a productive life, which I didn't have before I met him. If there is any way I can show support for Dr. Holden and his staff, please don't hesitate to write or call me.

Emma read a dozen letters and stopped, her face streaked with tears, her eyes red and puffy. She couldn't read a single line anymore. She went to the bathroom to wash her face before Ben returned home. She had to remain calm. She would sit at the computer and try to work. Everything at home should look as normal as possible.

She sank in the chair in front of the computer and stared at the screen for about an hour. Then she finally touched the keyboard and typed a few words, the ones she had never used in her entire life, even in her angriest moments.

Suddenly, the phone rang. It was their dear friend Tina, who also happened to be Ben's patient. From the tone of her voice, it was obvious Tina was upset. No, she was angry.

"Emma, I've read that blog on the Internet about the raid on Ben's office, and at the end of the blog the DEA agent left his phone number and suggested people call him with any information about Dr. Holden. I called. And I tried to tell him what an extraordinary physician Dr. Holden was. The man interrupted me and said that they were not interested in *this* kind of information. Can you believe it? What sort of investigation is it? Do they collect only the information they *want* to have? Do we live in North Korea? Or maybe in Mao Zedong's China?"

"Tina, please calm down. One agent doesn't comprise the whole legal system. There are others, and they will listen."

"Are you sure?"

Emma pondered the question.

"I hope they will," she said with slight uncertainty. "Tina, we have to believe that the system is fair. Otherwise..." Emma stopped. "Otherwise there is no hope."

"I know. What can I say? You are right. We have to believe."

Emma heard Ben's steps in the hallway.

"Sorry, Tina, I have to go. Thank you for your call to that agent. The DEA has to know what Ben's patients think about his treatments, even if some of them play deaf."

Ben walked into the room, his face lit by a happy smile.

"Emma, look at this." He handed her *Newsweek* magazine. "Look at the cover story! It's about treatment of wounded and injured American soldiers and modern ways to treat pain. The reporter describes a model pain clinic, and she practically describes our center! This is extraordinary! In *Newsweek*! Perfect timing! We have to send the piece to the Board of Medicine."

Emma took the magazine and got immersed in the article. It was well composed and it looked like the author had researched the subject thoroughly. The reporter described the wounded soldiers who had survived the battlefields of Iraq and Afghanistan. Ninety percent of them had left the battlefield alive, which was the highest survival rate in American history, but now when these injured soldiers came home, they practically overwhelmed VA pain clinics with their chronic health issues, including severe pain. There weren't enough places to take them, and there were not enough pain physicians to treat them.

Yet the article wasn't only about treatment of soldiers; it was about chronic pain, an affliction of millions of Americans. The number of patients who suffered from chronic pain grew as people got older, and so had our understanding of what pain was and how to treat it. Yet scientists didn't know why some people developed chronic pain after operations and injures while others didn't, and why some patients fully recovered after the most serious traumas while others never did.

Another question that made pain management even more complex was how to measure pain. There was no instrument for doing it. The best doctors could do was to ask patients to rate their pain on a scale from 1 to 10 and to trust their answers. But how objective was this rating, even if patients were not faking their pain? Some patients sometimes exaggerated their pain to get a more vigorous treatment, while others downplayed it to look tough. To complicate the problem even more, one patient's 4 could be another patient's 7 or 8. What one person could easily withstand for another might be agony.

As if this issue was not enough, ethnicity and gender also played a role in pain management. For example, women have about twice as many nerve fibers in the skin as men do and feel some types of pain more intensely than men.

But there was one thing all chronic patients agree about: constant pain could make a person's life a living hell. As one wounded soldier stated, "It is as if somebody is holding a knife in your back and twisting it against your nerves continually, never stopping."

By now, doctors and patients have learned than chronic pain can almost never be cured. It can only be controlled, although it is often quite a challenge to find the right treatment for it. As soon as pain is effectively and steadily controlled, patients are not liabilities; they are able to work and live normal lives, and once again are assets to society.

Emma finished reading the article and looked up at Ben.

"So, what do you say, Emma?" Ben asked impatiently.

"Pain management is becoming a hot topic. Everyone who reads *Newsweek* will learn how important your work is. If the Medical Board people haven't read it, they should, and DEA agents should, too."

* * *

Letters in Ben's and Julia's support were pouring in nonstop. At the end of the working day, Sandra would usually gather a pile of the new ones, split the pile into two smaller heaps, and along with Anita, move to the quiet corner of her front-desk cubicle, where she would read the letters, savoring every single line and then switching the piles.

"Anita, look at this one." Sandra handed her a letter from a well-known Boston physician, who was the department head in one of the big local hospitals.

Anita took the letter and started reading:

I am writing this letter in support of my colleague Dr. Ben Holden, who has devoted himself to one of the most challenging fields of medicine, pain management. I have personally known him for a number of years, and I would like to attest to his reputation of being a tireless, dedicated, knowledgeable, reliable specialist promptly responsive to his patients' needs. For many years Dr. Holden has been an active and valuable member of the local medical community. He is a compassionate, ethical specialist of impeccable integrity who will withstand unfounded allegations and distortions.

Anita finished reading and turned to Sandra.

"Well, what can we learn from these letters? And still... I actually feel kind of proud as if they are written about me too."

"Actually, they are about all of us. How could they handle this place on their own?"

Anita suddenly felt that someone was standing behind her and turned around.

"Oh, Julia, it's you. We are almost done. Read them. You won't regret it. Actually, here is a letter about you." Anita leafed through her pile. "And another one. May I read this one out loud? At least a few lines?"

"All right," Julia was too tired to argue. "Shoot."

I can't say enough about Julia Lander's care. It's the best care any patient can ask for. My back and knee injections helped me immensely. Without them I can't even imagine the pain I would be in.

"Not that I haven't been aware of Gayle's thoughts and feelings," smiled Julia. "But it never hurts to hear them again." Julia winked at Anita.

"Now listen to this." Anita opened the second letter.

If it wasn't for Ms. Lander, I wouldn't be able to take care of my children or even to function. She always finds new ways to help me physically and emotionally. In all my years I've never had any nurse or doctor who has given me as much attention as Julia Lander and Dr. Holden.

Sandra smiled warmly. "Every single word of this statement is true."

Chapter 7

On June 17, a Friday afternoon, about a month after the raid, a lengthy manuscript from the Board of Medicine was delivered to Anthony Minnelli, and by Friday night Ben received a copy of this two-hundred-page report. At the same time, he was notified by the Board of Medicine that he was invited to the board meeting for suspension of his license on Wednesday, June 22, at 10:00 a.m. He was given four days to read this two-hundred-page composition and prepare for the rebuttal.

Actually, he had only two days as on Monday and Tuesday he had a full schedule of patients, and he didn't want to cancel any of their visits. He couldn't let his patients down because it might be their last chance to meet with him as their doctor.

Ben sat on the couch and sank into the board's report. With every page that he read, he was feeling more and more nauseous. After a few hours, he stopped reading. He couldn't take it anymore. He could not comprehend all these lies and distortions.

A medical expert and an investigator had created this document, which was filled with incalculable allegations. Based on the review of thirty patients' charts, the medical expert concluded that none of Dr. Holden's assessments and treatments were correct. He also held Dr. Holden responsible for the death of six of his patients. Four of them died from overdoses of cocaine that he had not prescribed, one died from cancer, and one died from choking on food. Ben could not believe the ignorance of the medical expert and the gravity of his allegations. The report wasn't signed.

The investigator's allegations were based on two undercover agents' reports and interviews of a few of Dr. Holden's patients who had been discharged from his practice for their fraudulent behavior. The investigator's statements were a mixture of fuzzy quotes from anonymous sources and unfounded accusations. It seemed that the investigator's zeal to bury Ben alive had far surpassed his thoroughness.

* * *

On Wednesday morning, June 22, at 9:50 a.m., Ben, dressed in his favorite light gray suit, dutifully arrived for his meeting with the Board of Medicine. Anthony Minnelli, sharply clad as usual, showed up a few minutes later. When he saw Ben, he sent him a warm smile, but Ben could tell that the smile was no more than an awkward camouflage. They exchanged strong handshakes and moved straight to business.

"Things are not looking that good," started Anthony. "Over the past four days I've reviewed the allegations, and I believe that they are pure bullshit. The facts look twisted and misrepresented, and tons of contradictions are obvious. It's crystal clear they are trying their best to topple you. They threw all they could find into this boiling pot to burn you to the bones in hope that quantity will compensate for quality. The bad news is that they haven't given us any time to prepare for a rebuttal. Even for a top-notch expert, it may take at least a few weeks to analyze these thirty charts and come to any conclusions. Pump up your courage and be ready for the worst. One thing you have to promise me right now: no matter what happens, no matter what you are going to hear about your practice and yourself, don't say a word. I've prepared the strongest arguments in your defense, and I'll present them. Will they work? I don't know."

For four long hours, Ben and Anthony sat in the hallway, waiting to be invited to the hearing room. Ben, who hated being idle for more than a minute, continued to fight his growing frustration. Why did they summon him so early when they didn't have any intention to see him at the scheduled time? Four wasted hours! He could have spent them treating his patients.

Finally, they were invited into the hearing room and introduced to eight members of the Medical Board, which was comprised of physicians who were about to decide his fate. Oddly enough, none of these eight physicians specialized in pain management.

Ben and Anthony were offered seats at a small desk in front of the committee. Ms. Sharket and Mr. Beetle, the investigator, were sitting at another desk, right next to theirs.

Chairman Dr. Grave introduced the case and then offered the floor to Ms. Sharket. She stood up and looked at the members of the committee, her eyes livid—a greyhound ready to give chase. She was on a bloodthirsty mission. Her lips were noticeably twitching. Her hands were squeezed into fists. No, a "greyhound" was the wrong metaphor. A bulldog was better.

Over the next twenty minutes, Ben learned more about himself as a physician than he ever knew over his thirty year medical career. He was accused of being a major drug dealer, a murderer, a drug-pusher, and a pill-mill doctor, to name a few. A good number of the adjectives Ms. Sharket used to describe Ben's transgressions were most likely borrowed from paperback fiction and B-rated movies. Ms. Sharket obviously had a soft spot for this sort of entertainment. She repeatedly stressed that Dr. Holden presented a real and immediate threat to the general public. When she proclaimed "real and immediate threat" for the seventh time, Dr. Grave, looking slightly annoyed, informed Ms. Sharket that the committee understood her point.

Ben's memory suddenly flashed back to the methods used by Nazi Propaganda Minister Goebbels, who had proved that no matter how ridiculous some lies and accusations could be, if they were proclaimed repeatedly, most people would buy into them. Thank God, Ben thought, it was 2007, and they did not live in a Nazi state. He cast another glance at the board members and saw that their neutral expressions had become stern and unsympathetic.

Ms. Sharket finally rested her case. Attorney Minnelli was offered a chance to respond. He took about twenty minutes to list Ben's credentials and achievements in his medical practice. He passionately spoke of Dr. Holden's immaculate reputation and didn't forget to bring up the fact that over all the years of his practice not a single complaint about his treatment had been filed with the Medical Board and not a single malpractice claim against him had ever been filed either. The most reputable pain centers in Boston frequently referred their patients to Dr. Holden for his assessments and recommendations for treatment. Anthony also mentioned the fact that Dr. Holden was a frequent attendee of numerous medical conferences and workshops to enhance his knowledge and skills and to stay abreast of innovations in his field. He finished his speech, stating confidently that Dr. Holden in no way presented any threat to his patients.

"In fact," concluded Minnelli. "I wish there were more doctors like Dr. Holden, doctors as knowledgeable, passionate, and caring as he is; doctors who can devotedly treat this grossly undertreated patient population."

Ben looked at the board members, absolutely certain that they were impressed by the speech and shared Mr. Minelli's sentiments. Yet all eight members of the committee looked as if they'd just walked out of a funeral parlor. In dead silence, Dr. Grave asked Ben and Anthony Minnelli to leave the room and wait in the hallway for their decision.

Twenty minutes later, a policeman on guard ushered them back, and Dr. Grave announced the decision of the board: summary suspension of Ben's license.

Ben, dumbfounded, and Anthony, not overly surprised, left the hearing room. The investigator, Mr. Beetle, followed them. Not even trying to conceal his pleasure, Mr. Beetle walked up to Ben and demanded that he immediately surrender his medical license. Another man from the press release department informed them that the *Boston Veritas* planned to publish a piece on his suspension.

Ben felt he needed a breath of fresh air, immediately. They stepped outside.

"The whole procedure..." he stopped and exhaled. "It went so smoothly."

"Exactly," Anthony sneered. "Thoroughly staged and masterly performed."

"Like a perfect murder." Ben was silent for a long moment. "Anthony, let me tell you this—they've miscalculated. They have no idea how troubles affect me. I will not give up."

"Neither will I," said Anthony.

* * *

The news of the suspension was shocking to everyone in Ben's office. They knew that bad news was a possibility, yet each of them secretly believed that such injustice could never happen. The patients who had come to the office that day left subdued and sorrowful.

That night a reporter for Channel 25 announced the news, gloating over each of the allegations without any attempt to analyze them or verify if they were true. The next morning, the *Boston Veritas* joined the media execution squad. The lies of the investigator and distortions of the medical expert were repeated, blackening Dr. Holden's reputation and all but calling for tar and feathers.

* * *

Emma was sitting home, trying her best to concentrate on her writing. She was rereading again and again the last two paragraphs she had written a few days ago, but she didn't understand a word. Not a single line made any sense. Neither did sitting at the computer.

The phone rang, and she rushed to pick it up, and then stopped abruptly. More bad news? No, stop panicking. You can't live in constant fear. You have to answer the phone. It may be something important or, who knows, it may be good news."

"Hi, Emma, it's Michael." Emma heard a familiar voice and gently exhaled. Any phone call from a good friend was good news.

"I'm in New York now on business. How are you doing? How is Ben?"

"Nothing to brag about. Ben's license was suspended three days ago. He can't take patients anymore, but his colleagues are still working at the center. Ben's filed for an appeal. He is quite optimistic. How are you, Michael?"

"I'm all right." He paused. "I'm calling because... Emma, I just read an article that I think you both should read. It was published yesterday in *The New York Times Magazine*. I can e-mail it to you."

"Thank you, Michael. It's very kind of you."

"Oh, you read it first. You may change your mind about me being kind." Emma heard a long, weighty sigh. "But you *must* read it."

* * *

Emma printed out the article, snuggled on the couch, and plunged into the fourteen-page text.

The piece was about an elderly man, a devoted pain management doctor who treated his chronic patients with the utmost care. He gave them trigger-point injections, offered physical therapy, and designed exercise programs. He was able to reduce their pain to the lowest level possible and get better results than most doctors. On occasion, he also prescribed reasonable amounts of opioids to his patients that experienced severe pain.

Now this sixty-three-year-old man was serving a thirty-year sentence in a medium-security federal prison, convicted of drug trafficking. Some of his patients sold their pills, some abused them, and one of his patients died with an excessive level of opioid medication in his bloodstream, which happened to be the same type of medication this doctor had prescribed to him. The doctor was convicted in federal court of one count of conspiracy to distribute controlled substances and eight counts of distribution. The jury also concluded that the patient who died was killed by the drugs that the doctor prescribed. Now the doctor was serving concurrent sentences of twenty years for distribution of drugs and thirty years for dispensing drugs that resulted in his patient's death. His appeals to the U.S. Court of Appeals for the Fourth Circuit and the Supreme Court were denied.

Emma stopped reading. She swallowed hard. What did this doctor do wrong? He spent more time with his patients than most physicians did; he managed to relieve their pain much better than most other specialists, and where was he now? In a medium-security prison. Some of his *patients* sold their medications, some of his *patients* abused them, and now the *doctor* was paying the price! And what a price! Thirty years in prison! Why the doctor? What did *he* do wrong? Trusted his patients? Is it a crime to trust your patients? You can get thirty years behind bars for that?

Emma continued reading the article. It said that one in five adult Americans suffer from chronic pain. A Stanford University survey (2005) found that only fifty percent of people who suffer from chronic pain received sufficient relief. That's why Ben's office was growing so quickly, Emma thought. His center was that rare place where chronic patients *could* get adequate pain relief. And now what will happen to all these suffering people? Will Ben, like this doctor... She stopped herself and sank into the article, wanting to know more.

Every year, Emma read, more and more pain clinics were closed, and fewer and fewer doctors are willing to treat pain. Most doctors in the U.S. are now afraid to prescribe opioids and to treat chronic patients adequately because of fear of persecution. According to DEA records, in the previous year, *seventy one* doctors were arrested for diversion, or what the DEA defined as the leakage of prescription medicine into the illegal drug market. The DEA had opened 735 investigations of doctors. Any of these investigations alone could be enough to put a doctor out of business. Not only doctors were losing their licenses and practices, their homes, offices, and cars were seized, even if no federal criminal charges had been ever filed. Over the last few years, investigations as well as arrests had been rising steadily.

Emma could hear her heart beats like the strokes of an old broken clock, loud and maddening. It's a reputable magazine, isn't it? The author could not make up these facts. So the facts were true! But how could all this be happening in a democratic country! The government actions described in this article were obvious signs of tyranny and despotism. No, it must be some mistake.

A tender touch on the shoulder made Emma turn around. It was Ben. She didn't hear him entering the room. He kissed her gently on the neck.

"What are you reading, darling?" Ben's voice was his usual, tender and cheerful. "Something exciting?"

"I'm glad you are home," she said, pretending she didn't hear the questions.

Ben looked at her face inquisitively and asked quietly, "May I read this, too?"

Emma passed him the printed pages. Ben sat on the couch and immersed himself in the article. He read it silently, without a single interruption, to the very end. For a long ten minutes, he sat silently, deep in thought, while Emma waited patiently for him to say something. He *had* to say something.

"This article reminds me of the historic event we read about recently," he said finally.

"The historic event?" It took her a few seconds to understand. "You mean the notorious 'Doctors' Case' in Soviet Russia?"

"Yes, the 'Doctors' Case'. That witch-hunt during Stalin's regime."

"Another stain on Soviet history," said Emma. "You are right, some facts in *The New York Times Magazine* are not that different. Wrong treatments, conspiracy... Oh, there is one. Execution is substituted by thirty years in prison."

"Still, we can't be intimidated by this. We don't live under Stalin's regime. It looks like something is going wrong in this country, but the law is not abolished here..."

Ben stopped, not knowing what else to say. There must be something... something that would convince him too.

Chapter Eight

Three days later, Ben, Emma, Edward Gould, and Anthony Minnelli were sitting in Ben's office ready to start a strategy meeting. They were waiting for another team member, an invaluable adviser, to join them. Rachel Leigh had flown to Boston to make a presentation at a national pain management conference as well as to meet with Ben's lawyers and discuss the whole situation in person. As she walked in, Emma, who had never seen Rachel before and pictured her to be a middle-aged matron, was surprised to see a youthful woman, sprightly and attractive.

"First of all, we have to find top-notch experts to support the appeal," she began. "We need a medical expert and a pharmacologist, better yet a pharma-toxicologist. I know a few really good ones, nationally recognized experts. We just have to make sure they are available now."

All three lawyers got into a discussion of the strategies, and Rachel's knowledge of the medical issues involved—let alone the legal ones—was more than impressive. She was a save-the-doctor encyclopedia.

"I want to take a tour of your clinic, Ben," Rachel said when the meeting was over. "What do you say?"

"I would be honored." Ben smiled blissfully.

They passed through room after room, Ben introducing Rachel to his coworkers, and Rachel talking to each member of his staff for a few minutes. Her gaze was calm yet penetrating. She studied every single person. She explained to Ben and Emma later on that in almost every legal case similar to Ben's, someone in the office turned out to be either an undercover agent planted by the DEA or someone who agreed to cooperate with the authorities for one reason or another or even volunteered to do that. However, she couldn't spot anyone in Ben's office who raised her suspicion. To her relief, she found out that all the people who worked at the center not only loved their jobs but were very fond of Ben and devoted to him.

Because of his suspended license, Ben couldn't treat patients any longer, but a few who came to see other specialists or for their therapy treatments were quietly sitting in the waiting area, and the moment they learned that the woman on the tour was helping Ben, one after another they streamed to the front desk and begged Sandra to give them permission to tell her their stories. Rachel agreed to talk to a few of them.

The first one was Joe O'Reilly, a tall, brawny young man with a round face and a child-like smile.

"Ma'am, I have no idea what you know about Dr. Holden, but because of his prolotherapy injections and medications, I was able to go back to work, and my life is now as normal as it can be. He is the best doctor I ever met. I'll do anything for him. Just tell me what to do."

"Thank you, Joe," Rachel shook his hand and wished him well. "Who knows, maybe someday we'll need your help."

The moment Joe left, Mitch Forte, another patient who was impatiently awaiting his turn to tell his story, walked in.

"Mitch Forte, Dr. Holden's patient," he introduced himself with a broad smile.

"Rachel Leigh," Rachel smiled back and shook his slim but extremely strong hand.

"Ma'am, I'm forty-four and at least half of my life I've lived in pain. I had my first back surgery when I was only twenty-one. The surgeon promised that with the quick removal of a ruptured disk, within three weeks I would be a brand-new man. Guess what? After that first surgery, I had six more. I had two more disks removed and a spinal fusion with screws and plates at three levels. When this didn't work, the hardware was removed. I was in more pain than ever before, and they said that it was probably my sacroiliac joint that was killing me. They fused it too. What I called pain before was nothing compared to what I suffered after this second fusion. With all the Motrin and Naproxen I was fed, I developed a bleeding ulcer, and my kidneys were slowly failing too."

Mitch continued, "I was thirty-eight by then and couldn't remember the last time I'd made any money or did anything productive. My four years in college looked to me like a cruel joke. Between my surgeries, they also tried a morphine pump, a spinal-cord stimulator, and some other funky stuff, and it all failed. I'd gotten so disgusted with my life that I wanted to kill myself. Then my relative who lived in Boston told me about Dr. Holden. What the heck? I thought. What do I have to lose?"

Mitch Forte paused and took a deep breath.

"Dr. Holden was the first doc ever who looked at me and saw a live human being, not an object for another cut. He took time to explain to me the nature of my pain and the treatment options I had. I knew those seven back surgeries I had were seven too many, and my options were now pretty limited. We decided to try a course of long-lasting opioids to suppress my pain and give me a chance to function. In about six months my medications were adjusted, and not only could I function normally, I could work. For the last five years I've been a happy man"

Rachel, who had to learn a long time ago to keep her emotions in check, could barely do it now.

"Your story is incredible," she said softly. "Someday it might be very helpful."

"Please do something to get him out of this mess," Mitch pleaded. "He is a great doc, and a rare human being. I wish more doctors were like him. If you ever need my testimony, I'll go anywhere. I can't stand Dr. Holden being hurt like that."

"We'll keep that in mind, Mitch. And we'll do our best to get him out of the mess."

Rachel shook his hand, once again surprised by his exceptionally strong handshake.

* * *

The magistrate court appeal was scheduled for late August 2007, so there was not much time to find and hire a pain management specialist and a pharma-toxicologist with experience in the toxicological effects of drugs, especially opioids. Rachel called a nationally known specialist in Chicago, and he agreed to analyze and write a report on the deaths of Ben's patients and to respond to the allegations of the Medical Board expert. To find a good pain management expert was a harder job, and while Rachel Leigh and Ben's defense attorneys were searching for an expert, Ben launched his own preparation for the appeal.

Day and night, he reviewed the thirty medical charts that had been under scrutiny, trying to find errors and glitches in his diagnoses and treatments that could justify the accusations. He couldn't find anything alarming. All his initial diagnoses were confirmed by MRI, CT scans, X-rays, and other pain specialists, and all his treatments and prescribed therapies were working well. His patients were feeling better, could function better, and they were finally living normal lives.

Emma entered the room.

"Ready for lunch?" she asked uncertainly.

"Sure," said Ben, but his preoccupied look told her that he hadn't even heard the question.

"Emma, the more I analyze the files and this man's criticism of my practice, the more I'm coming to the conclusion that his expertise in the field of pain management is close to zero, unless he is intentionally blind. Why did the Medical Board choose this guy to write this baseless report? Why would they want to ruin our practice? Who will benefit from that? There are not many pain clinics left in the country. Why would they want to get rid of another one?"

"Ben, do you remember the article in *The New York Times Magazine*? They..." The phone ring interrupted her in mid-sentence.

Ben reluctantly picked up the receiver. He wasn't in the mood to talk to anyone now.

"Hi, Ben. It's Anthony Minnelli. How are you doing?"

Ben sighed. "I'm good. Thank you, Anthony. Any news?"

"Not just news, amazingly good news! Dr. Clemens, a knowledgeable and respected physician, agreed to analyze and write a report on the thirty charts for our court appeal. There is not much time left, but he said he would do it. Great news, right?"

"Couldn't be better, Anthony. I know him personally. A couple of years ago Julia and I attended one of his presentations. He has an excellent reputation. I'm so glad he agreed."

"Me too, Ben. It wasn't easy to find a good expert to do the job in such a short time. We are lucky. Are you still working on the appeal?"

"I've finished analyzing the charts, and I'm assembling a variety of medical articles that would confirm that my treatments were both reasonable and justified."

"Excellent idea, very helpful for the defense. Please make copies for me too."

Ben hung up and turned to Emma.

"Emma, Anthony found a medical expert for the appeal. I know him. He is a big name in Boston, and a really nice guy. Life is turning bright! Let's go and eat!"

* * *

Three days later, when Ben was in the middle of the article published in the *Pain Management Journal* that supported his prolotherapy treatments, he was interrupted by the ringing of the phone.

"Hi, Ben. Do you have a minute?"

"Sure, Anthony. More good news, I hope?"

"Sorry, Ben. Not a good one. Dr. Clemens won't write the report."

"Why not?"

"He happens to be a member of the Medical Board. So Ms. Sharket told him yesterday that he shouldn't write a medical evaluation of your charts because of a conflict of interest. She said that if he insisted on writing it, he would have to quit the Medical Board."

"Do you mean she's blackmailed him?" Ben asked incredulously.

"In my opinion, she has."

"So what was Dr. Clemens's response?"

"He sent us an apologetic letter. He had to make a tough choice. He is not retired yet."

Ben fell silent, still trying to digest the news.

"I don't blame him," he said finally. "How can a physician, even a reputable one, fight the Medical Board that can get him any minute they want?"

"I don't blame him either. I just can't believe the Medical Board is capable of such an unethical action. This Accalia Sharket..."

Minnelli didn't finish the sentence, but Ben could easily guess what he was about to say. "Listen," he continued, "there are only three weeks left, and we are back to square one." He paused for a long while. "Let me call Rachel Leigh. She may have some ideas."

Two weeks later, Minnelli called back.

"Ben, Rachel found an expert, William McGregory. He is a prominent pain management specialist from the West Coast. He is well known and highly respected across the country. But there is only a week left before the hearing in the magistrate court, and there isn't a chance he can thoroughly analyze the thirty voluminous medical charts and write a report in such a short period of time."

"Well, I'll appreciate even a summary report; whatever he can do in a week."

Dr. McGregory took a close look at the most damaging allegations of the Medical Board reviewer and wrote a detailed response, supported by scientific medical evidence, that refuted every single one of them.

* * *

"Hi, Ben, it's Anthony."

"Hi. Other good news?"

"Well... Ms. Sharket just called. She finally revealed the identity of the physician who reviewed the medical charts of your patients."

"Who is he?"

"A young doctor with only three years of experience in pain management, Sayyid Mustafi. I know some of the doctors who work with him. This fellow treats his patients exclusively with invasive spine procedures. Nothing else."

"Only three years in practice? Why him?"

"A dirty job. Not everyone is thrilled to do it. Yet some can't resist the temptation."

"You mean money?"

"Exactly. This guy's palm must be greased heavily. Besides, a few more of this kind of masterpieces, and he would probably be offered a seat on the Medical Board."

"But at the hearing, he'll have to get on the witness stand, right? Wouldn't he be embarrassed?"

"Actually, that's more news. The Medical Board won't put their investigator or their medical expert on the witness stand at the hearing. They will bring their affidavits instead."

"What about us?"

"If they want to bring affidavits only, we'll do the same. We have plenty of them, including Rachel Leigh's and Dr. McGregory's testimonies. And these two are very impressive. Rachel's has a sixteen-page résumé and a nineteen-page positive analysis of your practice."

"And Dr. McGregory's testimony?"

"There are about a hundred presentations on pain management around the U.S. and abroad and numerous articles in American and foreign medical journals. His conclusions regarding your practice are supported by solid scientific evidence and are remarkably positive."

"Thank you, Anthony. Let's hope the judge will appreciate all of it as much as we do."

* * *

By the morning of the hearing, Ben's attorney had a thick pile of persuasive affidavits and pertinent publications and was hopeful that they would convince the magistrate judge to restore Dr. Holden's medical license. He also prepared a fiery speech as his support. Antony Minnelli was primed for battle.

* * *

On the first day of the hearing, Ben, Emma, and Anthony arrived at the Magistrate Court around 10:00 a.m. Anthony was confident and excited while Ben was a little nervous and Emma was plainly jittery. They came early, and Anthony invited Ben into a small room next to the waiting area to discuss some last-minute questions, leaving Emma alone in the waiting area.

Medical Board Prosecutor Accalia Sharket showed up ten minutes later with a cortege of six young women who appeared to be more than cozy in the magistrate waiting room and were gleefully chirping, ignoring Emma's presence altogether.

Heading to any appointment, Emma never left home without a good book. But the court hearing was a new experience, and she found herself totally unprepared for it. Emma looked around and spotted a small stack of magazines. She picked one and began reading it. She scanned the first two lines of an article and then scanned them again. The result of the second attempt was exactly the same as the first one. Not only had she failed to comprehend the content, she couldn't read a word of it. The letters were slurring in line-long strings, and no matter how hard she tried, she couldn't separate them. Yet she continued staring at the page, her head light and empty. When will the judge arrive? she thought. And why are these women so cheerful and so loud? Do they expect a comedy show?

Ben and Anthony were now striding toward her, but Anthony's glance was directed at someone else. Emma turned around and saw a tall, middle-aged woman in a black robe entering the hallway. The woman greeted everyone with a nod and moved to the courtroom assigned for the hearing. She was the magistrate judge. Everyone in the waiting area followed her.

Anthony took a first-row seat right in front of the judge. Ben and Emma settled two rows behind him. Ms. Sharket took another first-row seat at some distance from Anthony while the remaining entourage occupied seats right behind her. Emma secretly examined the judge's face. The woman looked somber and respectable.

The hearing started with an opening statement by the prosecutor. Accalia Sharket took a sharp breath and launched into reading several pages from a thick pile placed in front of her. She delivered her speech with enthusiasm and swagger. "In multiple cases," "on numerous occasions," and "a danger to the public" were flying from her mouth in fervent competition. Ms. Sharket's passionate narration portrayed Ben as a totally incompetent physician and a brutal murderer of his helpless victims.

Ben, who had heard this presentation before at the Medical Board meeting, was listening to it with rueful amusement, and some revulsion too. Yet for Emma, Sharket's presentation was a first-time event. Was this monster's speech for real, or was she having the wildest nightmare?

Emma was sitting very close to Ben but was afraid to look at him. She instinctively slid her hand into his, as she often did while they were listening to music at a concert or watching a movie in a theater. Yet this time his grip felt different. Emma gave him a side glance, noting his stony gaze. She wished he looked angry instead.

The judge was listening carefully, her facial expression deadpan, although her chin twitched slightly with every negative phrase.

Finally Accalia Sharket finished her oratory. The silence in the room was thick and heavy. Emma sighed with relief and turned to Ben, her eyes and her whole body mute and tense.

"I've heard this before, at the Medical Board meeting," Ben said in a low voice and smiled sadly. "She didn't change a word. Quite impressive, huh?"

"No, it's repulsive." Emma looked at the judge. "What does she think about it? Does she believe it?"

The judge didn't make any remarks and seemed a little uptight. She turned to Anthony Minnelli and asked him to start the rebuttal.

Neither Ben nor Emma had ever heard Minnelli speak, but Ben had complete faith in his lawyer. Emma was edgy. Is Anthony well prepared?

Is he an eloquent speaker? How can anyone beat this colossal mound of accusations?

Minnelli's rebuttal speech turned out to be beyond reproach. The attorney described Ben's comprehensive pain center and the impressive results of his various treatments, and at the same time he described all of the Medical Board's transgressions, including their blackmailing of Ben's medical expert and their refusal to acknowledge the support letters from Ben's and Julia's patients and his fellow physicians. The judge seemed to pay close attention to his every word. She even looked sympathetic. Good sign, Ben thought. A truly good sign.

When Anthony finished his speech, the judge announced that the rest of the hearing would take place the next morning and headed to the exit. Anthony walked toward Ben and Emma, his glance an anxious question, "How was it?"

"Excellent job, Anthony. Thank you." Ben shook Anthony's hand.

"You were eloquent and ..." Emma paused for the right word, "utterly convincing."

"Thank you," Anthony lit up. "I thought it wasn't that bad, especially with so little time to prepare. You know I slept three hours last night. I hope it didn't show."

"No, not a bit," Ben smiled for the first time that day.

* * *

The minute they came home, Emma rushed to the bookcase and retrieved a big white envelope she had placed there the day before. It was a new pile of support letters that she had brought home from Ben's office. She was too tired last night to read them, but now she was eager to do it. All these board accusations were still revolving in her mind. This filthy residue had to be scraped away immediately.

The letter on the top was from a young physician she knew quite well. When he was a medical student, he had a four-week rotation at Ben's office. This young doctor was very capable but wasn't sure yet which area of medicine to pursue. A few weeks of Ben's contagious enthusiasm, and he made up his mind.

I met Dr. Ben Holden and observed his practice as a medical student on my four-week Physical Medicine and Rehabilitation rotation six years ago. He truly impressed me with his warm and bright

personality, and his enthusiasm and passion for the field of rehabilitation and pain medicine.

Dr. Holden's excellent communication skills enabled him to quickly establish rapport with his patients. He would spend a great deal of time learning about their concerns, previous and current treatments, fully evaluating them, and explaining the goal and rationale of his treatment plan. Hard working and professional, he was devoted to making a difference in the lives of his patients, enabling them to become more functional at work and at home.

Dr. Holden impressed me with his clinical knowledge and constant striving for improvement by participating in continued medical education. He would frequently bring the latest clinical research and review articles with him to the office to familiarize himself with most recent developments in the field of rehabilitation and pain management. He was a great teacher who inspired me to pursue residency training in Physical Medicine and Rehabilitation.

A great kid, Emma thought and grinned. No, Larry wasn't a kid anymore. He had a full-time job at one of the best local hospitals, he was married, and in a few months would be a father.

That tough afternoon of six years ago gradually surfaced in her memory. Ben had a ski accident and ended up with extensive shoulder surgery, performed at the hospital where his private office was at that time. Emma had spent the whole day in the hospital, waiting for the surgery to be over, and for Ben to recover from the anesthesia. By 8:00 p.m. she felt exhausted and hungry, yet she was unwilling to leave the waiting room even for a few minutes; she didn't want to miss the moment Ben woke up. She was falling asleep herself when someone touched her shoulder.

Emma looked up and saw a handsome young face with a friendly smile.

"You must be Mrs. Holden," said the young man. "Did I guess right?"

"Yes, you guessed right." She was puzzled.

"Sorry, I didn't introduce myself. I'm Larry. Last year, when I was a resident, I had a rotation with your husband. He was my attending physician. I don't know if he has ever mentioned me..."

"Yes, he has. He likes you. He said you would make a fine doctor. Nice to meet you, Larry."

"Nice to meet you too. Mr. Holden had surgery today, right?" Emma nodded. "How is he?"

"He is still in the recovery room. I'm waiting for him to wake up and say 'Hello, Emma. Why do you look so pale? Still recovering?'"

"Yeah, that's him. He loves joking and always with a straight face." Larry smiled. "Do you mind if I stop by later?"

"No, not at all. It's getting rather lonely here."

Twenty minutes later Larry came back.

"There wasn't much food left in the cafeteria, but I thought this would cheer you up a bit." Larry handed her a small carton and a plastic spoon. "I didn't know which flavor you like, but this was the only one they had. No tortuous multiple choices."

"Ice cream!" Emma felt like a little child surprised by a thoughtful parent.

"Thank you, Larry. Ice cream is exactly what I need. How did you guess?"

"If I may, it was written all over your face."

Emma laughed and uncovered the cup.

Fifteen minutes later, the nurse announced, "Your husband is awake and ready to go home. Please follow me."

"Mrs. Holden," Larry stood up. "If you don't mind, I'll help you to take Dr. Holden home. Trust me, it won't be that easy."

"Thank you, Larry. Let me look at him first and see how he is doing."

Emma walked into the recovery room, moved straight to Ben's bed, and almost gasped. His face was ghostly pale. He didn't look himself and didn't seem awake at all.

"Ben," Emma said softly. "How are you?"

Ben opened his eyes and moved his lips. Nothing but a feeble grunt.

"Ben, they want you to go home. Are you able to do that?"

Ben nodded faintly. He was heavily medicated and almost out of it. Emma shook her head. "Why do the hospital people want to discharge him when he is still so weak? Is it normal to release patients in such helpless condition?" Emma heaved a heavy sigh. Well, she knew that if he had a choice, Ben would rather go home and let her take care of him.

"Ben, Larry is here. He offered his help to take you home."

Ben nodded slowly.

* * *

If not for Larry, their trip home would have been a disaster. Ben was drowsy, weak, and looked like he had a horrible hangover. Larry put Ben in the car, took him out when they arrived home, and then helped Ben climb to the second floor straight to their bedroom. How could anyone forget that? Then he came to visit Ben the next day. And the day after. A noble kid. No, a noble young man.

Chapter Nine

Neither Ben nor Emma expected that the next day in the Magistrate Court would turn out to be so intense. The court session was nerve-wracking, every second of it.

The Medical Board emissary, Ms. Sharket, presented an affidavit from their medical expert, and Judge Muir accepted it. Now it was Minnelli's turn. The first affidavit he offered was written and signed by Ben's medical expert, Dr. McGregory. Minnelli started with Dr. McGregory's impressive credentials, including twenty years of experience in pain management, about a hundred presentations around the country and abroad, and scores of articles in respectable medical journals.

"Your Honor," Minnelli continued, "Dr. McGregory wasn't able to go through all thirty medical charts in question due to the lack of time, which we believe was caused by the Medical Board's blackmailing our original medical expert, Dr. Clemens." At the word 'blackmailing' Sharket turned red and furiously exhaled while the judge kept a poker face.

"Dr. McGregory had only a week to write his review," Minnelli continued, ignoring Ms. Sharket's breathing exercise, "yet he thoroughly examined the allegations by the Medical Board reviewer and wrote a detailed, scientifically based rebuttal to each one of them."

He barely finished the sentence when Accalia Sharket jumped from her seat and yelled, "This affidavit is not admissible! It's based on *nothing*!"

Exactly, thought Ben. What better way to define your expert's report? Nothing. What a shame he couldn't say it out loud.

Ben squeezed Emma's hand. Emma stared at the judge and silently pleaded, "Your Honor, please accept it!"

There was a long pause.

"Accepted," said the judge.

The minute Minnelli announced the next affidavit from Ben's assistant, nurse practitioner Julia Lander, Ms. Sharket jumped from her seat again.

"Not admissible!" she shouted. "She lost her license! She doesn't work anymore!"

Emma felt like jumping from her chair herself. She leaned forward as far as she could and, looking straight at the judge, whispered, "This is not true. She has her license. She is working."

Judge Muir couldn't hear her whisper, but it looked like she read her lips. She turned to Minnelli. "Are Nurse Lander's treatments mentioned in these thirty charts?"

"Yes, Your Honor," answered Minnelli.

"Her affidavit is accepted."

Minnelli held a thick pile of affidavits. They were from Dr. Holden's patients. The moment he presented them, Ms. Sharket sprang up and yelled again, "Not admissible."

This time Judge Muir ruled in her favor.

The next pile of affidavits was from Ben's fellow physicians, and Minnelli was certain that their unanimous support would make an exceptionally favorable impression on the judge. But for some inexplicable reason, Judge Muir didn't accept any of these affidavits either.

The next affidavit was from Ben's secretary and administrative assistant, Sandra. She had been working with Ben for about four years, and in her affidavit stated that she had never observed any conduct by Dr. Holden that, in her judgment, could in any way present an immediate or serious threat to the public. She wrote:

> ***Dr. Holden always had his patients' best interests at heart. Now while his license is suspended, I have the difficult task of informing the patients that they no longer can receive his treatments. Most of these patients can't find any other place to treat their pain, for there are very few specialists in the area who prescribe opioid medications or practice this challenging specialty. Some of the patients broke down in tears when they heard this news. I am frightened about what may happen to these people.***

Minnelli mentioned only a few points from Sandra's affidavit, and Judge Muir accepted it without hesitation. Ben and Emma sighed with relief.

The next affidavit was written and signed by Rachel Leigh. She was one of the most respected legal experts in the field of pain medicine, and her nineteen-page report along with her sixteen-page curriculum vitae was of vital importance. Her affidavit clearly stated that Dr. Holden always acted within the parameters of the law and medical ethics and had never posed any threat to the public. Ben leaned forward. Will the judge rule in his favor?

When Minnelli announced that his next affidavit was from Rachel Leigh, Ms. Sharket leaped from her seat.

"Not admissible!" she hollered. "I know Rachel Leigh! She is not qualified! She is a lawyer!"

Judge Muir reflected for a split second. "So are you," she replied calmly. "And so am I."

She paused. The silence in the room was unendurable.

"I accept it," she said.

Accalia Sharket glared furiously at Ben.

"I would love to put Leigh on the witness stand!" she blurted out.

So would I, Ben thought. He turned to Emma and caught her quick smile. He could bet she'd just visualized the same scene.

Minnelli stood up and handed Judge Muir their last affidavit. It was Emma's one-page letter, where she gave a brief account of Ben's persistent efforts to become a physician and to develop his pain management center. In the last lines of the letter, she pleaded with the judge to return Ben's license for the sake of Dr. Holden's patients, who were desperately hoping that their doctor would come back.

Judge Muir scanned the letter, looked at Emma apologetically, and began patiently explaining to her why she couldn't accept it. Emma was trying her best to grasp what the judge was saying, but she could barely hear her words. In any case, it didn't matter to her why exactly the judge refused to admit her letter; Minnelli had warned her earlier that there was hardly a chance the judge would accept it. What mattered to her at the moment was the judge's gentle, sympathetic tone and her effort to give her an explanation. It was a good sign. It meant the judge wanted to be objective. That was all that mattered.

The second day of the hearing turned out to be good. Judge Muir accepted the most important affidavits, put Sharket in her place when she objected to the Rachel Leigh affidavit, and even showed sympathy to Emma. The accusations by the reviewer for the Medical Board, who had no real expertise in comprehensive pain management, were completely refuted by the highly respected medical expert for the defense. Most likely, it wouldn't take the judge long to come to a sound decision. Things seemed to be looking up at last.

"I will inform both parties of my decision in four weeks at the latest," Judge Muir announced, and then left the courtroom.

* * *

The judge's decision arrived at Minnelli's office four weeks later. Minnelli called Ben and asked if he could stop by his place to discuss it. He showed up twenty minutes later and, without a word, handed Ben a two-page letter from the judge.

Ben and Emma sat down and silently scanned the pages.

"Is it possible that the judge hasn't read the documents we submitted?" Emma asked when she'd finished reading. "Is it possible?"

"I doubt it," Minnelli shrugged.

"So what does this rejection letter mean?" Emma swallowed hard. "Does it mean she ignored everything that Dr. McGregory, Rachel Leigh, and all the others wrote in their affidavits? She didn't even mention a single fact from any of these documents. Her decision is based exclusively on the opinion of the reviewer for the Medical Board! He's a physician who has only been in practice for three years. Why did he even agree to be an expert in such a complex matter? How could the judge reject Ben's appeal without considering both sides?"

"Politics," Minnelli sighed wistfully.

"Politics?!" exploded Emma. "Ruining a person's life based on groundless allegations is called politics? What kind of ..."

"Emma." Ben took her hand. "It's not the end. We'll fight it."

"We'll fight Judge Muir?" asked Emma.

Ben didn't answer.

"We thought she was a fair judge," he said finally, "but maybe ruling in my favor could somehow affect her career." He paused. "Anyway, I don't think it's over. She said in her report that I could have another hearing on the merits. Anthony, what does it mean in plain English?"

"It's a hearing with testimonies."

"You see? It's not a done deal. We still have a chance. I'm not giving up."

Chapter Ten

"So you are upset and still puzzled?" asked Edward Gould, Ben's criminal lawyer.

Ben and Emma were sitting in his office, where he had invited them to talk about the administrative judge's startling decision.

"To put your mind at rest, if such a thing is possible under the circumstances, let's start with the first issue," said Gould. "By now you should be aware of the fact that the government is conducting a criminal investigation of your office, right?"

"They mentioned something like that at the raid," Ben uttered uncertainly. "But they kept saying that there were no charges pressed, so I didn't pay much attention to this. I've never done anything criminal anyway."

"I believe you, but why do you think Rachel Leigh referred you to me?"

Ben didn't know what to say. He was so caught up in all these odd events of the past few months that he had never pondered the question.

"You think this pending criminal investigation could have affected the judge's decision?" Ben asked finally.

"I'm almost sure it did."

"Listen, if they haven't pressed any charges, it means they have no evidence that I am responsible for any wrongdoing. Then why would the judge base her ruling on something so groundless?"

"Politics, I guess."

"Oh, Anthony said the same thing. So politics can justify anything?"

"It should not. But it does."

Gould fell silent.

"In any case," he continued, "that was issue number one. Now let's move to the second issue. Do you remember the *Best Insurance Ever* incident you'd mentioned a while ago? It could play a certain role too. Actually, I would like to hear more about this story. It happened in 2005, right?"

"June 2005, to be exact."

"So what happened?"

"Two years ago, in June, I received an official notification from the *Best Insurance Ever* company informing me that my decade-long provider's privileges with them were about to be terminated and that I had thirty days to appeal."

"On what grounds?" asked Minnelli.

"Their expert had reviewed the medical records of twenty of my patients and concluded that *Best Insurance Ever* wasn't satisfied with the quality of my professional services. They sent me a thick folder with the medical expert's evaluation of the treatments that I had given to my patients. His report stated that my treatments were ineffective and below the accepted standards of care."

"What did you think of the report?"

"Either I was losing my mind or the person who had composed the review had lost his. These twenty patients had been under my care for a few years. All of them had documented evidence of severe chronic pain of different origins, and the results of their treatments were good."

"Can you be more specific?" asked Gould.

"Sure. While under my care, nine of them were able to keep their strenuous jobs. Four more managed to return to work after many years of disability. And the others, because of our treatments, were also able to maintain an active lifestyle."

"Who was their expert? Some experienced pain physician?"

"I have no idea. The name on the report was deleted and the signature was unreadable. Any credentials or hospitals' affiliations of this ghost-expert were nowhere to be found."

"Do you think this reviewer was intentionally blind or just ignorant?"

"I'm not certain. Could it be that he or she was a hired gun?"

"It's possible. Have you ever had any problems with *Best Insurance Ever* before that incident?"

"Never. Not a single problem with them or any other health insurance company and no complaints against my practice were ever filed with the Medical Board. I thought it was a mistake that would be straightened out in no time. These allegations were so easy to disprove. The results of our treatments spoke for themselves. After all, according to the Medical Board guidelines, the success of any treatment of chronic pain is measured by its ultimate outcome and the steady functional improvement of the patient. In other words, if under the doctor's treatment, the pain that patients suffer is less and they are able to function better than before, their treatments are successful. As simple as that."

"Did you file an appeal?" Minnelli asked with concern.

"I did, and I hired a lawyer, who'd dealt with insurance companies before, to help me with the appeal. He found a pain management expert, a medical director of a well-known pain clinic with a ten-page résumé and impressive credentials, to review the medical charts of my patients. His evaluation of our practice and the treatments of those twenty patients was extremely positive. At the same time, my manager asked these patients to write letters that would describe their experience with our practice and the results of their treatments and send them to the *Best Insurance Ever* administrators."

"Did they agree to do it?"

"None of them had to be asked twice. Their letters moved me to tears. I thought as soon as the insurance company received these letters, they would realize their decision was an unfortunate mistake, and they would fix it right away. Maybe even apologize."

"But it didn't happen?"

"No, nothing of the kind."

"How did the appeal go?"

"It was quite a show." Ben sighed. "Faultlessly orchestrated. The twelve members of the hearing committee included a pulmonologist, psychiatrist, pediatrician, social worker, ophthalmologist, and only one physician from our field, a young anesthesiologist. And even he had no experience treating chronic pain patients."

Ben recollected the faces of the committee members. Not a single pair of friendly or even curious eyes; everyone appeared to be hostile, suspicious, or simply indifferent. And the questions they asked indicated that they didn't have a clue about how chronic pain should be treated.

That meeting lasted over two hours. Ben had given honest professional answers to all the questions that the committee asked, no matter how provocative or foolish they were. Yet the meeting didn't appear to be the productive discussion Ben had hoped for; instead, it rapidly turned into a malicious interrogation.

At the beginning of the meeting, Ben wondered why these people were invited to serve on this committee. It wasn't their area of expertise. Their knowledge and experience in treating pain was sparse at best. Ben admired how diligently each member of the committee, like an experienced orchestra player, delivered his or her comments under the watchful eye and the stern baton of their "conductor," Dr. Russell. During the whole meeting, Dr. Russell was mostly silent, but his grim presence left no doubt about who was in charge. His brusque remarks and throat clearings could hardly be accidental, and none of them seemed to pass unnoticed.

Ben's attorney wasn't even given a chance to defend his client.

"So how did the hearing conclude?" asked Gould.

"The chairman said that they would scrupulously analyze the facts within the next few days, and the committee's decision would be delivered to me by the end of the week."

"And?" Minnelli leaned forward anxiously.

"On the very next morning a yellow manila envelope from *Best Insurance Ever* landed on my desk. It was a brief letter, stating, '*The Best Insurance Ever Company notifies Dr. Holden that his providing privileges are terminated with no option to appeal.*' The letter was dated March 6, 2006, the exact date of the hearing."

"It seemed that your fate was sealed even before these doctors showed up for that meeting." Gould shook his head incredulously. "So much for 'scrupulous analysis of the facts.'"

"You know, Edward, right after the hearing I made up my mind that no matter what their verdict was, it wouldn't change my philosophy of treating people in pain. It wouldn't affect my spirit or my professional conduct. Their privileges could be gone, but our practice was not."

Gould listened to the story with concern. It puzzled and worried him at the same time.

"Ben, who was your typical patient?" There was a disturbing tone to his question. "Can you describe a few of them for me? The diagnoses, treatments, and medications you prescribed."

"Typical?" Ben said. "Lev Tolstoy wrote in *Anna Karenina* that '*All happy families look similar, while each unhappy family is unhappy in its own way.*' That's how it goes for my pain patients. Let me give you a couple of examples from this past week. Both of them are rather typical."

"At the age of thirty-five, after his second unsuccessful back surgery about a year ago, a new patient comes to me totally crippled but still dreaming of getting back to his job. Pain commonly wakes him up a few times a night, and he gets up in the morning drowsy and tired. His right leg is always numb. How can he get back to his construction job when he can't even play ball with his six-year-old son and most likely never will?"

"Give me another one," asked Gould.

"Okay. A twenty-six-year-old woman, once a competitive athlete, had injured her back in a ski accident three years ago. She was promised a quick fix with a lumbar fusion. The procedure not only failed to relieve her sciatica but made her back pain and spasms much worse. Six months later, in her junior year, she had to quit college because one of her professors didn't like the fact that she had to stand up and stretch every fifteen minutes in his class. She was also discouraged from taking painkillers on campus and mocked by her former team members for being unfit. She is now obese, clinically depressed, and completely lost. Her chances to have a family are next to zero, and at this point, there's not much anyone can say or do to inspire her."

"She is young," said Gould. "I'm sure she will eventually get better."

"The sober reality is," said Ben, "that the vast majority of *any* chronic medical conditions are rarely cured and chronic pain is not an exception. By definition, pain is considered chronic if it lasts longer than twelve weeks, some say four to six months. This poor young woman had already been in pain for a few years, so her condition was definitely chronic. No matter how hard we tried, at best we could only hope to control the pain and spasms and to slow down the progress of her disability. That's all. No one could expect that she would ever completely recover. Unfortunately, for the overwhelming number of chronically ill people, including chronic pain patients, full recovery is usually not achievable."

"Why not?"

"Because the damage to their organs and tissues is beyond repair. All we are trying to accomplish is to alleviate their suffering and improve their functioning, which, by the way, is not an easy task either."

"Then what are these people's choices? What can they expect from a pain doctor like you?"

"Well, let me tell you about Steve M., one of my favorites. He is actually on the *Best Insurance Ever* list too," Ben started. "This man was thirty-nine when he injured his back and received his first spinal surgery fifteen years ago. He had to apply for total disability, and it was granted to him on his first application. Over the next few years he had six more surgeries. During the last one, the doctor inserted long titanium rods to stabilize his vertebra and prevent them from moving. As a result of this neurosurgical procedure, he became half-paralyzed. He was able to ambulate with two plastic ankle braces and had to walk with crutches."

"How long has he been your patient?" Gould interrupted.

"He came to my office four years ago after his pain doctor had retired. The man is fifty-four now and significantly obese. For the past three years, he has been working part time as a consultant for the company that he had once owned, the company he had to leave after his first surgery many years ago. I treat him with back injections of the natural medication Sarapin, a moderate amount of time-released opioids twice a day, and a small dosage of antidepressants. He is now totally satisfied with his pain control. Also, to his credit, Steve has finally come to terms with the fact that his pain will never go away completely and that he has to adjust to his permanent physical limitations. This understanding is critically important for any chronic pain patient."

"Did he have a choice not to?"

"Of course he did. Many pain patients believe they are victims; some of them have a good reason for that belief, and as a result, they give up on their hopes. Others accept the harsh reality of their condition and direct their efforts toward moving on with their lives. They try to make the best of the dire conditions they have to endure. My goal is to help them to choose this latter option, and it's the most challenging and probably the most rewarding part of our work."

"Ben, this man you just mentioned, was he one of your most difficult patients?"

"Not really," replied Ben. "But it's extremely rare that a patient would go back to work after so many years of disability. I'm very proud of him. Actually, I'm proud of most of my patients," Ben smiled broadly.

But Gould didn't return his smile. Something still bothered him.

"Let me ask you another question. You prescribe opioids, right? Are these medications safe?"

"An excellent question!" Ben smiled even broader. "And widely debated all over the country, especially lately. Are you aware that for the last four thousand years, maybe longer, in all parts of the world, narcotic medications or opioids have been used effectively to treat pain? They have an unmatched record of safety among all known prescribed medications, old or modern. If physicians use them *skillfully and judicially*, they can usually achieve adequate pain control for a broad spectrum of the most severe painful conditions, from traumatic surgical interventions to incurable cancers. Of course—and this is critically important—patients must act responsibly and not deviate from their doctors' orders. As an old saying goes, 'The same remedy may be a lifesaver or a poison; the difference is just a matter of dosage.' This is more than true for opioids."

"What about their side effects and other related problems? There should be some, right?"

"Like any other medications, opioids are not side effect free. In the early stage of the treatment, they may cause sedation, constipation, and occasional decreases of testosterone levels in men, but most of these side effects are usually manageable. A small percentage of pain patients can eventually become addicted, but this is a different story altogether. As I just said, when used the right way, both short and long term, opioids are much safer than most other groups of medications, including many over-the-counter drugs. Their benefits for appropriate medical conditions are practically unmatched and clearly override their risks."

"But some people also abuse them, don't they?" Gould frowned.

"Yes, some people abuse them, and it is a serious problem. Yet the majority of pain patients are honest and sensible people, and they need these drugs for their health conditions. They take their medications responsibly and have neither the intentions nor the need to do anything illegal."

"What about the impact of these drugs on the patient's life in the long run?" Gould asked cautiously. "My seventy-six-year-old aunt was started on Aleve for her achy back, and three months later she was diagnosed with an ulcer that she had never had before. Her kidneys started to fail too."

"Here is another advantage of opioids for people like your aunt. One can keep taking them for many years, and there would be no damage to the patient's liver, kidney, or bone marrow. No bleeding ulcer either, opioids just don't do that. Unlike Aleve, Motrin, and other similar drugs, they neither cause blood pressure to rise nor do they trigger fluid retention."

"Why is that important? Sorry, I'm quite ignorant about this stuff."

"Well, most people don't know much about the risks of these seemingly benign over-the-counter medications either. If you take them for a few days, they are quite safe and helpful. But taking them for longer periods of time is rather dangerous. In fact, that's how some people end up with a stroke or a heart attack."

"So for certain medical conditions opioids could be the safest alternative?"

"Exactly. For severe and lasting pain, especially if it's resistant to other treatments, they are the best option."

"Too bad my aunt's doctor disregarded this option." Gould took a long pause. "Fascinating group of medications," he said, yet he still looked concerned.

"Something still bothers you, right?" Ben asked.

Gould hesitated for a moment. "Could this *Best Insurance Ever* fuss be caused by the fact that you'd been prescribing opioids?"

"Why? The medications I've prescribed are all legitimate and FDA approved. As I just explained, for the right conditions, they are both safe and effective. They are also cost-efficient. They help patients to avoid risky, expensive, and, frankly, not always necessary surgeries. And, as I just said, these other over-the-counter remedies are not effective for severe, long-lasting pain, not to mention their general toxic effects. Many of our chronic pain patients, who over the years had tried other treatments, believe that opioids are the only medicine that keeps them both active and comfortable."

Gould gave Ben another worried look.

"Doctor, I'm not an expert in the field, but I heard that some physicians were in serious trouble simply because they'd prescribed opioids to their patients."

"I've read about that too, and I think it's outrageous. It will hurt so many suffering people." Ben paused. "But answering your question regarding *Best Insurance Ever,* I think that even if the company's administrators didn't understand the great necessity and usefulness of opioids, they should have realized that doctors who prescribe opioids were saving them millions of dollars that they would have spent on needless operations and costly procedures. Besides, if not for opioids, most pain patients wouldn't be able to work and pay their taxes. They would become a burden on our society, not to mention the emotional impact of living in pain."

"All right, Doctor. Your point is well taken." Gould couldn't help smiling. "So, despite the loss of your privileges with this insurance company, your practice was booming, right?"

"Well, we lost a few clients, but most *Best Insurance Ever* patients stayed. And we had a large flow of new patients, so we had to expand our services."

"Still, didn't it occur to you that the *Best Insurance Ever* attack was part of some bigger scheme? You had no idea that the government was investigating you?"

"I had no clue. We did everything by the book. Why would I even suspect that?" Ben paused. "Do you think the government might have pressed *Best Insurance Ever* into these actions? You think it could have been part of their ambush?"

"Well, let's look at the facts. You'd never had any problems with this insurance company. Not a single complaint against you had ever been filed with the Board of Medicine. You hadn't had a single malpractice case. The report of their medical expert wasn't signed, and you didn't even know who'd been its mysterious author. A respectable pain management specialist had concluded that your practice had met the standards of the State Medical Board, and the results of your treatments were its proof. On top of that, members of the committee who were assigned to evaluate your practice and to handle your appeal, with one exception, had never worked in the field of pain medicine and had very little knowledge of it. Moreover, their decision seemed to be made even before the hearing. Don't all these facts look odd to you, to put it mildly?"

Ben pondered the question.

"Yes, they seem odd." Ben frowned. "So you think it was the government's first blow?"

"Most likely it was. It didn't crush you, though. You didn't even pay much attention to it. You were too busy working, right?" Ben nodded in agreement. "And then there was this article in the local newspaper."

"Right. Some patient wrote a letter about our center to the local newspaper, and they sent a journalist and a photographer to investigate. Those two were curious about our practice, and also rather skeptical. After they talked to me and my staff, took a tour of the office, spent a couple of hours interviewing our patients, they left quite positive about their visit."

"Was their article favorable?"

"Yes, it was. And then we were featured on ABC."

"So, despite this *Best Insurance Ever* ordeal, the center continued to prosper? Things were looking up?" asked Gould.

"Right. We've become a comprehensive pain management clinic with diverse specialists who used a variety of nonsurgical treatments with patients."

"And then three weeks after the ABC production, seven agencies raided your office?"

Ben nodded.

"Smells Kafka." Gould fell silent. "Well, let's get back to the issue at hand. The judge has denied your appeal based on the *affidavits,* but she is willing to give you a chance to present your case in court with medical experts and witnesses." Gould's gaze turned grave. "Speaking frankly, I'm not sure this hearing makes any sense now. You are under criminal investigation, and I don't think the judge will be inclined to restore your medical license before these criminal allegations are resolved. But Anthony disagrees with me. So we can give it a shot. Do you want to go to the hearing and try to get your license back or do you want to voluntarily surrender it? It's your choice, Ben."

If Gould had known Ben Holden a little longer, he wouldn't have asked him that question.

Ben turned to Emma.

"Emma, what do you think?"

Emma was in no hurry to answer.

"I think," she said pensively, "that I know what your answer will be. And that will be my answer too." She gently squeezed Ben's hand and turned away.

"Edward, we are going to the hearing." Ben smiled and then noticed Emma's anguished look. "Don't you worry, honey, it will be fun."

Chapter Eleven

The morning after Ben had received Judge's Muir's rejection of his appeal, Sandra greeted the staff at the office briefly and somberly. Without a word, she handed Ben a copy of the *Boston Veritas* and pointed to an article, once again on the front page. The article featured a terrible photo of Dr. Holden and a string of accusations about his medical practice. However, to present some objectivity, the reporter squeezed into the last two lines a few words from her interviews of Dr. Holden's patients, praising him for his professionalism and good care.

Ben looked at Sandra, who was impatiently waiting for his reaction, her blazing eyes all but igniting the newspaper.

"Well, that's how journalists gain their fame," Ben said sadly. "But I'm not going to sue them, Sandra. I don't have either time or money for this; I'll be preparing for the appeal, which hopefully will turn out to be a much more productive step. Let this smear campaign be on the conscience of the instigators and this unscrupulous reporter. Please do not brood over this. It's not worth it."

A few days later, another article that mentioned Ben's name was published in a different local newspaper. A prominent Boston lawyer wrote about people who were accused of breaking laws that did not exist and of groundless accusations that destroy doctors' reputations and ruin their lives. The article was a breath of fresh air. The author was the first one who really grasped the essence of the matter, which was the criminalization of medicine, a tendency that could ruin its very core. Ben remembered the articles in *The New York Times* and *The New York Times Magazine* where reporters wrote about scores of doctors who had been arrested and prosecuted as well as hundreds of physicians who were under criminal investigation.

Ben sighed, "Who knows? There could be a few bad apples even among physicians, but how was it possible that hundreds of doctors were criminals? Does the government have the legal right or competence to decide how physicians should treat their patients? Physicians spend years studying in medical schools and going through internships and residency programs, and then during years of practice they accumulate more and more experience in treating people. Should they be patronized, judged, and persecuted by government officials, whose medical knowledge or medical experiences are nonexistent?"

There were no answers to Ben's burning questions. And there was another question that demanded his immediate attention. Could their pain management center survive now that his license had been suspended and he had to stop taking patients? He was the one who used to see new patients, refer them to other specialists in the office, and prescribe different therapies that they implemented at the center. It was he who recommended exercise classes, ALPHA-wave treatments, and other modalities. And it was he who paid the physicians, instructors, technicians, and secretaries, to say nothing of paying rent for the premises. The government had seized all the money from his business account on the day of the raid. And now when he couldn't make a penny, where would he get the funds to support his practice?

Ben took a deep breath and walked to the door next to his office. He had no choice. He had to tell his associates, in the most tactful way possible, that they had to start looking for new jobs.

This distressing task appeared to be a little less painful than he expected because most of his colleagues didn't believe they would be leaving the center for good. They all seemed sure he would win the appeal, and they promised to come back as soon as the ordeal was over.

* * *

Even though most of his coworkers were forced to look for other jobs, Ben didn't give up on his patients. He couldn't accept the fact that such an effective practice had to die because of an incomprehensible attack on it. He asked Dr. White to keep working at the center, and he asked Sandra to stay and take care of all the paperwork and the phone calls that were constantly coming through the unusually quiet waiting room of the office. Most of the patients were still certain that Dr. Holden would be back at his practice in a week or two.

These incessant, often frantic phone calls from patients were now the most upsetting part of Sandra's workday. Some patients sobbed and described their unbearable suffering, some sounded utterly lost, complaining to Sandra that they couldn't find another physician who would help them the way Dr. Holden had, and all of them begged her to call them as soon as the doctor had returned to work. Every single afternoon, Sandra left the office with an excruciating headache and a tight knot in her stomach, the last drop of energy drained from her body, longing for some good news, any good news.

Ben continued to come to the office every morning, which was quite painful for him without work to do, but he couldn't leave Dr. White and Sandra alone. He walked around the office, performing small, almost useless tasks and talking to Dr. White and Sandra, which was probably the main reason he showed up in the first place. But he couldn't stay long. He had to prepare for the appeal. Actually, even before that, he had to take care of another rather pressing issue.

* * *

For the past three months, it was getting harder and harder for him to walk even a few yards, and climbing stairs became a project. The recent events had afforded Ben little time to find out what was physically wrong with him. As a typical doctor, he hated to see himself as a patient and was looking for any excuse to delay it. Yet his limping was getting troublesome. He couldn't procrastinate any longer.

Now with some time on his hands, Ben finally scheduled an appointment with his primary care physician. The doctor examined Ben and, visibly alarmed, sent him for an urgent MRI. The results were both unexpected and frightening. The test showed a large tumor inside his spinal cord. Was it benign or malignant? It wasn't clear. Ben called the neurosurgeon who had operated on a few of his patients, and the very next day the doctor invited him for a visit.

"Ben, you need surgery as soon as possible," the neurosurgeon started without further ado. "You saw your MRI and already know that, right? Sorry, I can't perform this type of intervention myself. I simply don't have skills to do this particular surgery. The location of this tumor is too unique, and it takes a specially trained surgical team to remove it. But I know an excellent neurosurgeon at Mass General Hospital who does it. His name is Dr. Laurence Berg. I'll call him right away."

* * *

On June 24, 2007, three days after Dr. Holden received a notice of his license suspension, Julia Lander, the nurse practitioner, was notified by the Board of Nursing about the complaint filed by the DEA and the Department of Health and Human Services. The State Board of Nursing couldn't disregard the complaint, and in order to assess her practice, they hired a nurse practitioner gynecologist and a nurse practitioner ophthalmologist. Their reports were attached to the letter. Julia was offered an opportunity to respond to their allegations.

Neither gynecologist nor ophthalmologist had ever worked in the pain management field, and their ignorance of the subject was appalling. It didn't take Julia much effort to refute their allegations in her detailed, scientifically based response to the board.

Three weeks later, she received another letter from the Board of Nursing, this time with their preliminary decision, which was suspension of her registered nurse license and permanent revocation of her nurse practitioner license. Julia was stupefied. How could they do that? Haven't they read her response to all the allegations?

She called Peter O'Neil, her attorney; after the raid on the office, she had no choice but to hire a legal counselor.

"Peter, they suspended my registered nurse license, and they revoked my nurse practitioner license. I don't understand it. I thought my response to their accusations was—"

"Julia, calm down please. I saw their letter. I agree that it's appalling. But believe me, their decision has nothing to do with your rebuttal, let alone the quality of your work. The complaint to the board did not come from your patients. It came from the DEA and the Department of Health and Human Services. The board had to demonstrate its vigilance and had to take action. They had no choice. It's politics."

"Politics?"

"Yes, it's politics. And it's disgraceful!" Peter O'Neil pondered for a long while. "Let me think about what I can do. I'll call you back."

He called a week later.

"Julia, I've finally reached the board's attorney. She sounded reasonable. I explained to her your situation and asked if we could have a meeting with the chairman of the board or someone else who has the authority to reconsider the board's decision."

"What did she say?"

"She said she'd never heard anyone ever having this kind of a meeting with the head of the board, but she agreed to talk to him."

O'Neil called Julia two days later.

"Julia, we are on! The vice-chairman of the Nursing Board will meet with us in a few weeks. He is very busy. His assistant will schedule it and give me a call."

"Thank you, Peter. This is... I don't know what to say..."

"You don't have to say anything. Let's meet next Thursday at 3:00 p.m. to get ready."

* * *

The neurosurgeon called Dr. Berg right away, as he'd promised, and the next day Ben was scheduled to see him.

"Dr. Holden, I saw your MRI." Dr. Berg shot Ben a concerned look. "The exact nature of the growth in your spinal cord is not clear. The only way to find it out is to remove the lump, but I can tell you right away it's not going to be easy." He paused. "Let's first discuss the details of your surgery and the prognosis for recovery."

They talked about the specifics of the surgery, yet Dr. Berg was rather diplomatic regarding his prognosis. At the conclusion of the visit, he said, "Normally my operation time slots are completely filled for at least two or three months in advance, but I'll talk to my head nurse, and we'll see what we can do." He shook Ben's hand and shot him another worried look.

Dr. Berg's secretary called Ben an hour later.

"Dr. Holden, your luck is beyond belief. We just had a cancellation. Your surgery is scheduled three days from now, October 17. We expect you for a pre-op tomorrow at 2:00 p.m."

* * *

Ben's operation lasted eight hours. When it was over, the surgeon invited Emma to a small room in the waiting area. He looked a little pale but content.

"Mrs. Holden, the operation went well. Your husband's tumor looks benign, and we hope the biopsy will confirm that. But the tumor was huge and quite damaging to his nerves."

"Thank you, doctor. We are grateful for your promptness and certainly for the successful surgery."

Dr. Berg shook his head sadly. "If your husband had delayed his visit to his primary care doctor a little longer," he paused, and the half-minute pause seemed to last an eternity, "he would have ended up paraplegic. He was lucky he didn't."

Emma shuddered. If only Dr. Berg knew why Ben had gone to see his physician in the first place. She could bet Ben had done it only because he had some free time now. And he had that free time only because his license had been suspended. Was it a blessing in disguise? Quite a disguise.

* * *

Julia's meeting with the Nursing Board vice-chairman turned out to be even more astounding than the board's decision to agree to it. The vice-chairman asked Julia several questions about her job, all of them to the point and presented in the most affable manner. At the end of the meeting, he said that he had learned more about pain management from her than he had ever learned before. He even expressed his regret about the troubles Julia was going through.

"We can offer to reinstate your nurse practitioner's license, but in order to get it back, you'll have to take college courses and complete another internship. Can you afford that?" he asked with some hesitation.

"No, I can't." Julia shook her head.

"We can also reinstate your registered nurse license, with a year of probation and supervision. Is that something you would be interested in?" The vice-chairman smiled gently.

"I would be happy to get my license back. I have to work. I want to work."

The vice-chairman cracked a wider smile.

"So let's do it. Ms. Tobin, my assistant, will take care of the paperwork." He paused and gave another friendly smile. "Good luck, Ms. Lander."

Julia left the meeting room feeling slightly dizzy. This vice-chairman was understanding, courteous, and treated her with respect. After the past dreadful months, she'd gotten her first break. There was a chance now she could get her life back. Not entirely, but still...

* * *

Two days after the surgery, Ben, still in pain, talked his attending physician into discharging him from the hospital.

"Dr. Berg, there is not much you can do for me here. Believe me, I'll be better off at home," he insisted. Doctor Berg reluctantly agreed, although his standard protocol after this type of surgery was to keep patients in the hospital for at least five or six days.

Unfortunately, Ben's recovery at home turned out to be an ordeal of its own. Ben was lying motionless in bed day after day, agonizing pain piercing his body with every single movement. He couldn't sit at all—forget about walking—he couldn't get to the shower, he couldn't do anything. He was utterly helpless and utterly miserable. Emma was taking care of him the best way she could. Ben taught her a few nursing tricks, and she became his live-in nurse. She cooked his favorite foods and entertained him with funny stories, but none of her gentle ministrations seemed to be effective in speeding up his recovery. Ben's boundless and effervescent energy was gone. His lively nature seemed to be buried so deep inside his body, struggling with the pain, that no one could even glimpse it anymore.

One day Emma had a few minutes of respite while Ben was asleep. She was sitting in the kitchen, deep in thought. What could she do to change his mood? Was there a stand-up comedy course online that she could take? No, it would be useless, she didn't have a chance. Ben could have made a good comedian, he was a natural, but his condition and his mood were far from humorous now. Still, she couldn't show him any sign of concern. Just smiles, jokes, and funny movies, anything that had a chance to work.

The phone rang.

"Hi, Emma. It's Mitchell. Remember me?"

"Of course, Mitchell. How are you? How is Brenda?"

"We both are fine."

"And the baby?"

"A spoiled brat."

"And who has spoiled him?"

Mitchell laughed. He was Ben's colleague who hand worked with him for years.

"How is Ben doing? I heard he had major surgery."

"Holding up... Actually, not very well. He is in pain. His entire body hurts terribly."

"Listen, do you remember that special device that helps muscles to relax and reduces pain? An electric muscle stimulator. I'll bring it to your place. It may do the trick."

Two hours later the doorbell rang, and when Emma opened the door, a familiar face with a disarming smile moved through the threshold to give her a kiss.

"House calls are not popular nowadays, though they used to be a good tradition," he winked and followed Emma into the bedroom, a silver-gray box in his hand. In a minute his instructions for the use of an electrical muscle stimulator along with various doctor's jokes filled the room.

To operate the muscle stimulator was not rocket science. But in order for Emma to attach the sticky pads of the stimulator to Ben's middle back, he had to turn on his side, and for Ben that was a torment. Still he asked Emma for another treatment and then another. The next morning he was feeling a little better. In a few days he could finally get up by himself and shuffle step-by-step to the bathroom.

Two days later another phone call.

"Hi, Emma. It's Ellen Feldman. You may not know me. I worked with Dr. Holden a while ago. I've heard he had surgery. How is he?"

"Still struggling, but a little better than last week. Thank you, Ellen, for asking."

"Emma, I'm a massage therapist. And if you can believe my clients, a damn good one."

"I believe it. I've actually heard how good you are from a few of them," said Emma.

"Listen, I'll get straight to the point. I want to come to your place and give Ben a good, no, a super-good massage. Free of charge. I hope you don't think I give free massages every day, do you? I only do that on exceptionally rare occasions. First, I'm very busy and second, I don't want to spoil my clients. But Ben has a special place in my heart."

"In mine too," Emma couldn't help smiling. This woman's talk was Prozac to her ears.

"He is a fine physician and a noble man." She paused. "Is tomorrow night at six o'clock good?"

"Tomorrow night is fine. Better than fine."

The next day at six o'clock, a slender, dark-eyed, good-looking woman in her early forties arrived at their home, greeted Emma and Ben, asked a few professional questions, and in a few minutes performed the most skillful massage Emma had ever witnessed.

During the next several weeks, Ellen Feldman, whom Ben and Emma had nicknamed "a ball of fire," gave Ben a few more massages until Ben was finally walking. Still limping, but walking nevertheless—a silver lining in the thunderous cloud that was hovering over their lives.

Chapter Twelve

The criminal investigation, like Damocles' sword, was still hanging over Ben's head, and there were no signs of any closure to the case. Cagney, the prosecutor assigned to the criminal investigation of Ben's practice, told Edward Gould in June that he would be ready to discuss the case with him in late August. Now six months later, in February 2008, Cagney told Gould that he had nothing to say but would be glad to hear whatever Mr. Gould was willing to tell him. The only thing Edward Gould could tell him was that he had talked to Dr. Holden's staff, a number of physicians who knew him, and many of his patients, and he learned from them that Dr. Holden was a talented, experienced, and caring physician. None of those people could believe that Dr. Holden had ever been involved in any criminal activity. But these facts were apparently of no interest to Mr. Cagney.

A few active people in the community wrote a petition in support of Dr. Holden, demanding the return of his license, and within a week or so, more than five hundred people signed it, but it wasn't sent anywhere, for no one knew where exactly it should be sent. Still, some journalist learned about the petition and wrote an article about Dr. Holden's troubles and the local community's support for him. One of Dr. Holden's patients went to his congressman and begged him to help his favorite doctor; the congressman listened courteously to the man's plea but did nothing.

* * *

As if to prove the old saying that when it rains it pours, one night Ben, walking down the stairs, fell and hurt his shoulder badly. The MRI confirmed Ben's own suspicion about a torn rotator cuff. He was facing another surgery. A few days later, Ben experienced a painful flare-up of glaucoma, and he almost lost vision in his left eye. Three months later, he was diagnosed with another tumor, this time on his kidney. His blood pressure was also out of control.

Ben never complained and always had a humorous answer to his friends' questions about his health, yet it was clear that the events of the past few months took a toll on him. Still, any day he felt at least some surge of energy, he worked on the appeal.

Anthony Minnelli took the lead, and he and Ben planned to get together to discuss the rebuttal. Minnelli also asked Dr. McGregory and a renowned pharma-toxicologist from Chicago, Dr. Richardson, to evaluate Ben's medical practice and to write their responses to the allegations of the Medical Board's experts, especially in relation to the potentially inappropriate use of opioids.

Minnelli called Ben the day after he received their reviews.

"Ben, I just finished reading Dr. McGregory and Dr. Richardson's full reports. Both are exceptionally favorable. They speak highly of your treatments, and they are impressed by the results."

"What about the accusations of the Medical Board reviewer?"

"They both asserted that he'd distorted most of the facts, and they rebutted all his allegations."

"Glad to hear that. Thank you for the good news, Anthony."

* * *

The tumor on Ben's kidney was slowly enlarging, and the surgeon was debating whether to remove it or wait a little longer. The surgery was rather dangerous, and, considering Ben's other health issues, the doctor wasn't eager to rush into it. The back pain that continued to bother him and his poorly controlled blood pressure slowed down Ben's preparation for the appeal.

One afternoon, Ben was napping on the couch in the living room when he was awakened by Minnelli's phone call.

"Hi, Ben. It's me, Anthony." Minnelli paused. "More news of a different flavor."

"Judging by your tone, it's not butter pecan or rum raisin."

"Not even close. In their investigation, the Board of Medicine is using the materials received from the U.S. Attorney's Office."

"What kind of materials?"

"The ones they've collected for their criminal investigation."

"Is that a surprise?"

"No, it's not a surprise, but we need to have these materials for the hearing on the merits. In order to defend you, we need to see everything the board has."

"Will the Medical Board give them to you?"

"We can't ask them directly. We filed a motion to Judge Muir, requesting disclosure of these materials." He fell silent. "And the motion was denied."

"Anthony, how could the judge deny such a reasonable request?"

Minnelli didn't answer. "And we have another problem," he sighed.

"With the Medical Board?"

"No, with Judge Muir. We told her about your health problems and asked to postpone the hearing due to your health conditions. She denied this request as well. Ben, do you hear me?"

"I do."

"Ben, I'll talk to Gould tonight and will call you tomorrow. I hope you'll feel better."

* * *

The next morning, Ben was lying in bed reading a book that was meant to distract him from the pain and worrisome thoughts that had been bothering him lately. The last Grisham book was no help. Will he have enough energy to do well on the witness stand? Do they really have a chance to win the appeal? Isn't it ironic that after the raid and the assault of the Medical Board on his practice he is now suffering from pain, just like his former patients? And not only pain, but he was suffering from relentless fatigue, unbeatable insomnia, and even dark moods that had never visited him before. Was this irony? Or the inevitable result of the assault?

No, he had to stop these fruitless ruminations. They were like worthless trinkets that clutter your room and distract you from doing your work. He would start exercising more to regain his strength. They would win the appeal. He would get back to practicing medicine. He owed it to himself and to his patients. His patients alone were worth the fight.

The phone rang, and Ben, with some effort, reached for the receiver.

"Hi, Ben. It's Anthony. Bad timing? Did I wake you up?"

"Oh, no, Anthony, you didn't. I have been up since... Well, it doesn't matter. Any good news to add some spice to my life?"

There was a long pause.

"Ben, Edward and I have discussed the current situation, and we both think..." Anthony's voice was fading out. "We are both convinced that we have no chance to win the appeal. In cases like yours, a judge can find the slightest excuse to make a decision in favor of the Medical Board. And this judge... She's denied our motion to receive the documents crucial to our defense, she's refused to postpone the hearing because of your health issues, and she is most likely prejudiced..."

"Anthony, are you saying that all our work on the appeal and the medical experts' reports, all of this is shot to hell?"

"Ben, Edward and I see very clearly now that there is no real chance... The truth is you'll spend a fortune on this hearing, and you'll gain nothing."

Ben felt numb. Not a single thought was in his head. Say something. Anthony is waiting for your answer.

"So what should I do now?" Ben said finally, his voice unusually hoarse and low-pitched.

"You have to surrender your license."

"Surrender my license?" Ben felt blood rushing to his face. "I put my heart and soul into my practice! And now I have to voluntarily give up my profession?"

"Ben, listen..."

Ben was about to explode. Years of studies, countless tests and exams, scores of conferences, and equipment purchased to improve his treatments. All of this would go down the drain? What about his patients who were desperate and longing for him to come back? What would happen to them?

These crushing thoughts flooded his mind, but in an instant they were all gone, as if his brain was drained to the last drop. How could he fight the Medical Board? Hadn't the last few months taught him anything? He and his patients versus the *government*? David versus Goliath? David probably had a much better chance.

"Ben, listen, you'll have to sign an application to surrender the license."

"Sounds really tempting."

"But your application," Anthony continued patiently, "will be accompanied by our letter where we'll explain why you have to do it. You do it *not* because you consider your actions wrong. You do it because you have no choice. You have been forced into it. I'll show you the letter; it's already drafted. Believe me, we are not giving up on you. We just have to save our energy and money for the bigger battle."

"The bigger battle? What battle?"

"Your criminal case."

"Anthony, I've never done anything criminal in my whole life! How can they charge me with something I haven't done?"

Anthony sighed heavily.

"What can I say, Ben. It's a tough question even for a defense lawyer."

* * *

The moment Ben hung up, Emma walked into the room to check on him.

"Birds outside are chirping like crazy—" she started and stopped.

Still clenching the receiver, Ben was lying flat in bed, staring at the ceiling.

"Anthony called," he said, answering her silent question. "He and Edward are certain that we have no chance to win the appeal. They say I'll have to surrender my license. I have no choice."

Emma felt her gut clench. Her mind inadvertently rushed to the days when Ben was doing everything possible and impossible to become a medical doctor. He studied for countless exams from dawn till midnight, and during breaks he was looking for a job to supplement their meager income. But in those dire days of recession, he couldn't find any. Emma was lucky to get a teaching position, but her modest salary barely covered their rent and utilities, and every evening she babysat their neighbors' kids to earn a little more. Still, some nights they went to bed hungry. Then Ben finally found a part-time job delivering pizza, and they felt like the happiest people on earth. Even though this night job on top of the endless hours of studies took a toll on his health, Ben never regretted his efforts. When he opened his comprehensive pain management center, he knew that all of his hard work had finally paid off. Now the government had cornered him and was forcing him to give up the passion of his life.

Emma frantically searched for words of comfort or any reason to come to terms with this vicious blow. She could find none.

* * *

The next day Ben signed the application, and Minnelli mailed it to the Board of Medicine and to Judge Muir along with the letter, which read:

Now comes the respondent, Benjamin Holden, M.D., in the above-captioned matter and respectfully provides notice to this Honorable Court and to counsel for the Board of Registration in Medicine of his voluntary resignation. A copy of the respondent's letter of voluntary resignation is attached hereto as Exhibit A.

As grounds therefore, the respondent respectfully states that, given (1) the ongoing criminal investigation of him by the United States Attorney's Office, (2) the procedural facts and circumstances surrounding this disciplinary proceeding, and (3) his present medical condition, the respondent cannot effectively and properly defend himself against the above administrative prosecution by the board. The respondent's voluntary resignation is the result of the extraordinary position in which he has been placed; it is in no way an acknowledgment of wrongdoing or culpability.

That the respondent is the subject of an active and ongoing investigation by the United States Attorney's Office for alleged federal crimes is readily apparent from the pleadings in this case. As such, there is significant investigative material and information to which the respondent has no access and about which he knows nothing. Without such material and information, the respondent is unable to properly prepare an adequate defense and to properly confront and cross-examine witnesses at any hearing on the merits of the board's allegations. As importantly, the respondent's fundamental Fifth Amendment right to remain silent will be impacted at any administrative hearing. Moreover, as reflected by the medical records attached hereto as Exhibit B, the respondent, who is 57 years old, has suffered and continues to suffer from various ongoing medical issues.

In short, despite the rights and protections traditionally afforded by the Fifth, Sixth, and Fourteenth Amendments to the United States Constitution and Article XII of the Massachusetts Declaration of Rights, the respondent is nonetheless faced with the Hobson's choice of defending his license to practice medicine in these administrative proceedings or defending his personal liberty in any potential criminal proceeding. Absent a stay of these administrative proceedings (which request has been denied), he cannot effectively, professionally, or medically do both. Accordingly, the respondent respectfully submits the attached letter of voluntary resignation.

When they came back home, Ben had to lie down; his blood pressure had gone through the roof. Emma brought him a double dose of his medication and sat down next to him. His facial expression was an open book: he didn't want to talk. And what exactly could they discuss? His license was gone as well as his career as a physician. He would never be able to practice again, he would never be given a chance to find out what was wrong with his patients, he would never be able to alleviate their pain, he would never be asked for medical advice, and he would never watch people getting better because of his treatments.

Emma sat still, tormenting questions eating at her mind. Why has all this happened to Ben? How could it happen to a doctor who was so passionate about his work and so devoted to his patients? Could all these troubles be caused by his success? But hadn't his success been achieved because of his passion for medicine and devotion to his patients?

A long time ago, Emma had read a poem called "The Squares." She couldn't remember the poet's name or the exact verses of the poem. However, she still remembered the disheartening message. People live in invisible squares, and as long as they stay within the borders of these squares, they are more or less safe, but the moment they step outside the borders, they are in danger. They might even end up looking at the iron-bar squares of the windows in a prison cell. Yet she also remembered that the author of the poem lived in a totalitarian regime. Are we heading in the same direction? Emma wondered. Do we too have to stay within the borders of our invisible squares? Does success lead to vulnerability? Does it create desire for destruction? In a democratic country it shouldn't be the case. A grave, horrible mistake had been made by some incompetent people, but sooner or later other competent and considerate people might look into the matter, and this hideous error would be corrected. *But how soon and at what price?*

The phone rang, and Emma reluctantly picked it up.

"Emma? It's Tina. Listen, I have a stupendous idea!" Her best friend sounded excited.

"You do? What is it?" Emma heaved a soulful sigh.

"Your wedding anniversary is a few days away, and we, your close friends, want to celebrate it."

"On your own?" Emma couldn't help smiling.

"No, with you, guys."

"Tina, it's not a very good time—"

"It's a perfect time! Believe me." Tina was speaking fast, not giving Emma a chance to interrupt or object. "First off, it never hurts to celebrate, and secondly, we are dying to hear Ben's next version of how you guys met and got married. Remember, two years ago, when we celebrated it at your home? I laughed so much my belly hurt. Let's do it!"

Emma smiled at her own memories of that blissful evening.

"Maybe you are right. Maybe it's just what we need now. Close friends and funny stories." She reflected for a moment longer. "Let's do it."

* * *

Ben talked to Dr. White and Sandra and explained to them that his hope for returning to his work was gone with the Medical Board's decision. Now he had no option but to officially close his practice while Dr. White and Sandra had no choice but to look for a new job.

From the day Ben stopped working, debts were piling up. The money from his business account had been forfeited to the government right after the raid. Ben's attorneys sent a few requests to return the money, but despite the fact that no criminal charges were presented, the request was denied. Still, Ben had been paying his rent and Sandra's salary until the day he surrendered his license, draining his personal savings. He had also been paying for the leased therapeutic machines in the hope he would use them again once his practice was restored. Now he knew this day would never come. He had to return the equipment, pay the cancellation fees, and terminate his seven-year-long lease.

Ben had already returned the computers and the costly custom-made program for electronic recordkeeping to the vendor. However, the company demanded $65,000 for God knows what, and Emma had to hire another attorney to settle with the vendor. Their savings were melting like snow on a warm spring afternoon. When all their savings were gone, they borrowed money from the bank to pay the settlements with leasing companies and the attorneys' fees. At this point, they were totally broke and had no idea where else they could get money.

Ben was lying on the couch, gloomy thoughts swarming into his tired mind, when he suddenly realized that Emma was standing right next to him, and she was telling him something. He registered the upset tone of her voice but couldn't focus on a single word she was saying. He forced himself to concentrate.

"Ben, are you listening to me? I know it's something you wouldn't want to hear, but I have to say it. We don't have money to pay our mortgage any longer."

Ben shot Emma a frustrated look but didn't answer. What could he do about that at this point?

"Ben, we have to sell our house. And we have to do it fast."

"It won't take long, I guess. It's a pretty nice house."

"Yes, it is," Emma said quietly. "I know you love it. We both love it. But we have no choice."

"Well, as you said, let's do it fast," he gave her a wounded look. "Like... an amputation."

"Ben, one more thing we have to discuss."

"As pleasant as selling our house or even more exciting?"

"Much more important."

"I'm all ears."

"Ben, when your office was raided by all those agencies a year ago, we were stunned, and we thought it was just a nightmare that would be gone the moment we woke up. Now we know it *is* a nightmare, but there is no chance we can wake up and live the life we used to live. Not in the foreseeable future anyway."

"I know."

"We *have* to accept this new life. We have no choice. But we won't play by *their* rules. Whatever is going to happen, we will not feel sorry for ourselves, and we will not let these villains crush us."

"Amen," Ben smiled and kissed Emma on the cheek.

* * *

When the dust had more or less settled, Ben could finally see their present situation more clearly. Emma would be busy with selling their house and dealing with the creditors while the most urgent issue on his hands was vacating the office premises.

Because he had surrendered his license and his practice was closed, Ben notified his landlord that he wouldn't be able to rent his place any longer. The landlord wasn't happy about that, but he still had Ben's security deposit, a five-month payment. In any case, no matter how distressing it was, Ben had to clear out his office premises promptly; the landlord was looking for a new tenant, and his patience was running thin.

Every morning Ben arrived at this silent, empty place, once called his practice, and spent hours rummaging through the patients files'. The files that had been inactive for seven years or more due to the Medical Board guidelines could be destroyed. The rest of the files had to be kept for another seven years.

Ben was slowly going through the charts. The faces of his patients flashed through his mind as well as their sore backs, knees, shoulders. Ben opened the next file. The chart was of his favorite aunt, Sonia. Ben sighed mournfully. It had been more than eight years since Sonia had passed away.

When he was a medical student and lived far away from his family, Sonia, a schoolteacher, often invited him to dinners, and Ben had never refused her invitations—she was a marvelous cook. Firm and punctual, this woman always knew what was right and what was not, and none of her relatives dared to argue with her, except for Ben. The moment Aunt Sonia got upset, he would crack a joke, and her displeasure would evaporate at once. Ben closed the chart and sighed again. He didn't *have* to keep this one, but he didn't have the heart to destroy it either.

* * *

To speed up the process, Ben had to buy two powerful shredders at the local Staples and was spending hours getting rid of the inactive files. As soon as the shredders were full, Ben would fill a large garbage bag with the shredded waste along with other trash still left in the office, load the bag in his car, and drive to the nearest dumpster to dispose of it. He never expected that this tedious, tiring task could lead to some exciting developments.

Ben's office was the front building in a small business park with four other similar office buildings next to his. In the back there was a gigantic commercial dumpster shared by the neighboring offices. This industrial- size dumpster was strategically positioned in the very far corner of the parking lot so that the tenants and their vehicles could have easy access to it.

For the past few days, Ben had developed a rather close relationship with the dumpster, for he had to visit the place as many times a day as humanly possible to deposit all the remaining office trash to the welcoming belly of the giant. After all, dumpsters expected to be fed.

On that particular morning, Ben's customary visit with the dumpster was suddenly interrupted. He'd just driven his car to the dumpster, which at this early hour was almost empty, when something unusual caught his eye. Typically, this parking lot was empty as all the nearby buildings had underground garages. Most employees and clients preferred to park there, but not this time. A few nondescript sedans were parked along the perimeter of the lot.

The moment Ben opened the door of his car, as if by a silent signal, the other car doors opened too. From the womb of a Ford sedan, a thin, middle-aged woman clad in a dark gray suit swiftly emerged from the driver's side and crossed the lot in assertive strides, straight to Ben. When she was about ten feet away, she proudly flashed her brass.

"This dumpster is secured!" she declared.

Ben cast her an inquisitive look. He had no idea what deep meaning was hidden in the "secured dumpster" and why it should be secured in the first place. Was it a crime scene?

"You are Dr. Holden, aren't you?" The woman continued with the precision typical to someone used to incontestable obedience. Her complexion and raspy voice betrayed many years of heavy smoking, probably drinking, too.

"Yes, I am Dr. Holden. And could you please introduce yourself?"

"Detective McBride," the woman said dryly. She gave Ben a probing look. "What are you doing next to this dumpster?"

"Trying to get rid of the garbage from my office," Ben replied calmly. "I thought that's what dumpsters are for. Was I wrong?"

"Sir, I need to see what is in your garbage bags." It wasn't a request. It was a military order.

"No problem, officer," Ben awarded the detective with the most welcoming smile.

When the abrasive detective moved toward his car, he could finally reflect on what was going on. He could think of only two reasons for this absurdity. Either employees of the surrounding buildings noticed his frequent trips to the dumpster, got concerned, and reported them to police or he was followed. The latter seemed to be the case. The authorities probably hoped to finally discover proof of his criminal activity, and now they jumped at the opportunity to catch him in action. He was trying to get rid of all the incriminating evidence. What else could it be? Let's nail the bastard!

These thoughts amused him, and at the same time they infuriated him. All right, he'd play along. He had nothing to hide and nothing to lose.

"Officer, may I ask you what exactly you are looking for? Maybe I can help you to find it?" Ben offered politely.

He opened the trunk and placed the first box with garbage on the ground.

"We want to make sure that nothing illegal is going on here. We received a few complaints lately."

"Complaints?"

"Yes, there were complaints." The detective looked away.

"Complaints about what?" Ben insisted. "Does using a public dumpster constitute a violation of the city ordinance?"

"Just complaints." Ben's insatiable curiosity obviously annoyed her.

A uniformed police officer, who until that moment was patiently waiting next to another unmarked cruiser, decisively walked to the dumpster and bravely jumped inside.

This fellow is lucky if he doesn't sprain his ankle, flashed in Ben's mind. The man reappeared with the box that Ben had thrown away the day before, and fervently plunged into the investigation of its content. Outdated medical books and journals, scraps of paper, and broken pencils were neatly positioned on the ground and then carefully examined. "Damn it! Nothing illegal!" was written all over his face.

"Would you also like to take a look at the content of the boxes in my trunk?" Ben was becoming more and more entertained by the whole scene.

The officer nodded and rushed to Ben's car.

He won't be happy with the results of his search, Ben mused, but at least he might feel his "noble" mission was accomplished. Maybe after that I'll be allowed to go to my office and accomplish *my* noble task.

His thoughts were interrupted by rapidly approaching sirens and flashing blue lights. He must have underestimated the scale of the operation. Evidently, the troops were in need of reinforcements. This time a marked police car zoomed straight to the dumpster and parked behind

Ben's vehicle, blocking a possible route of escape, just in case this hard-core felon would stupidly resolve to flee. Now the whole crew was going through the contents of the remaining boxes and the large garbage bags they had dragged one by one from his trunk.

Ben had heard that the government's resources were big, but had no idea they were that big. It looked like there was nothing left for these public servants to accomplish. All major crimes were solved. Narcotics were not smuggled through the borders any longer, the drug warehouses and pharmacies had not been robbed, and schoolchildren were not seduced by drug dealers either. Now it was the doctors' turn.

Ben's reflections were once again interrupted, this time by a victorious shriek.

"Look at this!" A young plum-cheeked officer was holding a small plastic container, moving his triumphant glance from one of his superior officers to another. Even from a distance, Ben instantly recognized a bottle of multivitamins, most likely left by one of his employees. He moved closer and took another look at the bottle. Its label was half-torn, but it was just an empty bottle, a piece of recyclable trash.

"Look, look!" The young officer handed the bottle proudly to Detective McBride.

She carefully examined the bottle and ordered it to be filed as evidence.

"Are you going to arrest me for this?" Ben asked calmly, feeling anger stirring inside him every minute. The show didn't entertain him anymore.

"Arrest you? No, not at the moment," Detective McBride admitted with overt disappointment.

"Then, with your kind permission, I would like to get back to my work. Have a nice day." Without waiting for official approval, Ben turned around, got into his car, and drove away.

Chapter Thirteen

Monday morning Ben arrived at the office earlier than usual. His working plan for the day was to finish shredding documents and concentrate on the next task, packing "active" files into boxes to make them ready for storage. According to his estimate, eighty to ninety boxes might be needed to store the files. Where would he store them? They were selling their house, and he had no idea if they would have any space for all these boxes. The landlord expected him to clear the premises in the next few days, so the boxes had to be removed from the office without delay. Should he rent a large storage space? How much would it cost to store the files for another seven years? Emma was trying to save every penny now. She would be devastated by this new expense.

Deep in thought, Ben parked his car and was crossing the parking lot when he saw a tall African American man casually leaning on the hood of a blue Ford sedan. He was chatting with a young woman. Ben recognized both of them right away. They were agents who had invaded and trashed his office last May. Why were they here when there was nothing left to trash? Anyway, he'd try his best to be courteous. They were just foot soldiers, nothing more.

Ben headed to the Ford.

"Hello." He gave a friendly smile. "How can I help you?"

"The DA's office wants another thirty files to investigate," the man explained, skipping greeting formalities.

"Do you have a warrant?" Ben asked politely.

"No, we don't," the man said. "But we expect it any minute."

"As soon as you get it, you are welcome to come in and take the files." Ben walked into the building's lobby, opened his office, and locked the door behind him.

Two hours later, passing by the front desk, Ben glanced through the glass partition separating his office from the lobby and spotted a small crowd of agents behind his locked door. The agents were engaged in an animated conversation. A tall, beady-eyed man was definitely in charge of the pack. He was another familiar face. On the day of the raid, the man was among the intruders and was more obnoxious than the rest of them. His face and manners reminded Ben of a coyote.

All of a sudden, Ben felt uneasy. He reached for his cell phone and dialed his home number.

"Emma, listen, two DEA agents showed up this morning. They wanted thirty more files but didn't have a warrant. They said it was coming. Now there are five more of them, and I'm getting rather uncomfortable. My cell's reception is lousy here, so can you call Gould?"

"Sure. I'll call you back."

The sight of this unfriendly-looking group, congregating right behind the door, was disturbing. Besides, Ben hated uncertainty. He unlocked the door and walked into the lobby.

"Gentlemen, please step inside. You can wait for the warrant in our waiting area. Because you've showed up without a formal invitation, could you please introduce yourselves?" Ben asked politely.

The agents, except for Coyote, introduced themselves, shook Ben's hand, and some of them even offered him their business cards.

"And what is your name, sir?" Ben turned to Coyote and looked him straight in the eye. "My name is Joe," the man replied dryly and turned away, obviously implying that this "criminal" wasn't worth his attention, let alone his respect.

"Joe? And your last name...?" insisted Ben.

"O'Brien," Coyote mumbled with escalating irritation, his eyes blazing with contempt.

The other agents seemed to be slightly embarrassed by his behavior, but none of them said a word. At this moment the entry door opened and a lanky middle-aged man walked in. Although he was in civilian dress, Ben guessed he was another agent.

"Is this gentleman with you?" he asked.

"Yes, he is," replied one of the agents, a stocky man with a mustache.

"Please, come in, sir. Feel free to join our company." Ben offered an affable smile and held the door open. He wasn't nervous any longer, just amused.

"Don't pay any attention to him," snapped Joe O'Brien. "He's an asshole."

"Excuse me," Ben stared him down. "What did you say?"

"Nothing," muttered O'Brien.

"I clearly heard the word 'asshole,'" Ben said sternly.

"I was talking to him," O'Brien pointed to the newcomer.

"Oh, is this the way you greet each other?" Ben paused and cast Coyote another firm stare.

Awkward silence reigned in the room for a minute or two.

"Well, have a good day, everyone." Ben turned around and headed to his office.

"Mr. Holden, sorry to bother you," called the middle-aged agent. "What are these strips of paper on the floor?"

"My practice is closed. I have to vacate these premises. Due to the Medical Board's guidelines, I am allowed to destroy all the medical records that haven't been active for seven years or longer. So I'm shredding them."

"What are you planning to do with the remaining records?" The man was obviously curious.

"I'll have to store them for another seven years."

"Where are you planning to store them?"

"I don't know yet because we are selling our house. A friend of mine offered space in her garage. I have to think about it. Any other questions?"

His cell phone rang, and Ben hurriedly walked into his office to take the call. It was Emma.

"Ben, I finally reached Gould. He said, 'Don't let them in without a warrant. And don't talk to them. Not a single word.'"

Ben was silent.

"Is it too late? You talked to them?"

"Don't worry. We had a charming conversation and exchanged a score of pleasantries. No damage done."

"I hope so. How soon are you going to be home?"

"As soon as they bring the warrant, find the files, and leave. I hope their invasion won't last forever."

Eventually, the search warrant was delivered and presented to Ben. Eighteen months ago, the government had removed a thousand files from his office. Now they wanted more. Ben browsed through the list of the thirty names. He remembered most of these patients, except for the few whom he'd probably treated many years ago and for a short period of time. To speed up the search, Ben helped the agents locate the files, but their mere presence, not to mention their drilling glances, was wearing him out. He longed to go home.

* * *

As soon as he walked into the door of their ranch house, Ben greeted Emma, headed to the bedroom, and a minute later he was sound asleep.

Emma had been waiting impatiently for Ben all afternoon. The agents' visit to his office was disturbing. Why couldn't they leave Ben alone? If they found nothing criminal in the thousand medical charts they'd already taken, what did they expect to find in these other ones? The phone ring interrupted her thoughts.

"Emma? It's Edward Gould."

"Hello, Edward."

"Emma, bad news. Really bad."

"What's the matter?"

"The agents who showed up today at Ben's office to get thirty more medical charts..." Gould stopped and inhaled. Emma winced inwardly. "They reported to their superiors that Ben was about to flee the country. They discovered that he had been shredding important materials, and he was selling his house. Cagney called me a few minutes ago. They are sure Ben is contemplating an escape."

"Edward, this is ridiculous! We learned about their investigation more than a year ago. We are here, and we never even—"

"Emma, these people don't think like you and me. Their thinking is different."

"What is going to happen now?"

"They want to arrest him."

Emma felt her heart racing.

"Emma, do you hear me?"

"I do."

"I told them that they were wrong, but they didn't want to believe me. Tomorrow, first thing in the morning, you have to bring me Ben's passport. That's the only way to stop them. Do you hear me?"

"I do."

"Can you bring his passport to my office tomorrow morning?"

"I'll bring it."

"One more thing. Where are you planning to keep all these so called 'active' medical charts?"

"We don't know yet. We are selling our house, and we have no idea where we are going to live. We thought about renting some storage space, but to keep all these medical charts for seven years will cost us a fortune. Our close friend offered her garage—"

"Not a good idea," interrupted Gould. "Cagney said they had a storage place in the FBI building, and they can store all the charts there. Please talk to Ben about this suggestion and call me back. We have to solve this issue fast. We must reassure them that Ben is not planning to flee."

"But Edward... You know that he is not, right?" Emma was getting nauseous.

"Of course I do. I'm certain he is not planning to flee. But it doesn't matter what *I* know. We have to do what needs to be done and do it immediately." He wanted to add something else but changed his mind. "Sorry for the bad news. I'll see you tomorrow with Ben's passport."

Emma was sitting motionless, digesting the news, pondering the way she would deliver it to Ben. He never complained, occasionally even joked about their troubles, but she knew that this sickening suspicion would hit him hard.

"Why such a gloomy face?" Emma didn't hear Ben walk into the kitchen. "The chicken is burned? Or the neighbor's dog once again decorated our front lawn?"

"Nothing of that magnitude, thank God." Emma forced a smile and fell quiet.

There was no easy way to deliver the news.

"Edward Gould called. The agents who were in your office today misinterpreted what they saw and what you said about the shredded paper on the floor and your comments about selling our house. They convinced the prosecutors that you were planning to flee the country."

"Me? Flee the country?" Ben burst into laughter. "Why? Why would I flee?"

"I know you won't. But the prosecutors strongly believe that you will and demand that you surrender your passport. I'll have to bring it to Gould's office tomorrow morning."

Ben was silent for a long moment.

"It's my fault," he said finally, "I shouldn't have talked to them."

"Ben, what you did was normal. You were simply polite to them. In situations like that, honest people answer other people's questions, even if these people are government agents. You have never been in any legal trouble. And you have nothing to hide. How could you know that your words would be twisted and interpreted in the worst way possible?" Emma sighed wistfully. "Don't blame yourself. Just don't talk to them next time. That's all."

Ben didn't answer.

"How can I accept the fact that I haven't done anything illegal, yet the government considers me a criminal?" he frowned.

"You can't. And you shouldn't. But it's irrelevant now." She paused. "Anyway, we are not planning to go abroad at the moment. I'll bring them your passport. End of story."

The next morning, Ben's passport landed in Gould's office. Two days later an unmarked vehicle stopped by the building where the pain management center used to be, and eighty-seven boxes, filled with medical files, were taken away from the clinic to their new place of residence—the FBI facility in downtown Boston.

Their house was sold the day that it appeared on the market. The sale didn't bring a dime because the mortgage was still large. They had very little time to find a place to live, but they were lucky, and in a few days they rented a small house close to their parents and their children. And that was all that mattered.

* * *

They moved into the rented house in early November 2008, with their life up in the air and misfortunes bombarding them one after the other. Two years before, when Ben's practice was booming, he signed a seven-year lease for his office premises, and now when the landlord could rent out only half of Ben's former office, he demanded compensation for his losses. Emma begged him to accept a settlement, but the landlord's attorney insisted on a payment of $8,000, and Emma's fruitless negotiations had turned her life into a nightmare. On top of that, some of his former patients' families were now filing malpractice lawsuits. No one had ever sued Ben while he was practicing, but now when he was in trouble, the lawsuits were pouring in almost weekly. IIt hurt Ben to know that the relatives of those patients, who had never blamed him for the demise of their family members before, now joined in his persecution.

Every day they dreaded the arrival of the postman. Junk mail they used to hate was now a precious treat. It was harmless. It never brought bad news unlike the rest of the mail. Then later, in the middle of the night, Emma would wake up with an array of questions pounding on her brain: What new trouble could they expect tomorrow? Who else is suing Ben? To whom does he owe money? Who else wants a piece of him?

* * *

In December of 2008, nineteen months after the raid, Edward Gould invited them to come to his office for an important talk.

"New developments," Gould looked at Ben musingly, as if trying to predict what his reaction to the news would be. "We received a phone call from the DA's office. They have some documents in your case whose statutes of limitations are about to expire. Cagney wants you to sign a tolling agreement that will give them an extension on the usage of these documents."

"Edward, as we now know, they have been investigating me for the past six years, and seemingly found nothing. Now they want more time?"

"Exactly."

"How much time do they ask for?"

"Six more months."

"Why should I give them extra time? One good reason?"

"To show your cooperation and demonstrate that you have nothing to hide, for one." He paused. "Well, if you don't sign the tolling agreement, they'll go to a judge, and the judge will give them the extension anyway."

"So I have no choice?"

"No, you have a choice, but I would recommend signing it. Just read it first."

Ben read the agreement. Not only did it suggest an extension of the statutes of limitations, it listed their possible allegations, including conspiracy to defraud the United States, making fraudulent statements, participating in healthcare fraud, unlawfully distributing controlled substances, and money laundering.

"If my former patients ever read this, they would say, 'Who could imagine that this decent man was such a villain,'" Ben remarked bitterly.

"Ben, please," Emma stroked his hand gently. "None of them would believe this crap."

"Crap? Emma, you said 'crap'? Ben smiled broadly and turned to Gould. "She hates profanities and uses only the most refined words from the most refined classical literature."

Gould cracked a cryptic smile, thinking of his own wife.

"Emma, honey, you made my day. Let me sign this *crap*, and let's go and celebrate your entrance into a new speech era!"

Little did they know that six months later...

* * *

Six months later, in June 2009, the prosecutors asked Ben to sign another tolling agreement for another six-month extension.

"Edward, why should I sign it again?"

"Same reason. If they don't get the permission from you, they'll get it from a judge. Rules of the game."

Ben signed it for the second time.

Six months later, in December 2009, the same request from the DA's office, and Ben signed the third agreement in a row.

Six months later in June, 2010, which was three years after the raid, the prosecutors asked Ben to sign the fourth agreement, but this time he rebelled.

"Edward, there's no end to it! They have been investigating me for five years before the raid and for three years after the raid. Why do we have to give them extra time on top of all the years they have already spent on this wild goose chase? Could you ask them why they need these extensions?"

"We actually did."

"And?"

"They said they couldn't find a medical expert that would support their charges."

"So we are giving them extra time to find the 'right' expert?"

"Ben, as I told you before, they would get the judge's permission anyway. They always do. Please be patient. Time is on our side."

"What do you mean?"

"A delay of a criminal trial is generally beneficial to the defendant, at least in theory."

"I am not sure I get it. I always thought that the sooner the defendant cleared his name, the sooner his life got back to normal. Isn't it true anymore? And I don't need extra time on my side. I have something much more important on my side. The truth."

"Ben, we will get to this subject later, I promise. Meanwhile, we've asked them for something in return."

"What have you asked them for?"

"We've asked them to invite us for a talk before they press charges."

"Are you sure they will? I mean, are you certain they'll press charges? It looks like they have nothing to show."

"I doubt they will give up. They've already invested heavily in this case, with lots of manpower and tons of money... I don't think they'll back down. They almost never do."

"Edward, I'll sign this one, but no more."

"Ben, believe me, I don't think you have a choice." Gould sighed heavily. "Well, who knows, maybe there is a slight chance they won't press charges. But still..." Gould didn't finish the thought. "Let's wait and see what will happen."

* * *

Six months later, in mid-December 2010, Cagney called to announce the government's decision. The DA was finally ready to press charges. Cagney and Mike Lynch, another prosecutor recently assigned to the case, met with Edward Gould and showed him the indictment. Dr. Holden was charged with the deaths of six of his patients, and so was Julia Lander, the nurse practitioner. They were also both charged with conspiracy to distribute controlled substances.

"Ben, these charges are not official yet—"

"I can't believe they are doing it," Ben interrupted. "How are they going to prove criminal acts that never happened?"

"Ben, I told you before, they wouldn't back down no matter what. But we'll try to rebut these allegations before they are official. The prosecutors are willing to meet with us and to listen to our counter-arguments."

"Is there any hope it will work?"

Gould pondered the question for a long moment.

"There is a slight chance," he said finally. "They offered to meet, and we won't miss this opportunity." Gould paused. "One more thing, and it's very important. In case the government presses charges, and considering how grave these charges are, they may insist on your incarceration before the trial. Please ask your friends to write letters that will state that you are a respected member of the local community, you have strong ties to it, and you will not make any attempt to flee the country."

"Will these letters change the prosecutors' minds about me rotting in jail?"

"No, we are not trying to impress the government. These letters are intended for the federal magistrate judge, who will be making a decision to either keep you in prison before the trial or to set you free on bail," explained Gould.

"How many letters do we need?"

"Twenty or so will be good. Most likely we will not need them because you have never made any attempts to run away for these past four years, I mean, after your troubles started."

"It never crossed my mind."

"I don't doubt that. Still, I need these letters, just in case..." He paused. "And I'm calling Rachel Leigh regarding the rebuttal."

* * *

Rachel Leigh had followed the developments of the case from day one, and therefore developed an understanding of the issues of Ben's case, perhaps better than anyone else. Gould called her the same day.

"Rachel, we've had a call from the government. Cagney and company are about to press charges against Ben and Julia, but they are willing to meet with us to discuss them before they do so. No one can rebut their allegations better than you. They gave us three weeks to look at the charges and prepare a rebuttal. Three weeks! Can you believe it? They've spent years concocting the case, and they give us three weeks! The meeting is scheduled for January 6. Can you join me for this meeting? Is it enough time for you to prepare?"

"It's enough. Don't worry, I'll come, and I'll be ready."

* * *

A week later, Emma gave Edward Gould twenty-seven letters written and signed by twenty-seven couples. Each letter stated that Ben was a respected member of the local community, that he had strong ties to it, and that he hadn't any intention to flee the country.

"It looks like you still have some good friends." Gould smiled reticently.

"Surprisingly enough, no deserters yet," Emma smiled back.

* * *

The meeting on January 6, 2011, took a rather unexpected turn. Edward Gould and Rachel Leigh had scrupulously prepared for the talk, and using the scientific and factual evidence pertaining to the case, they explained to the prosecutors that their allegations were completely unjustified. To their surprise, the prosecutors seemed receptive, for it looked like they had no understanding that this crucial information, which was essential to the case, had even existed. They seemed perplexed and unprepared to respond.

"The information you presented is unfamiliar to us," Cagney finally admitted. "We have to think about it, and we'll let you know."

* * *

Ben wasn't present at the meeting. He was not supposed to be. He and Emma were at home, trying to occupy themselves with anything that would distract their thoughts from the meeting in progress. Nothing could. An hour passed, then another one.

The phone rang.

"Ben, it's Rachel. Edward will call you in a few minutes. Surprisingly, the meeting went well."

"Thank you, Rachel. I bet you and Edward did a splendid job. But what do you mean by 'well'?"

"They didn't have a clue about the information we presented. They listened, or at least it seemed they did. They looked puzzled. One of them said they had to think it over."

"What can I say? Sounds encouraging. Thank you, Rachel. I know that if it weren't for you and Edward—"

"Well, let's not get too excited," interrupted Rachel. "We did what we could. Let's see what happens. I feel more hopeful now... cautiously hopeful."

* * *

Six weeks later, in late February 2011, Gould received a phone call from the U.S. Attorney's office.

"Mr. Gould, it's Mike Lynch. I'm calling to say that we are going ahead with the charges."

"You are not convinced by the evidence presented at our meeting?" Gould paused.

"As I said, we are going ahead with the charges."

"Did you find any evidence that disproves the facts presented at the meeting?" There was another long pause.

"We are going ahead with the charges. I have nothing else to say."

Gould was not ready to give up. He called for a meeting with the prosecutors' superiors. He hoped he could get through to them. They couldn't be as stubborn as Cagney and Lynch. They would get the essence of Leigh's and his rebuttal. Perhaps there was still a slim chance that the charges would be dropped.

Gould called Ben right after the meeting.

"Ben, I went to the DA's superiors this morning and offered them all the facts that Rachel and I had presented at the meeting with Cagney and Lynch. I had hoped these people would be more sensible. I had hoped the facts would convince them. No luck. All they said was, 'You have your opinion, and we have ours. The indictment stands.'"

"Did they disprove any of the facts?"

"No, they didn't."

"But this is hideous. One of our friends said that they are persecuting me to advance their political careers. Is that possible?"

"What can I say, Ben? It wouldn't surprise me." He was silent for an instant. "When I first met you," he continued, "I had no idea who you were and how much I could trust your story. But then I visited your office, met your staff and your patients, and read their letters in your support. I examined the report written by that young doctor hired by the Medical Board and the response to his accusations by the highly respected expert. From all the facts that I'm aware of, the government's allegations are groundless. Do I think that what is happening to you and Julia is fair? Absolutely not! And that's why we will fight it. We won't give up, I promise."

"What should I do now?"

"Today is Monday... I need to see you and Emma on Wednesday, at 5:00 p.m. We have to discuss some specifics. By that time I'll be better informed."

The Wednesday night meeting wasn't long.

"Ben, the charges will be officially presented this coming Friday or next Monday. Tomorrow the prosecutors will give us a letter that will describe the conditions of your stay before the trial. They said that they do not intend to arrest you and keep you in jail. We'll discuss these conditions with Cagney and Lynch, come to a mutual agreement, and present that agreement to the magistrate judge at the hearing either on Friday or early next week. One more thing. The judge will most likely ask for bail. My guess is that it will be five hundred thousand or so. I know that by now you have nothing to offer. Is there any chance your relatives or close friends can post property as bail?"

"I'll ask."

"Call me with the name when someone agrees. You don't need to do anything else before the hearing. You don't need to prepare, and you won't say a word there. Just come dressed appropriately."

"No T-shirt or sandals?"

"Preferably not," Gould couldn't help smiling.

"Well, it's still too cold for that anyway," Ben said wistfully.

* * *

The same night Ben called Gould about the bail.

"Edward, my cousin Alex and my two close friends Tina and George offered their houses as collateral for bail. Both properties together are worth a little over five hundred grand."

"Great. We'll call them tomorrow. They'll have to sign some papers."

* * *

On a Thursday morning in early March, Emma woke up with a fearful thought that was swirling in her mind, not giving her a chance to grasp it to the full extent. For the past four years, they never lost the hope that the government would come to their senses and leave them alone. Now they had no doubt it had been wishful thinking. Ben and Julia were to be charged with grave allegations, would have to stand trial and, despite their innocence, might face years in prison. That was the reality, yet she was still struggling to accept it.

Emma got up and was about to plunge into the routine of the day when it hit her that there was a chance the hearing with a magistrate judge would be scheduled for tomorrow, and she would need a decent suit for the hearing. Ben, who used to be a spiffy dresser, often wearing a suit, a matching shirt and tie, and sometimes even matching socks, still had four suits. They were in good shape, unworn for the past four years, and they still fit him, so there was no worry about him looking presentable before the judge. But the last time she wore a suit was twenty years ago for her job interview. So no matter whether she was in the mood for shopping or not, she had to look for a decent suit right after breakfast.

The large department store was around the corner, and Emma easily found three suits to try on. The first one, which she liked best, fit her perfectly, and she was debating if she should even try another one when her cell phone rang.

"Emma," Ben's voice was slightly coarse, "Edward called and asked us to come to his office by noon. We have to leave in twenty minutes."

"I'll be home in ten."

Emma paid for the suit and rushed home.

* * *

Gould called Ben five minutes after Emma left shopping.

"Ben, it's Edward. I am calling you from my car and driving to the office as we speak. I just turned on the local radio station..." Ben couldn't hear Gould well, but his voice sounded a little shaky.

"Some unpleasant news? The Dow Jones dropped a few points?" Ben asked, puzzled by this early call.

"Much worse. This morning the government came forward with the official indictment of you and Julia at least a day earlier than they promised. And you both *will be* arrested. I can't believe it! We had a firm agreement that we would get together and discuss your and Julia's status before the trial and then present that agreement to the judge. And there wouldn't be any arrests! They gave us their word!" Gould was furious.

There was a long pause before he spoke again.

"Please don't go anywhere. I'll call you shortly."

"Don't worry. I'll stay put."

Ben slowly sank onto the couch. Was it a coincidence that the charges were presented earlier than expected and precisely on Thursday? Ben remembered their talk with Gould a few months earlier. Edward said that in Ben's case arrest was very unlikely because Ben had known about possible charges for a long time and never tried to flee. Yet Edward explained that sometimes prosecutors, even if there wasn't any danger of the defendants' escape, arrested them and sent them to jail for a few days, just to frighten them, to introduce them to the life they would lead in case they were found guilty. Prosecutors have the legal right to imprison the defendant for up to three days without any court order, even before the magistrate judge makes a decision on the defendant's status before the trial, and they often choose a particular day of the week for the arrest: Thursday. If the defendant was brought to court in front of a magistrate judge on Thursday, the judge would most likely have a packed schedule on Friday and would then schedule the hearing on the following Monday or Tuesday. So the defendant would not spend a day or two in jail, but at least four or five. Then it might be much easier to cut a deal with the defendant whether he or she was guilty or not.

Ben didn't need to look at the calendar. He knew it was Thursday.

Edward called fifteen minutes later.

"Ben, toughen up. Your voluntary surrender is scheduled for 1:00 p.m. at the FBI headquarters. Please make sure you arrive at my office not later than noon. We have a few things to discuss. And put on some comfortable clothes, perhaps jeans, an old sweater, something like that."

"Why at the FBI headquarters?" Ben was genuinely surprised.

"Two reasons. First, the case against you and Julia was built by the joint efforts of the state and the federal government, and the FBI was intimately involved in the case. Second, this is their favorite way to intimidate defendants, sort of 'precook' them. Not everyone views an invitation to the FBI headquarters as an honor."

"Well, I was always curious about what the place looked like," said Ben.

"You will have a chance to satisfy your curiosity in no time," Edward said soberly.

Ben hung up and suddenly realized that Emma was still completely unaware of what was going on. He had to call her right away. The FBI folk may get upset if he didn't show up for the arrest on time. Judging by the movies, they didn't take disrespect lightly.

* * *

"Ben, why does Gould need to see us today?" Emma walked in, looking concerned. "It's Thursday. He said the hearing would be on Friday or early next week."

"I'm going to meet with the FBI people..."

"Really?" Emma's heart pounded fast. Could it be, flashed in her head, that the FBI officials had a different view of Ben's case? What if they talk to Ben and then make the prosecutors drop their case. Maybe they've already reconsidered!

"Ben, I'll put on my new suit and be ready in five..."

She looked up at Ben and didn't finish the sentence. He wasn't prepared for the meeting at all.

"Ben, why are you wearing your old sweater and jeans? Is this an appropriate outfit for the meeting with the FBI agents? Please put on a nice suit, the gray one. It looks so good on you."

"Gould told me to wear something comfortable. And that's what I'm wearing."

"Are you sure he meant jeans and a worn sweater?"

"I'm sure. Please hurry up. We have to go."

Emma looked at Ben's feet. At least he wasn't wearing sneakers. His shoes were old too, but not worn. A few years back Ben bought them on clearance, and ever since then they had been his favorites.

* * *

They took a subway and then walked silently from the train station to Gould's office, where Ben stopped and took Emma's hand in his.

"Emma, you remember we planned to visit my father tonight to tell him about the upcoming charges? Could you please call him and tell him we are not coming?"

"We are not? Why? We have to prepare him... He is eighty-six. His second bypass was... what, two years ago? In case they press charges, do you want the news to hit him like an atomic bomb?"

"I can't go anyway. Maybe you could go alone."

"What do you mean? Why can't you go?"

"I'm going to the FBI... to be arrested."

Emma froze. She tried to say something, but the words stuck in her throat and wouldn't come out. And then they finally did.

"But they promised they wouldn't..." she said it so softly that Ben had to guess what she said.

"I know. They were probably joking. They have a peculiar sense of humor." Ben kissed Emma on the cheek and looked away. "Don't worry, I'll be all right."

Emma didn't answer. She kept walking, feeling lightheaded and devoid of any thoughts or feelings.

They entered Gould's office, and his secretary, Sally, a slender, affable woman in her late thirties, immediately offered them lunch. Emma stared at the salad and the sandwich placed in front of her, motionless. There was entirely different stuff to digest.

Edward Gould entered the room and greeted them warmly.

"Ben, before we go to FBI headquarters, I have a few important instructions," Gould said soberly. "If they ask you a question, please answer only 'yes' or 'no.' Do your very best to abstain from any kind of jokes. You have to realize that you are dealing with a totally different breed. They will not understand your jokes, and they will not appreciate them. Every word you say will be scrutinized. Any witticism or jest may be twisted and misinterpreted and then presented in the most unfavorable way. The best thing to do is to pretend you are mute," concluded the attorney.

Ben reluctantly gave him his word. Deep inside he was less than certain that under these unique circumstances he would be able to control himself. Who knows how soon he will have another opportunity to closely communicate with this group of people, whose sole mission is to place him behind bars for a century or so? Edward explained to him that he could get up to twenty years for each count of the seven charges, which was one hundred forty years total. Would he even last that long?

Finally Gould announced it was time to go. Ben kissed Emma goodbye and walked to the door. Then he turned around, quickly glanced at her, and walked out of the room.

Emma was still numb, trying to understand what happened and what she was doing in this room.

"Emma," Sally touched her shoulder. "Sarah, our paralegal, will take you to the courthouse. The arraignment is scheduled for 2:00 p.m. Please eat something. It could be a long day."

Chapter Fourteen

That afternoon in early March of 2011 was unseasonably warm. It was a ten-minute walk to the FBI headquarters, so Ben left his jacket at Gould's office. The two of them crossed the public square and entered the large FBI building. On that brief stroll, Ben and Edward maintained a light conversation, and they even exchanged a few jokes, but Ben could clearly sense his lawyer's hidden tension. Was Edward nervous because of Ben's somber future or was he concerned about Ben's unpredictable behavior under the stressful circumstances? Ben thought he looked more relaxed than his lawyer, but maybe he was kidding himself.

Strangely enough, Ben felt nothing but keen curiosity. The thought that this could be his last walk as a free man simply did not cross his mind. The gravity of the situation had not hit him yet, or maybe his mind refused to accept this event as reality. He perceived the whole affair as a farce and felt oddly detached, as if he were a spectator in his own life rather than a participant.

They entered an elevator and ascended to the seventh floor. From there they advanced along the dull-colored, poorly lit hallway toward the dim light at its other end. Ben spotted a small group of men congregating behind the glass door. When they approached, the door sprung open, the men stepped outside, and Ben and Edward were greeted enthusiastically with fawning smiles and handshakes. There was no overt hostility, only a slight inquisitiveness, if anything. To a naive bystander, this gathering could look like a business meeting of entry-level diplomats. Not that bad so far, mused Ben.

They were invited into a small waiting room that was separated from a much bigger office by a thick glass partition. Ben wondered if the partition was bulletproof or not, but his attention was distracted by what was taking place right behind the clear barrier. A dozen relatively young women and men were moving quickly back and forth, as if fulfilling vitally important tasks. What a surprisingly busy place it is, Ben observed.

When the formal introductions were over and pleasantries exchanged, Ben was instantly shackled. He certainly faced a day filled with new, exciting experiences. For the first time in his life, Ben learned the order for placing shackles: handcuffs go first, then leg irons, which had a surprisingly long chain that allowed him to almost walk normally, though at a slower pace. Jogging seemed to be out of the question.

Handcuffs were a totally different story. After a few minutes in handcuffs, Ben had a strong urge to wiggle his wrists but that led to severe pain, for his handcuffs were tightened to the limit. A little tighter, and they would cut his circulation. If he was holding his hands up front and thumbs up, he felt fine, but any attempt to move his wrists caused significant discomfort. Don't move your wrists, pal, Ben warned himself. You better learn this simple rule fast.

Then one of the agents wrapped an additional immobilizer, this time a heavy-duty chain, around his waist and connected it to the hand and leg shackles with vertical chains. The "headquarters," a steel box with a lock, secured all safety devices together. The chain between the box and the handcuffs was short, and when his forehead got itchy, Ben realized that he couldn't reach it; he couldn't reach his chin or nose either. His freedom was suddenly sharply curtailed.

The moment Ben was shackled, his position as an invited guest turned into something entirely different. He was surrounded by a group of fit but mean-looking men, most of them in their thirties or forties. The friendliness that these men had exhibited a few minutes ago had vanished into thin air. Ben sensed that, given an excuse, these guys would be more than happy to beat him to a pulp, most likely enjoying the process. Why did they look so fierce? He was handcuffed, and each of these men looked much heavier and stronger than him. What kind of threat could he pose to them? Maybe their hostility was part of a standard operational procedure to intimidate the detainee? But all of this wasn't important now; he had to focus on his immediate objective to absorb and memorize the whole procedure. He needed to register even the smallest details of the evolving events. That was the best way to preserve his sanity.

Ben was taken into a room that looked like a cross between a medical office and a clinical laboratory. He was informed that it was time to collect a sample of his DNA. His whole entourage gathered in the far corner of the room and discussed who the most skilled candidate was to collect this sample. John, a pale, brawny fellow with steel gray eyes, was clearly in charge. In his dark blue suit, with a military haircut, he looked like a poster boy for an FBI agent. Everyone, except for him, looked confused, but John promptly verified the assignments in his notebook and pointed to a redheaded man wearing old-fashioned spectacles.

With some effort, the agent put on a pair of surgical gloves and gently opened the DNA kit. The rest of the group watched with eager anticipation. After he had opened the kit, the redheaded agent carefully pulled out a device resembling a huge toothbrush. The tip of the brush was enveloped in a white cylindrical sponge. The agent carefully inspected this brush while the rest of the group nodded enthusiastically. The redhead admired the immaculate condition of the instrument and, holding it as if it were a national treasure, asked Ben to open his mouth. All his actions were accompanied by the grave silence of his colleagues.

Ben opened his mouth, but the redheaded agent froze in hesitation. Ben watched the agent with his mouth open and suddenly remembered his first surgical performance thirty-six years ago. His patient was peacefully asleep under general anesthesia, the operational field was sterile and draped, and the surgical nurse was ready to hand him a scalpel. Secretly ashamed of his own indecisiveness, he was still not sure how to make a simple skin incision. At that awkward moment, the chief surgical resident gave him an encouraging look and said quietly, "Go ahead, Ben. You can do it." And he did it.

"Young man," said Ben, unable to keep silent any longer. "Go ahead. No reason to be nervous. You can do it."

"Sir, you have nothing to worry about," the redheaded agent muttered. "I just washed my hands."

"Thank you. That is very comforting to know," Ben nodded approvingly. "And I swear, no matter what, I won't bite."

The agent did not respond, but his boyish face betrayed a deep sense of relief.

"Listen, Holden, besides your official last name of 'Holden' and your first name of 'Benjamin,'" John the facilitator asked him with a wry smile when the procedure was over, "are you known under any other names or nicknames?"

Gould had instructed him to answer all questions only with a "yes" or "no," a rule that he had already violated. How should he answer this question? As Oscar Wilde once said, "The only way to get rid of a temptation is to yield to it."

"As a matter of fact I am. Many people still call me Doctor Holden," said Ben.

John was done smiling. It was not the answer that he had expected. Ben scanned the rest of the pack. They looked somewhat perplexed—what was a respectable man doing in handcuffs and leg irons?

As soon as Ben's DNA sample was collected, he was brought back to the room where a little while ago his multiple photographs had been taken. It was clear now that his photo session hadn't been successful. The young woman, a technician, whose responsibility was to connect the camera to an aging computer with an antediluvian printer, seemed to have no idea how to do it. She was unable to get the ancient technology to cooperate, and under the pretense that they needed another set of pictures, Ben was now brought in for another photo session.

A spirited discussion of alternative options to their photography glitch turned out to be fruitless, and the crew called for a higher-tier specialist. In the middle of this crisis, Ben was left alone, and feeling tired, he politely requested permission to sit down. John gravely considered his request, nodded his approval, and pointed to a steel chair secured to the wall. Its metal seat was cold and its back uncomfortable. Still, Ben enjoyed a brief moment of rest. He leaned slightly backwards, and to get his circulation going extended his spent legs. To Ben's surprise, his position inspired a lively conversation.

"Nice shoes," John remarked with a tinge of envy. "Good taste, Doctor."

"Thank you," Ben nodded politely.

Ben had bought them a few years before, when they were on sale, quite cheap. Like almost everything else nowadays, the shoes were manufactured in China, but they were designed in Italy and made of genuine leather. It was good he'd chosen them over his sneakers. Emma had approved of them, and now John did too. The other agents, bored with these routine procedures, seemed thrilled to jump on a topic of fashionable footwear. If they were not joking, two of them were now planning a shoe shopping spree the coming weekend.

"Doctor, where do you like to shop?" one of them asked.

Ben was about to answer and then stopped himself. Should he reveal his favorite shopping spots or, considering his peculiar position and Gould's advice, keep quiet? Who knows where this new "bonding" could lead him? Nonetheless, he didn't want to appear impolite.

"Wherever the best sales are," he said with a half-smile.

* * *

Two hours later, the convoluted booking procedure was successfully accomplished. Immobilized by handcuffs and leg irons, Ben, following standard operating procedures, was loaded into a car waiting for him in the underground garage. The dark blue ford sedan matched the color of Ben's tatty sweater. Rick, an FBI agent that Ben remembered from the day of the raid, along with three other agents, was assigned to deliver Ben to the hearing at the courthouse.

Ben was strategically placed in the middle of the back seat while Rick positioned himself on his left and John sat on his right. The driver and the passenger in the front didn't introduce themselves—they ignored him altogether.

John instantly buckled up Ben, but both he and Rick left their seat belts unfastened. That is not right, Ben thought. He had seen many badly injured patients in his life, and quite a few of them were injured in car accidents.

"It's really dangerous to ride in a car without your seat belt fastened, especially in downtown Boston," Ben said casually.

The agents' jaws dropped at his fatherly comment.

"The statistics for car accidents are rather grim," Ben continued. "If you don't care about yourselves, think of your children."

They both instantly fastened their seat belts and exchanged astounded glances. It was one thing to transport a notorious criminal doctor and entirely another to deal with a perfectionist who might also be a lunatic.

Ten minutes later they arrived safely at the federal courthouse. They didn't park the car at the main entrance but proceeded toward an alley on the right side of the building and stopped in front of a barely noticeable door. This metal, arch-shaped door reminded Ben of medieval gates that were used to protect peaceful citizens from savage intruders, although in this case the gate served an entirely different purpose. In each upper corner of the door there were two small surveillance cameras, and on the left side there was a buzzer. The driver got out of the vehicle, approached the speakerphone, and whispered something to an invisible gatekeeper. The steel door moved upwards. The lifting stopped when the open space became large enough for the vehicle to pass through without scratching the roof antennas.

The car moved forward, entered a small, windowless space, and the door behind them promptly and quietly closed. They found themselves in complete darkness. A black hole, registered Ben. It's a shame Stephen Hawking can't share this stirring experience with me. A few seconds later the door in the far corner was unlocked from inside, and Ben's fellow passengers immediately sprang into action. Both left and right rear doors were opened. Rick on one side and John on the other jumped out of the car and, like royal guards, froze by the open doors.

John offered Ben a hand to get out of the car. Ben thanked him and politely refused. How could he, a rookie prisoner, know that the task was not as easy as he expected? Still, after a brief struggle with the handcuffs and leg irons, Ben crawled out of the vehicle. A tight phalanx was silently formed, with Ben once again positioned in the middle, with two guards in front of him and two other guards, John and Rick, behind him.

On the way to the door, Ben felt the steadfast, reassuring touch of John, his steel grip on Ben's right shoulder. Was he following the rules for preventing the escape of prisoners or was he genuinely concerned about his limited mobility? Ben would never know. There was no time to reflect on that, for they marched through the open door into a fascinating kingdom of marshals.

They entered a large but barely lit office packed with metal desks and file cabinets. Each desk had an old-fashioned monitor with constantly changing frames. Ben cast a glance at one of them and saw another vehicle waiting for permission to pass under the steel door they'd just passed a few minutes ago. No coffee breaks for the *Gates to Hell,* Ben surmised. He had read that this country had one of the highest rates of incarceration in the world. He didn't doubt it anymore.

Six or seven armed men dressed in uniforms were huddled in front of the computer monitors. They were dressed in gray shirts and jackets, gray pants, and black military-style boots, and on the back of each of their jackets appeared a sign, US MARSHAL. One glimpse at these men, and

Ben knew they had no need to work out at a local gym. They were all fit, and their faces bore a subtle warning, "DON'T MESS WITH ME, PAL."

Two of the armed men promptly positioned Ben between the tall, narrow file cabinets in the corner of the room for another set of pictures. If not for the gloomy milieu of the place, Ben could have imagined he was about to be featured on the front page of the *Improper Bostonian*. The marshals didn't strike Ben as particularly courteous. Their barking orders were not pleasant, although, to Ben's surprise, their demands regarding the aesthetic quality of his portrait exceeded all of his expectations. After multiple frustrating attempts to obtain his perfect image, Ben was finally upgraded to the next step of the booking process, which was data entry.

When data entry was finally accomplished with the help of an ancient computer, one of the marshals took Ben outside. They passed through a few metal doors and four large cells packed with detainees. People of various ages and ethnicities sat on narrow steel benches attached to the cell walls. In anticipation of their fate, they talked, laughed, or napped. Ben was brought to the last cell on the left. A thought zoomed into his head: the first prison cell in my life.

His handcuffs and other shackles were finally removed, and Ben massaged his wrists, exactly as he had seen it done in the movies. The guard demanded that Ben take off all his clothes. His instruction, however, was silent, using gestures only, which seemed to be the most common language in this place.

Having had his share of physical exams at his primary care physician's office, Ben could not recall a more thorough examination ever, even though it was the most humiliating one. The guard searched all of Ben's body cavities, and after he hadn't discovered any contraband, he desultorily gave Ben permission to get dressed. And here, as he was getting dressed, a painful question hit him hard. *Why is this happening to me? What have I done to deserve this debasing physical?*

A few minutes passed, and Ben then found himself in the company of an Ecuadorian man in his forties. Orlando's English was far from perfect, but he spoke fluently. On the verge of tears, he told Ben that he had a wife, three children, and a small plumbing business. The man looked frightened and upset, and Ben felt it was inappropriate to ask him questions about why he'd ended up in jail. Orlando didn't look like a brazen criminal. Most likely the man had gotten into this mess by a dreadful mistake, just like Ben himself, and Ben felt immediate sympathy for the plumber.

"Listen, Orlando, you shouldn't worry so much. Bad things happen to good people too. I bet your arrest is a mistake. They will sort things out in no time, and you'll be home before you know it." Ben had no idea where his reassurances came from.

Orlando nodded gratefully, his eyes full of anguish and doubt.

* * *

In about an hour, Orlando was taken away, and a few minutes later, it was Ben's turn to leave. His next guard, this time a young man, showed up in the company of a burly, cocksure colleague, both of them armed. Ben was once again restrained with handcuffs, leg irons, and waist shackles, and his companions led him out of the cell. All three of them entered an elevator that had an additional, one-person compartment, secured from the main chamber by thick steel mesh. The younger guard unlocked the inside door of the main chamber and thrust Ben into a dark, narrow space. Another "enlightening" experience, thought Ben. The guard locked the door, pushed the button, and the elevator went up.

It stopped at the fifth floor, and the whole procedure, only in reverse order, took place again. Ben was removed from the cage to the main chamber of the elevator and then placed in a small hallway. Across from the elevator there was another steel door with a painted black number 15 on it. Right underneath the number there was a sign: *To bring detainees inside the courtroom in shackles is against the law.*

Ben read the sign a couple of times. He could barely concentrate. Had they brought him for the hearing that Gould mentioned on the way to the FBI headquarters? Will Emma be there? Thank God, she won't see me in shackles. She's had enough excitement for the day.

Ben looked at his traveling companions to make sure they'd paid attention to the sign. He didn't want them to get in trouble. It seemed they were preoccupied with something else, so Ben silently pointed to the sign, and the young guard pulled out the key and removed the shackles. At the very same moment, the metal door opened from the inside, and Ben was led into the courtroom.

Ben couldn't spot Emma right away. She was in the far corner of the room, lost in the crowd of spectators. People were quietly talking to each other so that you might think this courtroom was their favorite hangout. Who knows? Maybe it was. They were FBI and DEA agents, the DA's attorneys, and local reporters, as he learned later.

Someone tapped Ben on the shoulder.

"How are you doing, Ben?" Edward smiled dolefully.

"Splendid," Ben smiled back. "I am allowed to joke with *you*, right?"

"Sure, but maybe not right now. The hearing will start in a few minutes, so let me explain the procedure."

Edward was in the middle of the explanation when two strangers walked into the courtroom and took seats at the table right next to theirs. Ben turned to Gould with a silent question, "Who are they?"

"Your prosecutors," whispered Gould.

Ben had never met them in person before and was rather curious. One of the men was of medium height, with sparsely graying hair, dressed in a dark brown, ill-fitting suit. He could easily pass for an accountant or an office clerk. He looked like an ordinary man showing up at his workplace.

His companion was a completely different type. His presence was felt a mile away. He was taller and much heavier. This well-nourished fellow, with a pendulous belly, was probably in his early fifties, and he did not have a single gray hair. His spiteful look and pompous manners screamed, "I'm in charge." This guy will probably swallow his victim without chewing, Ben thought gloomily.

"All rise!" announced the clerk. The door on the left side of the podium opened and Judge Fine, a slim, lively lady in her fifties, briskly entered the room. The hearing began.

In a well-practiced voice, the clerk announced the case number and then added, "The People versus Benjamin Holden and Julia Lander." The stout prosecutor, in a loud voice, listed the charges. The defendants were accused of causing the deaths of six of their patients and a conspiracy to distribute opioids illegally. The judge inquired if they pleaded guilty or not, and Ben and Julia's defense lawyers responded firmly, "Not guilty, Your Honor."

After their statements, the procedure switched to a rather heated argument between the prosecutors and defense attorneys. The prosecutors tried to persuade the judge that, considering the magnitude of the defendants' alleged crimes, both of them should stay in jail before the trial and throughout the trial procedures, while the defense lawyers demanded the immediate release of their clients with no or minimal restrictions, arguing that both defendants had known about possible charges for the past four years and never tried to flee.

"Can you submit proof of the defendants' good standing and be ready with bail by tomorrow?" Judge Fine asked calmly.

"Yes, Your Honor," Gould answered without any hesitation.

"Yes, Your Honor," said Peter O'Neil.

"All right then. The bail hearing will be tomorrow at 2:00 p.m.," concluded Judge Fine.

The DA's foolproof plan to keep the doctor and his nurse practitioner behind bars without a court order for four or five more days did not work. Ben saw that one prosecutor was biting his lip, and the burly one looked infuriated.

Four years earlier, the prosecutors had offered Ben an opportunity to "have a talk." He rejected it, and they gave up on him. But they went after Julia. The government offered her a deal, and in return they demanded that she testify against Dr. Holden, but Julia firmly refused the offer. Therefore, this day was probably the government's last chance to break these stubborn fools.

Judge Fine announced her decision about the next hearing and left the courtroom. Her departure served as a direct signal for Ben's guards to take him through the same door back to the familiar elevator. Ben's handcuffs and leg irons were promptly attached, he was loaded into the closet section of the elevator, and delivered without any delay to the same cell he had left an hour ago.

IN EFFICIENCY WE TRUST should be embroidered on the guards' uniforms in this place, Ben mused; and some people think government workers are lazy. What a shameful misconception, at least regarding the world of incarceration.

* * *

At the courthouse, Edward asked Emma to come back to his office and wait for him. He needed her help. Now she was sitting alone in a small office room, expecting him to appear at any minute. An hour passed, then another. Apparently something was keeping him in the courthouse. Sally, Gould's secretary, and other office people visited her every twenty minutes or so, offering her food, coffee, tea, anything she wanted. Emma politely refused. She wanted to talk to Edward, nothing else, but no one in the office knew when he would be back.

Six o'clock. She planned to rush to Ben's father and his wife to prepare them for the news about the arrest and charges right after her talk with Edward. But how soon would that be? It could be too late. They may learn the news from someone else. She needed help. Emma picked up the phone and dialed Ben's cousin's number.

"Hello?" Marion's voice sounded tense.

"Marion, it's me, Emma. Sorry to bother you. Ben was arrested. They pressed charges." Emma took a deep breath. "We didn't expect that. We planned to prepare Gregory and Martha tonight... I'm afraid Gregory may learn about the news before he is prepared for it. You know, his heart... Two bypasses... I wanted to come and explain everything myself. But I'm stuck in Edward's office. He asked me to wait for him. Can you..."

"Emma, I think it's too late anyway. It's been on the news since noon, probably even earlier."

"Since noon? But the charges were announced in court only at two..."

"All the local radio stations and local TV channels are having a field day with the news."

"Sorry I've bothered you, Marion. I'll call Martha right now. They don't watch TV much, and they don't listen to the radio. Maybe it's not too late."

Emma dialed Gregory's number and got lucky. Her mother-in-law, Martha, picked up the phone.

"Hello, dear," Martha's voice was unworried and cheerful. They don't know yet.

"Martha, did you watch local TV news today?"

"No, we didn't. Why?"

"Did anyone call you in the last few hours with any news?"

"No, is something wrong?"

"I wanted to come and prepare you both, but it's too late now, and I'm stuck in the lawyer's office. It's very bad news. Ben has been arrested and charged with terrible accusations. I can't get into it now. I beg you, don't let Gregory pick up the phone. Please tell him yourself... as gently as possible."

"I will. Don't worry, I'll talk to him. Call us when you can."

* * *

The minute Emma hung up, Edward Gould walked into the room, an apologetic smile on his tired face.

"Emma, sorry for keeping you late. I've had so many things to deal with. I need your help. Can you bring any of your relatives and friends to the hearing tomorrow?"

"I'll try. Most of them work, and I'm not sure they can take a day off, but I'll call them anyway. How many do we need?"

"Fifteen, twenty. The more the better. And we may need a bigger bail. Can you ask another friend or a relative?"

"I will."

"Please go home now, and if you find someone who can help with the bail, call me tonight. Oh, one more thing. Tomorrow at 10:00 a.m. you have to be at the courthouse for your interview with the probation officer."

"I will. Do you think Ben will be released tomorrow?"

"It's a possibility, but, as you know, it's the judge's decision, not mine."

"I was thinking... Will it help if I bring a letter from his primary care physician about his health condition? I'm not sure if you know, but for the past three years he has been totally disabled."

"Is it related to his back surgery?"

"Yes, it is. But it's not just his back. The latest tests show that his kidney tumor keeps growing. His blood pressure is out of control, and lately..."

"Something else?"

"He's rapidly losing his vision... His left eye is failing."

"Oh, God." Gould sighed and shook his head. "I had no idea. Sure, if you can get a letter from his doctor tonight, it can be very helpful."

"I'll call him right away. I know he works late on Thursdays."

Emma finally got home at 9:00 p.m. with a letter written and signed by Ben's primary care physician. The letter listed all of Ben's serious medical problems. But would the judge even consider them?

Chapter Fifteen

The moment Dr. Holden was returned to his designated cell, he was given a silent command to sit and wait. The gesture was simple and clear: the guard lifted his arm 30 degrees with his palm forward and then flipped his arm down. As Ben had noticed before, the habitual way of communication involved a language of hands and fingers, rarely heads, occasionally a bark. The guards reminded Ben of wild animal tamers, because he felt like a caged animal that wasn't given a choice about obeying their commands.

By the time Ben was brought back to his cell, Orlando, the plumber, was already there. He greeted Ben with a wispy "Buenas tardes, señor" and a sad smile. They had been sitting in the cell for about two hours silently, waiting for what would happen next, when both of them were commanded by a guard who wiggled an index finger to first exit the cell and then go outside toward a white van with a sign in capital letters on the passenger's side that read DEPARTMENT OF CORRECTION. The driver's seat was empty so they had to wait.

It was late afternoon, and with the sun gone and the air unpleasantly chilly, Ben's new amigo Orlando started to shiver. Ben was freezing too, fondly reminiscing about the jacket that he had so thoughtlessly left in Gould's office. The guards, also lightly dressed, might not enjoy the cold either, but their stoic faces didn't betray any signs of suffering.

Fifteen minutes later, the driver finally appeared. He was a wiry, dark-skinned man; his long, curly hair was turned into hundreds of braids, and he was mirthfully whistling an exotic tune. Another man, in uniform, who was short and completely bald, jumped into the passenger seat and fastened his seat belt.

A guard gestured to Ben and Orlando to get inside the van by pointing an index finger at the open door. However, performing this simple task in handcuffs and leg irons was far from easy. In order to transfer the maximum number of prisoners at a time, the benches in the van were placed very close to each other. As Ben and Orlando were the first ones to get on board, they had a choice about where to sit, and Ben took a seat in the first row next to the left side window. Orlando settled in the back. The driver's cabin was shielded from the rest of the van by thick bulletproof glass impregnated with steel mesh. All the windows were tinted and reinforced with solid mesh.

The van's engine roared, and as the van moved down the road, the driver immediately turned on his favorite radio station with music that Ben thought could shatter his eardrums. Well, no matter how deafening it was, it would hopefully remove his attention from his aching wrists. By then he had spent a few hours in handcuffs, and the original discomfort was gradually turning into real pain. Finally the van started to move, and the driver turned on the heat.

Ben positioned himself as comfortably as he could and stared out the window, observing life outside the van. It was getting dark, and the street lights were already on. Pedestrians were rushing toward their evening destinations, entering and leaving shops and cafes, and none of them paid the slightest attention to the white van passing by, let alone its occupants. The windows of the van were so heavily tinted that anyone peering inside wouldn't see a thing.

The van was moving at a snail's pace. They were catching all the red lights, the Bostonian drivers were doing their usual best at cutting each other off, and the evening rush hour in the city was in full swing.

Ben constantly reminded himself to observe these developing events as a spectator, someone who'd come to a show for a few hours and then would leave it and go back to his everyday life. To go through all of the occurrences of that day without losing his mind, he had to turn off his emotions and accept everything that was happening to him as an inevitable part of the show. Still, for a moment he felt an irresistible desire to jump out of the van, enter a coffee shop, and drink his favorite tea with maybe a lemon scone. Well, it looked like this wasn't an option today. All of a sudden Ben felt exhausted. The screaming voices of pop singers on the radio drifted away, and he gradually dozed off. In few minutes, he fell asleep.

* * *

Ben woke up much later when the van made a sharp right turn and approached a dark multistory building. The tall gate, covered with barbed wire, was electronically opened, and the van was allowed to enter the parking lot. Ben assumed they had arrived at their overnight destination and sighed with relief, but his naive assumption was short-lived.

The driver, a heavy metal fan, shut off the engine and, accompanied by the guard, hastily left the vehicle. The guard gave Orlando and Ben a verbal order to remain seated and wait. The air in the van was getting colder by the minute, but to balance the acerbic cold, an ear-splitting concert on the radio went into intermission, and they could enjoy a brief respite.

About an hour later, when Ben and his buddy Orlando felt like the van had changed from a refrigerator to a freezer, they were joined by a group of new detainees. There were ten or twelve of them, in handcuffs and leg irons, of all ages and ethnicities. In spite of the late hour and the circumstances, the men were clearly in high spirits. Without any assistance, like well-trained athletes they quickly filled the van. The engine came back to life, and Ben immediately discovered that the driver's favorite radio station was on 24/7. On a positive note, with the arrival of the newcomers, the temperature inside the van steadily rose, and Ben's fingers and toes slowly began to thaw.

The day had been filled with new educational experiences. Not only had Ben learned about the shackling procedures but he also discovered that these visually indistinguishable handcuffs and leg irons were the property of different law enforcement departments and had to be removed upon arrival at any new place and instantly replaced by identical ones that personnel at the place of destination owned. The preservation and safety of this government property was obviously one of the guards' highest priorities. A thorough examination, revision, and recounting took place at each stop, and Ben wondered if any of these shackles had ever been stolen, and if they had, under what circumstances.

When every new detainee was properly seated in the van, the driver swiftly left the barbed parking lot and drove into the darkness. The rumble of music, blaring from the radio, was now slightly subdued, and Ben could hear his companions' social exchanges. These newly arrived passengers were talking to each other in a calm and friendly manner. Ben knew he had to pay attention to their conversations. Here was his chance to learn from the incarceration masters. Their knowledge of prison life was immeasurable, and the ride turned out to be even more educational than the four-hour bus tour to the Grand Canyon that he and Emma took two years ago. The significance of their comments was hard to overestimate. For instance, Ben learned that the jail in Plymouth had a poor reputation, while the one in Walpole was much more respected and certainly preferred. They were unanimous that the worst correctional facility in the area was in Fall River, and decent people, like themselves, should stay away from that nasty place. Ben, whose personal knowledge of the subject was nonexistent, eagerly absorbed the views of his much more seasoned companions.

These people were from a different world, and in a way they reminded Ben of some of his former patients: ordinary working-class people who weren't well educated or especially well mannered. Some of them were street-smart, some simple-minded or childlike, but none of this mattered to him. They were his patients, and he felt respect and compassion for them regardless of their status, education, manners, or ethnicity. And now he felt inexplicable sympathy for these jailbirds too.

In the last row of the van, a heavily built man with a wisp of chin hair constantly interrupted the conversation with rounds of thunderous coughing. Every few seconds, his barrel chest convulsed with a barking hack, and between these attacks he groaned loudly. The man was clearly sick. In the best case scenario, Ben thought, the guy has a bad case of bronchitis, and in the worst case scenario, he may have bilateral pneumonia or even TB. Most likely the man had no idea how serious his condition was.

"Sir," Ben addressed the man with the utmost politeness, "I believe upon arrival at your destination you need to seek immediate medical attention."

The prisoners stopped talking.

"Are you a doctor?" An elderly, clean-shaven, dark-skinned man broke the silence.

"Yes, I am," Ben smiled awkwardly.

The old man's face took a pensive expression. He rapidly put two and two together.

"With all due respect, sir, are you that doctor they're talking about on the radio all day long?"

Ben hesitantly nodded.

His traveling companions looked at him with sudden interest and deference. For the first time that day, Ben seemed to be regarded as a person worth respecting.

* * *

Half an hour later, the van approached another large building, which Ben's new comrades instantly recognized as the Walpole Jail, which they greeted with enthusiastic cheers. Yet Ben and Orlando were the only ones that the guards allowed to get out of the van while their disappointed fellow travelers had to proceed to some other apparently less desirable destinations.

Before the van door was closed, Ben reminded the coughing man to see a doctor without delay. The man looked at Ben incredulously, thanked him for caring, and swore to follow his advice.

The minute Ben entered the jail, he was taken to the basement. The space was large with many cubicles separated by thick brick walls. With its low ceiling and grim appearance, the place resembled the cellar of a medieval castle. Ben was met by a few uniformly dressed guards, all of them armed. They didn't look overtly hostile, just unfriendly.

Ben scanned the room and immediately saw a gargantuan man in his mid-thirties. The tag on his chest read, *Simon*. Unlike all other prison personnel, Simon was in civilian clothing. Who was he? As it turned out, that night Simon was the sole representative of the medical profession. He was a nurse.

Simon invited Ben to his office, which was a real office, not a cubicle, and with a self-assured expression on his full-moon face, he performed a formal physical examination. He looked into Ben's throat, listened to his lungs and heart, and measured his blood pressure. By then Ben's blood pressure was high and read as 185/115, but these numbers didn't impress Simon, at least not noticeably. Maintaining the self-importance of a second-year pathology resident, Simon entered Ben's blood pressure data into his battered journal, and apparently satisfied with his professional performance, he pulled out a sizable sandwich and gingerly unwrapped it. Within the walls of this respectable institution, Ben noted, the guy had probably witnessed plenty of exciting incidents, including fatal ones, and to shake his serene composure seemed to be next to impossible.

"Simon," Ben asked, "by any chance, are any blood pressure remedies commonly prescribed here?"

"Benjamin, don't worry," Simon gave a paternal smile. "The night shift is about to start, and they will take good care of you. They always do."

How could Ben not trust this confident man with his impeccable bedside manners? What choice did he have anyway?

"Listen, Benjamin," Simon inquired in the most delicate manner, "by any chance, do you suffer from any major psychiatric disorder? Say, schizophrenia or bipolar?"

"No, I don't."

"Any attempts at suicide?"

"No."

"Borderline personality?"

"No, Simon. Nothing of the kind."

"Good."

"Simon, may I ask *you* a question?"

"Go ahead, Benjamin."

"Do people here often admit that they do have psychiatric problems?"

Simon's face lightened up.

"You won't believe how often my clients 'confess' their mental problems," he grinned. "And you won't believe how much you can gain by this 'sincere' confession."

"Like what?"

"You are treated less harshly by the guards and you are eligible for soul-calming remedies. Such remedies in places like this are in high demand. They are the popular local currency."

Gosh, what an ignorant man I am, Ben reflected. Why didn't they ever teach us anything about this in medical school?

* * *

Just like in the other facilities Ben had visited that afternoon, the guards used the same language of gestures. With his open palm pointed outward, a guard led Ben into one of the cubicles and ordered him to undress by using his index and middle fingers along with his thumb on each hand to form a pinch and then pulling aside the invisible lapels. The guard removed his shackles, with no resistance on Ben's part, and left him in his birthday suit. His body search was at least the third one in a row that day. They say practice makes perfect, and indeed by the third search Ben was perfectly aware of the specific parts of his body he should open, lift, or pull apart. This degrading procedure had become a routine, Ben thought glumly. The guard was so pleasantly surprised by Ben's efficiency that by the end of the search he looked almost jubilant.

As soon as his body examination was over, the guard gave Ben a large plastic bag and an extra-large bright orange uniform. In the past few years, after his spine operation and some other health problems, Ben's clothing size changed from large to medium, and when he saw this gigantic piece of clothing, he was a little confused. Why didn't they ask him about his size? Were these local garments "one size fits all"? This uniform would fit Nurse Simon perfectly, but him...

The struggle to put on the pants was fierce but relatively short, and then Ben almost drowned in the bright orange shirt. Thankfully, there was no mirror in the room and no time to care about his new look. A husky officer was already waiting for him to start another step of the booking procedure. The man approached the task with another ancient computer and his index finger. To every question that the officer asked, Ben responded with a polite answer, and by the end of the interview, the officer's manner became visibly softer. Exhausted by his mental effort, the officer unexpectedly announced his urgent need for a "bio break" and disappeared, leaving Ben unattended.

With nothing to do, Ben was about to explore the surroundings when his glance fell on a small brown paper bag sitting on top of the big plastic one that was handed to him along with the orange outfit. Somehow Ben had missed this small bag earlier, but now it drew his attention. He'd had a hunch there was something of real value in it. His last meal was an early morning bowl of cereal at home. Now it was long past dinnertime. Ben reached for the bag and opened it. There were two pieces of grayish bread in it with two anemic slices of bologna in between, and a tiny, plum-sized McIntosh apple for dessert. By the time the booking officer returned, Ben had devoured this delectable dinner.

With the heavy plastic bag hanging over his shoulder, Ben, feeling like a lonely pilgrim, followed the guard to the second floor. They had passed through two metal gates, secured with alarms, each of them opened remotely.

The second floor looked like a stadium, with myriads of steel barred gates that served as entries to the cells. In the far corner of this hall, hanging off the ceiling, was a large flat-screen TV. A few inmates occupied round tables in the middle of the hall: some of them were playing board games, others were reading newspapers or having cordial conversations. Everyone was wearing the same orange garments. They were of different ethnicities, and many of them were quite young. If I close my eyes, Ben mused, I could easily mistake the noise here for the racket of Grand Central Station.

A guard brought Ben to a tiny cell with a sliding gate decorated by thick iron bars. Identical cells covered the entire second floor. The lock clicked, the heavy gate slowly rolled to the right, Ben was led in, the gate rolled to the left, and Ben was finally alone. He surveyed his modest quarters with great curiosity. Along the right wall was an iron bed with a folded mattress and a thin, flat pillow. A small metal desk and a three-legged stool next to it were close to the opposite wall. The furniture was obviously considered as precious as the shackles, for every piece of it was securely welded to the floor. Opposite the gate was a shiny semi-oval steel sink attached to the wall. It was half-filled with opaque fluid of an unidentifiable age and of a mysterious chemical content. A pool of the same smelly fluid covered about one-third of the floor, spreading under the bed. I hope the local plumber, Ben thought, will show up more promptly than the one we use at home.

It appeared to be the time to get comfortable. Ben opened the plastic bag given to him during the booking. In the bag he found bed sheets and a pillowcase, seven polyester T-shirts, seven pairs of briefs, and seven pairs of white acrylic socks. Like his new orange outfit, all items in the bag were extra large. One size fits all, indeed.

In a separate small bag, Ben discovered a tiny toothpaste tube, a small toothbrush, a couple of pencils, a few envelopes, and a few sheets of paper. What a caring place. Ben stretched out on the bed. He felt dog-tired, but it was too early to fall asleep, and he rested quietly, going over the events of this past day. His glance suddenly fell on the cell entry, and he saw a smiley round face glued to the iron bars. A pair of curious blue eyes met Ben's half-dozing gaze. It was quite dark in the cell, and the unexpected visitor was peeking assiduously inside to make sure he was at the right place.

"Sorry to bother you, man. Is you that doc they talk 'bout on radio day an' night?" The visitor was apologetic for disturbing Ben's serene atmosphere, so Ben immediately forgave the uninvited guest. Wasn't it amazing that the jail's wireless communication system had no problem competing with the Internet?

"I am," Ben answered humbly. "Nice to meet you."

The amiable face of the stranger melted into a happy smile.

"I'm Anton. Bulgarian. Fifteen years I lived in Canada," he explained.

"How come you are here?" asked Ben.

"Long story, doc... Wanna hear?" Anton's eyes sparkled.

"Of course. As you can see, there is no line in the waiting room at the moment."

Anton's story was simple yet captivating. Living in Toronto and becoming bored with his uneventful life, Anton drove to the U.S. to visit an old friend. They had a jubilant reunion, and then, right after it, Anton felt inspired to check the safety and the content of the nearest ATM. The content of the ATM machine exceeded all his expectations. However, the functioning of the alarm system exceeded them even more. Anton was instantly apprehended, and his natural curiosity was rewarded with a four-year prison term.

Anton finished his story and waited for Ben's reaction. Ben was silent. He would have loved to show Anton his sympathy, at least as gratitude for his friendly visit, but he struggled to digest the startling conclusion he had drawn from the story. Anton had broken the law and was sentenced to four years behind bars. He *hadn't* broken any laws, yet he was facing one hundred and forty years in prison.

"Doc, don't worry," Anton interrupted his reflections. "It's not that bad here. Only one problem. You never guess."

"Please tell me," Ben smiled wistfully. "I don't think I have enough expertise yet to guess it right."

"Too many food!" Anton announced triumphantly. "Last two years I gained forty pound!"

"That's quite an achievement!" Ben gasped.

"Doc, I promise, same happen to you," Anton grinned gloomily.

"I hope not," Ben cringed at the idea. "I think you have to cut down on your carbs, if I may. Focus on fruits and vegetables. Drink more water..."

"Doc, you don't understand. Here you eat and eat and eat. All you can think of is food and sex."

"Anton, do you have a family?" Ben changed the subject.

"Yeah, wife and daughter," Anton admitted sadly. "Girl is five. They in Toronto. Wait for me."

"You probably weren't thinking of them when you checked that ATM?" Ben asked softly.

"No. Too much of Sliwowica, I guess." Anton's face suddenly wrinkled and his eyes slowly filled with tears, but he quickly composed himself. "Swear on my mom's grave, I'll never..."

Suddenly another face pressed against the bars.

"Doc, this is Punchy," Anton introduced the man with such regard that someone might think the guy was a war hero or at least a prominent scientist.

"Punchy? Is that your real name?" Ben inquired.

"My name is Moses, but all folks here call me Punchy," the man explained.

Ben got up, reached the door, stuck out his arm between the iron bars, and offered Punchy his clinched fist. Punchy's enormous fist gently bumped Ben's firm one, and Punchy beamed ear to ear.

"If you need anything, just let me know," he offered and vanished as swiftly as he'd appeared.

Ben turned to Anton, eager to ask him about Punchy, when he met his concerned look.

"Doc, you need good nourishment." Anton pronounced the last word with definite pride for his newly acquired knowledge. "I be right back." A few minutes later he returned with a small orange, a slightly wrinkled apple, and a bottle of water.

Ben remembered—he probably learned it from some movie—that according to the unwritten etiquette in jail, he could not accept anything offered by other inmates, but Anton's gifts were so sincere that Ben didn't dare reject them. He did not want to insult this generous man. He took the fruit and the water and thanked Anton.

"Doc, you have book to read?"

"No, I don't." Shocked by the question, Ben realized that the idea of bringing a book to jail didn't even occur to him.

"I bring you book," Anton said and was gone.

Three minutes later he returned with a battered paperback that he squeezed through the bars.

"I bet you like it. Very, very good!"

Ben looked at the cover. *The True Life of Vampires.*

"A great title!" Ben forced an approving smile. What could be a better subject to focus on for a doctor facing life in prison?

Anton honored Ben with a radiant grin. His mission was accomplished, at least for tonight. The doctor was now all set for his new life.

At 9:00 p.m., all the lights in the public areas were turned off, and the inmates promptly moved into their cells. All of a sudden, a racket of streaming water erupted all over the building. Was there an artificial waterfall in this jail like in a fancy mall? Ben arched his eyebrows. Then it hit him; it wasn't a waterfall, just hundreds of simultaneously flushed toilets.

In a few minutes all noise ceased, and nighttime tranquility descended.

* * *

At midnight, Ben, a light sleeper, was awakened by a night-shift nurse, accompanied by another heavy-set guard who, for a change, communicated with Ben verbally. Without unlocking the gate, the nurse invited Ben to come closer, thrust her hand through the bars, and placed a small pill into his mouth.

"A blood pressure pill, according to Doctor Simon's order," she mumbled.

"Your wake up time's 5:00 a.m.," croaked the guard. "At 5:30 we'll take you to the courthouse. Better be ready."

* * *

At 5:00 a.m. the guard arrived to wake Ben up, but by that time he was already awake. The guard confirmed the time of departure and granted Ben another thirty minutes to enjoy life in his cell.

At 5:30 a.m. the cell gate was unlocked and Ben was taken to the basement. This time he was placed in a medium-size cell with a small crowd of inmates huddled on narrow steel benches attached to the walls. The gate of the cell stayed wide open. Does it mean that we could leave the place at will? Ben pondered. Or is it just a test of our obedience?

Six men, still unchained, were peacefully sitting on the bench, talking. Ben had nothing to do, except for reading *The True Life of Vampires.* Well, he'll save the pleasure of reading that magnum opus for a rainy day. Now he would prefer something more entertaining, which was eavesdropping.

The most animated conversation around was taking place between a tall, robust, dark-skinned man named Eddie and his redheaded neighbor, MacManus. Eddie was trying to decide if he should be sad about the prospect of receiving undeserved punishment or to be thrilled it wasn't harsher.

On a sunny spring day, about a year ago, Eddie was sitting on the porch of his apartment building and smoking his last cigarette. He was in his usual mellow mood when he was accosted by a guy named Bill, whom Eddie barely knew. The guy looked a little drunk, but it was almost noontime, so by the local standards his condition was entirely acceptable.

The fellow asked Eddie for a cigarette, and Eddie replied with his usual politeness, "No disrespect, man, but my pack is empty." Bill wasn't discouraged by Eddie's reply and suggested that both of them should take a walk to the nearest convenience store. Agreeable by nature, Eddie accepted the invitation. That's how his troubled journey began.

At the convenience store, their tasks were divided. While Bill searched for his favorite Budweiser, Eddie stood in a long line to get to the cashier. Suddenly Eddie heard yelling and swearing coming from the far corner of the store. He recognized Bill's voice. Eddie rushed to his buddy and found him quarreling with a short, ghastly looking woman in her mid-thirties. A four-year-old boy, pressing himself to his mother, was watching the altercation in astonishment and dismay.

Names were exchanged and threats made, but eventually the halcyon atmosphere of this neighborhood store was restored. Eddie and Bill paid for the beer, and they left the store in high spirits. Crossing the parking lot, the buddies realized that they were about to be joined by a third party. From a rusty Jeep Cherokee parked nearby, a sizable bald man emerged with a baseball bat in his hand. He was followed by the ghastly lady who was pointing her index finger at Eddie and Bill and cussing like a drunken sailor.

The macho husband was hesitant so his sweetheart boldly rushed toward Eddie and his buddy. Eddie couldn't allow this woman to assault his bosom friend so he pushed the woman away. In a second, the woman found herself sprawled on the ground. Unable to tolerate this insult, her husband raised the bat and rushed to his wife's rescue.

This incident wasn't Eddie's first experience with brawling, so he pulled out his switchblade, which he always carried just in case, and the beefy husband instantly backed off. He even helped his trouble-making wife get up, and the whole family hastily retreated to their rusty Jeep. Slightly uncertain if the incident was over or not, Eddie and his buddy made a decision not to wait for the police and sprinted to Eddie's place to celebrate the victory with Budweiser and triumphant toasts.

The next morning, as on every last Tuesday of the month, Eddie went to the local welfare office to get his regular check. There was nothing seriously wrong with his physical health, but his past infractions with the law and occasional incarcerations had left him emotionally insecure and incapable of any productive work.

On that beautiful May morning, Eddie cheerfully approached the welfare office when the familiar Jeep Cherokee with the shameless bitch on board happened to pass by. The bitch recognized Eddie and immediately reported him to the authorities.

With an accurate description at hand, the policemen had no trouble apprehending Eddie even before he redeemed his small monthly check. His beloved switchblade was used as irrefutable evidence of his parole violation, and Eddie was placed under arrest. Seven months and two different jails later, the day of his hearing had finally arrived.

At the hearing, the emotionally distraught victim presented her own animated description of the events. She did not omit a single detail of the entire family's narrow escape from the monstrous goon. Her lawyer stressed the physical and emotional damage caused by the vicious attack; and testimonies about the permanent physical injury, submitted by two long-retired ophthalmologists, were legally filed. The multiple psychological traumas, including post-traumatic stress disorder, which her son had developed as a witness of his mother's near-death experience, were verified. Finally, the judge was asked to review the conclusions of a respected pediatric neurologist. The plaintiff's attorney also painted the wife's husband as an all-American hero; and to reinforce the evidence and ensure objectivity, photographs of the victim's cuts and bruises taken at the local ER were attached.

The judge ignored the timid inquiry of the public defender, who dared to ask why the pictures of the injuries were dated December when Eddie's alleged crime was committed in mid-May. The plaintiff's lawyer did a hell of a job, and five years behind bars for the assault and battery with an intent to murder looked like a fair verdict.

"Well, it could've been much worse," Eddie concluded pensively.

"Yeah, you're a lucky motherfucker," MacManus said with a sting of jealousy.

Ben didn't miss a word of Eddie's freaky story. What a bizarre and alien world. Ben had encountered this world only in books and movies, but never in person. Suddenly it hit him that if the government won his case, he would be thrown into this world, and it would become his *only* world for the rest of his life.

* * *

As Eddie told his story, MacManus did not make a single interruption or a single off-color remark. Now it was his turn.

Three years before, MacManus, an electrician by trade, finally started his own company. The new business rapidly took off. After six months he could afford to rent a bigger office, hire a second secretary, and even purchase two new vehicles: a brand new Dodge RAM truck and a used low-mileage Mercedes.

One Friday night, after an especially hard week at work, MacManus stopped at his favorite bar in Brockton for a well-deserved beverage, and that's where he met his sweetheart Jenny. She was a twenty-three-year old flirty blond who wasn't easy to resist. MacManus fell for her right away. He probably would have liked her a little less if Jenny had informed him about her cravings for cocaine. But she never did. She was a very private person. A month or so after their first encounter, Jenny and her only child moved in with MacManus.

That Thursday afternoon, MacManus took the rest of the week off, jumped into his beloved Mercedes, and went to visit his parents in Connecticut. Jenny was left home to take care of her son and the new Dodge. The very next day MacManus received a phone call. Jenny was in tears and told him about her minor car accident. His new pickup truck was a little dented, not a big deal, she said. She and her baby were fine, thank God.

Jenny didn't want to get into any specifics about the accident, but her speech was slightly incoherent, and MacManus became gravely concerned. A head or neck injury could be potentially disabling, and Jenny was a fragile creature. He wanted to drive home at once, but Jenny calmed him down, and he made a reluctant decision to stay with his parents for a few more days. Still, the next morning, just to make sure his sweetheart was feeling well, he called her. Her voicemail kicked in, and MacManus left a tender message with plenty of romantic overtures.

Meanwhile, Jenny, as he learned later from the police reports and witness testimonies, had been busy with a thoroughly designed project. She just couldn't stand the picture of the damaged front bumper of her boyfriend's truck and wanted to fix the problem. Her mind, fogged by cocaine, had brewed a brilliant, although not quite original, plan. Jenny came up with the brazen idea of trading the brand new pick-up truck for a Toyota Corolla. No cash back, no paperwork, just an old-fashioned handshake. Well, maybe a small additional payment, like a few plastic bags of fine white powder. Why not?

When MacManus finally reached his sweetheart on the phone, Jenny was exuberant. She informed him that she had exchanged the damaged Dodge RAM for a new Japanese jewel! Jenny did not forget to praise her trading skills and suggested that she might consider a new career as a salesperson at a Bentley dealership. Arguing over the phone was never MacManus's strong suit, and he decided not to make waves upon his arrival either. He'd already sensed a problem, but he hated conflict and was hoping for a peaceful resolution.

The whole event would probably have unfolded in a different way if Jenny had enlightened MacManus in advance regarding the details of his new possession. The object Jenny was raving about over the phone turned out to be a rusty, twelve-year-old Toyota Corolla with over 260,000 miles on the odometer and a broken tailgate light.

After coming home, MacManus made a reasonable request to see the accident report, yet his gentle inquiry made Jenny visibly upset. She felt insulted. With barely contained indignation, she accused him of mistrust and gender discrimination.

But her shrewd scheming became clear to MacManus only when he discovered that his new flat-screen Toshiba had disappeared from the bedroom in the company of his two-month-old Sony stereo system. Jenny failed to explain what had happened to these items; instead, she burst into tears, blaming MacManus for his poor fathering skills, to say nothing of how he had offended her, a poor single mother, for absolutely no reason. Heated up by snorting crack cocaine, which she'd recently purchased from a reputable dealer, Jenny had reached the next level of rage. She grabbed a hot pan of half-cooked beans and attacked

MacManus with all the might and bravery of a woman in "high spirits." MacManus would have been doomed, but the Almighty had his own plan. Trying to strike her "honey" on his head, Jenny tripped over the rug, lost her equilibrium, and hit the sharp edge of the couch. Thanks to the anesthetic properties of cocaine and her natural stamina, Jenny didn't suffer much physically or emotionally, yet she was so exhausted from the scuffle that she instantly fell into a deep sleep.

The next morning, while applying her favorite makeup, she discovered a small bruise just below her right temple. Without a minute of hesitation, Jenny called her attorney. The man was a well of conniving ideas, and he had proved his mettle before. Starting with her teenage years, he had arranged Jenny's transfer from jail to the drug rehab center. No doubt, the man knew how to fix things. Jenny gave her lawyer a "complete and unbiased" report of these events with particular emphasis on MacManus's jealousy, greediness, and lust. "This bastard was about to violate me, but, God bless, he is impotent," she explained to the lawyer. "A kind and loving person as I am, I can't forgive him for his shameless trading of my favorite pickup truck for some shabby Toyota Corolla! How, for God's sake, am I going to take my baby to a pediatrician if the boy gets sick? By public transportation?"

Jenny's lawyer delivered the folder with a list of all MacManus's crimes to the magistrate judge. The judge quickly issued an order for his arrest, and MacManus was apprehended. Without his close supervision, MacManus's business collapsed, and as if all these troubles weren't enough, his "first-rate lawyer" in no time sucked up all his savings. So at the moment, MacManus, who was probably naive but not stupid, contemplated his own defense. He had no choice. Despite all his misfortunes, the good-natured MacManus remained confident and optimistic. He knew that his tragic story would shock the jurors, so he was actually looking forward to his day of justice.

"Yeah, man, what can I say?" Eddie shook his head mournfully. "All our troubles are from women. Let's stay away from them."

"For the rest of my life, swear to God!" declared MacManus.

These eerie, self-inflicted tragedies upset Ben, and he wanted to do something really nice for these men in trouble. He would share his breakfast with them. That was the least he could do. His own problems at this moment seemed not even worth mentioning.

* * *

The very fact that on any given day at 5:00 a.m. hungry inmates may expect a free meal seemed purely remarkable to Ben. Similar service, with minor differences in the content of the food and its quality, could probably be found only on a cruise liner.

Ben opened the large plastic box and found it filled with brownish cereal, accompanied by two sizable bran muffins, a small carton of milk, and a tiny carton of apple juice. As dawn wasn't Ben's typical breakfast time, his decision to share his breakfast wasn't particularly painful. Still, the amount of carbs served at such an early time of the day was astounding. His new friend Anton definitely knew what he was talking about.

Meanwhile, another guard came in, and after verifying the inmates' names, reminded them of the exact time of their hearings. Among the people awaiting their transfers, Ben spotted the guy who had introduced himself as Gio the night before. The young man pushed his clinched fist through the bars, said, "I'm Gio" and marched away.

Next to Gio, on the cold metal bench, was Salvatore, an elderly fellow from Colombia. Salvatore didn't speak English and therefore remained silent. His inability to communicate with others was discovered as soon as the guard offered him a small paper cup with liquid medication, prescribed by the "attending physician," Simon. With well-practiced gestures, the guard was now trying to explain to Salvatore what his medical order was about and to make him swallow the remedy. Everyone else in the cell understood the purpose of the product in the cup long before poor Salvatore did.

Salvatore stubbornly refused to follow the guard's conventional instructions until the frustrated guard had a brilliant idea. He was now energetically moving his index finger from his mouth toward the rear end of his digestive system. The resourceful guard was also emitting loud noises, which no audience in the world would have trouble interpreting. Finally, enlightened Salvatore happily grabbed the cup and gulped its content. The spectators burst into applause and cheered while both Salvatore and the guard looked pleased with themselves. "Bueno, bueno," repeated the grateful Colombian, who'd finally gotten the flavor of free medical care.

If Ben's clinical estimate was accurate, the intended effect of the remedy had to start working at the exact time of Salvatore's hearing. Ben prayed that the poor Colombian would face the judge after him, not before. Who would dare claim the prison staff didn't have a sense of humor, even though it was jail-style humor?

Satisfied with his innovative approach, the guard left the cell to take care of other duties while two of his colleagues came in and wrapped everyone in familiar restraints. With handcuffs, leg irons, and waist shackles in place, the inmates were all ready to go.

The morning was cold and windy, and Ben was glad the guards had given him a winter jacket the night before. It was too early for the morning traffic, and arriving downtown turned out to be quick and easy. Another pleasant surprise was the musical taste of the new driver, who switched from ear-splitting heavy metal music to the much softer bluegrass. Was that a good omen?

Chapter Sixteen

THE WHITE VAN APPROACHED THE FAMILIAR gate of the courthouse, Ben was led inside, and the guards embarked on the next procedure, which involved unlocking and removing each and every restraining piece, property of the Walpole Jail, and promptly replacing them with the local, completely identical ones.

The procedure was going rather smoothly until the guard set about working on Ben's handcuffs. They were either poorly lubricated or the guard hadn't yet received adequate training in operating the devices, but the process of unlocking Ben's handcuffs stalled. After fingering the lock for a few minutes, the young guard gave up and called for backup. Help arrived half an hour later, but even two top-notch specialists in unlocking shackles could not defeat the unruly mechanism. The technicians' failure ignited a lively discussion about the maintenance of government property.

"Why do we need to lock and unlock them all the time?" The senior technical adviser looked gravely concerned about the inconsiderate use of this valuable merchandise. But his question went unanswered. The whole team continued to struggle with the stubborn mechanism, and their determination prevailed. The obstinate handcuffs finally announced their surrender with a tuneful squeak. The other handcuffs, property of the courthouse, were applied, and over the short interval of unlocking and locking them, Ben had a few joyful seconds of normal wrist circulation.

***

Back in the courthouse, Ben was moved into a cell, and with several hours to kill, he was happy to catch up on his sleep. He turned the winter jacket into a pillow and stretched on the cold metal bench. Yet a minute later, the cell door was hurriedly unlocked, and a new guard barged in.

"You can't have it here," he said sternly and pointed to the jacket. "Give it to me."

"Is it dangerous or illegal to keep a jacket here?" Ben asked politely.

"In this facility use of a garment for unintended purposes is prohibited." The guard cast Ben an austere look.

"That's a very sensible rule," agreed Ben.

The guard confiscated the improvised pillow, and order was restored. Lying on a cold metal bench was quite uncomfortable, Ben mused, but rules were rules, and nobody here was planning to bend them.

About an hour later, the sliding gate of the cell was unlocked, and an unsmiling female guard in her late twenties gestured Ben out of the cell.

Where is she taking me, Ben wondered. Why so early? My hearing is scheduled for much later. Ben was puzzled but didn't dare ask a single question—the woman's cold impenetrable look could frighten the Green Berets.

On the way to an unknown destination, Ben, preoccupied with his thoughts and tired after the sleepless night, missed the guard's silent motion to make a left turn and continued to walk down the hall. The female guard, who may have been warned about the doctor's potentially erratic behavior, grabbed Ben by his left shoulder with lightning speed, effortlessly rotating his body ninety degrees, and without a word, pushed him in the right direction. Ben, embarrassed by his disorderly conduct, apologized and explained that escaping from the courthouse wasn't in his plans. The guard burst into sardonic laughter. It was clear that she found the very idea that an inmate would have the chutzpah to escape under *her* watch simply hilarious.

Finally Ben was brought to a small, windowless room, divided into two sections by thin metal mesh. The female guard led him into the room and vanished. The heavy steel door behind him was rapidly locked from the outside, and Ben was left alone. He noticed that the heavy door had no knob and couldn't be opened from the inside. Ben looked around to get familiar with the setting. Two CCTV cameras were watching his every move. The only piece of furniture in his section was a round metal stool, securely attached to the cement floor. Then he spotted an identical stool in the other section of the room, which looked exactly the same except for a slight difference. The door had a doorknob.

It took Ben a minute to figure out that the function of the room was to conduct interviews and visitations. The door in the other section was opened, and Edward Gould walked in.

"How are you doing, Ben?" He looked concerned. "How was your jail experience? Any unpleasant encounters?"

"I'm good. The experience is unforgettable." Ben fell silent for a brief moment. "I've met some nice people. I mean, inmates. It looks like I've made a few friends. They said they would be waiting for my safe return."

Gould couldn't help laughing. "I hope they'll be disappointed," he smiled cautiously.

"That's my hope too."

"How would you evaluate your experience?" Gould passed Ben a penetrating look.

"What are the criteria?"

"Just on a scale from zero to ten."

Ben pondered for a minute. "I would say, nine."

Gould laughed again, this time lightheartedly.

"Listen," Gould was now serious, "in a few minutes you will have an important interview with a probation officer. He will determine if you can be set free on bail before the trial or if there is a danger of your escape. If he concludes the latter, you will be denied bail, and you will stay in jail until the end of the trial. The interview usually takes about half an hour. Then the officer will submit his conclusions and recommendations to your magistrate judge, and she will make the final decision."

"Do I have to prepare for it?" Ben asked.

"No, you don't. But what's tricky about it is that the officer knows most of the correct answers to the questions in advance. He essentially verifies the information you provide to him with his own data and evaluates your honesty and sincerity."

"So, I just have to tell the truth?"

"Right. Then, according to his assessment, the judge may impose a variety of restrictions on you, ranging from incarceration or house arrest to complete freedom to travel. The person who is granted bail is expected to follow all of the rules imposed by the judge until the end of the trial. The restrictions will be announced at the hearing, and they are not negotiable. And please refrain from making any jokes."

* * *

The interview was short and painless, but Ben had no idea what the probation officer thought of his answers. All Ben knew was that they were truthful. When the interview was over, a guard took Ben to his cell. No one bothered him anymore, and he fell into a deep sleep almost at once.

* * *

That night Emma got home around 9:00 p.m. All evening she talked with Gould on the phone or they exchanged e-mails. She went to bed at 1:00 a.m. and woke up at 7:00 a.m. She had an hour between 8:00 and 9:00 a.m. to call their friends and ask them if they could come to the hearing. Emma also asked a few of them if they could pledge their property to bail Ben out of jail. By 9:00 a.m., all seven couples had offered their homes as collateral. She couldn't predict how many relatives and friends would be able to come to the hearing because it was a weekday and for most of them taking a day off wasn't an option.

Emma reached the courthouse by 9:30 a.m. The traffic was light, and parking was effortless. But the interview with a probation officer didn't start at 10:00 a.m. or even at 11:00 a.m. She tried not to think about the time, but she was becoming more and more nervous. She had never met a probation officer in her life and was almost sure he or she would be tough and would most likely torment her with some tricky questions.

The interview started at noon and lasted about ten minutes. The probation officer, Tim McAleese, a tall, good-looking man in his forties, was respectful and didn't ask Emma a single tricky question. At the end of the interview, he shook her hand gently and offered the friendliest smile one could expect in a courthouse. Emma left his office almost euphoric when she remembered that the interview wasn't the main purpose of her visit and hurried to the lobby. A few of their relatives and friends were already there, and more and more were joining them every minute. By 1:00 p.m. there were around fifty of them, hugging and kissing Emma and each other. If they hadn't been in the lobby of a courthouse, it might seem like they were gathered together for a surprise birthday party.

About 1:30 p.m., Gould invited everyone to come upstairs and stay outside Judge Fine's courtroom. He pulled Emma aside, reached into his briefcase, and handed her a thick three ring binder.

"This is a copy of what we've put together overnight," he said. "The affidavits and letters of support are from the local physicians and Ben's patients, letters from your friends stating that Ben is an honest man and has no intention to flee, and our motion to let Ben remain free before the trial. This binder landed on Judge Fine's desk at 9:00 a.m. this morning. She has read it through and through. A little 'Molotov cocktail' for our dear prosecutors," Gould smiled broadly.

"Great." Emma nodded appreciatively. "Edward, here is the letter from Ben's physician."

"Thanks. I can't believe you could get it so fast." Gould scanned the letter, shook his head, and cast Emma a sad look. "In case the binder doesn't work, I'll pass the letter to the judge. Now let's go inside. The hearing is about to start."

* * *

Ben was still engulfed in weird dreams when a guard awakened him and gestured in the direction of the cell exit, the hallway, and the elevator. This time he was accompanied by several civilian-clothed FBI agents, and soon the whole detachment reached the fifth floor.

They arrived a little early, and one of the agents asked Ben to wait and allowed him to sit down. His companions moved a few steps away and dived into a discussion about their increased cholesterol and triglycerides. Clearly, each of them had his own ideas about how to fight the plague of the century. Ben, familiar with the topic both as a patient and as a physician, knew that he could easily participate in the debate and even give some valuable advice, yet sticking to Gould's instructions, he overcame the urge to share a few effective approaches to bring down scary numbers and forced himself to remain silent. Even if he offered his advice, would they take it?

To follow the posted announcement, the guards removed Ben's leg irons and other restraints. A few minutes later, they received a signal from the courtroom, and Ben and his somber entourage walked in. Julia Lander, his nurse practitioner, and her lawyer were already there. The room was packed with spectators. There were dozens of unfamiliar faces.

Ben was taken to the desk where his lawyer was patiently waiting for him. At the identical desk in the same first row, with their backs toward Ben and Gould, the two familiar fellows, the prosecutors, were conversing. Both of them looked glum. Gould reminded Ben about the purpose of the session. At the hearing, he noted, the judge would make her decision about whether to allow him to remain free before the trial. If she allowed it, then she would also announce the conditions of his freedom. The judge would also make the same kind of decisions regarding Julia Lander.

"Ben," Gould continued, "this morning at 9:00 a.m. we brought Judge Fine a binder with our motion to set you free before and during the trial.

In addition to the properties we already have as collateral in order to post your bail, your wife brought seven more couples, your friends, who are willing to pledge their homes too. I've never seen anything like that in my professional life as a lawyer!" He shook his head incredulously. "We arranged all the stuff overnight while you were having a good time in Walpole," Gould smiled demurely. "The prosecutors broke their promise not to arrest you and Julia, and last night they probably celebrated like crazy, certain that the arrest would crush your spirit. When they saw the contents of the binder, they became mad as hell. Now let's see if the judge's decision will cheer them up."

* * *

Except for Emma, Ben's cousin, and two of their friends who were the first ones to pledge their homes as collateral for Ben's bail, none of Ben and Julia's supporters, who took great pains to come to the courthouse, were allowed inside the courtroom. Instead, the courtroom was flooded with strangers. Why were *they* let in, Emma wondered. What connection do they have to the case? Judge Fine's arrival interrupted her thoughts. Then the door on the other side of the room opened, and Ben and Julia were led inside, Ben in a bright orange jail suit and Julia in a dark blue.

The case was announced. Judge Fine asked a few questions regarding the bail, listened to the answers, and said something to Gould. Emma, who was sitting in the back of the room, couldn't hear the conversation. Then the judge's voice got stronger, and she declared that Ben and Julia were free to go home today, and they were permitted to remain free on bail before the trial and throughout its duration. No home arrest, no curfew for coming and going, no electronic leg bracelet with a GPS, just a restriction to travel within state borders. The bail was set in the amount of $500,000, and the combined value of Ben's cousin's and their friends' properties turned out to be enough to cover it.

"Great job, Mr. Gould!" Ben turned to Edward and shook his hand.

"A well-deserved victory. A fair judge. A reasonable and fair probation officer. You see, sometimes justice prevails." Gould smiled happily.

* * *

Emma left the courtroom lightheaded, and suddenly she was surrounded by her friends' concerned, questioning looks.

"What happened?"

"They both can go free today and stay home up to the end of the trial. The only restriction is no traveling beyond the state borders."

Hugs. Smiles and tears. Sighs of relief.

Gould walked out of the courtroom, and Emma walked up to him.

"Edward, thank you... I don't know what else to say..."

"You don't have to. It's all over your face." Gould smiled.

"The three ring binder seemed to work like a charm."

"You know why? Judge Fine is sensible and fair."

"Where is Ben now? When can I take him home?"

"Very soon. Where is your car?"

"In the parking lot across the street."

"Go to your car and wait for my phone call. I don't want the media to tear Ben apart. As soon as he is ready to go, I'll give you a call and you can pick him up in front of the building."

The moment Emma left the courthouse, a swarm of reporters, a murder of crows, encircled her. What did they want from her? Edward asked her not to talk to them. Ever. They were not there to find the truth; they were there to find sensational news. Just be silent and keep going, Emma thought.

"Ma'am, what's your personal opinion regarding Dr. Holden's case?" A tall brunette moved forward with a microphone. She looked amiable. Actually most of them looked harmless. All of a sudden, Emma felt an urge to say something. These people already had been fed so many lies. This could be her only chance.

"Dr. Holden is an honest man and a talented physician." The words burst from her mouth uncontrollably. "He's never committed any crimes, and he will be acquitted."

She broke the circle of "crows" and walked rapidly toward the parking lot. She was mad at herself. Why did she talk to them? Did they really want to know how much Ben had cared for his patients and for everyone who ever asked for his advice or help? Or how excited he was about his work? If only she could say all of this and be heard!

Emma rushed to her car, suddenly feeling exhausted and totally devoid of her short-lived euphoria. Her cell phone rang. It must be Edward. She reached for the phone.

"Hello, Emma."

A woman's voice, quite familiar, but she couldn't recognize it.

"It's Molly."

"Molly?"

Molly was an attorney who had helped them obtain Ben's disability insurance after his devastating back surgery that they needed so badly to pay their debts. She was the most compassionate attorney one could imagine. They hadn't been in touch for months.

"I just heard that Ben was released. I'm so happy for both of you. How are you doing?"

Emma parted her lips to say she was all right, but the words didn't come out. The incessant stress that had been building over the past two days finally caught up with her. She swallowed, inhaled deeply, but still couldn't utter a word.

Their friend didn't rush her.

"Molly, I'm doing all right. I just... didn't expect your call. Thank you."

"Emma, let's get together one of these days. I miss you both. Best wishes to Ben. Good luck."

"Thanks, Molly."

Emma hung up and reached for the box with paper tissues. There wasn't much time left to get rid of these ugly traces.

Another call came in. This time it was Edward.

"Emma. We are coming outside. Move the car as close to the entrance as possible. I don't want the media to devour us."

"Edward, please don't go through the main entrance. Use the side one." Emma knew if *she* couldn't keep silent, there wasn't a chance Ben could.

"Emma, it's too late now; we are at the main entrance."

Emma moved the car up to the courthouse, watching the crowd of reporters and a man with a camera running toward Ben and Edward. Leaving them behind, Ben, head up, walked to the car, sat on the passenger seat, and kissed Emma.

"God bless Edward, his great team, and Judge Fine!" He took a deep breath. "Let's go home."

Chapter Seventeen

The charges were presented in early March of 2011, but only eighteen months later, in early September of 2012, Ben, Julia, their lawyers, and the prosecutors had their first meeting with a trial judge. Federal Judge Adler, who was appointed to their case, had to schedule the trial.

"Counselors," she turned to the prosecutors, "how long, in your estimate, will the trial last?"

"Two to three months, Your Honor," Lynch rose from his chair.

"Mr. Lynch, your medical experts were supposed to submit their reports with complete evaluations of Dr. Holden's practice by September 1. Do you have them?"

"No, Your Honor, we don't. Actually, the opinions of the medical experts in this case are far from critical because the case is not so much about medical treatments that Dr. Holden and his nurse practitioner provided as it is about their conduct, which the government perceives as ordinary drug dealing." He paused to stress his point. "In the government's opinion, the opioid medications that Dr. Holden and Nurse Lander prescribed were directly responsible for the deaths of six of their patients. So the drug suppliers, in this case Dr. Holden and NP Lander, should be prosecuted and punished by the same law that applies to drug dealers."

A twenty-year imprisonment for each patient's death, flashed in Ben's mind.

"It may take a while to present the entire case," Lynch resumed in his thundering tone, "but by the end of the trial, it will become clear that these two individuals are nothing but common criminals."

"Mr. Lynch," the judge looked slightly perplexed, "how many medical experts did you hire?"

"Five, Your Honor."

"Five?" Judge Adler arched an eyebrow. "Counselor, if according to your words the defendants are plain drug dealers and the opinions of medical experts are not relevant, why have you even bothered to obtain their testimonies and expertise in the first place?" The judge gave Lynch an inquisitive look.

Lynch mumbled something unintelligible in response, but nobody except for himself and his cocounselors could hear it.

"So, how soon can you submit the medical experts' reports? The court and the defense counselors need to receive them nine months before the trial. You know that, right?"

"We need five more weeks, Your Honor," Lynch replied.

"I'll give you six. By November 1 you will need to submit the reports to the court."

"Yes, Your Honor."

After five years of hunting, Emma thought, they'd finally found the experts.

"Now, does the defense have their medical experts' reports?" Judge Adler turned to Gould.

"Your Honor, we can't choose our medical experts before we see the reports of the government experts. We have to know what their conclusions are."

"That sounds reasonable. But you have to start looking for them; otherwise, your experts won't have enough time for the analysis."

"Yes, Your Honor, we will."

"Mary," the judge addressed her clerk. "Could you check our May schedule for the trial date?"

"May 13 looks good, Your Honor."

"All right, May 13, 2013, it is. Mr. Lynch, I expect your medical experts' reports by November first. Have a good day, everyone."

* * *

The November 1 deadline for the government's medical experts' reports passed, yet no reports were submitted. Finally, on November 6, with no formal excuse or apology, Gould's law firm received a long-awaited package, which included five reports by five experts who agreed to testify for the prosecution. The next day Ben received the whole set. He simply couldn't wait to dig in.

When Ben and the defense team learned the names of the government's medical experts, they wanted to find out as much as possible about them. Were they professionally qualified? Were they well known and respected in the medical community? Had they ever testified in court? If so, had they testified for the defense or for the prosecution, or for both? The most crucial question for Ben was how thorough and objective their evaluations were, and the only way to find out was to review the patients' files that the experts had evaluated, read their assessments and conclusions, and compare them with his own.

Emma walked into the room where Ben was going over the reports and met his puzzled look.

"Not as exciting as you thought?"

"Well, out of the five reports they gave us, four are brief summaries of what the experts plan to say, and all four summaries look like they were narrated by the prosecution."

"Did the fifth expert write a full report?" Ben nodded. "Who is it?"

"Dr. Jeremy Arnoldoff. He is actually well known. I met him more than once at pain management conferences. He is a fine presenter."

"He must be knowledgeable. I hope he tried to be objective."

"Me too," Ben said uncertainly.

"Who are the other pain physicians?"

"I've never heard of them, Dr. Finnegan and Dr. Michalek. They're both medical directors of local pain clinics."

"They must be expensive," said Emma.

"I bet they are."

"And they didn't have time to write reports?"

"No, their assessments are extremely evasive. They are more like general summaries with very few specifics to confront, but most importantly, their statements or conclusions are not based on any current medical literature, known policies, or regulations."

"Why?"

"Well, because at the time I was a pain doctor, such policies and regulations were not precise, to say the least. If a patient showed so called 'aberrant behavior,' most clinical decisions were left up to his or her physician. In each case, it was the doctor's judgment call, based on his or her medical expertise, an evaluation of the patient's history and health condition, and the risk/benefit ratio."

"What do you mean by that?"

"We always have to weigh the risks and benefits of our medical decisions. Let's say that my patient's urine test results showed he was recently smoking marijuana. Marijuana was illegal at the time, and using it was against our office's policy. Therefore, I had a reason to either discharge the patient or to stop prescribing opioids."

"And if you did?"

"If I did? Do you think the source of his pain would disappear and his need for pain relief would go away? No, it wouldn't. Is he going to be better off without the effective pain relief he's been receiving in the clinic? I doubt it. Most likely, he would be looking for other sources of pain alleviation and probably will end up buying street drugs, which is not safe, to put it mildly."

"So that's not the answer?"

"No, it's not. When patients came to my office for the first time, they were often suffering from uncontrolled pain, and their lives were miserable. With a variety of treatments and opioid medications, we got their pain under control, and they could live normal productive lives. If we stopped prescribing pain medications, or even worse, dismissed them from the practice, what choices would they have? They would be back to their misery or turn to street drugs for pain relief. Unfortunately, for many chronic pain patients deprived of professional help, that becomes a common way out."

"So, what's the solution?"

"To this day, there is no agreement among physicians about what to do, and there is no standard approach. Pain doctors have been haunted by this dilemma for years and still are. In each case, it's the doctor's judgment and the doctor's decision. I have no doubt that if the patient suffers from a serious health condition and needs pain medication on a regular basis, he would be better off under the supervision of his physician than left on his own."

"Sounds reasonable to me. But in our society drug addicts are often considered and treated as outcasts, right?"

"Unfortunately, they are, even by some physicians."

"Do you agree with them?"

"I think that most of these people haven't chosen to become addicts. But no matter what pushed them into this disaster, I strongly believe punishing these ill people, instead of treating them, makes this grave social problem even worse."

"So you're saying that addiction is an illness?"

"In my mind, it is."

Emma pondered Ben's response for a minute. "I wish more people realized that."

"Especially those people who believe addicts should be persecuted." Ben sighed. "Well, let me read these reports by the government's experts in more detail. I can't wait to see what they've come up with."

"Ben, listen, I'm completely baffled. Lynch said that at the trial they would easily prove that you and Julia were drug dealers. Why do they need five physicians to prove that?"

"That's the million-dollar question. Let's ask Mr. Lynch next time we'll see him."

Ben walked back to his desk and plunged into work. He had three different medical experts' reports to read, analyze, and rebut for starters. Out of the sixty patients' files the government planned to use at the trial, thirty five files were assigned to Dr. Finnegan, the same thirty- five files to Dr. Michalek, and the remaining twenty-five files were offered to Dr. Arnoldoff.

Even with the limited information that Ben could extract from Dr. Finnegan's synopsis, it became clear that Dr. Finnegan didn't try to be either thorough or objective. He overlooked or blatantly ignored many important facts, and his conclusions for each medical file that he reviewed appeared to be his personal and unsupported opinions on the matter. Moreover, this relatively young doctor wasn't even working in the pain field from 2002 to June 2007, the period of time considered in the indictment.

One of the critical points this medical expert for the prosecution tried to make was his assertion that on many occasions Dr. Holden ignored the results of the drug screening tests for his patients and continued prescribing painkillers, even if the previously prescribed medication hadn't been identified in their system by either urine or blood tests.

"I remember that the tests results at that time were not reliable," Ben muttered to himself, "but I will have to do some additional research to make sure."

He walked to the bookcase where he kept his medical journals, retrieved one of the latest issues of *Practical Pain Management,* and found a recently published article on the subject of drug testing. The article, written by a panel of well-known experts, clearly stated that as helpful as drug testing might be, the results of the tests are often inaccurate and misleading. The experts strongly recommended a cautious approach to drug testing and warned physicians that their misinterpretation could lead to devastating consequences for their pain patients. That was exactly what Ben discovered ten years ago when he started using drug testing in his practice.

Ben had just finished reading the article when the doorbell rang. He walked to the door, happy to have a respite. It was Emma's friend Danielle.

"Hi, Ben. Happy to—" Danielle stopped mid-sentence. "Are you alright? You look weary. Exhausted by hard labor?"

"Worse, by disconcerting reading."

"Then don't read it. If I hate the book, I just drop it."

"I wish I could drop *this* stuff, but I can't afford to do that."

"Listen, is Emma home?"

"No, but she'll be back in half an hour or so. Dani, can you do me a favor?"

"Well... Not now. I didn't have my lunch yet. I'm starving. If you treat me to something tasty..."

"Dani, everything we have in the kitchen is yours. When you're done canvassing the refrigerator, please stop by my study. I need your opinion."

Fifteen minutes later, Dani knocked on the door and, with a happy smile on her round face, walked in.

"Ready?" Ben asked impatiently.

"Happy to oblige. What's the task?"

"I need you to listen to my explanations of some issues. It's critical for the upcoming trial. If you understand them, I have a chance that the jurors will understand too."

"Do you mean if such a mentally challenged person like me can grasp..."

"Dani, please. Except for Emma, you are the most sensible woman I know."

"I won't disagree with that. After a scrumptious lunch, flattery is the best dessert. So what's the subject?"

"It's about the results of drug tests, and this issue is at the core of the government's accusations."

"The results of the drug tests is at the core? Why?"

"Basically, when a patient is given a prescription for an opioid, the medication is expected to be present in this individual's blood or urine. Ideally, if you test it, you expect to find it there. In theory its presence indicates that the patient is compliant with the medication regime the doctor prescribed while its absence implies its possible misuse or even diversion." Ben paused.

"You said, 'in theory,' so what happens in practice?" Danielle asked.

"In real life, there are multiple factors that can and do influence these results, and these factors could be confusing and misleading, and the conclusions based on the factors could be simply false."

"But pain management specialists still recommend using them?" Danielle looked perplexed.

"In fact, the results of the drug tests are often so confusing or misleading that many pain management experts strongly recommend that doctors be rather skeptical, even suspicious of them."

"Why?"

"Because jumping to conclusions based on the test results *alone* might lead to unforgivable injustice and harm to the patient," Ben said.

"Do you mean to say these tests are unreliable?"

"Exactly."

"But why?"

"Some laboratory tests might not be sensitive enough to detect a particular drug while others could provide physicians with false-positive results for medications that were never prescribed."

"So the testing technology is far from perfect. Any other reasons not to trust these tests?" Danielle was getting more and more curious.

"Quite a few. Most tests can't take into account a person's individual ability to metabolize medications faster than an average person."

"Can you be more specific?"

"Sure. For most people the time between taking some medicine and the moment when this substance can no longer be detected in blood or urine is quite similar. But in about ten percent of population, this interval can be significantly shorter."

"So what happens?"

"Patients may take their opioid medication exactly as prescribed, but because of their fast metabolism, which for them is completely normal, the residuals of the medication, when tested, will not be detected. They would be simply gone."

"And because of that, they may be falsely accused of its misuse?" asked Danielle.

"Precisely! Some overzealous doctors may suspect honest patients to be in noncompliance with their treatments, or even worse, in diversion of opioids, which is a crime."

"It's like accusing an honest person of stealing?"

"Exactly. And there is another reason. Many people do not always take their medications as punctually as they should. If someone takes her pills on a regular basis and then the night before her visit to the doctor feels well and skips a pain pill, the next day the drug test could be negative. Is it a sign of misuse or diversion? Of course not! Do you know anyone who *always* takes medications exactly as prescribed?"

"No, I don't. Even my mother, who has immeasurable respect for laws and rules, may easily skip a heart pill or two if she feels well. Or sometimes she simply forgets to take them."

"So if doctors don't take these and other similar factors into consideration, they could unjustly accuse innocent patients of unethical or even illegal actions and punish them for no reason. What could be worse than that?"

"Almost nothing," said Danielle. "Anything else that can cause an incorrect interpretation of the test?"

"Yes, another reason is the timing of the test. This government expert, Dr. Finnegan, didn't even bother to match the date of the medications prescribed with the date of the patient's follow-up appointment and the drug test."

"Why is it important?"

"Why? According to the DEA regulations, in most instances opioids should be prescribed as a thirty-day supply. In other words, in order to have a noninterrupted supply of their vital medicine, chronic pain patients had to come to our office for an appointment once a month to receive their regular prescriptions. But in reality, because of weekends, holidays and other issues, it isn't always possible to strictly maintain the thirty-day interval. That's why from time to time our patients were seen a couple of days later. When this happened, the patients would usually have run out of their supply at least a day or two before the appointment, which meant they hadn't taken their opioids for at least 24 hours or longer, and that made detection of the prescribed medications in their body fluids difficult or simply impossible."

"Did this Dr. Finnegan take any of these reasons into account?"

"Not a single one."

"Is it possible he didn't know about them?"

"Are you kidding? Of course he knew. They are the basics."

"But if he knows all these facts and ignores them in his evaluation, isn't his evaluation a lie by omission?"

"I think so."

"Will he testify as an expert at your trial?"

"Most likely."

"So if he repeats these lies on the witness stand, will it be perjury?"

"I believe that a lie under oath *is* perjury."

"But since he is a witness for the government, he probably feels fully protected, right?"

"I think so."

Danielle was silent for a moment.

"It just hit me, Ben. His accusations are directed not only at you but at your former patients too. As far as I know, most of them were honest people who never did anything illegal, and this expert portrayed them as crooks, addicts, and drug dealers."

"True."

"Well, he thinks he has an invincible backup." Danielle paused. "And I assume the government handsomely rewarded him for his efforts."

"Who knows, maybe he's volunteered his services out of pure enthusiasm," shrugged Ben.

"Ben, there is this question that I wanted to ask for a long time and never did..."

"Shoot, Dani."

"Did you have patients who abused painkillers?"

"I did."

"How about drug addicts?"

"I had a few of those people too."

"Was it easy to tell who was an addict and who wasn't?"

"Not at all. Over my many years of practice, I've learned that the diagnosis of drug abuse or addiction takes a long time to establish, especially in chronic pain patients."

"Why?"

"Their behavior very often may look quite similar to that of a drug addict, yet the difference between the two is critically important."

"What's the difference?"

"Well, no matter how hard the doctor tries to help addicts improve their health condition, they would always feel worse and would continue to ask for more and more opioids. Contrary to addicts, regular pain patients, if treated appropriately and if they stay in compliance with the medications prescribed, over time would feel better. Their sleep would improve, they would be motivated to get back to work or start working more hours, and their functioning in general would get better than before."

"So that's the major criteria? Not the drug test results?"

"The results of the drug test are only one piece of the puzzle. Physicians have to look at the whole picture."

"So if all these drug tests were not very reliable," pressed Danielle, "why would any doctor ask his patients to take them?"

"That's a good question. Here is the answer—all our patients were asked to sign a pain management agreement where they promised to take their medications as prescribed, not divert them, and never to take illegal drugs. So even the possibility of these random drug tests and the actual testing put patients on notice that we could check at any time whether they'd observed the office rules or hadn't."

"And what happened if the test was bad?"

"If the patient's test didn't show the prescribed drugs or it showed an illegal drug, I would have a serious conversation with the patient and would start more vigilant monitoring of his or her behavior. But I couldn't deprive people who suffered from severe pain of their pain medication only due to the results of their drug tests. It would be ruthless. Doctors have to judge the patient's behavior in its totality."

"That may be true, but that's not what doctors do now. As you know, I'm suffering from really bad back pain that can't be cured, so I went to a supposedly good specialist. He agreed I had a serious chronic condition and said that surgery wasn't my best option, but when I asked him for opioids to help me walk normally and get out of bed without the terrible pain I had in the past, he refused. I went to another doctor, but it was the same story. Three doctors, one after the other, refused to prescribe opioid medication to me, a respectable middle-aged lady with no drug abuse record or any bad record for that matter! Is it some kind of conspiracy?"

"I don't think so."

"And it's not just me. A few of my friends ran into the same problem. What's wrong with these doctors?"

"They are either scared of being scammed by their patients or scared of being persecuted by the government or possibly both. Many pain patients are collectively punished because a few dishonest ones fool their doctors and abuse or sell their pills."

"Some years ago in *The New York Times Magazine,* I read a story about this doctor, an elderly man with a very small practice, who was accused of causing the death of one of his patients. That man had been taking opioids for quite a while, felt well, and then for some reason he died. His insurance company blamed the doctor. He was charged with recklessly prescribing opioids. Several dishonest patients, who had deceived the doctor, were invited to testify against him as 'reliable' witnesses for the prosecution. He was found guilty and sentenced to thirty years in prison. Do you remember the story?"

"I do," Ben nodded.

"From what I read, the doctor was an honest, caring physician. He went to jail for no reason while his deceitful patients were conveniently used by the prosecution and never punished for their crimes. Isn't it horrible?"

"Yes, it is."

"Do you think something like that may happen..." Danielle didn't finish the sentence.

"I hope not," Ben frowned.

"Listen," Danielle changed the subject. "I still don't get what exactly this Finnegan is trying to prove?"

"Well, he doesn't question the legitimacy of my patients' problems, I'll give him that. But he constantly objects to my pattern of opioid prescription. I shouldn't have prescribed pain medication in this case, I shouldn't have prescribed pain medication in that case..." Ben paused, barely holding back his frustration. "He's never had a chance to see any of my patients, and he is sure he knows much better how I was supposed to treat them! Has he ever had a chance to physically examine my patients, talk to them, and ask them about their pain, their sleepless nights, their ruined marriages, and broken relationships? In his opinion, I never did anything right. Ever!"

"I bet those few who deceived you were really good at that. How could you know they lied? You are not a detective or a mind reader. You are a physician, for God's sake!"

"I always thought my professional duty was to treat those who suffer, but the government thinks otherwise. They are certain I *had* to know that the dishonest ones were lying to me. I just didn't care and did nothing to stop the crimes. I bet that will be their message to the jury."

"This Dr. Finnegan would probably make an excellent messenger." Danielle shook her head incredulously. "I can't believe this guy accuses your patients of being addicts and crooks without ever seeing them. That's preposterous!"

"And he doesn't show a speck of doubt in his report. You should see what he claims! Imagine this: over a three-year period, one of my patients was in two really bad car accidents. Each time the man brought a police report as proof, and Finnegan said that because the patient was in a car accident *twice*, he must be a drug addict. Another one was attacked on a street, beaten up, and his money and medication were stolen. He came to my office all black and blue and brought a police report as well. His attack and the robbery were documented, yet Finnegan is absolutely certain that this incident was an overt indication that this other man was also a drug addict. It seems this guy's motto is 'Don't believe anyone and suspect everyone.'"

"What can be a better motto for a physician?" Danielle couldn't repress her sarcasm. "I always thought that any doctor's relationship with a patient has to be based on trust, but this so-called expert states that it should be based on suspicion and mistrust. I don't envy his patients."

"Me either."

"Or his wife, for that matter," Danielle added musingly.

"Yeah, I feel for her," Ben echoed, and they both smiled. "So, were my explanations clear?"

"Yes, they were, but let's pray there will be at least one person on the jury that will be as sensible and open-minded as I am."

Ben grinned wistfully, "I hope that there will be more than one."

Chapter Eighteen

By the end of the week, Ben's analysis of Dr. Finnegan's composition was complete. Ben let himself relax over the weekend, and on Monday he reviewed the next government expert's report.

The second government expert, Dr. Larry Michalek, probably even a busier man than Dr. Finnegan, had chosen the easiest path and copied Dr. Finnegan's report almost verbatim. (Only much later, Ben learned that the prosecutors had drafted both reports and the experts had only slightly edited them.)

Unlike Dr. Finnegan, Dr. Michalek was a more seasoned physician. After reading his report, Ben decided to check if this doctor had published any previous articles on the subject in medical journals. There were quite a few of them. To Ben's puzzlement, most of Dr. Michalek's statements on pain management in his articles contradicted the statements that he made in his report on Dr. Holden's practice.

Ben picked up the phone.

"Hello, Edward Gould speaking."

"Hi, Edward, it's Ben. Are you ready for a thriller?"

"A thriller? Always."

"I just e-mailed you a few of Dr. Michalek's articles and highlighted his most riveting statements. I won't say more. Please call me after you receive them."

* * *

Gould called back two hours later.

"Ben, delightful reading. These greedy guys have no scruples whatsoever." He paused. "You know what? I've enjoyed the reading, but I'll enjoy cross-examining him on the witness stand even more."

* * *

The report that the third pain management expert, Dr. Jerome Arnoldoff, presented was totally different. Unlike the concise reports of the other two experts, his assessment was more comprehensive. Ben had met Dr. Arnoldoff before at several pain conferences and found him to be a fine presenter. He was truly perplexed why this knowledgeable doctor would write a report for the prosecution, but he hoped that at least *his* evaluation would be objective.

When Ben finished reading the first six pages of the report, he could hardly believe this opus was for real. Dr. Arnoldoff challenged and condemned almost every medical decision Ben had ever made and accused him of every possible wrongdoing one could imagine. Ben's blood pressure jumped so high that he had to take extra medication and lie on the couch to recover. He closed his eyes and gathered his thoughts. He had to learn how to read this report without losing his mind. Then he suddenly remembered that at one of the pain conferences he had purchased Dr. Arnoldoff's book and not only read it but followed a few of his recommendations. He had to find that book.

* * *

Ben found the book in no time, and by the end of the week he'd read it through and through. He highlighted one paragraph after another and flagged them for Gould when Emma walked into the room, looking sad and frustrated.

"Ben, what's going on? For two days in a row you've locked yourself in this room and completely ignored everyone, including me."

"I've been reading Dr. Arnoldoff's book. He's one of the experts."

"The book must be a work of genius," Emma shook her head incredulously.

Ben frowned. "In his book he recommends and supports practically everything we've done in our center, while in his report for the government, he *condemns* my treatments and practices, which are exactly the same treatments and practices that he's approved in his own publication."

"Do you think he was too busy to verify his conclusions with his previous statements?"

"Maybe he didn't care. Or maybe he assumed no one would ever discover that he had taken totally opposite positions on the very same subject in his book and in his assessment of my practice for the government, so he had nothing to worry about."

"But what is he going to say when called to testify in court? I can't even imagine—" Emma was interrupted by the familiar ringing tone. Ben reached for his cell phone.

"Who is it, Ben?" Emma whispered.

"Edward."

"Can you turn on the speaker?" Ben nodded.

"Hi, Ben. It's Edward Gould. How are you?"

"Pretty good, Edward. Thank you. I'm dissecting Dr. Arnoldoff's report."

"What do you think?"

"One surprise after another. All the treatments and policies that he denounces in his report on my practice he approves in his book."

"Couldn't be better!" Edward paused for a moment. "Actually, it could."

"You're kidding?"

"No, I'm not. We just finished Dr. Arnoldoff's background check."

"And?"

"He is a fascinating character. Did you know that he was prosecuted for corruption in our state, found guilty, and his license was suspended for a few years?"

"I had no idea."

"After this little blooper," continued Gould, "he moved to another state and currently has a private practice." Gould paused. "His practice is getting *scornful* reviews from his patients. You can read them on the Internet."

"Life is full of surprises." Ben heaved a wistful sigh. "I used to think he was a reputable physician... at least before I'd read his report. Who could imagine that behind the respectable facade..."

"He is also a very resourceful man," continued Gould. "It looks like he's made a spectacular career as a specialist in pain management, lecturing and joining all sorts of useful committees."

"I wonder if people on those committees are aware of his past."

"I doubt it."

"Now I see why he agreed to be the government's expert."

"How could he refuse?" Gould was quiet for a long moment. "I can't wait to see this guy on a witness stand and cross-examine the shyster. I wouldn't miss it for the world."

* * *

The next two reports that the prosecutors submitted were written by specialists in forensic medicine, commonly known as chief medical examiners. Considering that the prosecutors' most important objective was to directly connect the six patients' deaths to the prescribed opioid medications, these experts' opinions were absolutely critical. Before reading the reports, Ben once again thoroughly reviewed his own notes on the original autopsies and toxicology findings from the medical examiners in Massachusetts who actually performed postmortem examinations on the six deceased patients.

The defense team received these reports and passed them on to Ben a few months earlier. Ben wasn't a specialist in postmortem analysis, but he wanted to—he *had* to—get to the bottom of the matter. So he purchased a few fundamental books on the subject and studied the principles and rules of performing autopsies as well as standard ways to analyze their findings, particularly related to fatal drug overdose. Only after that, did he immerse himself in the reports. Ben also bought a volume, called *Disposition of Toxic Drugs and Chemicals in Man,* by the renowned expert in the field, Dr. Randall Baselt, and he studied the pertinent chapters of the book with utmost diligence.

The general facts of the reports were easy to comprehend. In four out of six of the deceased patients, the toxicological analysis indicated a combination of prescribed opioids and cocaine, and the medical examiners identified the cause of death as opioid overdose. In the fifth case, the cause of expiration was chronic heart disease, and in the last one, the cause of death was a cocaine overdose. But these explanations were only the medical examiners' conclusions, which could be either right or wrong. Armed with his newly acquired knowledge, Ben could now much more scrupulously interpret the facts that led to these conclusions, and the analysis of these facts appeared to be quite an exciting endeavor. When he was done, he sent the concise version of his findings to Edward Gould and Rachel Leigh. In these findings, which he titled *Summary of Errors and Guideline Deviations in the Medical Examiners' Reports,* Ben cited the following:

1. Blood toxicology: In five out of six cases, blood was collected from the heart instead of the femoral vein, which was *not* the way it should be done according to the CME guidelines.

2. In five out of six cases, toxicological tests for certain opioids were either not performed at all or were done without a mandatory GH/MS confirmation, which is much more accurate.

3. Despite the significant visual pathology of myocardium that was described in one case, a basic histological examination of the heart was never performed to rule out myocardial infarction as a possible cause of death.

4. In one case where the patient's actual height was 6'2", the report recorded it as 5'2", so Ben wondered if the autopsy was performed on the body of some other person who was not his patient.

5. In two cases, the toxicological analysis was dated *two weeks prior* to the actual person's death while in the third case the final autopsy analysis was dated *six months prior* to the patient's death.

6. In one of the cases, the autopsy wasn't performed at all.

7. The standard property list of the CME office indicated that the body of the deceased Mr. P. was removed from the body bag in *March 2004* when the man actually died two years later, in *March 2006*.

In addition to these errors, Ben cataloged many others and e-mailed them to Gould and Leigh.

* * *

Gould called him an hour later.

"Excellent job, Ben."

"Do you refer to the medical examiners?"

Gould laughed. "Not exactly."

"Edward, do you think the prosecutors haven't noticed all these flaws or they just don't care?"

"Could be either. Or both."

"Can we call any of these specialists to the witness stand?"

"We might, if it comes to that."

* * *

Ben reached for the report by another expert, the chief medical examiner that the prosecutor had hired.

"Well, let's see who the lucky author is. Gosh, Dr. Mitchel Bruton!"

For many decades, Dr. Bruton had been engaged in investigations of the most notorious murder cases across the country and even abroad, and usually testified for the prosecution but occasionally for the defense as well. He had more than forty years of experience in forensic medicine. His name was a trademark of expertise, and his opinion would be difficult to dispute, let alone to dismiss.

Ben opened the folder with Dr. Bruton's report and was about to start reading it when he was interrupted by a phone call.

"Ben, it's Rachel Leigh."

"Hi, Rachel," Ben said warily. He knew Rachel would never call for small talk.

"Ben, I have excellent news."

"Excellent news? Regarding what?"

"I found a court transcript with Dr. Bruton's testimony in Florida three years ago. The case was quite similar to yours."

"What was it about?"

"A pain doctor had a patient who was suffering from severe chronic pain and needed a significant amount of pain medication on a daily basis. The man was taking a modest amount of methadone for his pain and was doing fine until one weekend he got bored to death and in order to amuse himself took a generous portion of cocaine."

"Let me guess what happened..."

"I bet you guessed it right. The man died the same evening, and his postmortem toxicology showed a substantial amount of cocaine metabolites in his blood mixed with the methadone prescribed by his pain doctor."

"Sounds familiar."

"The government accused the doctor of directly contributing to his patient's demise. He was arrested, and the story was widely publicized in the local media."

"So the prosecution hired Bruton to testify?"

"Much better. The defense did."

"So what was his testimony?"

"I just e-mailed you the transcript. Enjoy."

Ben opened his e-mail and saw a two-hundred-page trial transcript. In his testimony to the court, Dr. Bruton explained:

> ***Although cocaine itself may be extremely toxic and frequently fatal, after the human body metabolizes it into more benign components, it typically becomes rather harmless. Typically, but not always. The amount of cocaine metabolites detected in the blood of the deceased patient was so high that no human being could survive it, and therefore, the prescribed pain medications, specifically methadone, had nothing to do with the tragic outcome. Cocaine was the culprit.***

When Ben finished reading, he ran to the living room to share the news with Emma.

"Ben, It couldn't be better! Aren't they crazy to hire him to testify against you?"

"Who knows? Listen, I've already researched this case on the Internet. It looks like this forensic expert's testimony in Florida played a huge role in its outcome. After a few hours of deliberation, the pain doctor was unanimously acquitted by the jury."

"Isn't it odd that the prosecutors have chosen him as their expert in your case?" Emma looked baffled. "The man is obviously on your side."

"At least he was three years ago."

* * *

As Ben read Dr. Bruton's report, his blissful mood started to fade. When he finished the last paragraph, he rushed to the phone and dialed Rachel's number.

"Rachel, have you read Dr. Bruton's report?"

"Yes, I have. Do you want my opinion?"

"Sure."

"Well, it's as predictable as any report for a prosecution can be. Are you surprised?"

"Am I surprised? In four out of the six deaths, the results of the blood toxicology showed substantial amounts of cocaine metabolites, exactly like in the Florida case. But this time around, Dr. Bruton claimed that cocaine had nothing to do with my patients' deaths because cocaine metabolites, by definition, couldn't be toxic. Has he forgotten his prior testimony?"

"Apparently so."

"Look what he writes, *'The main contributing factors in four death cases were opioid medications prescribed by the defendant, Dr. Holden.'* This is the complete opposite of his testimony in the Florida case!"

"Ben, you may not know this, but flip-flopping could be a well-reimbursed enterprise."

"Rachel, flip-flopping is not his only virtue. Look at this! In two other cases where cocaine wasn't found, his colleagues, who performed the original autopsies, stated that the patients' deaths were the result of natural causes. But Dr. Bruton adamantly disagreed with them and instead accused *me* of their deaths!"

"Ben, do you remember who hired him and who paid him?"

"Now, Rachel, listen to this," Ben barely heard her comment as he was getting more and more agitated. 'One of these six patients was taken to the ER, where they tried to resuscitate him but failed. While he was still alive, they found a fatal level of ethanol in his blood. The volume of alcohol detected...' That amount alone could kill almost anyone, but Dr. Bruton preferred to ignore that fact altogether. He never even mentioned it. In another case, the original medical examiner had performed the autopsy and identified the patient's health condition as severe heart disease and named it a direct cause of death. However, Dr. Bruton disregarded the opinion of his fellow medical examiner and concluded that the sole cause of the man's death was the medication prescribed by Dr. Holden."

"What can I say, Ben? Welcome to the world of doctors on criminal trial."

"This is really something to look forward to. Now I have to go over another report. This guy is not a celebrity, but maybe he wrote something more sensible than our TV star."

"Don't hold your breath, Ben."

* * *

The second expert in forensic medicine that the prosecution team hired was Dr. Smart. In his assessment of the forensic documents pertinent to the deaths of Dr. Holden's six patients, Dr. Smart, just like his renowned colleague, demonstrated that he was fully aware of the type of conclusions the government had expected to find in his report. Still, his conclusions grossly contradicted Dr. Bruton's conclusion. These two specialists presented several disagreements regarding the causes of these patients' deaths. In addition, their interpretations of the toxicology reports were different as well. They also deviated from the conclusions made by the medical examiners who had originally performed the patients' autopsies.

Ben shook his head in disbelief. Each of these medical examiners had an opposite opinion and a different interpretation of the most important findings, and none of them was in agreement with the others on almost every point, including the most critical ones. How could the prosecutors accuse him of his patients' deaths when their experts couldn't even come close to agreeing on the issues? Ben pivoted between anger and amusement. If the government put both of their CME experts on the witness stand, jurors' heads would be spinning.

* * *

The next pretrial meeting with Judge Adler in mid-May of 2013 was to schedule a Daubert Hearing—a battle of medical experts.

Daubert Guidelines were set up in 1993 during the trial of *Daubert vs. Merrell Dow Pharmaceuticals, Inc.* They established much higher standards for admissibility of scientific evidence. From that time on, the trial judge was responsible for making a decision about whether an expert's testimony in the upcoming trial was based on sound scientific research and methodology. The questions most commonly asked were: IS their testimony scientifically valid, supported by publications in respectable technical or medical journals? Is their testimony widely accepted in the scientific community and can it be properly applied to the merits of the case? If not, such testimonies may, and should be ruled as inadmissible in the court of law.

Judge Adler planned to order the defense and the prosecution alike to invite their medical expert witnesses to testify in front of her and to explain their reasoning and conclusions about the deaths of the six patients. The judge seemed genuinely interested in the essence of the matter and in becoming familiar with crucial concepts several months before the trial.

The judge's resolve to become educated in unfamiliar areas of medicine and to make sure the experts' conclusions were scientifically sound was truly commendable, at least in the eyes of the defense team and Dr. Holden. The prosecutors, on the other hand, had a different point of view.

"Your Honor," Mike Lynch leaped from his chair as soon as Judge Adler announced her decision to have a Daubert Hearing. "These defendants are nothing more than ordinary drug dealers; therefore the Daubert standard in this case is totally irrelevant."

"Really?" Judge Adler's dark brown eyes flickered in genuine surprise. "If this is the case, why have you hired five medical experts to support your position?" Judge Adler yielded a barely noticeable smile and cast Lynch a penetrating look.

Lynch muttered something incomprehensible and took a seat.

"Well, the Daubert Hearing will be scheduled..." the judge glanced at her clerk.

"June 25 is open, Your Honor," Mary finished for the judge.

"June 25 it is at 9:00 a.m. Who will testify on your side, Counsel?" the judge turned to Lynch.

"Dr. Bruton and Dr. Smart, Your Honor."

"And for the defense, Mr. Gould?"

"Dr. Kent, Your Honor."

"Good. See you on June 25."

Chapter Nineteen

The Daubert Hearing took place in late June, 2013 about three months prior to the scheduled trial. Two expert witnesses on the government's side and one on the side of the defense gave testimony. The first expert to testify for the government was the renowned Dr. Mitchel Bruton. After more than forty years of performing forensic autopsies, Dr. Bruton had acquired the reputation of a knowledgeable specialist, and his opinion was considered by many as the truth.

Ben and Emma arrived thirty minutes before the hearing and sat alone in the hallway, enjoying the ocean view through the huge window of the modern federal court building.

Ben had a lot on his mind, and when he met Emma's inquisitive look, he smiled ruefully.

"Is something bothering you, Ben?"

"I still don't understand why they've hired Dr. Bruton."

"Why not? You said yourself that he was constantly appearing on TV shows. The man is popular, at least."

"He is, but he is a medical examiner. He is not an expert in the matter at hand."

"How come?"

"No doubt this man is an expert in his area, but as far as I know, he is not qualified in interpreting laboratory results, which is the key here. It takes special knowledge and training to determine whether these six patients died because of the prescribed medication or because of other reasons. This case is primarily a toxicological issue and demands an expert in forensic toxicology, which he is *not*. Why haven't they hired a specialist?"

"Could it be that there is a shortage of toxicologists in the country?"

Ben just grinned broadly.

"Or could it be that over so many years of building a case against you and Julia, the federal prosecutors couldn't find a qualified forensic toxicologist who would concur with their agenda?"

"That could be the case," said Ben. "Anyway, let's see what venerable Dr. Bruton has to say. I'm awfully curious."

Ben reflected for a minute. "Can you believe our trial attracts such celebrities?"

"It looks like they can't win this battle with a pistol; they need heavy artillery."

* * *

In preparation for Dr. Bruton's testimony, Rachel Leigh obtained a few transcripts of Dr. Bruton's previous testimonies in court, and one of them was especially telling. About three years ago, Dr. Bruton was asked to be an expert witness for the defense in a case quite similar to Dr. Holden's.

A pain doctor in Florida was charged with the death of his patient. The man had received therapeutic dosages of opioids to control severe back pain when one day he overdosed on cocaine and died. The prosecutors tried to prove that prescribed opioids had played a central role in the man's demise while the defense argued that as long as the patient had followed the doctor's orders he felt fine, but as soon as he added cocaine to the prescribed pills, his life took an ominous turn.

Three years before, when the defense had called Dr. Bruton to the witness stand to testify for this case, this seasoned medical examiner had no problem explaining to the jury that the fatal outcome of the patient in question had absolutely nothing to do with the treatments that the doctor provided. Instead, the patient's death had been caused by an enlarged heart, which was a common complication for his systematic abuse of cocaine. "The death had nothing to do with the prescribed opioids,"Dr. Bruton declared.

During his testimony, Dr. Bruton explained to the court that any habitual use of cocaine sooner or later creates a serious heart condition. The size of the heart thus ultimately increases, and it often disrupts electrical signals across the heart muscle, known as the myocardium. At any particular moment, even during periods when a cocaine abuser stays clean, rapid, irregular heartbeats could kick in, leading to uncontrolled myocardial fibrillation and possible death.

The court reporter had meticulously documented Dr. Bruton's expert testimony. Ben and his lawyers were now curious what arguments Dr. Bruton would present when the circumstances of this case were almost identical, but his position was entirely different.

* * *

The hearing began at 9:15 a.m., and the first expert witness, a tall, elderly gentleman in old-fashioned glasses, sauntered to the witness chair.

Dr. Bruton's thinning, neatly combed snow white hair and regal posture may have impressed the audience even before he said a word. When he began testifying, it became clear that his deep, confident voice and impeccable manners could easily win him the affinity of judges, jurors, and spectators alike. There was no doubt that Dr. Bruton was aware of his formidable appearance, but he was obviously smart enough to keep this awareness to himself.

Lynch moved to the lectern.

"Dr. Bruton, could you please tell us about your work experience."

"Willingly." For the next ten minutes or so, Dr. Bruton described his credentials and his exceptional expertise in the field. During this slightly tiring introduction, the prosecutor looked as proud as if all the listed achievements were his own. Finally, Lynch moved to the direct examination.

"Dr. Bruton, are you familiar with the phenomenon of postmortem drug redistribution?" Lynch asked politely.

"Yes, I am," Dr. Bruton responded without hesitation.

"Could you please explain to us the essence of this phenomenon?"

"Of course," Dr. Bruton readily agreed. "Postmortem drug redistribution starts immediately after a person's death. It's a physiological motion involving certain substances in the body, which move from areas of higher concentration to areas of lower concentration. In a living body, some medications have a tendency to accumulate in large quantities in the lungs, liver, muscles of the heart, and some other organs and in significantly smaller quantities in the blood. Therefore, after death, substances move from these locations of high concentration areas to locations of lower concentration until equilibrium is achieved."

Dr. Bruton turned to Judge Adler to make sure his explanation was clear. Judge Adler nodded.

"That is why samples of blood for a postmortem analysis ideally should be taken from one of the peripheral vessels, usually from the femoral vein," continued Dr. Bruton.

"Why specifically from the femoral vein, doctor?" Lynch frowned.

"Multiple studies demonstrate that after death the concentration of medications and many other substances in the femoral vein are as close to the actual amount of drugs in the live body as it gets."

"So if you take a blood sample from the femoral vein, the result would be the most accurate, wouldn't it?" The judge asked.

"Exactly. However, most of the medical examiners still prefer to obtain their samples from the heart."

"Why?" Judge Adler looked perplexed.

"Technically, it is much easier and less time consuming. You see, taking blood from a femoral vein demands extra efforts; first, in order to locate the femoral vein, you have to make a deep incision; then you have to apply a ligature and only after that to aspirate some blood. More hassle, I would say."

"I see," the judge nodded hesitantly, obviously not fully convinced by Dr. Bruton's reasoning.

"Well, let's move to your conclusions, Dr. Bruton," Lynch said firmly. "Your toxicological analysis of the five out of six deceased patients revealed a very high amount of methadone in their blood, and as we know, in four of these cases, the blood was taken from the heart. So what did the test results show in your expert opinion?"

"They showed that the amount of methadone detected in their blood was consistent with a very high, potentially fatal level," Dr. Bruton said gravely.

"But isn't the heart one of those places where methadone has a tendency to accumulate in an artificially higher amount after death?" Lynch queried..

"Yes and no."

"Could you please elaborate, Dr. Bruton?"

"Sure. Although the blood in each of the four cases was obtained from one of the heart chambers, the discrepancy in the test results between this location and the femoral vein would make no difference."

"How come, doctor?"

"Because the amount of methadone detected was so high that even if we take into account the phenomenon of drug redistribution and subtract twenty percent of what the analysis showed, the amount of the methadone would still be very high and most likely toxic and fatal," the medical examiner concluded confidently.

"Dr. Bruton, did you come to your conclusions by referencing any scientific literature?" Lynch asked solemnly.

"Yes, I did. In fact, here is the book I used as a reference. In our line of work, we like to use a number of sources, but medical examiners consider this particular edition as a sort of a toxicological bible. It's written by the highly respected specialist Randall Baselt. His opinions in the field are considered to be the most valuable."

Dr. Bruton proudly lifted a heavy volume and showed it to the judge. The title of the book read *Disposition of Toxic Drugs and Chemicals in Man.*

Lynch's cold porcine eyes shone with satisfaction. The prominent expert's conclusions, especially supported by these indisputable sources, were impossible to refute.

"Dr. Bruton," he continued, "you mentioned that the concentration of methadone detected in the blood of the deceased was very high and likely fatal. Can you tell us how high it was?"

"Well, let's start with Patient D.," Dr. Bruton began enthusiastically, as if he had been waiting for the question for years. "His blood level related to the methadone was..." Bruton glanced at his handwritten notes, "540 ng/mL, which is way over potentially toxic limits."

"What is the lowest possible level considered to be toxic?" Lynch asked innocently.

"Anything above 400 ng/mL," Dr. Bruton reported.

"What about the blood level for methadone in Patient J.C.?"

"760 ng/mL," Dr. Bruton responded with increasing enthusiasm.

"What about Patient S.P.?"

"It was 640 ng/mL."

"And Patient D.D.?"

"570 ng/mL."

"And finally, what was the level in Patient C.B.?"

"About 900. Actually, it was 921 ng/mL to be precise," Dr. Bruton added victoriously.

"Doctor, would you agree that in all of these five cases the amount of methadone in the blood was way above the toxic level?" Lynch asked, stressing the last two words.

"No doubt in my mind it was," the expert responded firmly.

"Would you also agree that methadone was the cause of these patients' deaths?" Lynch asked, his voice escalating in pitch.

"Absolutely," Dr. Bruton nodded confidently.

"Now, let's talk about the last Patient, Mr. J.C.," suggested the prosecutor. "Do you remember his test results?"

"I do."

"What can you tell us about the cause of his death?"

"Well, this case is a bit different. Although he also had a very high level of methadone in his blood, another medication, fentanyl, was detected at a rather high level too."

"What's the significance of that, Doctor?"

"It means that not only his methadone level had increased and was definitely toxic, but this man also had a high level of another toxic substance in his blood."

"And?" Lynch slightly frowned.

"This substance — I am talking about fentanyl — could very well have contributed to his demise," the medical expert concluded.

"But would you agree, doctor, that in this case, just like in all the other cases, methadone played a major role in this tragic outcome?" Mr. Lynch asked cautiously.

This time Dr. Bruton wasn't as quick to answer as before. He chewed on his lip and looked rather hesitant. Judge Adler cast him an inquiring look. Heavy silence hung in the courtroom.

"In this case, I believe fentanyl could also have played a central role in the death of Mr. J.C.," Dr. Bruton finally concluded.

Lynch, turning defiant, opened his mouth to say something but instead took a long pause.

"Nothing further, Your Honor," he uttered slowly.

"Counselor," Judge Adler turned to Gould's second chair, Mark Daniels, "you'll have a chance to cross the witness after the break."

* * *

After the brief recess, Mark Daniels, a tall, slim man in a gray suit and a light blue tie, headed toward the lectern. He had just turned thirty-two and was relatively new to the firm. Gould had chosen him as the second chair for Dr. Holden's criminal case, and it was his first major assignment at the firm. Like everything else in his life, Mark approached the task with fervent determination and spared no time or effort in preparing for the hearing. Not only had he educated himself on the general issues of drug overdose and redistribution of methadone but he had also meticulously researched the most respectable scientific literature.

"Good afternoon, Dr. Bruton. My name is Mark Daniels. I'm Dr. Holden's attorney, and I have a few questions for you," Daniels began in a courteous manner.

The medical expert looked at the young lawyer indifferently, obviously not impressed. In his long career as a medical expert witness, he had met many experienced and even famous attorneys and was personally acquainted with quite a few celebrities. He knew rather well how the mind of a defense attorney, including the most outstanding ones, worked, and he didn't mind being cross-examined at all. He even enjoyed it, in a way. He was much more educated in his field than any of them would ever be, and he didn't expect to be caught off guard. As a seasoned master of his trade, he also knew a few tricks about getting out of the most delicate situations, and he expected no trouble in dealing with this rookie opponent.

"Dr. Bruton, in your explanation of postmortem drug redistribution, you strongly relied on the monograph of the eminent Dr. Randall Baselt, didn't you?" Daniels asked.

"I certainly did," the medical expert said proudly.

"We are talking about the book, titled *Disposition of Toxic Drugs and Chemicals in Man,* right?" Daniels asked and put his own copy of the heavy volume on the stand.

"Yes, we are," the medical expert agreed.

"My copy is the ninth edition. It's the same one you showed us before, right?" Dr. Bruton nodded in agreement.

"Very well, then we will definitely be referring to the same source," Daniels gave an inconspicuous smile. "Dr. Bruton, would you mind opening your copy to page 178 and looking at the second paragraph from the bottom?"

It took the medical examiner about a minute to locate the paragraph, but Mark wasn't planning on rushing him.

"Dr. Bruton, we are looking now at that twenty percent difference you mentioned during your direct examination by Mr. Lynch. In fact, would you mind reading aloud a few lines regarding the research that led to that twenty percent increase?" Daniels asked politely.

"'*Postmortem study performed on five corpses demonstrated about 20% discrepancy between the level of methadone in samples obtained from the heart and the femoral vein*,'" Dr. Bruton read and stopped.

"Thank you, doctor." The young lawyer nodded without confirming the quotation in his copy of the book as he was familiar with it. "So the study was performed on five corpses, right?"

"Yes, it was."

"Could you please read the next line, doctor?"

"'*Next study, performed on 106 corpses, revealed that the discrepancy in results between the heart and femoral blood could be as large as 300%.*'" Dr. Bruton read flatly.

"So the study on 106 corpses showed that the level of methadone was up to three times higher, taken from the heart rather than from the femoral vein, right?"

"Right."

"Could you please read the line below that one," Daniels continued without blinking an eye.

"'*Scientific research, performed at the University of Wisconsin, where 168 corpses were examined, confirmed that the difference between the results may reach as much as 600%.*'" With every word, the expert's tone of voice was becoming gloomier.

"In other words, when the study was done on 168 corpses, the level of methadone in blood taken from the heart was up to *six* times higher than in blood taken from the femoral vein? Six times higher..." Daniels paused for the effect, "means 600% higher, not 20%, right?"

"Right." Dr. Bruton's face had turned crimson.

"And finally, sir, could you please read the results of the most recent research involving about 300 postmortem cases where methadone was tested," Daniels said, his glance calm and poised.

"'*The latest study*,' Dr. Bruton was reading slowly as if he'd mastered reading skills just a few days ago, '*which involved the analysis of about 276 cases of suspected fatal methadone overdose, revealed that the difference between heart and femoral blood concentration may reach 900%, which constitutes a ratio as high as 9:1.*'" The expert sighed heavily.

"Dr. Bruton, could you please explain to us, in plain English, what this 9:1 ratio means in Dr. Holden's case?" Mark Daniels asked gently.

The medical expert licked his lips and kept silent.

"Well, let me help you. Isn't it true that this ratio means that the amount of drug, in this case the amount of methadone, if obtained from the femoral veins of Dr. Holden's six deceased patients, as the medical examiners guidelines strongly recommend, could be up to 9 times lower than in the blood taken from the heart?" Daniels said, his face deadly serious.

"Right," Dr. Bruton said so softly that everyone in the courtroom could only guess the answer.

"Would you be so kind as to remind us where the blood samples of five of these deceased were obtained from?"

Dr. Bruton was now surfing through the pages of his notes, as if his memory failed him entirely.

"From the heart," he muttered finally, and shot a frantic glance at the door.

"Does it mean, doctor, that if we divide the results of those tests by 9, the level of methadone would drop nine times, and the actual results would be far below the toxic level? Well, actually, it would be significantly below even the therapeutic level, right? And that means that the methadone prescribed by Dr. Holden or his nurse practitioner could *not* be the cause of these patients' deaths, right?"

For a minute or two Dr. Bruton remained silent, and then he looked up at Daniels and their eyes locked.

"I don't know..." The expert stopped in mid-sentence; everyone in the courtroom was waiting for the full response, but Dr. Bruton didn't utter another word.

There was no point in waiting any longer. Daniels continued the cross.

"Well, Dr. Bruton, let's move to a different topic. Can you explain to us the significance of an enlarged heart as a possible cause of death? Could you help us understand why a person whose heart is bigger than normal is at risk for sudden death?"

"Well, it's quite simple," the medical expert began in a lively tone, rapidly recuperating from the unforeseen blow. "The heart muscles, which we call the myocardium, should contract in synchrony as long as the propagation of electrical signals across its bulk isn't interrupted. The muscle fibers of a healthy heart work like an orchestra, where each musician knows when and how to respond to the conductor's signals. If, for some reason, this synchrony is disrupted, instead of the beautiful melody, we would hear an unbearable cacophony. In other words, different parts of the heart would be acting in total disarray and compromise the whole purpose of this organ, which is to efficiently pump blood through the body."

Daniels grinned at the comparison and nodded approvingly. Dr. Bruton, encouraged, gave a satisfied smile and continued.

"So when the size of someone's heart for whatever reason increases, the whole network of electrical signals is compromised. Getting back to our analogy, the orchestra musicians would have a hard time hearing each other and following their conductor. They would not be playing in accord any longer and would eventually stop. Something like that may happen when the heart is enlarged. As soon as the chaotic contractions of the myocardium begin, partial or even complete inefficiency of the organ follows. As a result, the heart stops pumping blood, and if the rhythm is not rapidly restored, the condition will very likely lead to death."

"So the enlarged heart can be the cause of death?" Daniels asked nonchalantly.

"Of course, but in all six cases, the size of the heart was normal so we can easily rule out myocardium-related issues as the probable cause of their deaths," Dr. Bruton concluded firmly, his self-assured posture reinstalled.

"Dr. Bruton, if you don't mind, what is an average weight of a man's heart?"

"Between 300 and 350 grams," the medical expert promptly replied.

"I have the same figure in my source too." Daniels pointed to the thick volume of the *Gray's Anatomy*. "Now, let's look at the autopsy reports and find the actual heart weight of each patient. Do you have the data in front of you?"

For a quick moment, the medical expert looked embarrassed, but then quickly regained his composure and looked up at Daniels.

"No, I don't have the data, counselor, but if you read them to me from the reports, I'll certainly take your word for it."

"I really appreciate your trust, Dr. Bruton, but we happen to have extra copies for you," Mark Daniels declined politely.

He respectfully asked the judge's permission to approach the witness and handed him a stack of papers; then he offered an identical pile to Lynch and his cocounselors.

"Now, Dr. Bruton, according to the documented measurements that the medical examiner took during the autopsy, what was the weight of Mr. C.B.'s heart?"

"275 grams, which is normal," the medical expert responded.

"Yes, it is," agreed Daniels. "Could you please look at the next report, J.C.'s autopsy? What was his heart weight?"

"It was..." Dr. Bruton stopped, a puzzled look spreading from his eyes all the way to his jaw. "It was 600."

"Which is about 90% more than the weight of a healthy heart, isn't it?" Ben could see tiny sparks hopping in Mark's dark gray eyes.

"Yes, it is." Dr. Bruton stifled a sigh.

"The next name on the list is Mr. S.P. How much was the weight of his heart, sir?"

"It was... It was documented as 510 grams," the medical expert declared in disbelief.

"Anything remarkable about his coronary vessels?"

"Coronary arteries have focal calcification," Dr. Bruton continued, reading from the report as if under hypnosis.

"What would be the explanation for that, Dr. Bruton?"

"It usually means that before he died, the patient had a condition called atherosclerotic cardiovascular disease."

"So, if this is the case," Mark Daniels paused, "would you agree that for a 36-year-old man, these findings are quite alarming?"

"Well, they are certainly not unique," Dr. Bruton said evasively.

"But still rather unusual and alarming, aren't they?"

"They might be," the doctor agreed reluctantly and cast Daniels a cold look.

"Here is the report on the next patient, Mr. D.D. What was the condition of his heart?" Daniels didn't give up.

"I am afraid we don't have any measurements because his autopsy was never conducted," Dr. Bruton said hesitantly.

"That's right; it was never done," agreed Daniels. "Do you know why?"

"I have no idea!" Dr. Bruton looked surprised.

"Neither do I. But, doctor, isn't it mandatory to conduct an autopsy in each and every case when foul play or a drug overdose is suspected?"

"Yes, that is correct," the medical expert nodded emphatically.

"So, in the case of Mr. D.D., we actually don't know what condition his heart was in, or, for that matter, his brain, lungs, liver, or his other organs, do we?"

"No, we don't," the expert agreed once again.

"So, isn't it true, doctor, that if an autopsy for the deceased has never been performed, it's practically impossible to determine with any degree of medical certainty the cause of his death?"

Dr. Bruton nodded reluctantly.

"The next patient is Mr. J.C. Do you have his autopsy report in front of you, sir?"

"Yes, I do."

"Could you please read the paragraph referring to his heart?"

"The weight of the heart is 300 grams," read Dr. Bruton and stopped.

"Could you please continue, doctor?"

"The left ventricle is concentrically enlarged..."

"Could you please explain to us in layman's terms what 'concentrically enlarged' means?"

"It means that when the person was alive, the biggest and probably the most important chamber of the heart worked harder, for whatever reason."

"And how long might it take for this chamber of the heart to concentrically enlarge? Months? Years?"

"A few months at least, possibly longer."

"Doctor, you just said that the left ventricle is the most important part of the heart muscle, so its *healthy* condition is critical, isn't it?"

"Yes, it is," agreed the expert.

"So if it's not healthy, the person could experience serious heart problems?"

"Possibly, but..."

"Doctor, I hope you are not implying that having an enlarged left ventricle for a twenty-six-year-old man is normal, are you?"

Dr. Bruton didn't answer.

"So, let's briefly review the evidence and your conclusions, Dr. Bruton," Daniels said in his usual tranquil manner.

"Number 1. Isn't it true that your conclusions regarding the cause of deaths of Dr. Holden's patients were based on unreliable toxicological testing that completely disregarded the phenomena of postmortem redistribution of methadone?"

Silence on the witness stand.

"Isn't it true and that the results of this unreliable testing could be up to nine times higher than the actual ones? Not to mention the fact that even based on these more than questionable results, the methadone found in the bodies of the deceased had never reached the toxic level?"

Dr. Bruton remained silent.

"Number 2. Isn't it true that in your analysis you totally ignored the toxicological evidence of chronic cocaine abuse, which by itself is fully capable of triggering potentially fatal cardiac disturbances in the form of ischemia or arrhythmia?"

No response.

"Number 3." Daniels continued since Dr. Bruton didn't even try to object. "In four out of the six cases, there is documented anatomical proof of substantial cardiac pathology, such as a grossly enlarged heart, and as you testified before, an enlarged heart is a time bomb, waiting to explode at any moment. In two cases, these grossly enlarged hearts were also accompanied by evidence of substantial coronary artery disease, which by itself is proof of considerable cardiac pathology. In fact, it is one of the leading causes of death worldwide, isn't it, Dr. Bruton?"

Bruton nodded reluctantly.

"Number 4." Daniels was on a roll. "In the particular case of patient D.D., the autopsy, contrary to all guidelines and regulations, wasn't even conducted, was it?"

"No, it wasn't."

"And finally, Dr. Bruton, Number 5," Daniels continued without pausing, "isn't it true that in all six cases, the mandatory, crucially important histological examination of the myocardium under the microscope was never conducted either? Dr. Bruton, can you tell us why this histological examination may be important? Sir?"

"It might confirm a fact of significant disease of the heart muscle," Bruton muttered.

"Including the evidence of past or recent myocardial infarction, right?" Daniels paused, waiting for an answer. But the best he could get from Dr. Bruton was a faint nod.

Mark Daniels deeply inhaled, and his face suddenly assumed a pensive expression.

"Well, actually, I have one more question for you, Dr. Bruton."

Daniels looked perfectly calm, but the rascally sparks in his eyes said to Ben that "here comes the bomb."

"Dr. Bruton, isn't it true that three years ago, when you testified for the defense of Dr. Green in Florida, you stated that it was impossible to determine which substance specifically caused the death of his patient. You explanation to the court three years ago was that ***'it was impossible because the postmortem toxicology had revealed not only the medication prescribed by Dr. Green but a few additional substances, including cocaine. And either of these additional substances, especially cocaine, could be potentially fatal.'*** Did I read your testimony correctly?" Daniels asked.

Dr. Bruton blushed profusely but didn't say a word.

"Doctor, I have the trial transcript in front of me. Would you like me to read the quote from your statement in the Florida case once again?"

"No need. I remember it."

"To the best of your recollection, was cocaine detected in four out of six of the deceased patients?"

"I believe it was."

"So isn't it true that your opinion in Dr. Holden's case is completely opposite of your opinion in Dr. Green's case?"

Dr. Bruton remained silent, but the rose color in his face got a shade brighter. He looked toward the door, his baby blue eyes betraying his one and only wish for this cross-examination to be over. Right this minute.

"I have no further questions, Your Honor," Daniels announced, and walked to his seat.

Chapter Twenty

Another witness for the prosecution who was expected at the Daubert Hearing the next day was Dr. Smart. He was also a prominent, out-of-state medical examiner and also a top-notch expert in drug overdoses. The prosecutors hoped that Dr. Smart would support their first medical expert's opinion and that he would instill in the jurors' minds the concept that methadone, prescribed by Dr. Holden and Julia Lander, had caused the deaths of those six patients in question. That would make the doctor and the nurse solely responsible for their demise.

"So tomorrow we are going to listen to Dr. Smart's testimony?" Judge Adler inquired as soon as Dr. Bruton left the courtroom.

Lynch reluctantly stood up and turned to the judge.

"Sorry, Your Honor, but Dr. Smart won't be able to testify tomorrow."

"Really? And why is that? What happened to him?" Judge Adler raised an eyebrow.

"Your Honor, Dr. Smart is a very busy man," Lynch gently emphasized the word "busy" but the judge didn't look impressed. "We called him a few times and tried to schedule his testimony, but he was extremely busy. He is either at a clinical conference or he is making a presentation or—"

"It's all very well," Judge Adler interrupted, "but he was notified about this hearing a while ago and had at least two months to rearrange his schedule. Wasn't it the purpose of this hearing to gather all the expert witnesses in this room and give them a chance to present their testimonies?"

"Yes, it was, Your Honor," Lynch agreed gravely.

"So why is he not here? Does he think his other assignments are more important than this one? Do I have to subpoena him?"

"Of course not, Your Honor!" exclaimed the lead prosecutor.

Judge Adler frowned and remained silent for a minute or two. She was obviously looking for the best possible solution.

"All right, I can have an additional hearing on July 28. Is this date good for everyone?"

Gould checked his electronic calendar.

"We have no problem with that date, Your Honor," he responded.

"Nor do we, Your Honor, and we'll do our best to bring Dr. Smart here," Lynch joined in.

"I hope you will," Judge Adler nodded somberly and turned to Ben's lawyers. "Mr. Gould, is your expert, Dr. Kent, ready to testify tomorrow?"

"Yes, Your Honor, he is."

* * *

Dr. Claude Kent, a prominent forensic toxicologist invited by the defense, was a tall, fit, gray-haired man in his early seventies. He looked confident and amiable. After being sworn in by the court clerk, he comfortably positioned himself in the witness chair, opened a thick folder with the documents and his notes, and was ready for the direct examination by Attorney Daniels.

Dr. Kent's credentials were quite impressive, and Daniels wasn't shy about presenting them to the judge. The defense strategy was to leave no doubt in the judge's mind that Dr. Kent was qualified to serve as a medical expert on drug toxicity.

"Dr. Kent, approximately how many toxicology results have you analyzed over your thirty-five-year career as a forensic toxicologist?" asked Daniels.

"I would say thousands," Dr. Kent answered.

"And how many of them, in your estimate, were drug overdose related?"

"About two thousand or so."

"Considering these two thousand toxicology results, is it common for such test results to reveal the presence of more than one potentially toxic substance?"

"It's very common. In fact, the vast majority of deceased individuals typically have a mixture of two or more substances on board," said Dr. Kent.

"And what are these typical substances?"

"Well, they may come in all variety of combinations, but typically they involve a mixture of prescribed medications such as oxycodone, vicodin, methadone, or benzodiazepines blended with alcohol or such street drugs as marijuana, heroin, methamphetamines, and PCP or cocaine, which is often one of the major culprits."

"Doctor, when such a complex combination of prescribed medications and street drugs leads to a fatal overdose, how easy is it for a forensic toxicologist to determine which one of the multiple substances has been the *major culprit*? For example, today, using available modern technology, can a specialist in the field confidently state which of the medications or street drugs has struck the final blow as the particular substance that caused the death?"

Judge Adler leaned forward, all ears.

"To say it's difficult to determine would be a gross understatement. In most cases, it is simply impossible," Dr. Kent said with no hesitation.

"And why is that?" Daniels persisted.

"First of all, people are different, and their reactions to the same amount of drugs or medication may be completely different."

Could you please explain what these different reactions depend on?"

"A variety of factors, such as the person's age, weight, general state of health, normal or abnormal function of his liver and kidneys, other medications he was taking, and so on. Even the level of stress can play a role."

"Are there any other factors?"

"Yes, other factors too need to be considered, truly important factors. For instance, the reaction of a human body to a certain medication, especially an opioid medication, very much depends on the person's recent experience with the substance. If someone is opioid naive or has not taken any opioid medication *recently*, yet rapidly consumes a rather large amount of it, the medication could turn toxic, potentially even fatal."

"So, the difference between an opioid-naive and an opioid-experienced patient plays an important, possibly vital role in the outcome. Is that what you are saying, Doctor?"

"I would say a critical role, yes."

"So what exactly can happen to these opioid-naive people?"

"First and foremost, they can suffer respiratory depression."

"And what is that, in layman's terms?"

"In response to a large amount of drugs in their blood, the command center in brain, responsible for breathing signals, is suppressed. As a result, the muscles of the chest wall may be blocked from receiving the signals that order them to contract and relax in a timely fashion."

"In other words, the body would simply forget to breathe?" Daniels asked.

"Exactly," agreed Dr. Kent.

"And what would happen?"

"A tragic scenario. The brain would die first, usually within a few minutes, and other organs, such as the heart, liver, and kidney, would suffer the same fate in short order."

"Dr. Kent, what is the role of opioids in this process, if any?"

"If someone has *not* been taking a substantial amount of opioids in the recent past, the respiratory center remains very sensitive to them. So, taking a large amount of these medications, especially at once, can be very dangerous. The greater the amount of opioids taken and the quicker they are consumed, the higher the risk," concluded Dr. Kent.

"And if the person is not opioid naive, will it make a difference?"

"It absolutely will. When someone has been prescribed opioids over a period of time, including the recent past, that person's brain rather quickly develops an immunity to the major side effects of the substance, especially to respiratory depression. This phenomenon is called opioid tolerance."

"Can you be more specific?"

"After taking opioids such as oxycodone, methadone, fentanyl, or other similar substances even for a relatively short period of time, let's say a couple of weeks, the danger of opioid related respiratory depression gradually subsides. Don't get me wrong; the risk of this complication wouldn't disappear completely, but it would take a much bigger amount of the same or similar opioid medications to place an opioid-tolerant patient at risk for ceasing to breathe."

"Thank you, Dr. Kent. Now, let's get back to the six deceased patients in question. Did you have an opportunity to read their medical files?"

"I certainly did."

"And based on the information in these files, how many of these six patients were opioid naive?"

"None," Dr. Kent answered determinedly.

"According to the data in these files, prior to their demise, were all of them prescribed opioids for a certain period of time?"

"Yes, they were. Reasonable and steady amounts of opioids," confirmed Dr. Kent.

"What do you mean by steady?"

"I mean that all of them received the same unchanged amount of opioids for months, in some instances for years," responded Dr. Kent.

"Does it mean that their respiratory centers were to a significant degree protected from the dangerous effect of respiratory depression?"

"Yes, it does."

"In other words, because they had a long experience with opioid medications, prescribed by Dr. Holden for their intense pain, their respiratory centers became tolerant to this common effect of respiratory suppression?"

"Yes and no. Patients, in general, are safe as long as they, under their doctor's supervision, take the same or slightly higher amount of opioids as prescribed. But mixing them with street drugs or alcohol, or drastically increasing their dosage in rapid succession, is still dangerous even for opioid-tolerant patients," explained Dr. Kent. "Unfortunately, some people become reckless or compulsive, they overestimate their ability to tolerate big dosages, and that's how many drug overdoses occur. Some of these episodes may lead to a person's death. Even an occasional use of certain street drugs, especially cocaine, can sooner or later create a significant dent in such vital organs as the heart or brain."

"And then what happens?" asked Daniels.

"The person turns himself into a ticking bomb."

"What do you mean by that?"

"Statistically, cocaine users quite frequently end up with a stroke. The accumulating damage to the heart muscle, caused by consistent or even sporadic cocaine use, predisposes the individual to such conditions as cardiac arrhythmia or cardiac fibrillation."

"Are these conditions dangerous?"

"These conditions are extremely dangerous. Cocaine is a notorious leader in triggering such life-threatening effects, especially among young and middle-aged people."

"Dr. Kent, isn't it true that the autopsy of four out of these six patients in question revealed significant amounts of cocaine metabolites in their systems?"

"Correct."

"But they were cocaine metabolites, not the parental cocaine?"

"That's true."

"Would you mind interpreting these results?"

"Sure. The mere presence of these cocaine metabolites demonstrates that cocaine was recently used, most likely within the last few days, possibly hours. However, cocaine continues disintegrating very quickly after death, and the chance of detecting pure, not metabolized cocaine in the blood of a deceased patient is very slim. Its detection is inversely proportional to the gap between the time of last cocaine consumption and the time of the autopsy. In other words, the longer the interval, the less likely it is that pure cocaine could be detected."

"So what about the intervals in these four cases, Dr. Kent?"

Dr. Kent conferred with his notes, keeping the judge and his little audience in suspense.

"Well, from what I have here, the shortest time between the death and the autopsy was 36 hours, and in the case of Mr. J.C. it was more than 54 hours."

"So the parental cocaine had enough time to metabolize and naturally disappear from their bloodstream, correct?"

"More than enough time. The average time for the complete degradation of parental cocaine is only about one hour or even less," clarified Dr. Kent.

"But let us assume, for the sake of argument, that pure cocaine wasn't present at the time of death because all of those four deceased patients had used it a few days before. How does it change the picture?"

"Actually, not much. The presence of cocaine metabolites most likely confirms the patients' habitual use of cocaine. As we discussed before, repeated use of cocaine, even if it's recreational, causes irreparable damage to the heart muscle, predisposing this vital organ to a variety of potentially fatal conditions."

"Such as cardiac arrhythmia?"

"Yes, but not exclusively. We can add accelerated atherosclerosis, myocardial hypertrophy, scarring of the heart muscle, and several others."

"Have you seen any evidence of these conditions in these four cases, Dr. Kent?"

"Yes, I have," the medical expert replied firmly. "And this evidence is absolutely critical because four out of six of the deceased patients were rather young men, whose heart conditions would be expected to be normal. Contrary to these expectations, most of the autopsy findings revealed advanced heart abnormalities."

"Were these abnormalities potentially dangerous?"

"Unfortunately, they were. When the fragile equilibrium of the damaged heart is somehow compromised or disturbed, Pandora's Box opens, and then the worst can be expected."

"Can habitual use of cocaine open this Pandora's Box?"

"Most scientists, including our prominent cardiologist, Dr. Steven Karch, believe it can. And I strongly agree with them," added Dr. Kent.

"Thank you, Dr. Kent. Now, let's change the subject and talk about the dose of medications, specifically the levels of methadone that were detected in the blood of the six deceased patients. How do you know if these medication levels were fatal?"

"Well, in theory, almost any pharmacological substance may have a toxic, potentially fatal effect," stated Dr. Kent. "The safety margin of drugs is determined by a few criteria, but the most important one is the range between the therapeutic and toxic amount. The wider the range is, the safer the medication is. For some drugs, this range is extremely broad, and for others, it is rather narrow."

"Dr. Kent, how safe, in your professional opinion, is methadone?" asked Daniels.

"Like any other opioid, methadone has no ceiling effect," stated the toxicologist, "which means that if the dose of methadone is increased slowly and carefully, in a matter of weeks or months, the patient may safely receive a much bigger dose than the initial one over time. When taken as prescribed, even with a much larger dose, the patient should be safe. As I just said, and this is critical, methadone should be taken only as prescribed. This is of paramount importance."

"And why is that?"

"The rate of methadone metabolism may vary greatly from person to person, and we, as physicians, have no way of knowing this in advance how this particular patient will be processing this medication," Dr. Kent said. "It means that if someone with a slow metabolism rate, contrary to the doctor's advice, starts taking methadone too often or too much at a time, this potentially effective pain reliever may accumulate in his or her system too fast. The medication will quickly exceed its safety level and may become toxic," concluded Dr. Kent.

"And then this effective pain reliever would turn potentially dangerous?" asked Daniels.

"Exactly," confirmed Dr. Kent.

"So what is the official toxic level of methadone, Dr. Kent?"

"It's very broad, between 400 and 1,800 ng/mL." The medical expert paused. "But in discussing the toxic or fatal levels of opioids, we always have to take into consideration whether the patient just started taking the medication or has been taking it for some time."

"So once again, you are talking about opioid-naive patients versus opioid-tolerant patients, aren't you?"

"Yes, I am, but here we have a caveat. In regards to methadone, the situation is a bit more complex. While the toxic dose of this drug for the opioid-naive person may range from 400 to 1,800 ng/mL, its official therapeutic range is between 400 and 1,100 ng/mL."

"Doctor, do you mean that the same 400 ng/mL of methadone may be therapeutic for one person, and toxic or even fatal for another one?" Daniels exclaimed.

"Unfortunately, this is true," answered the medical expert.

"Then how can anyone possibly determine the right dose of methadone for a patient?"

Attorney Daniels looked truly puzzled, and Judge Adler even more so. The issues at hand were getting more complex and confusing by the minute, and the judge clearly had a hard time grasping Dr. Kent's explanations. Ben was worried. If she can't get it, how would the jurors get it?

"Dr. Kent, let's make it clear," Judge Adler said impatiently. "Is the amount of methadone below 1,100 ng/mL therapeutic or toxic?"

"It depends. For many people, it would be therapeutic and safe, but for a few, it would be toxic and even fatal," answered Dr. Kent.

"How come? Aren't the *official* therapeutic versus toxic dosages designed to guide physicians so that they wouldn't prescribe too much or not enough?" Judge Adler inquired pointedly.

"Yes and no, Your Honor. They give us a reference concerning what not to exceed, but variations are too numerous to use as an official rule," Dr. Kent responded patiently.

"Doctor, you probably didn't quite understand my question," Judge Adler insisted with overt annoyance. "I need to know how much is too much? Specifically, was the amount of methadone prescribed by Dr. Holden sufficient to kill these six people or wasn't it? According to Dr. Bruton's opinion, it was. And you say—"

"Your Honor," Dr. Kent was now losing his patience too, but did his best not to display it. "As I already explained, to determine the cause of death, especially when the combination of drugs is involved, is extremely difficult. So many factors should be taken into consideration. In all of these six cases, the amount of methadone detected was *well within* the therapeutic range. And in all of these six cases, the patients had a long history with opioids prescribed by Dr. Holden and therefore none of them was opioid naive either."

Dead silence settled in the room.

"It's *critically important* to remember," Dr. Kent continued, "that before their demise, the patients' doses of methadone were stable and had not been increased, and they were not high doses in the first place. In four out of the six cases, I also found strong evidence of both remote and recent use of cocaine."

"But still, a significant amount of methadone was detected in their blood, wasn't it?"

"Yes, Your Honor, it was," agreed the medical expert. "But the methadone was legitimately prescribed, and its detection *should* be expected. I need to stress the following two factors. First, in all Dr. Holden's cases we are discussing here, the level of methadone *did not* exceed the official therapeutic range. Second, its level could be easily attributed to redistribution of the drug, because the blood was drawn against the rules, not from the femoral vein, as the guidelines required, but from the heart. This aberrant technique significantly exaggerates results of the tests and makes them questionable at best, if not invalid."

"Doctor, let me rephrase my question," Judge Adler forced a tiny smile. "Can you state, with a high degree of medical certainty, that the presence of methadone in the blood of the six deceased patients played no role in their premature demise? Can you do that?! Yes or no?"

Judge Adler rose from her chair and leaned forward.

The situation was definitely getting out of hand, and Gould could see that better than anyone else in the room. If Judge Adler didn't receive a straightforward answer immediately, she might lose her patience and who knows what the consequences would be. He had to do something about it, and he had to do it fast.

"Your Honor, can we have a five-minute recess?" Gould asked with the utmost politeness.

"All right, a five-minute recess it is."

* * *

In the hallway, Gould took Ben aside. "This doesn't look good." He shook his head in despair.

"If only someone could explain to the judge," Ben said in frustration, "that in medicine things are almost never black and white! How can we make her understand this vitally important point?"

"Let me handle it," Gould said, and walked to Dr. Kent.

"Doctor, in your professional opinion was the amount of methadone in these six people's blood toxic?" asked Gould.

"No, it was not!" exclaimed Dr. Kent.

"Then, doctor, please say it loud and clear. That's all Judge Adler cares about. We don't want to leave her confused or uncertain. It's critical."

That was exactly what Dr. Kent did after the recess. The moment Judge Adler heard his statement, she smiled approvingly, and the defense team sighed with relief.

Dr. Kent's cross-examination by Lynch was rather short and uneventful. Forty minutes later, the medical expert's testimony was over, and he promptly left the courtroom.

The hearing, however, wasn't adjourned. There was one more subject the judge planned to discuss, a significant one. This new and unexpected issue had to be resolved without delay.

Chapter Twenty-One

The issue that Judge Adler had in mind could affect the outcome of the trial dramatically. Ben and Emma learned about it the night before, when, exhausted after the long day in court and a short visit to Ben's relatives, they finally came home and were about to savor the few quiet hours left of the evening. The soothing silence of the house was interrupted by the persisting ring of the phone.

"Hello?" Ben answered reluctantly.

"Ben, its Edward Gould. Sorry to bother you so late, but we need to talk."

"Bad news?"

"I don't think so. Rather unexpected, I should say. The U. S. Supreme Court announced that in a few months the judges would consider an appeal filed on behalf of a certain Frank Burrage."

"A doctor? An identical case?"

"Not exactly."

"But similar?"

"Not quite." Gould paused. "A few years ago in Baltimore, a street drug dealer, Frank Burrage, was arrested and charged with the death of one of his regular customers."

"Edward, I'm not a drug dealer, and I can't imagine what his case has to do with mine."

"Ben, please listen to the rest of the story—you won't regret it."

"All right, I'm listening."

"This Burrage guy sold a drug user a few grams of heroin, which allegedly caused his customer's fatal overdose. He was charged with the death of his client, Mr. Banka, who was a long-time drug user. Mr. Banka died after an extended binge that, among other substances, included heroin, which he'd purchased from Burrage."

"Okay. But what exactly does all of this have to do with my case?"

"Burrage admitted that he had unlawfully distributed heroin but pleaded not guilty to the charges of his client's death. After medical experts testified at the trial that Banka might have died even if he had not taken the heroin, Burrage's attorney moved for a judgment of acquittal, arguing that Banka's death could have resulted from heroin use *only* if there were evidence that heroin was a solo drug in his system, dangerous for Banka's life."

"The judge denied the motion, right?"

"Yes, he did. He denied the motion and instructed the jury that the government only had to prove that heroin was a *contributing* cause of death. The jury convicted Burrage, and the court sentenced him to a mandatory twenty-year imprisonment. The Eighth Circuit Court upheld the District Court's jury instruction."

"And?"

"His attorney managed to bring the case all the way to the U.S. Supreme Court. The argument he used was simple but sensible. During the routine postmortem examination, including toxicology testing, the late Mr. Banka was found to have additional multiple illegal substances in his blood. Each of them could have been fatal, so if this man, Burrage, was charged with selling Mr. Banka heroin only, how could he be exclusively culpable for this man's demise?"

"Well, I hadn't sold anything to any of my six patients who died. But those of them, who had been subjected to autopsies, also had illegal, potentially lethal substances in their blood, drugs that I had never prescribed to them."

"Exactly my point."

"So the Supreme Court agreed to consider the case?"

"Yes, it did."

"Is the hearing already scheduled?"

"It's scheduled for mid-November, four months from now."

"Do you know if Judge Adler is aware of these developments?"

"No idea. We have to make sure she is. The Supreme Court ruling on Burrage's appeal can affect your case a great deal. It's only reasonable for the judge to reschedule your trial after the Supreme Court makes its decision. Otherwise, if your trial, God forbid, ends up with a guilty verdict and the Supreme Court rules in favor of Burrage, which also will be in *your* favor, Judge Adler will have to retry your case."

"She wouldn't want a second trial, would she?"

"I believe she wouldn't. Anyway, I'll speak to her tomorrow." Gould was silent for a long moment. "Ben, do you realize how serious this new development is and how it can affect your case?"

"I need at least a few minutes to digest it. But I have a gut feeling it's not a bad development for us. It's pregnant with hope."

"So let's pray for an easy pregnancy and a healthy delivery," Gould replied lightheartedly.

* * *

The next morning, on the last day of the Daubert Hearing, Gould informed Judge Adler about the news. Now, when the Daubert testimonies were over, the judge knew she had to deal with it. The Supreme Court hearing on Burrage's case was scheduled for November 12, 2013. Should she postpone the trial or not? On one hand, the case was already six years old and shouldn't be delayed any further. On the other hand, who wanted a second trial, especially as complex and lengthy as this one was going to be? Trials were also expensive, and judges had the responsibility to take that into consideration as well.

"Counselor," Judge Adler addressed Lynch. "You have been notified of the Supreme Court hearing on Burrage's case, right?"

"Yes, Your Honor."

"The ruling on Burrage's case can considerably affect this case. Would you agree with that?"

"It's possible, Your Honor."

"Well, I'm thinking about postponing the trial. What's your take on it?"

"Your Honor, we don't think it's a good idea. Our opinion is that the trial shouldn't be delayed any longer."

The judge considered the prosecutor's response for a minute or so.

"In your estimation, how long will the trial last?"

"About three months, Your Honor."

"Do you want to spend three more months in this courtroom retrying the same case after the ruling if the Supreme Court makes its decision in favor of Mr. Burrage?"

"Your Honor, I don't know... It's... we have to think about it."

"Let's reconvene tomorrow at 9:00 a.m. and discuss it. I have to make my decision soon."

* * *

When they left the courtroom, Ben turned to Gould. The attorney looked preoccupied.

"Edward, the judge is indecisive, right? Which direction do you think she is leaning?"

"Who knows?" Gould shrugged.

"The prosecutors had been dragging out the case for years. Now all of a sudden they are pushing for a speedy trial!"

"Ben, we did all we could. We notified the judge, but we can't force her to reschedule the trial. Let's not worry about it, at least until tomorrow."

* * *

The next morning, when Judge Adler walked into the courtroom, she turned first to Lynch.

"So, Counselor, have you made up your mind regarding the rescheduling of the trial?"

"Yes, Your Honor."

Lynch slowly stood up, but he wasn't rushing with a response. The silence in the room filled the torturous pause to the brim.

"The government is willing to wait for the Supreme Court decision," Lynch said finally.

A loud sigh of relief echoed his answer. Ben guessed it was Emma. He turned around and gave her a wink. Then he looked at Gould, and they both grinned broadly. Well, life was indeed full of surprises, and not always bad ones.

"What can I say?" Judge Adler looked almost as relieved as the defendants and their lawyers. "If both parties agree to wait, you only have to file a joint motion, and I'll do the rest. I think you realize that if the hearing takes place in November, the Supreme Court's decision will probably be announced in mid or late January 2014. To be on the safe side, I'll schedule our next pretrial conference in early February. I'll see you all in a few months."

* * *

When they walked outside, Emma pulled Ben toward the large hallway window facing the ocean. She couldn't wait to ask him the question that bothered her from the moment Lynch gave his unexpected consent to reschedule the trial.

"Ben, first I felt so relieved, but then I asked myself, 'Why did they agree so easily? Why? What's the catch?'"

"I don't know. And I don't think we'll ever know. Maybe it's just an order from upstairs. Maybe they expect the Supreme Court ruling to be in their favor."

"I pray the Supreme Court judges make the right decision." Emma walked a few steps down the hallway, then stopped abruptly and turned to Ben. "And what will happen if they don't?"

"If they don't? That's a tough question." Ben glanced at the calm water of the bay glittering in the morning sun. "Even if they don't, I think our situation won't be worse than it is now."

Emma fell silent and then with a pensive look turned to Ben.

"You know, it just hit me. The judge scheduled the next pretrial conference in early February."

"Right."

"And now it's late June."

"You are right again." Ben's eyes flickered with a tiny grin.

"Do you realize that the judge just treated us to a seven-month break! For the next seven months, we won't have to worry about what kind of nightmare is waiting for us tomorrow. We haven't had a gift like that for six years! A seven-month respite!"

"Yeah, a gift from heaven," Ben smiled for the first time in weeks.

"To be precise, from the Supreme Court and Judge Adler," Emma smiled back.

* * *

In mid-November 2013, Attorney Mark Daniels flew to Washington to attend the Supreme Court hearing, and when it was over, he called Ben from the capital.

"Hi, Ben. I'm calling to report about the hearing. It's over. I think it went well. Of course, no one can predict the judges' decision, but they asked extremely pertinent questions."

"No disturbing ones?"

"No, all their questions and comments were reasonable and to the point. I believe they were trying to get to the core of the matter, and that may be a good sign. But you never know..."

"Thank you, Mark. Have a safe trip home."

"Thanks, Ben. Make the best of your break."

"Believe me, we will."

Mark wished Ben good night and hung up.

"Emma, Mark Daniels just called from Washington. The hearing is over. The judges' questions were sensible and right to the point. Mark said that could be a good sign."

"If Mark said it..." Emma stopped, Ben looked worried. "You don't think they..."

"These Supreme Court judges rarely agree on anything."

"But maybe this time..."

"You are an unshakable optimist, aren't you?"

"Doesn't this odd trait run in the family?"

* * *

On January 27, 2014, Ben's cell phone was ringing madly in the closet when he finally located it in the pocket of his winter jacket. He looked at the display. Gould.

"Hi, Edward."

Emma heard 'Edward' and sank into the chair next to Ben.

"Yes, I can hear you well."

Ben was listening with unflagging attention.

"You think so?" Another pause.

Emma was trying to read Ben's face and failed.

"You're not sure it will happen?" There was a long pause. Emma was about to burst.

"Thank you, Edward, I really appreciate your call." Ben hung up and turned to Emma.

"What was it all about?" Emma asked cautiously.

"Dick Krokson, Lynch's second chair, just called him."

"And?"

"The Supreme Court announced its ruling."

Emma could barely breathe.

"What was it, for God's sake?"

"The Supreme Court made the decision in Burrage's favor. Unanimously. Edward said it was a huge victory. It means that if other toxic substances such as illegal drugs, like in our case, have been found in the body of the deceased besides the medications prescribed by the physician, the doctor *cannot* be held accountable for this person's death and *cannot* be charged with it."

"Does it mean that the prosecutors now have to drop all the charges? Their entire case is based on these six deaths, isn't it?"

"That's true, but Edward thinks that's unlikely. There is a chance they'll drop the death charges, but not the whole case..."

Emma's heart was pumping madly.

"They may drop the death charges?"

"They should now. It looks like they don't have a choice."

"If they drop the death charges, what's left?"

"I think nothing."

"Who will make the decision? Lynch and Krokson?"

"No, Krokson said they'll get the orders from Washington."

"Did he say how soon they would make that decision?"

"The judge gave the prosecutors thirty days to respond."

Ben opened the computer, typed *Burrage*, and there it was.

BURRAGE v. UNITED STATES CERTIORARI TO THE UNITED STATES COURT OF APPEALS FOR THE EIGHTH CIRCUIT No. 12–7515 argued November 12, 2013—Decided January 27, 2014.

The Supreme Court decided that at least where use of the drug distributed by the defendant is not an independently sufficient cause of the victim's death or serious bodily injury, a defendant cannot be liable for penalty enhancement under § 841(b)(1)(C) unless such use is a but-for cause of the death or injury.

* * *

The prosecutors called Gould exactly thirty days later. Either the government was working at a leisurely pace or the prosecutors were intentionally tormenting Dr. Holden, Julia Lander, and all those people who were rooting for them with intolerable uncertainty. The call from the DA's office came a few days before the pretrial conference that had been rescheduled for early March 2014. The message Gould received didn't surprise him a bit. Now he had to pass it on to Dr. Holden.

* * *

That night Emma was sitting in front of the computer, immersed in her work, and the ringing phone was an interference she couldn't bear at the moment.

"Ben, please get the phone!" Emma yelled. "I'm in the middle of a sentence."

"Sure." Ben walked to the desk and picked up the phone. "Hello?"

"Ben, it's Edward Gould. Krokson finally called. They dropped the death charges."

"Great news! Thank you, Edward."

"But not the whole case."

"No surprise here, huh?"

"No, no surprise. Sorry about that."

"Well, it's not your fault. It's politics, right? So what are the charges now?"

"Conspiracy with Julia to illegally distribute drugs and seven illegal prescriptions of methadone to six of your patients, given without a legitimate medical purpose," Gould explained.

"Seven prescriptions out of thousands!" Ben exploded.

"Yeah, that's their case. I agree, this is absurd, but—"

"But what?"

"But at this stage they simply can't afford to drop it. They've invested too much to back off."

"Tell me about it." Ben went silent. "Edward, we have to fight it."

"Believe me, we will."

* * *

On March 4, 2014, Judge Adler held the postponed status conference. The prosecutors announced their decision to drop the death charges and declared their new modified ones. The judge said that she would go over her schedule and would notify both parties about the date of the trial.

Two weeks later, Judge Adler's clerk called Attorney Gould and informed him that the trial was scheduled for June 23.

"Mary, could you please let the judge know that I can't start on June 23," Gould was dismayed. "I have another month-long trial starting May 10. According to my estimate, it would be over only two weeks prior to Dr. Holden's trial. How can I get ready for Dr. Holden's complex and lengthy trial in two weeks? Could you please ask the judge to move the date to early July? Please."

"I'll do my best," Mary sighed.

When Gould called Ben with the news, his voice betrayed ultimate frustration.

"Edward, don't get upset. Judge Adler seems to be a reasonable person. She will reschedule, or at least she ought to."

"Reasonable? Scheduling such a lengthy and complex trial without asking the lawyers about *their* schedules? You call this reasonable?"

"I don't believe the judge did it on purpose. I'm sure she'll reconsider the date."

And she did.

A few days later, Gould called him again.

"Ben?"

"Hi, Edward. Good news?"

"Beyond belief. Mary just called me. The judge rescheduled the trial. You know what the new date is? June 16! A week *earlier* than the first one! This is nonsense! It's humanly impossible to prepare for your trial in a week!"

"Listen, maybe you can call Judge Adler and talk to her? There might still be a chance she'll change her mind."

"To start the trial tomorrow? No, thanks."

"Listen, if there is nothing you can do, let it go. Get ready as much as you can, and who knows what will happen along the way? Life is full of surprises, right?"

"You bet."

* * *

On that bright sunny morning of May 20, Emma woke up rather late and in an inexplicably good mood. She made breakfast and called Ben into the kitchen.

"Ben, do you believe in premonitions?" she met Ben's puzzled look.

"Good ones or bad ones?" He grinned tentatively.

"Good ones."

"I am a big fan of them, especially lately."

"You know, this morning I feel a bit strange... as if something is in the air... as if I can smell..."

"No wonder, I bet the whole neighborhood can smell it. I mean, the aroma of your omelet," Ben quipped.

"No, Ben. I'm serious. It's something different. Something intangible, that—"

The phone ring cut her off mid-sentence. Ben looked at his wife apologetically and picked up the receiver.

"Hello, Ben. It's Edward."

Ben greeted his lawyer and felt his neck get stiff. "Another problem?"

"No, Ben, quite the opposite. I am calling to say that I'm done with my other trial. Two weeks earlier than I expected! I can start preparing for your trial right away."

"So life *is* full of surprises?"

"Apparently so."

"Thanks for the good news. You made my day."

"I made mine too. Please pass the news to Emma."

Ben hung up and turned to his wife.

"You won't believe it. Edward is done with his other trial. Two weeks earlier!"

"His trial is over?" Emma said incredulously. "Now he can start preparing for yours?"

"As of today, he said. It looks like that smell was not only from your omelet after all."

Chapter Twenty-Two

The trial of Dr. Holden and Nurse Practitioner Julia Lander began in Federal Court on June 16, 2014, with jury selection. Emma and Julia's husband, Arthur, were allowed to watch it. They were seated by the bailiff in the back of the courtroom, where they could see everything and hear nothing of what would be discussed by the judge, attorneys, and prospective jurors.

The first group of 160 people was brought to the courtroom, and the selection process, voir dire, began. In a few words, Judge Adler explained what the trial was about, told the potential jurors that the trial could last for two months or longer, and that she would need sixteen jurors for the case, including twelve regulars and four alternates.

"Please raise your hand if being in court for such a long period of time can become a financial burden to you," the Judge addressed the courtroom.

Myriads of hands soared up in the air.

"Please raise your hand if it may create a daycare problem for you."

A few hands were raised in response to the question.

"Please raise your hand if you may be prejudiced in matters concerning opioid prescriptions or overdoses."

About two dozen people raised their hands.

"Please raise your hand if you believe you are prejudiced against the government or the police."

Three hands went up in the air.

"Please raise your hand if you have a planned summer vacation, meaning that you've already purchased airplane tickets or paid for a cruise, not just planned something for the summer."

Fifty or so people raised their hands.

Emma's heart sank. It looked like almost everyone brought into the courtroom had one kind of excuse or another. However, a few people never raised their hands. One of them was a tall, skinny, dark-haired young man in a red T-shirt who hadn't raised his hand even once. She noticed two or three more people like him, probably model citizens, who were willing to fulfill their civic duty even though they had to sacrifice their whole summer to do that. But there were only three or four of them. How long would it take to select sixteen jurors? Emma wondered. A week?

"Since almost everyone present in this room has an excuse," Judge Adler scanned the courtroom, "I'll invite each of you to my bench, we'll talk, and then I'll make a decision whether you should be excused or not."

The court clerk started calling the numbers, and the potential jurors began forming a line.

I wish they would select a few young people, Emma thought, like that one in the red T-shirt. Young folks are usually open-minded. Emma cast the man an inconspicuous look. If only we could get twelve honest, reasonable people whose judgment wouldn't be clouded by any prejudice.

Judge Adler, joined by the prosecutors, defendants, and their lawyers, talked to the first potential juror. The conversation lasted about a minute, if not less. When it was over, Mary, the judge's clerk, handed her a piece of paper, and she left the courtroom with a smile on her face. The first potential juror was dismissed. The second potential juror followed the same scenario. He was gone in thirty seconds. The third person was also quickly dismissed; following a brief talk, the judge handed the man a piece of paper, and he left the room. Selecting sixteen jurors, thought Emma, might take forever!

Yet by the time Judge Adler had finished with the last person in line, twenty-one potential jurors were still left in the room.

After the lunch break, another pool was brought in. The judge gave the same speech and followed the same procedure. By 4:00 p.m. seven more candidates were tentatively selected for the trial. Now there were twenty-eight potential jurors to choose from. Emma sighed with relief.

During a short break, she walked toward Gould. "Edward, how many prospective jurors are you allowed to dismiss without any explanation?"

"By law our team is permitted to use five strikes, Julia and her attorney can dismiss five more, and the prosecutors can also get rid of five potential jurors they don't want."

"So if each team uses all its strikes, which is a total of fifteen, then we'll end up with only thirteen jurors. But Judge Adler wants sixteen, right?"

"She may settle for fourteen. In my opinion, twelve jurors plus two alternates should be good enough. We just need to select the *right* fourteen people, hopefully today. Judge Adler is eager to start the trial as soon as she can and finish it as early as possible. And so are we.

* * *

After the break, the selection went more or less smoothly. The prosecutors dismissed five prospective jurors, Julia and her lawyer Peter O'Neil dismissed another five, and Gould, Mark, and Ben dismissed four. Then Gould stumbled. The defense had one more strike left, and Gould had a strong feeling about whom he wanted to dismiss. However, if he followed his hunch, there would be only thirteen jurors left, which most likely wouldn't satisfy the judge, and she might demand to spend another day on the jury selection.

Gould took Ben aside and lowered his voice.

"This last prospective juror, this young woman, works at a large hospital doing medical research. I think we should let her go. I'm afraid she won't be objective. Who knows what kind of an attitude she's already developed regarding opioid treatments? Mark, what's your opinion?"

Daniels shrugged.

"I'm not sure."

"Ben, what do you think?" Gould turned to Ben. "You have the final word."

"I don't know." Ben paused. "If we dismiss her, we will get only thirteen people, and we'll have to spend another day on the jury selection. I'm already exhausted, and you are probably too. Besides, what kind of guarantee do we have with any of them?"

"That's true, we don't. Still, to have this young woman as a juror may be risky." Gould frowned.

"Edward, I think she is all right. She is young and looks shy. Most likely, she will follow the rest. They all seem quite intelligent. Most importantly, I was watching them closely when the judge was talking to them, and I didn't sense any hostility."

"All right, we'll let her stay," agreed Gould, but he didn't look fully convinced.

* * *

By the end of the day, jury selection was over, and Judge Adler seemed pleased with the outcome.

The selected jurors were asked to sit in their designated seats in the jury box. Emma assiduously scanned their faces. There were seven women and seven men. Out of the fourteen jurors, four were young people, including three men in their late twenties and a young woman. There were two elderly gentlemen, two more men in their forties, and six women in their late forties or early fifties. No mean faces, Emma registered with relief.

Judge Adler explained their roles and duties.

"Now, let me explain to you one of the most critical rules," the judge paused, and gave the jurors a pointed look. "You should not read any press about the case. You should not listen to any radio or TV reports or look for discussions of this case on the Internet. You shouldn't be influenced by any external opinions. Pay undivided attention to what's going on in the courtroom. The only important facts are the ones that will be presented here. You should base your conclusions and your decisions on them and them only. Please always come here on time. The session can't start if one of you is late. The sessions will go from 9:00 a.m. to 4:30 p.m. with a lunch break from 1:00 to 2:00 p.m., and we'll have a few short days because of my other obligations. You'll receive my schedule beforehand."

Emma left the courtroom and waited for Ben and Gould in the hallway. She wondered what they thought about the jurors. So much depended on them; in fact, everything depended on them.

"Edward, are you satisfied with the jury?" Emma rushed to Gould the moment he stepped outside.

"More or less. They look intelligent and rather amiable. I have only one concern."

"What is it?"

"I still have my doubts about the young woman. But we've spent the whole day on the jury selection. No one wants to spend another one. So we took a risk."

"Yes, it could be a risk," Emma agreed, "but I was watching this woman, and she didn't impress me as a strong-willed type who could lead others in the wrong direction." Emma paused pensively. "Nor did she look like a vicious person. Most likely she'll follow the crowd, which looks sensible and good-natured."

"Funny, Ben said the same thing." Gould gave Emma a half-smile. "Well, none of us is clairvoyant. Time will tell. It's so good we've wrapped it up in one day. Let's go home and relax."

* * *

The first day of the trial brought a big crowd. The courtroom was packed with all sorts of federal agents, lawyers, reporters, and spectators who arrived out of necessity or pure curiosity and occupied the back of the room. The first few rows were taken by those who'd come to root for Ben and Julia, whose lives had been hanging over the abyss for the past seven years. Now their drawn-out ordeal was reaching an apex.

The trial began with the prosecutor's opening statement. Krokson, Lynch's second chair, solemnly stood in front of the jurors and for a few seconds stared into their faces as if trying to gain their confidence and support even before his speech started.

"Ladies and gentlemen of the jury." His dulcet voice filled the courtroom. "From ancient times, every physician has taken the Hippocratic Oath, promising to treat their patients with all the knowledge, dedication, and best care they could provide. The cornerstone of this oath is 'Do no harm.'" Krokson stopped and cast a piercing look at the jurors. "Let me repeat. Do no harm! But these two individuals, Dr. Holden and his nurse practitioner, Julie Lander, shamelessly broke that oath. At some point the defendants imagined that they could be above the law."

Ben looked at the jurors. Krokson's enthusiastic tone had definitely caught their interest.

"Over many years in their practice, these two people again and again used opportunities to treat their patients with strong and dangerous narcotic medications. Many of their patients became addicted to these medications and to narcotics in general; some of them even ended up dead."

Krokson paused and shot a grim glance at the jurors. He wanted to make sure they hadn't missed his last pronouncement. They had not.

"During the course of this trial, we intend to clearly demonstrate that the main goal of these two medical professionals, Dr. Holden and Nurse Practitioner Lander, was to profit from some of their most vulnerable patients, providing them with a practically unlimited supply of extremely dangerous drugs. The defendants completely disregarded multiple 'red flags'—warning signs of abuse, addiction, and diversion of opioids—and therefore these two people broke the law. During this trial, ladies and gentlemen, you will hear from some of the former patients of Dr. Holden and Nurse Practitioner Lander, as well as the patients' friends and relatives, who will be telling you under oath what kind of horrendous experiences they had at Dr. Holden's medical office."

Krokson paused for effect, but when he looked at the jurors, he wasn't sure their faces expressed anything. By that time, he had gradually retreated to a flat tone, and everyone in the room could feel now that his ardor was sifting out of him by the minute.

"For example," Krokson continued, "you will hear directly from the brother of one of Dr. Holden's patients about his warnings in regards to his brother's addiction to opioids and how Dr. Holden essentially brushed him off. You will hear from the girlfriend of another patient, who had informed the defendants that her boyfriend had serious issues with narcotics—warnings which both Dr. Holden and Nurse Lander disregarded."

Emma knew that what was happening at the moment in the courtroom wasn't a harrowing nightmare. It was reality, but reality that was too hard to swallow. How could it be that the government attorneys were allowed to lie and distort the facts? Weren't they supposed to fight for justice?

"Now, let me say this," Krokson continued. "Although the government doesn't claim that every single medical decision these two defendants ever made was criminal or that every single opioid prescription they issued to their patients was outside the scope of legitimate medical practice, still, we will prove beyond a reasonable doubt that many of them were."

For the next thirty-five minutes, Krokson defamed their practice. And he totally disregarded the recent U.S. Supreme Court ruling, which stated that it was impossible to determine if any particular substance had caused the death of a person if the autopsy revealed the presence of several substances in its system. Instead, Krokson clearly implied that Dr. Holden and Nurse Practitioner Lander's prescription practices led to the deaths of six of their patients, and he promised to prove his assertions at the trial.

For the first ten minutes or so, the jurors paid close attention to the prosecutor's speech, but soon their faces began to betray indifference, if not boredom.

"Ladies and gentlemen of the jury," Krokson suddenly raised his voice as he moved toward his grand finale. "I have no doubt that by the end of this trial you will have a complete understanding of what kind of criminal enterprise these two defendants were running under the pretense of a medical practice. They acted as common drug dealers, and I am absolutely confident that you will have no difficulty in finding both of the defendants guilty as charged. Thank you for your attention," Krokson concluded and strode to his seat.

* * *

Now it was the defense's turn. Edward Gould walked up to the jury box. Dead silence settled in the courtroom, but Gould didn't rush to begin speaking. He wanted the jurors' full attention, and he got it.

"Members of the jury, good morning. My name is Edward Gould, and it's my privilege to represent Dr. Benjamin Holden, who is innocent of each and every accusation that the prosecutor has just made against him." Fourteen pairs of eyes instantly focused on his affable, lively face, and from that moment on they soaked up his every word.

Gould told the jury how at the age of eleven Ben made his decision to become a doctor and never gave up on it. He told them about Ben's deep unfailing empathy for people who suffer from one illness or another and his unstoppable thirst for new knowledge and new skills that would help him to make these people's lives as normal and as enjoyable as possible.

"Dr. Benjamin Holden was a board-certified physician in physical medicine and rehabilitation, and over the many years of his practice, he helped people suffering from pain put their lives back together both physically and psychologically. Now, in the time that I have this morning, it would be impossible for me to describe all of the various components of his practice, the ongoing efforts that he made to keep up with developments in his field, the seminars and lectures he attended across the country, and the talks that he gave to his colleagues. Still, I do want you to see some of the components of what Dr. Holden conceived and built. This is the floor plan of his office."

Gould put a sizable cardboard floor plan on a stand in front of the jury.

"As you can see," continued Gould, "Dr. Ben Holden built his practice as a multidisciplinary pain management center where patients could have access not just to him but also to a neurologist, a psychiatrist, an addictionologist, a pain psychologist, and an acupuncture specialist. He also employed a physical therapist and chiropractor working on site. The practice offered patients the Lordex decompression table for alleviating back pain, magnetic and alpha wave therapy as well as some other treatments, but I'll tell you more about that later on. Now, look over here. It's a big exercise room that Dr. Holden built for his patients. He hired instructors in Pilates, yoga, and tai-chi and encouraged his patients to take classes as often as they could. These classes were free of charge."

I wish the jurors could have spent a day in his office, Emma thought. If only they could see all of this not on a piece of cardboard but in action.

"When the government sent an undercover agent to his office," Gould paused for the jurors to digest the fact, "Dr. Holden, believing that the man was a legitimate patient, showed him all these treatment options and explained that it was his goal to treat patients and improve their ability to function, not just by using pain medications but by taking a holistic approach."

"Members of the jury," Gould's voice sounded brighter, "the evidence in this case will show that over the many years of his practice, Dr. Benjamin Holden always treated all of his patients in good faith and to the best of his ability. There were thousands of patients, not just the dozen or so that the government will present in this room. These people had been in accidents or had exhausted treatment options with their surgeons; people who told him that because of their pain they could not sleep at night and couldn't take care of their children and their spouses or their parents. Dr. Holden cared deeply about each of his patients and did everything he could to alleviate their pain so that they would live a normal life. He helped quite a few of them to go back to work or to start new careers more suitable for their health conditions."

"Let's be clear about something else." Gould moved a little closer to the jury box. "The government must prove that Dr. Holden abandoned the practice of medicine and became a drug dealer who knowingly and intentionally committed crimes by distributing drugs to his patients because he was a criminal and not because he believed these medications might help them."

Gould paused and scanned the faces in the jury box. The jurors were paying attention.

"Think about what the prosecutor said to you in his opening: 'Hey, we're not saying it was all bad. We're just saying some of it was bad. Some of it may have been legitimate.' Think about what he's telling you. Dr. Holden treated thousands of his patients as any good physician would do, but with a few of them, he acted like a drug dealer. Does this statement make any sense to you? Members of the jury, the evidence in this case, when you've heard it in its entirety, will demonstrate that the government's allegations are wrong and untrue."

Juror #1, a slender, well-dressed lady, leaned forward, as if she wanted to hear more.

"As you listen to the evidence, please use your common sense about what it means for a doctor to treat a patient. We go to doctors to tell them about our problems, usually in the privacy of a treatment room. Doctors are trained and ethically obligated to listen to their patients, to believe them, and to do the best they can to treat them. It's crucial, *crucial* to understand, although the prosecutor may wish it otherwise, that doctors are not police officers. They are not detectives. They are not DEA agents. They are required to treat patients who come to them with real and legitimate problems, even when the patients may have done something wrong, including smoking pot or even snorting cocaine."

A tall, stocky guy, Juror #4, smiled ironically and cast Gould a caustic look.

"These people have legitimate medical problems and even if, on occasion, they do those things, wrong as they may be, they are entitled to treatment, and when the prosecutor suggested to you otherwise, he was wrong," Gould concluded with passion.

"Members of the jury, when it is our turn to present evidence to you in this case, you will hear from a nationally prominent expert who has been working in this area her entire career; she will tell you that during the relevant time period and up to now, the medical community itself has been struggling with the questions of how the field of pain management should be practiced. Today, seven years later, many of the questions are still unanswered."

Gould caught a curious look from Juror #8, a thin, dark-skinned man in his late forties.

"For example, how does a doctor assess whether a patient needs prescription medications? How does a doctor assess whether a patient presents a risk of abusing prescribed medications? If a patient has these problems, how does the doctor respond to them? For all the years that Dr. Holden was in practice, there was no clear guidance given to physicians about these issues."

Ben noticed that Juror #8 exchanged glances with his neighbor, Juror #9.

"According to the pain management literature, chronic pain is an enormous problem that afflicts one in five adult Americans."

Gould paused for the jury to absorb that statistic.

"Medical studies have also confirmed the fact that opioids are extremely effective in the treatment of chronic pain. But no medical guidelines exist concerning what a doctor should do when a patient misuses opioids. Multiple studies also show that doctors shouldn't stop treating their patients based upon judgmental biases and reliance on so-called 'red flags' or warning signs. These 'red flags' may prove to be incorrect, especially when a patient in pain needs treatment."

"Now let's talk about the government's evidence. The government doesn't have a single piece of evidence of criminal actions by Dr. Holden but nevertheless accuses him of intentionally and criminally dealing drugs. They refer to a time period where the medical community itself could not agree on how to respond to the complex situations I just mentioned. Dr. Holden treated his patients exactly as the guidelines of the State Medical Board recommended. He trusted his patients, and he did everything he could to improve their lives. He never acted as a DEA agent trained to assume that every complaint of chronic pain must be a lie made by a drug-seeking criminal, who must be investigated and prosecuted but not treated."

Emma saw Juror #1 nod, almost invisibly. The others seemed to be attentive listeners, but their faces were unreadable.

"Now let's talk about the biggest challenge faced by a doctor practicing in this area. It is a fact of life that some people who seek out doctors are dishonest. Some of them are criminals, and some of them abuse drugs. These people know how to take advantage of the fact that a doctor has an obligation to listen to them, to believe them, and not turn them away when they are in need of care. Among Dr. Holden's patients, there were some who lied to him. But please ask yourself, if Dr. Holden were intentionally acting as a drug dealer, why would any of his patients find it necessary to lie to him in the first place? When these people testify in this courtroom, consider these simple questions: If they lied to Dr. Ben Holden in order to get drugs to misuse them or sell them, why aren't *they* the ones here being prosecuted? Why aren't *they* on trial?"

Two of the jurors grinned, the rest continued to keep poker faces.

"Now, members of the jury, how are you going to know that Dr. Holden acted as a doctor and not a drug dealer? Let me tell you about some of the evidence that you're going to hear in this courtroom, evidence that will make it crystal clear for you. First, doctors create and keep patients' medical records with the patient's history and a treatment plan. Dr. Holden did this each and every time. That's not something a drug dealer does."

Emma noticed another nod from Juror #1.

"Secondly, Dr. Holden made substantial efforts to objectively diagnose his patients by having them undergo X-rays, MRIs, EMGs, and other tests to confirm or rule out his diagnoses," Gould continued, his deep voice still passionate and unfaltering. "Drug dealers don't ask their customers to submit to tests which demonstrate that they need drugs."

"Another proof is that Dr. Holden made referrals to numerous physicians, including neurosurgeons, orthopedists, psychiatrists, psychologists, and others to evaluate his patients for further or alternative treatments that might help them."

Emma saw Juror #7 lean forward.

"And this is not all. Dr. Holden required patients to whom he prescribed opioids to sign informed consent forms, outlining the basic rules of using pain medication. Let me show you this form."

Gould handed a sheet of paper to each of the jurors.

"Please read the whole document later but let me quote to you just the first line: '*Taking your prescribed medication only as recommended by your doctor is an important part of your treatment.*' It means that his patients also had a responsibility to follow the rules and that Dr. Holden expected them to follow the rules. He had his patients read and *sign* this document. Members of the jury, drug dealers don't have their customers sign contracts promising to take their drugs only as directed and to rate how they feel when they are using those drugs. Dr. Holden and his staff stopped prescribing opioids to the patients who violated their obligations. Let me repeat that: Dr. Holden and his staff stopped prescribing opioids to those patients who failed to comply with their obligations. Members of the jury, drug dealers don't fire their customers."

The tall, chubby guy, Juror #4, smirked again.

"Members of the jury, this gentleman, Dr. Benjamin Holden, is a good man who did his best to treat a very difficult population—people suffering from pain day and night without hope of ever recovering. This is the essence of the case, and when I have an opportunity to address you at the conclusion of the evidence, I am going to ask you to find Dr. Holden not guilty of each and every accusation that has falsely been made against him."

Gould thanked the jury for their attention and unhurriedly walked to his seat.

* * *

Outside in the hallway, Ben, Emma, and their friends walked up to Gould.

"Edward, that was a very good start," Ben shook Gould's hand.

"Excellent speech, right to the point," joined in Emma.

"Thank you. But let's not get overexcited. We have a long way to go. Believe me, it's going to be a lengthy and rather bumpy road."

* * *

After the recess, Peter O'Neil stood in front of the jury to deliver his opening statement. He told the jury that at some point in her life, Julia Lander abandoned her successful career as a software engineer to pursue her lifetime dream of becoming a medical professional. For four years, Julia studied to become a registered nurse and then for the next three years, while working as a nurse, she enrolled in a master's degree program to become a nurse practitioner. Her job at Dr. Holden's clinic was her first introduction to the complex and challenging world of pain management.

"Ladies and gentlemen of the jury," concluded his opening statement, "can you possibly imagine how anyone, who spent so much time and effort on getting her license to practice medicine would risk everything, including her reputation and freedom, to become a drug dealer? During this trial we will be able to unequivocally prove that the government is totally wrong and Nurse Practitioner Lander is an honest, devoted, and caring medical professional, who never committed any crimes."

Ben could see that the jurors were closely listening to his speech, a few even nodded a time or two, but most of them were indecipherable. They were waiting for the evidence.

Chapter Twenty-Three

On the second day of the trial, the federal government's case against Dr. Holden and Nurse Practitioner Julia Lander began with the direct examination of Jake Donovan and his girlfriend, Lucille Flanagan. Both of them were Ben's former patients, but that wasn't the main reason why they were selected as the first witnesses for the prosecution.

At 9:10 a.m., Judge Adler entered the room, greeted everyone, and asked the jurors the same questions she would ask them every day of the trial, "Ladies and gentlemen, have you read anything about this case in the newspapers? Have you researched it on the Internet? Have you discussed it with anyone or with each other?" The jurors shook their heads in response to all the questions, and Judge Adler gave the signal to call the first witness.

A chubby man in his fifties slowly limped to the witness chair. By the time he was sworn in, the prosecutor, Mike Lynch, had already reached the lectern.

"Good morning, Mr. Donovan, how are you today?" Lynch started with a broad smile.

"Good morning, sir. I am OK. Thank you for asking." The man looked subdued and weary.

"Mr. Donovan, did you at some point become a patient of Dr. Holden?"

"Yes, I did."

"Why did it happen?"

"Well, I hurt my hip at work in 1998, when I was thirty-seven. The pain eventually became unbearable, and I was told by a few different doctors that I had bad arthritis and needed a hip replacement. The problem was my age. I was too young for it and the surgeons were reluctant to do it as artificial joints have a limited life span. It took us about five years to win the case. Meanwhile, something had to be done as I couldn't even walk to the kitchen to make myself a cup of coffee."

"How did you end up in Dr. Holden's office?" asked Lynch.

"I begged my primary care doctor for help, and she finally referred me to him."

"Did Dr. Holden help you?"

"Yes, he did."

"How exactly was Dr. Holden able to help you? Did he prescribe you any powerful medications like OxyContin or Percocet?" Lynch asked with wide-eyed curiosity.

Defense Attorney Edward Gould rose from his seat.

"Objection, Your Honor, leading the witness."

"Sustained. Please rephrase your question," said Judge Adler.

"What kind of treatments did Dr. Holden use to alleviate your pain, sir?"

"In the beginning, we tried physical therapy, some herbal shots, ibuprofen, and other stuff. Nothing really worked. I was just over forty and already had to use crutches. That was humiliating. That's when Dr. Holden said I needed something more effective for my pain and prescribed Percocet."

"And what happened? Did you get addicted?" Lynch asked casually.

"No, I didn't. The Percocet made all the difference in my life. I was sleeping better, walking better... I even gained a few pounds," replied Donovan with a shy smile as he glanced at his pot belly.

"How long did you remain under the care of Dr. Holden?" went on Lynch.

"I would say about two years or longer," said Donovan.

"Sir, what made you stop seeing Dr. Holden?"

Mr. Donovan dropped his head. He looked like he was about to cry.

"Mr. Donovan, I understand it might be a very hard question for you to answer, so if you need some time, please let us know, and we'll understand. Are you all right?" the lead prosecutor looked sympathetic.

"Thank you, sir. I am fine. You see, I had a baby brother. His name was Doug. Doug wasn't only my brother, he was my best friend. When I lost him, I was devastated, totally devastated."

Ben cast Jake Donovan a long gaze. His brother, Doug Donovan, was Ben's patient for four years, and on more than one occasion Doug had given Ben an entirely different picture. His relationship with Jake, he said, was rocky at best. Doug was angry with his older brother, who never believed that Doug's back pain was real and used to make fun of him for years. Doug could never trust him, and they had never been close friends.

"Do you mind telling us what happened to your brother, Mr. Donovan? If you need a moment, please let me know," suggested Lynch in a consoling manner.

"Thank you, sir." Donovan sent a grieving glance toward the jury.

"Mr. Donovan, let me help you a little. Was your brother Doug a patient of Dr. Holden as well?"

"Yes, he was. In fact, Doug was the one who recommended Dr. Holden to me and my girlfriend Lucille in the first place. And then I asked my primary care doctor for a referral. She knew about Dr. Holden too."

"Do you know what kind of problem brought your brother to Dr. Holden's office?"

"Doug had a very sore back for years," started Donovan. "He hurt himself while working at the Big Dig. Dr. Holden was giving him some pain meds."

"In your observation, Mr. Donovan, what effect, if any, did those narcotic pain medications, prescribed by Dr. Holden, have on your brother's well-being?" asked Lynch.

"Horrible," Donovan said softly and stared at his lap.

"Mr. Donovan, I realize this subject may be still agonizing, but can you be more specific?"

"Yes, I can. A few years after Dr. Holden started treating him, Doug became a different man. He lost weight, and he stopped shaving. He broke up with his girlfriend, he was falling asleep all the time, he..."

"Thank you, Mr. Donovan, we get the picture," intervened Judge Adler.

"Sir, did you ever talk to Dr. Holden about the changes in your brother's condition? Did you let him know what was going on with Doug?" pressed Lynch.

"Oh yes, sir, I did. My girlfriend Lucille talked to him too. We both told him that Doug was abusing his painkillers and shouldn't be getting any of them." Donovan was trying to sound incensed, but his feeble, monotone voice refused to cooperate.

"What was Dr. Holden's reaction to that, if you remember?"

"Well, he said that Doug had a really serious back condition and without his medications he would be totally crippled, possibly bedridden. But he promised to look into the problem. He said he would sort it out."

"Did Dr. Holden change his painkillers to something else after you talked to him?"

"Yes, I believe he did. On Doug's last visit, he replaced his oxycodone with methadone."

"Then what happened to your brother, Mr. Donovan?"

"One morning, in late February, I called Doug to check on him, but he didn't pick up the phone. I called again later, and there was no answer. At that point, I decided to go and visit him. I just had a bad feeling that something was wrong and wanted to make sure he was okay," Donovan's last words were barely audible.

"So what did you find out?"

"I had the key to his apartment. I climbed to the third floor and opened the door. Doug was sitting in the armchair. The window was wide open and the room was cold. Very cold. I walked up to him. Doug was still warm to the touch, but not breathing," Donovan was now almost whispering.

"What did you do then, Mr. Donovan?"

"I called an ambulance, but I knew it was too late. There was nothing they could do. Nothing." "Sir, did you tell Dr. Holden about your tragedy?" Lynch's tone was stern.

"Yes, I did. The next week, after the funeral, we, I mean my girlfriend Lucille and I, had an appointment. So we came to the office and told Dr. Holden that Doug was gone."

"What was Dr. Holden's response, if you remember?"

"He said, 'Well, he had problems anyway.' Like it's not a big deal."

Emma gasped. Dead silence filled the room. If only she could scream to the jury, This man is a liar! But screaming wasn't something the defendant's wife could afford to do in the courtroom. She would be instantly forced to leave. Her gasp was so loud that Mark Daniels turned around and mouthed, "You can't do that." Emma nodded in agreement. She should restrain herself. The trial had just begun, and who knows if this first big lie was the last one.

"Mr. Donovan, please excuse me for this harsh question, but do you know why your brother Doug died? Was it an overdose on the drugs that Dr. Holden prescribed?"

Defense Attorney Gould jumped up from his seat. "Objection, Your Honor, that question calls for speculation. Besides, there is absolutely no indication that the demise of Doug Donovan had anything to do with Dr. Holden's treatments!"

"Counselors, please see me at the sidebar," ordered Judge Adler.

All three prosecutors and the entire defense team, including Ben and Julia Lander, quickly approached the bench.

"Mr. Lynch, let me say this one time and one time only. In my pretrial conference, I already made a ruling on the inadmissibility of the death issue. I allowed the government to display the pictures of the deceased for the jury, but that's all I permitted. You can't disregard my ruling and directly connect Dr. Holden's treatments to the death of his patients. You cannot do this. Counselor, is this clear?"

"Yes, Your Honor, I understand," Lynch replied, slightly embarrassed.

Judge Adler turned to the jury. "Members of the jury, let me explain what this sidebar conference was about. During this trial, you will learn that some of Dr. Holden's patients died. Let me emphasize the fact that neither Dr. Holden nor Nurse Practitioner Julie Lander is charged with the deaths of their patients. Now, Mr. Lynch, you can proceed."

"Mr. Donovan, did you have a feeling that Dr. Holden was upset about this tragedy?" pressed Lynch.

"No sir, I don't think so. He looked pretty calm, which really pissed off both of us, me and Lucille. That was exactly why we decided not to see him anymore," Jake Donovan finished glumly.

"And you never did?" asked Lynch.

"Never," said Mr. Donovan, as if on cue.

"Thank you, Mr. Donovan. I have no further questions."

"Mr. Gould, are you ready for the cross?" Judge Adler turned to Ben's attorney.

"Yes, Your Honor."

"Let's have a fifteen-minute break, and then you may start the cross."

* * *

Outside the courtroom, Ben's friend Ron strode over to Gould.

"Edward, about this Donovan guy... Is he the government's star witness?"

"Apparently so. At least one of them." Gould caught Emma's gaze and turned to her.

"Emma, is something wrong?"

"Wrong is not the word for it. This guy is lying! Ben had been helping this man to lessen his suffering and to live a normal life, and now this liar has the nerve to portray Ben as a heartless person! After Doug died, Ben told me his story about the countless health issues he had and his ugly divorce. He also told me about the child support Douglas couldn't afford to pay and his deep depression after his mother died. Ben was helping him the best way he could, and Doug was truly grateful to him. He often confided his life troubles in Ben, even the most personal ones. He actually admitted to Ben that he had a *sour* relationship with his brother Jake for years. And now this man is shedding crocodile tears in front of the jury in order to prove how close he was to Doug. Ben would never say, 'He had problems anyway.' It's just not like him! Ben, what *did* you say to them? I know it a was long time ago, but maybe you—"

"Of course, I remember. How can I forget? Jake and Lucille showed up for their appointment that day and told me that Doug had died. I said to them how deeply sorry I was, and it wasn't mere politeness. I liked and respected Doug. He had been suffering from pain since he was a boy, but he was a fighter. I admired his courage and cared for him a great deal."

Ben paused for a long moment. "Actually, when Doug died, his blood toxicology revealed the standard amount of medications he was prescribed. They didn't find anything excessive or illegal. Still, for some inexplicable reason, no one bothered to perform an autopsy, so we never learned for sure what had really happened. In any case, Doug had a few serious, potentially fatal health issues, so I told Jake and Lucille that some of these medical problems might have caused Doug's death."

"Talking about an autopsy," said Alex, "I've read that all unexpected deaths should be investigated in full, especially when the deceased is young and a possibility of foul play is on the table."

"You are absolutely right," confirmed Mark Daniels. "The thorough investigation of any sudden death, including an autopsy, is mandatory."

"Ben, did you record your talk with this guy and his girlfriend in Doug's file?" asked Ron.

"No, I didn't. It was a private conversation with two of my patients. I didn't believe it should be documented in a medical file. I couldn't imagine that someday my words would be cruelly distorted."

"Unfortunately, there is no way to disprove this particular lie," Gould sighed resignedly, "so let's try to deal with the others."

* * *

They returned to the courtroom, and Ben's lead attorney started the cross-examination.

"Good afternoon, Mr. Donovan. My name is Edward Gould, and I represent Dr. Holden. Please let me offer my deep condolences to you and your family, sir."

"Thank you."

"Mr. Donovan, have you ever had a chance to review your brother's entire medical file?"

"I've never seen it."

"The government never showed it to you before you came to testify today?"

"No, sir."

"But you were aware that your brother was in treatment with Dr. Holden for quite some time, weren't you?"

"A few years, I think."

"And has the government showed you—"

"Objection, asked and answered!" interjected Lynch.

"Overruled," said the judge. "I haven't even heard the question."

"Has the government showed you the list of appointments that Doug had with Dr. Holden before you came here to testify?" continued Gould.

"No."

"May I show the witness this document, Your Honor? Exhibit 206-C."

"You may," said Judge Adler, and Gould put a stack of papers in front of Jake Donovan.

"Mr. Donovan, would you agree we're looking at about a three-inch-thick document?"

"Yes."

"Sir, did you ever attend any of Doug's medical appointments with Dr. Holden?"

"No, he never asked me to."

"So you have no idea what your brother told Dr. Holden during any of his appointments?"

"No, I have no clue."

"Would you agree with me that Doug saw Dr. Holden for a period of about four years and had about thirty visits?"

"I don't know how many times he'd seen him."

"Did you know that Doug underwent a series of MRIs?"

"No, I didn't."

"Doug didn't tell you that?"

"Doug wouldn't tell me anything."

"Did the government tell you that?"

"Objection, Your Honor!"

"Overruled," said the judge.

"Mr. Donovan, let's be clear about this. You met with Mr. Lynch to prepare to testify here, correct?"

"Yes."

"And he was going to ask you a number of questions about your brother Doug and your own medical treatment with Dr. Holden, correct?"

"Yes."

"And it wasn't just Mr. Lynch. I take it there were other attorneys and agents for the government in the room when you met, correct?"

"Yes."

"How many times did you meet?"

"Maybe three or four times."

"During these three or four meetings, did they show you any of Doug's MRIs or any other diagnostic test results?"

"No. They never showed me anything."

"Did they explain to you that as a result of his injury your brother had a large herniated disc in his lower back?"

"I don't believe they ever did."

"So, I take it, they didn't explain either that the disc in Doug's back compressed both of his sciatic nerves, causing a crippling, electrical-shock type of pain running down his legs?"

"Nope."

"That this out-of-place disc was triggering tingling and numbness, causing his legs to collapse under him once in a while?"

"Objection! Asked and answered!"

"Overruled."

"No, nothing like that."

"Are you aware that other specialists agreed with Dr. Holden's diagnosis and treatment of your brother Doug?"

"I am not aware of that."

"Did the government tell you that because of his unbearable pain Douglas had to apply for social security disability, which was promptly granted to him?"

"I had no idea," Jake Donovan shrugged.

"As you testified on direct, your brother was also your best friend, correct?"

"Yes, sir, he was."

"But the fact of the matter is that you knew absolutely nothing about Doug's serious medical conditions or his treatments with Dr. Holden, correct?"

"Correct."

"Now I'd like to ask you some questions about *your own* treatment with Dr. Holden that Mr. Lynch touched on briefly. Did you see Dr. Holden for the first time around January 2002?"

"Yes, that's right."

"Now, when you saw Dr. Holden, you told him that your pain was so bad that your life was pure misery. You said, and I quote, 'I was in so much pain that I didn't care if they cut my leg off. That's how much pain I was in.' Aren't these your words?"

"I don't remember."

"The statement I just quoted is from your testimony to the grand jury, sir."

"Maybe. It was awhile ago."

"Now, Mr. Donovan, when did you get your hip replaced?"

"In April 2005."

"So, between the times you first saw Dr. Holden in January 2002 and your hip surgery in April 2005, more than three years went by when you were suffering, correct?"

"No, I was suffering since 1998, when I fell and hurt myself at work."

"So, your pain wasn't a joke—you were in agony?"

"Yes, I was."

"Even before you came to see Dr. Holden, right?"

"Pretty much for five years, give or take."

"And Dr. Holden started to treat your pain since you first came to see him, correct?"

"Yes, sir, he did."

"He was giving you some herbal shots and sent you for physical therapy. Is that right?"

"Yes, he did."

"When those treatments failed, he prescribed Percocet for your pain, correct?"

"Yes."

"And when your pain got totally out of control Dr. Holden also prescribed OxyContin, right?"

"That's right."

"Because otherwise you were ready to cut off your own leg, right? At least that was your grand jury testimony, correct?"

"Yeah, my pain was really bad."

"And Percocet and OxyContin, which are both opioids, helped you to suffer less, didn't they?"

"They did. Very much so."

"And you told Dr. Holden, 'These medicines are helping with my pain,' correct? Isn't that what you told him, sir?"

"Yes."

"All right. Let's talk about something else. You told the grand jury under oath that Dr. Holden and his office staff had never asked you to sign a pain management agreement or informed consent form. Do you recall testifying to that to the grand jury?"

"He never asked me to sign anything."

"Could you please look at the document in front of you on page 33. Is that your signature? Tell me when you see it. I don't mean to rush you."

"I see it."

"The informed consent says, ***'I, Donovan, Jake, understand that pain medication is an important but not the main way to deal with my medical condition and to control my symptoms. I realize the importance of regular physical exercise, not smoking, diet modification, active lifestyle.'*** Have I read that correctly so far?"

"Yes."

Gould continued reading, ***'I also realize that pain medications, including narcotics, can interfere with my job performance, can impair my ability to drive, and can also be habit-forming or addictive. I will follow all conditions of Dr. Holden's pain management agreement and general treatment***

plan. I understand that the goal of this program is to increase my functional condition and improve the quality of my life.' "Have I read the rest of that correctly?"

"Yes, you have."

"That's the document that Dr. Holden and his office staff asked you sign in May 2003. In fact you signed it, right?"

"Yes."

"And yet you told the grand jury that when the prosecutors asked you questions and Dr. Holden and his lawyers weren't able to be there—"

"Objection, Your Honor!" Lynch's face turned beet-red.

"Sustained," said the judge.

"OK, I will move on," Gould resumed calmly. "You told the grand jury, 'I've never seen or heard anything like that.' That's what you said under oath in February 2009, right?"

"It's possible. I don't remember."

"Would you like me to show it to you?"

"No, that's all right."

"So, you testified to the grand jury under oath, and once again you did not tell them the truth, isn't that right?"

Donovan narrowed his eyes and didn't answer.

"You also told the grand jury in February 2009 that Dr. Holden never asked you to rate your pain while he was treating you. Do you recall saying that to the grand jury?"

"No."

"Do you want me to show your statement from the transcript?"

"No, I believe you."

"In fact, over these two years, when you were Dr. Holden's patient, you were repeatedly asked to rate your pain, correct?"

"I don't recall," Donovan said with annoyance.

"Well, let's go back to your medical file, sir. You have a complete copy of your own medical file in front of you. Mr. Lynch has the same copy as well. Please look at page 41."

"This is the first time I've seen my records."

"I understand that. No one showed them to you before, right?"

"Nope."

"Do you see your handwriting on that page?"

"Yes."

"Now, this is something called a pain map. And it has male figures on it. And you put those Xs on the figures, right?"

"I believe so."

"And then you circled number 7 to rate your pain. Do you see that?"

"Yes."

"And Dr. Holden asked you to do that because he wanted to know how bad your pain was while he was treating you, correct?"

"I guess so."

"Sir, you have to answer yes or no."

"Yes, he did."

"Using a pain scale from 0 to 10, when 10 is the worst pain possible, you circled number 7, which was pretty bad; isn't that right?"

"Yes," admitted Donovan grudgingly.

"And then did Dr. Holden also ask you to answer a series of questions about changes in your functionality, quality of your sleep, and so on, where you circled your own answers?"

"That's not my writing."

"The *circles* aren't your writing?" Gould's eyebrows shot up.

"No, it's not my writing."

Gould sighed heavily and turned to the judge.

"Your Honor, this might be a good place to stop for a break."

"Yes, let's continue after lunch," Judge Adler agreed, and adjourned the trial until 2:00 p.m.

* * *

"Good afternoon, Mr. Donovan," Gould resumed an hour later. "I hope you had a chance to eat your lunch."

"Yes, I did. Thank you."

"Did you also have a chance to look at your medical file?"

"I glanced through it." Jake Donovan gave Gould a wary look.

"I want to ask you just a few more questions about Dr. Holden's treatment of you. First, in addition to opioids, he prescribed a number of non-opioid treatments, correct?"

"No, I don't remember that."

"Let's see if we can refresh your memory. Do you recall, sir, that he gave you an injection of lidocaine and cortisone?"

"Yes, I remember that."

"And these injections helped you with your condition, right?"

"Well, not really. That was for my knee."

"Well, it was *your* knee that Dr. Holden was trying to help you with, not his knee, right?"

There was muffled laughter in the gallery, and a few jurors smiled.

"I know, but I was there for my hip, not my knee."

"Mr. Donovan, Dr. Holden couldn't do much for your hip at that point, remember? That joint was essentially gone and had to be replaced, but meanwhile he was trying to save your knee. He was doing that so your knee arthritis, which by then was also getting worse, wouldn't stop you from walking altogether, right?"

"I don't know. Maybe." Donovan shot Gould a long, rancorous look.

"Did he also offer you non-opioid treatments called Hyalgan injections?"

"Those five shots? I don't even know what type of medicine it was."

"Hyalgan. Organic medicine that works as a joint lubricant. Helps with pain too. Does that ring a bell, sir?"

"Sounds familiar, yes."

"It was a natural remedy for your bad knee, and it wasn't an opioid, right?"

"It does ring a bell, yes."

"Now, Dr. Holden also prescribed Gabitril for you because you were not sleeping well?"

"The only thing I got was shots. I always slept well."

"It's in your file, Mr. Donovan. Do you see it?"

"Umm, I see it, but he never prescribed it to me."

"Sir, the copy of the prescription is in the file. Isn't it a fact, sir, that you took a written prescription and got it filled?"

"I don't recall," Donovan said defiantly.

"I understand. After all, it happened almost ten years ago. All right, let's summarize the facts. You had been going to Dr. Holden for about two years, right?"

"Yes."

"He couldn't reverse the damage in your hip, but he could alleviate your suffering by giving you pain medications, correct?"

"He was giving me Percocet, correct."

"He was also treating your knees so that you could walk better. You had been coming to his office for more than two years, which means you were benefiting from his treatments, right?"

"I don't know about that."

"Well, let me ask you a few questions about your brother Doug. You know that since childhood, Doug was suffering from a serious blood disorder, correct?"

"Yes."

"Do you know which doctor treated him for that disorder?"

"No."

"What treatments he was receiving for his blood condition?"

"No idea."

"Do you know how serious it was?"

"No, I don't."

"Now, when you confronted Doug about what you said was his drug problem, he denied to you repeatedly that he had any problem of this sort, correct?"

"Yeah, he was pretty stubborn," admitted Donovan.

"He even became angry, correct?"

"Yeah."

"Doug also got mad at your girlfriend Lucille because she accused him of being a drug addict, correct?"

"I can't say. Probably."

"Well, haven't you testified to the grand jury that for about a year before Doug died, he'd stopped talking to Ms. Flanagan?"

"Yes."

"Because of the reason I just mentioned, correct?"

"That's right."

"Two more questions, Mr. Donovan. Your hip was replaced in the spring of 2005, nine years ago. Right?"

"Yes."

"And you still take opioids that allow you to function better, correct?"

"Correct."

"Now let me ask you about something else." Gould paused. "You're aware that the Donovan family filed a civil lawsuit against Dr. Holden and Nurse Practitioner Lander, correct?"

"No, I have no idea."

"You have no idea that there was a lawsuit filed by *your* family against Dr. Holden and Nurse Practitioner Lander that was dismissed?" Gould paused and looked at Donovan with puzzlement. "That's complete news to you?"

"Complete news. The first time I heard it."

"So you certainly had no financial interest in that lawsuit. Is that what you are trying to say?"

Donovan didn't answer, but gave Gould a hateful look.

"Thank you for your testimony, Mr. Donovan. I have nothing further."

Judge Adler turned to the jury.

"Have a pleasant evening, everybody. See you tomorrow at 9:00 a.m. sharp."

Chapter Twenty-Four

Judge Adler turned to the lead prosecutor. "Are you ready for the direct, Mr. Lynch?"

"Yes, Your Honor. The government calls Lucille Flanagan," announced Lynch.

A tall, elegantly dressed, fair-headed woman in her late forties walked into the courtroom and slowly moved toward the witness stand. She was obviously struggling with every step, but it was clear that she didn't want her efforts to be noticeable. Lucille Flanagan was Jake Donovan's girlfriend and another star witness for the prosecution.

"Thank you for coming, Ms. Flanagan," Lynch started his direct. "Where do you presently live?"

"In Maine."

"And are you in a relationship with anyone?"

"Yes."

"And who is that?"

"Jake Donovan."

"You need to speak louder so we can all hear you," interrupted Judge Adler.

"Okay, Your Honor."

"Are you partially disabled?"

"Yes."

"Did you previously work full time?"

"Yes, I did. I worked in a medical office."

"And what were your responsibilities in that medical office?"

"To make appointments, to deal with patients on the phone... usual office stuff, you know."

"Did one of the doctors in that practice prescribe pain medications to his patients?"

"Yes, he did."

"Including opioids?"

"Yes," the witness nodded firmly. She was looking more comfortable now.

"In that office, did you have an opportunity to observe people who were abusing opioids?"

"I object, Your Honor," attorney Gould intervened.

"Ms. Flanagan, you need to clarify," said the judge. "Was it something that was happening in your office?"

"Yes."

"So while you were working in that medical practice, did you have a chance to deal with people who were abusing opioids?" asked Lynch.

"Yes, with a lot of them."

"Were you able to observe their physical appearance?"

"Yes."

"Were you able to observe how they acted?"

"Yes."

"And how long were you in that medical practice?"

"Two years."

"Now, you've stated that you were involved... You're still involved with Mr. Donovan?"

"Yes, I am."

"How long have you been involved with Mr. Donovan?"

"Almost twelve years."

"And did you ever meet his family?"

"Only once, for five minutes. Before that, his brother Doug set us up on a blind date."

"And after you started dating Mr. Donovan, did you see more of Doug?"

"Yes, I did."

"Now, at some point did you observe physical changes in Doug that you thought were consistent with abusing opioids?"

"I object, Your Honor, leading," Attorney Gould rose from his chair.

"She's got experience, Your Honor," Lynch insisted.

"Overruled," responded Judge Adler.

"Yes, I saw changes," said the witness firmly.

"Could you describe to the jury what changes you saw in Doug?"

"Weight loss, not taking care of himself, not showering, started to just... just look very emaciated. Some days he looked... grayish."

"Now, at some point, did you become a patient of Dr. Holden?"

"Yes, I did."

"And how long were you a patient of Dr. Holden?"

"For two years. From 2002 to 2004."

"During that time, did you receive pain medications from Dr. Holden?"

"Yes, I did."

"Did you ever go to Dr. Holden's office intoxicated or high?"

"Never."

"Now, while you were going to Dr. Holden's office, did you ever observe other patients in the waiting room?"

"Yes."

"And was there anything about those patients that you thought was distinctive?"

"Yes, there was."

"Could you describe to the jury your observations of those people in the waiting room?"

"A couple of times there were some people who seemed like they were nodding off and going to sleep."

"Now, during the time from 2002 to 2004, were you aware whether Doug was seeing a doctor?"

"I knew he was seeing Dr. Holden."

"And at any point did you ever see anything in Doug's home that led you to believe that Doug could be abusing medications?"

"Yes, I did."

"And what did you see?"

"I saw a fentanyl patch, which was cut open, and there were empty pill bottles all over the kitchen."

"Now, at some point did you speak to Dr. Holden about your concerns regarding Doug?"

"Yes, I did."

"And what did you tell Dr. Holden?"

"I told him that I was scared because I didn't see any improvement and Doug was getting worse. And I... I actually was crying because I was scared for Doug, and Dr. Holden told me he would take care of the problem."

"And following your appointment in February 2004, at some point in that month, did Doug Donovan pass away?"

"Yes, he did."

"Prior to Doug's death, the day before, did you have a chance to interact with Doug?"

"Yes, I did."

"How did he look that day?"

"Doug actually looked well. He spoke to me. He joked... He looked like good old Doug." Lucille was about to cry.

"That's all right, Ms. Flanagan. Let me ask you another question. Following that day, at any point, did you go back to Dr. Holden's office?"

"Yes, Jake and I had a scheduled appointment. We went into an exam room to speak to him."

"And what did you discuss with the doctor in the exam room?"

"We asked Dr. Holden if he had heard about Doug's death, and he said, yes, he did."

"And did the doctor say anything else?"

"Yes, he did."

"And what was that?"

"He said, 'Jake, your brother had problems anyway.'"

"And did you ever go back to Dr. Holden's office after that?"

"I may have gone back another month to pick up a prescription until I found another doctor because I was on medication myself."

"No further questions, Your Honor," Lynch left the lectern with a satisfied smile.

* * *

"May I, Your Honor?" asked Gould.

"Yes, please," nodded Judge Adler.

"Good afternoon, Ms. Flanagan. My name is Edward Gould. I represent Dr. Holden. My sincere condolences to you and Mr. Donovan."

"Thank you."

"Let me ask you right up front about something that you just said. When you saw Doug on the Saturday before he died, he told you that Dr. Holden had switched his opioids to methadone, correct?"

"Yes."

"And that's what Doug *himself* told you after you brought these issues to Dr. Holden's attention, correct?"

"Yes."

"We'll come back to that in a few minutes. Respectfully, ma'am, you're not a doctor, correct?"

"No, I'm not."

"I don't mean anything insulting by that."

"No, I did not take it that way."

"You're not a nurse?"

"No."

"You're not an addictionologist, correct?"

"No."

"And when you talked about the medical office that you worked at, where one of the doctors prescribed pain medication, is it fair to say that you were the receptionist?"

"Yes."

"So all the observations you were making there, you were making not as a doctor, not as a nurse, not as an addictionologist, but as a receptionist, correct?"

"Correct."

"And all the experience you've had in that office was the experience of a receptionist, correct?"

"Correct."

"Now, I want to ask you some questions. You told the grand jury that before Doug died, you and Doug hadn't been speaking for a year, right?"

"Exactly."

"Did you know that Doug... and I want to ask this question with some sensitivity. So did you know that Doug was at some point suicidal?"

"I never knew that."

"You weren't aware that he had threatened to kill himself?"

"No."

"You did know that he suffered from a number of physical ailments, correct?"

"Only what he would say. I don't know for a fact what his ailments were."

"Have you ever seen any of his medical records?"

"No."

"Did you ever attend any of his medical appointments?"

"No, I did not."

"Did you know what diagnoses he carried as an individual when he was alive?"

"No, I did not."

"Did you ever learn that he had a relatively rare blood disorder called neutropenia?"

"I only knew that he had a blood disorder as a child."

"Did you ever go to any of his doctors' appointments or speak with any of his physicians about his blood disorder?"

"No."

"Do you know what, if any, medication he took for it?"

"No, I do not."

"Do you know anything about the medical nature of this disorder in terms of what someone who had this particular disorder might look like or suffer from?"

"No, I don't."

"Did Doug ever suggest to you that the blood disorder that he had compromised his immune system and could be potentially fatal?"

"No, he did not."

"I'm sorry to ask you such an obvious question, but when you say that his skin was changing colors or was grayish or that he lost weight, did you ever do anything to investigate whether it was his blood disorder that was causing those physical symptoms?"

"No, I didn't."

"I'm not saying that you should have, ma'am. I understand that you're not a doctor or a nurse, correct?"

"Absolutely not."

"And you weren't talking to Doug for the preceding year, correct?"

"No, I was not."

"Now, you were interviewed a number of times by the government in this case, correct?"

"A few times."

"For example, you went to the FBI offices in October 2008 to be interviewed, right?"

"Yes."

"And then you testified before the grand jury when you were under oath, correct?"

"Yes, I did."

"And you met with Mr. Lynch and lawyers from the U.S. Attorney's office before you came here to testify, correct?"

"Yes, I did."

"And in all of that time, they never showed you Doug's medical file with Dr. Holden, correct?"

"Never."

"And they never explained to you what his back MRI showed or what treatments he had, correct?"

"Objection, Your Honor, relevance!" Lynch exclaimed.

"Overruled," responded Judge Adler.

"And you have no idea whether Doug had suffered any injuries on the job, correct?"

"No, I don't."

"You have no idea whether he'd been involved in any type of accident that was causing him pain, correct?"

"No, I don't."

"But he did tell you before he stopped talking to you that he was, quote, 'in terrible pain,' correct?"

"He said he was in pain."

"Well, didn't you testify to the grand jury five years ago that Doug told you that he'd been in an accident and that he was in terrible pain when he was seeing Dr. Holden?"

"I don't recall at this time."

"Please take a look at page 16. It's the grand jury transcript from February 2011, when you and Mr. Donovan came into town to testify to the grand jury on the same day, right?"

"Yes, we did."

"Now, can you see your testimony? So Doug told you that he was in terrible pain, correct?"

"Yes, now that I see it, yes, I remember."

"Now let's focus on that day, Saturday, when you'd seen Doug for the last time. As you testified to the grand jury, it was the first time the two of you had spoken in a year, correct?"

"Correct."

"And you were glad about that, right?"

"Yes, I was."

"And in fact that day Doug was joking around like he used to joke around, correct?"

"Yes. He was making some jokes with his brothers and sisters and me."

"And as you testified to the grand jury, you liked what you saw that day; it felt good to see him acting like that, correct?"

"Actually, I said that he was... I was just happy that he was speaking to me again."

"Well, didn't you say under oath before the grand jury that it felt good to see him joking around and acting like his old self?"

"Yes."

"And he seemed alert, correct?"

"Yes."

"And he looked like his old self, correct?"

"Yes."

"And all of this happened the day Doug told you that Dr. Holden had started him on methadone, correct?"

"Yes, because Doug had an appointment with Dr. Holden a couple of days before that."

"Now, are you aware that the Donovan family filed a civil lawsuit against Dr. Holden and Nurse Practitioner Lander and that this lawsuit was dismissed?"

"Not at all."

"You had no role in that lawsuit whatsoever?"

"No, I didn't."

"Mr. Lynch also asked you about the fact that you were treated by Dr. Holden."

"Yes."

"I want to ask you some additional questions as a follow-up. You went to Dr. Holden because you were in very real pain, correct?"

"Yes."

"Other doctors had told you that your pain was all in your head, right?"

"Yes, they did."

"But you *were* suffering, correct?"

"Yes."

"And Dr. Holden believed you, didn't he?"

"Yes, he did."

"You've testified to the grand jury that Dr. Holden, according to you, 'was the *first* doctor that believed you,' correct?"

"Yes, he was."

"Can you describe to the jury the type of pain that you were in when other doctors wouldn't treat you?"

"I couldn't get out of bed, couldn't walk in the mornings. When I got up, I had to crawl to the bathroom."

"That must be terrible." Gould looked at Lucille Flanagan with sadness. "Dr. Holden treated you for your pain, correct?"

"Yes, he did."

"And you were thankful to him for helping you, weren't you?"

"Yes, I was."

"Now, you must have been suffering when people didn't believe you? It was probably humiliating?"

"Yes, it was."

"Are you still on pain medication today?"

"Yes, I am."

"Ms. Flanagan, you started taking pain medication about ten years ago?"

"Yeah, ten to twelve years ago."

"Ten to twelve years... Has it helped you?"

"Yes, it has. With opioids, I can live a normal life. My pain is bearable. I don't have to crawl to the bathroom anymore."

"Thank you, ma'am. I appreciate your coming in to testify," said Gould.

Chapter Twenty-Five

On the third day of the trial, the federal prosecutor, Dick Krokson, walked to the lectern and announced, "The government calls Hubert Snuffer." The witness for the prosecution, a short, plump, elderly man entered the courtroom. With the bearing of a celebrity, he positioned himself comfortably in the witness chair.

"Good morning, Mr. Snuffer," Krokson started his direct in his usual sweet manner.

"Good morning, sir."

"Are you working, Mr. Snuffer, or retired?"

"Presently I'm retired."

"Before you retired, what did you do?"

"I was a pharmacist."

"For approximately how many years?"

"I worked at the same pharmacy for forty-five years."

"Did you become an owner of that pharmacy at some point?"

"Yes, I did."

"Now, sir, while you owned your pharmacy, what were your responsibilities?"

"I filled prescriptions and did what was necessary to maintain the health of the patients who came to my pharmacy."

"Sir, if someone came into your store and presented you with a prescription for a controlled substance like an opioid, what were your professional obligations before filling that prescription and handing the drug to the patient?"

"My professional obligation was to check out and confirm the authenticity of the prescription, which involved calling the physician and verifying that it was legitimate. If I was in any doubt at all, I wanted to speak to the physician."

"And were you also ethically obligated to use your professional judgment before you filled these prescriptions?"

"Most definitely. That's the first thing that I did before filling any prescription. Yes, I used my professional judgment."

"And, sir, that doesn't mean that you yourself physically examined the patient and reached a medical conclusion, right?"

"Correct."

"What does 'using your professional judgment' mean? Could you explain it to the jury?"

"It means that in every instance I got an opioid prescription, I tried to find out what the patient's ailment was and I tried to find out to the best of my ability what the necessity was for the opioid and where the prescription came from, if it was a stolen prescription pad, and so on."

"Now, sir, over your more than forty years of practice as a pharmacist, did you have experience with people coming into your store who were either drug abusers or seeking drugs at your pharmacy for the wrong reasons?"

"Yes, quite often."

"Is that something you had to watch out for, sir?"

"Yes."

"Over time, in your professional judgment, did you develop an ability to spot potential trouble?"

"Yes, I did."

"Could you please explain generally how you did that?"

"Well, first of all, you don't judge a book by its cover, so I never judged the patients who were in need of these medications. Whether they were in casts or walking with crutches, or what they looked like, it didn't make a difference to me. I had patients from all the towns in the area."

"So you never judged the patients?"

"Never. I looked at the prescription, whether it was a duplicate, looked at the ink, whether it was altered, whether it was written for 10 mg and they changed it to 40 mg, or if there was a change in the handwriting. I also checked the one who wrote the prescription."

"You mean the physician?"

"Yes. I knew I had to be on the lookout for some doctors. Some prescriptions could be tampered with or a prescription pad could be stolen. I mean, I did my little investigation."

"Did you check the patients?"

"Of course, if the patients said they lived in my town, I could just open up a telephone book and see if they did live in my town. I asked for a driver's license to confirm who they were."

"Did you call the physician's office?"

"Of course. Usually, if it was a physician practicing for a number of years, I would speak to his secretary and confirm that the prescription was legitimate. I did everything possible to verify that, especially if I was in doubt."

"Sir, at some point during the operation of your pharmacy, did you start to come across prescriptions written by Dr. Benjamin Holden?"

"Yes, I did."

"Do you recall approximately when that was?"

"I think it was around 2002 that I became a little suspicious of what was going on."

"Sir, at some point, did you decide to stop filling prescriptions written by Dr. Holden?"

"Yes, I did. I believe I stopped filling prescriptions for him in 2004."

"Sir, let's first focus on the types of prescriptions, if we could. Did you notice any kind of pattern in terms of the types of prescriptions that were coming from Dr. Holden?"

"Umm, yes, I did. They were mostly opioid medications. There might have been Ambien with an opioid or some anti-anxiety medication, but there was always an opioid."

"Now, Mr. Snuffer, could you please tell this jury what the danger is in using these opioid drugs. Are they completely innocent?"

"Innocent? They are not innocent at all," grinned Snuffer. "Those drugs have a lot of dangerous effects and some of them might be lethal."

"Sir, would you mind listing their dangerous effects for the jury?"

"Not at all. The first and foremost danger of these drugs is addiction. People can become hooked on them and over time take more and more of them."

"And if addicted people can't obtain them on time, what would happen to them?" Krokson asked.

"They would suffer withdrawal."

"And what is that?"

"According to the medical literature, it's an extremely unpleasant experience. People start shaking; they have goose bumps, nausea, diarrhea, pain in every bone, and so on."

"And what would happen to the person who takes too many of these pills?"

"Are you talking about an overdose?"

"Yes, I am."

"The person could easily die. You see, opioids are able to suppress the respiratory center, and the victim of an overdose will simply stop breathing."

"I understand. Now let me ask you again about those drug prescriptions coming from Dr. Holden's office. Sir, was that pattern that you saw unusual, in your experience?"

"Well, it was unusual for one physician to keep prescribing that type of opioid derivative without prescribing other normal stuff such as antibiotics or anti-fungal creams. Most of the local physicians were specialists, such as ophthalmologists, ear-nose-throat doctors, or spinal injury physicians. Whatever they were, they would prescribe some opioids, but for this doctor, it was always an opioid."

"Sir, did you start to make observations about the types of people who were coming in to fill these prescriptions?"

"Objection, leading," Daniels rose from his chair.

"Overruled."

"The types of people I started to categorize and get a little inquisitive about were those people who concentrated more on what was going on in the surroundings rather than on their illnesses. They were looking at my diploma, at the pictures of my children sitting on my counter, and saying, 'Oh, your daughter's name is Amy. I think I went to school with her.' I mean... I normally don't judge people by their appearances, but some of those folks were really quite sketchy."

"But did you make any observations about these individuals in terms of their mannerisms or appearance?" continued Krokson.

"Well, some of them were nervous. Some were fidgety. Some were walking around the store."

"Sir, when the people would come in with a prescription, did you notice anything unusual about how they paid for those prescriptions?"

"Insurance. Everybody was coming with an insurance card."

"So, sir, you testified earlier that at some point you decided to stop filling Dr. Holden's prescriptions, is that right?"

"Right."

"Why?"

"I just didn't need that type of business. I didn't want that reputation in my town."

"So you stopped filling his prescriptions? And that was that?"

"Yes sir. End of story."

"Nothing further," said Krokson and moved back to his seat.

* * *

During the short break, Tina, the Holdens' close friend, walked hurriedly to Ben.

"Ben, what do you think?" she asked with concern. "A rather odd and disturbing testimony, would you agree?"

"I didn't expect him to sing my praises. This man reported me to the authorities."

"He did?"

"Yes, he did. I think people like him are as frightened to death to fill opioid prescriptions as much as many physicians are frightened to prescribe them," said Ben.

"Even if he was scared," Tina continued, "he just could have stopped filling prescriptions, but why should he rat on you?"

"It's always helpful to side with the people in power," Ron answered for Ben. "Just in case. What if some day Big Brother knocks on his door? No one is invincible."

"Well, let's go back and watch the cross," said Ben.

* * *

"Good morning, Mr. Snuffer. I'm Attorney Daniels, and I represent Dr. Holden."

"Good morning." The pharmacist raked his receding hair and nervously scanned the gallery.

"Mr. Snuffer, you're not a doctor, correct?"

"Correct."

"You're not trained in how *to prescribe* pain medication, correct?"

"Correct."

"As a pharmacist, it's not your job to diagnose patients' medical conditions, right?"

"Correct."

"So your job was to fill prescriptions written by physicians after they had examined their patients, taken their medical histories, looked at their diagnostic tests, and made diagnoses, right?"

"Right."

"You remember that you testified before the grand jury, and you testified under oath?"

"Umm, yes."

"And you told the grand jury that you made the decision to stop filling prescriptions for Dr. Holden's patients, correct?"

"Correct."

"When you testified on direct, you didn't say that you stopped filling Dr. Holden's prescriptions because you thought they were forged, right?"

"That's correct."

"People at your pharmacy called Dr. Holden's office and asked if those prescriptions were legitimate?"

"Correct."

"And they were told that the prescriptions were legitimate, correct?"

"Written by the doctor, yes."

"Now, when you made the decision not to provide the medication, you hadn't checked the medical history of any of the patients who were looking to have their prescriptions filled at your pharmacy?"

"No, I hadn't."

"You hadn't done a physical exam on a single one of them?"

"Right."

"You hadn't seen any of their medical files?"

"Right."

"None of their diagnostic tests?"

"Right."

"Because it's not in your job description, right?"

"Umm, true."

"So you had no idea why those medications were prescribed, or what conditions the patients were suffering from, correct?"

"Correct."

"You didn't know whether pain medications were prescribed to *stop* these people's suffering?"

"No, I did not know that," confirmed the pharmacist.

"You didn't know whether their pain, for which Dr. Holden prescribed the medications, was keeping them from sleeping or working, correct?"

"Correct."

"You didn't know if that pain medication that Dr. Holden prescribed was allowing them to walk to the bathroom so they didn't have to crawl from their beds, correct?"

"Crawl from their beds? I had no idea if they crawled or not."

"Nevertheless, you decided not to provide these people with their medications, correct?"

"I decided not to fill their prescriptions, yes."

"You made that decision because you thought those people looked sketchy?"

"No."

"That's not your word?"

"Well, it's more than that."

"Sir, can you please answer my question: you made the decision not to provide pain medications to these people because they looked sketchy?"

"That was one reason, yes."

"That's something to do with their appearance, right?"

"Yes."

"You judged them on how they looked, correct?"

"You have to make a judgment call."

"And you judged them on how they looked?"

"Among other things."

"You thought they looked like bad news, correct?"

"Some did, yes."

"And you testified that there were other reasons that you stopped filling the prescriptions other than they looked sketchy and were bad news, right?"

"Correct."

"Mr. Snuffer, do you remember that when you testified for the grand jury under oath, you only said that you stopped filling the prescriptions for Dr. Holden's patients because they were sketchy, looked like bad news, and came from other locations, correct?"

"Objection, Your Honor," interfered Krokson.

"Overruled."

"If you say so, yeah. I don't recall what I said back then."

"May I approach, Your Honor?" asked Attorney Daniels. "It's pages 11 and 12."

Mr. Snuffer's grand jury testimony appeared on the big overhead screen as follows:

Question: Did you make any other observations with respect to their demeanor or appearance that caused your concern, referring to patients who came to fill prescriptions from Dr. Holden?

Answer: *Yeah. They just looked like bad news. I mean, if you want to just nutshell it, they looked sketchy. And they looked... you know, like they took prescription medicine for... to get high. We just couldn't ignore the fact that, you know, the people coming in just looked like they were bad news.*

"Mr. Snuffer, do you recognize your testimony?"

"Yes, I do."

"And you didn't say anything in that testimony about any of the other reasons you talked about on direct, correct?"

"Correct."

"Now, as a pharmacist, do you decide not to fill a prescription because someone who is in pain and has been prescribed pain medication might not have showered or shaved?"

"No. There are a lot of different reasons why we wouldn't fill them."

"But you didn't testify about those other reasons before the grand jury?"

"No, I did not."

"You testified on direct about some ways in which opioids can be abused, correct?"

"Correct."

"But you didn't testify about their benefits, right?"

"No, I did not."

"But you are aware that opioids have benefits, right?"

"Yes, I am."

"You know that they're considered the most effective medicine for reducing pain, correct?"

"Yes, they are."

"They relieve most types of pain, correct?"

"Yes, they do."

"And they're safe when used appropriately?"

"When prescribed correctly."

"That wasn't my question, Mr. Snuffer. They are safe when used appropriately, correct?"

"In the right dose, yes."

"Sir, are you aware of *any* medication which would be safe if *not* prescribed or used in the right dose?"

Long pause.

"Hmm. I can't say I am."

"For example, opioids do not cause damage to internal organs when used appropriately, correct?"

"No, they don't."

"Which is different from non-steroidal anti-inflammatory drugs like aspirin, Motrin or Advil, right?"

"Yes."

"Especially when they are used over long periods of time, right?"

"Usually when you're taking too much, yes."

"And especially over long time periods, correct?"

"Yes."

"That's also true of Tylenol, right?"

"Yes, that's true."

"Because even over-the-counter Tylenol can cause organ toxicity. It can severely damage a human's liver, kidneys, and other organs, correct?"

"Yes."

"In fact, toxic effects of those OTC medications kill about 17,000 people a year, correct?"

"Probably."

"Unlike opioids, which don't cause significant organ toxicity, right?"

"I'm not sure of that."

"You testified a moment ago that when opioids are used appropriately, they do not cause organ toxicity, right?"

"I can't say... I can't make a blanket statement like that."

"Do you recall your testimony just a moment ago, that when used appropriately, opioids do not cause organ toxicity? Do you deny that you said, 'No, they don't'?"

"No, I do not deny that."

"And in fact, for a certain population of patients with severe pain, opioids have been found to improve daily activity, psycho-motor skills, and sustained attention and mood, correct?"

"Yes, that's true."

"In fact, for patients with chronic pain, opioids can attain favorable outcomes for prolonged periods, right?"

"Yeah, they could," the pharmacist agreed reluctantly.

"And, sir, although there are plenty of therapies available for pain management, opioids remain the cornerstone for the treatment of severe pain and are recognized by the World Health Organization as essential drugs for pain management. Are you aware of this fact?"

"Objection, Your Honor!" exclaimed Krokson.

"Never mind, I have no more questions, Your Honor," said Mark Daniels.

"Then let's have an earlier lunch," said Judge Adler. "See you all at 2:00 p.m."

* * *

On their way to the lunchroom, Ron and his wife, Elaine, caught up with Ben and his friends.

"Ben, can you explain to me," started Elaine, looking worried, "why this man insisted that you, as a pain doctor, had to prescribe 'normal' medications? Is there such a notion as a *normal* medication?"

"Funny you noticed it. The DEA and FBI agents who interrogated me during the raid seven years ago raised the same question. They kept asking me again and again why my office staff was writing so many prescriptions for opioids when all other specialists in the area were writing so few of them and many more prescriptions for other 'normal' stuff."

"And what did you say?" asked Ron.

"My explanation was simple: we pain doctors don't prescribe antibiotics, blood pressure meds, or inhalers because we don't treat people with infections, heart problems, or asthma. We deal with patients in pain. Opioids are exactly the medications that help these people the most."

"Did they get it?" asked Elaine.

"I don't think so. Actually, I don't think 'getting it' was in their plans."

"Ben, among your patients, there were those who abused opioids, right?" asked Elaine.

"Unfortunately, there were some, but they were a very small portion of our practice. The moment we realized who they were, we stopped prescribing to them and referred them to an addictionologist. But these people were our patients; Julia and I knew their health problems and their needs, and with each one we used professional judgment that was based on facts. What this overzealous pharmacist was practicing is collective punishment!"

"It's not just him," added Julia. "The government itself, on the pretense of fighting a war on drugs, actually implements the same collective punishment by intimidating physicians, especially pain doctors, and depriving millions of suffering people of effective pain relief."

"I don't think the government is winning the war on drugs," Ron said. "Judging by the media reports, today many more people are abusing them than ever before. I wonder why."

"Well, I can't vouch for everyone," said Ben, "but people who suffer from severe pain and are refused pain medications by their physicians or pharmacists often go to the street and buy whatever they can get to alleviate their suffering. Many of them buy cocaine or heroin, which, as known from the press, are now the cheapest products on the market. Either of these two substances can kill not only their pain but their poor souls."

"I wonder when the government will realize this," Julia said anxiously.

"I hope someday they will," said Ben.

Chapter Twenty-Six

When the lunch break was over, Krokson announced, "The government calls Roger Rafferty."

A blocky, redheaded man in his fifties, his face and arms splashed with freckles, moved down the aisle, rocking from side to side as if he'd just stepped ashore after a long sea voyage.

"I think in his other life he was a pirate," Gail, Emma's friend, whispered to her.

"I hope not a brutal one," Emma whispered back.

"Good morning, Mr. Rafferty," Krokson greeted the witness.

"Good morning, sir."

"Mr. Rafferty, were you ever a patient of Dr. Benjamin Holden?"

"Yes, I was," the witness said cautiously.

"When did you start seeing Dr. Holden?"

"I'm not really good with dates, but around 2002, I'd say."

"And why did you first go to see him?"

"Actually, first I was bringing my mother. She was Dr. Holden's patient."

"And at some point did you decide to ask him to examine you and help you?"

"Yes. I don't know how it came up exactly, but I think my mother said, 'Your shoulder bothers you. Why wouldn't you see Dr. Holden?' So we made an appointment, and that's how it started."

"So what was the problem with your shoulder?"

"It was dislocated many years earlier, and my arm pain was getting worse."

"And prior to seeing Dr. Holden, had you taken any pain medicine for your shoulder?"

"No, I had not," Rafferty answered uncertainly.

"Do you still currently have pain in your shoulder?"

"A little bit now and then."

"Did you ultimately have a shoulder replacement?"

"Yes, I did."

"Do you recall approximately when you stopped seeing Dr. Holden?"

"When they closed down."

"Was that approximately 2007?"

"I believe so, yes."

"So you saw him for a number of years during that time?"

"Yes, I did."

"During your time visiting the defendant's medical practice, did you receive prescriptions for pain medicine?"

"Yes, I did." Rafferty said calmly, but his fumbling fingers betrayed his growing nervousness.

"Sir, I know this is not easy to talk about, but at some point did you begin abusing drugs?"

"Yes, I did." The man's facial expression changed from neutral to tense.

"And was this while you were seeing the defendants?"

"Yes..." Rafferty stumbled, and for a split second, his eyes darted toward Dr. Holden.

"Did you consider yourself an addict?"

"Yeah, I did," the witness said with some hesitation.

"Did you, in addition to getting drugs from the defendants, start getting some drugs on the street?"

"Yes, I did." Rafferty lowered his eyes.

"What kind of drugs?"

"Percocet... and cocaine."

"And did you ever get drugs from another doctor while you were seeing the defendants?"

"Probably." Rafferty avoided looking either at the prosecutor or the jury.

"Do you remember what you got and how you got it?"

"Umm... not really, no."

"Do you recall, for example, getting Percocet from another doctor?"

"No, I was pretty crafty. If I got Percocet from Dr. Holden, I might have gotten Vicodin from another doctor." Rafferty sneaked an apologetic look at Ben.

"I'm sorry. I probably asked a bad question. Now, did the defendants ever talk to you about your drug abuse?"

"No, they didn't."

"Do you recall getting drug tested while you were in the defendants' office?"

"Yes, two or three times, not often."

"And you testified you don't recall ever talking to anyone about that drug test when cocaine in your urine was discovered, right?"

"Right. But I don't think cocaine was ever found in my urine."

"Okay. You mentioned that one of the drugs that you got from the defendants at some point was methadone, right?"

"Yes, it was." A rehearsed tone again.

"Did you also get methadone from someone on the street... I think you testified earlier you got methadone from someone on the street while you were seeing the defendants, is that right?"

"I would swap drugs with people I knew," Rafferty said in a weak voice.

"Say it again, because I can't hear you," demanded Judge Adler.

"I would swap. If I knew somebody else who was on that drug, I would get some from him if I ran out, or if they ran out of their drugs, I would give some to them."

"We're talking about methadone?" Judge Adler asked.

"Yes, and also Percocet and other stuff."

"Sir, while you were seeing the defendants, did you ever get free samples of any drugs from the office?" Krokson was carefully leading the witness through his charted course.

"Yes, I did."

"Could you please describe what you remember in that regard?"

"I was working at night at the time, and I couldn't sleep during the day, so I asked for some sleeping medication. Dr. Holden gave me samples of Ambien or Lunesta."

"Sir, one more question. Do you ever recall requesting testosterone from Dr. Holden?"

"Yes, I do."

"Could you please explain what happened with that?" The prosecutor broke into a wry smile.

"Well, because of my shoulder, I had lost a lot of weight and muscle mass, and I was just kind of joking, 'Could you give me some kind of testosterone?' I believe the following month, Dr. Holden gave me a prescription for testosterone cream. I was kind of shocked, but I took it."

"Why were you shocked?"

"Because I was kind of joking. I wasn't serious. I didn't think he would do that."

"Now, I want to talk about Dr. Holden: on average, approximately how long did your meetings with him last when you would see him?"

The witness took a long pause.

"Well, it was usually in and out, just 'Hi, how are you doing? What do you need?' He'd look at my file and give me the same prescription and 'See you later.' That would be it." Rafferty smirked, but his eyes betrayed fear and guilt.

"Do you recall how often he gave you a physical exam?"

"In the beginning, he did a couple of times, but later on it was just bending the arm, and that was it, not a real physical."

"Sir, how long did you usually wait for your appointment in the waiting room?"

"It varied." Rafferty looked pensive. "Sometimes it was five minutes. Other times it would be an hour and a half, two hours."

"And the times where it was long, was that because there were a lot of other people waiting?"

"Yes."

"Could you please briefly describe what the waiting room was like."

Rafferty paused for a very long moment.

"Well, the waiting room was..." he hesitated and then stopped, as if struggling to choose the right answer.

"Mr. Rafferty, if you need to refresh your memory, please take your time," suggested Krokson, with an encouraging half-smile.

"Thank you, sir. I think I've refreshed it." The witness shot a swift look at Ben and continued.

"Well, the waiting room was loaded with people," Rafferty was now back to his practiced tone, "and there were kids running around and people sleeping and...sweating. I mean, you could tell it was... It looked like... a drug clinic." Rafferty cast the prosecutor an inquisitive glance, as if seeking his approval.

"Objection, Your Honor," Daniels jumped in.

"Sustained," ruled Judge Adler.

"Let me ask you another, more-specific question," continued Krokson nonchalantly, as if Rafferty's description of Ben's practice as a "drug clinic" was impromptu. "You mentioned that you saw people sort of sleeping and nodding off? Is that what you said?" Krokson raised his voice a notch.

"Yeah..."

"And what other physical characteristics did you notice about these people?"

"I could tell some people were high or..."

"Objection!" Daniels jumped in.

"Sustained, because you need to lay a foundation," Judge Adler said and suddenly leaned forward: "Mr. Rafferty, when you would go to Dr. Holden's office, would you yourself be high?"

"I have been, yes," the witness said without blinking an eye.

Muffled laughter swept across the gallery while most of the jurors tried their best to stifle their smiles.

"So all your observations were made while *you yourself* were high?" Judge Adler looked at Rafferty with increasing amusement.

"Not all the time..." started Rafferty, yet the titters in the gallery didn't let him finish his sentence. "But I... I..."

"I think, Mr. Krokson, you need to move on," Judge Adler turned to the prosecutor with a telling smile and shook her head in disbelief.

"Yes, Your Honor," Krokson nodded agreeably and stared at his notes.

"Well, Mr. Rafferty, let me ask you a different question. Were there ever times when you actually sold your medication?" The prosecutor addressed the witness as casually as if his question was about a weekly forecast.

"Yes, I did." Mr. Rafferty emitted a heavy sigh.

"Are you a drug addict, Mr. Rafferty?"

"Yes, I am." The witness frowned and stared at his feet. "But in the last few years I am drug free. You see, I go to a methadone clinic every week. It helps my pain and helps me to stay clean."

"I have nothing further," declared Krokson, and sauntered to his seat.

* * *

After a short break, Roger Rafferty was back in the witness chair, and Mark Daniels replaced Mr. Krokson at the lectern.

"Good morning, Mr. Rafferty."

"Good morning, sir."

"My name is Mark Daniels, and I represent Dr. Ben Holden. I'm going to ask you some questions about your medical history. Here is a copy of your file for you to look at."

"Sure."

"As you just testified on direct, when you were receiving pain medication from Dr. Holden, you also got prescriptions from other doctors, correct?"

"Correct." Rafferty leaned back a little and swallowed. He knew that from this moment on, he had to be on his toes.

"And you used your disability insurance to see another doctor for that purpose, right?"

"Right."

"To intentionally get pain medication from another doctor other than Dr. Holden, right?"

"Right." Rafferty's voice was flat, but his small, bluish eyes were darting back and forth.

"And you intentionally *did not* tell Dr. Holden that you were seeing another doctor, correct?"

"Correct."

"As you testified on direct, you were pretty crafty, right?"

"I... I don't believe I said I was crafty, but I... I did see another doctor."

"And you sold some of the prescribed pills?"

"Yes."

"But you didn't tell Dr. Holden that, correct?"

"Correct, I didn't."

"And at a certain point, whether your pain was getting better or not, you would just lie to Dr. Holden to get medication, isn't that right?"

"I have always had pain in my shoulder. I—"

"Mr. Rafferty, I believe that you have always had pain in your shoulder, but at a certain point, though, even when your pain was getting better as a result of your treatment with Dr. Holden, you would lie to him to get more medication, right?"

"That is correct."

"Now, you just testified that you sold some of your pain medication, correct?"

"That's correct."

"You sold this medication on the street, right?"

"Yes, on the street."

"But the government didn't arrest you, right?"

"No, they didn't." Rafferty threw a desperate look at the prosecution table.

"Objection, Your Honor," Krokson interjected.

"Overruled."

"Sorry. Could you please repeat your answer because I didn't hear it," said Mark Daniels.

"No, I was not arrested for selling drugs," said Rafferty, this time without flinching.

"And they have not prosecuted you for selling drugs, correct?"

"No, they have not, thank God."

Mark shot a fleeting glance at Krokson. The prosecutor inconspicuously clenched his fists.

"Now, you came to Dr. Holden with shoulder pain that you'd had for a number of years, correct? It bothered you to the point that you were not able to work, right?"

"I... don't recall that. It hurt to work, but I... don't remember saying that."

"Mr. Rafferty, you're aware that Dr. Holden had notes in your medical file on his appointments with you, right?"

"Yes."

"Please take a look at the document in front of you. Do you see your name at the top?"

"Yes, I do."

"It reads, *'Mr. Roger Rafferty is a 42-year-old gentleman with shoulder pain which he's had for about 15 years.'* The note says you have a history of shoulder dislocation, and then the last sentence here states that *'The latest shoulder dislocation happened maybe two weeks ago, and it bothers him to the point where he hasn't been able to return to work yet.'* Does that refresh your recollection?"

"I don't remember that, to be honest with you, sir," said Rafferty.

"Is that statement true?" asked Judge Adler.

"Yeah, I would say it was true. I just didn't remember that," Rafferty said gloomily.

"And was your job at the time some kind of manual labor?"

"Yes."

"Dr. Holden also did a physical exam on you initially, correct?"

"Yes, he did."

"Now, you testified that sometimes in later visits, he didn't do a full physical exam, correct?"

"Correct."

"You weren't going to him as a primary care physician, correct?"

"Correct."

"So you weren't expecting a full physical when you went to see Dr. Holden, right?"

"I was expecting... help with my shoulder is what I was expecting."

"But he *did* look at your shoulder, correct? He checked the range of motion, and he evaluated the strength of your shoulder, correct?"

"Yes, he did."

"And that was the part of your body that you were complaining to him about, correct?"

"I guess so."

"Do you recall that you signed an informed consent from Dr. Holden?"

"No, I don't."

"Could you please take a look in your medical file in front of you on page 3."

"Put it on the screen," suggested Judge Adler.

"Do you see that it's titled as *Informed Consent*? And here is your signature, right?"

"Yes."

"And this document says that your pain medication is an important but not the only way to deal with your medical condition, correct?"

"Yes," reluctantly agreed the witness.

"So when you signed this form, you understood the importance of regular physical exercise, not smoking, diet modification, an active lifestyle, right?"

"Yeah, he was always lecturing me, 'don't smoke, eat healthy, exercise...'"

"And you signed the form titled *Pain Management Agreement*?"

"Yes, I did."

"Now, you talked about the pain medication that Dr. Holden gave to you, right?"

"Correct."

"Dr. Holden, though, treated you not only with pain medicine?"

"Well, he... He gave me a couple of shots, but..."

"Okay. And that was lidocaine and Sarapin? And it was more than a couple?"

"Maybe. I didn't know what it was, and I don't remember how many shots he gave me. I know it was some natural stuff, and I know it didn't get me high."

Daniels suppressed a smile.

"Dr. Holden also prescribed physical therapy for you, correct?"

"Umm, I remember some machine he put me on every visit, but not therapy."

"Do you remember that you testified before the grand jury that Dr. Holden had sent you to physical therapy?"

"Yeah, now I remember. I did do something in his office. He had a muscle stimulator, electronic gadgets that you hook up to wherever your pain is."

"Now, Dr. Holden also requested that you get an MRI on your shoulder?"

"Oh, yeah."

"And he explained to you that you had severe arthritis and torn ligaments, right?"

"Right," the witness agreed reluctantly.

"He also referred you to the shoulder surgeon, correct?"

"Yes, sir, he did."

"And you ended up with rather extensive shoulder repair, remember?"

"Yes, I do. I ended up with two shoulder surgeries."

"And in both cases it was Dr. Holden who suggested you to have it done, correct?"

"He told me I needed to have it done, right."

"Now, Mr. Rafferty, you testified for the grand jury that at some point after your first surgery, Dr. Holden told you that because your shoulder was in much better shape, he wouldn't be seeing you again, is that right?"

"That's correct."

"And you testified that you went back and continued to see him because you were in pain, correct?"

"No. I went back because I wanted more drugs."

"But you told Dr. Holden that you were in extreme pain, right?"

"Sure, I probably did, sure."

"On the pain map, you rated the pain in your shoulder as 8, which was pretty bad, wasn't it?"

"Yes, it was."

"Now, from time to time, you also filled out a survey for Dr. Holden that asked you questions about your general functionality. You recognize this form, right?"

"That is my handwriting, that's me."

"And on this form you said that your sleep, job performance, and family relationships were all improved, correct?"

"Correct."

"When asked about overall satisfaction with your pain management regime, your answer was *satisfied*, right?"

"Right."

"So in roughly two years that Dr. Holden had seen you, your life had gotten better, right?"

"Can I answer this question honestly without..."

"I hope all your answers are honest," interjected Judge Adler.

"Well, what I'm trying to say is..." Rafferty paused, pondering how to present this delicate matter in the most palatable way. "You know, I was trying to get... I wanted drugs. Of course I wrote down that everything was better. If he saw my pain was normally 8 but everything improved on the meds—"

"So what you're saying is," Daniels gently interrupted, "that you lied on this form in order to convince Dr. Holden that he should continue to give you pain medication?"

"Was I lying? No, I don't believe I was lying."

"So you weren't lying?" Daniels raised his eyebrows. "It means that your sleep pattern, family relationships, and daily living activities had all improved?"

"Objection, Your Honor. He's already said he doesn't remember this time period," interjected Krokson.

"Sustained," ruled Judge Adler.

"Okay, let's move on to another subject. You had two major shoulder surgeries, and after that second surgery you were able to return to work after not being able to do so for some period of time, correct?"

"Right. My right arm was useless."

"Were you working for a liquor distributor at that time and had to lift a lot of heavy things?"

"Yes."

"And you were able to do that, even with your repaired shoulder?"

"Yes, with the medication."

"With the medication, exactly!" Daniels said emphatically and smiled broadly. "So the pain medications prescribed by Dr. Holden did help you to get back to work?"

"Yes."

"Now, you knew that Dr. Holden sometimes discharged people from his practice for abusing pain medications or illegal drugs, correct?" Daniels queried.

"Sure."

"And you told the government that you saw Dr. Holden discharge people from his office based on the results of urine tests, right?"

"Yeah, I've seen people discharged from the office."

"Now, when Dr. Holden was treating you with pain medication, you were able to work, right?"

"Yes, I was."

"But after Doctor Holden's office was raided and closed, you had to quit your job because you couldn't obtain your usual pain medications anymore and the pain became too bad, correct?"

"That's right."

"Now, Mr. Rafferty, on a different topic..." Mark Daniels took a long, pondering look at the witness. "As you mentioned before, your mother was Dr. Holden's patient, correct?"

"Correct."

"And you drove her to her appointments with Dr. Holden, right?"

"Right."

"And your mother told Dr. Holden that she had an old-fashioned wheelchair, not an electric one, and she had been waiting for a long time to get an electric one, right?"

"R-right," Rafferty faltered, obviously wondering what direction the defense attorney was leading him now.

"And Dr. Holden made a few phone calls, faxed some papers, and three days later your mother had an electric wheelchair, right?"

"Yeah, that is true." Rafferty broke into a mini-smile. He seemed to be straying away from the charted course.

"And you were thankful for that, right?"

"Yeah, of course I appreciated that." Roger Rafferty suddenly softened up, and a wide, kindly smile lit his round, freckled face. "What can I say? I liked the guy."

He paused and emitted a long, weighty sigh.

"You know, I'm here to—" His eyes inadvertently met Ben's, and he didn't finish the sentence.

"Nothing further, Your Honor." Daniels gave the witness a final look and left the lectern.

Chapter Twenty-Seven

That night, when Ben and Emma were about to get some rest after a full day in court, their plans were interrupted by a phone call.

"Hi, Ben. It's Mark Daniels. Do you have a minute?"

"Sure, Mark. What's new?"

"Does the name 'Riana Bernardi' ring a bell?"

"Riana? Of course."

"What do you remember?" Mark's voice betrayed a hint of worry.

"She was a nice young woman who worked at the front desk for about six or seven months. She was hard-working and reliable. Everyone in the office liked her. Why'd you ask?" Ben was perplexed.

"The prosecutors plan to put her on the witness stand."

"They want her to testify on the government side?" Ben asked incredulously.

"Yes, they do. But she refused, and they had to subpoena her. Do you know why they want her on the stand?"

"No idea."

"Do you recollect any problems with her? Were there any confrontations?" Mark sounded concerned.

"Oh, no, we loved her. She was really sweet and hard-working... I don't believe we ever had any issues with her."

"So you don't think Riana could hold a grudge?"

"No, all the time she was working with us she seemed to be happy," reassured Ben.

"That's all I need to know. Sorry for bothering you so late."

"No problem, Mark. Have a good night." Ben hung up, feeling baffled and slightly upset.

Riana worked at their center more than eight years ago, but he remembered her very well. She started her secretarial job at Dr. Holden's pain center when she had just turned eighteen and was still a senior in high school. Her family was struggling at the time, and the money Riana made as a secretary gave her some independence. The girl planned to become a physical therapist, and Dr. Holden's clinic was her first experience with patients in pain. The office staff liked Riana, and the patients adored her. This beautiful girl was one of the most cordial and trustworthy employees he'd ever had. On the fourth day of the trial, Attorney Mike Lynch called Riana Bernardi as a witness for the government.

Over those eight years that Ben hadn't seen Riana, she'd hardly changed. She was still slender and beautiful, and her thick, wavy black hair still fell down to her shoulders. Riana wore a black dress with a wide, fashionable belt tied slightly below her waist. The young woman moved to the witness stand in a composed and dignified manner, but Ben could instantly feel the anxiety deeply hidden in her large, almond-shaped eyes as she passed by. When she reached the witness stand, her glance inadvertently moved from the jury to Dr. Holden. She sent him a shy smile, and he smiled back. This silent exchange didn't go unnoticed by Judge Adler, the jurors, and certainly by the prosecutors.

Lynch launched his direct. He started with questions about her background and how she happened to be hired by Dr. Holden. For a young woman who was testifying in federal court for the first time in her life, Riana appeared to be rather comfortable. Her answers were direct and confident.

"Miss Bernardi, could you please tell the jury what type of patients you'd observed while working in Dr. Holden practice?" asked Lynch. The benign part is over, flashed in Ben's mind.

"Well, Dr. Holden's patients were people from all walks of life. Most of them were middle-aged or elderly people. Many were using canes or walkers, and I even remember a couple of patients who had to be taken to the office on stretchers," Riana noted.

"Have you ever seen any young men or women in the waiting room who looked sleepy or were nodding off?" asked Lynch.

"Yes, I have. Some of Dr. Holden's patients were construction workers," Riana confirmed. "They would come to our office in the morning after their night shifts. They looked sleepy and tired. Some of them weren't very neat. They were still wearing their work clothes and dirty boots, but Dr. Holden didn't mind. He used to say, 'As long as these people are able to work, I don't care what outfits they wear,'" Riana added with a smile.

"Miss Bernardi, do you recall that some people in the waiting room behaved in a strange way?" Lynch stressed the word "strange."

"What do you mean by 'strange'?" asked Riana, obviously confused.

"I mean, were they drunk or high?" Lynch clarified with growing irritation.

"No, never!" Riana was astonished. "Many people who came to Dr. Holden's office didn't look well because they suffered from severe pain. You could read it on their faces. But they were not drunk or high. They were polite and very appreciative."

"Miss Bernardi," Lynch suddenly stopped and cast a swift glance toward the jurors. "Do you recollect any episodes when Dr. Holden's patients would call the office with reports of lost or stolen medications?" Lynch shot another quick look at the jury.

"As a matter of fact, I do. I believe it was my second week at work when I received a phone call from a lady who told me that she had been driving on the highway with the car windows open when her prescriptions were blown away. She was so upset, and so was I."

"And what did you do?"

"I rushed to Dr. Holden and told him what happened. I was so concerned about the lady."

"And what was his response?"

"He calmed me down and said, 'No, no new prescriptions for the lady. That's our firm office policy. No exceptions.' He was very busy at that moment but later he explained to me that such stories of 'blown away prescriptions or flushed down the toilet pills' were usually made up by patients who wanted to get more pain medication. He said, 'We give them as much as it takes to control their pain. And if someone needs more, this person has to come here and explain why. Don't let dishonest people fool you and take advantage of your kindness.' Maybe these were not his exact words, but that's what he tried to explain to me. At the end, he repeated, 'No exceptions.'"

"Huh, no exceptions," Lynch said with a smirk. "OK, let's move on. Miss Bernardi, to the best of your recollection, did you work at Dr. Holden's office on November 17, 2006?"

"Sorry sir, but I don't remember. It was more than eight years ago," said Riana.

"Let me remind you. Your Honor, government introduces Exhibit 44A." Lynch handed a piece of paper to the judge, the witness, and the defense. "Miss Bernardi, here is a handwritten note attached to the patient's medical record, and if you don't mind, I'll read it to you and the jury. It states: ***'November 17, 4:45 p.m. Received a phone call from a woman who claimed to be Mr. Richard G.'s wife. She said that the night before last, Mr. G. died of sleep apnea. She also said that Dr. Holden shouldn't have prescribed her husband the medications he had received.'***

The note is signed R. B. Are these initials yours, Miss Bernardi?"

"Yes, they are."

"Is this your handwriting?"

"Yes, the handwriting is mine too," confirmed Riana.

"That's exactly what I thought. Now, how soon after you recorded this message did you show it to Dr. Holden?"

"I don't remember." Riana said.

"Did you show it to him?"

"Sorry, but I don't remember. It was a long time ago." Riana was visibly upset.

"So you don't remember whether you showed Dr. Holden the note or not? And if you did, you don't remember his response to it?"

"No, I don't."

"How come you remember how nice and appreciative his patients were, and you remember what Dr. Holden told you about those 'blown away' prescriptions, but you don't remember any of this?" Lynch was barely able to contain his sarcasm.

"Objection, Your Honor!" interrupted Gould. "Asked and answered. The counselor is badgering his own witness!"

Judge Adler frowned.

"Sustained," she said austerely. "Please move on, Mr. Lynch."

"No more questions for this witness," declared Mr. Lynch, and he left the lectern.

Watching Riana on the witness stand, Ben admired her frankness, her affable presence, and her unruffled dignity. At the same time, with every consecutive question, he was feeling engulfed by frustration. Now the prosecutors' whole scheme had floated to the surface. With this brief handwritten note, the government was trying to plant into the jurors' minds the idea of Dr. Holden's callous attitude toward his patient's fate. Ben couldn't remember ever seeing this note. But was it of any importance to the prosecutors whether he'd seen it or not? For them, this note was just another nail in his coffin.

* * *

"Mr. Gould, are you ready for the cross?" The judge's voice interrupted Ben's disheartened reflections.

"Yes, Your Honor, I am," answered Gould, taking his place at the lectern. "Good afternoon, Miss Bernardi. My name is Edward Gould, and I represent Dr. Holden."

"Good afternoon, sir," Riana replied gingerly.

"Miss Bernardi, could you please tell this jury what it was like to work at Dr. Holden's office? What memories if any do you have about those times?"

Riana's face glowed with a smile.

"It was probably the best work experience in my life so far."

"What do you mean by that?"

"You see, at Dr. Holden's office, I always felt that I was part of something really important. Actually, I think everyone who worked there felt that way."

"Could you please be more specific?"

"Sure. At Dr. Holden's pain center we were dealing with ill people. They were coming for help every day. Some of them had been injured at work and others in serious car accidents; there were many patients with such bad arthritis in their backs or knees that they could barely walk. All of them were coming to us hoping to get better, and our doctors, Nurse Practitioner Lander, and other staff were trying their best to help them. I was part of their team, and it was rewarding."

"And what was your personal experience with Dr. Holden?"

"I think it wasn't just me... we all deeply respected Dr. Holden, and we all loved him." Riana turned to Ben and gave him a disarming smile. "We knew from the patients that he always took time to talk to them and to explain their problems and their treatments. He always had time for us too. I can't tell you how many times patients shared with me their personal experiences with Dr. Holden. They were so happy they'd found a doctor like him."

"Miss Bernardi, now let's talk about something else. Were you aware that Dr. Holden prescribed opioid medications to many of his patients?" asked Gould.

"Of course I was. The majority of our patients were in such poor shape that to relieve their pain without opioid medications would be impossible.

They came to us after failed surgeries and other treatments that didn't help them. Many of our patients couldn't have normal lives without painkillers. There were even those for whom opioid treatment was the only option left. Of course, Dr. Holden was monitoring them very closely..."

"What do you mean by monitoring?" gently interrupted Gould.

"We had a full-time laboratory, so everyone who received pain medications had to randomly submit his or her blood or urine for analysis."

"I see. Do you remember what Dr. Holden's actions were if the test came back positive for cocaine or some other illegal drug?"

"Well, as far as I know, if that sort of thing happened for the first time, he would usually talk to the patients and explain the risks of what they were doing. Dr. Holden would warn them that if this happened again, he would have to stop prescribing them opioids."

"And if the patient's test came back with illegal drugs again, what would he do?"

"He would refer the patient to an addictionologist."

"Were there any patients who refused to go?"

"Yes, there were. Then Dr. Holden would stop prescribing them any opioids. He didn't have a choice. He had warned them. I personally sent a few letters to some of his patients informing them that he wouldn't prescribe them opioids any longer."

"Miss Bernardi, do you think that Dr. Holden was a drug dealer?"

Riana gasped.

"Oh, no! He never was a drug dealer. He was a great doctor."

"Thank you, Miss Bernardi. I have no further questions," announced Gould and left the lectern.

Emma looked at the jurors. She saw that two women in the second row and a young man in the first row exchanged puzzled looks, wondering why this young woman was a *government* witness.

It was Friday, and the half-day session. The first week of the trial was over.

* * *

When they left the courtroom, Ben put his arm around Emma's shoulder and whispered in her ear, "What a witness!"

"A bright and noble girl," she whispered back. "Do you think we should award Lynch a bottle of scotch for his impeccable choice?"

"I'm not sure one bottle will be enough for him tonight." Ben grinned. "Well, it was a truly good day. I wonder if there will be any other days like that."

* * *

On the fifth day of the trial, the first witness for the prosecution was Tim Pantano, the close friend and confidant of Jason Cameron, Dr. Holden's former patient who had died of an overdose. This skinny, slightly bald young man with grayish skin and small, darting eyes sat in the witness chair and furtively scanned the gallery. He looked uncomfortable.

Attorney Dick Krokson cordially greeted him and immediately started his direct examination.

"Mr. Pantano, did you know Jason Cameron well?"

"Yes, I did." Pantano's voice was barely audible.

"Mr. Pantano, speak up please," Judge Adler asked politely.

"Yes, ma'am. I mean, Your Honor."

"How old were you when you first met Jason Cameron and how did you meet?" continued Krokson.

"Jason and I met in our freshman year at the Mass. College of Art. We were both eighteen. We knew many of the same people from the neighborhood, and we kind of clicked right away."

"Your Honor, may I publish Mr. Cameron's picture for the jury?"

"Yes, you may," said the judge.

A large portrait of Jason Cameron appeared on the overhead screen and the small screens in front of the jurors.

"Is it true that at some point Jason Cameron passed away?"

"Yes, it's true."

"From the day you met, did you hang out together a lot?"

"Almost every day. We were also roommates for a while. When Jason and I first met, we both felt like we had a lot in common. The same taste in everything. We painted together and did other things that normal eighteen-year-olds do."

"I apologize for having to ask you some of these questions, Mr. Pantano, but when the two of you were hanging out, did you abuse drugs together?"

"Yes, we did," Pantano agreed reluctantly.

"What kind of drugs?"

"A lot of crushed OxyContin, and, umm, we did... you know, cocaine and... only on occasion, some LSD. But mostly regular OxyContin. Jason liked to snort it, you know..."

"And why were you taking OxyContin?" Krokson persisted.

"Because I was addicted to... pain pills."

"At some point did you also abuse heroin?"

"Yes, I did."

"And do you still consider yourself to have a drug addiction problem?"

"Yeah. I consider myself a drug addict... probably till the day I die."

"Are you getting treatment?" Krokson asked with fatherly concern.

"Yes, I am. I go to the methadone clinic."

"Congratulations, Mr. Pantano."

"Thank you, sir."

"Now, where did you and Mr. Cameron get the drugs that you abused?"

"Umm, most of the time," Pantano started hesitantly, "I mean, we just got them off someone on the street, or from whoever... whoever we could get them."

"And sometimes did Mr. Cameron bring drugs that you would use?"

"Sometimes him, sometimes me. Whatever we had, we would always share it. We were really close, you know... He was like a brother to me."

"Mr. Pantano, is it true that you were friends with Jason Cameron for almost ten years?"

"Yes, that's true. We were very good friends."

"Mr. Pantano, may I direct your attention to March 9, 2005? Do you remember that day?"

"Yes, very well."

"Were you with Mr. Cameron that day?"

"Yes."

"Could you tell the jury what you were doing with Mr. Cameron that day?"

"Hmm, we had... Jason had come over to my house, and my son Brad was there, he was about six months old, and it was the first time that he had picked up my son, and..." Pantano stopped and pursed his lips. He was about to cry.

"Take as much time as you need, Mr. Pantano."

Pantano collected himself and signaled to Krokson that he was ready to go on.

"I assume it was a memorable day for you and your friend, Mr. Cameron," continued Krokson. "So what did you do that day? I know it may be hard on you, so please let me know if you need a moment."

"I'm okay," said Pantano. "As I said before, that day my son turned six months old, and we wanted to celebrate."

"And what did you and Mr. Cameron do that night, Mr. Pantano?"

"You see, sir, we had our favorite place where we used to go for years, a park next to Jason's digs. It was a neat place, with no foot traffic, if you know what I mean." Krokson nodded but refrained from any comments.

"So what happened in the park?"

"That day Jason brought some new stuff, and we..."

"Could you tell us more about that new stuff? Where did he get it?"

"Well, Jason got his meds from some doctor. Jason told him that his back pain was unbearable, and the doc prescribed him some painkillers. Then one day the doc said he wanted Jason to try some other pills that might work better for him, and he switched Jason to this new stuff."

"Do you know what that new medication was?"

"No, sir, I never heard the name before." Tim Pantano shrugged.

"Your Honor, at this time the government would like to introduce Exhibit 27J," announced Krokson. He reached into the evidence box and pulled out a small orange bottle, commonly used for prescribed medications. He placed it on the pad of the projector so that the jury could see its label.

Prescribing physician: Holden, B. MD.
Name: Cameron, Jason, Age 26
Medication: methadone 10 mg 60 pills
Take 1 pill two times/day

"Mr. Pantano, do you recognize the bottle?" asked Krokson.

"I think so," Pantano said with slight hesitation.

"Very good. Now, sir, do you remember what you did with the contents of this bottle?"

"I took a couple of pills, and Jason took a couple."

"And what did you feel after you took those pills, Mr. Pantano?" asked Krokson.

"Here is the thing, sir. I felt nothing. Neither did Jason. I mean, Jason and I did different drugs all our lives. We knew it might take some time to kick in, so we waited. We waited, and waited, and waited. Nothing happened!"

"So, what did you decide to do next?" asked Krokson.

"Well, Jason was very upset and disappointed. He said, 'What kind of stuff is it? It's just not working!' Jason got angry. Still, we thought, let's take a few more pills and see what happens. We took another six or seven pills, maybe more, but this new stuff simply wasn't doing anything."

"And what did you do after you realized that methadone wasn't giving you euphoria, Mr. Pantano?"

"Sorry, what did you ask, sir? Euphoria? Sorry, I don't know what this word means."

"I asked you if that medication, methadone, gave you a high?"

"That's what I'm talking about. We were not getting high. So we were taking more and more."

"Did you know that this medication, methadone, was dangerous?"

"No, sir. We thought it should be good, a real drug, but instead..."

"What do you mean by good?" Krokson interrupted.

"I mean, it came straight from the pharmacy, so the stuff should be clean and potent. People try to cheat a lot. They try to sell you junk—"

"Mr. Pantano," now it was Judge Adler who interrupted him. "You can tell us your exciting stories some other time. Now please answer Mr. Krokson's questions, and nothing else."

"Sorry, ma'am... I mean, Your Honor," apologized Pantano.

"Please continue, Mr. Krokson."

"Mr. Pantano, do you remember how many pills Jason took that day?" asked Krokson.

"No, sir. I took quite a few and passed out. Right there in the park. I have no idea how many Jason took. When I woke up, Jason was gone."

"Did you see him after that, Mr. Pantano?"

"No, I didn't. It was the last time I saw my friend alive," Tim Pantano cast a mournful glance at the jury.

"Thank you for your testimony, Mr. Pantano. No further questions," declared Krokson.

* * *

During the ten-minute break, Gail, Emma's friend, and Julia Lander stayed in the courtroom. Gail was definitely preoccupied with some troubling thoughts.

"Julia, why did the prosecutors bring this guy to testify?" she asked anxiously. "Isn't it insane for a grown-up person, a father of an infant, to act so thoughtlessly? And not just that. His friend Jason took ten times more medicine than he'd been prescribed, and this 'like his own brother' practically lent him a helping hand! And he is the government witness?"

"Yes, he did. But the government blames Ben for Jason Cameron's death," said Julia.

"They blame *Ben* for Cameron's death?" gasped Gail.

"Yes, they do. After the Supreme Court ruling, they can't charge Ben or even blame him openly, but that's exactly what they are trying to imply. This prescription for methadone to Jason Cameron is one of the eight counts. If the jurors agree with the prosecutors' insinuations that Ben is guilty, he will get twenty years in prison for this one count alone."

Gail turned pale and was about to say something, but Gould was already at the lectern to start the cross.

* * *

"Good morning, Mr. Pantano. My name is Edward Gould, and I represent Dr. Holden."

Tim Pantano nodded.

"First, let me express my sincere condolences about the loss of your friend," said Gould.

"Thank you, sir," Tim Pantano replied sorrowfully.

"Mr. Pantano, you testified that Jason Cameron was your close friend, right?"

"Yeah, he was my best friend. As I said, he was like a brother to me."

"So you cared about him a lot, true?"

"Very much so. We were very close."

"Had you ever thought about how dangerous it was to take medication in a way it was not prescribed?"

"I kind of knew it, but we wanted to get high."

"Mr. Pantano, let me show you some information that Mr. Krokson probably forgot about. Your Honor, defense would like to offer Exhibit 87-D."

"Objection..." jumped in Krokson.

"Your Honor," Gould didn't let him finish, "It's the same exhibit that the government introduced about thirty minutes ago."

"Proceed," said the judge.

Gould retrieved the same orange bottle that Krokson had shown to the jurors half an hour earlier, and the computer screen again revealed the same label of the prescribed methadone.

"Do you do recognize this label, Mr. Pantano?"

"Yes, sir, I do."

"Now, let us turn this bottle around to look at its other side."

A different image appeared on the screen, the one that the prosecutor had chosen not to show.

"Mr. Pantano, would you please read this other label out loud, so that everyone can hear you?"

Pantano cleared his throat and read, ***"Warning: take only as prescribed. If misused, this medicine can be dangerous."***

"Mr. Pantano, do you remember if on March 9, 2005, your friend Mr. Jason Cameron told you anything about the danger or possible side effects of this medication?"

"No, he didn't."

"Mr. Pantano, did you hold this bottle in your hands that night?"

"Yes, I did."

"Did you read the warning that night?"

"I don't remember."

"Did you see if Jason read the warning?"

"I don't remember. He probably didn't."

"Do you think it was important for you and your friend to read this warning?" pressed Gould.

Pantano was silent.

"Mr. Pantano, Mr. Krokson forgot to ask you, so I will: when you and your close friend Jason realized that medication prescribed by Dr. Holden didn't give either of you the high that you hoped for, did you take something else?"

"Objection Your Honor, relevance," interjected Krokson.

"Overruled," said the judge. "You may answer."

"Yes, sir, we did."

"And what did you take?"

"Well, I had a few bags of snow candy on me, so we both sniffed it a bit."

"Would you please explain to the jury what 'snow candy' means?" asked Gould.

"Sorry." Pantano shot an embarrassed look at the jury. "It's a street name for cocaine."

"Thank you, Mr. Pantano. No further questions."

* * *

"Ben, what do you think about this guy and his testimony?" Gail asked during the break.

Ben didn't answer right away.

"To tell you the truth," he said finally, "it's hard to believe that a twenty-six-year-old man with a wife and a little child could behave like a reckless teenager and have no clue that he was playing with his own life. Even now, ten years later, this man doesn't impress me as a responsible person. He is not ashamed of his past a bit."

"What was the purpose of his testimony anyway?" Gail turned to Mark Daniels.

"I believe the government wanted to show another example of careless doctors indiscreetly supplying young people with opioids and fueling a national epidemic of deadly drug overdoses," explained Mark. "So far that has been their theme all along."

"But didn't this man just admit that he and his friend took all kinds of drugs since their first year in college, long before Jason Cameron came to Ben? What does his addiction to drugs have to do with doctors?" Gail pressed.

"Nothing," said Daniels. "For most people, their first exposure to street drugs has nothing to do with doctors. Kids and young adults try all kinds of stuff offered to them on the street—pot, Ecstasy, cocaine, prescription pills, even vapors. They start it as 'fun' and eventually graduate to snorting, crushing pills, or shooting."

"But still, what does it have to do with doctors?"

"The DEA, which for years failed miserably to stop the flood of illegal drugs to the street, made doctors their scapegoats," explained Daniels. "Doctors do not hide in alleys and pose no resistance. The government can come and get them anytime and then present them to the public as culprits."

"But you can't deny that prescription drug overdose is a problem, right? I read it kills up to twelve thousand people a year," said Alex.

"It is true, and what is especially tragic, it kills mainly young people, leaving their parents, friends, and sometimes their children in inconsolable grief. But intimidating and prosecuting physicians for doing their job is not a solution."

"What is the solution?"

"I think it's education," said Ben. "Serious, consistent education, starting at a young age. And not only children and teenagers have to be educated, but adults too. I think that's the only effective way to prevent these tragedies." Everyone was silent for a long moment.

"Well, we can speculate on this subject for hours," said Daniels, "but it's time to go back to watch their next testimony."

Chapter Twenty-Eight

"The government calls Roger Ferranti," announced Attorney Mike Lynch, and a tall, burly, slightly stooped man walked to the witness stand.

Roger Ferranti, another former patient of Dr. Holden, was the most promising witness for the prosecution from the first day of the trial. Despite all the help he had received from Dr. Holden over the years, Ferranti held a grudge against him. More than that, the man carried a bucketload of bitterness and hatred for the whole world, and the prosecutors simply couldn't wait to have him unload it on the jurors.

"Mr. Ferranti, did you at some point become a patient of Dr. Holden?" Mike Lynch cast an encouraging glance at the witness.

"Yes, I did," Ferranti replied with bitterness.

"And what brought you to his office?"

"I told him I had a bad back for years, which was true. By the end of 2000, my pain was getting much worse. At that time, I was doing a lot of roofing, and climbing ladders was tough."

"How long had you been his patient?"

"About six years."

"So, you came to see Dr. Holden. And what happened?"

"He started to treat my back with narcotics and I got addicted. As simple as that." Ferranti's dark eyes turned grim.

"Sorry to hear that. Sir, had you used other drugs prior to seeing Dr. Holden?"

"In my past, I have, yes, in my youth and stuff."

"And while you saw Dr. Holden, did you use street drugs?"

"A few times."

"Sir, did you ever sell your pain pills, the ones you were getting from Dr. Holden's office?"

"At times, I did."

"And why did you do that?" Lynch frowned with the concern of a distraught parent who just caught his teenage son stealing beer from the fridge.

"I sold my meds because I'd missed work and didn't get my paycheck. I was too messed up, and I couldn't work."

"What do you mean by 'messed up'?"

"I would be either too high to go in, or I'd be too sick to go in."

"When you say 'sick,' was it an illness related to prescription drugs?"

"Yes, dope sick."

"Can you explain to the jury what 'dope sick' is?"

"You take too much of your medicine and then run out of it and go through withdrawals."

"And can you describe to the jury what happened when you would go into these withdrawals?"

"Sweats, chills, anxiety. You start panicking. Cramping legs are killing you... It was pure hell, I couldn't function at all."

"Sir, did you ever go to Dr. Holden when you were dope sick?"

"Yes, I did."

"When you went to see Dr. Holden while you were dope sick, were there times when you didn't go into his office?"

"Yes."

"But did you still receive your prescriptions?"

"Yes, I did."

"When you said you didn't go into his office, do you mean the building or his private office?" asked Judge Adler.

"I didn't go into the building," answered Ferranti.

"When you say you weren't in the office, sir, where were you?" continued Lynch.

"I was in my car in the parking lot. I was too sick to get out."

"Now, sir, you said you got prescriptions. How did you get prescriptions if you were in your car?" Lynch asked with a child's curiosity.

"I called up his office, spoke with him, and asked him if he... if he could bring it out to me."

"And did you get prescriptions?"

"Yes."

"And who brought them out to you?"

"Dr. Holden."

"Did he raise any issues when he brought out your prescriptions about you being dope sick?"

"No."

"Did he ask you why you couldn't come into the office?"

"No."

"Did you tell him why you couldn't come into the office?"

"Yes."

"What did you tell him?"

"Well, I... said that I was too sick and that I needed my prescriptions, and I couldn't wait. Then I just thanked him and left."

"Sir, what types of drugs did you get that day in the parking lot?"

"OxyContins, Percocets, you know..."

"What drugs were you addicted to?"

"OxyContin, Percocet."

"Did you tell Dr. Holden about your addiction?"

"He figured it out himself and switched me to methadone. But methadone didn't work for me, and he had to switch me back."

"So let's look at your medical note, Government Exhibit 31C, from February 26, 2004. Do you see that, sir?"

"Yes, I do."

"And it says in the treatment plan... that, *'Roger Ferranti came today still describing pretty severe lower back pain on the right side. He is about two weeks out of his medicine, which he forgot, according to the patient, in New Hampshire.'* Sir, had you claimed that you lost your medications in New Hampshire?"

"Yes, I had."

"Was that true, or was that a way to get drugs?"

"That was false."

"And Dr. Holden states this about giving you an injection, *'Then I also decided to start him on methadone, 10 to 20 milligrams twice a day. I suspect the patient was developing an addiction to OxyContin. I referred him to Dr. Warren, an addictionologist, for evaluation and possible treatment. He will be seen in two weeks.'* Do you remember being switched to methadone at some point, sir?"

"Yes, I do."

"Did you ever go to Dr. Warren?"

"No, I did not."

"Did Dr. Holden ever follow up with you as to whether you went to see this addictionologist?"

"No, he didn't."

"Did you continue to receive drugs after this?"

"Yes, I did."

"And, sir, just to be clear, it notes that your dosage was 10 to 20 milligrams twice a day. Did the doctor tell you that you could choose how many methadone pills in this range to take daily?"

"Objection. Leading," interjected Mark Daniels.

"Overruled," said the judge.

"I was..." hesitantly started the witness. "In the beginning I was prescribed 10 milligrams, and I was directed to take one of them two times a day. But over the years, he increased it to eight pills a day."

"Sir, did you at some point develop an addiction to methadone?"

"Yes, I did."

"Mr. Ferranti, did you talk to Dr. Holden about that?" asked Lynch.

"Yes, I told him."

"Is it your opinion that you became addicted to narcotic painkillers because you were regularly treated with this type of medication by Dr. Holden?"

"Yes, it is."

"Nothing further, Your Honor," Lynch's eyes glistened with contentment.

Emma felt her gut clench. What if the jurors believe Ferranti's accusations and the lies of the other government witnesses? If they do Ben will spend the rest of his life in prison. Emma stifled a groan. All of a sudden, the celebration of their wedding anniversary a month ago flashed in her memory. Their friends' humorous toasts about their happy twenty-four years of happy marriage and countless good wishes for another twenty-six. Was it the last celebration they ever had?

* * *

"Mr. Daniels, are you ready for the cross?" Judge Adler turned to Ben's attorney.

"Yes, Your Honor, I am." Daniels walked to the lectern and put a stack of papers on top of it.

"Good afternoon, Mr. Ferranti. My name is Mark Daniels, and I represent Dr. Holden."

"Okay." Roger Ferranti turned vigilant as he thought about his many experiences with lawyers. This one looked too intelligent for his taste.

But he was a shrewd fellow himself. Over the past fifteen years, he had submitted a few work injury claims, won all the cases, and was handsomely compensated in the end.

"Now, Mr. Ferranti, this isn't the first time that you've testified about this case, right?"

"No."

"You also testified before the grand jury, correct?"

"Correct."

"And you were under oath, right?"

"Yes, I was."

"And you were asked about all of your interactions with Dr. Holden, correct?"

"As far as I can remember, yes."

"You've also been interviewed a number of times about this case, correct?"

"A couple of times, yes."

"DEA agents interviewed you multiple times, correct?"

"A few times."

"You also spoke with the U.S. Attorney's Office about this case, right?"

"I spoke with people sitting here... yes."

"And in all those times that you testified before the grand jury, you never brought up the story that you just told this jury about getting prescriptions in a parking lot."

"Objection. Foundation," interfered Lynch.

"Overruled."

"So is it true that you never mentioned that incident before, sir?"

"Wrong. I did tell them." Ferranti shot Daniels a lethal look.

"You state now that you testified about those facts before the grand jury?"

"Oh, I don't know if it was for the grand jury, but I told the people in this office when they brought me in here."

"When you say 'this office,' are you referring to the U. S. Attorney's Office located on the ninth floor of this federal court building?"

"Yes."

"Okay. Now, we have heard in this trial, Mr. Ferranti, that people who abuse drugs sometimes have lapses of memory or difficulty remembering certain things. Has that been the case for you?"

"No, not for me," smirked Ferranti; no way was he going to fall into this trap.

"You've never had difficulty remembering something?"

"No, it has been a long time since all of this has happened, but I do recall this fact."

"Mr. Ferranti, please just focus on the question. You saw Dr. Holden from May, 14, 2002, through October 16, 2006, correct?"

"Correct."

"That's about four and a half years, right?"

"Yes."

"Although you testified on direct that you saw him for six years, right?"

"Yes, I didn't have the dates right."

"So you didn't remember that, right?"

"No." Ferranti shot another angry look at Daniels.

"And you actually stopped seeing Dr. Holden because he tapered you off your pain medication and then ceased prescribing your pain medication altogether, correct?"

"Wrong." Ferranti's eyes were now churning with fury.

"Okay. We'll get to that, Mr. Ferranti. Now let's move on to another topic. You testified on direct about selling your medication and buying illegal drugs on the street, correct?"

"Yes, I did."

"But you never told that to Dr. Holden, correct?"

"No, I didn't."

"And you hid it from Dr. Holden because you wanted him to continue prescribing you pain medications, right?"

"Yes."

"You were worried that if you told him about your illegal activity, he would stop prescribing for you, right?"

"I don't know what he would have done."

"I'm not asking what he would have done, Mr. Ferranti. My question is different. Did you hide your illegal drug activity from Dr. Holden because you were worried that if you told him about it, he would stop prescribing?"

"I'm not sure if I told him that or not."

"Mr. Ferranti?"

"I don't remember if I did or not."

"Mr. Ferranti, you testified just half a minute ago that you never told Dr. Holden about that."

"Okay."

"And we'll let the jury remember your testimony."

"Fine. I said that."

"So you hid these facts from Dr. Holden because you were concerned that if you told him about them he would stop prescribing to you?"

"No, I wasn't concerned about that."

"But you knew that Dr. Holden had discharged other people from his practice, right?"

"I knew of one. One that I saw."

"You were in the waiting room, and you personally saw it?"

"Right," the witness said with no apparent enthusiasm.

"And what did you observe?"

"A patient was angry. His drug test came back dirty, and the doc wouldn't prescribe the medication to him. So the guy got mad."

"And you heard Dr. Holden tell him..."

"Objection. Hearsay," Lynch rose from his seat.

"Overruled," said the judge.

"You heard Dr. Holden tell this man that he wouldn't prescribe pain medication to him?"

"Oh, I just heard... I didn't see Mr. Holden. He was behind the wall. The guy was yelling..."

"Who was yelling?" asked Judge Adler.

"The patient."

"So you knew that Dr. Holden discharged someone from his practice because he found the patient's drug results inappropriate, right?"

"Right."

"And you thought that it had something to do with the drug test, but your testimony is that you were not concerned that if he found out about *your* illegal activity he would have discharged you?"

"Correct."

"Now, Mr. Ferranti, let's talk about your care by Dr. Holden. I put some documents in front of you. If you go to the first page, you'll see a patient's information form with your name on it, correct?"

"Yes, I see it."

"And you see the question there: *'What is your major complaint?'*"

"Yes."

"It says *'Back pain, can't sleep at night and can't play with my kids.'* You wrote that, right?"

"I guess."

"Well, that's your signature at the bottom of the page, right?"

"Right."

"And your back was in pain, correct?"

"Not really."

"Oh, not really? So this statement was a lie to Dr. Holden that you had back pain, couldn't sleep at night, and couldn't play with your kids?"

"Yes."

"All right. So you were lying to Dr. Holden from your very first appointment, correct?"

"No, I take that back, okay. I'm sorry. I'm a little nervous here and a little messed up with all this going on. You know, I had been in the labor trade for many years prior to this, and I did have back pain, but I wanted to be checked out, you know, and he sent me for MRIs. I was just looking for help, and this is what I ended up with." Ferranti frowned.

"So you did not lie to Dr. Holden then about the fact that you had back pain, you couldn't sleep at night, and you couldn't play with your kids, right?"

"Yeah. I wasn't crippled. I could do things. But I was suffering from back pain, and I wanted to find out how bad it was."

"Mr. Ferranti, my question is different. Was your statement on that information form truthful?"

"That was the truth."

"And you went to Dr. Holden to address that severe pain, right?"

"Right."

"And you testified under oath to the grand jury that Dr. Holden asked you if you were taking meds before, and you told him you were taking Vicodin and Percocet, right?"

"Yes. It's possible. It was a long time ago."

"And Dr. Holden set up an MRI for you, correct?"

"Yes, he did."

"And this is your MRI. And Dr. Holden discussed it with you, right?"

"Yes. He said I had... a lumbar sprain."

"Now, let's look at your next visit from June 3, 2002. Dr. Holden wrote that the '*MRI came back negative for any obvious bone trauma. Today's examination revealed tender and painful to palpation spinous processes from L1 to L3.*' So at your second visit, Dr. Holden also physically examined you, correct?"

"Yes."

"Then Dr. Holden wrote, '*I had a lengthy discussion with the patient regarding the nature of his conditions and therapeutic options.*' Do you remember that conversation?"

"Yeah. He explained the treatment options to me. But it wasn't a lengthy conversation."

"Dr. Holden also writes, '*We decided to go ahead with a combination of lidocaine and dextrose injections in order to rebuild his affected ileosacral and ileolumbar ligaments.*' And you didn't object to having those injections, correct?"

"No, I thought the doctor knew what he was doing."

"Because you were in severe pain and wanted relief, right?"

"Right."

"Now, let's look at the survey you filled out on March 3, 2003, about 10 months after you started seeing Dr. Holden. You were asked about your sleep pattern, your job performance, family relationships, and daily living activities, and all of them you circled as improved, right?"

"Right."

"And in relation to your overall satisfaction with the treatments, you circled '*satisfied*', right?"

"Right."

"So in less than a year with Dr. Holden, all of these aspects of your life had improved, correct?"

"The pain medication helped, yes."

"It helped you to address the pain in your back, right?"

"At that time it did."

"Now, Mr. Ferranti, you recall on direct that you testified that Dr. Holden never gave you instructions about taking opioids, right?"

"He never spoke to me about taking them."

"But you signed an informed consent that also said, '*I, Roger Ferranti, realize that pain medications, including narcotics, can be habit forming or addictive. I will follow all conditions of Dr. Holden's pain management agree-*

ment and general treatment plan. I understand that the goal of this program is to increase my functional condition and improve the quality of my life.' And you read that statement when you signed it, right?"

"Yes, I read and signed it."

"And by the way, it says the goal of the program here is to increase your functional condition and improve the quality of your life. And in that survey, you reported that the quality of your life was improved, right?"

"Yes."

"Now, let's look at another note dated August 7, 2003, where Doctor Holden writes about your new injury. He wrote, *'Yesterday the patient fell on the railroad track and injured his back again.'* And the doctor describes your complaints and a possible diagnosis. You had that accident, right?"

"Yes."

"And you wanted Dr. Holden to treat your pain so that you could get back to work, right?"

"Yes, he was my doctor."

"Dr. Holden sent you for an MRI and then explained to you that you had an injury to your lumbar spine, right?"

"Yes."

"And in response to this injury, Dr. Holden injected your ligaments with lidocaine, Serapin, and 10 milligrams of cortisone?"

"Objection. Calls for speculation," interjected Lynch.

"I'm just reading the document," replied Daniels.

"He's reading the document," confirmed Judge Adler.

"And Dr. Holden wrote, *'I will start him on Celebrex.'* You knew that none of those medications were opioids, right?"

"Yes."

"Now let's look at the note dated August 21, 2003. This was about two weeks after that new injury, right?"

"Right."

"Dr. Holden wrote, *'To whom it may concern. Mr. Roger Ferranti has been under my care for the treatment of lower back pain,'* and he added, *'The patient is able to return to full duty starting August 30, 2003'*, right?"

"Yes."

"So after Dr. Holden's treatment, including the injections and the use of Celebrex, you were ready to return to work in about two weeks, right?"

"Yeah," Ferranti agreed reluctantly.

"And then you sign another informed consent. So this is a second time that you were provided with information about the potential risks of taking opioids, right?"

"Right."

I'm now showing you an office note marked February 10, 2004. Dr. Holden states that you were coming for your regular follow-up evaluation. *'The patient told me that he forgot his pain medication somewhere in New Hampshire, which is a three-hour ride from here. He was given samples of Gabitril to take at night and encouraged to go back to New Hampshire and find his medicine.'* You know that Gabitril is not an opioid, right?"

"Yes."

"So Dr. Holden *didn't prescribe* you opioids when you lied to him that you lost your pain medication somewhere in New Hampshire, right?"

"I guess not. Not this time."

"And as you admitted on direct, this story about leaving your medicine in New Hampshire was a lie, correct?"

"Yes, I lied to him."

"And Dr. Holden also wrote in his notes, *'I switched the patient to methadone, 10 to 20 milligrams twice a day. I suspect the patient is developing an addiction to OxyContin. He is referred to Dr. Warren, an addictionologist, for evaluation and possible treatment.'* So you testified on direct that Dr. Holden talked to you about a potential issue with addiction, right?"

"I talked to Dr. Holden about it, yes, and I asked him for help."

"And he referred you to Dr. Warren, right?"

"Not that I recall."

"Maybe because you didn't go to Dr. Warren? The copy of the referral is in your medical file. Do you see it?"

"Yes. But I don't recall him sending me to anybody."

"So you don't remember any discussion about going to an addictionologist?"

"No, we didn't discuss it. We didn't discuss anything."

"Okay. Now there's a March 9, 2004, note and Dr. Holden wrote again about you. '*Since his OxyContin was changed to methadone, Mr. Ferranti feels much better both physically and psychologically. He's able to work two jobs, sleeps well at night, and describes significant satisfaction with the pain control.'* That was true, right?"

Ferranti was clearly in no rush to answer.

"Yes or no, Mr. Ferranti?" Judge Adler asked impatiently.

"Yes," exhaled Roger Ferranti.

"Then over the next two years, you had a shoulder, a hip, and two elbow injuries. And all of those injures were rather serious, correct?"

"Yes."

"And Dr. Holden treated you for each of them and helped you to get back to work, right?"

"Yes."

"And then, at the very end, after you had your second elbow injury, Dr. Holden referred you to an orthopedic surgeon. In his notes he wrote, '*Besides patient's elbow injury, I believe he developed certain signs of addiction to methadone. I offered to refer him to an addictionologist, but he adamantly refused to go. Therefore, I decided to taper him off methadone, and he will be getting only 30 milligrams of methadone twice a day for the next week. The following week, he will be receiving 20 milligrams twice a day; and then a month from now he will be off methadone altogether, including off any other opioids. I informed Mr. Ferranti that he was welcome to my office for any other type of treatment, but no opioid medications would be prescribed to him from now on.*' And after that point, Dr. Holden reduced your methadone prescriptions, correct?"

"He never referred me to an addiction center. He did... He did lower my dosage..."

"You don't recall that Dr. Holden referred you to an addictionologist?"

"No."

"Well, you can't remember everything that happened more than eight years ago. Now, Mr. Ferranti, I don't want to go through your whole medical file, but isn't it correct, sir, that you had been Dr. Holden's patient for quite a few years and over that period you had five or six different rather serious injuries to your back, your shoulder, your left hip, and both of your elbows?"

"That sound accurate. I was working hard, so—"

"Mr. Ferranti, please focus on my question. And after each of your injuries you would file a new disability claim, correct?"

"Correct."

"You would also engage an attorney to represent you, because your injuries were real, correct?"

"Of course they were real; I was getting injured at work."

"I understand. But each and every time, Dr. Holden was able to quickly diagnose you with a new injury, and if necessary, he sent you to other physicians for consultation and also started an effective treatment, which would eventually bring you back to work, right?"

"Yes," Ferranti shot Daniels another cutting look.

"So, Mr. Ferranti, would you agree that Dr. Holden was really trying his very best and was helping you to get better?"

"And he also made me addicted to methadone," Roger Ferranti said sternly.

"Mr. Ferranti, according to the medical file, your last appointment with Dr. Holden took place in March 2006, correct?"

"Probably," replied Ferranti cautiously.

"Sir, can you tell the jury what exactly happened that day?"

"He fired me!" exploded Ferranti.

"Sir, Dr. Holden didn't fire you. He offered to let you use the services in his office, but he stopped prescribing you opioids any longer because your behavior suggested obvious signs of addiction, and you refused to go to an addictionologist, correct?"

"I don't remember any of that."

"He also gave you a small amount of methadone with detailed instructions about how to taper yourself off the opioids in a safe manner so that you wouldn't go into withdrawal, correct?"

The witness didn't answer. He looked angry and upset.

"And this was your last appointment with Dr. Holden, correct?"

"I have never seen him again," blurted Ferranti.

"Sir, what happened to you after you ceased to see Dr. Holden?"

"I was buying different drugs from people on the street for a while, but eventually I ended up in a methadone clinic."

"Sir, are you still taking methadone for your pain these days?"

"Yes, I am."

"So Dr. Holden was right when he suggested you had to see an addictionologist and refused to treat your pain until you did that, right?"

"He is the one who got me addicted," Roger Ferranti uttered doggedly.

"And you were the one who refused to be treated for that problem, denied the very existence of your addiction, and preferred to leave Dr. Holden's practice rather than to deal with this issue as Dr. Holden insisted you should, right?"

"No, it's not true!" Ferranti almost spat his answer.

"I have no more questions, Your Honor." said Daniels.

* * *

Outside, in the hallway, Gould hurried to Ben, Julia, Emma, and Arthur, looking upset and concerned.

"Not a good day. I would say this was the first bad day so far." He paused. "Ben, why does he blame you for his addiction?"

"I don't know. To be honest, at that time I was not completely sure he was an addict. He complied with all the tests and treatments I suggested, and with these treatments he was getting better and could get back to work. That's not typical for a drug addict. But when he 'lost' his prescription in New Hampshire, I thought that he could have been getting addicted to OxyContin. That's why I sent him to an addictionologist. I wanted the opinion of a specialist."

"But he refused to go?"

"Yes, and then eventually I had no choice but to taper him off." Ben was silent for a long moment. "Anyway, I think Mark did an excellent job."

"Yes, he did. But this Ferranti... he is so angry and vindictive. With all the help he received from you, there is no rhyme or reason to it."

"This man is angry at the whole world," said Julia. "We had patients who were struggling with horrible health issues and still preserved their dignity and even their sense of humor. They would arrive at our office with smiles and joke with me and Ben, but Roger Ferranti... he was always unhappy. He always looked grim and was never pleased with anything."

"And I bet," said Ben, "he is still suffering from his former injuries. His life must be wretched."

"Do you feel sympathy for him?" Gould arched an eyebrow.

"I do. Believe it or not, I feel sympathy for him even though I know that because of testimonies like his, I may end up in prison for the rest of my life. I'm still a much happier man than he is."

"Well, one thing's for sure," Gould grinned, "You never lose your sense of humor."

Chapter Twenty-Nine

The sixth day of the trial began with one of the most critical witnesses for the prosecution. This time it wasn't a patient who used to deceive Dr. Holden and sell the medications he'd prescribed, or a reckless friend. This time it was a full-fledged, decorated police officer, Mr. Adam Eves, a respectable member of the local community and probably the brightest star among all the government witnesses.

Matilda Hustler, the third prosecutor, moved to the lectern. This young woman, in her early thirties, was a new addition to the government team. At the DA's office, she'd already gained the reputation of a smart and capable prosecutor. She was tall and lean, with straight reddish hair dripping to her shoulders and a stern expression glued to her narrow face. During the first few days of the trial, Ms. Hustler was sitting quietly at the prosecutors' table, taking notes and eagerly listening to the occasional whispering of her neighbor, Mr. Krokson. Now she was finally given a chance to shine.

"Good morning, Detective Eves." Matilda Hustler blushed a bit. She felt honored to be trusted with such an important assignment but wasn't seasoned enough to conceal her pride.

"Good morning."

"Mr. Eves, would you please describe your educational background for the jury."

"I have a bachelor's degree in criminal science and a master's degree in criminal justice."

"Are you employed?"

"Yes, I am."

"Where?"

"By the Boston Police Department."

"And what's your current position?"

"I'm a detective in the Drug Control Unit."

"How long have you been with the Boston Police Department?"

"Approximately eighteen years."

Hustler nodded approvingly and paused for the jurors to fully appreciate the experience of the witness.

"And how long have you held the position of detective in the Drug Control Unit?"

"Nine months."

"What was your position prior to being a detective?"

"I was in the drug unit for approximately thirteen years total."

"At some point did you become involved in an investigation of Dr. Benjamin Holden?"

"Yes, I did. I was instructed by Sergeant Detective Peter Munich to initiate an undercover operation of Dr. Holden's office in 2003."

"And what was the purpose of the investigation?"

"The purpose was for me to receive a narcotic prescription from Dr. Holden."

"Did you use your real name when you went into Dr. Holden's office?"

"No, I did not."

"What name did you use?"

"Don Casey."

"How many times did you visit Dr. Holden's office in an undercover capacity?"

"Ten times in total."

"And were all those visits in 2003?"

"No, some were in 2004, and the last one was in 2006."

"Now, did you always see Dr. Holden when you had appointments at his office?"

"No, I saw Nurse Practitioner Lander too, three times."

"Do you recognize Dr. Holden in the courtroom today?"

"Yes, he is the gentleman sitting there with the blue tie."

"And do you recognize Nurse Practitioner Lander?"

"Yes, she is the female in the black blouse."

"When was your first visit with Dr. Holden?"

"It was on April 14, 2003."

"And when you arrived at the office, did you see Dr. Holden immediately?"

"No, I sat in the waiting area for about two hours."

"And what observations, if any, did you make while you were in the waiting room?"

"Over the course of two hours, I observed approximately seven to eight people who walked past the waiting room to the doctor's office and left a few minutes later. Practically in and out."

"Did you pay for this appointment?"

"Yes, I did."

"How much did you pay?"

"$150."

"Did you pay $150 cash for all your appointments with Dr. Holden?"

"Yes, I did."

"Now, when you met with Dr. Holden, what did you tell him about why you were there?"

"I told him that I had back pain for the last ten years, and that he was recommended to me by a friend."

"Now, when you went to visit Dr. Holden, did you actually have back pain?"

"No, I did not."

"What did you tell Dr. Holden about your occupation?"

"That I was a union carpenter, because at the time I was self-employed as a carpenter."

"Did Dr. Holden ask you any questions about your medical history?"

"Umm, yes. He asked me about sleeping and, umm, you know, about the back pain."

"Did Dr. Holden perform an examination on you?"

"Yes, he did. I lay down on an examination table, face down. He felt around my lower back with his hands. Then I was asked to turn over, and he performed a stress test. I would lift my legs, and he would apply resistance. And after that, I sat up, and he did the same to my knees. He also asked me to lift my legs and then my toes. The whole exam took approximately five minutes."

"What did you tell Dr. Holden when he asked if you had any pain?"

"I didn't reply. During the exam, he asked if there was any pain with that, and I had no comment."

"Did you embellish to make him believe you had pain at all?"

"No, I didn't."

"What *did* you say?" interrupted Judge Adler. "You said you had no pain?"

"Your Honor, I didn't comment. As the examination went on, he would ask me, 'Do you feel any discomfort there?' And I just... 'I don't have any pain.'"

"So you said, 'I don't have any pain?' persisted Judge Adler.

"Yes, Your Honor."

"That's not what he said before," objected Gould.

"So what did you say, after all?" asked Judge Adler.

"I just didn't comment."

"What happened after this examination?" asked Hustler.

"After the examination, he led me into his office, and he said, 'Good news. You don't need any surgery.' Then he recommended some herbal injections that could help, and he also requested that I get an MRI that could help him to see if it was long-term pain."

"What was your response to his recommendations?"

"Well, with the MRI, I told him I was self-employed, so I didn't have medical insurance at this time, so I wouldn't be able to get the MRI. I said I didn't know about the injections, maybe next time. Then I asked him if there was anything he could give me for the pain."

"What did he say when you asked if there was anything he could give you for the pain?"

"He stated that he didn't give out prescriptions on a first visit."

"Did he give you anything at all?"

"Yes, he did. He reached into his desk and gave me four boxes of patches. They were samples and the name on the box was Lidoderm or something. He explained to me that these patches were for pain, and he told me to apply them to my back overnight. He also gave me six packs of Celebrex, and that was for the inflammation."

"Now, you mentioned that he suggested you get an MRI. Was that something that he requested on a number of occasions throughout the time you visited him?"

"Pretty much every visit he would ask me if I had insurance to get an MRI."

"On your next visit in June 2003, did Dr. Holden ask you about your pain and if he did, what did you say?"

"I told him that the patches were working, and I felt better."

"Did you discuss the injections that he had suggested at the last visit?"

"Yes. I told him that I didn't want to do the injections at this time, and I asked him if there was anything else that he could suggest."

"Did Dr. Holden perform an examination of you on this visit?"

"Yes, he did. I sat on the examination table, and he gave me another test where I'd lift my knees and then my legs and toes as he applied pressure."

"How long did the exam last?"

"Approximately three minutes or so."

"And at any point in this examination, did you tell Dr. Holden that you had pain?"

"I did not."

"What happened after the test?"

"We went into his office, and I said I didn't want the injections, but I asked him for some pain relief pills, and he wrote me out a prescription for 60 pills of 5-milligram Percocet."

"Did he then introduce you to another person who talked to you about stretches?"

"Yes. He introduced me to a man who I believe was a physical therapist, and he talked to me about stretches and exercises I could do for my back."

"Did you often have to wait for your appointments to see Dr. Holden or Nurse Practitioner Lander?"

"Yes, the average wait was definitely over an hour."

"Did you ever bring anyone with you to your appointments?"

"Yes. I once went in there with Officer Jack Rogers."

"And why was Officer Rogers with you?"

"I introduced Officer Rogers to Dr. Holden."

"Was Officer Rogers also in an undercover capacity with you?"

"Yes, he was. We went into the examination room. I told Dr. Holden that I was making progress with getting an MRI, and then I introduced Officer Rogers."

"You introduced him as a friend of yours?"

"Yes, as a friend of mine."

"And what happened next?"

"So Officer Rogers said to Dr. Holden, 'I want the stuff that my friend has. I tried them, and they worked fine.'"

"And what was Dr. Holden's response?"

"Dr. Holden asked what was wrong with him, and he replied that nothing was wrong with him, that I just gave him a couple of pills and that he liked them."

"And what did Dr. Holden say to Officer Rogers in response?"

"He asked, 'Do you have any pain?' And Officer Rogers said no, he didn't."

"And what did Dr. Holden say in response?"

"He said, 'Then I can't help you,' and he turned his attention back to me."

"Did you at some point tell Dr. Holden that you finally got your health insurance?"

"Yes, I did."

"And what was his response, Mr. Eves?"

"Dr. Holden told me that he wanted me to take a urine drug-screening test and to get an MRI of my back."

"Did you take the drug-screening test?"

"No. He led me to the room where you would take that test, and I met with another gentleman. He asked me for my insurance card, but I told him I forgot it at home and would come back later that afternoon to take the urine test."

"Did you still get your prescription even though you didn't take the urine test?"

"Yes, I did get my prescription that day, correct."

"And did you go back that afternoon for the urine test?"

"No, I did not."

"Did you visit Dr. Holden's office again after the appointment you described?"

"Yes. I visited it on December 12, 2006, two years later. That was my next visit."

"Why did you visit after two years?"

"I visited his office because now it was a federal investigation, and they wanted me to visit Dr. Holden's office again."

"And who did you see during this appointment?"

"Dr. Holden."

"What did Dr. Holden say to you when you saw him for your appointment?"

"He asked what brought me back after two years of being away. I said that the back pain was pretty much better, but now it was hard to get out of bed and that I had stiffness in my back."

"Were you wearing a recording device at this appointment?"

"Yes, I was."

"What did you tell Dr. Holden about your employment situation?"

"That I was still self-employed; I was getting my carpenter's business going."

"Did Dr. Holden conduct an examination of you?"

"Yes, he did."

"And what type of examination did he perform?"

"Like the previous ones. I sat on the examination table, lifting my knees, my legs, my toes, and then bending over at my waist."

"Approximately how long was this test?"

"Just a couple of minutes."

"Did you tell Dr. Holden you were in pain?"

"No, I did not."

"And what happened after the test?"

"After the test, he gave me a paper; asked me to read it and sign it. It was called *Pain Agreement*. It said that I wasn't to give my prescription drugs to anyone else, that I needed to follow the treatment protocol, that sort of thing."

"What prescriptions did Dr. Holden give you at this visit?"

"He gave me a prescription for inflammation. I'm not sure what that medication was, and then he... He wrote out a prescription for Tylenol with codeine."

"And what did Dr. Holden tell you about these prescriptions?"

"Umm, I actually said, you know, previously we started with Percocet, so could you offer me anything like that? And he said, no, not until he saw the results of my MRI and my urine test."

"Did you take a urine test?"

"No, I did not. I would have taken it, but they wanted $225 for it, and I didn't have that kind of money on me."

"Did you try to negotiate the price?"

"Yes. We bartered for a little bit, but they were insistent; they said that I had to pay the money for the test, because it wasn't free. The girl told me that unless I took the urine test, I wasn't going to get my prescription."

"And what happened when you wouldn't take the test?"

"Umm, I left the office. They said that if I would come back in the morning and take the urine test, the prescriptions would be there waiting for me."

"Did you return to Dr. Holden's office the next morning?"

"No, I did not."

"And did you ever return to Dr. Holden's office?"

"No, I did not."

"No further questions."

* * *

Emma waited for Ben in the hallway. The detective's testimony was rather disturbing.

"Ben, do you think the jury found this man trustworthy?"

"Who knows?"

"Is he the one Edward was worried about?"

"Yes, he was worried about him, but not for long. Hey, *you* look worried!"

"You don't think I should be?"

"Be patient, and you'll see for yourself."

Chapter Thirty

"Good morning, Detective Eves. My name is Edward Gould. I represent Dr. Holden."

"Good morning, sir."

"Your visits to Dr. Holden's office were in 2003 and 2004, which is ten and eleven years ago, and then the last one was in 2006, eight years ago, correct?"

"Yes, sir."

"And I take it you've had a few cases since then, is that right?"

"Yes, sir."

"Hundreds?"

"It's fair to say, yes, sir."

"So you must have done something to refresh your recollection to testify here today, right?"

"Yes. I have my reports."

"We're going to talk about those reports, but you've met with counsel, right?"

"Yes."

"Ms. Hustler talked to you in the hall before you came in, right?"

"Yes."

"Objection, Your Honor," Matilda Hustler rose from her seat.

"Overruled."

"And you had met with the U.S. Attorney's Office previously?"

"Yes, sir, I certainly have."

"You also mentioned your reports, and I'm going to ask you about some of those, but just so it's clear for the jury, you've read all of the reports that you wrote about your visits to Dr. Holden's office, correct?"

"Oh, yes, and I went over them preparing for this trial, sir."

"Okay, let's explain exactly what a report is. As a police officer, after you left Dr. Holden's office, you'd actually type out a written report to your superior about what happened, correct?"

"Yes, sir."

"And you did it for each of the visits that you just discussed with Ms. Hustler, correct?"

"Correct, sir."

"And, as a police officer, it's important for those reports to be accurate, correct?"

"Yes, sir".

"And complete?"

"Yes, sir."

"Honest?"

"Absolutely, sir."

"And this was an investigation into a doctor's practice and then ultimately a doctor and a nurse's practice, and you knew that, right?"

"Yes, sir."

"So you knew that it was important to be accurate about what you told the doctor and the nurse in order to try to get pain medication, correct?"

"Yes, sir."

"In fact, that's why you were there, to try to get prescription opioids, right?"

"My objective was to find out if the doctor was doing illegal things or not."

"But you were there to try to get prescriptions, weren't you?"

"That was the objective, yes."

"And just so it's clear for the jury, it would be critical to include in your report everything that you told the doctor and the nurse in an effort to get those prescriptions, correct?"

"I would include anything that I thought was pertinent, sir, yes."

"Oh, did you make a decision that some things weren't pertinent and decide to leave them out?"

"No."

"So you understood that when you were writing these reports, it was critical to include everything that you said to the doctor in order to try to get prescriptions, right?"

"Yes, sir."

"Now, if your reports about those visits failed to include critical facts, then now, which is about ten years later, when you reviewed your reports to prepare for this trial, you wouldn't have a chance to refresh your memory about these critical facts, because they were still missing from your reports, correct?"

"I have my own memory too, sir."

"Well, putting aside your memory, you told us that you prepared for this trial by reading your reports, and if it's not in your report, it's not there, right?"

"Objection. Mischaracterization!" Hustler intervened.

"Overruled. Please continue."

"If you left something out of your report, sir, it was lost back in 2003, 2004, 2006, right?"

"No, sir."

"Well, let's start with the December 12, 2006, visit. You were working undercover, correct?"

"Yes, sir."

"Let's talk briefly about what that means. When you're working undercover, you assume a false identity, right?"

"Yes, sir."

"You make up facts about yourself, correct?"

"Correct."

"And you're trained in this regard? You're trained to lie about who you are, right?"

"I don't know if that's the word I would use."

"Making it up, if you're not comfortable with 'lying.' You're trained to make it up, right?"

"Yes, sir."

"Detective, when you go undercover, you know exactly what you need to get by way of evidence, right?"

"Yes, I do."

"Now, on December 12, 2006, you and your colleagues in law enforcement, in a joint state and federal government investigation, planned an undercover operation, correct?"

"Yes, sir."

"It wasn't just you. There were numerous people involved, right?"

"Correct, sir."

"You were wearing a wire, correct?"

"Yes, sir."

"And there were people in a van listening, correct?"

"Correct, sir."

"And this wasn't some spur-of-the-moment thing. This was a setup, correct?"

"Correct, sir."

"And your goal was to get a prescription for opioids from Dr. Holden, correct?"

"Yes, sir."

"And you wanted to have it recorded on tape in order to have evidence, correct?"

"Correct, sir."

"Because none of your other prior visits were recorded, were they, sir?"

"No, they weren't because—"

"Sir, just answer my question. None of them were recorded, were they?"

"The previous ones were not recorded."

"Who made that decision?"

"That would probably be my supervisor."

"You certainly had the technology to wear a wire to those prior visits, didn't you?"

"Objection!" Hustler interrupted furiously.

"Overruled," responded Judge Adler.

"No, I did not have the technology myself."

"The technology didn't exist for you to wear a wire in 2003 and 2004?"

"Well, back in 2003 and 2004, the Drug Control Unit in Boston didn't have electronic recording devices; however, we had a KEL, a listening device, that we would use in officer safety situations when we were going into the projects and stuff like that. So my limited—"

"Detective, is your testimony under oath that you were in the Drug Unit in the Boston Police Department in 2003 and 2004, and they had no electronic surveillance equipment at that time? Is that what you're saying?"

"Absolutely, that's—"

"You are saying," Judge Adler raised her eyebrows, "that the Drug Control Unit at that time didn't have recording equipment?"

"We didn't, Your Honor."

"Now, isn't it true that on December 12, 2006, there is a complete recording of what happened from the moment you met Dr. Holden until the moment you left that building?" asked Gould.

"Yes, sir."

"And this is the only recording of any of your visits, correct?"

"Correct, sir."

"And it is true that your undercover operation that day failed, is that right?"

"No, sir."

"You left without a prescription; isn't that right?"

"Because I didn't have $225, sir."

"Because Dr. Holden told you that he was not going to give you a prescription until you had an MRI and a drug test, isn't that right, sir?"

"Yes."

"Just to be clear, you failed to get a prescription for any type of opioids, correct?"

"Correct."

"You didn't get one for Percocet, correct?"

"No, I did not."

"You didn't get one for OxyContin or any other type of opioid, right?"

"Correct, sir."

"Now, when you left the building, you said to your fellow officers, 'Sorry, I tried,' didn't you?"

"Yes, sir, I did."

"Because you *did fail*, right?"

Eves didn't answer.

"Failed to get a prescription for opioids despite your best efforts, right?"

"To answer the question, sir, I think if I got an MRI or took a urine test —"

"You've testified a few times before, haven't you, sir?"

"I have."

"You know how to answer a question with a 'yes' or 'no,' don't you?"

"Yes, sir."

"Mr. Eves, were you interested in learning whether a crime had been committed or not?"

"Yes, I was, sir."

"Now, during your meeting with Dr. Holden on December 12, 2006, you specifically asked him twice to write you a prescription for Percocet, and he said 'no,' correct?"

"Correct."

"And that happened on your last visit that took place two years after your preceding visit, right?"

"Correct, sir."

"And Dr. Holden said, 'You have to get an MRI and a urine test, and then we'll discuss your treatment plan with you, but only after those things are done,' right?"

"Right, sir."

"Now, let's talk about that audio-taped visit. Dr. Holden examined you physically on that visit, correct?"

"Yes, sir."

"He asked you who your primary care physician had been over the last two years since he had seen you, correct?"

"Correct."

"And you supplied him with a name, correct?"

"Yes, I did.'

"Did you forget to tell that to Ms. Hustler when she was asking you questions?"

"Objection," Hustler uttered feebly.

"Sustained," ruled Judge Adler.

"Dr. Holden asked you about your employment, what your job was like, and how many hours you were able to work during the week, correct?"

"Yes, sir."

"He inquired whether your pain was causing you any difficulty sleeping, right?"

"Correct, sir."

"He asked about your general health, correct?"

"Yes, sir."

"He was professional, right?"

"Yes, sir."

"He was courteous to you?"

"Yes, sir."

"And he spent almost half an hour with you?"

"I think less, sir."

"How long do you think it was?"

"Umm, I think it was under 15 minutes."

"Okay. He talked to you about injections, right?"

"Yes, sir."

"He said that you needed to get an MRI to understand what was going on in your back, right?"

"Yes."

"Actually, during every visit, Dr. Holden told you that you needed to get an MRI so that he could figure out what was going on with your back that you were complaining about, right?"

"Yes, I complained about my back on the first visit, yes, sir."

"And you told him you had been having back pain for ten years, right?"

"Correct, sir."

"He also questioned you about what had happened two years before when you left without taking a urine test or getting an MRI, didn't he?"

"Yes, sir."

"Now, let me ask you about a couple of other things, since we have a tape of this particular meeting. Isn't it true that you told Dr. Holden during this last visit that your pain was excruciating, and you needed to earn a living for your family, and it was extremely tough for you to get out of bed in the morning?"

"To get out of bed, yes, sir."

"I want this to be crystal clear for the jury. You said all of those things to him in an effort to get a prescription on December 12, 2006, correct?"

"Correct, sir."

"And when you wrote up your police report, contemporaneous with that event, you didn't put any of that in your police report, did you? You left it out?"

"It's a summarized report, sir."

"Let's be clear: did you know any of these facts were not in your report?"

"No, I didn't write it word for word, sir."

"Let me see if I can get you to answer my question, Detective Eves. You know that the written report that you submitted to your superiors failed to include the fact that you said to Dr. Holden, '*My pain is so bad that it's tough to get out of bed in the morning. I need to earn a living for my family.*' You left that out of your report, didn't you?"

"I didn't say those words, sir. I said it was harder to get out of bed, sir."

"Well, we're going to listen to it in a minute."

"Yes, sir. I… I stated…"

"So you left out of your report the single most important fact for the doctor to consider in treating his patient's pain, didn't you?"

"Umm…"

"Yes or no, sir, did you leave it out of your report?"

"Yes, I left it out, sir."

"So the report that you filed was false, wasn't it, sir?"

"Objection!" interrupted Matilda Hustler.

"Sustained," ruled the judge.

"Detective Eves, you actually signed that report, right?"

"Yes, sir."

"Your Honor," Gould turned to Judge Adler, "I think it's a good time to take a break."

"Yes, let's have a lunch break and reconvene in an hour."

* * *

"Did you have a nice lunch, Detective?" Gould continued his cross.

"Yes, sir, I did."

"Then let's pick up where we've left off. Sir, do you believe as a police officer you have an obligation to be honest?"

"Absolutely, sir."

"To seek the truth?"

"Yes, sir."

"I am glad to hear that. Now, let's talk about a few other things. You told Dr. Holden that you needed medication so that you could work. You told a pain doctor that it was tough for you to get out of bed, and then you added, 'I need to earn a living to feed my family.' You wanted Dr. Holden to understand that your pain was so bad that you couldn't work and that your family was at risk, right? That's what you wanted him to believe?"

"Yes, sir."

"But you left that out of your report, right?"

"Yes, sir."

"Now, you were very careful to answer Ms. Hustler's questions by saying that during the physical examination you didn't say that you were in pain. So when Dr. Holden examined you that day, did you groan?"

"No, sir. I yawned."

"Oh, you yawned?"

"Yes."

"How many times did you yawn?"

"Approximately three or four times I yawned over the course of being in his office."

"Did you tell him that you had pain shooting through your legs?"

"Umm, I told him that I had stiffness down to my... to my butt."

"So that was another fact that you left out of your police report, correct?"

"I'm not sure."

"And you *directly* asked him twice to write you a prescription for Percocet, and he said 'no,' right?"

"Correct, sir."

"You didn't put that in your police report either, did you?"

"No, sir, I didn't."

"So you left out of your police report that Dr. Holden refused to write an opioid prescription in response to two direct requests from you? You didn't think that was important to include in your report? You just left it out?"

"I left it out, sir, yes."

"And he asked you questions about your sleep, and you said it was very poor, right?"

"Yes, he asked me that."

"And you left that out of your police report too, right?"

"Yes, sir."

"And he questioned you about why you left his office two years ago without taking a urine test, right?

"Yes."

"In fact, after you went for your drug test at the end of your very last visit, you didn't just say 'I'm not taking the test' or 'I don't have the cash' and leave the building; you actually talked to Dr. Holden again, didn't you?"

"That's correct."

"And he said to you that he was puzzled about what happened two years ago. You left without taking a drug test and getting an MRI, even though he asked you to get an MRI and take a drug test. That's essentially what he told you, right?"

"Yes, sir."

"And was there any particular reason that you didn't provide this information when Ms. Hustler asked you a question about what happened that day?"

"No reason, sir."

"Is there a reason that all these facts are not in your police report?"

"No reason, sir."

"So we only know what was really said on December 12, 2006, because there's an audiotape of that, and if we were relying on your police report only, we wouldn't have the truth, would we?"

"As I stated earlier, sir, it's a summary."

"See if you can answer my question. Your police report fails to capture each of the facts that I've just asked you about over the preceding 15 minutes, correct, sir?"

"Those items aren't in the report."

"So if you were a detective and you were reading your own police report and you didn't have the audiotape, you wouldn't have learned all the important information you'd missed in your report?"

"No, I wouldn't."

"And we don't have audiotapes for any of your preceding visits, correct?"

"Correct, sir."

"Were all those reports also just summaries?"

"Yes, sir."

"So for all we know, you left out critical details from your report on each and every one of those visits as to what you said to Dr. Holden, correct?"

"Umm..." The detective paused. "I believe I put pertinent facts in my summaries."

"The facts that you selected, right?"

"Yes, I—"

"So you insist that the facts I've just presented to you are *not* pertinent. Is that what you are saying?"

"Well..."

"You were equally selective in your prior reports as you were with the December 12, 2006, report, correct, sir?"

"Correct. I'm the person who decides what to write in my report."

"But you're the person who is working in law enforcement searching for the truth, right?"

"Yes, sir."

"Your Honor, I'd ask at this point that the audio recording of the December 12, 2006, visit be marked as Exhibit 172F and played," requested Gould. "Now, according to the recording, you waited for your visit not for an hour but for thirty-nine minutes, correct?"

"I believe it was longer, sir."

"So your memory is not always perfect, right?"

The detective didn't respond.

"Well, you were wearing a wire from the moment you walked in, right?"

"Yes, sir."

"So I'm going to start this digitally recorded disk. And just so the jury understands, your colleagues were in a van with their electronic equipment, right?"

"Yes, sir."

"All right, let's start. Andrea, could you please play that part where Dr. Holden performs Mr. Eves's physical exam," Gould asked his assistant.

Andrea was a bright young woman who had been working as a paralegal in Gould's office for a few years and had researched and accumulated evidence for Dr. Holden's defense.

With the push of a button, the recording came to life, and everyone in the courtroom heard Dr. Holden's instruction to Detective Eves to lie down on the exam table. The detective groaned loudly.

"Mr. Eves, do you call that yawning?"

"Yes."

"Let's play it again."

And once again everyone in the room heard harsh groaning.

"Well, I think that was quite distinctive. Let's move to another part."

Andrea pushed the button, and in the dead silence of the room, people could clearly hear Mr. Eves's complaints about his pain and his inability to provide for his family, followed by Dr. Holden's demands for an MRI and a drug test, and his refusal to give any prescription before these two tests were completed.

"Andrea, please stop the tape for a moment," Gould asked.

"So you told Dr. Holden your story of being in pain, and after his examination, you requested some Percocet, correct? The doctor's response to your request was 'I need to see the urine test first, and I need to see the MRI,' but the doctor's response didn't find its way into your police report either, right?"

"No, sir."

"Let's play the part where you argue with the lady at the front desk."

Andrea pushed the button.

'Sir, we will not give you a prescription without seeing the urine test and MRI.' 'But I need my meds!' 'Sir, if Dr. Holden said no, it means no.' 'Sandra, what's going on?' 'Dr. Holden, this gentleman insists on getting his medication.' 'Mr. Casey, I've already told you I need your MRI to figure out what's wrong with you and the results of your urine test before I can prescribe you any medication. Please do what you are asked to do.'

Gould signaled to stop the recording.

"And that's not in your police report either, is it?"

"No, sir."

"So finally you had to leave the office with no prescription for opioids in your pocket, right?"

"Right, sir."

"And after you left the office, you headed to the van where your colleagues were recording your visit to Dr. Holden, true?"

"True."

"Andrea, could you please hit 'Play' again," asked Gould.

She did.

'I'm sorry. I tried. I don't know if you guys were listening.'

That was the end of the recording.

"Mr. Eves, that's what you said, right?"

"Yes, sir."

"And that's your statement to your fellow officers as a result of your failed undercover operation, correct?"

"Correct. I didn't get a prescription."

"Nothing further, Your Honor," said Gould.

"Would you redirect, Counselor?" The judge turned to Matilda Hustler.

The prosecutor blushed and shook her head. "No, Your Honor."

"You may leave, Mr. Eves," said Judge Adler, and the detective, relaxed and unruffled, leisurely moved toward the exit, followed by the flummoxed glances of the jury and the gallery.

Chapter Thirty-One

On the seventh day of the trial, the first witness for the prosecution was Debora Renaldi, another former patient of Dr. Holden's. Yet Ms. Renaldi was invited to the courtroom not to testify about her debilitating injures or Dr. Holden's treatments. She was brought here for an entirely different reason.

A dark-haired lady—a wisp of a woman of indiscernible age—gingerly strolled to the witness stand. She stated her name, with some difficulty spelled it, and then cautiously took her seat.

"Good morning, Ms. Renaldi. How are you this morning?" Matilda Hustler started the direct.

"Tha-ank you, ma'am. I'm f-i-ine," Ms. Renaldi answered in a slightly sluggish manner.

"How old are you, Ms. Renaldi?"

"Me? I'm f-o-orty nine," said the witness hesitantly.

"You were the wife of Mr. Jeremy Callagan?"

"No-o, ma'am, I was his fia-a-ncé," replied Deborah, struggling to pronounce 'fiance.'

"And Mr. Callagan was Dr. Hoden's patient, right?"

"Ri-i-ight," said Ms. Renaldi.

"And at some point Mr. Callagan passed away, right?"

"Yeah, he p-p-passed awa-ay," stuttered Ms. Renaldi.

Her lower lip trembled as if she was about to cry, which was exactly what Matilda Hustler wanted her to do. But then the woman's features suddenly changed from upset to confused. She half-opened her mouth and glanced around the courtroom like a little girl who on the first day of school, overwhelmed by the new surroundings, wondered why she was brought to this unknown place and what troubles she may expect there.

"Ms. Renaldi, are you all right?" Judge Adler asked with apparent concern.

"I–I- I'm all- all- r-ri-ight," mumbled Deborah Renaldi, casting a confused look at the judge. Judge Adler studied the woman for a long moment and then turned to the jury.

"Members of the jury, may I ask you to leave the courtroom for a few minutes please?"

As soon as the jurors were gone, the judge turned back to the witness.

"Ms. Renaldi, are you drunk?"

"N-no-o, ma'am." The witness flinched and stared at the judge.

"Are you high?" Judge Adler asked austerely.

"No-o, ma'am," the witness mumbled a barely audible answer.

Judge Adler furrowed her eyebrows and shot Matilda Hustler a stern look that was easily read as, Why didn't you check your witness before bringing her here?

"Counselors, sidebar!" the judge ordered, and both teams immediately approached the bench.

Emma and her friend Gail sat right across from Ms. Renaldi. They couldn't hear the lively discussion at the sidebar, but they had a good view of the witness.

"Do you think she is drunk?" Gail whispered to Emma.

"I don't know," Emma whispered back, "but something is seriously wrong with her, no doubt."

Emma leaned forward to take a better look at Ms. Renaldi and was stupefied. The woman was now completely motionless. Her head jerked back, her eyes rolled up, and her mouth dropped wide open. She looked dead. Emma barely refrained from screaming when she noticed Ben moving fast toward Gould, who, along with the other attorneys, was still engaged in a heated discussion with the judge. Ben quietly pulled Gould aside and whispered something in his ear. Gould turned around, looked at Ms. Renaldi, then turned back to the judge and pointed to the witness.

"Your Honor, I am afraid the witness might be dead," Gould said quietly.

The judge and the attorneys at the sidebar looked at the witness and froze in astonishment.

"Ms. Renaldi, are you all right?" Judge Adler almost shouted as she recovered from her initial shock.

The woman in the witness chair jerked her head forward, slowly closed her mouth, and scanned the room in utter bewilderment.

"Ms. Renaldi, are you all right?" Judge Adler repeated even louder.

"Oh, yeah, I'm okay," answered the woman, slurring every word.

The judge shook her head. She was skeptical and truly concerned.

"Do you need a doctor?"

"No-o, ma'am," Ms. Renaldi replied with a faint smile. "I'm fi-ine."

"Mary," Judge Adler addressed her clerk, "could you please call for a nurse? I don't think Ms. Renaldi is well, let alone ready to testify. Bailiff, please take her to the witness room. I want to send her home immediately. What a start to the day!"

The judge turned to the prosecutors and gave Lynch a pointed look.

"Mr. Lynch, I'll ask the nurse to accompany Ms. Renaldi. Could you provide her with transportation?"

"Yes, Your Honor, but we thought... she is feeling better now. Maybe..."

"This woman is not testifying today, Mr. Lynch. She is ill... or even worse. Just send her home. We'll discuss her future testimony, if any, later on. Do you have your next witness ready?"

"No, Your Honor. We didn't expect..."

"You didn't expect?" Judge Adler was furious. "Well, you should have! How soon can you bring your next witness? We've just lost an hour of our court time. I don't want to lose the whole day."

"We need half an hour or so, Your Honor."

"Mary, please let the jurors know that they have a thirty-minute break, and we'll reconvene at ten sharp." Judge Adler shot a frustrated look at the prosecutors and left the room.

* * *

Outside, in the hallway, Alex, Ben's cousin, was waiting for Gould, totally perplexed.

"Edward, why did the prosecutors bring this poor woman to testify?"

"Well, it's quite simple. They wanted her to tell the jury how much she was missing her fiancé, Jeremy Callagan. He was Ben's patient for years and then died, most likely from heart failure. The prosecutors planned to imply that her boyfriend's death had been caused by Ben's treatment. They expected that Ms. Renaldi would cry, the jurors would be moved by her grief, and be outraged by the doctor's conduct."

"So the woman ruined their plans?" Alex shook his head, still baffled by the recent scene. "Ben, Julia, have you seen her before?"

"Many times," said Ben.

"Me too," Julia sighed wistfully.

"Many times? How come?"

"She was our patient."

"She was your patient? A difficult one?"

"No, she wasn't difficult," said Ben. "She came to me after an awful car accident. Her vehicle flipped over a few times on a slippery highway. She was fighting for her life. Severe head injury, many broken bones... She was looking for someone who could help her to get back on her feet. Both her legs were broken."

"How old was she at that time?" Gail asked Julia.

"I believe she was in her mid-thirties," said Julia. "She had two daughters and Jeremy, her disabled boyfriend. She called him 'my fiance.'"

Ben was quiet. He was thinking about the Debby Renaldi he knew a decade earlier. She was a model patient. He and his staff loved her. She was always polite and appreciative, and made a genuine effort to get better. Still, her severe head injury, aggravated by cluster headaches, was very hard to treat. In addition to physical therapy and pain medications, he gave her different trigger point injections, osteopathic manipulations, and occasional nerve blocks. All these treatments controlled her symptoms so effectively that Deborah Renaldi could finally live a normal life.

"Did your treatments help her?" Alex interrupted Ben's thoughts.

"Yes, they did. But everything changed when my office was raided and later closed."

"What happened?"

"Debby couldn't find anybody who would provide her with the pain relief she used to have."

"Why?"

"The doctors she called refused to take her as soon as they learned whose patient she'd been before. For the first few months after I stopped working, Debby kept calling my secretary and begging Sandra to let her know when I would return to practice. But then the office was closed, and there was no one to call, so I have no idea how her life turned out after that. Judging by her appearance today..."

"What do you think happened today?" Emma asked.

"My guess is that she is not receiving adequate pain treatment and buys illegal drugs to alleviate her pain. Who knows what kind of stuff they sell on the street?"

They all were silent for a long moment.

"Ben, do you think she has a grudge against you?" Emma asked.

"I don't think so. Our treatments kept her in the best shape possible, and she knew what good care I took of her Jeremy. She was truly appreciative of that and never too shy to tell me about it."

"Still," Emma turned to Gould, "they brought her here to testify against Ben?"

"They are using this suffering woman the way they are using everyone else. They want to crush Ben and Julia with any blow or trick they can think of."

"They just don't know how blow resistant we are, right, Julia?" Ben's eyes sparkled with a mischievous twinkle.

"They have no idea," Julia nodded in agreement.

Gould glanced at the peaceful view behind the large hallway window, and his thoughts raced in the direction they often did when he tried a federal case. He would never share these thoughts with anyone because his experience had taught him to stay away from any predictions of trial outcomes. Yes, Ben and Julia had been taking blow after blow over the past seven years and never caved in. But did they fully comprehend the magnitude of the fight? Did they know that when a criminal trial was over, less than one percent of defendants left the federal court free? Less than one percent! Were Ben and Julia aware of how minuscule their chances were? He wasn't sure.

"Well, that was a rather peculiar morning," Gould smiled wistfully. "Let me go back and find out who will be the 'lucky' replacement for the unfortunate Ms. Renaldi."

* * *

"The government calls Leandra Edwards," announced Matilda Hustler.

A tall, lean, peroxide blonde with greenish, bleary eyes leisurely strolled into the courtroom. She relaxed into the witness chair, and Matilda Hustler started her direct.

"Good afternoon, Ms. Edwards."

"Good afternoon," a raspy voice resounded through the courtroom.

"Ms. Edwards, do you have children?"

"Yes. Twin girls."

"How old are your twins?"

"They will be nineteen on June 19... no, June 20... or maybe 21. Sorry about that."

"Did you at some point become a patient of Dr. Holden?"

"I did. Around March 2004."

"And what brought you to his office?"

"I hurt my back. I was in a tussle with my kids' father, my twins' father. He pushed me down the stairs, and I wrenched my back."

"Was there any other reason that you sought the services of Dr. Holden?"

"Yes. I was looking for a prescription for pain meds."

"So what did you tell Dr. Holden when you first went to see him?"

"I told him what I just said, that I got into a fight with my kids' father and fell down the stairs and wrenched my back."

"Was it true that you had pain for which you needed painkillers?"

"Not at all. I was there to get a prescription. That was my excuse."

"Was it true, though, that you did in fact have a fight with the father of..."

"That was true."

"Now, prior to seeing Dr. Holden, had you ever used prescription drugs?"

"Never. I mean, I used prescription drugs, but I didn't have a prescription."

"So why would you use prescription drugs prior to seeing Dr. Holden?"

"Because I was... umm, I was an addict, I guess. I bought them on the street."

"Well, were you using prescription drugs recreationally before you saw Dr. Holden?"

"Yes."

"And were you addicted to prescription drugs before you started seeing Dr. Holden?"

"No, I wasn't."

"Did you have a history of substance abuse before you started seeing Dr. Holden, aside from recreational use?"

"No, I didn't."

"Did you have a history of alcohol use?"

"Here is the thing. My father was an alcoholic. We owned a barroom, so I started to drink at the age of nine."

"When you first met Dr. Holden, do you recall him performing any examination on you?"

"No, we had a talk about what had happened, and then I just pointed to where my back hurt."

"Did he ask you if you had any history of abuse of prescription drugs?"

"He never did."

"What did Dr. Holden do after you showed him where your back pain was?"

"He gave me a cortisone shot in my back."

"And did he give you a prescription for any controlled substances?"

"Yes, for OxyContin."

"Do you recall how long you saw Dr. Holden?"

"Umm, a few months."

"In that time, did you become addicted to the prescription drugs he prescribed for you?"

"I did."

"Did you ever sell the drugs that Dr. Holden had prescribed to you?"

"I did."

"Did you ever tell Dr. Holden that you sold the drugs he'd prescribed to you?"

"No way."

"Did Dr. Holden ever confront you about the fact that you sold these drugs?"

"Nope."

"Do you recall ever taking a drug test at Dr. Holden's office?"

"Only when he kicked me out. That was the only one I remember."

"It was on June 7, 2004, correct?"

"I believe so."

"And can you describe your last visit for the jury?"

"Hmm, he said that the test had come up positive for methadone and cocaine, I believe."

"And what was your response?"

"I said, I didn't know why it came up positive."

"And as a result of this drug test, what did Dr. Holden tell you?"

"Umm, that he was not going to give me a prescription."

"And what was your response?"

"I got angry."

"And what did you say to him?"

"Umm, I basically said, 'Go fuck yourself. I am not fucking leaving your office unless you give me something.'"

A choked laugh rolled over the gallery. A few jurors exchanged wry smiles. Judge Adler flinched and raised her eyebrows, but didn't say a word. Ms. Hustler's jaw dropped, but she quickly recovered and continued in her usual flat tone as if such an answer from a witness was nothing special.

"Ms. Edwards, can you look at the last page in the stack of the documents I gave you. What do you see?"

"I see a prescription for OxyContin. 10 milligrams. 60 pills a month."

"Did you receive this prescription before or after you had this blowup with Dr. Holden?" asked Judge Adler.

"I believe after we had the blowup."

"So it was your last visit with Dr. Holden, is that right?" asked Hustler.

"Yes."

"What happened to you after you stopped seeing Dr. Holden?"

"Hmm, when I finished my last OxyContin, I got sick because... well, I coached cheerleading for my twin girls, and it was my turn to carpool, and..."

"You're not going off into cheerleading land, Ms. Edwards, right?" interrupted Judge Adler.

"No, I'm just trying to explain. That day I was physically sick and couldn't drive my girls, so I sent a friend to find OxyContin in the neighborhood, and... she brought back heroin, and—"

"So you didn't have OxyContin, and you switched to heroin?"

"Yes."

"Are you sober now?" continued Matilda Hustler.

"Yes, I am."

"Congratulations on your sobriety, ma'am, and thank you for your testimony. No further questions, Your Honor."

* * *

Outside the courtroom, Emma met Ben with a smile.

"What a character! Plenty of fun with a patient like that?"

"A little too much, to my taste."

"And you prescribed her painkillers even after her outburst?"

"Could you guess why?"

"I think so. You didn't want her to suffer from withdrawal."

"You hit the mark. I had to taper her off, and I certainly explained to her how to do that."

"Ben, I've been coming to your trial day after day," said Alex, "and I think I see a pattern."

"What pattern?"

"Most of your former patients—the government witnesses—admitted that they abused drugs long before they came to see you. Not just prescribed opioids, but all sorts of drugs, including illegal ones. However, they did their best to hide it from you."

"That's true."

"So how can the prosecutors imply that it was you who turned them into drug addicts?" asked Gail. "I've been here every day too, and I didn't hear a single piece of evidence that would prove that."

"Still, that's the essence of their case," said Ben. "They want to blame me and Julia for our patients' drug abuse and portray us as drug dealers."

"But that's a lie!" Gail exploded.

"Unfortunately, when a lie comes from the DA's Office," said Alex, "some people buy into it."

"On the other hand," Gail said with concern, "most of those patients who testified had real pain, right, Ben? They weren't shy talking about it either."

"Yes, they did have pain, but maybe for some of them it wasn't as severe as they claimed. And if it wasn't, did they use the opioids we'd prescribed to treat their pain or to divert them? Or both? I don't think we'll ever know that."

"How about legitimate pain patients with *no* prior history of problematic drug behavior? Do they often abuse opioids?" asked Gail.

"No, they almost never abuse opioids or get addicted to them. They *depend* on them to feel better, but it's not addiction. They use opioids as prescribed because they are not interested in getting high. Their 'high' is life without pain, and they don't want to jeopardize their well-being by doing something irresponsible, let alone criminal."

* * *

After the lunch break Mark Daniels began his cross.

"Good afternoon, Ms. Edwards. My name is Mark Daniels, and I represent Dr. Holden."

"Good afternoon, sir," Leandra Edwards nodded politely.

"Now, you just testified about a drug test that you took on June 7, 2004, correct?"

"That's correct."

"And that drug test came back positive for methadone and cocaine, correct?"

"Yes."

"And that day you had an argument with Dr. Holden about that test, right?"

"Yes."

"And Dr. Holden told you that he wouldn't be able to prescribe you opioids anymore, correct?"

"Yes."

"And he released you from his practice, correct?"

"Not immediately. We had words. You know what I mean?"

"I know exactly what you mean, Ms. Edwards," Daniels could hardly suppress a smile. "Now, let's go back to your first appointment with Dr. Holden. You went to him because you wanted to get prescription pills to get high, right?"

"Yes."

"And as you testified on direct, you had been using unprescribed opioids and alcohol long before you ever saw Dr. Holden, right?"

"Incorrect. I'd never had a drug problem."

"Objection, Your Honor!" interrupted Matilda Hustler. "He mischaracterizes..."

"Overruled," said Judge Adler. "Continue please."

"I didn't say that you had had a drug problem," clarified Daniels, "but, as you said, you had used drugs, including opioid medications, like OxyContin, before seeing Dr. Holden, right?"

"Alcohol was more my thing," said Edwards, with some playfulness in her tone. "I did drugs only recreationally, not—"

"But even recreationally you did use pain medications like OxyContin before ever seeing Dr. Holden, correct?"

"Umm, no, incorrect. I used Vicodin and Percocet."

"Ms. Edwards, do you recall that in the last few weeks you had a meeting with some of the lawyers sitting at this table?"

"Yes."

"Do you remember that you told the government that as a teenager, you began occasionally abusing a variety of street drugs? You were sober for a while when your twin daughters were born, but then began drinking alcohol and occasionally taking a variety of drugs that were never prescribed to you, including barbiturates, OxyContin, oxycodone, and methadone, correct?"

"Objection," Hustler jumped from her seat again, "he's reading from a letter written by a lawyer."

"Overruled," said the judge, telling Daniels to continue.

"It's mischaracterizing what was stated," shouted Hustler, disregarding the judge's ruling.

"Your Honor, I'm reading the letter from the United States Attorney's Office," explained Daniels.

"Ms. Edwards, is this something you remember saying?" asked Judge Adler.

"Yes."

"And you went to Dr. Holden because you wanted to get more pain medications, right?" asked Daniels.

"Right."

"But you didn't tell Dr. Holden that you went to him just to get pain medications, correct?"

"No."

"You told him that you'd hurt your back and you were in pain, right?"

"Yes."

"And you were limping when you went to see him, correct?"

"No, I wasn't."

"Ms. Edwards, you have your medical file in front of you. Please turn to page 2. Your first visit is March 3, 2004. Do you see it?"

"Yes."

"If you take a look at the physical examination, it says, '*A pleasant 34-year-old lady who limps on the right side,*' and so on. Does this quote refresh your recollection?"

"No, it doesn't."

"Well, you told us you had a physical fight with the father of your kids, right?"

"Yeah. We had a tussle."

"You had a tussle, and you fell down some stairs?"

"Correct."

"That's pretty dramatic, right?"

"But I wasn't limping."

"Could you please take a look at the form titled *Patient Information* that you filled out in Dr. Holden's office. Do you see it?"

"Yes."

"Do you recognize your signature?"

"I do."

"And do you see what you filled out for your major complaint?"

"Yes."

"You wrote, *'Back pain on right side, swelling, crippling leg pain.'* So you told Dr. Holden that you had crippling leg pain, correct?"

"Yes."

"And on direct you said that there was no physical exam at your first visit, right?"

"No... just the cortisone shot, and I explained where it hurt and why I was in pain."

"Could you please turn back to page 2. Do you see where it says, *'Right-side radiculopathy. Examination revealed somewhat limited and painful spine range of motion with grossly positive straight leg raising on the right side.'* And then the detailed description of all findings revealed during the physical exam? Does that refresh your recollection?"

"Uh-huh."

"Then Dr. Holden came up with a treatment plan for you, right?"

"I guess."

"Do you see the section with the heading *'Assessment and Plan'*? It starts with, *'1. Right lumbar spine and right knee MRI, electrodiagnostic study, electrical muscle stimulator for home use, physical therapy, Lidoderm patches, Celebrex, 200 milligrams twice a day.'* By the way, you know that Celebrex is a non-opioid medication, correct?"

"I have no idea what any of this is. I've never seen this document."

"Ms. Edwards, Dr. Holden treated you in ways other than prescribing opioids, correct?"

"No."

"Well, he gave you a cortisone shot, right? You've already testified to that."

"Correct."

"He also sent you to physical therapy, correct?"

"Yes, that was part of... yes."

"He also sent you for an MRI, correct?"

"I don't remember."

"Please go to page 4. The MRI result is in your file," Daniels said patiently.

"Now I see it."

Do you remember that Dr. Holden gave you some Lidoderm patches that weren't opioids to help you with your pain?"

"I remember that."

"Now let's look at your follow-up visit on March 13, 2004. *'She feels progressively better with the therapy and medication. Her sleep is improved, and she is able to take care of her twin daughters.'* So you told Dr. Holden that your sleep was improved, and you were able to take care of your daughters, right?"

"I'm sure I did. I... don't remember the conversation, but..."

"You also signed a form titled *Pain Management Agreement* at your first visit with Dr. Holden, correct?"

"I don't remember."

"Please take a look at page 3. Now you remember?"

"Yes."

"And one of the rules in this agreement is that if you break it, Dr. Holden might stop prescribing pain control medicines, correct?"

"Yes."

"And you knew from this agreement that you shouldn't sell your pain medication, correct?"

"Yes."

"You also knew that you were not to take illicit drugs that Dr. Holden did not prescribe to you, correct?"

"Yes."

"But you did all of those things, right?"

"Yes, I did."

"And you never told Dr. Holden that you sold some of your pain medication or did some other illegal things, right?"

"No."

"Because you knew that if he'd learned about that, he would have stopped prescribing you pain medication, correct?"

"Correct."

"And you have never been arrested for selling your pain medication, correct?"

"Objection!" Matilda Hustler yelled angrily.

"Overruled," said Judge Adler. "You may answer."

"No, I have never been arrested."

"And the government isn't prosecuting you for selling your pain medication, correct?"

"Objection!" Ms. Hustler yelled even louder.

"Overruled," responded the judge.

"No, they are not prosecuting me."

"Nothing further." Daniels gathered his notes and unhurriedly walked back to his seat.

Chapter Thirty-Two

Day 8 of the trial began when Matilda Hustler announced, "Your Honor, the government calls Agent Janet Finnerty."

A short, stout blonde in her early thirties carefully positioned herself in the chair. She looked neither comfortable nor confident, and her pallid eyes betrayed fretful anxiety.

"Good morning, Agent Finnerty," Matilda Hustler smiled encouragingly. "Will you please describe your educational background for the jury."

"Sure. I have a master's of business administration and a master's degree in tax from Suffolk University, and I'm a licensed certified public accountant in Massachusetts."

"Are you currently employed?"

"Yes."

"Where?"

"I work for the Internal Revenue Service, Division of Criminal Investigation."

"What's your title?"

"Special agent."

"How long have you been a special agent with the Internal Revenue Service?"

"Since September 2005."

"What are your duties as a special agent with the Internal Revenue Service?"

"I investigate potential criminal violations of the Internal Revenue Code, such as tax evasion, money laundering, and others."

"At some point in the course of your employment with the Internal Revenue Service, did you become involved in an investigation of Dr. Benjamin Holden?"

"Yes, in May, 2006."

"In the course of this investigation, did you interview Dr. Holden?"

"Yes."

"When was that interview?"

"May 17, 2007."

"Where did you interview Dr. Holden?"

"At his business location."

"Did you and Dr. Holden discuss the number of patients that he sees each day?"

"Yes, we did. He said that he and his nurse practitioner saw between 45 and 50 patients a day."

"And did you and Dr. Holden discuss how many of those patients he personally saw each day?"

"Yes. He said that he saw approximately 25 patients per day."

"Did you and Dr. Holden have any discussion about how long his typical patient visit was?"

"Yes. During the initial visit, he saw them for approximately 20... excuse me, 45 minutes."

"Did he explain why that first visit was longer?"

"Yes, he would go over their medical history. He would get medical records, if they had them, and then he would request a urine screening."

"And did you and Dr. Holden discuss whether subsequent visits were shorter?"

"Yes. He said that... that the subsequent visits were... were not 45 minutes."

"Did you and Dr. Holden discuss how he got patients?"

"Yes, he said that most of his patients were referred by word of mouth," the witness said softly.

"You need to speak up," interrupted Judge Adler. "We all need to hear what you said."

"Sorry, Your Honor." Agent Finnerty blushed and raised her voice a bit. "Most of his patients were referred by word of mouth, by relatives or friends."

"Did you and Dr. Holden discuss how his patients paid for their appointments?"

"Yes, he said that most of his patients had medical insurance, and those who didn't paid by cash and credit card."

"Did you write a report of your interview with Dr. Holden?"

"I did."

"Was that report a transcript or was it intended to be a summary of the interview?"

"A summary of the interview."

"Did you and Dr. Holden talk about other people who worked in his office?"

"Yes, he had four full-time employees, including an office manager, two secretaries, and an individual who took urine samples."

"Did Dr. Holden talk about any other physicians who worked in his practice?"

"Yes, he said he was trying to make his practice like a one-stop shop, so he had other specialists, and they all treated the patients."

"Did you discuss whether or not he had a nurse practitioner working with him?"

"Yes. His nurse practitioner was Julia Lander, and she also saw patients."

"And did you and Dr. Holden discuss her role with the patients?"

"She saw patients daily. She did not make any decisions about their prescriptions—whether to increase or decrease—without consulting with Dr. Holden."

"Did you and Dr. Holden discuss at all whether Ms. Lander saw new patients?"

"Yes. She did not see new patients."

"Did Dr. Holden make any statements about whether or not he prescribed narcotic medications to patients on the first visit?"

"Yes, he said he did not prescribe narcotics on the first visit."

"What did Dr. Holden tell you about the percentage of patients for whom he wrote Schedule II narcotic prescriptions?"

"He said that approximately 90 percent of his patients received these types of medications."

"Did you and Dr. Holden have a discussion about whether in his experience patients tried to get medications from him without a legitimate need?"

"Yes, he said that some patients tried to get opioid prescriptions without a legitimate medical need, but he would refuse to prescribe them."

"Did you and Dr. Holden discuss how easy or difficult it was to fake particular injuries?"

"I object, Your Honor," said Edward Gould.

"Sustained," responded the judge.

"Did you and Dr. Holden have a discussion about diagnosing patients?"

"Yes, he said that knee pain was easy to diagnose, but with back pain, it was hard to tell if the patient was actually in pain or not."

"Now, did you and Dr. Holden discuss what..." Hustler suddenly turned to Gould, who was fidgeting slightly in his seat, her eyes burning with irritation, "Will you let me finish the question?"

"I haven't objected yet," replied Gould.

"Did you and Dr. Holden discuss any precautionary steps he took with his patients?"

"Yes, he stated that for new patients he would get their medical history, request urine samples, and do a medical exam himself."

"Do you recall the conversation that you and Dr. Holden had about urine screens?"

"Yes, he said that he would frequently send his patients for urine screening."

"And what would happen if there were bad results on a urine screen?"

"I'm not exactly sure what he told me. Can I look at my notes?"

Matilda Hustler handed the witness a stack of papers.

"Let me say it for the record," Gould rose from his seat, "the witness is looking at her *typewritten* notes, not the *handwritten* notes she took during the interview."

"Does this refresh your recollection?" continued Hustler, ignoring the comment.

"Yes. If the patients had bad urine screens, he would stop prescribing opioid medication for them. But sometimes he would give them a one-time pass."

"Did he use a specific example?"

"Yes. If a person tested positive for cocaine, he would stop the opioid medications."

"Did you discuss whether any of his patients ever used or purchased illegal drugs from someone on the street?"

"Yes, he said that he was aware that some patients did purchase street drugs."

"Did you discuss his prescribing practices for methadone?"

"Yes, he stated that the majority of his patients were on low doses of methadone, and only a couple of patients were on higher doses."

"Did you and Dr. Holden discuss whether any of his patients had died?"

"Yes, he said he knew of three patients who had died."

"Did he use their names?"

"Yes. He recalled that one patient was Steve Porter. Another one was Jeremy Callagan, and another person had an Italian last name, but he couldn't remember it."

"Well, we'll take these in turn. What did he tell you about Steve Porter?"

"Steve Porter, he said, may have been a drug abuser. He had gone to an addiction center and then left it and overdosed."

"And what did Dr. Holden say to you about Jeremy Callagan?"

"Jeremy Callagan, he said that... he was overweight, with a lot of health problems and he... he died of a heart attack."

"And do you recall if Dr. Holden said anything else about the man with an Italian last name?"

"Yes, he had tested positive for cocaine, and Dr. Holden had dismissed him from his practice, and then three or four months later, he learned that this man had died from an overdose."

"Did you and Dr. Holden discuss whether primary care physicians would prescribe opioids?"

"Yes."

"What did he say to you on that subject?"

"He made a direct comment that... I'm not a hundred percent sure, but he said something like, as a rule, primary care physicians do not prescribe opioids."

"Did he give you a reason?" A small, taut smile flashed across Hustler's lips.

"Yes." Agent Finnerty checked her notes. "Well, he said, 'because doctors are afraid of people like you. I am not.'"

"Thank you, Agent Finnerty. No further questions." Hustler left the lectern with a victorious air.

Judge Adler, looking tired, turned to Gould. "Counselor, are you ready for the cross?"

"Yes, Your Honor, any minute."

* * *

Gould walked to the lectern. "Good afternoon, Agent Finnerty."

"Good afternoon."

"My name is Edward Gould, and I represent Dr. Holden. I've placed copies of two documents in front of you. One is your typewritten report. Another one is your handwritten notes. Do you see them?"

"Yes."

"I'd like to talk about the interview and the two documents you are looking at now. This interview took place on May 17, 2007, correct?"

"Yes."

"For the moment, would you just turn those two documents over. I'm very interested in your memory. May 17 is the date that you took notes, correct?"

"Yes."

"However, you drafted and typed this report on June 14, 2007, correct?"

"Yes."

"Four weeks later or twenty eight days later, correct?"

"Yes."

"And when Ms. Hustler asked you to refresh your memory, she showed you your typewritten report that was prepared four weeks later, not your original handwritten notes, correct?"

"Correct."

"Now, are you aware that the FBI has a rule that you're supposed to type up a report of your handwritten notes within five business days. Do you know that?" asked Gould.

"I was not aware of that."

"And you're not an FBI agent. You're an IRS agent, right?"

"Correct."

"You're an accountant, right?"

"Yes."

"We'll come back to that. But when an IRS agent participates in a criminal investigation, do you have any similar rules that you're supposed to type up your report within *five* business days?"

"No."

"Now, as defense lawyers, we had received your typewritten report only but had to *request* your handwritten notes, right?"

"Correct."

"Agent Finnerty, would you agree with me that this is an important case?"

"Yes."

"And it's critical that you be accurate, and it's critical for your report to be complete, correct?"

"Yes."

"When you interviewed Dr. Holden, you knew he was the target of a criminal investigation, correct?"

"I did."

"Therefore you needed to be one hundred percent accurate about what he said, correct?"

"Based on my notes and my memory—"

"Ma'am, please answer my questions. In your report, you needed to be one hundred percent accurate?"

"I guess so."

"Well, did you have a lower standard than that?" Gould asked.

"No."

"Now, could you please listen to what I'm about to say, and then I'll ask you a question about it. I want you to assume that you're investigating a bank robbery, and I'm your suspect. You have an opportunity to ask me some questions. So you ask me, *'Did you commit the robbery?'* and I answer you with three different responses. *'I was in the bank at the time of the robbery,'* is my first response. My second response is *'I didn't commit the robbery.'* My third response is *'They got away with millions.'* Did you hear all three of these responses?"

"Objection, Your Honor," interjected Hustler.

"I don't know what the question is other than did she hear it or not," said Judge Adler.

"Did you hear what I just said?" asked Gould.

"Yes."

"So what's the question?" asked Judge Adler.

"Agent Finnerty, would you agree with me that it would be completely unfair to write a report about your interview of me by including the first response and the third one, but not the second?"

"Objection."

"Overruled."

"I… I really don't understand the relevance of this."

"Well, whether you understand the relevance or not, ma'am, with all due respect, could you answer my question? Would you agree that to omit the second response, the one that says, *'I didn't commit the robbery,'* would be unfair and in gross disregard of your responsibility as a federal law enforcement agent?"

"Correct."

"Now, when you created your report twenty eight days later, you literally omitted the middle sentence of what Dr. Holden told you. Remember, Ms. Hustler asked you a question about whether Dr. Holden said anything to you about his patients who got their medications, but later it turned out that these patients' urine tests were bad. Do you recall her asking you about that?"

"Yes."

"And there were two sentences in your notes on page 3 of your handwritten notes, but I'm not asking you to look at it yet. Didn't Dr. Holden immediately say, *'We used to give them a second chance, but lately we changed our policy and after the first strike, they are automatically discharged'*?"

"I don't know."

"And didn't he then tell you that he had all those patients sign a form titled *Pain Management Agreement*?"

"His patients signed an agreement with him."

"Well, in paragraph 16 of your typewritten report you wrote, *'Holden stated some of his patients who do not have legitimate pain are just looking for drug prescriptions and have received drugs from him. All patients who receive narcotic medication sign an agreement stating that they will take their medication as prescribed.'* That's paragraph 16 of your report, correct? The very same report that you typed twenty eight days later, correct?"

"I object!" Hustler was out of her seat. "If he wants to ask her a question about her notes, he has to at least let her look at those notes."

"Do you need to see your notes, Agent Finnerty? That's what you wrote in your typewritten report twenty eight days later, correct?" asked Judge Adler.

"Yes, Your Honor."

"You put those two sentences together, and you made it one typewritten complete paragraph, right?" asked Gould.

"Yes."

"But your handwritten notes show that Dr. Holden said something in between those two sentences, correct? He used the words 'automatically discharged,' right? And you wouldn't have written those words down unless Dr. Holden said that, correct?"

"Yes."

"And so these were your notes, and twenty eight days later, when you went to prepare your typed report, those notes became this paragraph with nothing mentioned about 'automatically discharged,' correct?"

"Because that is not—"

"Ma'am, just focus on my question. You left that out of your typewritten report, correct?"

"This is not in my typewritten report."

"And that's the only document Ms. Hustler was showing you to refresh your memory, right?"

"Yes."

"Now, the effect of what you did was to change something that Dr. Holden said which was favorable to him to something that was unfavorable to him, correct?"

"Objection!"

"Overruled."

"That's what you did?"

"No."

"So you're telling this jury that leaving those words out didn't change something that was favorable to him to something unfavorable to him. Is that your testimony?"

"Repeat the question, because I didn't get it."

"I will be happy to do that. Did you or did you not know that when you left those words out you were changing something favorable to Dr. Holden to something that was unfavorable to him?"

"No, I was not aware..."

"And until I just pointed that out, no one from the government told you that the words 'automatically discharged,' which are in your handwritten notes, were omitted from paragraph 16 of your typed report, correct?"

"Correct."

"Now, you were involved in that interview because the United States Attorney's Office was executing a search warrant on Dr. Holden's office, correct?"

"Yes."

"In that twenty eight-day period, were you in touch with any of the agents that were working with the U.S. Attorney's Office on this investigation or any of the lawyers at the U.S. Attorney's Office?"

"Yes."

"And after you interviewed Dr. Holden, did you show them your handwritten notes?"

"I may have."

"So did any of the prosecutors tell you what *you should* and *should not* include in your report?"

"No."

"Agent Finnerty, did anyone use a video camcorder or some other monitoring device while you interviewed Dr. Holden?"

"I don't recall. There could have been."

"So you could have recorded this interview if you wanted to, correct?"

"I... I... you know what... I don't..."

"I'm just asking you, Agent Finnerty, you could have recorded this interview, correct?"

"I suppose."

"Well, let's talk about the interview itself. This was a raid on Dr. Holden's office, correct?"

"It was a search warrant."

"It was a raid, wasn't it?"

"It was an enforcement action, a search warrant."

"Do you have trouble with the word 'raid'?"

"Objection, Your Honor. She answered it. It was a federal search warrant."

"Overruled."

"It was a raid, wasn't it?"

"If you want to say a raid, yes, it was a raid."

"I don't want to say anything. I want the truth. It was a raid, wasn't it?"

"It was a search warrant."

"Okay. We'll go with your word. When you were executing the search warrant, it was a surprise, wasn't it?"

"Yes."

"And there were three dozen or so agents in different uniforms carrying weapons who descended upon Dr. Holden's office, correct?"

"Yes."

"And nevertheless, Dr. Holden agreed to sit down and talk with you, right?"

"Correct."

"And he did that voluntarily, right?"

"Yes."

"And he didn't say, 'Hey, wait a minute, I've got to call a lawyer,' did he?"

"I don't recall. I... He would have been..."

"If he did, you would have made note of that, wouldn't you?"

"Yeah, he could have called an attorney if he asked for one."

"Well, let's be clear here. If Dr. Holden had said he wanted to call a lawyer, if things were being done correctly, everything would have ground to a halt, and there wouldn't have been an interview until he exercised his right to do so, correct?"

"What are you asking?"

"He didn't call a lawyer, did he?"

"I... No, he did not call a lawyer."

"So he sat with you and Agent Ulmer voluntarily from 10:51 a.m. to 1:17 p.m.—about two hours and twenty minutes, correct?"

"That sounds about right."

"So in the midst of—and we'll use your words 'execution of a search warrant'—Dr. Holden sat down and voluntarily answered all of your questions for two hours and twenty minutes, correct?"

"Yes."

"He didn't refuse to answer any questions, correct?"

"Correct."

"He was professional, right?"

"Yes."

"He was courteous, correct?

"Yes."

"Your Honor, I think it's a good point to take a break."

"I agree. Let's have a lunch break and reconvene at 2:00 p.m."

* * *

An hour later Gould was back at the lectern.

"Good afternoon, Ms. Finnerty."

"Good afternoon, sir."

"Now, at the time you were asking questions and documenting Dr. Holden's answers, what training did you have in the area of pain management?"

"I am not trained in pain management."

"So you knew nothing about it, right?"

"I knew about it from my... from starting this case."

"And you're not a narcotics agent, are you?"

"No, I am not."

"You don't work with the DEA; you're not involved in diversion, right?"

"I am not."

"And your background is as a CPA, right?"

"Yes."

"I mean this is not something you typically do, right?"

"Pain management? No."

"You didn't ask any of the questions of Dr. Holden, did you? Agent Ulmer did, right?"

"Yes, Agent Ulmer asked the majority of the questions, yes."

"Because you didn't really know very much about that subject when you took these notes about it, right?"

"Right. I don't have a background in pain management or DEA or diversion, no."

"By the way, the government has brought *no* tax charges against Dr. Holden, have they?"

"No, they haven't."

"Agent Finnerty, do you know the difference between dependence and addiction?"

"No."

"I also want to ask you about some things that Ms. Hustler didn't ask you. Her direct examination of you was about 40 minutes, while Dr. Holden's interview lasted two hours and twenty minutes, right?"

"Correct."

"Well, I want to ask you about the other hour and a half of it. So when Dr. Holden—"

"Objection! I'm objecting to him asking questions about what I didn't ask this witness!" Matilda Hustler jumped from her seat.

"Overruled."

"Are you with me so far, Agent Finnerty?"

"Yes."

"The very first thing that you asked Dr. Holden was about the legitimacy of his patients, correct? One of the first things he told you was 'that he prescribes legitimate medicine only for legitimate reasons,' correct?"

"Yes, that's in my notes here."

"Then he was asked by Agent Ulmer about an overview of his business, correct?"

"Yes."

"And he explained that he sees pain patients, people who have a history of pain, who have been through multiple surgeries, and treatments elsewhere, and he diagnoses them to help them feel better. That was the second thing he told you, right?"

"Yes, he explained... but this is not everything he said to me."

"Oh, I get that."

"I couldn't transcribe every single thing that came out of his mouth, or what came out of my mouth, or Ulmer's mouth. They are just notes."

"They're just notes, but they're all we have, right?"

"Yes, and our memories."

"And we don't have the benefit of a tape-recorded interview, do we? Although the tape recorder *was* there and *could have been used*, but for some unknown reason it wasn't, correct?"

"We didn't use it, correct."

"And what you wrote in your notes wasn't verbatim, right?"

"It was not verbatim, no."

"Even though this gentleman was the target of a criminal investigation, you didn't take verbatim notes, right?"

"No, I don't know shorthand. If I knew shorthand, maybe I could get every single word—"

"So when Ms. Hustler asked you questions, it's fair to say that your responses did not refer to anything that was in quotation marks, right?"

"There may be."

"You know that there isn't anything, don't you?"

"No, I don't know."

"All right. Then Dr. Holden told you that he had decided to specialize in physical and rehabilitation medicine, correct?"

"He was in... physical and rehab medicine, yes."

"Do you know what a PM&R doctor is?"

"No."

"I see. Then he was asked whether he was surprised by your intrusion into his office that morning, correct?"

"Yes."

"And his answer was, 'I'm surprised but not scared because I'm not aware that I have been doing anything wrong,' correct?"

"Yes, he said that."

"Then he described his practice and the nature of the patients' maladies, right?"

"Yes."

"He told you that he saw patients, some of whom had had multiple surgeries, correct?"

"Yes."

"And they were at an end result because more surgery couldn't help them anymore, correct?"

"He may have said that, yes."

"And that they were suffering with severe pain and that he treated them, correct?"

"He said they were in pain, and he treated them, yes."

"And then when he was asked about any patients who may have gotten prescription drugs without legitimate pain, he pointed out that some people tried to scam him, correct?"

"Yes."

"And so he was explaining to you one of the difficulties about practicing in this area, namely, that some people scam their doctors, correct?"

"Yes."

"And he said to you that when he finds out about it and has evidence that someone is scamming him, he dismisses them from his practice, correct?"

"He said that at one point, yes."

"He also said that he would send his patients for urine drug tests as often as he could, correct?"

"I don't recall his words exactly, but he would routinely send his patients for urine tests, yes."

"Now, you were asked some questions by Ms. Hustler in regards to your conversation with Dr. Holden about what happens if someone has a positive cocaine test, correct?"

"I remember discussing it."

"You testified that Dr. Holden said he 'gives patients a pass' in response to a cocaine test, but in reality he never said anything like that, did he?"

"I can't say never."

"Well, it's not reflected anywhere in either your notes or your report, correct?"

"What are you asking again?"

"You didn't write down anywhere in either your notes or your typed report that Dr. Holden responded to you that 'sometimes he gives people a pass.' That's the words you used when Ms. Hustler was asking you questions. That's nowhere in your report, is it?"

"No, it says he gives them a second chance."

"Now, he explained to you the difficulty that a pain physician has when someone comes to him or her with multiple surgeries and is suffering in pain, but may be abusing street drugs, right?"

"Yes."

"I mean you're not a doctor. You don't know how to deal with these kinds of patients, do you?"

"I'm not a doctor."

"And before you or Agent Ulmer asked these questions, had anyone explained to you the concept of pseudo-addiction?"

"I'm not familiar with the term."

"So someone sent you into an interview with a pain management doctor to inquire about the legitimacy of his care without telling you what pseudo-addiction was. Did anyone explain to you the difference between dependence and addiction?"

"Never."

"When Dr. Holden was talking about the difficulty that a pain management doctor has in dealing with drug tests, he explained to you how unreliable these tests were, didn't he?"

"He only said they may not be accurate," said Finnerty.

"And that was a concern for him as a doctor before he made a decision not to continue treating someone. He explained that to you, correct?"

"I mean we discussed it. We didn't go into a ton of detail about it, no."

"Well, you were investigating Dr. Holden for crimes. Didn't you think it was important to get the details right?"

Finnerty didn't answer.

"Well, let's move on. He explained to you during the interview how he went about adjusting patients' pain medication and decreasing their dosage in order to taper them off narcotics at an appropriate time, correct?"

"He discussed increasing and decreasing their doses."

"But one of the things that he explained to you was how he would decrease dosages for patients when he was tapering them off narcotics, correct?"

"I don't recall that."

"Let's take a look at the top of page 5 of your notes. Do you see the words *'decrease doses'*?"

"Yes."

"And then he gives you an example of a hypothetical patient who is on Percocet, correct? Didn't he explain to you that even with regard to patients who may be abusing drugs, you cannot stop them cold turkey; instead, you have to taper their dosages off so as not to harm them?"

"I do not recall that conversation."

"And, again, as someone who's not familiar with pain management at all and hadn't been educated about it before, but still went in to do the interview, would those words have had any meaning to you as a CPA? When you were taking notes, isn't it true that because of your background, you really weren't sure what to write down and what not to write down?"

"I wrote down what I thought was appropriate, what I thought was important, yes."

"But there were things that you determined were *not* important, and you just didn't write them down, right?"

"I'm sure there were things that I did not write down."

"So it's fair to say that you didn't have the background to know what might be important and what might not be important, right?"

"I guess so."

"Now, Dr. Holden made the statement to you about him prescribing drugs only if he genuinely believed that the pain was legitimate, right? Could you take a look at the seventh line on page 5?"

"Yes, that's what I wrote down, yes."

"But that statement didn't make it into your typewritten report, did it?"

"I don't know."

"Dr. Holden also told you that he sent his patients for MRIs and X-rays to help him figure out whether the pain his patients were describing was legitimate or not, right?"

"Yes."

"And he used diagnostic nerve conduction tests, right?"

"Yes, I believe so."

"I don't mean this to be a memory contest, but he went into some detail about the source of the information that he would seek so that he could form a genuine belief that the pain was legit, right?"

"Yes, he would get the patient's history. Yes."

"And while he was telling you about the initial patient visits, he explained to you that some of the people who came to see him were desperate. That's the word he used, right, 'desperate'?"

"Yes."

"And they were desperate because they were suffering, right?"

"Yes."

"And he was just trying to explain to you what his job was like and the population he was dealing with, correct?"

"Yes."

"Now, he also told you that when he would see patients who were desperate, he would ask them questions about what had happened to them, correct?"

"I believe so, yeah. He would get their history."

"He would find out whether they had another doctor who'd referred them, and what treatments they'd already had and what had helped them and what had not, right?"

"I don't know if he said that to me, but I assume he said that to his patients."

"And the reason that you say you assume that is because that's what doctors do—legitimate doctors. That's what they do, right?"

"Right."

"They do it when they're practicing good legitimate medical care in the usual course of medicine, correct?"

"Correct."

"You've said a number of times that there may be things that you didn't write down in your notes, right?"

"There may have been, yes."

"And you're a professional, right?"

"Yes."

"And in this situation you were involved in talking to a target of a criminal investigation, and even then you left out some things from your notes, right?"

"I did not write everything down."

"You're a trained criminal enforcement agent for the IRS, and even you can't do that, right?"

"Right."

"Now, Dr. Holden then went on to explain about the examination that he conducts on an initial visit with a patient, correct?"

"Yes, he went over that."

"Okay. Did you learn anything?"

"Yeah."

"Did he impress you as a doctor who actually cared about his patients?"

"Objection!" exclaimed Hustler.

"I'll allow your impression," ruled Judge Adler.

"I think he did, yeah."

"Sorry. You said that he did care about his patients?"

"Yes, he cared about them."

"Now, he explained that his center was an integrated medical practice?"

"Yes."

"And he explained to you some of the equipment that they had in the office, correct?"

"He did."

"Do you remember the names of any of that equipment?"

"I don't recall the names of the equipment, no."

"Well, you didn't put any of the names in your notes so I'm going to try to help you here. Do you know what a lumbar-decompression table is?"

"No. I'm not saying he didn't tell me. I just... I don't recall those names, no."

"Did he explain to you that if you walked down the hall you would find a room that had some equipment in it, and one of them was a machine that helped strengthen people's backs?"

"I believe there was... yes, I think there was a discussion about that."

"And did you go down the hall and see the machine?"

"I probably did. I just don't recall that."

"And you didn't put that in your notes, did you?"

"If I went down the hall or not? No."

"I see. He explained to you some of the other things that the office offered such as acupuncture, for example?"

"Yes, I believe he mentioned... aca... acopuncture."

"And there was an exercise room, and he also talked about physical therapy, correct?"

"Yes."

"And he explained to you that he offered these treatments to his patients to help them function better, correct?"

"Yes, he did."

"And when he did that, he impressed you as someone who actually cared about his work, correct?"

"Objection, Your Honor," Hustler jumped from her seat, fuming.

"I will allow her impression."

"My impression was that he wanted to offer his patients all these opportunities."

"He also talked to you about other specialists that he worked with, correct?"

"Yes."

"And during your direct examination on the topic of someone becoming addicted, Dr. Holden said that there wasn't much more he could do for them. Is that what you said to Ms. Hustler?"

"He said that, yes."

"But he explained to you that he referred those people to other physicians who were addictionologists and psychiatrists, correct?"

"I don't recall. I remember a psychologist that he referred people to."

"Do you know the difference between a psychologist and psychiatrist?"

"It is not my area of expertise, no."

"Well, on page 6 of your notes, you wrote that he sent his patients to Dr. Koselsky, a psychiatrist who treats people for addiction. That's what he told you, correct?"

"I believe he did."

"Do you know what an addictionologist is?"

"No. It's not my expertise, no."

"And Dr. Holden told you that he had recently brought a neurologist into his practice, right?"

"He brought a neurologist into his practice, yes."

"Dr. Holden also explained to you that he monitored those patients to whom he prescribed opioids?"

"I believe so."

"He said that he saw those patients once a month, sometimes even more frequently, if he wanted to keep an eye on them, right?"

"I believe so."

"Let me change the subject, Agent Finnerty. When you arrived to conduct an interview with Dr. Holden, had you ever been involved in anything like that before?"

"Yes."

"Do you remember some specifics about those search warrants?"

"Yes, I do."

"But, clearly, it is not much you remember about this case, do you, Agent Finnerty?"

"I just... I was... I was trying to... "

"Thank you, Agent. I have nothing further."

* * *

"Edward," Ron stopped Gould in the hallway, "Can you tell me why the U.S. Attorney's Office chose this particular agent to testify?"

"Sorry, but I'm the wrong person to ask," Gould suppressed a smile. "You can try to get the answer from Mr. Lynch."

"And what do you think about the interrogation itself?" asked Elaine. "Why didn't they use a tape recorder?"

"It looks like, without a recording," interjected Ron, "as we've seen in Detective Eves's testimony, agents can make up their reports any way they like, according to their skills and objectives."

"But this is fraud!" exclaimed Elaine. "Are government agents allowed to commit fraud?"

"Well..." Ron paused for a brief moment. "If I may paraphrase an ancient Roman saying, 'What is not permissible for an ox is permissible for Jupiter.'"

Chapter Thirty-Three

Day 9 of the trial began when Prosecuting Attorney Lynch called John Thorn to the witness stand.

A tall, hefty man, with his right arm supported by a black sling, sauntered to the witness stand. His old-fashioned spectacles and goatee made him look like a respected college professor, but the grim expression on his large face hinted at dissatisfaction either with his present role or life in general.

"Is your arm broken?" Judge Adler asked with genuine sympathy.

"No," laconically responded the witness.

"What's wrong with it?"

"Nerve damage," was another terse answer.

"Nerve damage, I see. Then don't raise your hand while you are sworn in," offered the judge.

"Thank you, Your Honor."

Mr. John Thorn was sworn in and he sank in the witness chair, with apparent reluctance.

"Sir, would you please state your name," Lynch requested.

"John Salvatore Thorn."

"Sir, how old are you?"

"Sixty years old."

"Mr. Thorn, are you presently incarcerated?"

"I am."

"And where are you incarcerated?"

"Bristol County House of Correction."

Elaine leaned toward Emma. "If I met him on the street, I would take him for a professor of English literature," she whispered.

"On what charges are you in jail, sir?" continued Lynch.

"Identity fraud."

"Were your charges for identity fraud in any way related to prescription drugs?"

"Yes."

"Could you explain to the jury how they were related?"

"I had a Vicodin addiction, and I wrote some prescriptions in other people's names."

"Sir, at some point did you go to Dr. Holden's office?"

"Yes."

"Why did you choose to go to Dr. Holden's office?"

"A relative recommended him."

"Sir, how long did you go to Dr. Holden's office?"

"Four and a half years."

"And at some point did you stop going to Dr. Holden's office?"

"Yes."

"Why was that?"

"The office was suddenly closed."

"Sir, during the time that you went to Dr. Holden's office, did you ever sell any of your prescription drugs?"

"I would take some and sell some."

"Why did you sell the drugs you were getting?"

"At that time workers' comp stopped paying me. I needed money to live. I sold some so I could eat and pay rent."

"Did you have a gambling addiction too?"

"Yes, I did. For years."

"Did you use any of the money from selling your prescriptions to pay your gambling debts?"

"Yes."

"Sir, what types of drugs did you get from Dr. Holden's office?"

"80-milligram OxyContins and 10-milligram Percocets."

"Sir, did Dr. Holden ever give you physical examinations?"

"Yes, he did."

"How many times?"

"Almost every time he would give me injections."

"Okay. Where did you have pain when you went to Dr. Holden?"

"My right shoulder and the neck area, and my arm, all the way to my fingertips."

"When you went to Dr. Holden's office, would he physically examine your shoulder?"

"Yes, he always did."

"Now, sir, before you went to Dr. Holden, did you have any previous abuse issues with Vicodin?"

"Yes, I had them for many years."

"Do you remember signing a form titled *Pain Management Agreement* with Dr. Holden?"

"Vaguely."

"Did you understand that those were the rules you had to abide by at Dr. Holden's office?"

"I did."

"Do you remember whether he ever spoke to you about you taking too much medicine?"

"Yes."

"And what did he tell you?"

"That somewhere down the line he was going to cut it down."

"And do you remember what he said to you when you told him that you were doubling up on your OxyContin?"

"He sort of scolded me for taking extra, saying it was a very strong medication."

"Do you remember whether he sent you to an addictionologist?"

"I do not."

"Or referred you to another physician to deal with any potential issues?"

"Yes, he did, and I was very grateful for that."

"Who was that physician?"

"Dr. Baron at Saint Vincent's Hospital in Worcester. Dr. Holden wanted someone else to look at me."

"Sir, do you remember whether you ever went to Dr. Holden earlier than you should to get more prescriptions?"

"I did it once."

"And why did you do that?"

"Gambling habit."

"Did Dr. Holden speak to you about why you'd come back two days earlier to get more prescriptions?"

"He did. He was sort of reluctant to refill the prescriptions."

"Did he give you prescriptions two days before he should?"

"He did."

"What did you do with those drugs, sir?"

"I sold them to pay my gambling debts."

"Excuse me," interrupted Judge Adler. "What did you tell Dr. Holden? Why did you say you needed them earlier?"

"I told him that I was in severe pain," explained John Thorn.

"Sir, do you remember whether there were other times when you would go to Dr. Holden's office a couple of days earlier to get more prescriptions?"

"I don't recall any others except for that one instance."

"Did Dr. Holden or Nurse Practitioner Lander ever send you for blood or urine drug tests?"

"Yes, a few times."

"Sir, did you take steps to try to meet the requirements of the drug test?"

"Yes, I did."

"What would you do?"

"I would save a certain portion of the medication for the day or two days before my scheduled appointment."

"In order to test positive for what you were supposed to be taking?"

"Exactly."

This time Emma leaned toward Elaine.

"He is smart. No wonder he looks like a college professor."

"Sir, do you remember ever being tested positive for amphetamines?" continued Lynch.

"Yes, I do. I was prescribed some other medication by my primary care doctor, which could show as amphetamines in the urine."

"But you never told Dr. Holden about it, did you?"

"Not until he found it in my urine."

"But in spite of your gross violation of the pain management agreement, Dr. Holden never stopped prescribing you those opioid medications, did he?"

"No, he never did."

"Mr. Thorn, in all those years, what did you do with your prescriptions?"

"I sold most of them."

"Besides receiving opioids, did you ever go to any physical therapy treatment?"

"Yes, many times. In his office."

"And did you pay for that?"

"The insurance company paid."

"When you got injections, did those cost you money?"

"No, the insurance company paid."

"And when you did urine tests?"

"I never paid for any."

"No further questions," declared Lynch.

* * *

Outside the courtroom, Alex joined a group of Ben's friends.

"If I met this guy on the street," he started, as Emma and Elaine exchanged humorous glances, "I would take him for a CEO of a big pharma company or... a hedge fund, nothing less."

"I think," Julia smiled, "either of these positions would fit him like a glove. Well, let's go and watch the cross."

* * *

"Good afternoon, Mr. Thorn. My name is Edward Gould. I represent Dr. Holden. Can you hear me well?"

"Yes," Thorn replied, and stared at Gould with his dark, stinging eyes.

The attorney took a long look at the witness. "I want to clear up any misunderstanding that may have been created about your last drug tests at Dr. Holden's office. You do recall that Dr. Holden confronted you about the issue of finding amphetamines in your urine, correct?"

"Yes."

"Your test demonstrated the presence of amphetamines, and Dr. Holden accused you of being on an illegal drug—something that he had not prescribed, correct?"

"Correct."

"And he was quite upset with you?"

"Yes."

"It was pseudoephedrine, legitimately prescribed to you by your primary care physician, right?"

"Yes."

"So Dr. Holden made you do a number of things to prove that it was a false-positive result on the test, correct?"

"Correct."

"He made you contact the pharmaceutical company that makes the drug, correct?"

"Yes."

"And, by the way, you did this because you were in serious pain and needed the medication, right?"

"True, my pain was unbearable."

"He also made you contact your own primary care physician, who got in touch with Dr. Holden about the drugs he prescribed for you, correct?"

"Correct."

"And you knew very well that if your primary care doctor hadn't confirmed that, Dr. Holden would have stopped prescribing your medications to you?"

"Most likely."

"Well, let's move on. Nowhere in the two hours that you've been asked questions by the prosecutors did they ask you about brachial plexopathy or RSD, which I understand stands for reflex sympathetic dystrophy. You're familiar with those terms, aren't you?"

"Unfortunately, I am."

"I don't mean to call out attention about your personal matters, sir, but it's important. It's more than twelve years since you injured your shoulder and arm, and it's still in a sling now, right?"

"Correct, I can't even take it off."

"So let's talk about this injury that you suffered. Dr. Holden explained the diagnosis to you and other doctors have confirmed it, correct?"

"Yes, they have."

"And RSD is one of the most painful nerve conditions that you can have, correct?"

"Correct."

"And you experience extraordinary pain with that condition, don't you?"

"At times. Not all the time but at times, yes, the pain becomes horrible."

"Sometimes it runs down your arm from your neck to the tips of your fingers, right?"

"Correct."

"And sometimes it leaves your arm throbbing so that you're in agony, right?"

"Yes, it does."

"And you're not making that up, right?"

"No, I'm not."

"And when you told Dr. Holden and Nurse Practitioner Lander that you were in agony, you weren't making that up, so they would prescribe you enough opioid medications to relieve it, correct?"

"No, that was all true."

"Yet you would sell them to someone on the street rather soon, right?"

"I had to sell some meds, like I stated."

"Well, you didn't tell them that. You told them that you were in agony, right?"

"Yes."

"Mr. Thorn, when you first sought out treatment from Dr. Holden in March 2003, you already had a serious injury, and you were in substantial pain, and you weren't making that up, correct?"

"No, I wasn't."

"You were in need of medical help, including strong pain medications, correct?"

"No doubt about it."

"And you had seen a series of doctors before and they had tried a number of things with you, like physical therapy and some small amounts of painkillers, and they really didn't help, true?"

"Absolutely, they did nothing for my pain."

"So Dr. Holden wasn't the first doctor to prescribe opioids for you, correct?"

"No, he wasn't the first one."

"How many doctors had you seen before you ever met Dr. Holden?"

"I would say four."

"And they all prescribed opioids to you but you were still having enormous pain, correct?"

"Yes."

"And when you arrived in Dr. Holden's office, do you recall that one of the first things that the staff asked you to do was to fill out some forms?"

"Yes, they did."

"And you were asked the question, 'What is your complaint?' and you said, 'Right upper back and neck pain, right shoulder, arm and hand numbness, tingling, sharp shooting pain, work injury,' because you were injured on the job, right?"

"Right."

"And then you listed OxyContin, oxycodone, Vicodin, Prilosec, Ambien and other medications that you were taking. That's your handwriting, correct?"

"Yes, that's what I was taking before, correct."

"Now, Mr. Lynch asked you about this document, 688G, the *Pain Management Agreement,* in relation to the chronic use of opioids, and that's your signature at the bottom, correct?"

"Yes, it is."

"You understood that Dr. Holden asked you to read and sign this document before he'd agree to prescribe opioids to you, correct?"

"Yes, I knew that."

"And Mr. Lynch asked you whether you violated it, right?"

"Yes, he did."

"And you testified that you were selling drugs. So you violated it, right?"

"Yes."

"But you never said to Dr. Holden, 'I'm violating your pain management agreement, right?"

"Of course I didn't!"

"You deceived him, right?"

"Right."

"You wanted him to believe the exact opposite, which was that you were complying to the letter of this agreement, correct?"

"Yes, that's true."

"Because you had a gambling addiction to support, right?"

"Yes."

"So you were highly motivated to deceive your doctors?"

"Yes, I was."

"And one of the ways that you would deceive them is that you knew when you needed to take your medication in order to have a good drug test, correct?"

"Correct," Thorn said with barely hidden pride.

"Now, there were other drug tests that Mr. Lynch didn't show you, and those were good, right?"

"Yes, those were good."

"Sir, is it true that Dr. Holden sent you for a few nerve conduction tests?"

"Yes. They all revealed severe nerve damage."

"And he constantly checked the intensity of your pain, correct?"

"Yes, he did."

"Did he also treat you with non-opioid injections?"

"Yes, he did."

"And did he always discuss your current condition with you so that he and you together could design a treatment plan based on what was working for you?"

"That's true. He did."

"At some point, Dr. Holden was concerned about you taking opioids for a number of years, and he talked to you about tapering your OxyContin, right?"

"He did."

"He had tried all sorts of alternative therapies that didn't seem to help you, correct?"

"Correct."

"So in May 2006, Dr. Holden suggested tapering you off opioids and having a procedure done at a hospital in an attempt to block the pain through surgery?"

"Yes, he certainly did."

"He sent you to a leading expert in the area, a doctor in Worcester, to consult about this procedure, correct?"

"Yes, he sent me to see Dr. Baron for that."

"But the doctor told you that, unfortunately, you were not an appropriate candidate for this treatment, right?"

"Yes, he said that in my case that procedure would be too risky."

"So without that as an alternative, you went back to Dr. Holden, right?"

"I never left Dr. Holden."

"And your pain hadn't gone away, had it?"

"I have had it 24/7 for years."

"In addition, Dr. Holden referred you to the Mass. General Hospital Pain Center for consultation and a second opinion, correct?"

"He did."

"And that other physician confirmed the seriousness of your condition, correct?"

"Correct."

"And based upon the recommendations of that other physician, you continued to be treated by Dr. Holden, correct?"

"As I said, I was with Dr. Holden right to the end."

"Mr. Thorn, let me ask you a few questions on a different topic. Isn't it true that you were an avid gambler, and although from time to time your pain was unbearable, you sacrificed your body and sold some of your medication to pay your gambling debts?"

"That's true."

"And you deceived Dr. Holden and Nurse Practitioner Lander by not disclosing to them your gambling addiction and selling pills?"

"Yes, I deceived them."

"And I want to ask you a couple of questions about what it is that you're in jail for. In 2009, 2010, and 2011, it wasn't just a matter of writing a few prescriptions with other people's names that you were caught doing and ultimately found guilty of, is that right?"

"You could say that."

"As I understand it, you were convicted of 50 counts of identity fraud?"

"Correct," Thorn answered without batting an eye.

"And another 45 counts of fraud for obtaining and possession of non-prescribed controlled substances?"

"Right," Thorn said with conviction, as if he were going through a job interview and was attesting to his recent performance.

"You tricked CVS into giving you the names of 50 CVS customers, didn't you?"

"I didn't trick anybody."

"Well, did you get the names of 50 CVS customers?"

"More like 500," Thorn said with conspicuous pride, and for the first time broke into a half-smile. "But if you say 50, that's fine by me."

"500? Okay. And you used that information, right?"

"You better believe it."

"I don't want to belabor it, but you're 60 years old now?"

"Yes."

"And that wasn't the first time that you had engaged in activity like that, correct?"

"Not at all."

"And you have convictions going back to the year after you became an adult for things like writing forged checks, right?"

"Yes, I do."

"Larceny by check?"

"Correct."

"Other instances of identity fraud?"

"Most definitely."

"I don't want to go through all of them, but on your record there are over 100 crimes, right?"

"Maybe more."

"There may be more that you committed, but you didn't get caught, right? So when you showed up at Dr. Holden's office in 2003, you were quite practiced in the art of deception, weren't you, sir?"

"Probably," smirked John Thorn.

"Well," Gould gave Thorn an acerbic look, "I have no more questions."

Elaine turned to her husband. "Ron," she whispered, "a convicted felon is brought in as a reliable government witness? Is this their normal practice?"

"I don't know," Ron whispered back. "I've never worked at any U.S. Attorney's Offices."

Chapter Thirty-Four

That Thursday morning, which was day 10 of the trial, the prosecutors called their most respectable witness, whose testimony they hoped would fortify their case against Dr. Holden and NP Lander and lead to the government's victory in this case.

"The government calls Dr. Chuck Finnegan," announced Prosecuting Attorney Dick Krokson.

A slim, medium-height man in his forties, clad in a perfectly tailored dark gray suit, comfortably positioned himself in the witness chair. Accustomed to public esteem, this expert cast a relaxed, self-assured glance at the courtroom audience in apparent expectation of approval when he suddenly stumbled over Emma's resentful look. He winced. Confusion and embarrassment flashed in his small, bluish eyes, and he instantly shifted his gaze from the gallery to Krokson. By that time, the prosecutor was already shuffling papers at the lectern across the room.

"Good morning, Dr. Finnegan," Krokson smiled courteously.

"Good morning, sir."

"Dr. Finnegan, could you please introduce yourself to the jury."

"Sure." The expert cleared his throat. "I'm Chuck Finnegan, a pain physician and the division chief of pain medicine at V. I. Medical Center."

"Dr. Finnegan, I want to talk to you first about your background and your training. Let's start with your formal education. Where did you go to college?"

"I graduated from Harvard with a BA in sociology. Then I finished Yale Medical School and had a surgical internship in New York, and after that I moved to Boston for surgery residency and got my medical license. Then I went to Wharton Business School and got my MBA."

"And what did you do after that?"

"I did a couple of years of venture capital investing in some biotech companies."

"But it was always your intention to go back to medicine, is that right?"

"One hundred percent. I returned to medicine in 2004 as an emergency medicine resident. Then later I did a fellowship in pain medicine, and in 2009 I got my Board certification."

"Now, sir, let's talk about pain medicine a little. What is the practice of pain medicine?"

"Don't forget," interrupted Judge Adler, "you're talking not about today, but about the time period from 2004 to 2007."

"Ending in May 2007 to be precise," added Edward Gould.

"Yes, ending in May 2007," confirmed the judge.

"Understood," said Dr. Finnegan.

"All right. What is the practice of pain medicine, Doctor?"

"The practice of pain medicine is trying to use all the treatments and diagnostic tests that we have available to treat patients' pain; to come up with a plan to safely and effectively treat their pain and try to improve their level of functioning. We do it because pain, certainly when it's severe, will interfere with the patient's level of functioning; if we can treat their pain and improve their function and do that safely, that's our goal," the expert raced through his speech, then stared at the jurors.

"Sir, you started with surgery, and then you moved to emergency medicine," continued the prosecutor, "but then you chose pain medicine as your field. Why?"

"If you think about what brings patients to a doctor or to a hospital, one of the principal things is to try to get relief for their pain, and I wanted to learn how to do that in the best possible fashion. I wanted to treat patients with acute pain and chronic pain and try to get them good relief and good return of function. I also wanted to learn how to do that in a safe way."

Emma shook her head. Isn't he here to drown two innocent people who had been doing exactly what he'd just described?

"All right," Krokson continued. "Now, when you began working in pain management in the summer of 2007, did you take on a leadership position?"

"Yes. In 2008, I became the director for the clinical trials at the center."

Alex turned to his wife, Susie, and whispered, "I wonder how he's achieved such a meteoric rise in his career."

"Sir, what type of patients did you see when you were the director? I mean in a socioeconomic sense."

"We saw the whole range, including homeless people, billionaires, and royalty. We saw them in the same place, and we treat them in the same way."

"So you were also serving as a director of clinical trials there, right?"

"Yes, for the first year, and then I was asked to serve as the director of the whole center. I was also running weekly conferences on interventional techniques."

"Sir, in addition to your administrative responsibilities, do you also teach?"

"Yes, I do. I am an assistant professor of anesthesia at Harvard Medical School."

"And do you participate in workshops and presentations and conferences?"

"Yes, I do."

"Do you belong to any professional medical societies, Dr. Finnegan?"

"I do. I belong to the American Medical Association, the Massachusetts Medical Association, the Anesthesiology Society of America, the International Spine Intervention Society, the North American Spine Surgery Society, and the American Society of Regional Anesthesia."

That's odd, reflected Ben. We have so many different pain organizations that help us to keep abreast with the latest developments in the field, and he, a medical director of a pain center, isn't a member of a single one?

Over the next twenty minutes, Krokson gave Finnegan ample opportunity to talk about editing and reviewing scientific articles for medical journals and about writing his own articles and chapters for textbooks. As if his administrative duties, teaching, and writing weren't enough for this busy man, he also served on quite a few important committees.

Does he have any time to see his patients? Ben wondered.

"So, Doctor, is it fair to say you're a busy man?" A broad smile of approval and admiration lit the prosecutor's face.

"I would say that's fair."

"Is the government compensating you for your time in working on this case?"

"Yes," responded Dr. Finnegan, with an awkward smile.

"Dr. Finnegan, what are the goals of pain management?" Krokson switched to another subject.

"The goal is to alleviate pain and by doing that to improve the patient's function."

"So Doctor, when patients first come in, they tell you what's going on, right?"

"That's right."

"And is part of your job as a doctor to try to assess the credibility of what it is they're telling you?" asked Krokson.

"Absolutely."

"Are there some unique issues in the field of pain management when it comes to assessing the credibility of what the patient tells you?" A trace of concern clouded Krokson's sugary voice.

"In pain medicine, there are some unique issues because we certainly encounter patients addicted to medications, in which case they lie to you because they want to get the medications that they are addicted to. They crave those medications. So, by definition, they would lie to you to try to get you to prescribe them. Part of the work is to be aware of that and to have the utmost vigilance for signs of abuse or addiction that might be taking place."

"Anything else, Dr. Finnegan?"

"Yes, doctors need to consider diversion, where patients are trying to convince you to prescribe narcotics, not so that they can take them but so they can sell them. Narcotics are very valuable, so for somebody on a limited income, that could be a source of money. Or they might take those medications and trade them for illegal drugs or for something else that they want."

"Counselor," Judge Adler addressed Mr. Krokson. "We have to finish earlier today. Are you about to finish your direct?"

"No, Your Honor, I'm not even close."

"Then let's resume it tomorrow."

"Sure, Your Honor."

* * *

The next morning was Day 11 of the trial.

"Now, Dr. Finnegan," continued Prosecuting Attorney Krokson, "As a medical doctor, could you please tell us, generally, what your obligations are with respect to your patients?"

"The first obligation is to do no harm. That's a fundamental principle of medicine that every physician learns in medical school. When you're looking at any treatment, your initial obligation is to say, 'Should we first make sure that we're not hurting the patient?' That actually dates back to the Hippocratic Oath. The next obligation is to make an informed diagnosis, with as much due diligence as you can, to form a treatment plan and to monitor the patient."

"What does a physician need to do in order to prescribe narcotic drugs?"

"Well, in order to prescribe narcotic drugs, also called opioids or controlled substances, a physician has to get a special certificate from the DEA, or the Drug Enforcement Agency."

"Now, Doctor, there are some substances that even physicians can't prescribe, right?"

"That's correct."

"Like heroin, for example. You can't prescribe that even if you're a doctor?"

"That's right. Heroin cannot be prescribed legally."

"Now, Doctor, there are risks and dangers that come with prescribing narcotic medicine, right?"

"That's correct. The DEA states that because of your training and expertise, you've been given the power to prescribe narcotics that have risks and are subject to abuse; with that comes the responsibility to make fully informed decisions about when it is appropriate and safe to prescribe those medications, and when it is not. You're getting a lot of responsibility with that authority, and that authority is not granted to you lightly."

"Doctor, could you list the types of drugs that are currently available for treating pain?"

Dr. Finnegan listed them at length, including opioids, commonly referred to as narcotics.

"Doctor, could you please explain to the jury what an opioid is?"

"An opioid is a class of pain medications that act to block pain signals transmitted through the spinal cord into the brain. They also can trigger reward centers in the brain. When this rewarding effect happens, people get a sense of euphoria. As a result, they often develop a craving for euphoria and, eventually, an addiction to that substance that can trigger it. Opioids are the most common substances that can cause addiction."

"Doctor, when you said 'euphoria,' did you mean the high that you can get from opioids?"

"That's exactly right, the high."

"So in addition to this high that opioids can cause, do they also create any other types of effects on the body?"

"Yes, they can make you sleepy. At excessive doses, they also can suppress your breathing. There are some other side effects too, including nausea and constipation."

"And when you say they can suppress your breathing, you mean they can kill you?"

"They can kill you."

Like any other medication if taken inappropriately or in excess, thought Ben, barely refraining from saying it out loud.

"In general, Dr. Finnegan, what role do opioids play in treating pain?"

"In cancer pain, which tends to be very severe and progressive, opioids are typically the cornerstone of treatment. In acute pain, for a short time, opioids will also be typically a main part of treatment. It's significantly more complicated in chronic pain because that condition is going to go on for a long time. So there are some instances where opioids are appropriate, and some when they are not. They have some significant drawbacks."

"By the way, a minute ago we talked about heroin being an illegal drug that doctors cannot prescribe, right?"

"That's right."

"But heroin is an opioid, right?"

"Yes, heroin is an opioid."

"Okay. What are the different types of opioids out there?"

"Those opioids that come from the opium poppy are natural, but some are man-made or synthetic."

"Now, Doctor, let's look at some opioid labels and inserts that come with these prescribed medications. Let's start with an oxycodone label from 2002. Could you please explain the call-out that is here on the screen?"

"It says, '***Drug abuse and dependence addiction: oxycodone products are common targets for drug abusers and drug addicts.***'"

"So regardless of the usefulness of these medications, this is something that, as a physician, you need to pay particular attention to?"

"Yes. The idea of these black box warnings is to give you a highlighted alert about a risk associated with a drug."

"Now I'd like you to take a look at another portion of that black box warning for OxyContin."

"Sure." The medical expert continued: ***'OxyContin tablets are to be swallowed whole and are not to be broken, chewed, or crushed. Taking broken, chewed, or crushed OxyContin tablets leads to rapid release and absorption of a potentially fatal dose of oxycodone. The drug is intended for oral use only. Abuse of the crushed tablet poses a hazard of overdose and death.'***"

"Is OxyContin a time-release medication?"

"Yes, it gets slowly released when you take it. People who are addicts will crush the pill and then either sniff or inject it so they can get the release of the entire drug in a short time period to get more of the euphoria or high."

"And you can potentially die from doing that, right?"

"Yes."

"Okay, let's look at another portion of the label that says, ***'Such drugs are sought by drug abusers and people with addiction disorders and are subject to criminal diversion.'*** What is diversion?"

"Diversion is when a patient is prescribed a medication, but rather than consuming it as it was ordered, he or she either sells or trades it, typically for other legal or illegal drugs. That's called diversion."

"As a doctor, why is that a problem?"

"With these medications, you're making a judgment about what's a safe dose for a given patient to take. You're most commonly prescribing a month's supply of the medication with the assumption that the patient is going to take it over the course of the entire month. If that medication gets subverted, you've passed a month's supply of it to a person you don't know. Therefore, you have no idea how this individual is going to take it. There's certainly a high risk that it will be abused and that the entire month's supply could be taken all at once, which would be extremely dangerous, even fatal."

"And just to be clear, diversion is not only the selling of the drug but also giving it to others or trading it, right?"

"Diversion could also be trading. It doesn't have to be selling."

For the next two hours, the prosecutor asked the medical expert endless questions about dangers of other drugs, such as fentanyl and methadone, and the necessity of extreme vigilance, especially with the patients to whom the doctor prescribed opioids. In Dr. Finnegan's opinion, vigilance was the cornerstone of pain management and the indisputable navigator in opioid prescription.

Dr. Finnegan glided through Krokson's direct like an ice skating champion in the Olympics finals. He never stopped even for a second to ponder his answers. His high-velocity performance seemed to make the prosecutor shine while most of the jurors, who at first were impressed by the man's credentials and polished presentation, now were yawning and nodding off.

All of a sudden, Krokson took a long pause, swiftly turned to the jurors and shot them a somber look that clearly read, Now, honorable members of the jury, pay attention!

"Doctor, one of the drug labels described this vigilance with respect physicians, right? Could you please describe the concept of vigilance and how it applies to you as a doctor when you are making decisions about whether to prescribe opioids to someone."

"Sure. As I said, we have to recognize 'red flags,' signs that a patient is abusing or addicted to medications. We also have to identify risk factors even before the patient has been exposed to those medications. So our job in making these decisions is to be very vigilant, to be looking for that sort of information, and then if we find it, weighing it into our decisions. We *have to* be vigilant. We have to know the red flags and studiously look for them. In whatever decision we make, we have to weigh those risk factors and red flags versus the patient's condition and potential benefits, and then we need to make the best reasoned decision that we possibly can about what's in the best interest of that patient."

The theme of "vigilance" became the linchpin of Dr. Finnegan's testimony.

The finale of Dr. Finnegan's direct examination by Krokson was devoted to his analysis of Dr. Holden's thirty medical files. Finnegan asserted that in twenty-nine out of the thirty medical cases he analyzed, Dr. Holden was not vigilant enough and was missing one red flag after another. All these red flags, according to Dr. Finnegan, had obviously pointed to opioid abuse or diversion. The patient who was involved in two car accidents over the five years of his treatment was, in Finnegan's opinion, definitely a drug abuser. The fact that another patient claimed that he worked two different jobs was a clear sign of abuse or diversion that Dr. Holden also missed. According to Dr. Finnegan, another patient was also a drug addict because he was attacked on the street, robbed of his money and medication, and then showed up at Dr.Holden's office the next day black and blue, and on Dr. Holden's request, provided a police report.

Then there were a few patients whose urine tests showed cocaine or marijuana. As drug addicts typically do, each of them swore it was a one-time blunder, but Dr. Holden still prescribed them opioids. In Dr. Finnegan's mind, it was another grave mistake. No, not a mistake, it was a crime. Their pain medications should have been stopped, and the patients should have been sent to an addictionologist. Instead of doing that, Dr. Holden gave them a second chance, which was further proof of his criminal actions.

In other cases, when the patients' urine tests didn't show the medications prescribed by Dr. Holden or NP Lander, that was an obvious sign of diversion. Dr. Finnegan certainly knew that there were a few legitimate reasons why medication would not be detected in the patient's urine, but he preferred to ignore them.

Dr. Finnegan didn't deny that all of these thirty people were legitimate pain patients, and he didn't rule out the fact that they could be in severe pain. He didn't even criticize any of Dr. Holden's treatments, but that wasn't the point. The point was that Dr. Holden didn't exercise vigilance in the required capacity. Therefore, in each of the twenty-nine out of thirty cases, including the six that were listed in the indictment, Dr. Holden prescribed opioid medications *that were not within the scope of the usual professional practice and not for legitimate medical reasons.* That was Dr. Finnegan's firm conclusion and, if accepted by the jury, Dr. Holden would end up in prison for the rest of his life.

Ben locked eyes with Finnegan and felt his stomach grinding. This witness wasn't a rookie IRS agent, who had no clue about pain management, or a detective, who had been sent to his office as an undercover agent and then in his report "accidentally" skipped all the facts that testified to Ben's honesty, professionalism, and good faith. Neither was this witness one of his former patients who had sold their prescribed medications and whose credibility was more than questionable. No, this time the witness for the prosecution was a well-educated physician with an impressive background and a prestigious administrative position at one of the best hospitals in the area. The jurors—at least those who by the end of the direct examination weren't napping—probably believed his every word.

"Nothing further," announced Krokson with a smug half-smile.

Emma turned around and looked at the clock over the exit. Ten minutes left before the end of the session. It looked like Krokson's slow pace wasn't accidental. He was intentionally dragging out his direct so that Gould didn't have a chance to start his cross. No doubt, this testimony was a smashing blow to the defense. Everything good that had been said about Ben, Julia, and their practice before was just wiped out by this expert's accusations. Emma looked at the jury box. She could not read a single emotion on their faces. The jurors would now be dismissed for the weekend, and they would leave this room with an image of Ben as a drug dealer. This hideous image, implanted in their heads by the government expert, would take root within the next two days...

"Mr. Gould," the judge's voice broke through her despairing thoughts, "we still have nine minutes left before the end of the session. Would you like to start your cross?"

"Yes, Your Honor."

* * *

Gould rose from his seat and hurried to the lectern.

"Good afternoon, Dr. Finnegan. My name is Edward Gould. I represent Dr. Benjamin Holden along with my colleague, Mr. Mark Daniels."

"Good afternoon."

"Dr. Finnegan, you told us that you were the chief of the pain medicine division at the V. I. Medical Center, correct?"

"Correct."

"Now, that medical center has a name, doesn't it?"

"It does."

"And the name is Westwood Medical Center, isn't it?"

"Yes, it is."

"So the center is named after Dr. Karen Westwood, right?"

"Correct."

"You regard her as one of the most prominent figures in pain medicine in the nation, don't you?"

"She's a well-known pain medicine specialist."

"And has been for years, correct?"

"She's been well known for years."

"Including the time period that we're talking about in this case, correct?"

"Yes, she was well known during that period."

"Dr. Westwood actually founded the first pain clinic in the area thirty years ago, correct?"

"Correct."

"She is also a national and international authority in the field of pain management, who for decades has extensively lectured on the subject of pain both in this country and abroad, correct?"

"Correct."

"In addition, did you know that Dr. Westwood has hundreds of publications in the most prestigious medical journals and magazines and her pain management textbooks are translated in more than thirty countries?"

"I wasn't aware of that, no."

"Now, Dr. Westwood is sitting right over there, correct?"

"Yes, she is."

"In fact, at some point she was your mentor, wasn't she?"

"Yes, she was."

"She's someone that you know personally, correct?"

"Correct."

"And you know that she is also Dr. Holden's and Nurse Practitioner Lander's medical expert in this case, correct?"

"I do."

"And you know that she's reached the exact *opposite* opinions of the ones you've been giving over the last two days, correct?"

The medical expert's face turned white. He involuntarily clenched his fists.

"I… I don't know all of her conclusions," he muttered. "But I… I assume that they might be significantly different from mine."

"Dr. Finnegan, you're entitled to your opinion, but that's what you are expressing here, just your opinion, right?"

"I believe I'm expressing more than my opinion. I believe I'm expressing a consensus view in the field of pain medicine because it's based on risk/benefit and on 'do no harm,' which are concepts that have been present for many, many decades."

"Well, we'll get to 'do no harm,' hopefully before my seven minutes expire, but you do realize that there's a significant difference of opinion between you and Dr. Westwood regarding this case?"

"Yes, I do."

"And that difference of opinion includes the validity of certain red flags, correct?"

"I don't know her opinions on the red flags," Finnegan's eyes flashed with malice.

"The government hasn't told you?"

"Not specifically about the red flags."

"You have a difference of opinion as to how a pain physician during the relevant time period should have responded to someone with legitimate pain who also shows signs of diversion or abuse, correct?"

"Yes."

"And you know that this issue was being hotly debated in the medical community during the relevant time period, right?"

"I can't answer it with a simple yes or no."

"Do you deny that there was a debate going on in the pain management community during this time period as to how to handle someone who is suffering from legitimate pain who also presents evidence of misuse or diversion? Please answer yes or no, sir."

"I'm very happy to answer the question, but I can't answer it with a simple yes or no. There are always debates in fields of medicine."

"No, no." Judge Adler gave the witness a stern look. "You've got to answer the question."

"Yes, there were debates at that time in pain medicine about the fine points of how you would treat one patient with a given condition, but not regarding the issues that we're talking about here."

"Okay, we'll spend some time on that later. Now let's talk about what you were doing during the relevant time period. You've already testified that you know Dr. Westwood actually practiced in the area during this time period, correct?"

"Correct."

"Now, as I understand it, during 2000, 2002, and 2003, you weren't even in the field of medicine, were you?

"No, I wasn't."

"You were a senior associate at a venture capital firm. You were a venture capitalist, right?"

"That's correct."

"And in 2001 and 2002, you weren't even in the country. You were abroad, correct?"

"That's correct."

"And you didn't even start your fellowship in pain medicine until July 2007, a month after Dr. Holden's practice was raided and closed, right?"

"That's correct."

"So you did not work in pain management during the relevant time period, correct?"

"Correct."

"Now, you've testified a lot about 'do no harm,' and I think it's important that before the jury goes home for the weekend we talk about what was being said about 'do no harm' in the context of pain medicine. You're familiar with the book *Responsible Opioid Prescribing, a Physician's Guide* by Scott M. Fishman, M.D., correct?"

"I am."

"This book didn't come out until 2007, correct?"

"Correct."

"And this particular book is one of the three sources that you cited in your 150-page affidavit that the government prepared for this case, correct?"

"Correct."

"Actually, this 150-page affidavit that you signed and presented as your report on this case was not originally written by you, correct? It was written by the government, right?"

"Correct, I didn't write it," Dr. Finnegan agreed with some hesitation. "But I made some corrections."

"That's nice. But for now I'd like to read for you the opening words from Dr. Fishman's book that you cited in your affidavit. By the way, Dr. Fishman is a respected person in the area of pain management, correct?"

"He is."

"You wouldn't have cited him in your affidavit, would you, if he wasn't respected?"

"That's correct."

"On the direct, you talked about the Hippocratic Oath and the first rule of medicine, right?"

"I did."

"So here is the quote from Dr. Fishman's book.

Hippocrates' seemingly straightforward directive to "First do no harm" is anything but simple in today's medical practice. Nowhere

is its complexity more evident and vexing than in pain management with controlled substances—particularly with opioids. Patients in pain who rely on opioids for analgesia and improved function deserve access to safe and effective medication; to deprive them of optimal pain relief certainly does them harm.

Yet these same life-restoring medications carry the potential to do grave harm to patients who may be at risk for addiction and abuse. Significant quantities of prescription opioids are delivered into an illegal black market that puts millions of non-medical "recreational" users at risk of addiction and death—many of them young adults and teenagers.

Very few physicians are complicit in this criminal diversion, and there are no proven methods for preventing patients from deceptively acquiring prescriptions—pain, after all, is a subjective symptom for which there are no foolproof diagnostic tests.

"Are you familiar with those statements in Dr. Fishman's book?"

"I am." Dr. Finnegan's eyes darted to the clock above the door.

"Do you agree with them?"

The expert paused and fidgeted in the witness chair.

"Umm... not entirely."

"Well, you expressed such certainty about your opinions, but isn't it true, Doctor, that the Hippocratic Oath, the rule of 'Do no harm' is a little more complicated when it comes to pain management because of the various ethical issues involved for a doctor?"

"I think 'First do no harm' can be complicated in many different fields of medicine."

"Well, I'm asking you about the field of pain medicine, sir, which is what we're talking about here. Would you agree with me, as Dr. Fishman says, that nowhere else is the problem more vexing and difficult than in the area of pain medicine?"

"Oh, no. I would actually disagree with that," Finnegan's facial expression turned stony.

"Well, Dr. Westwood actually agrees with Dr. Fishman and disagrees with you." The expert, his jaw clenched, treated Gould with an implacable look. "Now let me just go to the last paragraph of Dr. Fishman's book.

Obviously, the content of this book cannot substitute for the commitment to relieve suffering. There is no debate among public health experts about the undertreatment of pain, which has been recognized as a public health crisis for decades. The cost of undertreated pain in dollars is astronomical, but the cost in human suffering is immeasurable. Turning away from patients in pain simply is not an option.

"That's the last paragraph, the ultimate conclusion of Dr. Fishman's book. Do you agree with that, sir?"

"I do," grudgingly admitted Finnegan.

"Is it time, Your Honor?"

"It's time," nodded the judge.

"I appreciate the nine minutes. No further questions at this point. Have a nice weekend, everyone. I look forward to continuing our discussion on Monday, Dr. Finnegan."

"We'll see you on Monday, Doctor, right?" Judge Adler turned to the expert witness.

"Yes, Your Honor," Finnegan's pale blue eyes flickered with uneasiness.

* * *

When the jury was dismissed and everyone but the defense team left the courtroom, Ben, smiling from ear to ear, walked to Gould and shook his hand.

"Thank you, Edward. These last few minutes were..." Ben paused, looking for the right word. "They were lifesaving."

"At least we tried to change the direction of the ship. I hope that this weekend the jurors will have food for thought not exclusively served by Dr. Finnegan."

Chapter Thirty-Five

Those people who watched Gould's ten-minute cross-examination of the government's expert before the weekend apparently had spread the word, and on Monday morning—day 12 of the trial—a much bigger crowd gathered in the courtroom to witness the next stage of the cross.

"Good morning, Dr. Finnegan," Gould opened the cross.

"Good morning."

"When we left off on Friday, we were talking about 'Do no harm.' Do you recall that?"

"I do.

"Now, you had talked during your direct about keeping the patient safe, and that's the important part of the 'Do no harm' concept, correct?"

"That's correct."

"And part of keeping the patient safe is keeping them as healthy and functional as possible, correct?"

"That's correct."

"So I want to talk to you about the effects of chronic pain on an individual. That's something you've seen during your career, correct?"

"It is."

"Is someone who is in chronic pain at risk for sleep disturbances, anxiety, and depression?"

"They can be."

"They're also at risk for loss of normal body function, correct?"

"They can be, yes."

"And it can be extreme? Some people, for example, can barely get out of bed in the morning as a result of chronic pain, correct?"

"That can happen, yes."

"And it can be so extreme, that left untreated, someone can be at risk of suicide, correct?"

"There's some chronic pain conditions that are associated with a higher risk of suicide."

"So if someone who is in chronic pain and is suffering from anxiety or stress or depression, part of the 'Do no harm' is to help them avoid those negative outcomes, correct?"

"If possible, yes."

"And it also means protecting their families against some of the negative consequences of those outcomes, correct?"

"Correct."

"So, let's get 'real world' about this. If the father or mother is in chronic pain and is undertreated and can't work, the family might not have money for food, and it could be that they have to go on welfare. So there's a societal interest in treating chronic pain, all as part of this 'Do no harm' concept, right?"

"Right."

"Dr. Finnegan, would you agree that all you've done in reading the files of Dr. Holden's patients is that you read cold files?"

"I read the medical records."

"You never talked to any of these patients or put your hands on them?"

"That's correct."

"You never interviewed any of his patients about their pain, right?"

"Right."

"You never talked to their families about these patients' lives at home and whether they could get out of bed in the morning, correct?"

"Correct."

"You didn't examine any of the thirty patients whose records are in that box, did you?"

"I did not examine those patients, no."

"Well, I'm asking you, Dr. Finnegan, because last week you kept talking about the need to investigate before you make a treatment decision, right?"

"For the decision how to treat the patient, yes."

"So, even without examining any of these patients and without interacting with them or their families, you formed opinions about how they should have been treated, right?"

"I wasn't... I'm not the physician who was treating those patients."

"That's true. Still you came here to this courtroom and rendered your opinions without doing any of the investigatory things that I've just listed, correct?"

"Objection, Your Honor!" jumped in Krokson.

"Sustained," said the judge.

"Now, let me ask you, Doctor, to assume the following hypothetical situation: a 35-year-old man has been involved in a serious car accident and, as a result, he suffers two herniated disks with nerve involvement. Are you with me so far?"

"I am."

"Would you agree that suffering two herniated disks with nerve involvement is a painful condition?"

"Yes, I would."

"Now, the individual goes to the emergency room initially and is given a two-week supply of Percocet. He works as a cabdriver and is the sole support of his wife and three children, so he needs to go back to work. Are you with me so far, Dr. Finnegan?"

"Yes, I am."

"Now, after his initial two-week supply of Percocet is exhausted, this man buys Percocet from someone on the street because he is in pain. Under your definition of abuse, that would be abusing the drug, correct?"

"Correct. A patient who is illegally buying the drug..."

"Doctor, all I needed was 'correct.' You told us on direct that that was your definition of abuse. One day, six weeks after the accident, the man can't take it anymore, so he goes to a pain doctor. He brings his medical records from the emergency room visit confirming that there was an accident, and he tells his doctor the whole story, including the purchase of Percocet on the street. He also tells the doctor that he is in severe pain and that Percocet is really helping him. Are you following me?"

"I am."

"Now, is it your opinion, Doctor, that the physician cannot prescribe Percocet to that patient?"

"No, Percocet can be prescribed only if the doctor puts in place a meticulous system for vigilantly monitoring that patient, including frequent test results, pill counts, and short-term visits. So the doctor could either not prescribe him opioids or could prescribe them in the setting of a meticulous, well-documented monitoring plan."

"Now, Doctor, prior to 2007, cite a single peer-review article that says that."

"This was the consensus in the field, as seen—"

"That's not my question, Doctor. Tell the jury a single peer-review article prior to May 2007 that says what you just said."

"I would point to the guidelines from the Federation of State Medical Boards about opioid treatment."

"Okay. I'm glad you did because there is nothing that you just said either in the Board of Registration in Medicine or in Federal Model Policy Rules, right, sir? Nothing!"

"I disagree."

"Could we have Exhibit 128, please? *The Massachusetts Board of Registration in Medicine Prescribing Practices, Policies and Guidelines as of August 1, 1989, amended December 12, 2001.* Do you see it?"

"Yes."

"It says, '***Where the physician has reason to suspect the patient's motives but the physical examination and patient history indicate that the patient's complaint may be based upon a legitimate physical or physiological condition, the physician can lessen problems of noncompliance by prescribing the smallest possible amount of the drug pending confirmation of the patient's ailment.***'

"It's a provision endorsed by the American Medical Association explicitly in the Board guidelines, and there isn't a word about any of the measures you insisted on, right?"

"Still, it calls for vigilance."

"But it looks like your interpretation of vigilance is entirely different from theirs. Now, are you familiar with the concept of pseudo-addiction?"

"I am."

"Would you agree with me, sir, that in the hypothetical I gave you, the individual who bought Percocet from someone on the street for a legitimate problem would fit within the definition of pseudo-addiction?"

"That would seem the most likely explanation, but in a setting of possible pseudo-addiction, you would always increase your level of vigilance."

"The man seems to be obsessed with 'vigilance,' Ron whispered to his wife Elaine. "Why in the hell has he chosen a medical career? He would have made a perfect DEA agent."

"He still can," Elaine whispered back. "He's changed his careers before."

"Now, let's go back to the 'Do no harm' concept, continued Gould. "With Percocet on board, this hypothetical patient is feeling much better than before; he works full time and his family relations have improved. Over the next few months he takes a couple of urine drug tests and they are good, but then a year later his urine test shows cocaine. The man swears that it was a one-time slip and insists that he is not a drug addict. He begs his doctor not to stop his pain medication. What would you do?"

"I would taper him off the medication."

"But he needs it to work and to provide for his wife and three kids. So you think it's in the best interests of the patient at this point to take him off opioids and send him back into the street to buy Percocet? Is that how you understand 'Do no harm'? Is that your testimony, sir?"

"Yes, it is."

"And now, let's say, Percocet isn't available on the street. You've left that person at risk for buying other street drugs, like heroin. Is that an acceptable risk to you as a physician who's charged with doing no harm?"

"Objection!" Krokson interjected.

"Overruled," said Judge Adler.

"Yes, I would insist on tapering him off his Percocet because it is too dangerous to continue to take it."

"But another doctor might consider it much more dangerous to send someone out on the street to find medication to self-medicate because they have two herniated discs with nerve involvement and a wife and three kids to feed. You'd agree with that, wouldn't you, sir?"

"I'd agree that a different doctor might make a different judgment from the first doctor."

"And that decision could be made in good faith, right?"

"Right."

"And that's because we are not talking about cold files now, but about real human beings."

Dr. Finnegan didn't reply.

"Well, in some situations like our hypothetical one, Dr. Holden gave his patients a second chance. Yet you accuse him of not properly documenting his reaction to his patients' infractions because, in your opinion, everything that happens during the patient's visit has to be documented, correct?"

"Correct."

"So if Dr. Holden met with my hypothetical patient, that 35-year-old cabdriver and had a conversation with him after his test came up positive for cocaine, and the individual was in tears saying, 'Doctor, I'm not a drug abuser. It was a onetime thing because the pain meds wore out. I needed something to help me with my pain. Please, please continue to treat me with the opioids,' and Dr. Holden didn't write down the fact that the man was in his office crying, that might be an error in his documentation, right?"

"Correct."

"Yet the fact that it's not documented in a treatment record doesn't mean that it didn't happen, correct?"

"You're saying that just as a statement about the world?"

"I'm saying it as a statement about your testimony, Dr. Finnegan. The fact of the matter is that just because Dr. Holden didn't write down the fact that the person was crying in his office and begging to treat him with pain medications so that he could go back to work doesn't mean it didn't happen, right?"

"Correct."

"It means it just didn't make it into his record, right?"

"Correct."

"Now, Doctor, didn't you testify under oath in your own affidavit that there were no specific written regulations, guidelines, or standards prescribing how medical practitioners should respond to a particular patient presentment? It's in paragraph 31 of your affidavit, correct?"

"Correct."

"So, you are accusing Dr. Holden of violation of laws and regulations that didn't exist, correct?"

Dr. Finnegan pursed his lips, his eyes smoldering with fury.

"Now let's go to the document titled *The Massachusetts Board of Registration in Medicine Prescribing Practices, Policies and Guidelines* and see what it says about prescribing opioids. The Drug Enforcement Administration has issued these general guidelines for prescribers of controlled substances, Schedules II through V. These guidelines have been endorsed by the American Medical Association. *'Guideline No. 1: Controlled substances have legitimate clinical usefulness, and the prescriber should not hesitate to consider prescribing them when they are indicated for the comfort and well-being of patients.'* Have I read that correctly?"

"You have."

"So the very first guideline is to tell physicians that, where needed, they should prescribe opioids, correct?"

"Correct."

"It also says, '*Prescriptions for controlled substances in all schedules should be prescribed and filled pursuant to the professional judgment of the practitioner and the pharmacist, in good faith, and in the usual course of professional practice and treatment.*' So it's a judgment call, a professional judgment call, right?"

"That's correct."

"And, by the way, the word 'vigilant' doesn't appear in that sentence, does it?"

"Not in that sentence, no."

"And if the doctor suspects their patients of abuse or diversion, they don't recommend cutting them off from their medication; they recommend giving them small dosages of it, pending confirmation of their ailments, right?"

"Right."

"Now, Doctor, you know from those patient files that Dr. Holden repeatedly sent patients to reconfirm their diagnoses through diagnostic testing, correct?"

"He did."

"He did it through MRIs, nerve conduction tests, and X-rays, correct?"

"That's right."

"Sometimes sending his patients to orthopedic surgeons to get another opinion, correct?"

"Correct."

"Sometimes referring them to a psychologist or a psychiatrist to see if there was an emotional or psychiatric genesis to the problem, correct?"

"Correct."

"And those are all things that physicians do in the usual course of medical practice in good faith, correct?"

"Those are some of the things that physicians do in the course of usual practice and good faith, yes," Dr. Finnegan agreed.

"And that's what the Board of Registration in Medicine said to do in the provision that I just read to you, correct?"

"I think you and I have a different reading of the Board of Registration in Medicine," said Finnegan.

"I have no doubt about that. But let me read a little more.

> ***Notwithstanding progress to date in establishing state pain policies, recognizing the legitimate medical uses of opioid analgesics, there is a significant body of evidence suggesting that both acute and chronic pain continue to be undertreated. The undertreatment of pain is recognized as a serious public health problem that results in a decrease in patient's functional status and quality of life and may be attributed to a myriad of social, economic, political, legal, and educational factors, including inconsistencies and restrictions in state pain policies.***

"And that's something that the Board of Registration was telling doctors as of 2004 when it adopted this model, correct?"

"Correct."

"Then the Medical Board goes on to say, ***'Circumstances that contribute to the prevalence of undertreated pain include, number one, lack of knowledge of medical standards, current research, and clinical guidelines for appropriate pain treatment.'*** Do you agree with their statement?"

"I do."

"Let's read more: ***'Number two: the perception that prescribing adequate amounts of controlled substances will result in unnecessary scrutiny by regulatory authorities.'"*** Do you agree that this is an issue?"

"I do."

"And just to translate, this statement means that sometimes doctors are afraid to prescribe opioids because they're afraid of being prosecuted, right?"

"Correct."

"And that's a problem in medicine, isn't it, doctors acting on fear rather than on what's in the patient's best interests?"

"It's a problem if a doctor who is appropriately and conscientiously prescribing is afraid to do so."

"So it wouldn't be appropriate and conscientious to make a treatment decision based upon a fear of being prosecuted, right, as opposed to the patient's actual medical needs?"

"Correct."

"Now let's read the next page. It says, ***'The revised policy notes and the state medical board will consider inappropriate treatment, including the undertreatment of pain, a departure from an acceptable standard of practice.'*** So doctors practicing during the relevant time period, when they looked at these written guidelines, would say to themselves, Holy mackerel, I better not undertreat pain. The Board is telling me that undertreatment could be a deviation from the standard of care, correct?"

"That is one point in the document."

"And I don't mean to be repetitive, but just since it's mentioned in a second place in the same paragraph, the guidance to physicians says, ***'Pain should be assessed and treated promptly, and the quantity and frequency of doses should be adjusted according to the intensity, duration of the pain, and treatment outcomes.' And also, 'Physicians should recognize that tolerance and physical dependence are normal consequences of sustained use of opioid analgesics and are not the same as addiction.'*** Have I read that correctly?"

"You have."

"And this is something that Mr. Krokson didn't read to you on direct?"

"No, he didn't."

"Mr. Gould," interrupted Judge Adler. "Would you mind if we break for lunch now?"

"Not at all, Your Honor."

* * *

The day was too pleasant to spend their lunch break inside, so they brought their sandwiches, salads, and drinks to the lawn in the back of the courthouse. Ben quietly watched the tiny silver waves of the bay rustling back and forth beyond the green as he sank into memories of his last fishing trip to the Cape, the trip that had a big chance to actually being his last one.

"Ben, is it true that in the past few years most of the pain clinics in the country stopped prescribing opioids for their pain patients?" Alex interrupted his reminiscing.

"Yes, most of them did. Doctors are too frightened to prescribe. They don't want to lose their licenses or worse, end up in prison. So many pain patients are now left without desperately needed pain medications."

"It's a shame." Alex pondered that thought for a moment. "But if opioids are out of the picture, what else can pain clinics offer? Cortisone shots?"

"Not only shots. Many clinics are now focused on invasive procedures, such as implantation of morphine pumps, electrical spinal cord stimulators, radiofrequency nerve ablation, and some other stuff. In the last few years these treatments have replaced almost everything else they'd used before."

"Do these procedures help?"

"Like most other treatments, sometimes they help and sometimes they don't. All of them have significant risks associated with the intervention itself, such as a possibility of infection, bleeding, and nerve damage. Technical malfunctions can happen, too."

"And if the procedure fails, then what?"

"If it fails, the patient's suffering is usually much worse than it was before the procedure."

"Wait a minute," Ron turned to Gould. "Edward, didn't Dr. Finnegan say that he was an intervention specialist?"

"Yes, he did."

"Does it mean he is doing all these procedures that Ben has just listed?"

"Yes, he is focused primarily on these invasive treatments," Gould nodded.

"So Finnegan performs procedures that are not always effective and quite dangerous, yet on the direct he expressed his deep concern for his patients' safety!" Ron exploded.

Alex shook his head, "Well, friends, it looks like we have to do whatever it takes to stay healthy."

* * *

"Now, Dr. Finnegan," Gould continued his cross, "do you remember what Dr. Fishman said in his book and that you cited in your affidavit and I quoted before, about how to tell the difference between a legitimate pain patient and an addict?"

"Not exactly."

"He says that the key thing in differentiating between a legitimate pain patient and an addict is assessing improved functionality, correct?"

"He said that improved functionality is important in pain management, but he didn't say it particularly regarding addiction."

"Are you sure about that?"

"Sure."

"Well, let's read what Dr. Fishman wrote in his book.

> ***When given adequate pain relief, persons in chronic pain can gain or maintain function in their lives. Addiction, on the other hand, involves drug use that causes dysfunction in one or more spheres of a person's life. Addicts have a disease that impairs their ability to control or modulate their use of a drug despite the dysfunction and harm that it incurs. In the setting of active addiction, function does not improve with exposure to the drug.***

"Have I read that correctly?"

"Yes, you have."

"So, what he's telling a practitioner, like Dr. Holden, is that, you know what, those who are addicted, when you give them opioids, they don't improve. They don't go back to work. They can't get out of bed in the morning and go to the bathroom without crawling. Their functions deteriorate. But a legitimate pain patient's functions improve. Do you agree that this is what he's saying?"

"Yes, but it's only one of the patient's assessments, and none of the assessments is perfect."

"Nothing in this world is perfect, Doctor. We can agree on that. Now, let's talk about the thirty files that you were given to analyze. You didn't select those files, did you?"

"No, I did not."

"You are aware that the government possesses approximately 2,200 files from Dr. Holden's practice, aren't you?"

"I knew there were a lot of files. I didn't know the number until you said it."

"But, nevertheless, those files were selected by the prosecutors, correct?"

"Correct."

"And you have no idea what criteria they used to select those files, correct?"

"Correct."

"Did you ask?"

"No."

"I believe you said on direct that in order to understand what's going on with a particular patient, you have to gather as much information as you can."

The medical expert shot Gould a grim look and didn't reply.

"Well, did you think it was appropriate before coming here to give an expert opinion on behalf of the government to understand the criteria that was used to select those files?"

"No, I didn't think it was necessary."

"Really?" Gould shook his head. "Now, you told us on your direct examination that if you had a question about toxicology, you'd pick up the phone and call a toxicologist. Did you do that with regard to these thirty files?"

"No, I did not."

"Now, let's talk about the report that you gave in this case, Dr. Finnegan. It's actually titled *Affidavit of Chuck Finnegan, M.D.* Do you have that in front of you?"

"I do."

"And it is 151 pages long, excluding your CV, correct?"

"Correct."

"And I think that you told us that you read every word of this before you put your name on it and signed it under penalty of perjury, correct?"

"That's correct."

"Now, you didn't write this report, did you?"

"No, I did not."

"The U.S. Attorney's Office wrote the report *for you,* correct?"

"That's correct."

"I'm going to put on the screen a letter from the U.S. Attorney's Office sent to us before this trial. Isn't it true, sir, that there were pages in your affidavit that had to be corrected?"

"That's true."

"Would you agree with me that it is inappropriate to form an opinion based upon suggestions from the U.S. Attorney's Office as to what your opinion should be? Yes or no?"

"Objection," interfered Krokson.

"Sustained," said the judge.

"Would you agree with me, Dr. Finnegan, that your opinions in this case are only as good as the information provided to you?"

"Yes, I would."

"Now, the government didn't provide you with any of the grand jury testimony of the witnesses or their own interviews with them in this case, correct?"

"Correct, they didn't."

"As part of the investigation of Dr. Holden and Nurse Practitioner Lander's treatments of these patients, did you ask to see those materials before you formed your opinion?"

"No, I did not."

"Well, during your direct examination, you said repeatedly that there might be a benign explanation to something that you saw in the files, but it had to be investigated further, right?"

"Correct."

"Did you try to investigate any of these instances?"

"No, I did not."

"For example, I'm talking about people who may finish their medication several days early because they doubled up for a few days since they were in severe pain. That happens all the time, doesn't it?"

"It's a known red flag, which you have to look into as a possible sign of abuse or diversion."

"Please focus on my question, Dr. Finnegan. Red flag, green flag, or purple flag, it happens all the time, doesn't it?"

"It doesn't happen all the time. It happens on occasion, yes."

"And one explanation for a drug test that doesn't show the presence of prescribed opioids is that a patient finished the prescription early, right?"

"Yes, but that is also a sign that the patient—"

"Okay, thank you, Doctor. We don't need to argue."

"Doctor," interrupted Judge Adler. "We're trying to get through your testimony, so if you can answer yes or no, please do that."

"Now, do you know that out of the thirty patients whose files you reviewed, seven of them were discharged from Dr. Holden's practice?" asked Gould.

"No, I did not know that."

"That information wasn't provided to you by the government, right?"

"No, it wasn't."

"Well, they probably forgot. Now, let's talk about patients who scam their doctors. You know about this problem concerning opioids, right?"

"Do I know that patients lie to their physicians in order to get drugs? Yes. I know it."

"And it is an issue because doctors are trained to believe their patients, aren't they?"

"No. Doctors are trained to listen to their patients, but they should also verify their statements with independent information where appropriate."

"Well, Doctor, am I correct that you were at Mass. General Hospital for a period of time?"

"Yes."

"And you'd agree with me that it's one of the finest hospitals in the world, right?"

"I would."

"Are you familiar with the document titled *The Massachusetts General Hospital Handbook of Pain Management, Second Edition*?"

"I am."

"It is written by Jane Ballantyne, M.D. She's someone whom you cited earlier, right?"

"Correct."

"I'll post page 74 on the screen, which states that ***'The assessment of pain can be challenging and intensive, but it is an essential component of pain management, and it allows the pain physician to devise optimal treatment for some of medicine's most complex patients.'*** Do you agree with that statement written by Dr. Ballantyne and her colleagues?"

"Yes, I do."

"Then it goes on to say, ***'The patient must be treated as a complete person and not just at a painful location. Believing the patient and establishing rapport are of the utmost importance.'*** So this was in the guidebook at Mass. General Hospital while you were there, right?"

"It was."

"And it's written by someone whom you respect, Dr. Ballantyne, right?"

"I respect her, but I disagree with her on that point."

"So there can be disputes among doctors about how to approach this issue of trust, right?"

"Right."

"And this is an area where you and Dr. Ballantyne part company?"

"Yes."

"Okay, Dr. Finnegan, would you agree with me that no matter what safeguards pain management doctors put in place, they can still be scammed by their patients?"

"Yes, I would."

"And to protect themselves from scammers, doctors physically examine their patients, send them to take diagnostic tests, to consultations with other physicians, and so on, right?"

"Right."

"And from the files you've analyzed you know that Dr. Holden did all of that, correct?"

"Correct."

"More than that, if the patient didn't have health insurance, he called the MRI center and asked them to perform the MRI at a very low cost. Did you see that?"

"I did not know that, no."

"Dr. Holden also referred his patients to chiropractors and physical therapy offices, and he offered them quite a few non-opioid treatments and exercise classes right in his center. Did you see that?"

"Yes."

"And if Dr. Holden assumed that some of his patients were abusing drugs, he referred them to an addictionologist, and if the patients refused, he discharged them from his practice, correct?"

"In some cases, yes."

"Now, we've talked a lot about what you did and did not find in the patients' records of Dr. Holden and Nurse Practitioner Lander and how you essentially relied on what you could see, right?"

"Right."

"Now, you'd agree with me that each and every one of the drug tests that you've discussed on your direct was actually in the patient's file, correct?"

"Yes, the ones I've discussed were in the patient's file."

"They weren't destroyed?"

"They were not destroyed."

"They were actually put in the patient's file, and that's why you were able to see them, right?"

"That's right."

"Dr. Finnegan, with regard to urine drug tests, would you agree that during the relevant time period there was disagreement as to how they should be interpreted and used?"

"That's true, but that's different than the topics that came up in the thirty cases that I reviewed."

"Well, the debate had to do with whether they were reliable or not, and if they were not, could they produce an inaccurate or false results about the patient, correct?"

"Correct."

"So all your testimony regarding the drug tests could be based on unreliable results of these tests, correct?"

The medical expert opened his mouth to respond and paused, lost for words.

"Which means that so-called 'bad tests' can have alternative benign explanations, correct?"

"Whenever you see a red flag, you look into it; there are possible benign as well as non-benign explanations. That's what I've said repeatedly."

"But whenever you saw a bad drug test in the files of Dr. Holden's patients, you always assumed abuse or diversion, right?"

"Yes."

"By the way, are you familiar with Dr. Larry Michalek?"

"I am."

Ben and Mark Daniels exchanged swift glances. Dr. Michalek was another medical expert expected to testify for the prosecution, but at the last moment the prosecutors figured out that he shouldn't testify because of the statements in his signed affidavit. Michalek's statements were precisely opposite of the ones he'd made before in his presentations or medical publications.

"And is Dr. Michalek someone whom you regard as an authority in the area of pain medicine?"

"He's a respected pain physician, absolutely."

"Do you follow his articles and contributions to the field?"

"I do."

"Well, let me just show the article where he is the lead author, published in February 2007 in *The Clinical Journal of Pain*. Did you read this article?"

"I did. I'm familiar with this article."

"Okay, let me post it on the screen. So you see these lines about the fact that pain afflicts one in five adult Americans and accounts for twenty one percent of emergency room visits and twenty five percent of annual missed workdays? Then the author states that several studies have confirmed the usefulness of opioids in the treatment of chronic pain. Do you agree with those statements?"

"Yes, I do."

"Now, if you turn to page 177, you'll see that Dr. Michalek cites some studies and comes to the conclusion that judgmental biases and reliance on red flags to predict opioid misuse may prove to be wrong. Do you see that?"

"Yes, I do."

"Dr. Finnegan, on your direct you were asked numerous questions about red flags, drug tests, and prescriptions, but not a single question about how Dr. Holden's treatments helped his patients to improve their functionality and live better lives, correct?"

"Correct."

"By the way, none of those things are reflected in your 151-page report either, correct?"

"Correct."

"So let's just be clear. When your 151-page affidavit was drafted by the government based upon your 'very careful' input, did you make the decision to leave out any mention about the patients' diagnostic tests and their results and any mention of their improved functionality? Who made that decision?"

"I made that decision because—"

"You've answered my question, Doctor. Thank you. Nothing further, Your Honor. Tomorrow morning Mr. Daniels will take over."

* * *

"Edward, I don't get it," Ron said to Gould when they all walked outside. "How come this rather young medical expert dares to disregard the opinions of the most respected medical professionals in the field, especially with his minimal experience in pain management at the relevant time?"

"Well, the government recruited him to slander Ben and his practice, even if it means to disagree with the commonly accepted views of the national authorities in pain management. His job is to implant in the jurors' minds the prosecutors' agenda. Unfortunately, no matter how unfounded the government's accusations might be, many people believe that if the federal government charges someone with a crime, it has to be trusted on that. This perception is very hard to shake, let alone to reverse."

"Edward, I think you are doing a great job rocking it to its foundations."

"Who knows if it works? Thank you for the compliment anyway. Please come tomorrow for Mark's cross. You won't regret it."

* * *

The next morning, which was day 13 of the trial, the government's medical expert was back for the cross by the Defense Attorney Mark Daniels.

"Good morning, Dr. Finnegan. My name is Mark Daniels, and I represent Dr. Benjamin Holden."

"Good morning."

"Doctor, on the direct, you said that ceasing to prescribe opioids to a patient who exhibits drug-aberrant behavior is an indication of good faith, right?"

"Yes, I did."

"You also testified that in very carefully reviewing Dr. Holden's files, you didn't find any indication that he or Nurse Practitioner Lander tapered off and ceased prescribing opioids to quite a few of their patients, correct?"

"In some specific cases?"

"Yes, in some specific cases. If you had found that Dr. Holden had ceased prescribing opioids even to one of these thirty patients, you would have put that in your affidavit, right?"

"I... I might have."

"There were seven cases like that, among those thirty files you analyzed, but you didn't report any of them in your affidavit, did you?"

"I... I didn't include every single point of information in my affidavit."

"But ceasing prescribing opioids to a patient with an aberrant behavior is a major event in the physician/patient relationship, correct?"

"It can be a major event, yes."

"And, as you testified, it's relevant to the consideration of whether or not a doctor is acting in good faith, right?"

"It would be relevant information, yes."

"Now, as an example, let me show you an office note from Mr. Ferranti's file written at the very end of his relationship with Dr. Holden. He writes, *'The patient will be taking Ambien at night and Advil or Motrin during the daytime. No more opioids will be prescribed.'* Do you see that?"

"I do."

"And you know that after this point, Dr. Holden never prescribed opioids to Mr. Ferranti, right?

"Right."

"And you know that he did that in response to what had been apparently aberrant drug behavior exhibited by Mr. Ferranti, correct?"

"I believe that he did do it in response to that behavior, yes."

"But neither the government nor you included this fact in your 151-page affidavit, right?"

"Correct."

Then Daniels methodically reviewed the other files where Dr. Holden ceased prescribing opioids to other patients who showed aberrant drug behavior, demonstrating to the jury how Dr. Finnegan failed to report that fact again and again in his affidavit.

Daniels then discussed the thirty patients, including the six patients who died, mentioned in the indictment. Daniels asked Dr. Finnegan questions about the severity of these people's injuries, their inability to sleep or work, and their depression and declining relationships with their spouses and children, which were all caused by unbearable pain. Dr. Finnegan reluctantly agreed that following Dr. Holden's treatments, all of these thirty patients, who had been cherry-picked by the government, could sleep better and perform daily activities, and almost all of them eventually went back to work.

Step by step, Daniels forced Dr. Finnegan to admit that Dr. Holden's treatment of his patients testified to his good faith. However, no matter what Dr. Finnegan was talking about, he just couldn't refrain from playing his favorite tune again and again. Never trust your patients. If they said they were sleeping better, it could be a lie. If they said they were feeling better, they could have deceived you. The patient said she was satisfied with the treatments; she possibly tried to scam you. Essentially, anything the patients said could be a lie, as their ultimate goal was to get more opioids, and that's why nothing the patients said should be trusted.

"Doctor, I believe you saw in some of these thirty files that, whenever possible, Dr. Holden reduced the dosage of his patients' pain medications, right?"

"I did."

"And that's also an important indication of a doctor acting in good faith, right?"

"That could be, yes."

"Because every physician prefers having his patients on as low a dose as possible while still effectively keeping their pain under control and improving their functioning, right?"

"Correct, that's one of the goals."

"Also, if a patient agrees with the doctor's reduction of his pain medication and doesn't fight him regarding it, that's also an indication that this person isn't a drug seeker but a legitimate pain patient just looking for legitimate medical treatments, right?"

"Objection, calls for speculation," interjected Krokson.

"Overruled."

"It could indicate that. It could indicate many other things as well."

"Dr. Finnegan, would you agree that all thirty patients that we discussed had legitimate, wel-documented, and rather severe medical conditions?"

"I would."

"Doctor, would you agree that all those painful conditions required adequate medication treatment to alleviate them?"

"Most of them might."

"And would you agree that as a result of Dr. Holden and Nurse Practitioner Lander's treatments, including non-opioid medications for insomnia, anxiety and depression, all of these patients were able to live normal lives, sleep better, and perform daily activities, and almost all of them eventually went back to work?"

"I would." The medical expert replied under his breath and shot another glance at the clock above the door.

"And despite these facts, do you still insist that the discussed treatments, including prescriptions for opioid medications, were not issued for legitimate medical purposes and not within the course of legitimate medical practice?"

"Yes, I do," Dr. Finnegan stubbornly muttered.

"Nothing further, Your Honor." Without another look at the witness, Daniels collected his notes and left the lectern.

* * *

Outside in the hallway, Ron approached Daniels, "Mark, could you please explain to me what's going on here? I'm stunned. I know that drug abuse is a serious problem in our country. I also know that because pain doctors prescribe opioids, they become a tempting target. It looks like they are now nothing short of scapegoats. I've known Ben for years, and he is not just my close friend, he used to be my doctor. He helped me a great deal. Every time I came for an appointment and sat in the waiting room, I would hear stories that his patients told—"

"What were they saying?" asked Daniels.

"They said that Dr. Holden saved them from unnecessary surgeries, got them back to work, and helped them to avoid disabilities."

"Well, we've interviewed many of his patients, and that coincides with what they said. So what is your question?" said Daniels.

"It's very simple. In his three-day testimony, Dr. Finnegan portrayed Ben as a monster who willingly harmed so many people. It was nauseating. Why would he do that?"

"The government didn't start this trial to present Dr. Holden with a Doctor of the Year award," Daniels stated sadly. "And they didn't call Dr. Finnegan to the witness stand to sing Dr. Holden's praises. Since the start of their investigation, it was never their intention to find anything good about him or his practice. Their objective was to find evidence of his criminal activity, but when they found none, they had to find somebody who could portray Dr. Holden and Nurse Practitioner Lander as reckless, malicious criminals. So they invited Dr. Finnegan, who disregarded the facts that testify to Ben and Julia's good faith and offered his personal opinions as proven and accepted professional standards, blatantly disregarding the views of the most respected specialists in the country."

"Do you think the jurors have bought into his distortions and misrepresentations?"

"I hope they haven't. But who knows?"

"Mark, how do you explain this war on opioids? They were successfully used by physicians all over the world for thousands of years to treat all kinds of pain, and then in a flash they became pariahs?"

"That's exactly what happened."

"But as a general practitioner, I know that after many years of observing the benefits and side effects of opioids, their major side effect, addiction, was estimated as one percent or less, which is by any standard extremely low. Over the last twenty years, the most respected pain physicians have recommended opioids for pain."

"That's also true. I read that their significant benefits were confirmed by extensive research presented in numerous publications."

"Exactly. Then, almost overnight, opioids were proclaimed villains and essentially labeled as poison. Doctors and patients, stay away! How come?"

"Welcome to the world of politics, my friend," Daniels sighed dolefully.

"If the government continues this witch-hunt," said Julia, "there won't be any doctors left who will agree to provide people in pain with legitimate and effective help. Then what choice would they have? In their frantic search for pain relief, they will go to people on the street and buy cocaine, heroin, or other dangerous stuff and face the risk of overdose or even death."

"True," Ben agreed. "They will either suffer unbearable pain or do just that. They know that this stuff can kill, but they are at the end of their rope and don't see any other way out."

"Or, as I read in the *NY Times* and *The Guardian*," Eileen added quietly, "they commit suicide, and that number is more than those who suffer from diabetes, heart disease, and cancer combined."

They all fell silent and started moving to the elevator, suddenly craving fresh air.

Chapter Thirty-Six

It was Day 14 of the trial. That cool summer morning, Ben and Emma arrived at the courthouse later than usual, and when they approached Judge Adler's courtroom, on the bench right next to the entrance, Ben saw a familiar figure. He slowed down and stopped, dumbfounded like he was a traveler in the desert, startled by an optical illusion. This man couldn't be a witness for the prosecution. Or could he?

"Ben, we have to hurry," Emma gently pulled his sleeve. "It's five minutes to nine."

The man on the bench offered Ben an inconspicuous smile and a nod as a silent greeting.

"Who is he?" Emma asked when they entered the courtroom.

"He's my former patient." Ben frowned. "It's a long story. I'll tell you later."

The judge entered the courtroom, the jurors filled the jury box, and the trial session began.

"The government calls Alexander Singer," announced Lynch, and a tall, dark-haired man in his late thirties slowly limped to the witness stand. Leaning on a cane, he was forcing his every step. With visible difficulty, he lowered himself into the witness chair.

"Good morning, Mr. Singer." The prosecutor shot his own witness an unusually stern look.

"Good morning," the man replied with a cold stare.

"How old are you, Mr. Singer?"

"Thirty-nine."

"Are you presently employed?"

"No, I am totally disabled."

"Sir, I'm going to apologize for the next few questions, but we just need to move through them. Are you recovering from a drug addiction?"

"Yes."

"And what were you previously addicted to?"

"Painkillers, cocaine, alcohol."

"Are you taking something to help with your addiction?"

"Yes, I take Suboxone."

"Does this Suboxone affect your ability to testify?"

"No, it doesn't."

"Sir, you just testified that you had some prior issues with opioids?"

"I did because I had severe back problems."

"Sir, is it true that you believe that Dr. Benjamin Holden helped you?"

"Yes, absolutely."

"And how did he help you?"

"He tapered me off pain meds."

"Off your addiction to pain meds?"

"I was... I was overmedicated by my former doctor."

"And then Dr. Holden took steps to help you with that?"

"Yes, he did."

"And how did he do that?"

"He slowly tapered me off."

"And what kind of drugs was he tapering you off?"

"OxyContin, Valium, Percocet. I mean, I was really overmedicated."

"So at the time that you came to Dr. Holden, you were overmedicated?"

"Yes."

"And who was the doctor that treated you before Dr. Holden?"

"Dr. Lidia Ambrosi."

"And what was she treating you for?"

"Chronic back problems. I was addicted within months."

"And what were you addicted to?"

"I think the first thing I got addicted to was OxyContin. If I ran out, I'd feel it physically."

"And was it OxyContin that you were abusing when you were seeing Dr. Ambrosi?"

"I started to abuse it, yes."

"And how were you abusing it?"

"I would chew it sometimes."

"Now, sir, when you were chewing the OxyContin pills, did you understand that chewing them could be dangerous?" Lynch looked at the witness with parental concern.

"I did understand it was dangerous, but it relieved my pain much faster."

"Did you understand it could kill you?"

"Yes."

"Yet you kept doing it?"

"I understood that if I took too much it would kill me, but if I didn't take enough, it would not help my pain, so I had no choice. It helped the pain at that time, and that was all I cared about."

"Did Dr. Ambrosi share her office with any other doctor?"

"Yes, with Dr. Holden."

"At some point, do you remember whether Dr. Ambrosi tried to wean you off opioids?"

"It didn't happen. One day she said, 'That's it. I'm not treating you any longer.'"

"Did she tell you why she was dropping you?"

"She dropped me like she dropped every single pain patient she had in that office. She left to work at another place."

"So you went to a new doctor?"

"Yes. Dr. Holden knew my issues. He'd seen me too. He talked to me, and he talked to my father. My father would sometimes bring me in a wheelchair to see Dr. Ambrosi because that's how bad my pain was. Dr. Holden knew my diagnosis. He knew I was crippled. He knew I wasn't there for recreational pain meds. In the beginning, I was there for my pain only."

"At that point, though, you were addicted to pain meds, correct?"

"Yes."

"And do you remember telling Dr. Holden that you were overmedicated and wanted to be weaned off them?"

"Yes."

"When you saw Dr. Holden for the first time, did you and he discuss why you'd been discharged by Dr. Ambrosi?"

"I don't remember. But I do remember that he was very considerate and compassionate toward me. He understood that I was going through a tough time. That's why I think he took me in. He saw that I was suffering."

"Did part of that tough time involve your overmedication?"

"Yes."

"Did he talk to you about tapering you down on that first appointment?"

"We had a conversation about weaning me down, yes."

"Your Honor, I think Mr. Singer has some serious back issues, and he may occasionally need to take a quick break, or probably stand up for a minute or two," suggested Lynch.

"I have no problem if you stand." Judge Adler gave the witness a friendly look.

"I have neuropathy. Sitting and standing are quite difficult for me. I can bear pain as much as I can, but sometimes it gets excruciating..."

"Stand up and stretch any time you need to, and if you need a break, we'll have a quick one. I don't want to keep you here for another day," said Judge Adler.

"Thank you, Your Honor, I'll do that."

"Do you remember your first meeting with Dr. Holden?" continued Lynch.

"Like it happened yesterday."

"Okay, do you remember being drug tested at Dr. Holden's office?"

"Yes."

"Did you ever discuss the drug tests with Dr. Holden?"

"We probably did, but I don't remember; it was more than ten years ago."

"Do you remember if he ever referred you to some treatment program at Faulding Hospital?"

"Yes, he did, and as soon as I was discharged from it, I wanted to see Dr. Holden."

"So sir, I think you stated that you'd been weaned off all opioids at that point?"

"While at Faulding? Yes, which I shouldn't have been. They did it without my consent and without Dr. Holden's knowledge."

"And when you went to Dr. Holden, did you talk about your time at Faulding?"

"I told him that I was in much more excruciating pain when I got *out* of that program than ever before. After I left, that program was closed down within months because many patients complained about it. I wound up in a nursing home for three months after it. The Faulding doctors should have at least done my MRI and blood work. That would have helped them to find out that I had a disk infection that whole month. When I got out of that program it was a nightmare."

"When you went to Dr. Holden that day, what did you talk about?"

"I don't remember the entire conversation, but Dr. Holden immediately saw that there was something very wrong with me because I could barely walk. He instantly sent me to Newton-Wellesley Hospital for an MRI, and they found out that I had a large abscess in my spine. A few more days of delay and I would probably be dead."

"Did you say that at Faulding you'd been weaned off opioids?"

"I was completely weaned off them, yes. I had a big abscess in my spine, and all they did was take me off pain medications. They didn't even bother to send me for any diagnostic tests."

"Now, sir, you mentioned that because of the treatment in the Faulding Program you ended up in a nursing home for three months. While you were there, did you receive opioids?"

"Yes, because my pain was unbearable."

"Okay. And were you receiving opioids over that whole period?"

"Of course."

"Do you remember how long you were going to Dr. Holden's office?"

"Until the middle of 2006."

"And over that time period, you continued to receive opioids from Dr. Holden, correct?"

"Yes, but much less than before. I went from a high dose of OxyContin to methadone. In my eyes, that's a way of tapering off slowly."

"Sir, at some point, did your family take steps to send you to a drug rehab program?"

"Yes. It was a tough psychological period for me."

"Did you discuss that period with Dr. Holden in relation to receiving opioids?"

"Sure. We talked a lot about my life and my health and, of course, my pain."

"Were you allowed to take drugs in that program?"

"In that program? No."

"And when you got out of the program, did you go back to Dr. Holden's office?"

"I think I came back once."

"Did you get drugs?" Lynch's features hardened.

"I think for one month."

"And what did you get?"

"I think he gave me a few methadone pills to get by. I was still in *severe* pain."

"Nothing further," Lynch frowned and left the lectern.

"Let's have a fifteen-minute break and then reconvene for the cross." The judge turned to Mark Daniels, "Are you ready, Counselor?"

"Yes, Your Honor."

* * *

When the judge left the courtroom, Ben turned to Daniels, who was still scribbling notes on his legal pad, and waited until he finished.

"Mark, do you have any idea why the prosecutors brought Alex Singer to testify? He didn't say a single bad word about me or our practice. What was their intent?"

"To fortify our defense?" Mark suggested with a straight face.

* * *

"Good afternoon, Mr. Singer. My name is Mark Daniels, and I represent Dr. Ben Holden."

"Good afternoon, sir."

"Mr. Singer, are you in pain today?"

"Yes, I am."

"Can you describe your pain?"

"It's torture. I have neuropathy. I had two back surgeries, and they messed up on the first one and damaged my sciatic nerve. I also have diabetic neuropathy and arthritis in my joints, and my feet swell up, so I'm in constant pain."

"And you went to Dr. Holden to treat that pain?"

"Yes, to treat it better than it was treated before and, at the same time, to reduce the opioids."

"Mr. Singer, when did you first have issues with your back?"

"When I was seven years old. I had a traumatic event."

"What happened?"

"I went to... I don't know if anybody ever remembers Brett Gillari's Karate Schools..."

"I do," said Judge Adler.

"The very first week at Brett Gillari's, I landed on my back, and I was almost paralyzed. I couldn't bend my back for half a year. I was seven years old. Growing up after that, I had chronic back pain. Then one day when I was fifteen, I was shoveling snow and I hurt my back. My MRI showed a tear in my lumbar disc. My pain became even worse. I tried to live with it, but it was unbearable, and eventually I went to see Dr. Lidia Ambrosi."

"And then later you went on to see Dr. Holden to treat your pain?"

"Yes."

"Do you believe that Dr. Holden was doing his best to treat you medically at every visit?"

"Yes, one hundred percent."

"And what is that belief based on?"

"I respected his professional way of treating me. He diagnosed me with a very serious back condition. He knew... he knew that I was... I was very sick."

"And you actually credit Dr. Holden with saving your life, right?"

"Absolutely."

"Why is that?"

"Because of what he did for me. Dr. Ambrosi just kicked me to the curb, and he picked me up. When I started seeing Dr. Holden, I wasn't ready to be taken off the pain meds. I simply couldn't. But I was addicted to them not because of Dr. Holden, but because of me. He helped me to stop. You know, I tried but... fighting my addiction is one of the hardest things I've ever done in my life."

"Why do you say that?"

"Because it's physically and mentally... unbearable. It gets to the point where you feel hopeless. But I did it somehow. When Dr. Holden helped me, I was clean from opioids for about three years. Then I hurt my back and had another operation. That's the reason I'm on Suboxone."

"So Dr. Holden was treating your pain but also helping you to slowly taper off your pain medication, correct?"

"Yes, absolutely, especially off OxyContin."

"And you knew that it was very difficult to taper down your pain medication, right?"

"Yes."

"Why was that?"

"Once I was in physical pain, I also was in mental pain and became addicted to pain meds. I mean, it's like a vicious circle, like chasing your own tail."

"How did your pain impact your functionality on a day-to-day basis?"

"Severely. I couldn't do things when I was in pain. I couldn't take care of myself. Some days I couldn't even get out of bed."

"Did you ever tell Dr. Holden anything about your drug abuse?"

"No, I would never do that. I was in so much pain. I hid it. If I told him I was addicted to cocaine and alcohol, he wouldn't have prescribed me the pain medication that I needed."

"When you first went to see Dr. Holden, you had trouble even walking around, right?"

"Yes, I could barely move."

"At some point you began to use a wheelchair, right?"

"Actually, I was bedridden. I couldn't even get out of bed. I went to physical therapy for three months to learn how to get from my bed to a wheelchair and from the wheelchair to a walker. It was before I went to Dr. Holden. I was only twenty-eight years old then."

"And when you first started seeing Dr. Holden, were you working?"

"I don't think I was."

"Here is an office note dated May 28, 2005, which states: *'With pain medicine on board, Mr. Singer is able to work part time and perform his daily activities.'* This was sometime after you'd started being treated by Dr. Holden, correct?"

"Yes."

"Was doing part-time work and performing daily activities an improvement in your life?"

"Yes, definitely, especially compared to what I could do before."

"And in general your back and leg pain also decreased, correct?"

"Yes, no doubt about it."

"Let me read a bit more from another office note of that period: *'Alexander Singer was diagnosed with severe left-side radiculopathy. His pain is well controlled, and he's able to work 30–40 hours a week, sleep well at night, and ambulate well without a cane.'* Do you recall that by the summer of 2005 you were also able to walk without a cane?"

"Yeah, I was."

"And that's also a substantial improvement after Dr. Holden started treating you, right?"

"Big time."

"As you testified on direct, at some point you spent three months in a nursing home, correct?"

"Yes."

"And doctors at that nursing home prescribed you opioids, correct?"

"They didn't hesitate to do that. They knew exactly how much pain I was in."

"And that pain medication enabled you to function on a day-to-day basis?"

"Yes. Nothing else worked."

"So it is fair to say that after all those surgeries and therapies, opioid medication was the only thing that controlled your pain and allowed you to work full time and lead a normal life?"

"At that point in my life, pain medication was the only thing that allowed me to get out of bed. I couldn't survive without it."

"You also said that by the end of your treatment with Dr. Holden, he had significantly tapered down your pain medication, correct?"

"Yes, sir, he did."

"And you were still able to work?"

"Yes, and I was a happy camper those days."

"Mr. Singer, in general would you agree that while under Dr. Holden's care your life became much better?"

"One hundred percent," Alex Singer answered.

"No further questions," Daniels gathered his notes and returned to his seat.

Judge Adler dismissed the jurors and left the courtroom. So did the prosecutors. Alex Singer awkwardly rose from the witness chair and moved into the aisle, leaning heavily on his cane. Yet instead of heading to the door, he slowly walked to Dr. Holden, gave him a gentle smile, and shook his hand.

* * *

That afternoon, Ben and Emma's friends, who showed up in the morning, had to leave by the lunch break. Ben, Emma, Julia, and Arthur went to the cafeteria alone, bought sandwiches and bottles of iced tea, and walked outside to savor their lunches in the open air. The day was warm and pleasant, and right in the middle of the large lawn adjacent to the back entrance of the courthouse, a guitarist was playing familiar pieces. Soothing melodies accompanied by the light breeze from the bay were soaring over the green. An unanticipated treat.

Twenty minutes later their short respite was over, and they headed back to the courtroom.

"A good trial day so far," Ben took another glance over the glittering ocean and walked inside.

"You mean Alex Singer's testimony?" asked Julia.

"Yeah."

"I think the whole trial is going well," said Arthur. "All the testimonies sooner or later turn out to be in your and Julia's favor."

"That's true, but the trial is not over yet." Ben paused. "Still, a good day is a good day."

They entered Judge Adler's courtroom and instantly sensed something askew. The session had not started yet, but the judge was already on her bench. All the defense lawyers and prosecutors were at the sidebar, and Lynch's face was raspberry-red. Krokson and Hustler looked tense and dismal. Gould noticed Ben and Emma and hurried to them, his expression a mixture of amusement and concern.

"Edward, what happened?" asked Ben.

"One of the jurors found a copy of the *Boston Veritas* in the jury room, with a reader's letter about you and the trial. The newspaper was left on the table, and the piece was circled."

"Have you read it?"

"Yes, I have," he said, a twinkle in his eye."It mentions you and argues that the government shouldn't persecute good doctors and leave pain patients suffering."

"That's why Lynch is angry as a raging bull. Can I read the piece?"

"Judge Adler has the newspaper, and I don't think she plans to give it to the defendants at the moment. She is trying to figure out how to deal with this rather peculiar situation. The prosecutors may demand a mistrial. I wouldn't be surprised if they do."

"A mistrial? We'll have to start all over?"

"Ben, calm down. The judge didn't make up her mind yet."

"Mary," Judge Adler's voice interrupted their talk, "please call the juror who found the newspaper. I want to hear the whole story."

The alternate, Juror #13, a heavyset woman in her early fifties, entered the courtroom.

"Ma'am, please tell us what happened this afternoon," said the judge.

"I saw a newspaper on the table in the jury room, with an article circled. I saw the headline... It looked like it was about this trial so I took the paper and brought it to the bailiff."

"Have you read the article?" asked Judge Adler.

"God forbid, no!"

"Have you discussed it with anyone?"

"No, I have not."

"All right. You may go."

When the woman left, Judge Adler turned to her clerk.

"Mary, I want to interview all the other jurors, one at a time."

One after another, the jurors were invited into the courtroom and asked the same questions: "Have you read the circled article in the newspaper? Has anyone discussed it with you?" Looking Judge Adler straight in the eye, all thirteen jurors answered 'no' to both of her questions.

After the last person left the courtroom, Judge Adler turned to the counselors.

"So what should we do?"

The prosecutors remained silent. Ben turned to Emma and met her fearful gaze. He could read her thoughts. If the judge declared a mistrial, everything that had been achieved so far would be lost. They would have to start all over. Where would they get the money for a new trial, let alone the stamina to endure it?

"Your Honor," Gould interrupted the silence. "If none of the jurors read the article, I think we should proceed with the trial."

Judge Adler didn't answer. She looked contemplative and was in no rush to make her decision.

In the silence of the room, Ben heard someone's hefty sigh.

"Well, after all," the judge paused for a very long moment, "I don't see any legal reason to declare a mistrial." She turned to the prosecutors. "Mr. Lynch, who is your next witness?"

"Miles Moore, Your Honor," muttered the lead prosecutor.

Chapter Thirty-Seven

A chubby man with thin grayish hair guardedly sank into the witness chair.

Miles Moore was a friend of another former patient of Dr. Holden, Ted Daley. Morbidly obese and totally disabled, Ted Daley was treated by Dr. Holden and NP Lander for over three years and then unexpectedly died at the age of forty-nine. None of his relatives were invited to testify for one reason or another, so his buddy, Miles Moore, was offered the honor.

"Good afternoon, Mr. Moore," prosecuting attorney Lynch began his direct.

"Good afternoon, sir." Moore fidgeted in the witness chair.

"Mr. Moore, are you recovering from a drug addiction?"

"Yes, I am."

"Sir, are you in treatment for that?"

"I'm in a methadone clinic, but I also have back injuries, so I was told to take methadone for my pain, and I get it from my doctor."

"Now, while you were abusing opioid drugs, where did you get the pills?"

"I bought them on the street."

"And did you ever buy any pills from an individual you knew as Ted Daley?"

"Yes."

"Sir, I'm showing you what's been marked as Government's Exhibit 121-D. Do you recognize the person in that photo, sir?" Lynch pointed at the blown up portrait of Daley on the overhead screen.

"I recognize him. It's my friend, Ted Daley."

"At some point did you make contact with Mr. Daley to get his pills?"

"I did, yes."

"And what did he sell to you?"

"He sold me OxyContin, Percocet, I think 10-milligram tablets, and fentanyl lollypops."

"Approximately how long did you get those types of drugs from Mr. Daley?"

"I would say for about two years."

"And while you were with Mr. Daley, did you ever see him take prescription drugs?"

"Yes, I did."

"What types of drugs did you see Mr. Daley take?"

"OxyContin, Percocet, fentanyl, whatever he was prescribed."

"Sir, you stated that Mr. Daley was selling you OxyContin, Percocet, and fentanyl, right?"

"That's right."

"Were you aware whether Mr. Daley also had multiple injuries?"

"Yes, I was well aware of that."

"And you were aware that he took pain medication for that?"

"Yes. He had a serious back injury and some other pains too."

"Did you take Mr. Daley to his last medical appointment?"

"I did, unfortunately... Ted couldn't drive by himself because of his bad knees."

"And do you remember where that appointment was?"

"Yes, it was in Dr. Holden's office."

"And how did you become involved with taking him to his last appointment?"

"Ted told me one day that he had an appointment coming up, and he asked me if I could drive him, and I said I could. I picked him up and brought him to the medical office."

"And what did you do once you went into the office?"

"I waited for Teddy until he came out."

"And what did Mr. Daley say to you after he came out?"

"He said, 'The nurse wants me to provide a urine sample, and my urine is dirty. Can you give me some of yours for this?' That's what he said."

"And when he asked you about the urine sample, did you say anything to him?"

"Yes. I said, 'Listen, mine isn't clean either, because I'm taking methadone. I go to a clinic, you know that.' And he said something like, 'Well, it's still better than what I have in my system. I have...' I think he said heroin and cocaine."

"Did he say how he was going to explain methadone in his urine if he was asked?"

"Yes. Teddy said that he could always say he ran out of his regular Percocets because his pain was too bad, so a friend gave him a few of his own methadones."

"So he asked you to take a urine test for him. Did you do that?"

"Yes, I did."

"Can you describe to the jury how that switch took place."

"Teddy walked out of the examination room, like I said. He had a cup in his hand, and we both went into the men's room, and I took the cup into one of the stalls and urinated in it."

"Now, was anyone supervising the urine test?"

"No."

"Do you know whether Mr. Daley got any prescriptions that day?"

"Yes, he did. He got a prescription... Well, he was very upset because he didn't get what he usually got. He didn't get the OxyContin. He got, I think, his regular Percocets. Again, my memory may be failing me, because it was quite a while ago. Anyway, they changed Teddy's OxyContin to methadone because they found he had methadone in his system."

"But in fact it was the methadone that you were taking, right?"

"Right, right."

"And did you go to a pharmacy that day?"

"Yes, we did. He got methadone and Percocet tablets, I believe."

"Were you present when Mr. Daley did anything with those Percocets?"

"He sold the whole bottle."

"Where did he sell it?"

"On the street."

"Now, while you were in the vehicle after he filled the prescriptions, did you and he have any discussions about methadone?"

"Yes, we did. Teddy was very upset because he didn't want methadone. He wanted the OxyContin that he used to get. And I told him, 'There's nothing you can do about it.' And then he started taking them."

"Did you see how many of those methadone pills he took?"

"Five or six at a time, at least."

"Did you make any statements to him about methadone?"

"I told him that methadone was a pain medication people should be very careful with."

"And how did you know about the danger of methadone?"

"Well, many years ago, before they took my license away, I was a pharmacist, so I knew."

"At some point, Mr. Moore, did you agree to help Mr. Daley sell the methadone pills?"

"I told him that I could probably sell them for him."

"And did you take some of those pills yourself?"

"I took only ten. I didn't swallow them, though."

"At that point, sir, you were getting methadone from your treatment program?"

"Yes, for my addiction, not for my pain."

"Did you drive Mr. Daley back to his residence?"

"Yes, I did."

"And the next day you learned that your friend died, correct?"

"Correct."

"No further questions," Lynch concluded his direct.

Judge Adler announced a short break and released the jury.

* * *

In the hallway Ben, Julia, and their friends gathered near the window facing the bay. These gatherings, which often included lively discussions of the trial, were becoming a tradition.

"Ben, Julia, this witness is mystery to me," said Alex. "What exactly did the prosecutors intend to prove by his testimony?"

"This man's friend, Ted Daley, was one of those six patients who died," explained Julia.

"Those six patients whose deaths the government blames on Ben and you?"

"Yes."

"But now, after the U.S. Supreme Court ruling, the law forbids them to do that, right?"

"Right, but the prosecutors never gave up on the idea of blaming us, even indirectly, for these people's deaths. That's the only reason they brought Daley's friend to testify."

"But if we can trust this witness," said Gail, "his friend's reckless behavior could be the direct cause of his death. This Ted Daley probably didn't even bother to check how many pills a day he was prescribed to take. He just took one pill after another."

"I think you are right. He simply didn't listen to our instructions or check the warning on the pill bottle," said Ben. "In addition, his blood toxicology also revealed the presence of large amount of cocaine metabolites. His autopsy report showed a grossly enlarged heart, damaged lungs, and morbid obesity. The exact cause of his death was far from clear."

"The guy had serious health problems, right?" said Alex.

"Quite a few. He fell from the roof, broke a few bones, and ended up with nine surgeries that left him badly crippled and in severe pain. That was before he came to see me. Then, two years later, while crossing the street, he was hit by a car, which wrecked his knees."

"Then a few months later," added Julia, "Ted was helping his friend mow the lawn, and he tripped over something, broke his shoulder, and perforated his lung with two broken ribs. He spent three weeks in ICU and barely made it. Yes, his pain was very real, and we treated him the best way we could. Time and again he would say to us how grateful he was. But he never brought up the fact that he supplemented his prescribed pain medication with illegal drugs."

"Did you have any suspicions?"

"None," said Ben. "Ted never missed his appointments, went to each and every consultation and test I'd referred him to, and agreed to all the treatments. By the way, other doctors who treated him before me never questioned his disability either, and they also prescribed him opioids. We thought he was an honest man. How could we know that he was a cocaine user and that he was selling some of the prescribed pills on the street?"

"So he'd cheated you out of his last prescription for methadone, and now this prescription may send both of you to prison?" asked Alex.

"It may," Julia frowned. "This particular methadone prescription actually appears in two out of the eight government counts. One count for Ben and one for me. Twenty mandatory years in jail for each count. Not a laughing matter."

Heavy silence filled the hallway.

"As they say, no good deed goes unpunished." Ben turned to Emma and met her strained gaze. "Okay, let's go back," he smiled awkwardly. "Maybe we still have a chance to survive."

* * *

Judge Adler turned to Julia Lander's defense attorney. "Counselor, are you ready for the cross?"

"Yes, Your Honor, I am." Peter O'Neil took long strides to the lectern. "Good afternoon, Mr. Moore. My name is Peter O'Neil, and I represent Nurse Practitioner Lander."

"Good afternoon." Moore wriggled in the witness chair, slight agitation in his watery-grey eyes.

"Sir, was methadone prescribed to you because you were addicted to opioids?"

"Yes, it was."

"So when you were initially prescribed methadone, it was in a drug treatment program, right?"

"Yes. It was at the VA clinic. I'm a veteran."

"Now, let's talk about your testimony regarding your friend Mr. Daley. You said that he had injuries that you were aware of, correct?"

"Correct."

"Do you know what originally happened to your friend, Mr. Daley?"

"I… I remember he fell off a roof and broke many bones in his arms and legs."

"And for those injuries Mr. Daley had surgeries—nine of them, to be precise, right?"

"That's what he told me."

"And you're aware that Mr. Daley weighted over three hundred pounds, right?"

"Teddy was obese, yes."

"And, in addition to his broken bones, he also had a back injury, correct?"

"Yes, his back was a mess too."

"And sometime later, after he was hit by a car, his knees were badly damaged as well, right?"

"No question about it. Teddy could barely walk. I mean, in the first couple of years after that fall, he used two crutches, but later on his doctor switched him to a cane."

"And you were convinced that he suffered from real pain, correct?"

"He suffered all right, yes."

"And did you believe that he had a need for narcotic pain medication to treat his pain?"

"I would say so, sure."

"Now, it sounds like you were aware that Mr. Daley abused drugs above and beyond the limits of what was prescribed to him, is that correct?"

"That's true."

"For example, you testified that on the day that you drove him to the pain clinic for his last appointment, he told you that he'd been taking heroin and cocaine, correct?"

"Correct. Sometimes his pain was very bad, so he had to."

"Did you ask him if Dr. Holden or Nurse Practitioner Lander were aware of that?"

"No, I did not, but at some point Teddy said that if either of them learned about it, he would be in trouble. Big trouble."

"Did he say what kind of trouble that would be?"

"He said they would most likely stop prescribing him any opioids or even dismiss him from their practice altogether. He said he saw with his own eyes how some people were dismissed because of their dirty tests."

"Did you know that on his last appointment your friend Ted was seen by Nurse Practitioner Lander?"

"Not specifically, no."

"But you knew that he didn't want that person to know that he had heroin in his system?"

"No question about it."

"Sir, let me ask you this: you actually agreed to be an accomplice in a scheme to mislead the people at Dr. Holden's office, right?"

"By giving the false urine sample?"

"Yes, by giving your urine sample instead of Mr. Daley's."

"Yes, I did."

"Because you knew that if Mr. Daley had given his own urine sample and it showed that there was heroin and cocaine in it, he wouldn't get his prescription, correct?"

"Objection, calls for speculation," Lynch intervened.

"Overruled. Tell us what you knew."

"I... I can't say I knew that for a fact."

"Well, what did you think was the reason why Mr. Daley was and saying to you, 'Hey, Miles, I can't give my urine for the drug test because I've taken heroin and cocaine'?"

"That my urine would be cleaner than his, I guess."

"And if he submitted yours, he had a chance to get the prescriptions he wanted, correct?"

"Correct."

"And you knew that he planned to lie, right?"

"Yes, I knew that."

"You knew that this lie was intended to deceive these professionals into thinking that the sample was Ted Daley's urine, when actually it was Miles Moore's urine, right?"

"Yes, I knew that."

"Now, you have experience dealing with street drug dealers, right?"

"Drug dealers?"

"Like people on the street who sell drugs illegally?"

"Objection, relevance," said Lynch.

"Overruled."

"Yes, I know some of them."

"And what kind of drugs have you bought illegally?"

"Opioids."

"Heroin too?"

"Umm, no, not me."

"Cocaine?"

"Thirty years ago."

"And whenever you dealt with these drug dealers on the street, did they demand that you take a urine test?"

"Objection, Your Honor, relevance!" Lynch jumped from his seat.

"Sustained."

"When you deal with drug dealers on the street, do they normally ask you whether you're taking illegal drugs?"

"Objection, your Honor, relevance."

"Sustained," ruled Judge Adler.

"Now, one thing you didn't do, Mr. Moore, after you gave your own urine sample to Mr. Daley, was that you didn't go and tell the people at the front desk, 'Hey, by the way, I just gave my urine as a sample to Mr. Ted Daley.' You didn't do that, did you?"

"Of course not. I'm not that stupid," Moore grinned broadly.

"And you didn't say those words because you knew that if you said them, Ted wouldn't have gotten the prescription that he wanted, right?"

"Yes, sir, that's right."

"So you were part of this scheme to mislead Dr. Holden's office, right?"

"Yeah, I guess."

"Now, you've been on methadone for a while, correct?"

"Correct."

"Are you on methadone today?"

"It's in my system from yesterday."

"And can you function normally when you're taking methadone?"

"Yes. I've been on it for a decade, and it works for me."

"So you're able to think clearly?"

"Yes, I am."

"Speak clearly?"

"Yes."

"Can you function well? If you'd had a job today, you could have done it while on methadone, correct?"

"Yes, I could have."

"You can live a normal life on methadone, correct?"

"Yes, I can."

"And does methadone help you with your pain?"

"It sure does."

"So as far as you're concerned, it's a good medication?"

"For my back pain it works best."

"When taken properly, it actually gives you a better life, correct?"

"It does, yes. If taken properly, it helps a lot."

"And it is the U.S. government program in the VA hospital that approved your methadone prescriptions for the last ten years because with methadone you can live a normal life, correct?"

"Yes, sir, this is correct. It's much cheaper for them too."

"Nothing further, Your Honor," Peter O'Neil concluded his cross.

Chapter Thirty-Eight

Day 15 of the trial had now begun.

"Do you know who is the government's first witness today?" asked Alex when he, Emma, and Ben headed to the courtroom next morning.

"I believe it's Saad Habib," said Ben.

"Why do you think they called him?"

"Beats me." Ben shrugged. "He was my patient for two years and then was discharged from my services. He never tested positive for anything illegal. Actually, he never tested positive for anything prescribed to him at all. Ben pondered. "He was a likable guy, polite and appreciative. Why the prosecutors have chosen him as their witness is a mystery to me. But I bet they will solve it in no time."

* * *

"The government calls Saad Habib," announced Prosecuting Attorney Matilda Hustler, and a short, plump man in his mid-fifties, in a bright orange outfit, escorted by a bailiff, strolled into the courtroom. He positioned himself in the witness chair with elegance and ease.

"Good afternoon, Mr. Habib," Matilda Hustler started soberly.

"Good afternoon, ma'am," the witness said, and a shy smile lit his round, amiable face.

If he weren't in a jail uniform, Emma mused, this man, with his pleasant features, well-mannered demeanor, and old fashioned glasses, could easily pass for an elementary school teacher or, better yet, for your friendly neighbor—a baker at a family diner.

"Mr. Habib, are you presently in a federal prison?"

"Yes, I am."

"Why?"

"Drugs and weapons."

"Were you convicted of felonies?"

"Yes."

"Were you a drug dealer?"

"Yes."

"What type of drugs were you dealing?"

"Pills. OxyContin, Vicodin, and stuff like that."

"How long have you been in federal custody?"

"Seven years."

"Have you previously served as an informant for the government?"

"Yes, I have."

"To be clear, you did not serve as an informant to the government in this case, correct?"

"No, I did not."

"Have you been offered or made any promises or inducements for your testimony today?"

"No."

"Have you ever been a patient of Dr. Benjamin Holden?"

"Yes, I believe about ten years ago."

"In 2004?"

"Yes."

"For what purpose did you start seeing Dr. Holden?"

"To get pills. I had to support my wife's drug habit."

"When you first became a patient at Dr. Holden's office, do you recall what you told him about your symptoms?"

"Yes, I said I had a few back surgeries and that I had bad chronic pain."

"Did you actually have chronic back pain?"

"Yes, I was in pain, but I learned to live with it."

"And what about your back surgery?"

"Yes, my first back surgery was performed in 1997. I had two more after that."

"I'm going to ask you some personal questions." Matilda Hustler cast an apologetic look at Mr. Habib. "Have you ever had any substance abuse problems?"

"Yes, I was a heroin addict."

"In the time that you were a heroin addict and later, did you also abuse prescription drugs?"

"Yes, I did."

"What type of prescription drugs did you abuse?"

"Percocet, Vicodin, some others."

"You're clean now, right?"

"Yes, I'm clean," the witness unleashed a cordial smile.

"Congratulations, Mr. Habib," Matilda Hustler nodded approvingly. "Now, I want to talk a little bit about your appointments with Dr. Holden. When you saw Dr. Holden, did he conduct any type of examination on you?"

"He asked me to bend, to see how far I could do it, and then felt my back and asked me if it hurt."

"Did he do any physical therapy with you?"

"Yes, he did."

"Do you have any specific memory of your first appointment with Dr. Holden?"

"I'm not sure if I brought my medical records the first time, or he asked me to get them. I can't remember."

"There's a statement at the very top of your first office visit that says, *'A 46-year-old gentleman with complaint of lower back pain.'* Did you tell Dr. Holden that you had back pain?"

"Yes."

"For what purpose?"

"To get prescriptions for drugs."

"Did Dr. Holden write you any prescriptions for opioids at his appointment?"

"I'm not sure exactly what he prescribed for me, but I got them from him."

"Did Dr. Holden ever explain to you the dangers of the drugs that he prescribed to you?"

"No, he didn't."

"What did you do with these drugs?"

"I gave some to my wife and then sold the rest to get more drugs for my wife."

"Who did you sell them to?"

"Just different people on the street."

"I have no more questions for this witness," said Matilda Hustler.

Judge Adler turned to Julia Lander's attorney, "Mr. O'Neil, are you ready for the cross?"

"Yes, I am, Your Honor," said the lawyer, and moving to the lectern.

"Good afternoon, Mr. Habib. My name is Peter O'Neil, and I represent Nurse Practitioner Lander."

"Good afternoon," the witness gave a taut smile.

"Sir, how did you become involved in this case?"

"I was contacted by FBI agents a couple of years ago."

"Where did they come to visit you?" continued O'Neil.

"At the Beaumont Jail in Texas."

"You were incarcerated there, correct?"

"Yes, I was."

"And when they came to visit you, what did they say to you?"

"That Dr. Holden was under investigation for giving prescriptions to people who passed away."

"When did they notify you that they wanted you to testify against him?"

"They told me that they were thinking about it."

"And what ran through your mind when they said they were thinking about asking you to testify?"

"Well, I didn't want to testify. I just don't want to be in this position."

"But you're in jail right now, correct?"

"Yes."

"And how much more time do you have to serve in jail?"

"Six more years."

"And do you like being in jail?"

"No."

"Do you want to be there for six more years?"

"No."

"You understand, sir, that there's at least the possibility that because of your testimony in this case, the government could make a motion to reduce your jail time. Isn't that true?"

"I don't know. We never talked about it."

"Well, you know that, sir, because you're in a federal prison with a bunch of other federal prisoners, and there is a law library there, and just about everybody there wants to get out, right?"

"Yes."

"And they talk about getting out all the time, right?"

"Yes, they do."

"Objection, Your Honor," Hustler intervened.

"Overruled."

"And you know that the prosecutors sitting at this table right in front of me can make what's called a Rule 35 motion to reward you for your testimony here today, and that may result in a judge reducing the remainder of your sentence. You know that, don't you?"

"Objection!" Hustler instantly rose out of her chair.

"Overruled."

"No, we never talked about it," responded Habib.

"But you know that from jailhouse gossip, right?"

"I believe my testimony here is... I'm just telling the truth... about what happened. I'm not here on anybody's side or nothing. Do you know what I'm saying?"

"Yeah. You just came here to tell the truth, that's all?"

"Yes."

"Well, we'll get to that. But you do know about certain possibilities from being a guy who has been in jail more than once, right?"

"Yes."

"You have been in federal prison more than once, correct?"

"I was on federal probation once before."

"And you have been the beneficiary of a government motion to reduce your sentence because of your cooperation with the government, right? You've already experienced that benefit, haven't you?"

"Yes."

"So you know that if you help the DA's attorneys, they can give you a shorter sentence, right?"

"It never crossed my mind."

"It never crossed your mind?"

"No."

"Okay. So let's go back into your history a bit. You mentioned to Ms. Hustler that you've committed some felonies, correct?"

"Yes."

"Sir, you've committed a lot of felonies, haven't you?"

"Yes."

"Do you know how many?"

"No, not exactly."

"In fact, you've been convicted of more than a hundred felonies, right?"

"Somewhere around there. I'm not sure."

"And you've admitted in the course of your FBI interview that you committed crimes that you've never been convicted for, right?"

"Yes."

"For example, you admitted that when you were down in Florida, as part of an OxyContin smuggling scheme, you were involved in falsifying identifications in order to get prescriptions fraudulently from pharmacies. You were involved in that, right?"

"Yes."

"And you were not convicted of that, right?"

"No, I wasn't."

"And you told the government about that, and nobody has charged you with that, right?"

"I think that it all came together with the whole case in Florida."

"So let's run through some of the hundreds of crimes you've committed. You committed assault and battery with a deadly weapon, correct?"

"Yes."

"You have been convicted many times of distributing controlled substances, correct?"

"Yes."

"You've been convicted of writing false checks numerous times, correct?"

"Your Honor," Hustler argued. "I object to the extent that he's not clear as to what the time period is for these convictions."

"That could take some time, but we can do that," O'Neil responded calmly.

"You're not going through more than hundred of them, are you?" Judge Adler looked concerned.

"No, Your Honor, I'm just going to give the jury a taste," explained O'Neil.

"But do you actually have the dates on them?"

"Sure, they are all there, Your Honor. You were convicted of assault and battery with a deadly weapon on July 30, 2003, in Chelsea District Court, correct?"

"Yes."

"You were convicted of possession and distribution of a Class A narcotic in Suffolk Superior Court on March 21, 2001, correct?"

"Yes."

"You were convicted of resisting arrest in Chelsea District Court on January 18, 2001, right?"

"Yes."

"You've been convicted of armed assault in Peabody District Court on January 11, 1999, right?"

"Yes. That was thrown out though."

"Larceny in Suffolk Superior Court on April 26, 1994, correct?"

"I guess, yes."

"Writing a bad check in Chelsea District Court on February 8, 2000, correct?"

"Yes."

"True name violation. What's a true name violation?"

"Giving my name wrong."

"Giving your name wrong to police officers and convicted of that crime in Wrentham District Court on May 31, 1990. Do you remember that?"

"Oh, yes, I remember that one."

"You gave a bogus name to the cops because you wanted to get away with criminal conduct, correct?"

"Yes."

"That time you received a ten-year sentence but served only four. Can you tell us why?"

"I promised to stay away from illegal drugs, and I also informed the DEA and FBI about some bad people I knew."

"So they trusted your promise and once again petitioned the judge to release you early, right?"

"They wanted me working for them." Habib shrugged and offered a sheepish smile.

"Obviously they did, because that was exactly why they set you free early. But eleven months later, you managed to bribe a state official, Oliver Peppe, who at that time was working as an officer at the Boston Police Department. First, you paid him $8,000 to let you out of jail, right? Officer Peppe eventually became your associate in crimes and is presently serving a twenty-year sentence for selling half a kilo of cocaine to an undercover agent, right?"

"Right. He was such a greedy guy," smirked Habib.

"Now, let's go back to the beginning of your treatment by Dr. Holden. Actually, let's go back before your treatment. Let's look at the history of your spine illness. You were diagnosed with severe lower back degeneration, and you had multiple MRIs to confirm that. Do you understand that severe degenerative osteoarthritis is a chronic condition that doesn't go away? It gets worse over time, right?

"Yes."

"Did you ever have surgery to correct that?"

"Yes, I had three of them."

"And did it correct it?"

"No."

"Do you still suffer from severe degenerative osteoarthritis in your back?"

"I get back pain."

"Did you tell that to Dr. Holden when you first met with him?"

"Yes."

"And you told him that because you wanted him to believe that your pain was real, correct?"

"Correct."

"So that he could write a prescription for pain medication for you, right?"

"Sure."

"But you didn't want these pills for yourself, correct?"

"Of course."

"But you never told Dr. Holden that part, did you?"

"No, I didn't."

"You didn't do that because you knew if you did, Dr. Holden wouldn't write a prescription to you for anything, right?"

"Right."

"And you wanted Dr. Holden to believe your back pain was severe, correct?"

"Naturally."

"Now, one of the questions that Ms. Hustler asked you on your direct examination was if Dr. Holden ever explained to you the dangers of the drugs that he was prescribing to you, right?"

"Yes."

"And you said 'no,' didn't you?"

"Yes, I said 'no.'"

"But that's not true, is it, sir? Is that your signature on the document called *Informed Consent*?"

"Yes, I signed it."

"And it spells out the dangers of the drugs that were prescribed to you?"

"Yes, it says that."

"And Dr. Holden expected you to read this form before signing it, correct?"

"Right."

"And it explains in detail the risks associated with the medications that were prescribed to you, correct?"

"That's what it says here, yes."

"Dr. Holden also asked you on that same date to sign a document titled *Pain Management Agreement,* right?"

"Yes."

"And that document included a litany of promises to Dr. Holden that you would not engage in any inappropriate behavior involving drug use, correct?"

"Correct, it did."

"And you signed that as well, did you not?"

"Yes, sir, I did."

"And you knew that all of those promises were lies, correct?"

"I just signed on the dotted line."

"But you knew that you were trying to get prescriptions to give the drugs to your wife?"

"Correct, yes."

"And sell the rest, correct?"

"Correct."

"But you didn't write on this form, '*I promise to do all the things except for the drugs I'm going to give to my wife and sell to my friends.*'"

"No."

"You knew that if you did that you never would get any prescriptions from Dr. Holden, right?"

"Probably not."

"Also, on your first visit, Dr. Holden asked you to indicate where your pain was, correct?"

"That's what it says here, yeah."

"And do you see that you rated your pain at between 9 and 10, correct?"

"Yes."

"You wanted Dr. Holden to believe that you were in excruciating pain, didn't you?"

"Yes."

"In February 2005, you told Dr. Holden that you were suffering from severe post-traumatic arthritis, and you were experiencing severe pain in your right forearm at that time, didn't you?"

"Yes."

"In March 2005, you told him about tingling and numbness in both legs, as well as a sensation of weakness in your legs, correct?"

"Correct."

"And Dr. Holden prescribed for you conservative non-opioid treatment on a lumbar-decompression table, do you remember that?"

"Yes."

"Did you actually get that treatment?"

"Yes."

"Did it aid your pain?"

"I guess. I don't know."

"Do you remember also having a brain MRI around this time?"

"I might have."

"Do you remember Dr. Holden getting a report that you had a neurological problem?"

"Oh, yes, that was back in 2001. I had a brain abscess."

"In May 2005, you were diagnosed with post-surgical failed back syndrome, and you described progressively worsening lower back pain with tingling and numbness in your left leg, correct?"

"Correct."

"Did you actually experience that pain?"

"Not that severe pain, no."

"So you exaggerated it to get drugs, essentially lying?"

"Yes."

"And you're telling the truth today, aren't you?"

"Yes."

"Thank you. Nothing further, Your Honor."

* * *

Peter O'Neil returned to his seat, while Edward Gould headed to the lectern to finish the cross.

"Good afternoon, Mr. Habib. My name's Edward Gould. I represent Dr. Holden, and I want to clarify something up front. Mr. Habib, you have a very extensive medical record, right?"

"Yes."

"And over the years you were trying to take advantage of that fact by lying to Dr. Holden because you knew that your previous record would show that you had been seriously injured, right?"

"Yes."

"In fact, all of these documents are in Dr. Holden's file, right in front of you, right?"

"Yes, they are."

"Here is the report signed by Dr. Richard Whitehead, M.D., and just in case one wasn't enough, there is another one signed by two other doctors, right?"

"Yes."

"You are a clever liar, aren't you? This wasn't a matter of you going into Dr. Holden's office and saying, 'Oh, my back hurts, can I have some OxyContin,' was it?"

"Not at all."

"You had a scheme because you knew that there was a thick medical record out there, and Dr. Holden and Nurse Practitioner Lander were going to see it, right?"

"Yes."

"And you knew that to any healthcare provider you would look like a real pain patient, right?"

"True. That worked for me before."

"When you met with the government people in this case, did they tell you that they regarded what you did to Dr. Holden and Nurse Practitioner Lander to be illegal and in violation of federal law?"

"They never did."

"They didn't tell you that you were violating the criminal narcotic distribution statutes passed by Congress?"

"No one ever did."

"They just asked you to come here and testify, that's all?"

"Yes, come here and tell the truth, that's all."

"Really?" Gould repressed a minuscule smile and paused. "Now, sir, are you currently incarcerated in prison in Beaumont, Texas?"

"No, I'm now in the Wyatt Detention Center. I was in Brooklyn, New York, on my way to the prison in Danbury, Connecticut, and I got re-routed here."

"Well, let me scroll back a little bit. You said two FBI agents came to see you in the Beaumont prison?"

"That was a couple of years ago."

"In connection with this case, right?"

"Yes."

"So the agents, working with the counsel at this table, flew all the way from Boston to Texas to see you a couple of years ago about this case when you were in the Beaumont prison, right?"

"Yes."

"When they talked to you about becoming involved in this case, did they discuss your criminal history?"

"I'm not sure what they discussed."

"Did any of them express any reservations about your capacity for truthfulness?"

"I can't recall that either, but I don't believe they did. Not to the best of my knowledge."

"Now, when you lied to law enforcement in the past, did they always catch on within a day or two as to what you were doing? I am asking you about your deceptions."

"I'm not sure when they caught on my lies."

"Didn't it sometimes take them months or years to figure out that you had lied to them?"

"Yes, sometimes they were pretty slow," smirked Habib.

"Because you're a good liar, aren't you? You were able to fool law enforcement, weren't you?"

"A couple of times, yes," admitted Habib with a shy smile.

"Well, let's talk about... and I want to say this respectfully, but let's talk about the lawyers involved in this current case."

"Objection," Hustler and Lynch jumped out of their seats simultaneously.

"Overruled," said the judge.

"Have you met with them previously? I am asking about these three individuals sitting at this table?"

"I met with one of them."

"Which one?"

"Miss..."

"Ms. Hustler?"

"Yeah, Ms. Hustler. I'm sorry."

"And where and when did you meet with Ms. Hustler?"

"In one of the rooms in this building."

"And where did you reside at that time?"

"At the Wyatt Detention Center."

"Which is in Rhode Island?"

"Yes."

"So you were brought up from Rhode Island to meet with Ms. Hustler in this building, right?"

"Yes."

"How long ago?"

"This past Friday."

"Did you go over your criminal history with Ms. Hustler on that date?"

"I'm not sure exactly what was said. I mean she knows... she must know my criminal history."

"I'm not asking whether she knows it or not. I'm asking you whether you went over your criminal history with Ms. Hustler last Friday?"

"Not in detail."

"Did you go over some of it?"

"Maybe a couple of things were mentioned."

"And when Ms. Hustler had a conversation with you this past Friday about your coming testimony in this case, did she express any reservations about your lack of capacity for truthfulness?"

"No, she didn't."

"I have nothing further," said Gould, and returned to his seat.

* * *

Outside in the hallway, Alex approached Gould. "Edward, this Habib was quite a character," he grinned wryly. "How many more crooks like him will we have the pleasure to see on the witness stand?"

"No more," said Gould. "The government's last witness is Ken Bertoldi's mother."

"Sounds like they've run out of convicted criminals as their trustworthy witnesses," Alex shook his head. "I wonder what the prosecutors planned to accomplish by bringing all these shady characters to testify in court? I mean, one was a decorated police officer who did his best to trick Ben into illegal actions, failed miserably, and then falsified his reports to accommodate his superiors, right? Another one was an IRS agent who was assigned to record Ben's interrogation with no basic knowledge in pain medicine or medicine in general. More than that, this agent conveniently forgot to incorporate Ben's most critical statements in her report that testified to his good faith because, according to her own admission, she considered them unimportant or irrelevant, didn't she?"

"That's true."

"And, also," joined in Elaine, "the agents did not videorecord the interrogation, so that no one would ever have an opportunity to nail her and her colleagues for dishonesty."

"That's right."

"And how about the other witnesses?" continued Alex. "For instance, this young man—the father of an infant—who was a drug addict, and took part in his close friend's poisoning. His friend was prescribed methadone for his serious back pain—not to get high. But these two grown-up men were so itching to get stoned that they didn't even bother to read the warning label on the bottle. They kept gulping the pills like candy..."

"They were reckless," said Ron, "but the prosecutors want to blame Ben for his friend's death?"

Gould didn't answer, just sighed heavily. He knew it was a rhetorical question.

"Now, how about Miles Moore?" asked Alex. "The man committed a felony by substituting his friend's urine with his own and couldn't stop his buddy from overdosing. As a result, his buddy ended up dead, and this 'true friend' was brought in to portray Ben and Julia as villains."

"Talk about government witnesses..." Ron shook his head in disbelief. "Some of them, such as your former patients, were doctor-shopping or selling drugs, or both, but they were never arrested and never prosecuted. Are they now 'credible' witnesses for the government?"

"But if they were at some point selling drugs and got caught," said Alex, "and most likely they were, how could they refuse to testify against their doctor and their nurse?"

"They could not." Ron paused and shook his head again. "And what do you think about the two career criminals who managed to fool not only their physicians but a number of law enforcement officials, including DEA and FBI agents? Now both of them were brought from their jail cells to testify against Dr. Holden? What are these crooks' testimonies expected to prove?"

"Your guess is as good as mine," said Gould. "Maybe these crooks are the best witnesses they could produce."

Chapter Thirty-Nine

After the lunch break, Judge Adler turned to Lynch. "Is this your last witness, Counselor?"

"Yes, Your Honor."

A small, neatly dressed elderly woman took her seat in the witness chair. Mrs. Follain's son and Dr. Holden's former patient, Ken Bertoldi, had died of cocaine overdose at the age of thirty-six. His mother's testimony, as the last witness for the prosecution in the case against Dr. Holden and NP Lander, wasn't accidental. The prosecutors were sure that this woman's grief-stricken look would break the jurors' hearts and fill them with rage and disgust against the physician who, in the minds of the prosecutors, personally contributed to the demise of that unfortunate young man. "Good afternoon, Mrs. Follain," said Lynch gently.

"Good afternoon," replied the woman, obviously familiar with the man at the lectern.

"How old are you, Mrs. Follain?" Lynch continued.

"I just turned seventy-six."

"Mrs. Follain, how many children do you have?"

"I had five sons, but now I have four," Mrs. Follain sighed heavily.

As Ben looked at the fragile lady, his thoughts drifted to her son Ken, who was always well dressed and good humored but who had a most hopeless shoulder condition. On his first visit, Ken told him that he had four older brothers and two of them, like Ken, had suffered the same rare, debilitating shoulder condition. As a result of an odd genetic mutation, they had developed intense pain in their shoulders and by the age of fifteen were regular visitors at different orthopedic clinics. By the age of thirty, all three of the brothers were considered totally disabled. They were put through a battery of diagnostic tests and conservative as well as surgical treatments, but none of them worked.

"Mrs. Follain, could you please tell us what happened to one of your sons?" asked Lynch.

"My youngest son, Ken, died about nine years ago," Mrs. Follain said quietly. A tear glistened in her eye. She opened her purse, retrieved a small pack of tissues, dabbed her eyes, and sighed.

"I am very sorry about your loss, ma'am, but could you tell us what actually happened to Ken?" continued Mr. Lynch sweetly.

"Ken was a drug addict since he was a teenager. Almost ten years ago, when Kenny was thirty-six years old, he overdosed on cocaine mixed with heroin and died," the woman said softly.

"Mrs. Follain, did, at some point, Ken become a patient of Dr. Holden and Nurse Practitioner Lander?"

"Yes, he did."

"Do you see that doctor or his nurse in this room?"

"I never met Dr. Holden," said Mrs. Follain.

"Do you see his nurse here?" said Lynch, and turning Julia Lander.

Mrs. Follain followed his glance and nodded. "Yes, she is here."

"Thank you, Mrs. Follain. Now, could you tell the jury what brought you and your son Ken to their office and when that happened?" asked Lynch.

"That year, I think it was 2003, pain in both of Ken's shoulders became unbearable. It was bad for years, but then it got to the point that I had to help him wash his face and feed him."

"What do you mean, to feed him?" Lynch arched his eyebrows.

"Yes, I had 'to feed him,' because sometimes his shoulders gave in, and he couldn't use them, especially the right one. On those days, I had to feed him as if he was a little baby."

"But Ken also had serious issues with street drugs, didn't he, Mrs. Follain?" asked Lynch.

"Yes, sir, he did," agreed Mrs. Follain. "He started using them when he was only fourteen."

"So, when your son became a patient of Dr. Holden and Nurse Practitioner Lander, he was already a drug addict, and both of them knew it, correct?"

"Objection, Your Honor. Argumentative," interjected Gould. "There is no evidence in Mr. Bertoldi's medical file that Dr. Holden or Nurse Practitioner Lander had ever been informed of this issue."

"Overruled," Judge Adler dismissed his objections. "You may answer the question."

"I believe so," nodded Mrs. Follain.

"And to the best of your knowledge, what exactly did either of them do to help your son to stay away from street drugs?"

"I am not aware of anything, sir," said Mrs. Follain.

As the testimony continued, Ben recalled that he had learned about Ken's drug addiction upon reading the discovery that the prosecuting attorneys submitted to his attorneys. The young man hid this information from him and his staff very skillfully, and Mrs. Follain, who was well aware of her son's addiction, never shared her knowledge with his medical caretakers. The woman worked as a nurse for over forty years and knew how reluctant most physicians were to treat drug-addicted patients, no matter how serious their other health conditions would be, including pain.

"Mrs. Follain, is it correct to assume that, in spite of the clear signs of your son's heroin and cocaine addiction, both of these medical professionals provided your son with opioid prescriptions for over two years, including prescriptions for methadone?"

"Objection, Your Honor. Leading the witness," interrupted Gould.

"Sustained," said the judge. "Please move on."

"OK, let me ask you a different question." Lynch paused and pursed his lips. "You said that you'd never met Dr. Holden, but have you ever had any personal interactions with Nurse Practitioner Lander?"

"Once." Mrs. Follain suddenly turned sour.

"Could you please tell the jury about that encounter?" asked Lynch.

"Sure. That day Ken and I had to see a shoulder surgeon. I don't remember his name. We came to his office, a nurse greeted us at the door, and she led us into a small, dark room."

"Into a small, dark room?" Lynch slightly flinched as if he'd never heard the story before. "And what happened there, in that dark room, Mrs. Follain?"

"Well, she brought both of us into this dark room in the back of the office and said, 'Give me $200 cash, and I'll give your son a prescription.'"

"So what was your response to that, Mrs. Follain?"

"What could I do? Ken needed his prescription so I had to pay." The old lady sighed wistfully.

"On that particular day did your son leave the office with a prescription for methadone, Mrs. Follain?" Lynch asked sternly.

"I think... I think he did," the woman said with some vacillation.

"And the nurse who took you to the dark room was Nurse Practitioner Lander?" Lynch pointed to Julia.

Mrs. Follain squinted at Julia and somberly nodded.

"I have no further questions," declared Mr. Lynch, who triumphantly moved to his seat.

"Let's take a fifteen-minute break." announced Judge Adler.

* * *

"Did you know that Ken was a drug addict?" Emma asked Ben when they walked outside.

"No, I never even imagined he was. He always looked so neat and appropriately dressed. He was such a likable guy... 'A straight shooter,' I used to call him. Not to his face, of course. Ken had two older brothers who suffered from similar shoulder arthritis, but Ken's condition was the worst. It started when he was just a kid, and at the age of twenty-eight, he was granted a total disability."

"Was he married?"

"Yes, by the time he turned thirty, Ken already had three daughters. But his marriage was rather rocky. A few months before he died, he told me they were on the brink of separation."

"Poor man." Emma reflected for a moment. "I just couldn't stop thinking about why his mother said you knew that her son was a drug addict even though she testified that she had never met you."

"Who knows? Maybe she is confused."

"And what is this weird story about the small dark room? I don't remember any small, dark rooms in your clinic."

"There weren't any. And I can't believe anyone in our office would demand cash for a prescription. Not Julia, not anyone else. Besides, Kenneth had full health coverage. Mrs. Follain must be confused. An elderly woman, still mourning her son..."

"But the jury may believed her and imagine awful things about Julia and your office, right?"

"I don't know if anything can be done to disprove her statement. The jurors feel sympathy for her, and I doubt they would question her truthfulness. But let's see what will happen on the cross."

* * *

After the break, Mrs. Follain returned to the witness chair for the cross-examination.

"Good afternoon, Mrs. Follain. My name is Edward Gould, and I represent Dr. Holden." Gould paused. "First of all, let me express my deepest condolences about your son's death."

"Thank you, sir," responded Mrs. Follain flatly.

"Mrs. Follain, would you please tell us what your son's life was like before he became a patient of Dr. Holden?" asked Gould.

"To tell the truth, he didn't have much of a life. When Ken was a teenager, he was all in sports. His favorite was windsurfing. He was also a hard-working boy, but by the age of twenty, that was all history. His shoulder pain became so bad that Ken had to quit his job in construction."

"I see. Mrs. Follain, do you think your son's drug addiction was somehow caused by the pain and disability he had been suffering for years?"

"No doubt, it was. Each time Ken had a flare-up of his pain, I knew what would follow."

"Do you mean he would resort to his drug habit?"

"He most definitely would. You see, Ken knew that if he took a drug, his pain would be gone, at least for a while. He would buy heroin, Percocet, morphine, whatever he could get. Ken knew it wasn't the right thing to do, but his pain was so bad, he didn't care. He told me once that he would rather be dead than continue living in such misery." Mrs. Follain bit her upper lip.

"Now, ma'am, could you please tell us what happened after he became Dr. Holden's patient?"

"Well, by that time, other doctors gave up on Ken. They said he was too young for shoulder replacements. Over the years, none of the other treatments worked for him either. But when he came back from his first visit to Dr. Holden, he said, 'The doc sent me for an MRI. He said that he would try his best to help me. Finally someone is taking my pain seriously.'"

"And that someone was Dr. Holden?"

"I think so."

"And did Dr. Holden help your son?"

"Yes, he did."

"Did he prescribe any pain medication for your son?"

"Yes, sir. There weren't any other treatments that could help him anyway. You can't believe how terrible his pain was. His life was a nightmare."

"Mrs. Follain, on the direct examination, the counselor asked you about methadone. Do you remember your son Ken taking methadone?"

"Yes, he did. I remember it clearly. Ken was very happy that Dr. Holden prescribed him methadone. He said that, unlike other drugs he'd tried before, methadone didn't make him drowsy. Each time he took it, he would stay pain free longer."

"Mrs. Follain, would it be accurate to say that after Ken had been prescribed methadone, he suffered less pain and his life had improved?" Gould asked gently.

"Objection, Your Honor, leading!" intervened Lynch.

"Overruled," Judge Adler leaned forward. She seemed genuinely interested in the witness's reply. "Please answer the question."

"Yes, that's what Ken told me," Mrs. Follain cast a guilty look at Lynch.

"Mrs. Follain, isn't it true that before your son became Dr. Holden's patient he was totally disabled, yet six months after he'd started his treatments with Dr. Holden, for the first time in twelve years, he was able to work?"

"Yes, this is true."

"Do you remember what type of work it was?" asked Gould.

"Ken was offered a position as a foreman. It was a union job. He received full benefits, paid vacations, you know... He was very happy," explained Mrs. Follain.

"Could Ken return to some athletic activities too?"

"Yes, he could. I remember about a year after he started his treatments, Ken went to the attic, found his old windsurfing board, and went to the beach. He was so excited he could do his favorite sport again. After so many years of doing nothing..."

"Do you mean that Ken could get back to windsurfing?"

"Yes, he could, and he did! He even called Dr. Holden's office to tell him about it. He was elated, like a little boy."

Emma still remembered how happy Ben was when his patient told him he could get back to windsurfing. She didn't know then that the patient was Ken Bertoldi because Ben never mentioned any of his patients' names, but she remembered the story.

"And then, a few months later, something tragic happened, right?" asked Gould.

"A terrible thing happened." Mrs. Follain paused, her look turned mournful. "Ken's life was getting better and better, and I thought that he finally had a chance to recover from his addiction, but one night he went out with his friend Jim... and I never saw him again. Not alive." Mrs. Follain fell silent.

"Mrs. Follain, I really feel deep sympathy for your tragic loss," Gould said gently.

"Thank you," the woman muttered under her breath, and her look went blank.

"Thank you for your testimony, Mrs. Follain." Gould turned to the judge. "Nothing further."

"That was your last witness, Counselor?" Judge Adler asked Lynch.

"Yes, Your Honor. The government rests its case."

* * *

The next morning, even before the alarm clock had a chance, a phone call woke Ben up.

"Hi, Ben. It's Mark Daniels. Sorry to wake you up, but we got a message from Judge Adler's clerk late last night. The judge wants us all in the courtroom at least half an hour earlier. Something unexpected happened last night. We don't know the details yet. Can you be at the courthouse by 8:30?"

"No problem, Mark. Do you have any idea what all this fuss is about?"

"No, I don't, but we'll find out shortly. See you at 8:30."

* * *

It was now Day 16 of the trial. By 8:20 a.m., the defendants, their attorneys, and all three prosecutors had gathered in the courtroom. Judge Adler arrived and went straight to the point.

"Mr. Lynch, could you please tell us what happened last night?"

"Yes, Your Honor. At about 10:20 p.m., our office was contacted by the FBI officer, Agent Grimm. He sent us an e-mail and then told us personally that he'd just had a phone conversation with Mrs. Cathleen Follain and—"

"Your last witness, right?" clarified Judge Adler.

"Yes, Your Honor, that's her," confirmed Lynch. "According to Special Agent Grimm, Mrs. Follain told him that during her direct examination yesterday she got confused, and she wanted to change her testimony."

"Her entire testimony?" asked Judge Adler.

"No, a specific statement, Your Honor. Mrs. Follain said that the nurse who demanded a cash payment for the prescription in the small, dark room wasn't the nurse she saw in the courtroom yesterday. The entire episode most likely happened in some other office, not in Dr. Holden's office."

"Your Honor," Gould raised from his seat, "I think the jury has to be notified of this statement immediately."

"Counselors, do you agree?" Judge Adler turned to the prosecutors.

"Yes, Your Honor," nodded Lynch.

The jurors were called in and presented with Mrs. Follain's changed testimony. Judging by the flat or confused expressions on their still sleepy faces, some of them had already forgotten her original statement while others may not have paid much attention to it in the first place.

"All right, Counselor." The judge turned to Edward Gould. "Since we've taken care of Mrs. Follain's restatement, let's get back to our business. Is the defense ready to present its case?"

"Yes, Your Honor, we are."

Chapter Forty

The first witness for the defense, a stocky man in his late fifties, labored to the witness chair.

"Good morning, Officer Barkoff," Mark Daniels began the direct.

"Good morning."

"Sir, are you currently working?"

"No. I'm retired."

"What was your occupation when you were working?"

"I was a police officer with the Boston Police Department. I was a street cop," explained Barkoff.

"For how many years were you a police officer?"

"Thirty-four years."

"And at some point, you became a patient of Dr. Holden, correct?"

"Yes, in 2001 or 2002, I don't remember exactly."

"And for what injuries did you go to see Dr. Holden?"

"I had injuries to both my shoulders, both knees, my lower back, my elbow, and my arms. I've had numerous injuries throughout the years and numerous surgeries."

"How did you come to suffer those injuries?"

"Through scuffles at work. There were a number of things that caused those injuries."

"Did you miss time from work because of those injuries?"

"Yes, I did. Some of it was due to physical rehabilitation, others due to surgeries and rehab."

"Did Dr. Holden help you to get back to work?"

"Yes, he did."

"How?"

"Well, on my first visit, he assessed my injuries and suggested that we would start off with physical therapy. He said that if that didn't work, I would need an MRI, and in case I needed surgery, he would refer me to a surgeon."

"And what treatment, if any, that Dr. Holden provided was most effective in helping you return to work?"

"Well, it depended on the injury. I had shoulder injuries where I had injections to my shoulder. I had a few different types of injections to my knee, which got me through that. I had several physical therapy treatments. At some point, I was prescribed anti-inflammatories and other medications, and I was able to go back to work."

"Were you also prescribed opioids?"

"Yes, I was prescribed oxycodone."

"And did those opioids allow you to return to work?"

"Yes, absolutely. I was taking them when I had a problem with my sciatica and my back pain."

"You mentioned that you had knee injuries as well, right?"

"Yes."

"And was that a chronic issue for you?"

"Yes, until today."

"And you mentioned back problems too?"

"Yes, I have had a bad case of sciatica for years. The pain would come across my back, down my right leg to my knee, and it would be almost a stabbing pain, and it would cause a numbing effect in my leg all the way down."

"And did that keep you from being able to work at times?"

"Oh, yes."

"What, if anything, that Dr. Holden treated you with enabled you to get back to work?"

"Good physical therapy, some injections, and also medications."

"Including opioids?"

"Yes. Without taking them, I would be crippled, no doubt about it."

"You also mentioned some surgeries. Did Dr. Holden refer you for those surgeries?"

"Yes, he did."

"Were those surgeries helpful?"

"Very much so. I could get back to work."

"Did Dr. Holden give you instructions about your pain medication?"

"Yes, he did."

"What instructions did he give you?"

"Well, there were written instructions that I had to read and sign. He also consistently explained to me that opioids could be addictive, and he wanted to know how I was taking them, and he always asked me how they were helping, and if I still needed them."

"When, if ever, did you tell Dr. Holden that your pain medications weren't needed anymore?"

"Objection, leading," interrupted Krokson.

"Overruled."

"When the pain had subsided, either through therapy or surgery in some cases, I didn't need them anymore."

"On those occasions, did Dr. Holden continue to prescribe you opioids?"

"No, he stopped them right away. He was actually very happy to hear that my pain subsided."

"Let's look at one of Dr. Holden's office notes, written on March 20, 2001: *'Mr. Barkoff is a 51-year-old police officer who recently returned to work on a full schedule after being treated for a few months.'* Is this one of the occasions on which Dr. Holden helped you to get back to work?"

"Yes, that's true."

"Let's look at another office note. On June 22, 2001, Dr. Holden wrote that you'd gotten into a scuffle with a criminal who'd tried to escape after a robbery. He wrote, *'As a result of a big fight, Officer Barkoff injured his left shoulder and elbow. He hasn't been able to return to his duties since the day of the confrontation and cannot even hold a cup of coffee because of his elbow and shoulder pain.'* Do you remember how severe that pain was?"

"I remember that vividly. I had no strength in my arm or my hand at all. If I tried to grasp a cup of coffee, I would lose hold of it."

"How did Dr. Holden treat you for your shoulder and elbow injury?"

"He referred me to a physical therapist, who did electrical stimulation, massage, and exercise. Dr. Holden also treated me with prolotherapy injections."

"Was the prolotherapy helpful?"

"Yes, it was."

"Did Dr. Holden explain to you what prolotherapy was?"

"At the time, yes. He explained how it worked and what I could expect from those injections."

"Were there injuries after which Dr. Holden got you back to work without opioids?"

"Absolutely."

"Were there other times when opioids were necessary to get you back to work?"

"Yes, there were."

"On October 7, 2003, Dr. Holden writes, *'According to the patient, he was regulating traffic in downtown Boston when a cabdriver, who was passing very close to him, knocked him down. The patient was spun around, hit the pavement, and was taken to the hospital by an ambulance. He complains of left shoulder pain and left knee pain. His left knee is swollen. X-Rays were taken at the hospital, and he was sent home. Officer Barkoff could not return to his job as police officer thereafter.'*

"Do you remember that?"

"My pain was so debilitating, it would be difficult to forget."

"And Dr. Holden eventually had to send you to surgery, right?"

"Yes, he did."

"Was the surgery helpful?"

"Yes."

"Do you know whether this was the point at which you were having difficulty walking on uneven surfaces and up and down stairs?"

"Yes. My knee pain was so bad that I could hardly walk for a while."

"And did taking OxyContin help you with your mobility?"

"Yes, and it also helped me at night when the pain was especially bad."

"Sir, we just spoke about your medical history. What was a typical visit like with Dr. Holden?"

"Well, on a typical visit, we'd go over how I felt that day compared to the last time I was in the office. If I was in physical therapy, how it was helping or not helping and if my pain was still the same, worse, or better. He also wanted to know if I was planning to go back to work and how soon."

"Did Dr. Holden consistently perform physical exams on you?"

"Yes, he did it on every visit."

"How long did your appointments with Dr. Holden typically last?"

"About 15–20 minutes or so."

"Could you describe his office?"

"Well, it was a big office with a lot of equipment. It had a professional look."

"How long did you typically wait when you came for your appointments to see Dr. Holden?"

"Maybe 20–25 minutes or so, sometimes longer."

"What observations, if any, did you make about people whom you saw in the waiting room?"

"Objection," interjected Krokson.

"Counselor?" Judge Adler raised her eyebrows. "You've asked your witnesses the very same question on multiple occasions. Overruled."

"Well, there were various people there," said Mr. Barkoff. "Young people, older people. I saw people in wheelchairs. I saw people with crutches. Some people were in business attire, other people looked like construction workers."

"Did you ever see anyone nodding off in the waiting room?"

"Nodding off? No, I didn't."

"Officer, given your decades of police experience, have you had experience with drug addicts?"

"Yes, I have."

"Did you ever see anyone in the waiting room who you thought was a drug addict?"

"Objection!" Krokson rose from his seat.

"Overruled, you opened the door to this topic yourself, Counselor," Judge Adler responded.

"No, I never saw anyone who looked like a drug addict."

"Did Dr. Holden ever explain to you what his practice was and what he was trying to do?"

"Yes, he did."

"What did he say?"

"He told me his practice was pain management, and he tried to manage patients' pain the best way he knew how."

"Officer Barkoff, how would you describe your experience with Dr. Holden?"

"Dr. Holden was a very professional person. I went to him to avoid surgery at all costs, if I could. When the therapy and injections and everything else didn't work, that's when I was referred to a surgeon. Over the years that I saw him for various injuries, we not only had a doctor-patient relationship, but it became a little more personal. I could talk to him about different things. He was a very responsible doctor. He explained everything to me every time I was in his office, and that's why I kept going back to him."

"Thank you, Officer Barkoff. No further questions."

Daniels left the lectern, and the prosecutor, Dick Krokson, took his place.

"Good morning, sir." A taut smile flashed across his face.

"Good morning."

"I only have a few questions. It shouldn't take more than five minutes. First of all, you testified on direct that you were a police officer for 34 years?"

"Correct."

"Thank you for your service, sir. Dr. Holden knew that, right?"

"Pardon me?"

"He knew that you were a police officer?"

"Yes, he did."

"And the fact that you were a Boston police officer, you were open about that, right?"

"Yes, I was."

"You went to the defendant's office because you were injured on the job several times, right?"

"Correct."

"So there were several times where you'd get injured, and then you'd go see the doctor, and then maybe you'd go back to work, and later on you'd get injured again, and you'd come back to see the doctor again, right?"

"Correct."

"You testified on direct that you did not get opioids on a regular basis from Dr. Holden, right?"

"On a regular basis? No."

"And in fact, as you testified on direct, you got them sporadically?"

"Correct."

"You would get them for a short period of time after you were either injured or you had surgery, right?"

"Correct."

"So, for example, when Mr. Daniels showed you that note about getting OxyContin in 2004, you only got it for one month, right?"

"One month it was."

"And there were times when you didn't get a prescription for opioids for almost a year, right?"

"Correct."

"And that's consistent with what you've been saying, right, that you didn't get very many opioids from Dr. Holden?"

"Correct."

"Sir, you testified on direct that you had a number of different injuries while you were on the job, right?"

"Correct."

"You got hit by a car once, right?"

The witness nodded in affirmation.

"And you sometimes got injured either when dealing with people that you were trying to apprehend, or in the course of your work as a police officer, right?"

"Right."

"And some of those injuries were really painful, weren't they?"

"They were."

"So your back pain and sciatica was a chronic issue as well, right?"

"It became constant, yes."

"Sometimes it kept you up at night?"

"Yes, it did."

"Sometimes it kept you out of work, right?"

"Once in a while, yes."

"But you never got a prescription for methadone, did you?"

"No, I didn't."

"You were a police officer, is that right, sir?"

"Yes, for about thirty-four years."

"No further questions," proclaimed Krokson.

"Anything for redirect?" Judge Adler asked.

"Very briefly, Your Honor," responded Mark Daniels.

Judge Adler sighed impatiently.

"Officer Barkoff, just a few questions. Did Dr. Holden ever give you opioids when you said that you didn't need them or that your pain was controlled?"

"Never."

"Did Dr. Holden frequently talk to you about how to approach your pain needs?"

"All the time."

"And following up on what Mr. Krokson asked you, just to be clear, you *did* get opioids when you told Dr. Holden you were in pain in addition to the other treatments, right?"

"Yes, I received opioids."

"Thank you, Officer Barkoff. No further questions," said Daniels.

Judge Adler turned to Krokson, a question mark in her glance.

"Any recross, Counselor?"

"Your Honor, just one question, if I may," said Krokson.

"Sir, is that correct that you had a lot of different conversations with Dr. Holden?"

"Yes, we did."

"And you said on direct that your relationship went from a professional one to being something more than that, is that right?"

"Somewhat."

"You considered him a friend, right?"

"Yes, I did."

"You consider him a friend today, right?"

"I do. And I always will."

"No further questions, Your Honor," concluded Krokson.

"Thank you for coming in, Officer." Judge Adler broke into a smile. "Let's have a lunch break."

* * *

Following the lunch break, an elegantly dressed, attractive woman in her early fifties walked into the courtroom, and Mark Daniels began his direct.

"Good afternoon, Mrs. Shamarian."

"Good afternoon." Ben's former office manager unwittingly touched her wavy auburn hair.

"Is this your first time testifying?"

"Oh, yes, and I hope the last time." The witness rendered a tentative smile.

"Are you a little nervous?"

"Yes, I am."

"Mrs. Shamarian, are you currently employed?"

"Yes, I am."

"Where are you employed?"

"I'm a program coordinator for the cardiovascular division at Longwood Hospital."

"How long have you been working there?"

"Since August 2007."

"Did you work with Dr. Holden before that?"

"Yes, I did."

"When did you start?"

"In February 2002."

"What were your job responsibilities?"

"At the beginning, I mostly did a front desk job."

"While doing this job, what, if any, observations did you make about Dr. Holden's patients?"

"Our patients had different painful conditions, and many of them were in really bad shape—"

"Objection, calls for speculation," interrupted Lynch.

"Well, tell us what you saw," suggested Judge Adler.

"I saw patients coming in pain, often using crutches, walkers, or canes. Some wore slings or casts, and others were limping. A few of them were in wheelchairs. Our waiting area sometimes looked like an emergency room."

"Objection, Your Honor."

"Overruled," said the judge. "I am interested in hearing that. Please go ahead."

"They were all coming to see Dr. Holden or Nurse Practitioner Lander with the hope of getting some relief."

"Mrs. Shamarian, you started with Dr. Holden when he had a small office, right?"

"Right."

"And then you moved to a bigger one, correct?"

"Yes, in January 2003 we moved."

"Do you know what the purpose of the move was?"

"We were getting more new patients so we needed a bigger waiting room, and Dr. Holden planned to include new services for his patients."

"What were those services?"

"He hired a psychiatrist, a neurologist, a chiropractor, and a specialist in acupuncture. He purchased various physical therapy equipment, including a Lordex machine for spinal decompression. For those who had severe back pain, it worked wonders," beamed Mrs. Shamarian.

"Do you remember any other services or equipment?"

"Right after we moved, Dr. Holden arranged to build a large exercise room where our patients could have yoga, Pilates, and tai-chi classes, free of charge. He also hired an acupuncture specialist, Ms. Marcus, who was great!" Mrs. Shamarian paused. "We had rooms for bioelectrical and electromagnetic treatments and a room assigned for back massage therapy using electrical waterbeds."

"Anything else you remember?"

"Later on we started alpha-wave treatments, supervised by our pain psychologist, Dr. Satriani. She was an excellent specialist and a compassionate person."

"Were you personally a patient of Dr. Holden?"

"Yes, I was. I had a bad knee and a herniated disk in my lower back. He practically cured my knee arthritis and helped me with my back pain. That Lordex machine was a marvel."

"Mrs. Shamarian, were you present at Dr. Holden's office on May 17, 2007?"

"Yes, I was."

"Do you remember what happened?"

The witness frowned and was silent for a long moment.

"It's hard for me to even talk about it. Many military-looking people rushed into our center that morning. No one in the office knew what was going on. They were yelling, 'Don't move! Don't talk! Don't do anything!' It was terrible. I was frightened. I thought some terrorists had planted a bomb—"

"Objection, Your Honor. Move to strike," yelled Lynch.

"No, I want to hear her side of the story," overruled Judge Adler.

"That's fine, Your Honor, I can move on," said Daniels. "Mrs. Shamarian, did you like working at Dr. Holden's center?"

"Yes, I liked it. I liked Dr. Holden. I liked working there because it was an exciting, challenging, and rewarding job. Dr. Holden was constantly improving the services, and he cared about his staff. We had good health insurance and paid vacations."

"Mrs. Shamarian, what is your impression of Dr. Holden as a doctor?"

"Objection, relevance."

"Your Honor, she was his patient," Daniels reminded the judge.

"I'll allow her to say what her personal experience was with him as a doctor," ruled the judge.

"Based on your personal experience, what was your opinion about Dr. Holden as a doctor?"

"He was a great doctor, very professional, very caring, and that's not just my opinion."

"Thank you, Mrs. Shamarian. Nothing further," concluded Daniels as he left the lectern.

Wasting no time, Lynch took his place and for the next twenty minutes tried to force Dr. Holden's office manager to denigrate his patients. But he failed miserably.

Chapter Forty-One

THE TRIAL HAD NOW ENTERED ITS seventeenth day.

"The defense calls Dr. Karen Westwood," announced Attorney Gould.

A tall, attractive woman in an elegant light-beige suit entered the courtroom and took a seat in the witness chair. The combination of her royal posture and her agile, cordial features was enthralling. She was in her early sixties, but her lively, glowing eyes made her look much younger.

"Good morning, Dr. Westwood."

"Good morning."

"Dr. Westwood, how long have you been a doctor?"

"Almost forty years."

"Has your professional career focused on any particular area of medicine?"

"Yes. It's focused on pain medicine."

"And, in your own words, how would you describe the field of pain medicine."

"Well, pain medicine is a specialty that deals with helping diagnose and treat people with all types of pain. We treat patients with acute pain, which is pain after an injury like a broken leg or pain after surgery. We treat patients with cancer who have unremitting pain, and we also treat patients with chronic pain, which is probably the largest group of patients that we treat."

"Dr. Westwood, were you hired by the defense counsel in this case?"

"I was."

"And were you given an assignment?"

"Yes, I was asked to describe the practice of pain medicine during the period between 2002 and 2007, and I was also asked to review a number of medical records."

"And have you in fact reviewed the same thirty files that Dr. Finnegan reviewed?"

"Yes, I have. I actually reviewed a total of seventy six of Dr. Holden's medical records."

"And were you here for the direct testimony of Dr. Finnegan, the government's witness?"

"I was."

"Have you reached the opposite opinions of Dr. Finnegan in this case?"

"I have."

"Do you agree with Dr. Finnegan's description of the guidance given to physicians practicing pain medicine during the relevant time period, 2002 to May 2007?"

"No, I don't agree with him at all."

"Were you actually in the field at the time?"

"Yes, I was."

"Now, could you please describe your educational background?"

"I went to Tufts University, received a bachelor of arts in mathematics and a bachelor of science in mechanical engineering. After that, I attended Tufts Medical School, graduated in 1976, and did an internship in surgery and a residency in anesthesiology at Massachusetts General Hospital. I completed a fellowship in a variety of areas, including pain medicine, and then in 1980 I started the first multidisciplinary pain center at Harvard Medical School."

"Do you consider the practice of pain medicine to still be an evolving medical field?"

"Yes, it's still evolving."

"Dr. Westwood, are you Board-certified in any particular area of medicine?"

"Yes. I'm Board-certified in anesthesiology and also in pain medicine."

"Could you please give us a description of your teaching experience, just in summary fashion?"

"Sure. I'm currently a full professor at Harvard Medical School."

"Were you actually the first woman full professor at Harvard Medical School?"

"Objection, relevance," Lynch interjected.

"Overruled."

"I was the first woman to hold an endowed professorship at Harvard Medical School. Today I teach at Harvard Medical School, and I have taught in the field of pain medicine all over the world. I've written a number of textbooks on the subject that are widely used in this area. I developed the largest pain training program in the world. I have trained many fellows and residents who are out there practicing pain medicine today. And I lecture regularly nationally and internationally in the area."

"And were you doing that during the time period from 2002 through May 2007?"

"Yes, I was."

"Did you see patients as well?"

"Yes, I did."

"Have you received any awards during your career?"

"I've been elected to *Best Doctors in America* several years running, and I have received awards from Tufts University."

"Have you ever testified for the government?"

"Yes."

"Now, do you agree to testify in every case in which you're asked to testify?"

"No, I don't always testify when I'm asked. My decision depends on whether I agree with what the doctor did or disagree."

"Now, you were here when Dr. Finnegan testified for the government, and I take it that you heard he wasn't practicing pain medicine during the relevant period of time, correct?"

"Yes. I believe he was working for a venture capital company, not in pain medicine."

"Now, in your experience, Doctor, is it possible for someone to have expertise about the practice of pain medicine during the relevant time period when they *weren't* practicing?"

"Objection," interrupted Lynch.

"Overruled."

"No. I believe it's impossible to have true expertise, especially in pain medicine, if the physician wasn't working in the field during that time."

"Why not, Doctor?"

"The field of pain management had changed so much. It's totally impossible for a doctor who hadn't even started training in that area during that period of time to have true expertise in the area."

"Now, Dr. Westwood, could you please tell us what chronic pain is?"

"Well, there isn't any agreed-upon definition of chronic pain. Some say it's pain lasting more than three months, others say it's pain lasting more than six months. Some say it's pain that outlasts the expected time for tissue healing while others say it's anything that is not acute or cancer related."

"Now, what are the risks to an individual if chronic pain is left untreated or undertreated?"

"There are a number of risks. If you are left suffering in pain, your blood pressure goes up, your pulse goes up, and this is not good for your heart. So if you have any heart problems and you're left suffering in pain for a long period of time, you can have a heart attack or stroke."

"Any other risks?"

"Well, people who are left in pain don't want to move. If you have pain in your back and every time you move it hurts, you want to just lie in bed. And if you don't move, you're more likely to get blood clots in your legs, a pulmonary embolism, or other serious problems. Lastly, if you don't move around and you don't take deep breaths, you can get pneumonia. So there can be very serious effects in your body, and very serious psychological issues can occur as well."

"Could you please name them?"

"People who are left in chronic pain often become depressed, even to the point of suicide. I've seen this in a number of patients with unremitting severe pain. They lose their jobs and their income. They lose their families. It can become a very serious physiological and psychological problem."

"Dr. Westwood, have you spent a good deal of your career trying to educate doctors about the risks of untreated and undertreated pain?"

"Yes, that's been the thrust of my practice."

"Is chronic pain in this country adequately treated?"

"No, it's undertreated."

"In your view, was there undertreatment of pain in this country from 2002 to May 2007?"

"Yes, it was definitely a problem. Many patients were left suffering. It was a very serious issue."

"Now, Dr. Westwood, are there a variety of ways to treat someone in chronic pain?"

"Yes, there are a variety of ways."

"And one way is through the use of opioid medications, correct?"

"Yes."

"Is it true that the use of opioids has been the cornerstone of pain management for a long time?"

"Yes. Opioids have been around for 4,000 years, which is really a testament to the fact that there have never been better painkillers than opioids. These medications are able to really transform patients and allow them to function much better, to be able to sleep, to get back to work, and to enjoy their lives with their families."

"Dr. Westwood, during the forty years that you've been in the pain medicine area, have you observed a wide variety of approaches in the use of opioids to treat chronic pain?"

"Yes, I have. When I started in the pain field in the early 1980s, they were not very widely used. Then in the late 1980s and the 1990s, pain specialists basically said, 'Why aren't we using these great medications to treat patients suffering from horrible pain?' Before that time, doctors were often uncomfortable using opioids or they were afraid of them. So in the 1980s and 1990s, there was a huge push in the medical community to use them more widely for patients with chronic pain."

"Was that taught in medical school?"

"Absolutely. Medical students were taught that patients should not be left suffering in pain and that these are the best medications we have. We are very familiar with their side effects or the problems they may cause, so we know what to expect, and we should use them for patients who are suffering with pain. Over the relevant period of time, more and more physicians began using these drugs to treat pain, not only pain management physicians but general practitioners too. We taught these doctors to use these medications more readily because leaving patients in severe pain was really detrimental to them."

"And what were the discussions about using opioids to treat patients who have a legitimate source of pain but who have exhibited potential drug-aberrant behavior?"

"The teaching was that patients who have aberrant drug behavior also can have severe pain, and they are really the most difficult group of pain patients to treat. But these patients may need pain medications. There wasn't any teaching that said you should never give opioids to patients who have aberrant drug behaviors. The teaching has been that these patients should not be left to suffer. You need to investigate each of these patients individually, and you need to determine on an individual basis if a patient has real pain, and if that is the case, choose the most appropriate ways to treat him or her."

"Was that true during the time period we're talking about here, from 2002 to May 2007?"

"Absolutely. There was never any dictum that said you should never use these drugs on patients with a history of aberrant behavior or a history of substance abuse or a history of addiction."

"Was there ever any dictum that you could treat this kind of patient only by utilizing an addictionologist?"

"Absolutely not. There was never any dictum that said you have to send these patients to an addictionologist. Sometimes that was appropriate, sometimes not. If patients tell you they're in pain, you should treat them in the best way you can."

"Dr. Westwood, a few minutes ago, you mentioned that some doctors are afraid to prescribe opioids. Could you describe for the jury the source of that fear, as you observed it?"

"Objection, Your Honor," interfered Lynch.

"Overruled."

"In my experience, and also in speaking to doctors all over the country, during the period of time we're talking about, from 2002 to 2007, there was tremendous fear in the medical community about prescribing opioids, and I think that fear has become worse and worse over the ensuing years because it is a fear of being sanctioned. There are many physicians out there who refuse to prescribe opioids because they have heard about legal sanctions put upon some physicians for prescribing them, even for cancer patients. So there are many physicians, who on one end of the spectrum, who never prescribe opioids for any of their patients, and there are other doctors who prescribe them. So, sadly enough, there are many patients out there left in severe chronic pain."

"Now, Doctor, let's talk about addiction. We've heard from a number of Dr. Holden's former patients on the witness stand that they were addicted. Could you tell the jury, please, from the perspective of a doctor in the medical community, what addiction actually is?"

"Well, there's a lot of confusion around the definition of addiction, even among physicians. Addiction is really a psychiatric diagnosis. It's an insatiable craving, for which drug addicts will do anything: lie, cheat, and steal to procure and take drugs. They lose control and, most importantly, their function declines. They lose their jobs, and they are not able to get out of bed in the morning. They don't have control over using drugs."

"Has there ever been a surefire way for a pain doctor to diagnose addiction?"

"Absolutely not."

"Why not?"

"There have been questionnaires to help doctors to diagnose addiction, but unfortunately there has never been a foolproof way of deciding whether a patient is addicted or not. Any of us who have worked in the field of pain medicine long enough have been fooled by patients who become addicted. So I'd have to say 'no.' To this day, there's absolutely no foolproof way to determine addiction."

"Dr. Finnegan talked about so-called 'red flags.' Are you familiar with that term?"

"Yes, I am."

"During the relevant time period, was there any consensus about red flags that provide a definitive diagnosis of addiction?"

"All we knew about them was that these red flags by no means definitively meant someone was addicted. For example, one of the red flags might be a history of a psychiatric illness, but as I said earlier, almost everyone who's in chronic pain long enough becomes depressed. Does that mean that this person should never get painkillers? Of course not. So none of these red flags individually, or even taken in a group, definitively proves this patient is an addict and should never get those medications."

"What problems does that fact pose for a doctor practicing in the area of pain medicine?"

"It becomes a big problem because it's very difficult to determine which patients are addicted and which patients are not. The only way you can guarantee that you're never going to prescribe to a patient who is addicted is to *never* prescribe this medicine to anyone. And I think that's a huge disservice to patients who are in real pain."

"Dr. Westwood, do those who are *not* addicts but who cease taking opioids go through withdrawal, even though they're not addicts?"

"Oh, absolutely, and the reason is physical dependence, which is very different from addiction. Physical dependence means that if I give someone enough opioid medication for a long enough period of time and I suddenly stop it, they're going to go through a withdrawal phenomenon, which is a very unpleasant condition. Your body gets used to having the drug around, and if you stop it, you'll go through withdrawal. You can be physically dependent without being addicted. And I would say the vast majority of patients we treat with opioids over a long period of time become physically dependent, pretty much all of them do, but they are not addicted."

"And if for some reason a patient has to stop taking opioids, could he or she stop abruptly?"

"No, you have to taper it over a couple of weeks, maybe a month, because if you stop it, you are going to have a withdrawal phenomenon."

"Your Honor, I think it's a good point to break for a short recess," suggested Gould.

"All right, let's reconvene in fifteen minutes," Judge Adler agreed.

* * *

When Ben and his friends walked outside, Ron said, "While Dr. Westwood was talking about patients that fool physicians in order to get opioids—and most of them, I believe, were drug abusers or drug addicts way before they came to their doctors—I was thinking about this war on drugs that the government declared a while ago. It looks like, despite this war, drug abuse is getting worse and worse. For years our schools and colleges had been getting practically unlimited supplies of legal and illicit drugs, and they essentially became breeding grounds for drug abusers and addicts."

"Tragically, that seems to be the case," agreed Ben. "Kids think that smoking pot and drinking alcohol is just a part of growing up. But then some of them graduate to benzodiazepines, opioids, or neurostimulants, such as cocaine."

"And then quite a few of them overdose," said Elaine.

"Some die," Julia added dolefully.

"But what does this problem have to do with doctors who prescribe opioids for legitimate patients in pain?" asked Elaine. "Doctors don't prescribe all this stuff to these teenagers and college students. They get these drugs from dealers, right?"

"Exactly," said Alex. "But the government, which can't seem to offer any effective means to stop this drug exposure in schools and colleges, has chosen to blame the drug overdose epidemic on doctors."

"And we can see it firsthand," said Ron. "It frightens most physicians, and they stop prescribing opioids to those people who really need them, who then have no choice but to go on the street and buy whatever they can get to alleviate their pain, which is illegal and dangerous. So guess who eventually profits from all of this? Who is the winner in this war on doctors?"

"Drug dealers," Alex stated glumly. "Everyone else loses."

* * *

"Dr. Westwood," Gould continued the direct, "now back to Dr. Holden's patients who stated that they were addicted to opioids. Based on your analysis of their medical files, do you think all of them were addicted?"

"No, the issue of opioid addiction in pain patients is very confusing, even for physicians. Many people who are on opioids for a long period of time become physically dependent on them, but they think that they're addicted. They say, 'Oh, I need this medication all the time, I must be addicted to this drug. But they're not addicted; they're physically dependent. Only a small number of them become truly addicted."

"Dr. Westwood, when doctors talk about opioids, they use the term 'tolerance.' What is that?"

"Tolerance means that over a period of time, some patients may need more opioids to give them adequate pain relief, and that's why the drug dose will need to be increased. You can be tolerant without being physically dependent or physically dependent without being tolerant. You can be addicted without being tolerant. These are three separate entities."

"Are they all interrelated?"

"Well, they're interrelated in the sense that they can all occur after someone is on opioids for a long period of time, but you can have any one of them without the other two."

"And just as a practical matter, when a doctor, like Dr. Holden, is in his examination room seeing a patient for a fifteen- or twenty-minute visit, are these the concepts that a pain doctor must struggle with to figure out what's going on with the patient?"

"Certainly they are. You have to take them into account. But I think the best way to understand what's going on with your patients is to examine them, talk with them, and make an effort to know them. There's no substitute for that."

"Is there a judgment call involved?"

"Absolutely. When you have a patient before you, you have to decide: Should I continue this medication? Do the pros of continuing it outweigh the cons? Should I use other medications? Should I use other methods? These are all things that go through your mind."

"What are the appropriate responses of a pain doctor who's treating a patient with a diagnosed source of legitimate pain and sees that the patient has become tolerant to a particular medicine?"

"Generally, the response is to increase the dose and to observe the patient's response."

"And what about rotating to a different pain medication?"

"Sometimes rotating to a different pain medication is appropriate. For example, if you become tolerant to methadone, you might switch to the fentanyl group or vice versa. That's called 'opioid rotation,' and it's a way to minimize the side effects and minimize the effective dose of the new drug."

"Is it also a way to maximize the analgesic effect?"

"Absolutely."

"Doctor, was the rotation of opioids something that was commonly done by pain doctors during the relevant time period?"

"Yes, it was."

"Now, let me ask you, Doctor, what is breakthrough pain?"

"Well, breakthrough pain is sharp, unexpectedly increased pain. So if patients are on long-acting medications, they can take one pill in the morning, and it will last for twelve hours, and then they take another one at night, and it will last all night. But if they take one of those pills at eight o'clock in the morning, and then at eleven o'clock in the morning their pain has unexpectedly increased, they don't want to take another one of those twelve-hour pills because it's still too early for that. So for that breakthrough pain, doctors generally prescribe a short-acting medication that acts faster and effectively alleviates this sharp pain."

"And during the relevant time period, was it common for pain doctors to prescribe some short-acting medication along with the time-released medication to deal with breakthrough pain?"

"Yes, it was."

"Was it a requirement that the patient take that breakthrough medication?"

"No, if the patient's pain broke through, then she would take it, and if it didn't, she wouldn't."

"And who would make that judgment?"

"The patient would be solely responsible for that decision."

"Dr. Westwood, we've heard this term 'pseudo-addiction.' What is it?"

"Let's say a patient was in the hospital, and a hernia operation had been done. The patient said to the nurse, 'You know, I was given one Percocet tablet for my pain and that just wasn't enough for me. Please give me more pain medicine.' Sometimes the nurse would think, Oh, this patient must be addicted. He is asking for more pain medicine. But this patient is not addicted. He is in pain. This is pseudo-addiction."

"Any other examples?" asked Gould.

"Sometimes the patient might say, 'I've just had two Percocets. They haven't helped my hernia incision at all. You know, the last time I was in the hospital, they gave me a different drug called Dilaudid, and that worked really well for me. Could I have that drug for my pain?' The nurse might think, Oh, the patient is asking for a specific drug. She must be addicted. But this patient wasn't addicted either; she was simply in pain. If the pain medicine doesn't work, it's normal and quite common for someone to say, 'It's not working. I need more,' or, 'It's not working, but in the past another medication helped.' And that's called pseudo-addiction."

"Any other scenario?"

"Sure. A patient is told to take four pills a day, and he takes five a day because he is in more pain. That's also called pseudo-addiction."

"What about a patient who's on OxyContin but goes out to the street and purchases methadone? Would that fall under the category of pseudo-addiction?"

"Absolutely, if they're purchasing methadone to relieve their pain."

"What about a patient who finishes his medication early and comes to his doctor early? Would that fall under the definition?"

"Yes, it would."

"Are there other instances that might look like addiction but might possibly be pseudo-addiction?"

"Yes. Let's say a chronic pain patient was in more pain than usual, finished his medication early, using more than was prescribed, and then found in his wife's medicine cabinet some Percocet left from the time when she had her wisdom tooth out. So he takes one of those and then says to his doctor, 'I took one of my wife's Percocets, and that really helped the pain much more than this other stuff.' This is also behavior that is indicative of pseudo-addiction."

"And was the term and concept of pseudo-addiction known in the pain medicine community during the time period from 2002 to May 2007?"

"Yes, it was."

"So when Dr. Holden was in a room with a patient for his visit on a monthly basis, would he have had to consider pseudo-addiction along with addiction, dependence, and tolerance?"

"Yes, he would. These are all things you consider when you're sitting across from a patient trying to determine in good faith what to do for that patient's pain."

"Is it fair to say that that's a complicated judgment?"

"Very complicated."

"Now, when a pain doctor is faced with a complex situation—a possible aberrant behavior of his patient, does the patient's functioning play some role?"

"Well, in the pain management field, it became obvious early on that the patient's functionality really was the most important factor. Many physicians in pain medicine think functionality is even more important than these pain scores that we get. So if a patient tells you, 'I'm taking this medicine, and I'm able to go back to work,' or, 'I'm able to get up and play with my children,' or, 'I can do some sports activities I couldn't do before,' you can see that the pain medicine is doing them good."

"And what is the basic goal of pain medicine?"

"Well, the basic goal is relieving the pain so that people can get back to living their normal lives: to sleep through the night, get back to work, and for some of them, it's just a matter of being able to get out of bed, being able to interact with their families, not being grumpy all the time because they're in constant horrible pain."

"Was that true during the relevant time period as well?"

"Definitely."

"And how important is the patient's functionality when you're trying to determine whether your patient is a drug addict or not?"

"As I mentioned earlier, one of the definitions of addictive behavior is that your functionality gets worse. The person continues to take opioids despite the fact that it's ruining his or her life while the person using opioids for his or her pain is getting better. So functionality is very important in that regard. Addicts won't tell you, 'On this drug I'm able to go back to work.' They will typically lose their jobs, because their functionality will go down."

"Now, let's talk about a legitimate medical purpose for prescribing opioids that is within the usual course of professional practice. Are you familiar with that standard?"

"Yes, I am."

"Could you explain to the jury, please, the different levels and standards that existed in the practice of medicine during the relevant time period?"

"Sure. Within the umbrella of the standard of care, there are different types of practice. There's the best possible practice, which we should all try to attain. There's an average practice, which is what your average physician out there practices. Then there's not-so-great practice but still within the standard-of-care practice. And way, way below is a practice that we won't even call a medical practice."

"And what is a legitimate medical purpose?"

"Each patient has to have a diagnosis because that's a reason for providing him or her with pain relief. Doctors base their diagnoses on what their patients tell them, on the physical examination, and on the diagnostic tests, such as MRIs, X-rays, or others. Sometimes physicians get old medical records and sometimes they send their patients out for consultation, and they base their opinions as to the diagnosis on all of those things."

"Do red flags eliminate a legitimate medical purpose?"

"No, they do not. For example, someone's MRI shows she has a broken back, and then the doctor finds out that the patient is using her medicine more quickly or the doctor gets a report that this patient was using her friend's medication. That doesn't negate the fact that this patient has a legitimate medical purpose. So red flags really have nothing to do with a legitimate medical purpose."

"What about drug addicts and drug abusers?"

"There are people who are drug abusers who have legitimate medical pain, and they should be treated. They shouldn't be left suffering in pain because they have a substance abuse problem."

"So what does it mean that the doctor acts outside the usual course of professional practice?"

"It means," said Dr. Westwood, "that a doctor isn't acting as a doctor but as a drug pusher. For example, the doctor doesn't ever do an examination of the patient or take a medical history or anything like that and just prescribes opioids. Or at a party, a doctor is asked, 'Can you give me a prescription for Percocet?' and the doctor gives this person the prescription. That's outside the usual course of practice. That person is not this doctor's patient, he's never done his examination, never sent him to any diagnostic tests, but he hands this person a prescription. That's outside of the usual course of practice, even if that person has legitimate pain. Or prescribing when a patient says, 'I don't have any pain. I just want this medication to get high. I'm addicted to this medicine.' That's not prescribing for a legitimate medical purpose. That would be outside of the usual course of medical practice."

"Now, Dr. Westwood, does the doctor have to stop prescribing pain medication and even discharge a longtime patient from his practice because he or she has a bad drug test result showing use of a street drug?"

"No, of course not. You still have to treat that patient."

"Does the doctor have to stop prescribing pain medication if a patient asks to come in early for an appointment or reports a stolen prescription?"

"No, the doctor still needs to determine what the right course of action is for that particular patient, weighing the pros and cons. As I said before, a judgment call is needed."

"Now, Dr. Finnegan suggested that in the face of the behaviors that I've just described, during the relevant time period, a pain doctor had only two choices: to taper the patient off opioids or to utilize the services of an addictionologist and increase monitoring. Based upon your experience and your actual involvement in the pain management community during the relevant time period, were those the only two options?"

"No, Dr. Finnegan was wrong about that. There were many other options."

"Could you describe them for the jury, please?"

"First of all, you can continue to prescribe the medication for that patient. If you know the patient has a legitimate pain diagnosis for which he needs the medicine but he also happens to have gone to a party the night before and used cocaine or something else, you can determine that that was an aberrant behavior, but the patient still needs the pain medicine that you are prescribing. You can increase the frequency of the urine drug testing and have the patient come back earlier, and maybe you give them prescriptions for a briefer period of time. There are many options available there. One option is to get an addictionologist involved, but I must admit, in my practice I can count the fingers on one hand for the number of times I've gotten an addictionologist involved because even at a big hospital it's not easy to get an addictionologist appointment. By the time this patient sees the addictionologist, he or she would have a withdrawal and would also be in a lot of pain. Sure, one of the options would be to discontinue the pain medication, but then one has to wonder what's going to happen to that patient whose pain is not controlled anymore?"

"And again, this is a judgment call?"

"Absolutely. This is a judgment call on the part of the physician who's sitting there facing the patient and having to make a very difficult decision. Patients with severe pain who also happen to have a substance abuse problem are some of the most difficult patients to treat. Do you want to stop their pain medication and risk that the patient is going to go on the street and buy illegal drugs because they're in horrific pain? That's a risk. Or do you want to continue the medication with the understanding that there are other risks involved?"

"Doctor, is it true that the Massachusetts Board of Registration in Medicine in its Model Policy actually provides physicians with a strong and clear recommendation to adequately treat pain?"

"That's correct."

"Why is that?"

"Because I think physicians all over the country, including the state of Massachusetts, understand what scares doctors away from treating pain with the appropriate medications. So they put this statement up front that says, 'By having these regulations or guidelines, we mean that you *should* be treating patients who are suffering in pain.'"

"Thank you for this clarification, Doctor. Is there anything in those guidelines that tells doctors during the relevant time period what their judgment *should be*, given a particular set of facts?"

"Absolutely not. The guidelines are just guidelines, and the decision as to what a doctor does when a particular red flag, for example, comes up is always a judgment call on the part of that doctor. There's *no* law, there's *no* regulation that says: if this happens, do this or do that."

"Now, Doctor, are you familiar with the issue of patients who fool the doctor?"

"Unfortunately I am."

"Something that gets talked about at conferences?"

"It does, and I'm smiling because I've been fooled by patients myself. I think any doctor who prescribes opioid medications is sometimes going to be fooled, and we all understand that. The only way to prevent that would be to never prescribe these medications, and that would mean that there would be a lot of people out there suffering horrible pain because we were unwilling to take that risk. I haven't met a doctor that prescribes opioids who hasn't been fooled occasionally by a patient. Some people become extremely good at deceiving doctors."

"And how do they do that?"

"They know how to fake the physical exams, they make up their medical history, and they fake their symptoms. I've even heard about people who cut and paste somebody else's MRI report and bring it into the office and say, 'Here's my MRI, see how bad it looks.' People like that will do anything to get opioids. So, all of us have been fooled at one time or another by patients who are trying to get these medications, not for pain, but for recreation or their profit."

"Now, Dr. Westwood, is it part of medical training for a doctor to believe their patients?"

"Absolutely. This is the fundamental core of the doctor-patient relationship."

"I want to ask you, and I asked Dr. Finnegan about this, are you familiar with the *Massachusetts General Hospital Handbook of Pain Management* written by Dr. Jane Ballantyne?"

"Yes, I am."

"And is it true that it says that believing the patient and establishing rapport with the patient are of the utmost importance?"

"Yes, and I completely agree. We teach our residents and fellows that if patients say they're in pain, they're in pain. There are no laboratory tests or any other ways to determine how much pain any patient is in. It can't even be determined by diagnostic tests. We always teach our doctors this: if your patient says, 'I'm in severe pain and this medicine or this treatment isn't helping me,' you believe them."

"Doctor, does the practice of pain medicine in part rely upon the good faith of the patient?"

"Certainly."

"It relies upon patients being honest with the doctor?"

"It relies upon patients telling you the truth and you believing them."

"Does it also rely upon the patient following the doctor's prescribing advice in terms of when to take the medication and how much to take?"

"Yes. The patient's responsibility is to fulfill their obligations and take the medication as the doctor prescribes it."

"Does medicine presume that people are out to deceive the doctor and abuse their medications?"

"No, such an attitude was never discussed in the medical community at any time. It was never taught in medical schools either."

"Now, Doctor, you heard Dr. Finnegan testify about the 'Do no harm' concept, correct?"

"Correct."

"Do you agree with Dr. Fishman's statement in his book, *Responsible Opioid Prescribing,* that Hippocrates' directive to 'First do no harm' is quite complex and vexing in pain management, particularly with opioids?"

"I couldn't agree more. It's often very difficult to determine what the appropriate thing to do is with some patients. If you don't treat pain, they can have high blood pressure and suffer heart attacks, and they can get blood clots, pneumonia, and depression. But you also understand there are potential risks from the medications you're going to prescribe. So you're really walking a fine line between trying not to do this kind of harm or that kind of harm, and you have to weigh all the pros and cons and say, 'Do I leave this patient suffering in pain, or do I treat this patient with this medication?'"

"Doctor, do you think that Dr. Fishman's book attempts to be a practical guide as to how to deal with these judgment calls?"

"Yes."

"And it didn't come out until 2007, practically after the relevant time period?"

"Correct."

"Doctor, what do you mean by being vigilant?"

"In my opinion, vigilance is when the physician sits across from the patient and in good faith thinks, 'What's the best thing to do for this patient at this moment in time?'"

"Are you aware of any requirements that doctors write down every aspect of that thought process every time they go through it?"

"Absolutely not. A doctor couldn't possibly write all that down in the time frame of a visit."

"And during the course of your forty-year career, have you reviewed records and office notes written by other doctors?"

"Yes. I've done peer reviews for other hospitals and medical centers, private practices, and academic centers across the country where they've asked me to look at their records to see if they're doing things the right way."

"Now, you said that you looked at seventy six records from Dr. Holden's office. So based upon your review of the records from Dr. Holden and Nurse Practitioner Lander, where do they rate in terms of the range of doctor notes that you've seen in your forty years?"

"Oh, I think they are more legible and there's more information in their records than in most of the notes that I've read."

"And in the medical records that you reviewed from Dr. Holden and Nurse Practitioner Lander, what, if any, observations did you make about the dosages of opioids prescribed, just as a general matter?"

"I would say the doses that Dr. Holden started his patients with were low. He also titrated them up appropriately, exactly as the teaching at that time suggested."

"Mr. Gould," interrupted Judge Adler, "let's stop at this point and have a lunch break."

* * *

The second floor cafeteria of the federal court was famous for its good-quality food and for its unhampered seating arrangement, as prosecutors and defense teams could sit at the neighboring tables and hopefully didn't ruin each other's appetites. Still, the cafeteria was large enough for both sides to keep some distance for the sake of privacy, mainly to avoid eavesdropping.

Ben, Emma, and their friends took seats around a big aluminum table, and as soon as they started eating, Alex interrupted the silence.

"The more I listen to the testimony of Dr. Westwood, the more I become convinced that most of Ben's patients who testified for the prosecution were not addicted. They were dependent on opioids. They simply couldn't function normally without them."

"Can't agree more," said Ben.

"And those few patients who abused prescribed opioids and were addicted," added Ron, "admitted themselves that they were exposed to them and to illegal drugs, way before they started their treatments with Ben or with any other doctor prior to him. As we said before, opioids and illegal drugs, such as cocaine, Ecstasy, and heroin, are available in almost every high school or college."

"Maybe instead of persecuting physicians, who are helping suffering people live normal lives," offered Elaine, "the government should concentrate on this issue. Isn't this experimenting with legal and illegal drugs in adolescence one of the main causes of further drug problems?"

"I think it is," agreed Ben.

"Then maybe, instead of targeting doctors, government agencies should work in cooperation with them."

"I believe it would be much more productive," said Ben. "It may become one of the solutions to the drug abuse problem and especially to this epidemic of drug overdose."

Chapter Forty-Two

"Dr. Westwood," Gould continued his direct examination after the break, "could you please tell the jury: during that time period between 2002 and 2007, to what extent did physicians practicing pain medicine use drug testing in connection with prescribing opioids?"

"I would say it was very uncommon. Even in 2012 the data showed that only ten percent of physicians who prescribed opioids used urine drug screening."

"Could you explain why during the relevant time period physicians weren't using drug testing?"

"Well, drug testing is extremely confusing. It's confusing for the patient; it's confusing for the physician. I think it's even confusing for toxicologists. It's a can of worms, and I'll tell you why. If you are a drug addict or a drug pusher and you're trying to get opioids from a doctor, you know how to falsify those urine drug tests. You can go on the Internet and it will show you how to do it."

"Were those Internet sites available between 2002 and 2007?" asked Judge Adler.

"Yes, definitely they were available at that time. You could buy devices such as a hat with a 'bladder' under it where you put somebody else's urine, and there was a tube that came down your arm. So even if someone actually witnessed that person urinating, it was someone else's urine. There are all kinds of ways to obviate those tests. If you weren't taking the drug you were supposed to take, some people used to put a little piece of the drug under their fingernail so that when they urinated, they would drop a little into the collecting container, and it would come out positive."

"Were there any other problems?" asked Gould.

"Yes, the second problem was that the tests were notoriously unreliable and often misleading."

"Doctor, on your review of Dr. Holden and Nurse Practitioner Lander's patient files, were you able to find drug tests?"

"Yes, I found many tests."

"Dr. Westwood, why would doctors use them in the first place if they were unreliable?"

"Well, the most common reason is to determine whether there is some illicit substance present and to determine if the drug you're prescribing is there at all."

"And would that be another piece of information a doctor would need to factor in when charting out a game plan if, for example, a positive cocaine test was detected?"

"Certainly."

"And during the relevant time period, would an appropriate response to a test showing cocaine be to talk to the patient?"

"Yes."

"Why is that?"

"Because people who experiment with or use cocaine at parties also may have pain, and these patients are difficult to treat. So let's say that after the urine drug test comes back positive for cocaine, the patient says, 'You know, I don't usually do this, but I was at a party the other night and I took some cocaine.' This patient had never shown any signs of abusing the opioids you prescribed. Now you have the decision to make: Do you stop prescribing opioids to this patient who has a legitimate medical condition and suffers from pain? Do you send him off, or do you counsel him and repeat the drug test the next month? It's a judgment call on the part of the physician, and it really depends on the individual patient and the individual situation."

"Doctor, based upon your knowledge, during the relevant time period, did some pain physicians continue to prescribe opioids to legitimate pain patients who had had problematic drug tests?"

"Absolutely."

"Why?"

"For some patients, this option is appropriate. If you have patients with legitimate pain complaints who've been suffering from horrible pain and you give them medication that you know has helped them with their pain, and they have gone to a party and used some drug, the appropriate response may not be to suddenly stop that drug and say, 'Oh, you know, too bad. I'll never prescribe you pain medication.' I don't think that's an appropriate response. But it's the individual physician who has sat with that patient who really knows what the appropriate response is for that patient in that situation."

"Doctor, have you recently reviewed all thirty files that Dr. Finnegan testified about?"

"Yes, I have."

"Could you tell the jury, please, what your conclusions are regarding these files?"

"My conclusions are that Dr. Holden and Nurse Practitioner Lander acted within the usual course of professional practice. They took the patients' medical histories, asked them about their pain, and did physical examinations on all of these patients. They established a diagnosis for all of these patients. They used informed consent and pain management agreements. They used many non-opioid treatments and non-opioid medications, such as anti-inflammatory drugs, antidepressants, anticonvulsants, and many others. They used local anesthetics. So there was this combination of many different types of treatments that they used for their patients. Drug dealers don't do that. In my opinion, Dr. Holden's practice was an absolutely legitimate medical practice."

"Please tell us what else you observed," Judge Adler asked.

"I observed a lot of important, in fact, critically important things. Dr. Holden referred quite a few of his patients to neurosurgeons, orthopedic surgeons, psychiatrists, and psychologists. He ordered physical therapy. As I mentioned, he used non-opioid treatments, he gave different types of injections, and recommended different types of physical therapy and nerve stimulation therapies. He also referred some of his patients to addictionologists and to a number of other providers. His patients underwent random drug testing. Dr. Holden tracked his patients' functionality. I saw many notes in the charts where he asked patients about their functions. Drug dealers don't do that."

"What else did you observe in the files you looked at?" continued Gould.

"I saw that his patients' functionality often improved. Several of his patients could go back to work, and quite a few patients reported improved sleep and improved relationships with their family members. I also saw pain assessments, and I saw evidence that Dr. Holden and Nurse Practitioner Lander regularly adjusted their patients' medications and quite often lowered their doses. That's another sign of a legitimate medical practice. Dr. Holden used diagnostic tests. He ordered nerve conduction tests to determine which nerves were damaged and causing the pain. Numerous MRIs were ordered. There were a number of blood tests. Not just *drug* blood tests but blood tests about patients' blood counts, liver and kidney functioning, testosterone levels, and that sort of thing. Drug dealers don't do that. It was a legitimate medical practice."

"Anything else?"

"He stopped prescribing opioids to a number of patients when he felt it was not appropriate to continue prescribing them. Drug dealers don't dismiss their clients."

"And when you say 'stopped prescribing,' do you mean he tapered some of his patients off their medications?"

"Yes, that is precisely what I am talking about."

"Why is that important?"

"If you're treating patients for pain and they're on opioids for a long period of time, and then for some reason you decide that this is no longer the best thing for those patients, rather than stopping them and having them go through a withdrawal phenomenon, it's best to taper the drug off over a long period of time so they don't experience horrible withdrawal symptoms. In addition, when two of his patients came in and said, 'My medication was stolen,' Dr. Holden required a police report, which is something I think of as above and beyond, and that evidence certainly shows that it was a legitimate medical practice. Drug dealers don't do that."

"So, Dr. Westwood, let me just pick up on the last thing you said, 'above and beyond.' Based upon your review of the files, did you observe evidence that put Dr. Holden and his practice ahead of the curve in terms of what was going on during the relevant time period?"

"Yes, I did. Based on my experience during that period between 2002 and 2007, I think, compared to most of the other pain doctors, Dr. Holden conducted urine drug tests, whereas most physicians did not, and he used them frequently. He employed pain maps, and he used follow-up questionnaires. He required police reports for lost prescriptions. I don't know of anyone else who was doing that. Using pain management agreements and informed consents, I think, was way ahead of the curve. He referred his patients to chiropractors and acupuncture specialists. He used nerve conduction studies that showed which nerve was damaged and might be causing the pain. He ordered general blood work, liver function tests, and many other diagnostic tests. Dr. Holden was using quite a few alternative treatments, such as prolotherapy and osteopathic treatments; he used muscle stimulators, the Lordex decompression table, and magnetotherapy as well as other treatments."

"Now, Dr. Westwood, I would like to ask your opinion regarding those thirty files that Dr. Finnegan has testified about in this courtroom. What is your professional conclusion about these files?"

"Based on my knowledge and experience, I consider that all thirty of these people were legitimate patients who suffered from pain a great deal and who were treated for legitimate medical reasons and within the course of legitimate medical practice. All thirty of them."

"Thank you, Dr. Westwood. Nothing further, Your Honor. My second chair, Mr. Daniels, will take it from here tomorrow."

* * *

The next morning, which was Day 18 of the trial, Daniels continued the direct by asking Dr. Westwood questions about specific treatments of the thirty patients in question, including the six that were mentioned in the indictment. Dr. Westwood's testimony was not limited to drug tests and prescriptions as it was with Dr. Finnegan. She described the severity of their injuries, their failed surgeries, their unbearable pain, the hardships they endured because of these afflictions, and the variety of treatments offered to them by Dr. Holden. She also noted that these patients were gradually feeling better and that some of them went back to work. All of them were able to live normal lives, which was not possible, in her opinion, before Dr. Holden treated them.

It was obvious that Dr. Karen Westwood felt true empathy with the patients she described. To Ben she appeared to be fully aware that these people not only suffered from incurable physical traumas but also faced daunting challenges caused by the pain they had to endure day and night. Ben thought she came across not only as a top-notch expert in the field of pain management but as a human being who understood what people in pain went through.

* * *

As soon as the prosecutor, Mr. Lynch, started his cross-examination, the atmosphere in the courtroom changed dramatically. His cross was aggressive and rude as he tried to dismiss or distort everything that Dr. Westwood said on direct. In his desperate attempts to discredit Dr. Westwood, Lynch used every trick he had up his sleeve, but the harder he tried, the more skeptical the jurors seemed to become.

* * *

Ben thought that the last two hours of cross-examination were almost grotesque. Lynch, who probably ran out of dirty tricks, essentially lost it, as Dr. Westwood warded off his attacks, unshakable and utterly composed. But at the point when the prosecutor's rudeness reached its apex, Edward Gould had enough and rose from his seat.

"Your Honor, could you please ask the counselor to stop harassing the witness," he addressed the judge.

"I agree. Counselor, please refrain from badgering Dr. Westwood." Judge Adler cast a grave look at Lynch, and the prosecutor, who most likely was accustomed to getting away with his obnoxious manner, paused in puzzlement.

An awkward silence hung in the courtroom, and Ben saw a few wry smiles in the jury box.

"I have nothing further," the prosecutor unexpectedly muttered and hurried to his seat.

* * *

The jurors were dismissed. Another court day was over. The prosecutors, the FBI agents, and other government personnel reported to their headquarters on the ninth floor while Ben, Emma, Julia, and their lawyers and friends gathered in the hallway to discuss the events of the day.

"What do you think of Dr. Westwood's testimony?" asked Mark Daniels, not addressing anyone in particular.

"I think she was beyond reproach," said Alex, and everyone nodded in agreement. "Highly professional, sincere, and unlike Dr. Finnegan, empathetic to people suffering from pain."

"A physician of the finest caliber with the stamina of a Navy SEAL," added Emma, and noticed Ben's smile—his first smile of that grueling day in court.

"And what do you think were the jurors' reactions?" asked Gould.

"I saw a few pained glances when Lynch questioned Dr. Westwood," said Elaine.

"Two of them sneered when the judge asked Lynch to stop harassing the witness," added Ron.

"What about that young girl, Juror #12, the one I was hesitant to select for the jury?" asked Gould with concern. "How did she react?"

"I think she looked neutral," said Emma. "But that's probably her regular facial expression."

"I don't believe her opinion will be crucial," said Ron. "She looks much younger than most of the jurors and doesn't impress me as a leader or even a strong personality type."

"Well, we have a few more days to go, and it's not the right moment to make predictions—if such moments ever exist," grinned Gould. "Today was a tough day, but despite the gloomy atmosphere—thanks to the ceaseless efforts of Mr. Lynch—it was a good one, at least in my estimation."

Chapter Forty-Three

THE NINETEENTH DAY OF THE TRIAL began.

"The defense calls Ed Parker," announced Julia Lander's attorney, Peter O'Neil.

A tall, lean man in his fifties slowly entered the courtroom and lowered himself into the witness chair with conspicuous difficulty.

"Good morning, Mr. Parker. I'm Peter O'Neil, and I represent Nurse Julia Lander."

"Good morning."

"Sir, do you suffer from pain?"

"Yes, I do."

"Are you employed?"

"No, I am not. I'm on disability."

"I see. Now, did you previously work?"

"Yes, I did."

"Did you own your own business?"

"Yes, sir, I did. I owned Parker Construction Company."

"Sir, what were the events in your life that led to your pain?"

"I was involved in a very serious car accident in July 1992."

"Were you a patient of Dr. Holden and Nurse Practitioner Lander?"

"Yes, I was their patient from 2002 to 2006. I'm not sure of the exact dates."

"Do you recall if August 9, 2006, was the day of your last appointment?"

"Yeah."

"Tell this jury what happened on that occasion?"

"Dr. Holden terminated my relationship with him for pain management. I tested positive for cocaine, and they had to discharge me."

"We will get back to that, but first I want to ask you a few more questions about your injuries. You said you were in a car accident?"

"Yes, sir, I was. There were multiple fractures in my pelvis, torn soft tissue in my lower back, nerve damage down my left leg, broken ribs, and internal bleeding. I had a lacerated bladder and intestines, and a few broken vertebrae too."

"It sounds as if it was a serious accident?"

"Yes, very serious. I almost died."

"Were you hospitalized?"

"Yes, sir, I was in the hospital for almost three months and had a few surgeries."

"Focusing on the time period from 1992 to 2002, before you became Dr. Holden's patient, did you receive any medications for your pain?"

"Over those years I got a small amount of Percocet from my family doctor and some other doctors, but that did nothing for my pain."

"Did your pain affect your interactions with your family?"

"Absolutely. My sex life was extremely diminished due to severe pain. You know, my attitude was not the happiest. When you're in pain, you're not a happy camper, so to speak."

"And it affected your ability to work?"

"Without taking pain medications, I was literally crippled. I could do nothing at all."

"During this time period before you became a patient of Dr. Holden, did you ever seek drugs from someone on the street in order to help your pain?"

"Yes, I did... I had to."

"Why do you say that?"

"I had a difficult time. During those years I had seen multiple doctors. They would put me on painkillers for a short period of time, and then take me off, and I'd be right back where I started. It was a big roller coaster ride."

"How did it make you feel having to go on the street to find drugs to treat your pain?"

"Nerve-wracking, to say the least."

"Why is that?"

"Well, obviously it's illegal. I had a family, a home, a business to run, and it was a risk. But the pain... was so severe... I had to take that risk."

"So is it fair to say that in 2002 when you became a patient of Dr. Holden, you were suffering from severe back pain and other pain?"

"Yes, I was hurting all over."

"And how did you come to be Dr. Holden's patient?"

"My brother-in-law referred me to him, because Dr. Holden helped him a lot."

"Do you recall your first visit with Dr. Holden? Can you describe what it was like."

"Like most doctor's appointments, I had an extensive examination: range of movement, pain levels, and what not. Dr. Holden asked me about my pain. It was between 9 and 10."

"Did he appear to listen to you?"

"For the first fifteen minutes, I was talking, and he was listening. And after Dr. Holden examined me, he explained his plan for treating my pain. Actually, he suggested a plan for other aspects of my life too."

"Were you eventually able to get to a point where you felt some relief for your suffering?"

"Yes, definitely! My construction business was steadily improving; I started to make a good living. I thought my dark times were finally over."

"Do you recall that from time to time Dr. Holden would ask you to rate aspects of your life, such as daily living activities and how your pain impacted different areas of your day-to-day life?"

"Yes, he did that quite often."

"During the time when you were Dr. Holden's patient, did you have an occasion to observe other patients in the waiting room and to interact with other patients?"

"Yeah, I had conversations with some people."

"What did you observe?"

"It was similar to any other waiting room." Parker reflected for a long minute. "I mean, there would be people in the waiting room just like myself. People would talk about their injuries, ask about mine, share war stories and what not. Just like in any other doctor's office."

"And did you have an occasion to take urine drug tests while you were a patient?"

"Oh, yeah."

"Do you recall approximately how many occasions?"

"Two or three times. I don't remember. It was many years ago."

"And you testified earlier that you were actually discharged when you tested positive for cocaine, is that correct?"

"Yes, I was."

"Did that positive cocaine test happen more than once?"

"Twice. The first time it happened in 2005."

"Mr. Parker, did the treatments that were provided by Dr. Holden and Nurse Practitioner Lander, including opioid medications, help you with your pain and your life in general?"

"No doubt. They made my life bearable. I was able to work and to provide for my family."

"Do you recall the second time that you received a positive test for cocaine?"

"Oh, yes, I do. It happened sometime in the summer of 2006. I tested positive, and Nurse Practitioner Lander asked me to come in and see Dr. Holden. Dr. Holden gave me a two-week prescription and discharged me."

"How did you feel about that decision?"

"I was angry and ashamed of myself."

"Why?"

"Because I knew I was going to be in severe pain, would likely lose my business, and neither one is any fun whatsoever."

"Did you understand his decision?"

"Yeah. It was my mistake. I... I made a stupid mistake. I screwed up."

"Did you ask Dr. Holden to reconsider?"

"Yeah, of course I did."

"Were you successful?"

"No, Dr. Holden said, 'I'm sorry, Ed, I already gave you a chance, and now I can't help you.'"

"Prior to the discharge, how did you feel about the care that you were provided by Dr. Holden and Nurse Practitioner Lander?"

"I was very satisfied. They turned my life around, and that is not an exaggeration."

"Are you still taking opioids to this day?"

"Yes, sir, I am."

"And who is prescribing them for you?"

"My primary care doctor, but I don't get enough. I am still in a lot of pain."

"Thank you, Mr. Parker. I have no more questions for you," concluded Peter O'Neil.

"Ms. Hustler, how long would you need for your cross-examination?" inquired Judge Adler.

"About five minutes, Your Honor."

"Okay, so we'll try to get you out of here by our break time, Mr. Parker," said the judge.

"Oh, we'll be done by the break," agreed Hustler. "Good morning, Mr. Parker."

"Good morning, ma'am."

"Now, you started seeing Dr. Holden in November 2002, is that right?"

"Yes."

"And you saw him on a monthly basis, correct?"

"Yes, I did."

And every month you received prescriptions for opioids, correct?"

"Yes, I did."

"Now, you just testified that you took urine tests two or three times, is that right?"

"Something like that, yeah."

"Have you ever reviewed your medical records from Dr. Holden?"

"Not in any extensive way, no."

"So I'm holding your medical file from Dr. Holden's office. If I told you that the only urine drug test results in this file were from August 2005, and August 2006, would that surprise you?"

"Yes, it would... Actually, it's like I said, two times."

"Well, let's talk about your August 2005 test. You testified that you tested positive for cocaine. This was the first test that was found positive for cocaine, correct?"

"Yes."

"So let's look at the note from that date that Mr. O'Neil just showed you, August 29, 2005. It states, *'On today's visit, a urine test was performed, and cocaine and marijuana were found. I prescribed him Percocet three times a day, and the patient will be back for close follow-up in two weeks.'*"

"Yes."

"Now, did Nurse Practitioner Lander tell you on this day that she and Dr. Holden have a zero tolerance policy for cocaine use?"

"I don't recall that, no."

"Did she tell you that, in her view, it was illegal to prescribe narcotics because you tested positive for cocaine?"

"No."

"Did she refer you to an addictionologist?"

"No, she didn't. I wasn't a drug addict. I was running my business and supporting my family."

"Other than coming back in two weeks, was there any other increased monitoring of your prescriptions?"

"No. I don't believe so."

"And you continued to receive narcotics at each appointment after this, correct?"

"Yes."

"And the next test that we have in your file is from August 2006. That's the one you just testified about, right, where you again tested positive for cocaine?"

"Yes."

"And you saw Dr. Holden on that day?"

"Yes, ma'am. It was my last visit with either him or Nurse Practitioner Lander."

"Nothing further, Your Honor," declared Hustler.

Ed Parker limped to the exit. Emma rose from her seat and followed him into the hallway.

"Mr. Parker!" she called.

"Yes?" The man stopped and gave Emma an inquisitive look.

"I'm Mrs. Holden," Emma offered a handshake.

Ed Parker shook her hand and smiled gingerly, another question mark in his glance.

"I just wanted to thank you for your honest testimony. It was truly noble on your part."

Parker gave Emma a sad look.

"He was the best doctor I ever had, and I screwed up."

"Do you see a doctor now?"

"Yes, I do. But it's not the same. I'm constantly in pain. We crippled folks..." He stopped mid-sentence. "The doctors now are scared to treat us the right way. Your husband was different..." Parker was silent for a moment. "And now he is paying the price." He paused and shook his head in despair, as if to say, I can't believe such injustice has been done to him.

"I wish all the luck in the world to Dr. Holden and to you too, ma'am." He gave a soulful smile.

"Thank you, Mr. Parker."

Ed Parker turned around and slowly hobbled toward the elevator.

Chapter Forty-Four

"Your next witness, Mr. Gould?"

"Yes, Your Honor. Defense calls Sandra Learner."

A slender, attractive woman in her late thirties took her seat in the witness chair. Dr. Holden's devoted and reliable front-desk assistant, Sandra Learner, was smart, capable, had an incredible memory, and could handle the most demanding patients with the ease of a tiger tamer.

"Good afternoon, Ms. Learner," Gould began his direct.

"Good afternoon, sir." Sandra had never testified in court before, and she looked a little nervous.

"Would you like some water?" asked Gould.

"Thank you. I'm all right."

"Ms. Learner, are you presently employed?"

"Yes, I am."

"Where do you work?"

"I work in a family care medical group in Needham."

"And what do you do there?"

"I am a front desk assistant for a group of three doctors."

"Ms. Learner, have you ever worked in Dr. Holden's pain management center?"

"Yes, I have."

"And what was the position that you were hired for?"

"A front-desk secretary job."

"Could you tell us a little bit more about your job duties at the center."

"I answered the phones and made appointments, greeted patients, made sure that the charts were prepared for Dr. Holden and Ms. Lander, and collected co-payments if necessary. When patients were leaving, I would be responsible for making follow-up appointments and referrals, if needed."

"Would you ever take messages for Dr. Holden or Nurse Practitioner Lander?"

"Yes, I would."

"Were you ever involved in referrals to other medical providers?"

"Yes, we referred a lot of patients to neurological studies. Many of our patients were sent for MRIs, CT scans, and X-rays. If it was necessary, patients were also referred to neurologists, psychiatrists, or psychologists. If some of them needed surgery, they were referred to surgeons."

"How about referrals to addictionologists? Did you ever see those?"

"Yes, I did. There were patients who were referred to addictionologists."

"So, in Dr. Holden's center, where did you physically sit?"

"My desk was located in the center of the office. To my right there was a large waiting room."

"So you had an opportunity to interact with patients who came to the practice, right?"

"Of course. I was the first person to see them and interact with them."

"You greeted them, processed their paperwork, and had a view of them in the waiting room, correct?"

"Correct."

"How would you describe the patients that you saw coming into the practice?"

"Objection!" interrupted Lynch.

"Mr. Lynch, you were the first one who raised this issue on a few occasions, so the objection is overruled," said Judge Adler. "Ms. Learner, please go ahead."

"I would say the majority of the patients were regular working-class people."

"Did you observe people who appeared to be in pain?" Gould asked.

"Yes, almost all of them were in pain."

"How could you tell they were in pain?" asked Gould.

"You can see that by their facial expressions, by their movements... Pain can change people's appearances. I remember a patient who used to come to our center often, but one day, he came after a recent accident and I *did not* recognize him. This is how pain can change a person."

"Did you observe people whose pain appeared to get better over time?"

"Yes, on many occasions," Sandra Learner said firmly.

"Who was responsible for admitting new patients to the practice?"

"Dr. Holden personally evaluated new patients and ordered diagnostic tests, if necessary."

"Based on your personal knowledge, on average, how long did his patients' visits tend to last?"

"If it was the patient's first visit, it would last forty minutes or so, and if it was a follow-up then, I would say the visit lasted at least fifteen minutes to twenty minutes. Sometimes longer."

"Do you remember how many patients Dr. Holden and Nurse Practitioner Lander would see in a day?"

"I would say probably twenty–twenty five patients per person, sometimes less."

"And do you know how large the patient population was in total?"

"I would estimate it as between two and three thousand, but I don't know how many exactly."

"What types of treatments were offered to patients in Dr. Holden's center?"

"Dr. Holden was an expert in muscularskeletal problems, so he used different types of injections and osteopathic treatments. We also had a physical therapist, a neurologist, a psychologist, and a psychiatrist. Dr. Holden hired tai-chi and Pilates instructors, and a specialist in acupuncture."

"Anything else?" asked Judge Adler.

"We had an electronic spine decompression table and some other unique physical therapy machines. And there was a clinical laboratory, where the lab technician collected samples for the general blood and urine tests."

"Did you have any additional staff for administering urine drug tests?"

"Yes, we did. We had a person in charge of collecting the samples, and I was one of those who would receive the faxed results of the urine tests and go over them to see if any illegal substances were detected. If any of these tests were problematic, I would highlight their results and put them on Dr. Holden's or Nurse Practitioner Lander's desk for review."

"Before the patient's appointment?" Judge Adler asked.

"Usually before, Your Honor. Or if the patient had already left, and we received the test results a couple of days later because the laboratory had some delays, I would put them immediately on Dr. Holden's or Nurse Practitioner Lander's desk."

"Did Dr. Holden or Nurse Lander ask you to do that?" asked Gould.

"Yes, we had discussed it, and I was assigned this responsibility."

"Do you know what Dr. Holden or Nurse Practitioner Lander would do with those results?"

"Objection, calls for speculation," interfered Lynch.

"Did you personally see what they did with the results?" Judge Adler rephrased the question.

"Yes, Dr. Holden came up with an idea to send letters to the patients who tested positive for illegal substances. The letter informed them that their tests came back positive for illegal drugs. I would mail a letter to the patient, make a copy, and put it into the patient's file."

"Do you know if patients were ever discharged because illegal drugs showed up in their blood or urine tests?"

"Yes, especially if it was their second violation of the office policy. The letter that I just mentioned actually notified patients they had broken our rules and that their narcotic pain medications would not be prescribed any longer. They could still come for other treatments, but they would not receive prescriptions for any opioids. They were also offered a consultation with an addictionologist."

"Ms. Learner, did you ever witness patients becoming disruptive or unruly in the practice?"

"Yes. Some of the patients were very unhappy about Dr. Holden's decision to stop prescribing opioids to them."

"Do you recall any specific instances where a patient got upset about being told that they could no longer receive opioids?"

"Well, one sticks out... This patient, I don't remember his name, had cocaine in his urine test for the second time, and when Dr. Holden told this patient that he couldn't prescribe him opioids any longer, he got really angry and verbally abusive. He started swearing and made Dr. Holden really upset. That's why Dr. Holden made a decision to send each of them a confidential letter with an explanation about why they couldn't receive opioids any longer rather than confronting them in the office."

"Ms. Learner, do you recall Dr. Holden or Nurse Practitioner Lander ever telling you to call the police?"

"Yes, on a few occasions."

"Can you describe some of those occasions, please."

"If the patient was disruptive and demanded drugs, I would call Dr. Holden or Ms. Lander, and they would tell me to contact the police and ask them to come over."

"Do you recall an incident in 2006 when Dr. Holden was not in the office, and you received a call from a pharmacist who suspected that a female patient had forged her prescriptions?"

"I don't remember exactly, but we had an incident when Dr. Holden was not present at the office, and Ms. Lander received a phone call about stolen prescription pads."

"And do you recall Nurse Lander instructing you to call the police?"

"Did she tell you to call?" asked Judge Adler.

"Yes, she told me to contact the police immediately."

"Do you remember a female patient being arrested after leaving the practice on one occasion?"

"I didn't see anyone arrested, but I saw how the police escorted patients out of the office."

"Oh, you did see the police escort people out of the office?" queried Judge Adler.

"With my own eyes, yes."

"You actually saw that?" Judge Adler arched a brow.

"Yes, Your Honor, I did see the police come into the office and escort patients out of the office. Were they arrested or let go? I don't know."

"Perfect. You're getting the hang of this evidence thing," Judge Adler remarked, her comment accompanied by a hushed laughter in the courtroom.

"Do you believe that Dr. Holden and Nurse Practitioner Lander cared about their patients?" asked Gould.

"Objection, relevance!" Lynch jumped up from his seat.

"Overruled," said the judge.

"No doubt about it. Absolutely. I—"

"You meant to say 'yes,' suggested Judge Adler.

"Sorry, Your Honor, it was my unconditional yes."

"Ms. Learner, why do you think that?" asked Gould.

"Objection!" Lynch could barely stifle his anger.

"Describe it, please, based on what you've seen," said Judge Adler.

"I remember a couple patients who were actually cancer patients. One of the patients... I'm going to be kind of..." Ms. Learner paused and inhaled. "One of the patients came in and said good-bye to Dr. Holden and thanked him for everything. This man was so ill that his adult son had to wheel him in." Sandra stopped, her eyes were filled with tears, and she breathed deeply to compose herself. "For so many years, Dr. Holden had been helping him so much..." Sandra halted again, "and he really, really appreciated it. It was the last time this patient came, and it was...

it was heartbreaking." Sandra quietly sobbed. "And then this lady with lung cancer... she too came over to say good-bye."

"Objection, Your Honor," Lynch interfered, but not as forcefully as before.

"This is what you personally saw?" Judge Adler asked.

"This is what I saw. Dr. Holden's patients, dying of cancer, came to the office just to say thank you and good-bye."

"Do you need a tissue?" asked Judge Adler.

"Yes, please." Sandra took a tissue offered by the clerk, thanked her, and dabbed her eyes. "I'm sorry."

"That's all right," Gould replied and cast Sandra a kindly look. "Take your time."

There was a long silence in the courtroom, and then he continued.

"Ms. Learner, were you ever a patient of Dr. Holden or Nurse Practitioner Lander?"

"Yes, I was."

"Why?"

"I had a car accident. An eighteen-wheel truck hit my car, so I experienced frequent and severe headaches and neck spasms. Because I valued Dr. Holden's expertise, I asked him to take care of me."

"What types of treatments did you receive?"

"I had regular shots of Sarapin to my neck muscles, trigger point injections to different areas of my head, and osteopathic treatments. Dr. Holden also suggested that I have acupuncture and physical therapy."

"What is Sarapin?" asked Judge Adler. "I never heard about it."

"Your Honor, it's an extract from a pitcher plant that blocks pain. It has no side effects, even if used frequently," Sandra explained. "Those shots were very helpful."

"Did you improve under the care of Dr. Holden and Nurse Practitioner Lander?"

"A great deal. I was able to work full time at the office. I was able to take care of my daughter and my home. Without these treatments, my headaches were debilitating."

"Did you ever refer anybody else to Dr. Holden's center?" asked Gould.

"Objection."

"Overruled."

"Yes, I did. I personally referred to him quite a few of my friends."

"Ms. Learner, you said you now work at a family care medical group?"

"Yes, I do."

"Is it a reputable medical practice?"

"Yes, it is."

"And you said you work as a receptionist at the front desk?"

"Yes, I do."

"Are your duties there similar to those you performed at Dr. Holden's center?"

"Very similar, and my work experience with Dr. Holden was very helpful for my present job."

"In your experience, is the medical practice that you are currently working at similar to Dr. Holden's center?

"Very similar. I would say extremely similar."

"Thank you, Ms. Learner, I have no further questions," concluded Gould.

* * *

Attorney Lynch moved to the lectern, a wicked sparkle in his eyes foretelling a harsh cross.

"Ms. Learner, I have a few questions. First, let me show you the document that has been put in evidence, Exhibit 816A. Do you see it? It's on the screen too."

"Yes, I do."

"This notes a number of cash payments here, correct?"

"That is correct."

"And a number of patients paid for their visits by cash, correct?"

"That is correct," said Sandra.

"And when patients showed up, they paid up front, correct, before they had their visits?"

"Patients were informed about the insurance that Dr. Holden accepted, and they were also informed that if they didn't have insurance or if we didn't accept their insurance, they had to pay a certain amount of money. It's normal practice."

"And they would pay before they saw the doctor or the nurse, correct?"

"That is correct."

"And was the reason for this office policy that if they didn't pay first and they didn't get a prescription for opioids, they might not pay on their way out?"

"No, that is not correct. It's absolutely not correct, because it's normal practice at the place where I work right now to collect a co-payment or cash payments *before* the visit."

"Okay. Is it normal practice at the clinic you're at now to call the police on multiple occasions to remove people from the office?"

"Sir, in Dr. Holden's office we didn't call the police on *multiple* occasions. It happened only two or three times over the years, and Dr. Holden explained to me that, unfortunately, every pain clinic has its share of abusive patients. As for the place where I work now, our doctors do not prescribe any opioids because they are afraid of the DEA. They are afraid of being prosecuted for doing their job."

"So you can remember *some* occasions where the police were called to remove people from the office, right?"

"Yes."

"Do you remember the fact that you had confrontations with people because they weren't getting the medications they wanted?"

"Yes, I do."

"And that happened weekly, correct? Actually, daily?"

"No, it happened a few times in the course of several years. Not weekly and not daily."

"And you remember at least sixty or seventy patients were cut loose because of positive drug tests?"

"Between 2004 and 2007, yes."

"Now, Ms. Learner, you stated you were a patient of Dr. Holden for approximately four years?"

"Yes, I was."

"Did you receive any opioids?"

"No."

"In fact, at no point in those four years, despite your pain, did you receive any pain medications, correct? No opioids were prescribed to you, right?"

"That's right, because I'm highly allergic to them. I told Dr. Holden about it."

For fifteen minutes, Lynch continued to ask Sandra Learner questions about drug tests and letters in patients' files, looking more and more frustrated and worn out. Sandra never buckled under his onslaught, and the jurors seemed to enjoy every instant of the duel.

Lynch, exhausted by his futile attacks, finally gave up and moved to a new topic.

"Now, you spoke about the doctor and the nurse seeing patients. Was every minute of every day spent seeing patients?"

"Yes, it was."

"They were constantly seeing patients?"

"That's what they both did all day long, sir."

"Okay, and they never did anything else?"

"They went to the bathroom. It takes a few minutes."

A few smirks flashed in the jury box. Even Judge Adler couldn't repress her smile.

"Ms. Learner, you stated that you would receive phone calls, and you would take notes and put those notes in the files if they were related to patients, is that correct?"

"Yes, I would receive phone calls and put notes in the files."

"And also occasionally write things on file covers?"

"Yes."

"Did you also bring those to the attention of Dr. Holden or Nurse Practitioner Lander when they—"

"I didn't need to bring it to their attention. If *any* important information about patient's health condition was received, they would make a decision right away. After that, I would put a sticker on the file cover. Dr. Holden made these medical decisions, and I just flagged them. That's the way it should be, and that's how it was in our office, sir."

"You spoke in general that you would write notes, correct?"

"I would write notes after I was told to, but I would not make any decisions."

"No, I'm not asking that. Your Honor, I'm just going to... I don't want to publish this note to the jury. I just want to show it to the witness. Can you see us at the sidebar?" Lynch asked.

"Okay, come over," agreed Judge Adler.

"Is that your writing?" Lynch asked, showing Ms. Learner a handwritten note.

"No."

"Do you know whose writing that is?"

"I cannot guess, but it's not my handwriting."

"I see. Now, Ms. Learner, you said you were the one who sent out the letters, correct?"

"I would, but if I was not in the office, someone else would send them."

"Would you speak to Nurse Practitioner Lander or Dr. Holden before you sent the letter?"

"I stated before that it was *their* decision to send the letters."

"Was it *their* decision for each individual letter?"

"For each individual letter, it was their decision. Sir, I think I told you that at least three times already," said Ms. Learner.

Still, for twenty more minutes Lynch peppered Sandra Learner with questions about the correspondence that Dr. Holden sent to his patients and the drug test results that she put in the patients files. Sandra parried each of his questions with an instant answer, but they definitely were not the answers that the prosecutor tried to squeeze out of her.

Judge Adler became annoyed.

"Please, we've got to finish this today!" she finally exclaimed in frustration. "Mr. Lynch, let's change the topic! Move on please."

Completely drained, Lynch suddenly uttered, "Nothing further, Your Honor."

The judge turned to Ben's attorney.

"Anything for redirect, Mr. Gould?"

"Very briefly, Your Honor," said Gould. "Ms. Learner, let's just try to clear up the confusion."

"Let's do it," Sandra Learner nodded approvingly.

"Whenever it was, in late 2005 or early 2006, when letters were mailed from the office, that was something that you were involved with, correct?"

"That is correct."

"And you would do that when either Dr. Holden or Nurse Practitioner Lander would tell you, 'A patient won't receive opioids any longer. Please let him or her know about it by mailing the letter,' correct?"

"Finally someone got it right! Yes, sir, that is correct," said Sandra.

"But even before that, were there occasions where Dr. Holden or Nurse Practitioner Lander would ask you to make a notation in the chart: *'This person has violated our rules and should be discharged'* or *'This person won't get opioids any longer'*?" asked Gould.

"Yes, I would write on the cover of the file, *'No more appointments with Dr. Holden'* or *'No more opioids.'* Always in big letters so that it wouldn't be missed," she added.

"And that was during the pre-letter period?"

"I couldn't say it better myself. Yes, it was during the pre-letter period. That's what it was."

"So at some point, your office procedure changed from the doctor's verbal instruction to an official notification letter, right?"

"Yes! Exactly."

"Okay. Can I just ask you generally, was this a busy practice?"

"It was a very busy practice, and when our office got raided... oh no, I am not going into... I value your time. I'm sorry."

Judge Adler smiled and shook her head.

"Don't worry, Ms. Learner," Gould gave an inconspicuous grin. "Your testimony is over. Thank you. No further questions."

"Nothing for recross," echoed Lynch.

"Thank you, Ms. Learner." Judge Adler offered Sandra another gentle smile. "By the way, is this your first experience testifying in court?"

"Yes, Your Honor." Sandra heaved a deep sigh.

"Oh, you did well," the judge smiled a little broader. "But I hope it's the last one."

"Me too, Your Honor."

Chapter Forty-Five

Day 20 of the trial, the last day of the defense case, started with the testimony of Dr. Janine White, a neurologist, who had joined Dr. Holden's practice about a year before the DEA and FBI raid. She soon established herself as a knowledgeable and caring specialist and became a valuable team member, equally respected by the office staff and her patients.

During Mark Daniels's direct examination, confident and composed, Dr. White talked about her personal and professional experience at the pain clinic that Dr. Holden directed. She described her most complex and challenging patients, who suffered from various painful conditions, and stressed that as a result of her observations, she believed that Dr. Holden had a legitimate practice, and his staff did their best to help people in pain.

Under the cross by Matilda Hustler, Dr. White demonstrated the same self-control, and in spite of the prosecutor's intense questions, she stuck to her favorable opinion of Dr. Holden, Nurse Practitioner Lander, and their medical practice. During her testimony, Ben noticed a few approving nods from the jurors.

When her testimony was finished, the judge turned to Ben's lead attorney:

"Mr. Gould, if I'm not mistaken, the next witness is your last one?"

"Yes, Your Honor." Gould turned to Mark Daniels.

"The defense calls Mitch Forte." Daniels moved to the lectern and placed his notes on the stand.

A middle-aged man with a round face and large blue eyes took his seat in the witness chair. "Good morning, Mr. Forte," began Mark Daniels.

"Good morning, sir," Mitch Forte answered with a humble smile.

"Mr. Forte, where do you currently live?"

"Nashua, New Hampshire."

"With whom do you live?"

"I live with my wife and my two boys."

"Are you currently employed?"

"Yes, I am."

"What's your job?"

"I work as a senior product planner for a medical company in the renal dialysis industry."

"Mr. Forte, do you currently take opioids?"

"Yes, I take oxycodone and I use a fentanyl patch."

"Mr. Forte, at some point did you injure your back?"

"Yes, in December of 1999, we had a heavy snowstorm, and I was shoveling the driveway. I felt a pop in my back and immediate pain, stabbing, burning... really sharp pain going down my legs."

"What happened next?"

"A couple of days later, I called my family doctor, and he suggested that I see a specialist because I wasn't getting any better. We tried some anti-inflammatory pills, but eventually I ended up going to a specialist."

"Did this specialist give you a diagnosis?"

"Yes. He said it was a herniated disk. He started me on steroid injections and physical therapy, but they did not help me more than for a few days, if that."

"How, if at all, did your pain impact your ability to work?"

"The more the day progressed, the worse the pain got, so staying at work was torture."

"Did you ever consider seeking disability?"

"No way. I have a family. Two boys to put through college. I had to work and I wanted to."

"Sir, what else did doctors try to relieve your back pain?"

"A lot of conventional things and also some new techniques: epidurals, the facet joint injections, a Racz catheter, and a few other things, but nothing really helped."

"Did you eventually see a surgeon?"

"Yes, the surgeon took out a big chunk of my lumbar disc."

"And what happened after the surgery?"

"For about six months I felt great, and then the pain came back, and it was worse than ever. So I went back to my family doctor, had an MRI, and then he said, 'You need to go back to the surgeon.'"

"And did you have another surgery?"

"I did, unfortunately."

"And what happened in that second surgery?"

"They took out ninety percent of that disc, but I still had very serious pain."

"Did doctors start prescribing you opioids, including oxycodone and Actiq?"

"Oh, yes, they did. I simply couldn't function anymore without them."

"Sir, what is Actiq?"

"It is an oral form of fentanyl. You use it as a lozenge in case of severe flare-up, and it lessens the pain almost immediately."

"How did these medications work for you?"

"Well, at that point I couldn't do anything. The pain would just stop me dead in my tracks. Actiq took away that breakthrough pain. It would settle me down. I was finally able to sleep. Then, later on, Dr. Holden started me on methadone."

"And did methadone help you as well?"

"No doubt about it. Compared to the other medications prescribed to me before, methadone didn't sedate me, and I could also take a much smaller dose with a greater effect."

"Sir, did methadone give you any significant euphoria?"

"Sorry, what is euphoria?"

"Euphoria is a sensation of being high or feeling excessive elation."

"I don't believe I ever experienced that sensation... Maybe on my wedding day, or our honeymoon in Aruba. Not in the last ten years, for sure. Not after my first back surgery anyway."

"Objection, relevance," interjected Lynch.

"Sir, please just answer the questions. I don't think we have time to listen to your honeymoon experience." Judge Adler smiled.

"Sorry, Your Honor," blushed Mitch Forte. "I'll stick to the questions."

"Sir, did you need all of those pain medications in order to function on a day-to-day basis?"

"When all other treatments failed, those pain medications were the only thing that really helped. They gave me a chance to live and work, and that's all I was looking for."

"So at some point did you begin seeing Dr. Holden?"

"Yes, I did."

"Who referred you to him?"

"Actually, a nurse at the ER where I was admitted referred me."

"Could you please describe what your first appointment with Dr. Holden was like?"

"It was a full physical examination. He was looking at my mobility, where my pain was, my history with other doctors, and what type of treatments I was getting from them. I believe I had my records sent over to him so he could see my medical history. Then he said, 'Okay, let's have a plan. We'll start with different types of herbal injections, prolotherapy, and some new treatments, and also a special course of exercises.' So I made another appointment, and we went forward."

"Can you tell us a little about some of these new treatments that Dr. Holden offered to you?"

"Well, he had that Lordex decompression table in his office. After a few treatments, I felt much better."

"Given your history with other doctors, can you compare the first appointment with Dr. Holden with the first appointments you'd had with the other physicians you'd seen for your pain?"

"Objection, Your Honor, relevance," intervened Lynch.

"I'll allow it. Just tell us what you remember about that day," ruled Judge Adler.

"You know, when you go to see a doctor, you can always tell when you're having a good exam or not. Dr. Holden was very attentive. He listened to what I was saying, what my pain level was, what I went through, and then he examined me and designed a plan and discussed it with me in every detail. I was comfortable with him right away."

"Did Dr. Holden give you any instructions about how to take pain medications, especially methadone?"

"Oh, yes, he did. Just like with any medication, you have to follow the instructions. Methadone is an opioid, and it has to be taken very seriously. So, yes, he did. Absolutely."

"Apart from the injections and the opioids that we've talked about, in what other ways, if any, did Dr. Holden treat you?"

"He used some machinery for my therapy. I don't remember the name. With these injections, the medication, and the machinery, I was doing really well. I would go for physical therapy in the morning, driving down from Nashua at 6:30, arriving at his office by 8, and having it done. That really helped. With all the treatments, and, sure, with the medication, we finally got a good handle on it."

"Mr. Forte, you just mentioned prolotherapy injections. Did Dr. Holden's prolotherapy treatments help you in addition to the pain medications?"

"Yes, they surely did."

"I saw in your medical file that you were also treated by a pain psychologist. Did Dr. Holden refer you to her?"

"Yes, he did. I was becoming very irritable. My wife and my two boys noticed something was wrong with dad... Well, to make a long story short, I told Dr. Holden about that, and he sent me to a pain psychologist. She was a nice lady, and very professional too."

"Did at some point Dr. Holden begin decreasing your pain medication?"

"Yes. When I got more control over my day-to-day pain. That was the plan from the very start."

"Based on your personal experience and all your interactions and treatments with Dr. Holden, what was your overall experience with him as a doctor?"

"It was very good. I got results. I was able to work every day. That's all I was asking for. I didn't want to be disabled and go on disability. I wanted to work to support my family. I was not planning hang gliding or parachuting. I just needed to provide for my family, as simple as that."

"And overall what was your experience with Nurse Practitioner Lander?"

"The same as with Dr. Holden. You know, she was very caring. She helped me reach my goal, which was to work, and I was able to do that."

"Thank you, Mr. Forte. No further questions," said Attorney Daniels.

Judge Adler turned to the jurors. "Do you want to stand up and stretch before Mr. Lynch starts his cross?"

The jurors nodded with appreciation and got up from their seats.

* * *

"Good morning, Mr. Forte," Lynch began his cross. "I'll try to get this done as quickly as possible. Please turn your attention to your first visit note that was shown to you by the defense counsel. Do you remember you testified that you had an extensive physical examination?"

"Yes."

"And do you remember getting prescriptions for opioids from Dr. Holden?"

"Yes."

"Sir, in your prior testimony, you said that before you came to Dr. Holden you hadn't gotten the amount of opioids that Dr. Holden gave you, correct?"

"Right. Other doctors I'd seen gave me some, but that was never enough, because I was in constant pain."

"Okay. Now, during your direct examination by Mr. Daniels, you said that you understood that you had to take your medications carefully, correct?"

"Yes."

"You understand that those medications could be potentially dangerous if you mixed them?"

"Absolutely, they should be taken only as prescribed, yes."

"You've been told you have to take the drugs as they're prescribed?"

"Correct, Dr. Holden told me that a few times."

"Sir, do you remember at one point requesting your medical insurance to cover the Actiq lozenges from Dr. Holden?"

"Yes, I remember that."

"Sir, are you aware that Actiq should be prescribed for cancer pain only?"

"Dr. Holden told me that. He also told me that it was an excellent medicine for breakthrough pain, which I had many times a day."

"Sir, did Dr. Holden or Nurse Practitioner Lander ever wean you off any drugs?"

"Yes, they did."

"They told you they were going to wean you off?"

"Well, they said to me, 'Mitch, we're going to start gradually reducing the amount of pain medicine you are taking.' Gradually, they said."

"And still at some point they gave you a prescription for methadone, didn't they?"

"Yes, that's true."

"Did they discuss with you the dangers of taking methadone?"

"I don't remember if Dr. Holden used the word 'danger,' but he explained to me how to take it and told me to use regular precautions. At that point, my back pain was out of control again, and my usual pain meds didn't work. So Dr. Holden wanted me to try this new stuff, methadone, and it worked wonders. Yes, he told me to take it only as prescribed."

"How about Nurse Practitioner Lander? Did she ever give you any directions regarding methadone?"

"Nurse Lander? Of course. She was as vigilant about that stuff… as a hawk."

"No further questions," said Lynch, casting a disappointed look at the witness.

"Mr. Daniels, redirect?"

"Yes, Your Honor." Mark Daniels rose from his seat.

"Mr. Forte, since the accident in December 1999 and before you saw Dr. Holden and Nurse Practitioner Lander, had you ever gotten sufficient relief from your pain?"

"No, never, that's why I was getting those surgeries."

"But they didn't help you either, did they?"

"They made my back pain worse than ever, that's what they did."

"Before Dr. Holden prescribed opioids, were you able to function on a day-to-day basis?"

"No, I was practically crippled."

"And are you still receiving powerful opioids?"

"Yes, and I'm working full time, and I've had that job for over nine years. I'm functioning as an ordinary human being, not as a cripple… I can be a good husband and a good father."

"Last question, Mr. Forte. Mr. Lynch told you that the pain medication Actiq should be prescribed for cancer pain patients only, remember?"

"That's what he said. Dr. Holden explained to me that Actiq was designed for cancer patients, but he said that physicians all over the country also prescribe it for noncancer patients when their pain becomes unbearable, and it works for them very well. We tried it, and it really helped. It was my salvation. I could sleep at night and work during the day, and I could even go fishing with my sons."

"Nothing further," Daniels concluded his redirect.

"Thank you for coming in," said Judge Adler.

"At this time the defense rests," declared Gould.

"Very well, in that case we should conclude our day," Judge Adler said with discernible relief. "I will see you all in the morning for the closing arguments."

* * *

On the last day of the trial, the closing arguments attracted a full house. Ben and Julia's relatives and friends filled row after row, competing with government agents and other eager spectators from the U.S. Attorney's Office. It looked like people on the ninth floor had dropped their busy routines and rushed to support their colleagues. They occupied more than half of the courtroom in rapt anticipation of the grand finale. Their mood was on the verge of festive—all handshakes and smiles.

Lynch went first. He painted Dr. Ben Holden and Nurse Practitioner Julia Lander as two ruthless drug dealers, destroying the well-being of innocent citizens who had the misfortune to become their patients. In a theatrical and grotesque manner, he tried to convince the jury that under the pretense of valid medical care, these two individuals fed their patients addictive drugs for years, and as a result, their families were ruined, and their lives shattered. A guilty verdict for each of these common criminals, Lynch insisted, was the only one that would fit the bill. The jurors looked attentive, at least for the first ten minutes of his closing argument, Ben noticed, but after that most of them seemed lost to him.

Then it was Gould's turn. In an eloquent, thoroughly prepared closing argument, armed with facts and quotations from the national medical experts and the witnesses' testimonies, he refuted one after another of Lynch's statements. He stressed that Dr. Holden, while practicing in one of the most challenging fields of medicine, did his best to help thousands of suffering people to live better lives. As a practicing frontline physician, he always followed the existing regulations and guidelines and was never involved in any criminal acts.

"The government is trying to punish Dr. Holden for breaking the rules, which at the time of his practice didn't even exist. Dr. Holden is an honest man and a devoted physician, and should be found not guilty on all counts."

To Ben, it looked like the jurors were listening closely, and five or six of them even slightly nodded in agreement a few times. By the end of Gould's speech, one of the jurors, a middle-aged lady in the first row, was teary-eyed.

Peter O'Neil, Julia Lander's attorney, followed. His closing arguments were thoughtful, persuasive, and straight to the point. He too demanded a not guilty verdict for Nurse Practitioner Lander, whom he described as a caring and highly professional nurse, who never committed any illegal acts and who put her heart and soul into helping those patients who suffered from intense pain.

Then, as the court rule allowed him to do, Lynch presented his accusatory conclusions to the jury. Because he couldn't offer anything new, Ben observed, the prosecutor hammered away at him and Nurse Practitioner Lander with his accusations, his swaggering enthusiasm compensating for the lack of convincing facts.

In about four hours, the trial was over. The judge declared a break before giving the jury instructions, and the main participants, along with the gallery crowd, poured into the hallway.

"Edward, your closing arguments were superb... and truly moving. Are you pleased?" Ben smiled broadly.

"You know," Gould grinned wistfully, "I am never completely satisfied with my work."

"You may not be, but I am. We all are."

"Thank you, Ben."

"Did you see that by the end of your speech Juror #1 was about to cry?"

"I noticed."

"So, what do you think? Do we have a chance? My friends and relatives who have observed the entire trial think we do."

"Ben, I don't have any clairvoyant abilities."

"Are you always that cautious?"

"I have to be." Gould gave a world-weary smile. "You see, after my closing arguments in some trials, I was totally sure I'd won the case, and then the jurors found the defendant guilty, while there were other times when I was confident I'd lost the battle, and the defendant was found not guilty. Eventually I said to myself, no more predictions on my part."

"Well, I'm quite sure we won." Ben thought for a moment. "Okay, let's have a bet. On Monday, the jurors will start deliberations, right?" Gould nodded. "If they don't come back with a not guilty verdict in less than two hours, I'll buy you a bottle of any whiskey or brandy you like. A deal?"

"A deal. Too bad I don't drink much. And if they do?"

Ben shrugged.

"What else can I wish for? I'll buy you a bottle anyway."

"Sounds good," Gould grinned widely. "Well, our bet aside, starting Monday, you and Emma have to stay in our office from nine to five. We all have to be close to the federal courthouse. Not more than fifteen minutes away. We have to be there at once when the jury is ready with the verdict."

* * *

They were driving home in silence when Emma turned to Ben, looking tired and preoccupied.

"Ben, it keeps bothering me..."

"What particularly?" Ben smiled.

"We knew it from the beginning, but now I think it's clear to everyone who watched the trial that the prosecutors didn't have a shred of evidence of any illegal activities either on your or Julia's part. They have been investigating you both for years, and there is no chance they didn't know that. Actually, in the documents they submitted before the indictment they admitted that they couldn't find any evidence of your illegal activity. Do you remember that line?"

"I do."

"Then why didn't they drop the case? Why did they go ahead with the charges? Why did they put you and Julia through this nasty, humiliating experience in prison and this long, distressing trial?"

"Some of our friends think they did it to advance their careers," Ben said.

"But how could it be that the prosecutors, who are supposed to be honorable and professional, are willing to send two innocent people to jail for the rest of their lives just to climb their career ladders?"

Ben didn't answer.

"Do you hate them?"

"No, I don't."

"Ben, they robbed you of the job you loved, of your income, and your home, they trashed your reputation and ruined your health, and you don't hate them?"

Ben fell silent for a moment.

"No, I don't. I'm appalled and grossly disappointed, but I don't hate them. I just want the whole ordeal to be over. And I want to get back to our normal life... and to see my patients again."

"Do you think you can get back to work if you are acquitted? With all your health issues?"

"No, I probably can't. Just wishful thinking. But even if I were healthy enough to work, the Medical Board will never let me. Seven years ago, they forced me to surrender my license, and they'll never give it back to me."

"These seven years," echoed Emma, "feel like an eternity."

Chapter Forty-Six

For weeks, if not months, before the trial started, Emma had tried to visualize the trial procedures, preparing herself for the most horrible moments. She was concerned that the facts would be twisted and that the witnesses would lie under oath while the prosecutors would do everything to portray Ben and Julia as ordinary criminals. Yet beginning with the cross-examination of the very first witness, when Jake Donovan's lies were disproved and the truth restored, her dread of the trial slightly subsided. Many of the scenes unveiled before her eyes were dramatic, often disturbing, but still, they were bearable because they were the part of the relentless action: new questions and new answers that perhaps were more truthful. In a way, it was like watching a compelling play that draws you in so intensely you forget it's a play, with the only difference that at the end of this particular "play" there wouldn't be a storm of applause. There would be a verdict.

Now their days in court were over. There was no more testimony to watch or digest. All they had to do was wait for the verdict, and at the beginning, it didn't seem to be such a grueling task. The trial went so well that she and Ben were certain it would take the jurors no more than a couple of hours to come to the obvious conclusion that both defendants were innocent. A couple of hours of suspense and anxiety seemed manageable.

* * *

On Monday Ben and Emma were in Gould's office by 9:00 a.m. sharp. They were allocated a small, vacant office, and the law firm's friendly staff was especially cordial to them, offering them coffee, tea, anything they needed.

Emma and Ben brought books to keep themselves busy and tried to focus on their reading. Minutes ticked by, and then an hour passed. Eerie silence settled in the room. Another thirty minutes passed. Nothing. Just unhinging disquiet. Emma tried to focus on her book, but in a few minutes, a wave of crashing anxiety hit her even harder. Then it sank deep inside her and refused to leave.

Two hours passed. No verdict. Ben had lost his bet, but Gould didn't show up to claim his prize.

Four hours passed. Nothing. At 1:00 p.m. the jurors took a lunch break.

"We can relax for an hour." Emma looked at Ben, who was staring blankly at his book, deep in thought. "Let's go outside and get something to eat."

Ben nodded and forced a smile.

"Do you think it will take them another couple of hours?"

"With my limited experience..." Ben's voice was now tense and low. "I would say it might."

"I think they will be ready by the end of the day," Emma ventured uncertainly.

"After losing my bet," Ben said with a joyless smile, "I'm not into predictions anymore."

* * *

After the lunch break, around 3:00 p.m., Mark Daniels rushed into their room.

"The jurors have a question for the judge. We have to be there. Let's go, Ben."

"Mark, should I go too?" Emma asked uneasily.

"Oh, no, only the attorneys and the defendants need to be there. We'll be back soon."

"Is it a good sign that they've asked a question?"

"It could mean they want to get to the core of the matter. Usually it's a good sign. Usually..."

"I thought the evidence at the trial had already served that purpose."

"Well, what we see and hear may differ from what the jurors see and hear. They are probably looking for clarification on some technical or legal issues. In any case, we will know soon."

Mark and Ben left, and Emma forced herself to relax. It seemed unlikely that in the next hour or so the jurors would have enough time to reach a verdict.

Ben returned fifty minutes later.

"What was the question?" Emma leaped from her seat.

"It wasn't a question. They asked for the Medical Board guidelines for prescribing opioids."

"Oh, that's good. They'll see one more piece of evidence that proves you're both innocent."

Ben kept silent.

"Do you think this request confirms that the jurors are thoughtful?"

"Could be."

At 5:00 p.m. Daniels stopped by their room to let them know they could leave. The first day of deliberations was over. No verdict.

* * *

Tuesday passed uneventfully. No questions from the jury. Their silence was getting harder to endure.

No verdict.

On Wednesday, the jurors asked another question about some minor specifics of the case; otherwise, nothing happened. The wait for the verdict was getting harrowing.

On Thursday afternoon, Ben stopped even pretending he was reading. He put his hand on Emma's wrist and looked at her intently. "I have this gut feeling today we'll get a verdict."

"That makes two of us," Emma answered. "They just needed more time to sort things out."

The fourth day of deliberations went by. Not a word from the jurors.

* * *

By midday on Friday, looking slightly nervous, both Gould and Daniels popped into the room with the prediction that by the end of the day the jurors would definitely reach a verdict.

Both of them turned out to be wrong.

Ben and Emma left Gould's office upset and relieved at the same time. They couldn't believe that the jurors were still struggling with their decision. On the other hand, for the next two days—the weekend—they wouldn't have to think about the verdict. At least not every single moment of the day. Nights were a different story altogether.

The following Monday dragged by even slower than the previous days.

"Is this torturous wait the start of my future sentence?" Ben asked with a half-smile. "Will it count as time served?"

"Ben, that was the most tasteless joke you've ever made." Emma frowned and turned away, fighting unbidden tears.

Gould was getting edgy too. In his twenty years of criminal law practice, he had never encountered such a long deliberation. And he could not remember when he had ever taken a case so personally. Mark Daniels and their younger colleague, Helen, stopped by the room to cheer up Ben and his wife. Andrea, Gould's aspiring paralegal, and Cathy, Gould's personal assistant, also found a moment to say hello, give them a supportive wink, and offer to get anything they needed. Their sympathy and support were moving and truly appreciated, but none of these caring people could deliver what Ben and Emma needed now more than anything else—a not guilty verdict.

* * *

On the seventh day of deliberations (the ninth day from their start), when Ben and Emma had barely settled in their assigned room, Mark Daniels hastily walked in, greeted them, and handed Ben a piece of paper.

"Please read it right now. We are taking off for the court in five minutes."

"What is it, Mark?"

"A letter from one of the jurors. It was passed to Judge Adler first thing in the morning. We just received a fax from Judge Adler's clerk and then a phone call with the demand to be in court as soon as possible. Please read it. We can't afford to be late."

Ben and Emma started reading the letter, moving swiftly from line to line in glum silence.

August 5, 2014

Your Honor Judge Adler,

I am kindly asking your permission to be removed from the jury deliberations process. I understand that this is a serious matter and my resignation can cause a delay in delivering a verdict, but the stress and anxiety I experience every day of deliberations are affecting my physical and mental health.

This harmful experience is caused by two reasons: I feel bullied by the other jurors, and in my opinion, the deliberation process is edging towards misconduct. For instance, some jurors suggested vote-trading in order to be unanimous on two of the counts. They know it's inappropriate, but all of them, except for me, voted for trading.

Five of the jurors were switching back and forth without any serious reasons. One of them said that he didn't want to stay here till mid-August, another said she "had to switch," the third offered some lame excuse while two other jurors simply refused to explain why they had been switching.

I also feel upset as I am bullied by some of the jurors. A few of them accused me of not being open-minded. I've spent almost the whole weekend writing up examples to explain my thinking to the other jurors more clearly. After the weekend, I asked if I could present my examples and thoughts. The jurors agreed, but only if it would take five minutes or less, although most of them were not interested in hearing what I had to say at all. I felt disrespected and upset.

Then I stayed up all night writing other examples that I hoped most of the jurors could relate to in order to illustrate my logic and thought process based on the evidence presented. I brought the paper in and asked if they would read it. I didn't want to present it anymore, because last time they made me rush through my presentation. Only four people bothered to read what I wrote, and the rest just dismissed it. They were definitely frustrated with me and didn't even want to listen to my ideas.

I understand that the deliberation process is difficult, and everyone is tired by the end of the day, but the situation has seemed to escalate. Yesterday at the end of the session, one of the jurors started yelling at me, and I left the courthouse thinking that I would rather break a toe than spend another day stuck in that room with the other jurors. Whenever someone in the room gets irritated, I become the scapegoat.

Thank you for considering my situation.

Sincerely, Juror #12

The moment they finished reading, Mark tapped Ben on the shoulder. "We have to move. Let's go."

Ben passed the letter to Mark, and they left for the courthouse. Alone in the room, Emma stared at the table in bewilderment. *12 Angry Men?* No, that was different. There wasn't any vote-trading or anything else inappropriate. No one wrote letters to the judge begging to be dismissed from the jury. What side was this woman on? The letter wasn't clear about that. During the trial, it appeared that most of the jurors were on their side. So this woman must believe Ben and Julia were guilty. Still, the others shouldn't have bullied her, and they shouldn't have traded votes. That was sickening.

She looked at the clock: 10:30. Ten thirty. Ben and Mark had left around nine, and they were still not back. Another hour passed. No phone calls. No messages. No one stopped by. She had to do something, but what? Emma paced the room like a panther in a cage, desperate for freedom. Another thirty minutes passed. Not a word. Dead silence was her only companion, not an enjoyable one.

Then it hit her. Mark often checked his e-mail. She reached for her phone, wrote, "Mark, what's going on?" and pressed Send. "We are in the cafeteria. Come over," he wrote back almost instantly.

Emma ran to the front desk.

"Diane, does anyone know walking directions to the courthouse?"

"Could you wait a few minutes? I'll find out." Diane, the sweetest secretary Emma ever met, left and a minute later brought Cathy, Gould's personal assistant.

"Emma, I'll walk you there," Cathy said firmly.

Emma, infinitely grateful, didn't dare reject the offer. In her state of mind, even with detailed directions she could hardly find her way to the office restrooms.

On the route to the courthouse, to keep her anxiety in check, Emma asked Cathy about her family, her childhood, and her hobbies—anything to distract herself from worrisome thoughts. Talk, talk, and talk. No pauses.

At the entrance to the courthouse, Emma thanked Cathy and was about to say good-bye.

"I'll walk you to the cafeteria." Cathy looked at Emma as if she were a child who shouldn't be let out of her mother's sight for a minute.

"Cathy, I'll be all right." Emma took a deep breath. "By now I can find my way in this building with my eyes closed."

"No, I'll go with you." Cathy opened the door with such fervor that Emma could do nothing but follow her.

* * *

In the cafeteria, Ben and his defense team sat around a large table, sharing it with Julia Lander and her close family. Cathy said hello to everyone, exchanged a few words with Gould, and left. Emma scanned the faces around the table, trying to read them. Everyone was somber and quiet. But Helen London... From the day this young attorney had joined the firm, she worked on the case day and night: interviews with the witnesses, tons of research, and everything else essential to prove Ben and Julia's innocence. Now she was tense and ashen as if her close relatives' lives hung by a thread.

"What's going on?" Emma leaned to Ben and asked softly.

"We discussed the juror's letter with the judge, and Edward moved for a mistrial. Judge Adler denied the motion and called the jury in. The foreman said they'd tried really hard but couldn't come to a unanimous decision. The judge said, 'Vote your conscience and bring me a verdict. You can do that.'"

"That was a few hours ago, right?" Emma asked.

"Yes, around 9:30 a.m. Believe it or not they are still deliberating. It's 1:00 p.m. now. It's lunchtime, our sacred hour for food consumption. Would you like a bite?" Emma shook her head. "Nothing will happen until two anyway. We can relax a little."

"We can try. Want your favorite cream of mushroom soup?"

"Sounds good. Who knows if they serve this soup in the pen?" Ben smiled sadly.

"Do you expect the verdict today?" asked Emma, pretending she didn't hear his last remark.

"Everyone thinks it may come any minute."

* * *

After the lunch break, Gould began to compulsively check his phone for text messages almost every minute. At 2:50 p.m. he rose from his seat. "Let's go. The jury is ready."

They all rushed to an elevator with hurried steps in taut silence. The courtroom was already flooded with FBI and DEA agents, and other spectators from the U.S.Attorney's Office. Plenty of strangers, flashed in Emma's mind, and only a handful of us. If she had known the verdict was coming today she could have called their relatives and friends. Now it was too late.

Ben, Edward Gould, and Mark Daniels took their assigned seats at the table in front; Lynch, Krokson, and Hustler settled at the next table to their right. Julia and Peter O'Neil sat in the second row, right behind Ben and his lawyers. Julia's husband, Arthur, their daughter, Lila, and son-in-law, Ned, sat right next to Emma in the third row.

"All rise!" hollered the clerk as Judge Adler swiftly entered the courtroom.

"Please be seated," she said. "Today is the only day when you will sit while the jury will stand."

The jurors slowly marched to their seats but didn't take them.

"Members of the jury, have you reached a verdict?" asked the judge, veiled anxiety in her voice.

"Your Honor," the foreman started and faltered. He was that tall, skinny young man in a red T-shirt, who unlike many others, seemed eager to serve on the jury. "Your Honor, we... His voice faded. "We couldn't reach a unanimous verdict."

Judge Adler's face turned stiff. Silence engulfed the room for what seemed to be an eternity.

"I have no choice but to declare a mistrial," she finally uttered and turned to the jury box. "Members of the jury, thank you for your sincere efforts. This court is adjourned. You are dismissed."

The jury departed from the courtroom. The judge, her face impenetrable, turned to the prosecutors. "Counselors, if you decide to have another trial, let me know immediately."

"Yes, Your Honor," Lynch replied somberly.

Julia turned around and her eyes met Emma's, reflecting the same pain, confusion, and disappointment. What had happened? The trial went so well. Each and every testimony proved their innocence. Why is it a mistrial? What went wrong?

Ben turned to Julia, "It's not what we expected."

"No." Julia sighed gravely. "I don't even know what to say. It's... inexplicable."

Ben walked in long strides toward Emma.

"Let's go outside. I'm getting tired of this place." He took her hand, and they headed out of the courtroom.

In the hallway, Edward Gould, Helen London, and Mark Daniels quickly caught up with them, but before they reached the elevator, a perky brunette in her forties accosted the lawyers and introduced herself as a reporter for the *Boston Veritas.* No one had seen her at any of the trial sessions; she was obviously sent only to cover the verdict.

"Mr. Gould, what's your opinion of the trial, in general?" she asked with a charming smile.

Gould didn't rush with an answer. "We tried our best to prove Dr. Holden and Nurse Practitioner Lander's innocence, but it was a very complex case," he said calmly.

"Thanks. Sorry, I have to run." The reporter offered another dazzling smile. "I'll try to catch up with the jury." She disappeared with the breeze, before anyone could wish her good luck.

* * *

Ben and Emma stood in the lobby of the courthouse waiting for their lawyers when they noticed three of the jurors headed toward the exit. Emma looked them straight in the eye in a pointless attempt to figure out what had really happened in the jury room. The first two jurors, the middle-aged woman who almost cried at the end of Gould's closing arguments, and the slender, affable man in his fifties, caught her gaze and turned away with a hint of discomfort while the third juror, a tall, burly young man, shot them both a long, rancorous look. Ben met his gaze without flinching, while Emma was aghast. What's wrong with him? During the trial, he exchanged quite a few scornful glances with other jurors when the prosecutor's schemes were exposed, and he nodded approvingly each time the truth about Ben and Julia was revealed. Why did he look hostile now? Could it be that he was simply frustrated and tired of this lengthy trial and the draining deliberations?

"Emma, let's go outside," said Ben, interrupting her thoughts. "It's getting claustrophobic in here."

They stepped into the street and bumped into the reporter they had met minutes ago.

"Ma'am, did you have a chance to talk to the jury?" Emma asked anxiously.

"Only to one of them. The others refused to say a word."

"What did the juror say?"

"She told me they voted eleven to one. That's practically all I could drag out of her."

"Did you ask her which way—"

"I did. She said, 'You can guess yourself,' and refused to say more."

"Oh, I'm sure the eleven voted not guilty," said Emma with conviction.

"Why do you think so?" the reporter asked curiously.

"All the testimony proved the defendants' innocence. We watched the jurors' reactions. They were getting it right."

"You think so?" The woman shot Emma a quizzical look. "Anyway, I have their phone numbers. I won't give up. I'll get more. Sorry, I have to go. Bye." She vanished into the street crowd.

Gould, Daniels, and Helen emerged from the courthouse, weary but definitely in a good mood.

"Edward, do you have any explanation for what happened?" Ben asked soberly. "What do you think happened in that jury room?"

Gould pondered the question for a long moment.

"I can only guess, but let me tell you something. Of course, we all hoped for a much better outcome. Still, you can't imagine how lucky you and Julia are even with this verdict. You were up against Goliath. You may not fully grasp that, but almost *no* defendants leave this courthouse without handcuffs. One percent, at most. In government cases, mistrials are practically unheard of, and today you and Julia are that one percent." He smiled gently. "Take Emma home, and relax and celebrate. You are a free man."

"Edward, wait," Ben didn't give up. "You just said that not more than one percent get acquitted. What happens to the rest?"

"Well, about ninety-five percent of those indicted by the government, including the innocent, agree to plea bargaining, and only five percent go to a trial," explained Gould.

"Why would innocent people go for a plea bargain?" Emma asked incredulously.

"First, they are intimidated by the government. Second, most of them are financially ruined and psychologically crushed, so they don't have stamina to fight it. Not everyone is as resilient as you two. Or Julia and Arthur. For the past seven years, you've fought for your lives day and night and you never gave up. Not many people are capable of doing that."

"And probably not many people have such strong support as we do," said Emma.

"You are right. Even if an innocent person is able to overcome all obstacles and go to a trial," continued Gould, "there is no guarantee that the jury will return a not guilty verdict. You just experienced it firsthand."

"That's true," Emma said quietly. "We knew it was an enormous risk to go to trial, and we should feel lucky that Ben and Julia are leaving the federal court as free people, but I also wonder, if both of them had been found not guilty today, would the prosecutors have been punished for concocting such a bogus case?"

"I doubt it. At worst, they would have gotten a slap on the wrist from their boss. Our judicial system makes them essentially immune from any punishment," explained Gould.

"Sounds like the government perfected its means of securing a conviction as well as getting away with unfounded accusations," Emma paused, and then gave Gould a worried look. "Edward, can they retry the case?"

"Well, theoretically, they can. But they practically never do that. It's awfully expensive and, trust me, they've already spent millions on your case. Not to mention the fact that most of their witnesses testified in Ben and Julia's favor. So I don't think you should worry about another trial. Go home and enjoy your well-deserved freedom."

* * *

On their ride home, Ben was gloomy and silent. Gould's speech about their rare luck was somewhat comforting, but the mistrial was not the acquittal they all anticipated.

"Ben, we were childishly naive. We expected a miracle," said Emma, as if reading his mind. "But the only thing that matters now is your freedom. I think Gould is right. Let's have a little celebration with our relatives and friends. What do you say?"

He smiled resignedly. "Okay, let's celebrate."

* * *

The next morning, they could finally sleep late—no more court sessions, no more elbowing cars on the Mass Pike, and no more tormenting anticipation of the verdict. They were having a leisurely breakfast when the phone rang. Reluctantly, Ben picked up the receiver.

"Ben, it's Edward Gould. Sorry to interfere. There is an article about your case in the *Veritas*. I've sent you a link. Please read it when you can and call me back."

"Thanks, Edward. I will." Ben frowned.

"Is something wrong?" Emma swallowed a lump in her throat.

"I don't know. Edward asked us to read some article in today's *Veritas*. His voice was... Well, let's finish breakfast first."

There was no doubt that the article was written by the same feisty reporter they'd met in the courthouse the day before, the one who didn't come to a single court session, didn't hear a single piece of testimony, and had no clue about the case. Her superficial, mindless review of the trial was faultlessly in line with the fashionable trend in modern journalism. The most important facts were omitted, while those that found their way into the article were grossly distorted. She quoted a juror, most likely the woman who agreed to talk to her, and the juror finally admitted that eleven of them had voted guilty. This juror also bitterly complained about the "bullheaded holdout," the one juror whom the rest of the pack couldn't turn around.

Ben and Emma stopped reading and exchanged silent glances.

"Ben, it's insane. Were these eleven jurors deaf? They were taking notes, they seemed to be listening, they—"

"You just said it. They *seemed* to be listening, they nodded at the right moments, and they snickered when the prosecutors' schemes were exposed. But we have no idea what was behind this nodding and snickering, do we?"

"What about that woman in the first row, who by the end of Gould's closing arguments was teary-eyed? Was she feigning her feelings? Ben, were these eleven people simply enjoying the 'show'?"

"Could be. Some days it was nothing short of a farce."

"Yes, in a way, it *was* a farce. But your life and Julia's life were at stake, and these eleven jurors... they didn't give a damn about it. They ignored all the evidence! They were thinking only about their own convenience. They wanted to be done with their deliberations and go home. Vote for the government side, ruin the lives of two innocent people, and then go on with your own lives as if nothing happened. For God's sake, who are these people?! Heartless pretenders?"

"Emma, please calm down. People bring their prejudices to the jury box, and there is nothing we can do about that. Let's finish reading."

They returned to the article and found out that, to her credit, the reporter quoted some fragments from the letter written by that stubborn holdout, the letter that described the jurors' misconduct and bullying.

"So the woman who wrote that letter..." Emma faltered. "She is the one who voted not guilty."

"From the letter it was hard to say which side she was on, but now I have no doubt it's her. She was fighting for her principles against the rest of them."

"Do you know who she is?"

"I remember the letter was signed by Juror #12..." Ben stopped, stupefied. "It's that young woman that we were concerned about... on jury selection day."

"The one Edward was hesitant about because she worked in the medical field?"

"Yes, it's her. He wasn't sure he wanted her on the jury. Actually, he was almost sure he didn't. He thought it was a risk. But we took a chance..."

"Ben, she saved you and Julia from jail." They fell quiet.

"Can you imagine..." Ben shook his head in disbelief. "We could have dismissed her."

"True." Emma paused, deep in thought. "How was she able to stand up against their pressure and bullying? She must have had real guts to do that."

"Judging by her letter, there were a few others who'd been on our side at first, but they caved in. She was the only one who had dignity and stamina to stick to her guns. I'll be grateful to her to the end of my days." Ben fell silent. "Anyway, let's read this shitty article to the end."

They finished reading the article and looked at each other, dumbstruck. The last line of the article was a bombshell. The reporter quoted the U.S. State Attorney, Calvina Cortes, who announced her firm decision to retry the case.

* * *

"Hi, Edward. It's Ben. I've read the article. What do you think about the vote?"

"It's not as shocking to me as it probably is to you. Jurors are just ordinary people, and they commonly bring to the courtroom their convictions and prejudices. As I said, many of them think that the government is always right, and it's virtually impossible to persuade them otherwise. In your case, there were at least a few of them who by the end of the trial were clearly on your side. Unfortunately, they were not scrupulous enough to defend their views—"

"Unlike this brave young woman," said Ben, finishing Gould's sentence.

"Exactly."

"Well, I don't think your explanation is extremely comforting, but it probably makes the cut."

"I know, Ben. You are upset and disappointed, and rightfully so, but you can't imagine how many phone calls I've received from my colleagues with congratulations on the victory. It's not a full-fledged victory, but trust me, it is a big victory."

"I understand. Listen, Edward, we appreciate everything you and your team did for us, we really do. And we accept this outcome... considering the alternatives."

Gould thought he heard a heavy sigh on the other end of the line.

"Ben, we need to talk."

"I had a feeling you would say that."

"Can we meet tomorrow in my office at 10:00 a.m.?"

"We'll be there."

Chapter Forty-Seven

On the way to Gould's office, Ben was subdued.

"What do you think about this second trial?" Emma asked cautiously.

"There won't be any second trial," Ben said flatly.

"There won't be another trial? What do you mean?" Emma was confused.

"The first one went as well as it could, and look what happened. What chance do we have to win the second one? None. Zilch. Where will we get the money to pay for it? We are broke."

"Ben, we can borrow..." Emma started uncertainly. "You remember our friends offered to have a fund-raiser for us... We refused before, but now maybe—"

"Fine! They'll do fund-raising, we'll borrow a lot of money somewhere, and then what? Another mistrial at best, or... much worse. Is there a chance that there would be another courageous juror who would stand up for us?"

"So what do you suggest?" Emma frowned—she knew too well what the other option was.

"I think I should consider a deal with the government."

"Ben, how can you even..."

"I'll agree to go to prison but on one condition only."

"And what would that condition be?"

"They have to drop all charges against Julia. They have to leave her alone!"

"Ben, they will never go for that. It's naive to expect it. They'll gladly send you to jail for twenty years, but they will never leave Julia alone. And then as a result of your sacrifice, she'll have to fight them without you, on her own. And something else to consider: in order to have a deal, you have to admit your guilt. What exactly are you guilty of? Helping suffering people?"

He didn't answer.

"Ben, I know you're shocked by the outcome of the trial. I am too. But over these past seven years, you've never considered any concessions. Ever. Don't do it now! I beg you, don't do it."

* * *

Gould met them with a warm smile, but he didn't appear relaxed or joyful.

"You've read the article," he said after greetings. "So what is your plan?" He cast an inquisitive glance at Ben.

"We are going to the second trial," Emma fired off before Ben even opened his mouth. "But at this new trial, our case has to be presented even better than at the first one. Right, Ben?"

Ben slowly nodded and shot Emma a look that only she could understand.

"It won't be cheap, Emma. You know, I can recommend to you a young lawyer who will not charge you as much as our firm. He is very good. Would you like me to give him a call?"

"No, Edward." Ben swallowed hard. "If... If we go for it, we want you, Mark, and Helen, your entire team."

"Edward, don't worry. We'll get the money," Emma caught Gould's glance and held it, unshakable. "We'll do whatever it takes to get it."

"All right, but under one condition: no bank robberies, please, and no tunnels to Fort Knox." Gould gave them a thin smile.

"No bank robberies, promise," said Emma.

"Well, if this is your final decision, let's do it. As they say, there is always room for improvement." Gould turned serious. "We will start discussing our new strategy in a week or so. All suggestions are welcome." He shook Ben's hand. "Onward we go."

* * *

Emma borrowed money from their close relatives and friends, yet it was far from enough for the trial. Then their close friends started fundraising. The response was beyond belief. Personal checks from relatives, good friends, people they'd met just a few months before, and Ben's former patients poured into the fund every day to cover the arduous work of the defense attorneys, their assistants. and all other services involved in the preparation for the trial. By late March, they were ready for the second trial.

* * *

On March 31, 2015, Ben Holden walked into the courtroom he had left a few months ago with a startling feeling of ease and composure he had never felt during the first trial. It was jury selection day. He and Emma came early, and the only person in Judge Adler's courtroom was her clerk Mary.

"Good morning, Mary. Only God knows how much I missed this place," said Ben with a straight face that obviously didn't fool the clerk.

"I can only imagine," Mary grinned humorlessly, pouring water into the pitcher on the defense's desk. "Welcome back, Doctor."

* * *

By 3:15 p.m., jury selection was complete. Twelve jurors and four alternates were seated in the jury box, and the trial began.

It started, as usual, with the prosecution's opening statement, and Krokson made the same opening arguments he'd made at the first trial. With eight months between the two trials, Krokson had plenty of time to work on his new opening statement, but he didn't bother to change a word. The federal prosecutor was apparently confident that his former arguments were powerful and persuasive enough that he didn't need to make any improvements. His sugary voice and slow pace, Ben noted, were in stark contrast to the aggressive content of his speech. He implied over and over that Dr. Holden and Nurse Practitioner Lander were simply dealing drugs. It didn't matter, he said, that most of their treatments were legitimate, because even one illegal prescription was an indication of their criminal conduct. In his monologue, Krokson hadn't even bothered to mention their patients' horrific injuries or unbearable pain, both physical and psychological. Instead, he focused on the epidemic of opioid abuse that he argued was fueled by unscrupulous medical professionals like Dr. Holden and his accomplice, Nurse Practitioner Julia Lander. Listening to Krokson's argument, uninformed jurors could easily conclude that these two perpetrators were solely responsible for the national drug abuse catastrophe.

Gould's opening statement was next. He'd also used his old version, but only as a base. He made important changes to his statement because he knew it had to be even more powerful than the first one. He described the difficulties and controversies related to the field of pain management in which Dr. Holden had been practicing for years with obvious success. He also described the enormous impact of poorly controlled pain on the lives of those who suffered and their loved ones. He promised the jury that during the course of the trial, he and Mark Daniels would disprove all of the government's allegations.

As Emma watched them, not a single juror showed any signs of boredom nor were they staring impatiently at the courtroom clock. Even Juror #9, a weary old lady, wasn't shifting much in her seat.

Peter O'Neil's speech about Nurse Practitioner Lander was short, to the point, and also drew the jurors' close attention.

The first day of the trial went without a glitch.

* * *

The next morning, the Honorable Judge Adler didn't look happy at all. She invited both sides to the sidebar and announced that she'd just received a handwritten note from juror #8, notifying her that he couldn't serve on the jury because after two years of unemployment he was finally offered a job, and he was expected to start tomorrow at 8:00 a.m.

"I can't force this man to stay." Judge Adler frowned. "That would be neither ethical nor legal. Fortunately, we have three more alternates, although I have to admit that this sort of thing makes me really anxious."

The second day of the trial didn't go exactly as the prosecution had planned. Their star witness, Jake Donovan, didn't impress anyone as a reliable witness this time around. He had apparent difficulty remembering the facts and answering the prosecutor's questions, except for the most damaging one about Dr. Holden's reaction to his brother's death. Donovan repeated his previous statement that Dr. Holden said, "Jake had problems anyway," which was impossible to disprove. But during Gould's cross, he wasn't as defiant as before, and he even said a few good words about Dr. Holden and his practice.

Donovan's girlfriend, Lucille Flanagan, on the other hand, on the direct played the role that the government expected, although on the cross she admitted again that Dr. Holden was the first physician who believed her pain was real, and the first one who treated her effectively and helped her live a normal life. And then, at the end of the cross, something entirely unexpected happened.

"Ms. Flanagan, do you remember the day when you and Jake Donovan came to Dr. Holden's office and told him that Doug had died?"

Ms. Flanagan's expression instantly changed.

"Yes, I do." She lowered her head. "I remember it very well." Her face twitched with grief, and her eyes got blurry.

"Do you remember what Dr. Holden said when he heard about this sad news?"

"I do." Lucille Flanagan paused, and her glance suddenly met Ben's. "He said... He said he was truly sorry," she finished softly, her eyes welling up with tears.

Lynch, his teeth clenched, his eyes dead cold, was up out of his chair and then instantly back. He didn't dare object. The government's portrait of Dr. Holden as a heartless man had been shattered by their own witness. This bulletproof piece of evidence was going up in smoke.

* * *

The next morning, Judge Adler stormed into the courtroom, her face pale and unyielding.

"Counselors, sidebar please," she ordered, after an atypically curt greeting.

"I just received another request for dismissal!" her face flushed. "This elderly woman, Juror #9, claims she can't physically sit through the trial because she has severe pain in her lower back."

Gould, Daniels, and O'Neil exchanged telling glances. A woman who suffered from pain would understand the issues of this trial better than anyone else.

"Your Honor, we totally share your concern..." started Gould. "But we are sure something can be done to accommodate her discomfort. A back pillow, more frequent breaks..."

"We disagree, Your Honor," Lynch interrupted fervently. "We think it would be simply merciless to allow this suffering old woman to sit through such a lengthy trial."

"Your Honor, the trial may last more than two months," Krokson protested. "God forbid, something bad should happen to her."

"Well, I certainly don't want to expose this elderly lady to any harm." Judge Adler stopped and frowned. "But I would really hate to lose another juror. It's only the second day of the trial, and we've already lost one!" The judge was absorbed in thought for a minute. "This woman has a medical appointment regarding her back this morning at 10:00. I will request an official note from her treating physician. Because we don't know whether she'll serve on the jury or not, we'll have to delay today's session. I'll contact her doctor around 10:30 a.m. and we'll reconvene at 11 a.m."

At 10:30 a.m. Judge Adler personally called the juror's physician, and ten minutes later her clerk received a fax.

To whom it may concern: Ms. Virginia Price is a-seventy-six-year-old woman who suffers from two acute compression fractures of her lower thoracic spine. Her condition is extremely painful and, in order to keep her comfortable, the patient requires periodic bed rest and a significant amount of opioid medications as needed. Lifting, leaning forward, or long sitting are strictly contraindicated as these activities may severely aggravate her condition. Please call if you have further questions. Amanda Stroll, MD

"This woman has to be dismissed," said the judge, frustration in her voice. "Now we are down to only two alternates. I am not happy about it, but we have to move on."

* * *

To Ben's puzzlement, the next witness for the prosecution was Detective Eves. Ben thought that after the detective's testimony at the first trial, when he was exposed as a shameless liar, they would never call him back. But the government's pool of potential witnesses was probably so murky and depleted that they had no choice. At least he didn't sell pills on the street or have a rap sheet longer than Pennsylvania Avenue.

Just as at the first trial, Detective Eves looked collected and self-assured. He didn't seem to be the least bit ashamed of his previous lies and distortions. On direct, questioned by Matilda Hustler, Mr. Eves, like at the first trial, explained to the jury how under the pretense of having severe back pain, he went to Dr. Holden's office as an undercover agent to observe his illegal activities and support a criminal investigation of Dr. Holden's practice. His testimony wasn't especially damaging even on direct. However, during the cross, Gould, with the help of the audio recording of Eves's last visit, once again successfully demonstrated to the jury the failure of the detective's mission. "Sorry, guys, I tried," was his last line on the recording, when Eves entered the FBI surveillance van. The moment it was played in the courtroom, Ben saw astonishment in the eyes of Jurors #4 and #7 while Juror #3, an elderly man, who hadn't missed a word of the detective's testimony, leaned forward with his jaw so tight that Ben was afraid the man would crush his molars. The last thing we need now, Ben shook his head with concern, is an excuse note from the orthodontist's office.

* * *

"I think it was a good day," said Elaine, walking to Gould in the hallway. "Your cross was superb."

"During your cross, if any reporter from the *Boston Veritas* or the *Boston Herald* was present," Ron shot a wide grin, "I bet tomorrow we'll see the headlines, 'Detective Nailed for Falsifying His Reports' or 'Police Officer Implicated in Records Doctoring.' Or something else along those lines."

"Ron, don't overestimate the press," Emma gave a rueful smile. "We've seen them in action. But I agree, it was a really good day."

* * *

Ben's cell phone rang at about 11:00 p.m.

"Hi, Ben. It's Mark."

"What's up, Mark?" asked Ben, half asleep.

"Sorry to disturb you so late, but I've just received an e-mail from the judge's clerk. Something happened. Judge Adler expects us tomorrow in her courtroom at 8:00 a.m. sharp. Please be on time."

"I will. Mark, do you know what it's all about?"

"No clue. Sorry. See you tomorrow at 8:00 a.m." And the line went dead.

* * *

At 8:05 a.m. Judge Adler, her face ash gray, entered the courtroom.

"Mr. Lynch, would you like to inform this court about what happened yesterday?" she asked.

"Yes, Your Honor," Lynch took a deep breath. "Last night our office received a phone call from Detective Eves." The prosecutor swallowed hard. "He told us that yesterday afternoon, on his way from the courthouse, he was approached by Juror #3, and—"

"What happened?" interrupted Judge Adler.

"Juror #3 wanted to talk to our witness, Detective Eves, but Mr. Eves said that it was inappropriate."

"And?" Judge Adler was getting truly impatient.

"According to Detective Eves, Juror #3 simply conveyed his personal appreciation of the detective's public service and wanted to shake his hand, that's all."

"That's all?" Judge Adler arched an eyebrow.

"Yes, Your Honor, that's all. Nothing else."

"And what does the government think about this encounter?"

"Well, as awkward as it looks, Your Honor, we don't see this event as a big deal... We really don't. The man was just trying to—"

"With all due respect, Your Honor," interrupted Gould. "I adamantly disagree with Mr. Lynch. Besides the fact that this man completely disregarded your instructions and came into direct contact with a witness, which by itself is a grave violation of the court rules, his action was also evidence of bias against our clients."

"This is a crucial consideration, Your Honor," added O'Neil. "Apparently Juror #3 had already formed his opinion about the case. There is no chance he will remain impartial through the trial."

"Well, we think this man only tried to show his personal feelings," said Krokson. "That's all."

"All right, I've got the picture." The judge briskly turned to her clerk. "Mary, as soon as Juror #3 arrives, bring this man here. Right away."

Thirty minutes later, a short, elderly man, dressed in a black T-shirt and dust brown wrinkled pants, walked into the courtroom and approached the judge.

"Good morning, sir." Judge Adler cast the man a piercing look.

"Good morning, ma'am," replied the juror.

"I believe you are retired, Mr. Pock, correct?"

"Yes, ma'am, I mean Your Honor, I am."

"What type of work did you do before you retired?"

"I was a car mechanic for over twenty-five years, fixing all types of vehicles for the Boston Police Department," Mr. Pock said proudly.

"I see. Can you tell us briefly what kind of conversation you had with the witness yesterday? I'm talking about Detective Eves."

"Well, to tell the truth, ma'am, not much was said. The detective is a distinguished man, and I only wanted to shake his hand, nothing else. Not a big deal, I think."

"Did you say anything to him, Mr. Pock?"

"No, ma'am, I didn't," Mr. Pock blushed and looked away.

"I see." The judge frowned. "Mr. Pock, I believe I have no choice but to dismiss you from your jury duty. Have you left any belongings in the jury room?"

"My jacket, Your Honor."

"Please wait outside the courtroom, and we'll bring it."

When Mr. Pock left the room, Judge Adler turned to the bailiff.

"Mr. Drummer, would you mind going to the jury room and bringing Mr. Pock's jacket? I don't want that man getting back there even for a moment." Judge Adler glared across the room with overt exasperation. "We lost another one. What's next?"

Gould leaned into Ben, "It's our good luck," he whispered, "that the guy showed his true colors now, not during the deliberations. It's a gift from heaven."

"I don't think the man even understands how prejudiced he is," Ben whispered back.

"Have you ever met anyone who does?"

* * *

During the first two weeks of the second trial, the government paraded the same witnesses they had brought to the first one, using exactly the same scripts they had used before. Still, quite a few unforeseen incidents interrupted the prosecution's case. At the end of the direct by Krokson, Dr. Holden's former patient, Mr. McBride, suddenly rose from the witness chair and, looking straight at Dr. Holden, profoundly apologized to him and Nurse Practitioner Lander for his deception and betrayal of their trust. The scene was so dramatic that most of the jurors looked truly bewildered.

At the end of the third week, the prosecutors called their most important witness, Dr. Chuck Finnegan. The medical expert was wearing the same meticulous iron gray suit and projected an aura of unshakable confidence. On the first day of his testimony, he arrived to court a few minutes early and had an amicable chat with two FBI agents. Watching their cordial conversation, Ben thought that one could assume the three of them were childhood buddies having a long-awaited reunion.

Dr. Finnegan's direct examination followed the same familiar script, yet Finnegan was less categorical than eight months before, and his statements were much more cautious.

Gould's cross this time was even more effective than the one at the first trial. He demonstrated to the jury that Dr. Finnegan's allegations against Dr. Holden were nothing more than his personal opinions. They were not supported either by any professional publications or scientific research or by any existing laws and regulations. In fact, the opinions of the most respected experts in the field on the subject of treating patients in pain were exactly the opposite of Finnegan's opinions.

Gould had used these facts at the first trial as well, but right before the second trial he discovered new evidence, and the government medical expert was now in for a surprise.

"Dr. Finnegan, you had a chance to testify in the similar proceedings about eight months ago, and you most likely recollect saying that you hold pain physicians to much higher standards for prescribing opioids than general practitioners?"

"Yes, and I still do," confirmed Finnegan.

"And that is because pain doctors have better knowledge and education in this area, right?"

"That is right," agreed Finnegan.

"Very well. At some point you also agreed with Dr. Westwood and other leading physicians that for many chronic pain patients opioids are the most effective way to alleviate their suffering, correct?"

"This is correct."

"According to the World Health Organization, opioids are essentially the gold standard for treating severe pain, correct?"

"Yes."

"So, you agree with the *National Pain Management Guidelines*, which say the same, correct?"

"Yes, I do."

"Your Honor, with your permission, the defense offers exhibit 111-C." A website page appeared on the screen. "Sir, please look at the screen, and tell us if you recognize this page. Isn't it the first page of your pain center website?"

"Yes, it is," confirmed Finnegan.

"And you, as medical director of the center, have approved it, right?"

"Yes, I have."

"This website has four pages, and it's designed for prospective pain patients, correct?"

"Yes, it is."

"Let's get to the bottom of the first page. Sir, could you read it out loud for the jury. Just the last paragraph, please."

"Objection, relevance," interrupted Krokson.

"Overruled," responded Judge Adler. "I am curious myself."

"If our physician determines that your pain should include management with opioid medications," Finnegan stopped, as it finally hit him. *"You will be"*—there was a long, awkward pause before he continued reading—*"referred back to your primary care provider, who would be solely responsible for prescribing them to you on a regular basis."*

"Now, sir, would you mind reading the last paragraph found on the second, third, and fourth pages? Or shouldn't we bother because they are exactly the same?"

Finnegan didn't answer.

"Now, Dr. Finnegan, I assume you have no problems with this statement, correct?"

"What do you mean?" Finnegan's eyes darted desperately to Krokson.

"I will tell you exactly what I mean. I simply wonder why one of the largest pain clinics in Boston refuses to prescribe opioid medications to the most vulnerable pain-patient population while, according to its own medical director as well as other medical experts in the field, these medications are considered the gold standard for treating pain."

Finnegan remained silent.

"I am also curious," continued Gould, "why, in spite of your admirable knowledge and expertise in prescribing opioids, you, sir, shift these responsibilities to primary care providers. Didn't you claim that, unlike pain doctors, general practitioners are far less qualified to prescribe opioids?"

"We... We... We simply want to deter drug-seeking people," Dr. Finnegan mumbled. "But sometimes we prescribe."

"Sometimes?" Gould's eyebrows rose. "Thank you, Dr. Finnegan. I have no more questions for this witness, Your Honor."

Ben glanced at the jury box. A few jurors looked perplexed, a few others disgruntled.

CHAPTER FORTY-EIGHT

THE NEXT MORNING WHEN BEN AND Emma arrived at the courthouse, the first person they saw on the bench next to Judge Adler's courtroom was Ben's former patient Alex Singer. He greeted them silently and offered an almost imperceptible smile.

"Ben, what's going on?" Emma asked softly. "The prosecutors brought him back?"

"Yeah, they did."

"At the first trial, he praised you and your treatments. And now...?"

"Maybe they think this time he'll be more 'cooperative'?"

"Alex Singer? Last time, after his testimony he went straight to you and shook your hand. It's a pity the jury didn't see that."

"Do you think it would have changed their votes?"

"Who knows?"

Alex Singer, heavily leaning on a cane and painfully forcing his every step, slowly moved to the witness chair. Because the sitting position aggravated his pain, the judge allowed him to stand up whenever his suffering became more than he could tolerate.

The direct wasn't much different from the one they heard eight months before. Lynch was trying his best to coerce the young man into admitting that Dr. Holden's treatments were damaging to him, but Alex Singer stood his ground and, instead of defaming his former doctor, spoke highly of him.

"Is it true, Mr. Singer, that the Faulding Center weaned you off the drugs you were addicted to, but then you went to Dr. Holden, and he prescribed you opioids again?" fumed Lynch.

"They lied to me!" Singer could barely hold his anger. "They promised to relieve my pain, but instead they simply weaned me off any medications. I was in excruciating pain and pleaded with them to send me for an MRI, but they did nothing for a whole month. When I came to Dr. Holden, he immediately saw that something was wrong with me and sent me to Newton-Wellesley Hospital for an MRI, and they found out that I had a large abscess on my spine. A few more days of delay and I probably would be dead. He cared about me, and he helped me."

Lynch looked grim. Singer's testimony was exactly the opposite of what the prosecutor wanted. He couldn't control his own witness. Lynch went on and on, increasing his pressure on Singer, but his efforts were shot to hell.

Around 11:00 a.m. Judge Adler declared a short recess.

The jurors left, but all the attorneys and Judge Adler were still in the courtroom when Alex Singer, overcoming his pain, stepped off the witness stand, walked to Dr. Holden, and respectfully shook his hand.

Ten minutes later, the recess was over, the jury was called in, and Lynch was back at the lectern.

"Mr. Singer, I couldn't help seeing that a few minutes ago, you approached Dr. Holden and shook his hand, didn't you?" Lynch asked with poorly masked contempt.

"Yes, I did," admitted Singer.

"Mr. Singer, why did you do that?" The courtroom became dead quiet.

"I shook Dr. Holden's hand, because he is a very good man, and he saved my life."

One of the jurors gasped. A few others exchanged incredulous glances. Lynch turned the color of an eggshell.

"I have no more questions for the witness," he said abruptly, and hurried to his seat.

"Is it my imagination or did Matilda just have hiccups?" Gould turned to Daniels.

"Yes, she did," Mark smiled.

"Pinch me," Elaine whispered to her husband. "Was it for real? Or did I just see it in a dream?"

"For real," he whispered back, "But I can pinch you anyway."

"Gosh, the scoundrel couldn't have asked a better question. Do you think he is planning a new career?"

"Who, Lynch? Who knows? Life works in mysterious ways."

* * *

"Mark, who is the next witness for the prosecution?" Ben asked when the session was over. "Is it the lovely Mr. Habib?"

"You mean the guy with a hundred convictions?" Ben nodded. "No, they are not bringing him this time. Even by the government's standards, his testimony at the first trial was too embarrassing."

"I bet Matilda Hustler is still blushing at the sound of his name," Ben shook his head. "It's a shame he is not coming. What a character! Any new witnesses?"

"Actually, tomorrow morning they plan to bring a brand new one. Your former patient Catherine Fitzgerald. Do you remember her?" asked Daniels.

"Catherine? Oh, she is hard to forget." Ben gave a cryptic smile.

"What exactly do you remember about her? I'll be doing her cross tomorrow."

"Well, Catherine came to my office with intractable back pain. Three years before, she had a car accident. Soon after that accident, her back and leg pain became too much to bear. A neurosurgeon offered Catherine a quick cure. During the next three years, she survived one minor and two major spinal surgeries. The second one put her into a wheelchair and made her totally disabled."

"Why?"

"At her second surgery, they placed large titanium rods in her back. They were designed to fuse her damaged vertebra. But, just like after her first surgery, after this one her pain became even worse. Much worse. The titanium rods had to be removed. Catherine was thirty-six at that time, and she was left to live in agony for the rest of her life. Surgeons were not interested in her any longer." Ben sighed. "Unfortunately, her story is rather typical."

"And then she came to see you?"

"I would say, 'came' is not the right word—she arrived in a wheelchair."

"Could you do anything to help her?"

"Yes, we could. After a few months of different treatments, her pain became quite manageable. Her sleep improved, and she wasn't as depressed as before. I remember once she said to me, 'Doctor, I can hardly believe it, but now I can dress myself and I can do shopping! I am walking again, and I am able to play with my daughter!'"

"Why do think they want her testimony?"

"At some point she left my practice."

"Why would she do that?"

"I believe that she'd been treated in our clinic for about three years when one day we sent her for a urine test, and it came back positive for cocaine. I had a serious talk with Catherine, and I warned her that if she had another bad test I would stop prescribing her opioids. After that all her tests were good, at least for a while, but then something else happened."

"By the look on your face, I would say it was pretty dramatic."

"Dramatic indeed. About a year later, my office received an anonymous letter, in which some woman accused Catherine of selling her prescription drugs to the woman's daughter. This sixteen-year-old girl allegedly overdosed and almost died."

"What did you do?"

"The letter was anonymous. No name, no return address or phone number to verify. Nothing. So there was no way to contact the woman. Still, the letter was so alarming that I simply couldn't ignore it. At Catherine's next visit, I confronted her and demanded an explanation."

"What did she say?"

"She burst into tears and swore on her mother's grave she'd never done it. She thought the letter was written by her neighbor as revenge. Catherine was now seeing this woman's ex-boyfriend. 'My pain medication is my whole life,' she was sobbing. 'If I don't take it, I can't even get out of bed.'"

"Did you believe her?"

"Yes, I believed her. After all, she'd never deceived me before. So I decided to give her a second chance and to keep an eye on her. Two weeks later we invited her into our office for a pill count, to check how many pain pills she had left of her monthly supply."

"And?"

"She had exactly as many pills as we expected her to have. But two months later, I sent Catherine for another random urine test, and it came back positive for cocaine again. Now it was her second time. I told Catherine that, as I'd warned her before, I couldn't prescribe her opioids any longer. She was welcome to have our other treatments, but not narcotic medications. I liked her and felt sympathy for her suffering, and we had a truly good relationship, but because she'd broken our pain agreement for the second time, I simply had no choice."

"Did she come back for other treatments?"

"No, it was her last visit."

"Do you think she is still angry with you?"

"I wouldn't be shocked if she is. But who knows?"

* * *

The next morning, Catherine Fitzgerald was the first person they saw in the hallway right next to Judge Adler's courtroom; a tired-looking woman sitting on a wooden bench, deep in thought.

She's gained some weight, Ben remarked to himself, but she was still good-looking. The woman heard their steps, looked up, and instantly recognized her former doctor. She rose to greet him, but Ben shook his head, as if to say, "We are not allowed to do that here." Ms. Fitzgerald slowly settled back onto the bench and cast Ben a shy smile.

* * *

Matilda Hustler, who was assigned to handle Catherine Fitzgerald's direct, didn't waste time on pleasantries.

"Ms. Fitzgerald, at some point you became a patient of Dr. Holden, correct?"

The witness suddenly rose from her seat.

"I want to say something. I am here to tell the truth. Not to say bad things about Dr. Holden."

Judge Adler's eyebrows shot up, but she refrained from making any comments.

"Ms. Fitzgerald," Hustler promptly regained her composure, "Did Dr. Holden prescribe narcotic drugs for you at some point?"

"I was in severe pain. I simply couldn't get out of bed without taking them," Ms. Fitzgerald replied defiantly.

"Ma'am, that wasn't my question. Did Dr. Holden ever prescribe narcotic drugs to you? Yes or no?" Hustler repeated impatiently.

"Yes, he did."

"Now, at some point in 2003, someone sent a letter to Dr. Holden's office accusing you of selling drugs. Do you remember that?"

"Yes, I do. I remember that day like it happened yesterday. Dr. Holden was very upset and disappointed, but I told him I never did that. And it's the truth."

"And what was his response?"

"He believed me because I never lied to him, and he knew that," Ms. Fitzgerald added softly.

"Your Honor, at this time the government would like to offer exhibit #209-B. May I put it on the screen?" asked Hustler.

"You may."

"Ms. Fitzgerald, here is Dr. Holden's handwritten note from your medical file, where he asks you to come to his office for a pill count. This note is dated March 17, 2003. Ms. Fitzgerald, did you come to Dr. Holden's office for a pill count that day?"

"I'm not sure."

"Ma'am, yes or no?" Hustler said fretfully.

"I don't know. I'm not sure. It was twelve years ago."

"Ms. Fitzgerald!" Hustler barely held her temper. "Do you remember that in May 2008 you were interviewed by two special agents from the FBI, Agent Faber and Agent Cabbie? When they asked if you'd ever gone for a pill count, you answered no. Do you remember that?"

"Sorry, but I don't recall that, because it was long ago." Ms. Fitzgerald looked confused and upset.

"Then in August 2011, at the U.S. Attorney's Office, you met with Special Agent Molloy who asked you the same question. Once again, you denied ever being called for a pill count, right?" Hustler turned purple-red and was almost gasping for air.

"Ma'am, I simply don't remember that. I don't even know what *pill count* means," Ms. Fitzgerald was almost in tears.

"Oh, you don't!" snarled Hustler. "Then why, only three weeks ago, at your last meeting with the U.S. Attorney, did you confirm that in 2003 Dr. Holden never summoned you for a pill count?"

"Ma'am, I was probably confused. As I said, I have no idea what pill count means. But let me tell you this: I always, always did what Dr. Holden asked me to do." Ms. Fitzgerald dabbed her eyes.

"And still in December 2004 he stopped prescribing you any opioids altogether and dismissed you from his practice, did he not?" almost screamed Hustler.

"He stopped prescribing me opioids, but he didn't dismiss me. He asked me to come for other treatments."

"Why did he stop prescribing you opioids?" the prosecutor ignored the witness's last comment.

"My urine test showed cocaine for the second time."

"Did you use cocaine?"

"Yes, I did use it occasionally. I was going through a very difficult period in my life. I was getting divorced, and I had to sell my house... My life was a mess, and at times my back pain was unbearable, even with the medications Dr. Holden prescribed to me."

"You said that Dr. Holden offered you other treatments, but you never returned to his office after that, correct?" pressed Hustler.

"It's true. I never did."

"Could you please explain why?" the prosecutor asked wryly.

"I was too embarrassed." Ms. Fitzgerald cast Dr. Holden a guilty look. "Dr. Holden trusted me, and I was ashamed to face him. I let him down. I just couldn't go back," Ms. Fitzgerald said quietly.

"Nothing further," announced Hustler, still boiling with indignation.

"Mr. Daniels, are you ready for the cross?" Judge Adler asked, looking slightly perplexed.

"Yes, Your Honor."

* * *

"Ms. Fitzgerald, how old are you?" Daniels asked gently.

"I'm forty-eight."

"And how old were you when you had your first back surgery?"

"Thirty-three."

"Ms. Fitzgerald, Ms. Hustler probably forgot to ask you this question, so I will. How many back surgeries did you have?"

"I had one small and two extensive surgeries on my lower back and one major surgery on my neck."

"Could you describe briefly what was done to your back, please?"

"First they removed one of my lumbar discs. That didn't work, so later on, the doctors placed titanium rods and plenty of screws into my back."

"Did that help?"

"I wish it did! It made my back pain much worse. It became so bad that a few months later they had to scrape out all this hardware, and after that, I was left on my own."

"Did you experience any kind of pain after your last surgery?"

"Oh, gosh, I did. I still do. I suffer day and night. I feel like it owns me. It shoots down both of my legs; my right leg is constantly numb and feels dead. I can't sleep, I can't even lift my granddaughter. I can't do anything. I... I even need help to take a shower." Ms. Fitzgerald brushed away her tears.

"Ma'am, do you need a moment?" Judge Adler looked genuinely concerned.

"Thank you kindly. I'll be all right," Catherine Fitzgerald said softly.

"Ms. Fitzgerald, Ms. Hustler asked you earlier if Dr. Holden had prescribed opioid medications for your pain, and you said he did, correct?"

"Yes, he did."

"And your pain wasn't a joke, was it?"

"No, sir, it wasn't a joke. It was a nightmare that never ends."

"Were those prescribed medications helping you to suffer less?"

"They turned my life around. I could finally sleep, I could cook, do dishes... My life became... almost normal. I even got a boyfriend." Ms. Fitzgerald smiled.

"Over the three years of your treatments with Dr. Holden, did you find him to be a caring physician?"

"Dr. Holden was always caring and professional. He did his best to help me. He is a good man."

"Did you trust his judgment?"

"Yes, I did. He never gave me a reason to doubt it."

"Nevertheless, on two occasions, despite your pain agreement with Dr. Holden, you used illegal substances, specifically cocaine, didn't you?"

"Yes, sir, I foolishly did, and I paid a dear price for that."

"Now let's clarify something. When your urine test showed cocaine for the first time, Dr. Holden had a serious talk with you, right?"

"Yes, sir, he did. We had a serious conversation, and it wasn't pleasant."

"Then two weeks later he asked you to come to his office and bring your remaining pain pills that he'd prescribed to you on the previous visit. It's recorded in your medical chart. Do you remember this?"

"Vaguely..." She paused. "I think it was something like that. If Dr. Holden asked me to do that, I did it for sure."

"I believe you, ma'am. *That* was a pill count. You just didn't know it was called that. Now, let me ask you a different question. Were you angry at Dr. Holden because he'd stopped prescribing you opioids?"

"No, I was mad at myself. I've never been angry with him. It was my own stupid mistake. Dr. Holden is not to blame for it." Her eyes welled with tears.

"That was my last question for you, Ms. Fitzgerald," said Daniels. "Thank you for your testimony."

"Thank you, ma'am. You are free to go," Judge Adler said with a trace of sympathy.

Lynch rose from his seat.

"Your Honor, the government rests its case," he announced.

"All right." The judge turned to the jury box. "It's around 1:00 p.m. Let's have a lunch break. I'll see you at 2:00 p.m."

The moment the jurors left the courtroom, Judge Adler turned to the attorneys.

"Counselors, can I see you all at the sidebar?"

The prosecutors, defense attorneys, and defendants approached the bench.

"Mr. Lynch, was it your idea to bring this woman here as a witness for the prosecution?" The judge shot the lead prosecutor a sardonic smile. He opened his mouth to respond, but before he could utter a word, the judge waved her hand dismissively. "Well, counselors, I have a problem here. Actually, I am confused. I've been working as a judge for only twenty-six years, so can somebody explain to me on which side this witness was testifying?" The judge was now staring at Hustler.

"Your Honor, I was planning to treat her as a hostile witness, but—"

"Ms. Hustler, she *was* a hostile witness since the first minute of your direct. Even the most myopic juror could see that." Judge Adler shook her head in disbelief. "Well, thank you for a surprising experience anyway. Have a nice lunch, everyone."

Chapter Forty-Nine

The case for the defense was going smoothly, just like it went at the first trial, even though on the cross, Ben observed that the prosecutors went out of their way to trick the defense witnesses into admitting that he and Nurse Practitioner Lander were common drug dealers. So far, none of the defense witnesses took the bait or caved in even once. Office staff insisted on describing Dr. Holden's surpassing dedication to his work and his unfailing efforts to advance his practice while the patients kept saying they were always treated by Dr. Holden and Nurse Practitioner Lander with professionalism and care that finally gave them a chance to lead normal lives.

On more than one occasion, Ben observed that Lynch was on the verge of losing his temper; however, he reached the peak of his arrogance during his cross-examination of Dr. Westwood, the medical expert for the defense and one of the most respected specialists in the field. Lynch was rude and disrespectful to her to the point that Judge Adler finally curbed his enthusiasm. Ben noticed that some of the jurors couldn't hide their shock and disgust at the prosecutor's unruly behavior.

To the prosecutor's utter frustration, Dr. Westwood completely ignored his crude behavior. Only once, when Lynch had brazenly twisted her explanation, she politely asked him not to put words in her mouth. She was dignified, composed, and answered each of the prosecutor's questions with competency and assurance, refuting the prosecutor's distorted facts. And she stated with full confidence that Dr. Holden and Nurse Practitioner Lander had followed all accepted regulations to the letter and their medical practice was legitimate and effective.

* * *

The last witness for the defense was Steven McGovern, one of the most good-humored and likable patients Ben had ever had. Heavily leaning on his cane, his every step labored, the chubby man with a sunny smile slowly moved to the witness chair. I wish, Ben thought, the jurors knew how much it cost this man to smile. Ben turned around, and his glance met Julia's. He could bet the same thought crossed her mind. McGovern slowly settled in the witness chair, and Daniels started his direct.

"Good morning, Mr. McGovern."

"Good morning, sir."

"How old are you?"

"I'm forty-seven."

"Are you currently employed?"

"I'm not. I'm totally disabled."

"What's the cause of your disability?"

"Years ago my disks collapsed. I have titanium rods and about a dozen screws in my spine."

"Are these titanium rods and screws from your back surgery?"

"Yes, they are. I had three surgeries."

"And when did you have your first one?"

"I was thirty-two. Almost eleven years to date."

"At some point in the past, have you been employed?"

"Oh, yes."

"And what was your employment?"

"My last employment... I worked for a program called Strive."

"Very briefly, what's that?"

"It's an attitude-adjustment program. The judge might have heard of it. It's for inner city youth, basically for kids with bad attitudes who are trying to get back on their feet, whether they're just getting out of jail or they simply don't know what to do with their lives."

"I see. Mr. McGovern, are you taking opioids today?"

"Yes, I take them every day."

"And what was the original reason for your back pain?"

"I was in a severe car accident about fifteen years ago. Then I had back surgery, and after that I couldn't walk right. I was completely hunched over. I couldn't sleep, and I had nightmares. I couldn't do anything. I couldn't even walk to the bathroom." McGovern stopped and took a deep breath. He wasn't smiling anymore. "It was very difficult for me and my wife."

"Did you become a patient of Dr. Holden at some point?"

"I did. The director of Strive was his patient. He saw what I was going through and suggested that I see Dr. Holden."

"Did Dr. Holden help you?"

"Yes, he did. By the time I came to him, I'd tried everything I could and was desperate. He listened attentively to my story, and then he put his hand on my shoulder, and he said, 'Steve, I will try my best to help you, but you're going to need to follow my instructions, and here we have rules.'"

"What did he mean by that?"

"He gave me a Pain Management Agreement to sign, and then he said, 'It's not going to be just pain medicine. You'll have other treatments too.' The very first day he gave me an electrical massage machine to use on my back at home, a special pillow, and some rubber bands with which to exercise. We were going to rebuild the muscle around the injury. It was exactly what I wanted."

"Did Dr. Holden's treatments keep you working?"

"Yes, they did. I received different therapies, herbal injections, and pain medicine, all of that."

"Did Dr. Holden ever change your pain medicine dosages?"

"Yes, in the first few months, we tried various combinations. He wanted to find out what would work best for me."

"Did you ever make any observations about people you saw in Dr. Holden's waiting room?"

"His waiting room? Oh, they had a nice fish tank there. I mean, it was a very nice office."

"What did he say, a fish tank?" Judge Adler couldn't help smiling.

"Yeah, that's what I noticed. He had a nice office. It was a very comfortable place to come to."

"Do you remember anything about the people who were sitting there with you?" asked Judge Adler, curious sparks in her eyes.

"Yes, Your Honor, I do. I remember a police officer, a college professor, and some construction workers." McGovern paused. "And a few people from my neighborhood. I mean, Boston is a small town, and I was born and raised here, so I knew a lot of people, but I don't know anybody on the jury." McGovern looked at the jury box with a disarming smile. A few jurors smiled back.

"Did you ever see anyone nodding off in the waiting room?"

"No, I never saw anyone doing that."

"Mr. McGovern, did Dr. Holden or Nurse Practitioner Lander ever ask you to take a drug test?"

"Yes, on a regular basis."

"Have you had any problem with that?"

"Not at all. Why should I? It was a part of our pain agreement."

"Did you at some point move to Florida?"

"I did, but I couldn't find a good pain doctor there so I was flying to Boston to see Dr. Holden."

"Did you eventually move back to Boston?"

"I did. It was too tough to fly back and forth every month, and too costly."

"Sir, throughout the years that Dr. Holden was treating you, were you able to work?"

"Yes, I had a full-time job, and I was very happy about that."

"Did Dr. Holden also help you to quit smoking?"

"Yes, he referred me to a famous hypnotist in Brookline. I forgot his name, but people call him Mad Russian. Quite a character, I should say." McGovern smiled widely. "He helped me a lot. Now I am a smoke-free man. I still have his number, if anyone is interested..."

The witness stopped mid-sentence and turned to the judge, smiling apologetically. "Sorry, Your Honor."

"All right, let's move on, Mr. Daniels."

"At some point, did you learn that Dr. Holden's office was closed?" continued Daniels.

"Unfortunately I did."

"How did you learn that?"

"I actually came to see Ms. Lander on the day when their office was raided. I've seen all those DEA and FBI agents, police... state troopers too. There were people in blue jackets running around like no tomorrow, some with guns. It was insane."

"What happened to you after Dr. Holden's practice was closed, Mr. McGovern?"

"I was left on my own. No one was around to help me anymore. I tried to find another doctor, but... none of them would take me," McGovern grinned humorlessly.

"What happened then?"

"I ended up buying OxyContin on the street, and methadone too."

"Did you eventually find a doctor who prescribed opioid treatment for your pain?"

"Eventually I did, but it took a long time. Now I'm taking the same dose of opioids that Dr. Holden used to prescribe for me eight years ago.

Even though the difference between now and then..." McGovern fell silent. "I lost my job and became totally disabled."

"Mr. McGovern, did your treatments with Dr. Holden improve the quality of your life?"

"Sure. I could work, and my life was pretty good. I was a happy man. I'm truly grateful to him."

"I have nothing further," said Daniels.

"Mr. Krokson, ready for the cross?" Judge Adler turned to the prosecutor.

"Yes, Your Honor, I am." Krokson walked to the lectern. "Mr. McGovern, I have only a couple of questions for you. The first one is about your trips from Florida to Boston. You said you were flying back and forth to see Dr. Holden. Were you coming to Boston to get your opioid medications?"

"No, I could get plenty of these medications in Florida. I was coming to Boston for his treatments." McGovern shot the prosecutor a stern look.

"All right. Let's move on. You said you are taking now the same medications that Dr. Holden used to prescribe to you, correct?"

"Correct."

"In the same dosage?"

"Yes, in the same dosage."

"Mr. McGovern, do you work now?"

"No, I don't. I can't work at an office. It's too hard for me now, but I privately help people to write their résumés. If you need assistance, sir, I can write one for you," McGovern smiled broadly.

A hushed laughter rolled over the courtroom.

"I may need that," Krokson muttered under his breath. "Nothing further," he added out loud.

"Mr. McGovern, thank you for your testimony," Judge Adler smiled gently. "You may leave."

"Your Honor," Gould rose from his seat. "Mr. McGovern was our last witness. The defense rests."

"Very well, Mr. Gould. I'll see you all on Monday for closing arguments. Enjoy the weekend."

* * *

Steve McGovern was walking slowly to the elevator when Emma caught up with him.

"Mr. McGovern, thank you for your testimony. It was... It was truly helpful." The man gave her a curious look. "Sorry, I didn't introduce myself. I'm Emma, Dr. Holden's wife."

McGovern smiled from ear to ear and gave Emma a big, lingering hug. While holding her in his arms, he whispered to her, "Don't worry about a thing. I watched the jury. Everything will be all right."

"Thank you," Emma smiled back wistfully and shook her head, as if to say, From your lips to God's ears. And before she could add another word, McGovern disappeared behind the elevator doors.

* * *

For the closing arguments, the courtroom was packed. Ben and Julia's relatives and friends filled the first few rows of the gallery while FBI and DEA agents and other spectators from the district attorney's office occupied the remaining seats in eager anticipation of another grand finale.

Lynch went first, and his speech was a replica of the closing arguments he delivered at the first trial. He looked like a ferocious fighter, his eyes smoldering with spite and indignation. Ben watched the jurors. They seemed attentive. Were they buying his lies and distortions?

Gould went next. He had been assiduously working on his closing arguments for the past two days, staying up way past midnight. His speech was passionate and, in Ben's opinion, truly persuasive. He could see that the jurors looked engaged. Yet, unlike at the first trial, not a single juror was teary-eyed. Which side were they on? His and Julia's lives depended on the answer to this question.

Gould finished his speech, and Julia's attorney, Peter O'Neil, took over. His statements, as always, were right to the point. However, the jurors' reactions were again indecipherable.

When Lynch, due to the trial rules, came back for his concluding arguments, he revealed a talent he'd never shown before. The prosecutor moved to the jury box as close as he could and, like an opera soloist giving himself wholly to his climactic aria, delivered his venomous proclamations, alternating them with theatrical whispers that no one except the jurors could hear. Piling the government's allegations against Dr. Holden and Nurse Practitioner Lander, he was diligently hammering the final nails into the coffin. By the end of his speech, Ben thought that a few of the jurors looked dismayed. Done with his performance, Lynch, with the air of an indisputable winner, sauntered back to his seat.

The judge announced a short recess before giving the jury instructions, and everyone moved toward the exit. Julia turned around and saw Emma holding in her arms her daughter, Faye, who was quietly sobbing. Julia rushed to them and instinctively shielded Faye from the crowd. "Please don't cry," she said softly. "They shouldn't have the pleasure,... They shouldn't see our tears."

"How could he?" Faye turned her anguished look toward Lynch. "How could he say all these despicable lies? He is not talking about some soulless objects, he is talking about human beings! He lied and lied and lied with one purpose only, to ruin your lives!"

"He had another one in mind too," Emma said somberly, "to advance his career."

The show was over. Most of the spectators had left. The judge read her lengthy, elaborate instructions for deliberations to the jurors and dismissed them until the next day. This time neither Ben nor any of his friends made any predictions. They had learned their lesson.

* * *

The next day, Tuesday morning, Ben and Emma arrived downtown around 7:30 to get street parking before all the office people took over. It was the first day of jury deliberations, and this time they had no hopes for an early verdict. No one could foresee how long the wait would be, but the experience of the first trial had taught them that the wait for a verdict could make the courtroom sessions look like a picnic. Every day and every minute would be torture, as at any single moment they could be told, "The jury is ready with a verdict. Let's go." They longed for this moment to arrive as soon as possible, and at the same time they dreaded it.

At this early hour, before the deliberations started, they could relax, at least to some extent, and have a nice breakfast at a nearby coffee shop. They left the coffee shop forty minutes later and were strolling to Gould's office when Emma saw an old homeless woman in a shabby, colorless coat sitting tiredly on the sidewalk. The woman looked sick and fragile. She sat quietly, didn't ask for change, and from time to time followed pedestrians with a sorrowful gaze. Ben and Emma were already a few yards past her when Emma stopped, opened her handbag, reached into her purse, grabbed all the coins she could find, turned around, and walked back to the woman.

A middle-aged man in a business suit was ahead of her, dropping two dollar bills in a small tin dish hardly visible from afar. The woman thanked him with a faint nod. Emma bent down to drop the change, but as soon as the coins were in the tin, the woman grabbed her hand. Emma tried to pull it away, but the woman clutched it with the strength of a wrestler, pushed something into Emma's palm, squeezed her hand into a fist, and only then let her hand go. Emma flinched and shot the woman a stunned look. Then she turned around, saw Ben patiently waiting for her at the corner, and hurried to catch up with him.

"Emma, what's wrong?" Ben's face creased with concern. "You look like you were just mugged."

"No, I wasn't. Quite the opposite. This homeless woman..." Emma inhaled deeply. "She gave me something."

"She *gave* you something? What did she give you?"

"I don't know. I didn't look."

"You didn't? Can you look now?"

Emma opened her palm. She saw a tiny white cotton sack, tied with a string. Emma stared at the sack and couldn't make herself open it. She cautiously fingered the soft fabric. Three pieces of something. Oval, smooth.

"Perhaps you should have refused to take it." Ben's eyes sparked with curiosity.

"I don't think so."

"Will you open the sack?" Ben shot his wife a teasing look.

"I will." Emma pondered for an uncertain moment. "But not now. Not before the verdict."

"Emma, that's crazy." Ben shook his head. "You have never been a superstitious type."

"No, I am not. But this is different." Her baffled eyes met Ben's puzzled look. "Have you ever received a gift from a homeless woman?"

"No," Ben grinned with bemusement. "Not even from a homeless man."

"Maybe..." she stuttered a little, "Maybe she gave it to me for a reason."

"For a reason? Congratulations, you met your match. I think both of you are a bit crazy." Ben winked and smiled. "Anyway, it's almost 9:00 a.m. Let's go."

Emma put the cotton sack into her handbag and shook her head in disbelief: wasn't she the one who always mocked superstitions?

* * *

For the next four hours, they sat in a small office at Gould's firm. It was the same room they used ten months before, and they both stared fruitlessly into their books. Gould's assistant, Cathy, and front desk secretary, Diane, stopped by now and then, making sure they had everything they needed.

At 1:00 p.m., when the jurors had lunch, they were able to have a break of their own. They'd chosen a small cafe on a side street and, as arranged the day before, their old friends Michael and Eileen drove downtown to spend an hour with Ben and Emma. The day was warm and sunny, and they sat outside.

"Any news?" Michael feigned cheerfulness.

"No, the deliberations started this morning. It's too early," said Ben. "How was your trip? How is Ethan?"

"Oh, he is good, still likes his job, met a nice woman."

"That's pleasant news," Emma winked to Eileen.

"You know, right before we came to visit him, Ethan had bought this new book about Rabbi Schneerson, and he couldn't stop talking about it."

"An interesting book?" asked Ben.

"Fascinating. The stories it tells about the man are mind-blowing," Eileen smiled widely. "The Rebbe—that's what everyone called him—was a legend, and he still is. People from all over the world used to seek his advice. Some of them would come to him with the toughest problems, practically unsolvable, and sometimes he would suggest solutions that seemed—"

"Totally unattainable," finished Michael, "but the Rebbe would encourage to proceed anyway, with the belief that their goals could be achieved against all odds."

"Against all odds" echoed in Emma's head. Isn't that what they'd been doing for the past eight years, fighting against all odds?

"So even if the goal seemed almost impossible to achieve, the Rebbe believed it could be achieved?" Emma asked.

"Yes, he believed that," said Eileen.

"Like in a fairy tale?" Ben rendered a skeptical grin.

"I know it appears that way." Michael didn't seem discouraged. "But those who followed his advice accomplished the impossible. The author of the book describes real stories. They may sound like miracles, but they are true."

"Maybe that's what we need." Emma cast Ben a pensive look. "A miracle."

"No, Emma, what we need is justice."

"But it looks like in your case justice *is* a miracle."

* * *

At 2:00 p.m. they were back at Gould's office. They spent three more hours in the small, cozy room making futile attempts at reading. At 5:00 p.m. Helen stopped by and let them know that the first day of deliberations was over. No verdict.

* * *

The next day, Wednesday, at 9:15 a.m., Mark Daniels walked in, his eyes ablaze with excitement.

"Ben, let's go. The jurors have a question."

Emma stayed in the office, calming herself down with one cup of tea after another.

* * *

Gould was driving to the office when he received the message about the jurors' question. He immediately called Mark Daniels.

"Mark, I've got the message, but I'm stuck in heavy traffic and won't make it on time. You, Helen, and Ben go. You'll have to handle it on your own."

"All right, I will."

Gould hung up and dialed Peter O'Neil's number.

"Peter, have you received the e-mail about the jurors' question?"

"Yes, I have."

"Are you in the office?"

"No, I'm on a bus. Stuck in traffic. You?"

"Me too. Do you know what the question is? I can't read it while driving."

"Yes, I do. *'If a doctor was aware that his pain patient was also abusing drugs, was it legal to continue prescribing him opioids?'* That was the question."

"Thanks. See you in a bit."

Gould felt his anxiety soar through the roof. The question was about the very essence of the trial. It was the most critical question the jurors could ask! That was the core issue the first jury was supposed to address eight months ago, but they never did. Gould dialed Daniel's number again.

"Mark, go to the courthouse, but do whatever you can to put it on hold until I get there."

* * *

Gould arrived at the courtroom and instantly felt the tension that filled it to the brim.

He walked straight to Daniels. "Did Judge Adler give the answer?" he whispered.

"She said that the answer was 'yes.' Lynch is furious."

"Your Honor," Gould turned to the judge, "Sorry for being late, I got stuck in traffic. I believe the answer to the jurors' question is in your jury instructions on page 28."

"How about another place in the instructions?" Lynch shot Gould an infuriated look. "Regarding willing blindness."

Judge Adler found page 28 and read the answer to the jurors' question out loud.

"Your Honor, with all due respect," said Gould, "they asked only this specific question, and I believe they should be directed to the answer in the instructions. The answer is very clear."

"This time I have to agree with Mr. Gould," said Judge Adler. "But to satisfy your request, Mr. Lynch, I'll tell the jury that they are welcome to reread all of the instructions."

* * *

Mark and Ben returned to the office in about two hours.

"What was the question?" Emma rushed to the door.

"They asked whether it was legal to continue prescribing opioids if the doctor was aware that a patient was abusing drugs," said Mark.

"What did Judge Adler say?"

"She said it was legal."

Emma sighed with relief.

"And Edward reminded her that the answer to this question was in her jury instructions."

"So if they asked this question, it means they had an argument about it?"

"Most likely. I can't think of any other reason." Mark reflected for an instant. "I believe there is a chance of another mistrial." He paused. "As for an acquittal... we need a miracle."

"A miracle..." Emma pondered. "Mark, the jurors asked the most critical question, and they received the clearest answer. Do you think they are about to reach a verdict?"

"It's hard to say. They may need a little more time. Maybe tomorrow."

* * *

At 5:00 p.m. Mark stopped to tell them they could leave. Another deliberation day was gone. No verdict.

When they walked outside, the color of the city had turned soft yellow-orange. The most beautiful time of the day in Boston.

"Ben, do you believe in miracles?"

"Many moons ago, when I was a kid, my uncle David insisted that from time to time miracles do happen. After the first trial, I don't know what to believe in." He sighed. "In good luck at best."

"I hope they'll reach a verdict tomorrow. This uncertainty is killing me. I think there are very few things in life that are worse than waiting for a verdict."

Ben grinned sadly. "Can't agree more."

* * *

Thursday, the third day of deliberations, had come and gone. No questions from the jury. No verdict. They were driving home in silence, the ghostly image of the first trial lurking at every turn, a disturbing reminder of what could lie ahead. The jurors received the answer to the most crucial question, and they were still arguing. What does it mean? Another four or five days of deliberations? Another hung jury? Or worse?

Chapter Fifty

The next morning, exhausted after a sleepless night, Ben and Emma were sitting in the room, staring at the pages of their books, unable to focus on anything.

"I can barely stand it." Emma turned to Ben, pale and drawn, dark circles under her eyes. "It's already Friday, and not a word from the jury. I can't even imagine what Julia and Arthur are going through." They fell silent and went back to their fruitless reading.

At 11:30 a.m. Mark barged through the door.

"Let's go! They are ready with a verdict."

* * *

Outside, the sun was blazing insanely, turning mid-May into late July. Ben was sweaty, and the brisk walk to the courthouse in a business suit wasn't helping. The last thing he wanted was the people around him to think he was nervous. The streets of Boston looked surreal, and Ben couldn't get rid of the thought that it was *not* entirely impossible he was walking these streets as a free man for the last time in his life. In fact, it was the more likely alternative. His lawyer's words about the government practically never losing federal cases were ringing in his head with relentless persistence.

Edward Gould was striding side by side, and both of them were quiet.

"Well," Gould finally broke the silence. "I really don't know what people are supposed to say in moments like this."

Ben pondered for a moment.

"Don't worry, Edward, by the time we head back to your office, you'll figure it out," he said with an encouraging smile, and silently added, But will I be walking with you to hear it?

They covered a few more yards in silence when Ben, preoccupied with a troubling thought, turned to Gould.

"You know, Edward, even though I haven't been practicing medicine over the past eight years, I've never stopped reading pain journals and everything else on the subject of pain, and the current trend in the field frightens me. The regulations regarding prescribing opioids are getting stricter by the day, and more and more physicians are afraid to prescribe them even to those who suffer from the most severe pain. I hear these heartbreaking stories from my colleagues and my former patients all the time. I can only guess how our verdict could affect pain doctors or any doctors."

"Do you think there is a chance this trend will reverse?"

"Even if it does, it won't happen tomorrow. Nowadays it looks like an open season on pain doctors and pain patients. And it's only getting worse."

Emma was walking to the courthouse, thinking about the past eight years of their life that brought them to this fifteen-minute walk. How did they survive them? This was the question so often asked by their closest friends. How did they survive the smearing of Ben's reputation by the media, the assault by the Medical Board, and the revocation of Ben's license that ruined his practice? How did they survive the dragging government investigation and two lengthy trials? But primarily, how did they survive this dark, perilous cloud that hung over their heads every minute of the past eight years and bombarded them with one trouble after another? Still, the real possibility of Ben's imprisonment for the rest of his life was worse than anything else.

Could it be, Emma thought, that they survived because they knew that Ben and Julia had never done anything illegal, and they both had stayed strong and unbeatable through all these disastrous years? Could it also be because they were supported by their families and many good friends and never felt like victims. More than that, they enjoyed every good moment that life had offered them over these tough years. Under these dire circumstances, they never lost their sense of humor and had been as happy as any loving couple could be.

At the entrance to the courthouse they met Julia, her amiable face ghostly pale, and Arthur, quiet and composed. Julia forced a pained smile, hugged Emma, and they all silently moved into the courthouse.

* * *

The defendants, their attorneys, and the prosecutors took their seats in the front rows, while Emma and Arthur sat behind the defendants. In a few minutes they were joined by Julia's and Arthur's daughter Lila and her husband Ned. Both of them worked downtown, and they were the only ones on the defense side who could make it to the verdict announcement on time.

The rest of the room was packed with DEA and FBI agents and people from the district attorney's office, who didn't even try to hide their excitement in anticipation of a verdict. They looked as if they were about to receive Academy Awards or at least Christmas bonuses. U.S. State Attorney Calvina Cortes, who hadn't shown much interest in the trial, had joined their ranks to celebrate the upcoming victory. Over the last twelve years, from the day the investigation of Dr. Holden's office was initiated, her troops had worked tirelessly to make it happen, and now they were about to reap the fruits of their labor.

Emma glanced at the prosecutors. They were chatting jauntily, now and then exchanging cheerful smiles. Could it be that they already knew? Emma swallowed the lump in her throat.

"All rise," declared the clerk.

Judge Adler entered the courtroom, her expression more somber than usual.

"Good afternoon, everyone. Please sit down and remain seated," she stated, and turned to her clerk. "Please invite the jury to come in."

The jurors walked in. They looked solemn, their faces unreadable.

Judge Adler turned to the jury box, "Members of the jury, have you reached a verdict?"

"Yes, we have, Your Honor," answered the foreperson, a tall, dark-haired woman in spectacles.

"Was it unanimous?"

"Yes, Your Honor."

The juror handed the verdict to the clerk, and Mary passed it to the judge.

"Please present the verdict." Judge Adler gave the document back to her clerk.

"Count #1," started Mary, "Conspiracy to distribute controlled substances: methadone, oxycodone and fentanyl." A short pause. Emma's anxiety spiked through the roof.

"Dr. Benjamin Holden. Not guilty. Julia Lander. Not guilty." Mary's voice was firm and loud.

Julia's daughter heaved a loud sigh.

"Count #2," continued Mary, "distribution of methadone and fentanyl, Doug Donovan, February 12, 2004." Another short pause. "Benjamin Holden. Not guilty."

Another palpable sigh from the first row of the gallery.

"Count #3. Distribution of methadone and oxycodone. Jason Cameron. March 26, 2005. Benjamin Holden. Not guilty."

Emma glanced at the prosecutors: their postures turned stiff, their faces tense.

"Count #4. Distribution of methadone and oxycodone. Ted Daley. July 14, 2005. Benjamin Holden. Not guilty. Julia Lander. Not guilty."

"Four more to go," flashed in Ben's head.

"Count #5. Distribution of methadone and oxycodone. Ted Daley. August 16, 2005. Benjamin Holden. Not guilty. Julia Lander. Not guilty."

Ben glanced at the jurors. Their faces were grave and indecipherable.

"Count #6. Distribution of methadone and oxycodone. Jeremy Gallagan. October 26, 2005. Benjamin Holden. Not guilty." Ben shot a swift glance at Gould, his face taut and flushed.

"Count #7. Distribution of methadone. Ken Bertoldi. Benjamin Holden. Not Guilty."

One more left. Emma's heart was pounding through her chest. She inhaled and froze, afraid to breathe. The last one. The last one...

"Count #8. Distribution of methadone and oxycodone. Simon Peterson. September 10, 2006." Mary paused. Dead silence filled the courtroom for an eternity.

"Benjamin Holden. Not guilty," announced Mary.

Emma squeezed her fists to restrain herself from yelling, Yes!

Eight years of relentless battle, and they were finally free. The age of miracles was not past. Their brightest and most dedicated attorneys had done the impossible and won a federal case! Justice had finally prevailed.

Ben turned to the jury box and bowed his head in gratitude. Barely moving his dry lips, he said "thank you." A few of the jurors smiled back.

"Members of the jury," announced Judge Adler, "thank you for your service. You may be dismissed. This court is adjourned. The defendants are free to go."

Smiling from ear to ear, the defense attorneys shook hands and hugged Ben and Julia. Then both Ben and Julia rushed to their spouses and Julia's children. More hugs and smiles... and sighs of relief.

When a few minutes later they turned around to leave the courtroom, they found it empty. No prosecutors, no DEA or FBI agents, no people from the DA's office or their leader, Calvina Cortes, not a single person from the blood-thirsty crowd that was sneering and snickering a little while ago in eager anticipation of a victory. They all quietly vanished, as if licked away by a mute ocean surf. Thirteen years of their ceaseless, vigorous efforts and millions of taxpayers' dollars spent on a witch-hunt went up in smoke.

In the hallway, Emma reached into her purse, retrieved the tiny cotton sack, untied it, and discovered three white sugar candies. A gift from the homeless woman. Emma smiled. Was it the last missing ingredient for their victory?

* * *

At the courthouse front-desk, Emma and Ben received their cell phones, and the calling marathon began.

"Mom, not guilty on all eight counts!"

"I knew it!"

"Dad, not guilty on all eight counts!"

"Say it again, I can't hear you!"

"Not guilty! On all counts!"

They walked back to Gould's office called their relatives and close friends, one after the other. Some screamed with joy, some sobbed. Then they saw Edward Gould and Mark Daniels at a distance, in the middle of the bridge, jumping up, thrusting their fists in the air and yelling, "Ye-e-s!" Bystanders stared at them stunned and then smiled.

They finally reached the office building and walked into the elevator. Still smiling from ear to ear, Gould, Daniels, Helen, Ben, and Emma were waiting for the door to close when a slightly stooped, balding man in his fifties, clad in a navy business suit, walked in. The elevator was about to stop at the next floor when Gould suddenly turned to the stranger and pointed at Ben.

"This man," he started, blissful twinkles in his eyes, "was just acquitted in federal court."

The man in a navy blue suit gave Ben a quick perplexed look.

"That's nice," he said, and stepped out of the elevator.

Gould shook his head in amusement. "Yeah, that's nice," he repeated, and they all burst into laughter.

Epilogue

The next morning when they thought they could finally sleep as long as they pleased, the phone rang at about 9:00 a.m. Ben, half asleep, picked up the receiver.

"Good morning, Ben, it's Edward. Hope I didn't wake you up."

"You did, but that's okay. Good morning. Don't tell me we've overslept, and Judge Adler will scold us for being tardy."

"No, Ben, she won't. The trial is over."

"I still can't believe it."

"I have a hard time believing it myself."

"So, what's up?"

"Judging by your sleepy voice, you didn't have a chance to see today's *Boston Veritas*, did you?"

"No, I didn't. Is our victory front page news?"

"Keep dreaming." Gould laughed. "It's not even in the metro section."

"It doesn't surprise me a bit."

"Me neither. Still, this morning's issue is worth reading."

"Let me guess: Dr. Finnegan's clinic had a change of heart and started prescribing opioids?"

"You have quite an imagination. No, nothing like that."

"Then you'll have to tell me what it is. The day the *Boston Veritas* smeared my name, I canceled my subscription."

There was a long pause at the other end of the line. Ben could feel this pause didn't foretell anything good.

"Yesterday, right after you and Julia were acquitted, another local pain doctor was charged with the same crimes. The Medical Board has already revoked his license."

Ben was at a loss for words.

"I know it's not good news," said Gould, "but I thought you had to know. Remember our talk on the way to the courthouse? It seems you were right."

"I wish I weren't," Ben said quietly. "Do you know anything else about this doctor?"

"The man is over sixty; he had a tiny practice. According to the testimonials, he, like you, was highly respected by his patients." Ben remained silent. "Sorry for the bad news."

"As you said, I needed to know it."

Gould's voice turned tense. "Ben, you never asked me this question, but I think it's the right time to answer it." He took a long pause. "The evidence at the trials proved that you and Julia were honest, caring professionals who did their very best to help people in pain. The government investigated you for years and was totally aware of that, and yet they knowingly put you both and your families through hell on earth, ruined your careers and your lives, and the lives of so many of your patients." Gould took a deep breath. "And now I'll answer the question I believe you will ask me sooner or later. Will they apologize to you or recompense you for your losses? No, don't expect an apology or any compensation. You will not get either."

Ben was silent for a long time.

"It's upsetting," he said finally. "But we'll survive. The persecution is over, and that's all that matters." Ben reflected for a moment. "Edward, are you willing to defend this doctor?"

"If he asks me, I'll certainly look into his case," said Gould. "Well, sorry for messing up your serene morning. Anyway... enjoy your freedom."

"Thanks, Edward. Thank you for all you did for us."

Ben hung up and turned to Emma.

"Bad news?" she asked with concern.

"Another pain doctor has just lost his license and is facing criminal charges. I pray he'll have courage and stamina to survive it."

"I wonder how many more fine doctors have to be sacrificed before the public will be outraged?" Emma asked quietly. "Isn't it frightening that these self-serving careerists keep destroying the lives of dedicated physicians and millions of suffering people?"

"It is frightening, but I hope that someday conscientious people will find a way to put an end to this shameful war on doctors and their patients."

"And doctors won't have to choose between their freedom and helping those who suffer."

"Wouldn't that be great?" Ben smiled. "And then those who are in pain will get the effective help they desperately need and deserve," he added earnestly.

"Do you think we'll live long enough to see it happen?"

"I hope we will. As you may have noticed, life works in mysterious ways."

Acknowledgments

It took me quite a few years to write *Pain on Trial,* and I'm grateful to many people who helped me to stay strong through these difficult years of my life and certainly to those who helped me with writing the book.

Many thanks to my caring, devoted mom for her unfailing support and encouragement and to my lovely sister Irene, who put countless hours into reading the book and came up with many valuable ideas and suggestions.

I'm especially grateful to my good friends Judy Pfeffer, Madelaine Botti, George Karounos, Garry Polyakoff, Bob Brooks, Marina Lokshin, Margarita Epshteyn, Barbara Cooper, and Terri Rumpf, who were so generous with their time in reading the book and making very important suggestions. Their help was absolutely priceless.

Also my thanks to my dear friends Tanya, Yuri, Michael, Nelli, Victor, and Galina for their suggestions and support, and to my good friend Mila Ma for her infallible encouragement and advice.

I'm especially indebted and grateful to my editor, Deanna Boddie, whose superb work and generosity are impossible to overestimate.

I would like to make particular mention of my book designer, Natali Cohen, my proofreader David Yerganian and my publisher, Michael Minayev, who was helpful in so many ways.

And lastly, a very special thanks to my loving husband, Joseph, my inspiration and my most loyal supporter, who never lost faith that one day I would finally finish this book. I'm infinitely grateful for his precious ideas and immeasurable input. In my opinion, this book is as much his as it is mine.

Made in the USA
Columbia, SC
30 December 2017